A GRAND ConspIRACY

A SEQUEL TO *THE COUNSELOR*

BY

CURTIS TAYLOR

ASPEN BOOKS

A Grand Conspiracy is a work of fiction. Names, characters, places, and incidents either are the product of the author's imagination or are used fictitiously. Any resemblance to actual persons, living or dead, or events, is entirely coincidental.

Other works by Curtis Taylor
(Most recent to earliest)

Fiction
A Grand Conspiracy
American Grace
The Counselor
Rolling Home
(Originally published as *The Dinner Club*)
The Invisible Saint

Nonfiction
The Burning Within, by Ranelle Wallace with Curtis Taylor
Embraced By The Light, by Betty J. Eadie with Curtis Taylor

Boys Books with Todd Hester
The Adventures of Mark Heroic: CyberDeth
The Adventures of Mark Heroic: MegaBlast
The Adventures of Mark Heroic: Flash Point
The Adventures of Mark Heroic: Treasure Hunt
The Adventures of Mark Heroic: The Not-So Private Eyes

Screenplays
The Review
American Grace

Acknowledgements

Originally, this tome was nearly a thousand pages long; then, after wise counsel from concerned people who loved me, it was whittled down to its current length. No doubt it could have been whittled further, but my "delete" finger (right ring) became bruised after days of hammering.

My son, Andre, came to the rescue and joined our little firm, bringing good perspective and technical skills. His advice for his often forgetful and sometimes clueless father was almost always appreciated—and should have always been followed.

As always, many thanks to my loving and tenacious wife, Janet, for multiple readings and too many late-night discussions. I am especially grateful that somewhere along the way she mastered the art of nodding sagely while entering REM sleep—and then of continuing to sleep while I pounded away on a keyboard not ten feet from her head.

My thanks also to those who reviewed, guided, and gently corrected this work, especially Tai Priebe, our oldest daughter, who understands motivation and story better than many editors. Also, to Roger Hoskins, who, over a cup of Wendy's excellent chili, nonchalantly gave me the original idea for this book. When I heard that operatives from the Smithsonian had looted the Kincaid Cave in 1909, my blood began to race, and I asked for permission to begin writing. For some reason, this excellent writer gave it.

I must also give credit to Stan and Polly Johnson, whose amazing book *Translating the Anthon Transcript*, pioneered the first possible translations of the characters in Joseph Smith's Anthon Transcript. I have every reason to believe they are on to something important, and no reason to disbelieve their exhaustive work. Now, if we could just find a few more plates to translate. (Anybody up for a stroll in the canyon?)

Also, thanks to Tina Taylor, who again saved me from embarrassment by correcting a multitude of typos, lapses in logic, and other incomprehensible renderings. As Roger often says: "There are two kinds of people—the humble and those who are going to be." As long as Tina keeps proofing my work, I will remain

Your humble servant.

Prologue
The Big Fog

It didn't steal in on little cat feet. It didn't saunter in off the Pacific, ooze over the bay, or roll into the valley. It had nothing to do with the ocean or the mists that masquerade as fog along the coast. This was a vise. This was a smothering nullity that birds disappeared in, the homeless hid from, and long lines of motorists wrecked in. The ocean-borne fog of the San Francisco Bay is gray and gentle, indeed creeping in "on little cat feet," as the poet once said. But this was the dark empire of fogs. This was tule (too-lee) fog, a dank atmospheric phenomenon that rose from the Great Central Valley's wet, fecund soils to strangle entire counties in its grip. It moved neither right nor left, north nor south, but simply existed and squeezed—*squeezed*—until the life of the valley seemed wrung out from the dripping air.

Precisely at 2:00 a.m., just as he had been instructed, Keith Nelson stood under the dripping canopy of a large live oak. Exactly how large, he couldn't tell, as he could barely make out the dripping leaves that had just brushed his face. There was no motion, no sound, not even the murmuring of Dry Creek which he knew was less than twenty feet away. He put his hand out before him, not to judge the visibility, which was virtually zero, but to find the trunk. He glanced down and realized that he couldn't see his feet. Vertigo rocked him, and he sought more urgently for the solidity of the tree. The fog had been a problem while driving to Beard Brook Park, but down here by the creek it was a 3-dimensional wall. He extended his hand deeper into the mist, causing it to disappear about two inches above his wrist. Poof. Gone. Another wave of vertigo rocked him, and for a thrilling second he was lost. Then his fingertips brushed the coarse bark and he latched onto the solid two-foot-wide trunk.

The text said that he was to come alone and stand under this tree until the man with the money showed up. He was to bring nothing but a bag with the artifacts.

His right shin became angrier, throbbing where it had struck against a concrete bollard in the parking lot when he got out of his car. He had heard that homeless people made the willows near the creek their haunt, but as he listened for movement he heard only wisps of ambient noise from Highway 99, where desperate travelers braved the soup, no doubt praying that nobody had stopped in front of them and that no speeders were racing up behind them. Death lurked in the big fogs.

"I could kill you right now, and you'd never know who did it."

The voice might as well have been the Voice of America coming from nowhere, everywhere. Keith angled his head toward the trail he had come down, seeking sonic placement.

"You really can't see me, can you?"

"No," Keith said uncertainly. "Are you on the path? How do you know where I am?"

The deep, masculine voice chuckled. "Infrared. The fine folks at Flir turned my iPhone into a heat-seeking camera. I watched you walk down here from your car."

"Does it show you concrete posts too?" Keith asked, the growing knot on his shin barking louder.

"Nope. They're as cold as the fog, but I saw you trip over something up there. Do you have the artifacts?"

"They're in my bag. Do you have the money?"

"Of course." The man snapped a compact flashlight on, turning the mist into an incandescent bubble. The man opened his own bag and focused the light inside, revealing stacks of $100 bills and an iPad with a short cable. He closed the bag. "Satisfied?"

"Yes." Keith was tempted to smile. He had made it clear that he wanted American dollars, not some cryptocurrency. But now that he had seen the cash, he was growing wary. The man, though Keith couldn't see his face, was obviously much taller than his own slender five-eight—and something about the man's guttural voice, a thickness in the consonants, reminded him of a Semitic tongue. The last thing Keith needed was to deal with a potential terrorist. Keith himself was in good shape for his age, having just scaled some of the steepest, tallest cliffs in America, but he wasn't going to win a physical contest with this monster.

2

"Okay," the man said, "very carefully, so I know you don't have a weapon, show me each artifact, then, slowly, place it back in the bag."

The huskiness in the voice again evidenced a *very* large man. Holding his bag with one hand, Keith reached in with the other and pulled out a heavy bracelet constructed of silver, copper, and gold. A one-inch, circular turquoise stone hovered in the center the way a pond can seem to hover over a meadow at dawn. In the illuminated mist, the simple piece was breathtaking.

"It will do," said the rumbling voice behind the light. "Now, very carefully, show me the next piece."

Keith slowly replaced the bracelet and pulled out a necklace. A long braid of silver and gold lace was encrusted with dozens of blue stones. An orangish-red stone, perhaps jasper or agate, served as a clasp and would have hung just below the throat. A fire deep within the stone rose and fell with the movement of the light. But the buyer seemed more interested in the bluish flecks set in the braid.

"Are those sapphires?" He moved the light from side to side, examining the gems.

"Yes. They scratch quartz but not rubies."

Keith's vision had begun adjusting to the light, and he was able to make out the man's smiling face above him. The man must be pushing six-five. His short dark hair glistened in the fog, but, surprisingly there was no beard. In fact, in the light, the man's face appeared almost Oriental, or perhaps Native American.

"Very good," he said. "Now the diadem."

Keith put the necklace back and pulled out the *piece de resistance*, an articulated gold headband inlaid with rows of garnets, amethysts and turquoise. As he brought it out he placed the band's centerpiece in his palm—a center clasp of pure gold carved into a Herakles knot. As always, the diadem's weight surprised him.

A soft exclamation escaped the buyer's lips. "And all this is from the cave in the canyon?"

"Yes. I sent you the pictures of the cave, but I can show you again." Keith slowly set the diadem back in the bag and pulled his phone out of his pocket. In moments he brought up the gallery of photos from his time in the canyon. The man took it from him and slowly scrolled through the photos, examining each.

"They may have been Photoshopped. I need to check the metadata."

3

Keith understood. Anyone could use software to create photos of virtually anything, but the metadata embedded in each shot would prove its true provenance. The man reached into his bag and brought out the iPad with a digital connection kit. He quickly inserted the free end of the cable into Keith's phone and waited a moment for the proper screen to come up. He hit two buttons on the iPad, and in seconds a black and white screen of metadata appeared from the current photo. The man studied it then scrolled through the remaining photos, checking each.

Keith waited patiently, though still wary. He glanced at the man's bag.

All that money.

But the fact was, Keith had done almost everything in his power not to be here. He had tried to meet the man in a restaurant, but the guy had insisted on total privacy. Since this was the only buyer he had found on the dark peer-to-peer site who mentioned serious dollars, he had to follow his instructions. The man had offered $100,000 for the artifacts if Keith also gave him directions to the cave. Though many had considered Kinkaid's cave a hoax, this man, whoever he was, had seen through the online clutter and *believed.* But of course the guy needed to verify that this wasn't an ICE sting operation trying to catch him illegally buying Native American artifacts—if that's what they were. Keith wasn't sure of their provenance himself, though he knew they were ancient and hadn't been disturbed in centuries.

Earlier that night the man had told Keith to show up at two other locations, and each time when Keith got there, the man texted him to go somewhere else, obviously looking for cops in tow. Moments ago, when the buyer actually showed up here, just above the confluence of Dry Creek and the Tuolumne River, Keith was more surprised than relieved.

The hundred grand wasn't what he had been hoping for, but it would have to do. Thousands of people had spent nearly a century searching for Kinkaid's cave in the Grand Canyon, but only he had been successful, because only he had the documents from "Kinkaid's" own hand to take him to exactly the right location. No, a hundred thousand dollars was peanuts for these relics—and for the greater knowledge of the cave's location—but, again, it would have to do, as he knew that retrieving more jewelry would be risky, if not impossible. After all, the federal government had actually sealed off that part of the canyon, not only from the public, but from the park rangers as well. They wanted *nobody* in there. He knew that he only had to be caught once with the artifacts to be prosecuted to the full extent of the law. People didn't play around with Immigration and Customs Enforcement or with NAGPRA, the Native American Graves Protection and Repatriation Act. If you wanted to spend a dozen years in a federal penitentiary, getting caught with stolen artifacts from sacred burial sites, especially from the Grand Canyon, was a good way to get there.

The man disconnected the cable from Keith's phone. "The photos look legitimate. And so do the artifacts." He handed the phone back to Keith.

"Of course they look legitimate. They are legitimate. And there's a lot more where they came from. Give me the money, and I'll tell you exactly how to find them."

"First, who else knows about this?"

"Nobody. That's what I told you in the email. I haven't told anybody."

"What about your wife? What about your family?"

Keith laughed. His ex-wife was the last person this guy needed to worry about. "I'm divorced, and she lives out of state. I hope she—and her lawyer—never find out about any of this. They'll squeeze all the money they can out of it."

"And your children?"

"I have one daughter. She lives in Virginia with her husband. She only talks to me when her mother wants something from me. Nobody knows about this. Telling people would be a little, shall we say, counterproductive. It's just you and me—and I don't even know who you are."

The man gently set the iPad back in his bag then reached behind his back. When his hand came out, it held a black handgun. "I was sent by Washington. You never should have gone in the cave."

Keith froze. "Are you from ICE?"

"No, from a group much older and much more powerful."

Keith thought about running, but the man still had his infrared-enhanced phone and could easily follow him as he flailed through the fog.

"Out of curiosity," the man said, "how did you get in the cave? It's supposed to be sealed."

"You're right. Actually, I couldn't get in. These are fake. I bought them on the rim, from a Hopi medicine man." Keith tried to chuckle, but couldn't really pull it off. "The poor old fool didn't even know what he had. He couldn't even—"

The big man's left fist shot out and struck Keith across the chin. Keith's eyes rolled back and his body collapsed to the carpet of leaves, then, gradually gathering momentum, it rolled down the steep bank toward the water.

"They call that the Whislin' Claw," the big man muttered, but Nelson didn't respond, lying head-down by the water. The fog was so thick that the big man couldn't even tell if Keith was actually in the water or not.

Not that he cared. He had no great affinity for his own people, but he often surprised himself by the way he responded to insults against them. Using his infrared camera, he found the heat signature of Keith's phone in the grass. He checked the recent calls and texts, then he put in his pocket. He peered down the bank and saw that Nelson still wasn't moving. Sometimes the big man's left fist was more potent than he wanted it to be. He made his way down the muddy bank.

Oops, Nelson's head was face-down in the water. The man grabbed Nelson's ankles and dragged him up the slippery bank. Through the swirling fog, he saw rivulets of water draining from Nelson's mouth.

Not a good sign.

He applied compression to Nelson's back, forcing more water out, then he scooted down and put his ear to the man's mouth. Silence. He checked the carotid artery. No pulse. He put his ear to the man's chest and listened for a heartbeat.

More silence.

Nelson was dead.

The large man stood up to check for witnesses. He heard nothing and knew that nobody could see him. He looked down at Nelson. With the head still positioned below the body, the face was already growing purple as blood pooled into it.

Not my fault. I only wanted to punish him for his lies—and for his ridicule of my people.

He had never murdered intentionally. Yes, in battle he had taken lives, but that was in defense of his country. And there was that time in Texas, but that had been an accident too. Maybe some smart cop would connect the dots, and they'd start calling him the Accidental Killer.

Heavy rains two days before had swollen the creek, increasing the current. There was nothing the big man could do about Nelson, so he gave the body a little shove back down the slick bank into the water. The body drifted off and disappeared in the shroud of swirling fog. He raised his camera and watched the yellow glow of the body fade to orange then red then violet as its warmth dissipated in the dark water.

Chapter 1

Encircled About in a Fearsome Place

A man of woes. That's what I was. A man of woes crawling home through the thickest fog I'd seen in years.

Actually, work was going well, it seemed, since I was making money, but the price was high. People say the problem with money is that it costs too much. No kidding. I was a financial counselor, so I dealt with this cost on a regular basis. Too many of my clients were willing to sell their souls for a life of luxury and impunity. I say impunity because that's how they treated people around them, me included. Sometimes I wished I could make a living helping them get poor again.

Then there was my health. A word of caution: Don't get Lyme disease. Mine had been misdiagnosed for years, and by the time a diligent doctor tracked it down, it had crossed the blood-brain barrier. That meant it was sealed off from antibiotics, meaning its effects would probably be lifelong. As if this weren't bad enough, as a result of my lowered immune system, a gaggle of viruses had also entered my system, like Epstein-Barr, cytomegalovirus, and HHV-6. Here's another word of caution. Don't be misled by these exotic-sounding names—they are deadly serious. I could usually work around the flu-like symptoms they caused, but I had to be careful when the brain fog hit. If I didn't stop what I was doing immediately, I tended to make poor decisions.

And here I was, exhausted, driving through fog that could drown a person. But as long as I kept a set of taillights fifteen or twenty feet in front of me, I was okay.

My mind latched onto another woe: the 12-year-old genius that my wife, Anna, and I were raising. He could do math at the college level, solve ridiculous Sudokus, and play the guitar both left-handed and right-handed. He remembered *everything*, and, just to make things fun, he seemed to have a mischievous streak in him. Just recently, for example, he solved a chronic problem at our stake center. The building is located on the outskirts of town, and a pack of starving feral cats had taken up residence in the bushes. If they had stayed there, we might not have had the problem, but they kept slipping into the building when people propped the doors open, and some of them took up residence under the stage. Any number of removal methods had been tried. All had failed.

Then Kevin, our son, came to the rescue. He borrowed my key to the building before dawn one Saturday, rode his bike to the church, scared all of the cats out from under the stage with an ultra bumpbox (a modern boombox) and my old megaphone. I can't imagine what the decibels were. After the frantic felines had scrambled out the door for relief, he shut the door and set up a small cage near the bushes. In the cage was a small mouse he had caught in a nearby field. He hid behind a tree about thirty feet away. Actually in retrospect, I think it was his patience that alarmed me. As the starving cats, lured by the mouse's pitiful pawings and squeakings, emerged from the bushes and began attacking the cage, Kevin began picking them off with a Wrist Rocket. The slingshot sported a stabilizer, counter balance, and fiber optic sight. Kevin had 500 rounds of 9mm steel shot ammo balls. The cats never had a chance. He had been practicing, evidently, and rarely missed. After each kill, the cats would scatter, then a few minutes later would be lured out again by the even more frantic eeks and scratchings of the terrified mouse. It took until noon, but Kevin eventually dispatched all the cats and tossed their flea-ridden bodies into the dumpster behind the church. He set the mouse free in the field where it came from. It was the putrefying carcasses in the dumpster that did him in a few days later, and the rumors that he was bragging to other deacons about his "big game expedition."

Our bishop, Robert Quinn, and I both discussed our concerns with the boy, I in my way and he in his. My way included volume, threats, and the confiscation of the wrist rocket, steel shot and all. Bishop Quinn's way included, I learned later, a few scriptures and an appeal to a talk by President Kimball about killing birds. The stake president, good man that he is, only asked if "the problem" was solved. I assumed he meant the cat problem, and I assured him that it was. There was no way I could assure him of anything concerning my son.

To prevent temptation from rearing its ugly head again, I kept the wrist rocket and its forearm stabilizer, counter balance, fiber optic sight, and 450 or so steel shot ammo balls, in my car where, theoretically, the young fiend couldn't access them.

Yes, I had woes, but rich people and Kevin's genius were mere annoyances compared to my larger problem.

I served in the stake high council, which meant that I served the stake presidency and gave talks in different wards each month. I considered the calling an honor and wanted to magnify it as well as I could. But sometimes my other problems got in the way.

My beautiful and brilliant wife, the powerful defender of yours truly in a highly publicized murder case years before, didn't believe in one of the foundations of our religion, actually, in the very keystone of our religion. Although a member of the Church, she didn't believe in the *Book of Mormon*. For that matter, she didn't believe in the *Doctrine & Covenants* or *Pearl of Great Price* either. Oh, she thought they contained some rather excellent teachings, and for the most part she was amazed at the young prophet's genius in "composing" it all—but she never accepted that they were revealed gifts from God. This was a problem, not just because in my calling I was expected to have a believing family at my side, but because I loved her dearly and wanted *her* at my side eternally—along with my first wife, Marsha. This may sound scandalous, but the fact was I loved both women deeply and, I hoped, eternally. Sacred experiences had shown me that Marsha approved of the former Anna Kohlberg as the new mother of our two children, the renegade Kevin, and his twin sister, the sweet and adoring (of her father) Kalley. I sensed that things were different on the other side, that jealousy didn't play havoc with our better judgment, and that people loved each other in ways we barely understood here. But my faith also led me to believe that living eternally with a spouse who didn't believe the basics of a gospel that I was willing to sacrifice all for might be problematic.

I'm not saying that she wasn't a wonderful wife and mother. Anna could not have been more loving of Kevin and Kalley and our two children together, Lucas, 6, and Mia, 4. And, ironically, she was very active in the Church. She had always had a strong set of personal values, and she believed that the gospel provided a great environment for raising children, so she and our long-term nanny, Rosemary Skiles, made sure the children participated in every Church activity available. These two women had become good friends before our marriage and had worked out a system of teaming up on the children from morning to bedtime. As often as possible, this included Anna coming home early from her law firm to be with them. The system was so seamless that I often wondered where I fit in.

I turned onto the quiet road leading to my house, and the lack of traffic actually made driving more iffy—no taillights to follow. I slowed down to a crawl, which was dangerous not just because a car might hit me from behind, but because even at this pace I could damage a fire hydrant or hit a parked—

I jerked my wheel to the right and just missed an oversized pickup half blocking my driveway. I stopped in the street and gazed at the unknown vehicle, a lifted, silver Ford F-150, 4x4. There was just enough room that I might be able squeeze into one side of the driveway. Who had done this? My side window was glazed with mist, so I rolled it down, letting in a rush of cold air. In the distance I heard a faint metallic, wrenching sound. I shot a glance at my rearview mirror but saw no lights. The sound came again, a creaking, twisting sound that I now realized was coming from the side of my house. The truck blocked my view, so I backed up and saw a diffused glow on the wall of my house above the side gate. The light moved, and I realized somebody was pointing a flashlight at my surveillance camera above the gate.

Years ago my home had been broken into by somebody who had disabled that same camera. I quickly pulled my car around the truck, into the driveway. I knew Anna wasn't home yet, and I knew Rosemary, our nanny, now 53, had never bothered with a surveillance camera in her life. The other likely possibilities were Kevin or an intruder. The light seemed to be positioned close to the camera, which meant it was being held by a very tall man or somebody on a ladder. I couldn't imagine why Kevin would be on a ladder in the fog, but that meant little. I couldn't imagine why Kevin did most of the things he did. I opened the door, paused, then reached back in and picked up the Wrist Rocket with stabilizer, counterweight, and fiber optic sight. I also dumped a handful of steel balls into my pocket.

As I mentioned, when I got tired I tended to make poor decisions.

The gate, set about ten feet back from the front of the house, was obscured by fog, but I could still see the light above it illuminating the surveillance camera. Then I saw a large hand reach up, grab the camera, and angle it away from the house.

Somebody was trying to alter the camera's field of view.

I could faintly make out a shadowy, tall figure standing on our black, heavy-duty garbage can. The brazenness astonished me, incensed me. I stood by the corner of the house, 15 feet away, grabbed a steel ball from my pocket, loaded it into the kangaroo leather pouch, stepped around the corner, and fired.

I should mention that the bands of the slingshot were warm from having been under the heater in the car. Heated bands, counterintuitively, create a faster contraction, increasing their velocity—in this case up to three or four hundred miles per hour. I might also mention that I only intended to scare the intruder, rather than hit him. I certainly didn't need a court case hanging over my head, all-star attorney of a wife notwithstanding. So, I aimed for the garbage can. Third, I should mention that I am, evidently, a poor shot, because the scream of pain suddenly issuing from the intruder indicated a sure miss—of the garbage can. He fell to the ground, and the light tumbled under some bushes, plunging us both in darkness.

Sensing that he might be upset, I reloaded, pulled back as hard as I could, and waited.

Or so I thought.

New shrieks of pain gave me to understand that I had actually fired again. The Lyme disease, no doubt, had deadened both my awareness and judgment. In self-defense I loaded again, something I was getting faster at.

And now a strange fact occurred to me, indicating, certainly, that my mind was beginning to suffer: *If the Yanks had been armed with these handy devices in the Revolutionary War, they would have won long before very many people got hurt.*

I was suffering from brain fog and actual fog *simultaneously*. I called out: "Are you hurt?"

There was a pause. Then the voice said, "Travis?"

I pulled back again. Hard.

The fallen man said: "Travis, are you having an episode? Do you feel sick to your stomach?"

I have always been susceptible to the power of suggestion, and no sooner had he said the words than I felt my stomach churning, rising, preparing for release.

"No, Travis, not this way!" Evidently he could see me.

My lunch, whatever it had been, spewed forth, arced through the fog, and landed somewhere in his direction. Sudden nausea had plagued me since I got the Lyme disease, but it rarely projected so far. Indeed, this may have represented some sort of record.

"Ahhh! What's the matter with you? It's me, Ross!"

Now I recognized the voice. "Ross? Is it you? Did I get you?" I stepped forward but for some reason kept a little distance.

"Yes—to both. What were you shooting?"

"You mean with the slingshot—or, you know? . . ."

"Slingshot. What was in it?"

"Um, just some ball bearings."

"Ball bearings?"

"Did they hurt?"

"I'm bleeding!"

"Sorry. It's Kevin's—but, you know, I'm not blaming him. What were you doing? I thought you were in Utah—wait, what were you doing to my camera?"

"Just a minute. I'm going to try to stand up. Can you see me?"

"Just barely."

"Okay, let me get my phone."

The light, which had fallen upside down under some roses by the fence, bobbled again as he picked it up. I stepped closer and saw his face, which was, indeed, Ross Keller's. Something viscous was hanging from his jacket.

"Travis, what'd you have for lunch? This really stinks."

"Um, I don't remember."

He turned the light on the slingshot. "Is that thing legal?"

"I don't know. Again. Are you okay?"

He shined the light on his jeans, and I saw two holes in the right leg. Both were dark with blood.

"Oh, I'm so sorry. Lucky I didn't aim for your heart—I probably would have hit your head."

He turned the light on my face, almost blinding me. "I think you need to go inside. You're definitely sick again."

"Yeah."

We walked around the fallen garbage can to the gate, then to the front door. I may have felt worse than he did.

"The red light was out," he said, "so I was trying to make sure it was working."

"Huh?"

13

"On your camera."

"Oh, I got new ones. They don't have red lights, but why were you turning it away from the house?"

"Well, when I got up there, it looked like the wind had pushed it down too much. I was just trying to set it back in the right place. We don't want what happened before to happen again."

"No. Definitely not."

We went in the house.

Rosemary was in the kitchen putting dishes away. When she saw Ross, she literally shouted for joy, threw her dishtowel onto the counter and ran and kissed him. Frankly, I was glad to see this, because ever since the fiasco of several years ago, when my first wife was killed and Ross and I blamed Rosemary for it, she seemed to hold a grudge. Evidently, all was forgiven, at least toward Ross.

"Ross! It's so good to—" She stepped back and eyed him. "Are you okay? You look ill."

"No—I just need to get these ball bearings out of my leg."

"*What?*"

He lifted his pant leg, revealing two streams of blood oozing into his sock. One ball had hit him just above the sock, and the other had struck him a little higher, closer to the knee.

Rosemary screamed. "You've been shot? Who did it?"

Ross looked at me.

I looked away.

She saw the wrist rocket, still in my hand.

"Travis!"

A surprising amount of malice was contained in that word.

"I thought he was a prowler."

"So you *shot* him!"

"My bad."

"*What?*"

A pounding of feet on the stairs rattled the house. Ross let his pant leg down, much to my relief, and four children rounded the corner, led by Kevin and Kalley, the oldest.

"Uncle Ross!" they shouted in unison. Kalley ran into his arms and hugged him. Kevin pulled up short and stared at the wrist rocket with stabilizer, counterweight, and fiber optic sight, still dangling from my hand. I really needed to lose that thing. His eyes met mine. "Out hunting?" he asked.

The kid was twelve.

"Yes," Rosemary hissed. "Hunting Ross!"

Lucas and Mia watched the commotion around Ross but didn't really understand it. He had been gone most of their lives, but Kevin and Kalley knew him well. Kalley, my precious twelve-year-old daughter, said, "What? He was hunting Ross?"

Ross pulled up his pant leg again. It couldn't have been orchestrated better if they had practiced the routine for weeks. The children saw the blood, and Kalley looked up at me.

"You *shot* him?"

"I didn't mean to. I just . . ."

Somebody was pulling the wrist rocket out of my hand.

Rosemary.

Somebody else was battering my chest with both hands.

Kalley. "How could you shoot him? You made him bleed!"

I tried to hug her, but she pulled away. Kevin studied the wounds then said, "Man, Dad, those things can kill people."

Lucas, six, and Mia, four, were caught between trying to hug Ross and trying to see his leg better.

Ross attempted some reconciliation. "Your dad didn't mean to shoot me. He's just feeling sick again."

Kevin didn't buy it. "I just hope he doesn't try to *not* shoot us. He'd prob'ly wipe us all out."

The front door opened and Anna came in. Ross's pant leg was still up, exposing the blood, and I decided to surrender to the full brunt of fury.

She came into the kitchen. "Travis, there's a truck in front of the driveway, and you didn't leave enough room for me to park—" She yelped in glee, ran toward Ross, then noticed his leg and put her hands out, as if trying to stop her momentum. "Oh my! What happened?"

"Daddy tried to wipe him out," Kalley said, echoing the sentiments of her twin brother.

Rosemary held the wrist rocket up for Anna's inspection. Anna speared me with new malice.

"You *shot* him?"

I was tired of the question. I was also sick. I had just vomited on my friend. "I don't feel good," I said. "I'm gonna go to lie down." As I trudged to safety in the living room, Kevin said, "What stinks?"

The family cleaned Ross up while loudly examining my inadequacies as a human being. The steel balls had broken the skin but hadn't really entered the flesh, not seriously anyway. As soon as this was discovered, Kevin ran outside with a flashlight, then he came back with two 9mm balls.

"Numbers sixteen and forty-two," he announced, showing them proudly. He had numbered each round with a Sharpie fine point so he could learn which shot had killed which cat, though why this was important, I couldn't fathom.

Ross didn't want to go to the emergency room, which was likely spilling over with fog-victims anyway, so the two women washed and treated his wounds, fawning and cooing all the while. In minutes he was walking as if nothing had happened. On the other hand, I, who actually presented with a chronic disease, nay, *diseases*, was *persona non grata*.

Still on the couch in the living room, I heard Anna ask why Ross was in town in the first place, and not in Utah where he had been living for the last four years.

"Didn't Travis tell you?" he said, surprised. "I'm here so he can help me invest my money. I sold my company."

"What? When?" asked Rosemary.

I opened my eyes, now remembering. Yes, he had told me some days ago that he had sold his company—and yes, I had forgotten. I also remembered that he had mentioned something about coming out here so we could create a customized-tax shelter for him. Because I took the call while driving and not at work, I forgot to put it in my planner, then I forgot altogether. A weighty silence issued from the kitchen, and I sensed more abuse coming. I stopped studying the ceiling and quickly closed my eyes.

"Travis, did you know Ross was coming out?" The voice was assaulting me from somewhere above.

I wanted to feign surprise, but no words came out. I could think of nothing to acquit myself, not even a good old-fashioned lie.

"Travis, sometimes you're so—"

She must have seen our four children watching and learning from her example, which ceased the imprecation.

"Here's your mail," she said. "You forgot to get it again." She flicked some envelopes onto the coffee table and departed. It was my duty to walk across the street to the neighborhood mailbox to get our mail each evening, but of course I was handling burglar duties at the time.

Troubles aplenty.

My stomach had settled, and the pressure in my head, one of my myriad ailments, had receded, so I reached over and picked up the mail. There was a plastic bubble mailer big enough to hold a manuscript, but it felt like it only contained a few papers. It had a return address but no name. I set it down and sorted through the other letters. Nothing of consequence. I closed my eyes again—when I remembered that it was Thursday and I had a stake high council meeting at seven. With heart racing, I checked my watch. It was 6:35. Saying a silent prayer of gratitude for the prompting, I ran upstairs to change my clothes, my stomach somehow maintaining equilibrium.

When I came back down, the family was waiting at the dinner table, but of course I had to leave. I kissed Anna then squeezed Ross's shoulder to say good-bye.

"Ow!" he cried, pulling away.

I was mortified. Had I shot him there too?

"Just kidding." He gave Kevin a wry smile.

"We'll talk when I get back," I said gravely.

I was out the door before the laughter died down.

Chapter 2

A Great Spewing Forth

Ross and I were more like family than friends, which made my shooting him all the worse. Marsha, my first wife, and I had taken him in when he was an orphaned, rowdy teenager. After his parents died, he had lived with his older sister for a time, but that hadn't worked out. With us, he was able to straighten out his life, save some money, and leave on a mission to upstate New York. His mission was interrupted, though, when he was called back to Modesto to answer questions about my first wife's murder, which had happened shortly before he had gone to New York. For a week or so he was a suspect, as was I, but together we were able to track down the killer, who then promptly tried to murder me. If Ross, all six-foot-three and 200 pounds of him hadn't been there, my own children would have been orphans, if they had survived.

Shortly after finishing his mission, he tried to get in BYU Provo. It had been over five years since he'd had a mark on his police record, which consisted only of misdemeanors, so he thought he might have a chance. But before he heard from them, another issue came up. He couldn't discover which of his classes at the local junior college would transfer to BYU. He thought there might be a website that would tell him, but in the end he had to call people at each department at BYU to find out which classes would transfer. In sharing this experience with his friends in the YSA, he found that nearly all of them had suffered the same experience, so he decided to do something about it.

After teaching himself how to write code, he opened a new website and started making hundreds of phone calls around the country to learn which classes transferred to which colleges. It was tedious, mind-numbing work. There are over 2,400 four-year institutions in America, and over 1,600 two-year colleges. Creating nexus points between each of the 4,000 different institutions alone was a monumental challenge. That's 4,000 times 4,000. In other words, 16 million nexus points. Then, learning which classes in each institution transferred to each of the other institutions meant creating a website with literally hundreds of millions of nexus points. And each fact had to be gleaned by calling each department of each school and asking which class transferred to which. He made many enemies of department secretaries, but as he persisted, some department heads began to see the value of his work and tried to help. Fortunately most departments kept lists of which classes they deemed transferrable from local institutions, so they sent that information to Ross, who was quickly overwhelmed with data. To mitigate this, he hired two data-entry people to work at home, and to pay them, he squeezed a member of our ward to get a fairly high-paying job at the Lawrence Livermore Laboratories, about fifty miles away. Then, by living with our family and keeping his expenses to a minimum, he managed to cover his new company's expenses. But he needed more typists. So, seeing his dedication to the project and its potential for success, I invested fifty thousand dollars, which allowed him to hire more typists and a couple of people to make phone calls. Then I persuaded two of my clients to invest another fifty thousand. Each.

He advertised on every college sports discussion board on the internet, and within a few months his website, which was loaded with other people's advertising, began getting some hits. Within six months he was making money. When the original investment ran out a few months later, he seamlessly started paying his employees from the site's income. That was a great day. He was meeting his own expenses. Unfortunately, as the company swelled with employees, he never did make it back to school. Three years later he moved everything to Utah, hoping, perhaps blindly, to find his eternal mate. Instead, he found himself working more hours than ever. The site was getting over a million unique views a month, nearly twenty million total hits a month, and he had to keep hiring people and buying new equipment.

As his company grew, he somehow found time to start dating, and about six months later he was engaged to a beautiful girl who was attending the Y. He was madly in love with her, and she with him, he thought, until she called it off. A missionary she had been waiting for had come home and re-wooed her.

Ross took the blow in stride, sobbing for hours on the phone. He didn't date again for two years. Then, last year, he found another "soul mate." Of course, he took things slower this time, and they almost made it to the altar, but two weeks before the big day he received a text from her. It had come by mistake, having been intended for her best friend, to whom his fiancé boasted of Ross's net worth, his monthly salary, and the credit limits on the platinum cards she expected to have soon.

To my knowledge, he hadn't dated since.

Then last week he sold his company, Dotsee.com (Database of Transferrable Classes) for a little over $10 million. After splitting the profits with his investors and allowing for capital gains taxes, he cleared something over $5 million. Even after tithing, that meant he would have enough to set him up for life if he invested wisely.

And that's where I supposedly came in, if I could just remember anything.

I didn't get home from high council meeting until late, so we met the next morning after family scriptures.

He limped into my home office and took a seat across the desk from me.

"Ross, I'm so sorry about last night. How's it feel?"

"Oh, no problem. Anna and Rosemary fixed me up pretty good."

"But you're still limping."

"Aw—" He waved me off. "How are *you* feeling?"

"Good. Sleep always does wonders." I reached across the desk, and we shook hands. "All right, then, let's get to work."

I asked about his goals and expectations. Did he want growth or income? Did he want conservative or aggressive picks? As we talked, I began thumbing through the previous night's mail. His desires were pretty much what I expected, and before we got very far I presented a plan to him: a new all-weather portfolio I had pioneered for some of my larger clients. Had I started this fifteen years ago, its income would have grown faster than any other investment tool I had. It hedged against all likely environments, including recessions, stock implosions, and even war (as long as we won). I explained how its ten asset classes would protect him in all kinds of inclement weather and even pay him $5,000 a month after taxes. He waved a hand.

"It sounds great, Travis. Just do it."

I stared at him.

"I know you're good at what you do, even when you're sick. And I trust you. So where do I sign?"

"Wait a minute." I put the mail down. "You drove out here to discuss this with me face to face, to learn the liabilities and risks. You have an obligation to yourself to hear all points of view, even to ask around. I'll put you in touch with some other clients who are in this portfolio."

"Naw," he said again. "I just came out to be with you guys. It's been too long. We could've done this on the phone. I just like being here. Heck, I like you guys more than my own brother and sister." He reddened. "Sorry. I shouldn't have said that."

"So, you come out here," I said, maybe a little offended that he wouldn't let me give my whole spiel, "and I shoot your leg all up, and you still trust me?"

"Well, when you put it that way, I guess you could still talk me out of it."

"Great! Okay, listen, I want you to see some of my . . ."

He waved me off again. "C'mon, just make it happen. I've got a few bucks stashed away from my salary, so I don't even need the five grand a month. Why don't you just reinvest that too?"

"No, you'll keep that extra money and like it. You're a young man with expenses."

"Wrong. I'm a young man with *no* expenses, especially if I'm staying with you guys, but, whatever." I was his financial counselor, and I was supposed to counsel, and I hated it when my reputation denied me the fun of making the sale. The fact was, though, this had already proven to be a pretty good portfolio.

"All right," I said, "let's transfer the funds and I'll start placing the buys right away. Here." I gave him a card with my firm's bank information on it. "You can do it now."

He took his phone out. It would take a few minutes, but I was always amazed by how quickly millions of dollars could change hands.

While he was doing that, I picked up the small bubble mailer and opened it. A single typed page fell out with another, smaller manila envelope. It wasn't sealed, so I blew it open and a key and a slip of paper fell out. A client's name was printed at the bottom. I had visited with him a week or so before, but I wasn't expecting anything from him. In our meeting, he had asked about my faith, and I had shared what I thought was appropriate, focusing on my belief in the Book of

Mormon. He had seemed interested at the time but didn't pursue it further. Waiting for Ross to complete the transfer, I began reading:

Dear Travis,

I am writing this because you're the only person I can trust. If you haven't gotten a call from me by the time you receive this, please try to call me. You have the number. If I don't answer, or if I don't get back to you right away, please go to my home. If I'm not there, I'd like you to do something.

Please call my ex-wife, Claudia, and ask her what her maiden name is and where she was born. You will find her number in the little envelope with the key. She will probably give you the information because she always liked you and Marsha. (She still watches Marsha's movies.) I am not writing the information here in case this letter falls into the wrong hands. Then please take the key and the other information I've included (a code) to where it belongs. What you find there should answer your questions and hopefully help you find justice for me.

I know this sounds strange, but if you need to use the key, something very bad has probably happened to me.

By the way, I really liked our talk last week and have been thinking a lot about it. I hope you're right about the Book of Mormon, even if you-know-who doesn't believe it. Wouldn't it be great if something really does exist on the other side?

Keith Nelson

Ross was looking at me. "Something interesting?"

I didn't answer.

"When you sit like that and your eyebrows go in, I know you're focused on something."

I didn't realize until then that I had been leaning forward, almost on the edge of my chair.

"Did you transfer the funds?" I asked.

"Yep, they should be there soon."

"Okay, I'll start making the buys at work. Thanks—and, I'm sorry again for your leg." I stood up.

"Hey, do you want some company today?"

I usually worked alone. "No, but thanks. I guess you're on your own today. Oh, and nice truck out there. Get it in Utah?"

"Yep. They know trucks in Utah."

I casually looked down at the bubble envelope to find a date. The post date was two days ago. I should have opened the letter last night when I saw it. Another mistake.

"Ross, I need to make some calls. Can you give me a minute?"

"Yeah, sure." He glanced at the letter then left.

I called Keith's number. It went to voicemail. I left a message then clicked off.

I looked at the return address on the envelope. It was just a couple of miles away, but I had a busy day planned; after some calls, I had two consultations, one during lunch and one in the afternoon, then I needed to place Ross's funds, which would take some time. I got in my car, a used Lexus, and drove across town. It was still foggy, but it didn't seem as dense as before. Actually, this was late for fog—the middle of February. We usually had daffodils and almond blossoms by now.

I hadn't been to Keith's home before, though I had sent him a number of packages. I was surprised when I parked in front of the yellow and brown stucco single-story home. It had middle class written all over it. Most of my clients were professionals, upper middle class at least. Keith, it appeared, lived frugally. Of course, he did go through a divorce several years ago which must have hit him pretty hard. I walked up to his door, trying to remember the salient facts about him. He had owned two used car lots but sold them and invested the profits in distressed real estate during the recession. To the best of my knowledge, he now made most of his income from about twenty duplexes in a poorer part of town. Over eight years he had invested a total of $75,000 with me. His average annual return on that money had been a little over 11%, which was solid—but we had been helped by a rising market as the country came out of the recession.

The house looked dark. I rang the doorbell.

For some reason I had not only shared my faith in the Church and Book of Mormon with him the week before, I had also mentioned that my wife didn't completely share that faith. He found that interesting. He had known her before I did in her capacity as a rising defense attorney, and he laughed and said she was probably right and that I should listen to her. In my defense, I shared some "proofs" of the Book of Mormon, as I had so many times with Anna. They were mostly literary elements, like chiasms and other Hebraisms in the book that Joseph Smith couldn't have known about. I also told him about the coincidences of Central American myths and Book of Mormon teachings as well as the idea that the American Indians were probably descendants of the ancient Book of Mormon people. Although Keith's interest seemed piqued, he wouldn't accept a challenge to read the book and find out for himself if it were true.

Nobody answered the door. I peeked through a front window. Yep, dark. The driveway was empty. I went around to the side and looked through a partially curtained garage window. No car inside. I went back to the front and tried the door.

Locked.

I went back to my car and pulled the little envelope with the key out of the bubble envelope. On the slip of paper inside was his ex-wife's phone number. I had only met her once, when the two of them needed to sign documents for a joint real estate investment trust. As I recalled, she had asked about Marsha, who had just gone missing at the time. Half the country thought she had run away with a private detective. Her body would be discovered nine months later in a grave by the Stanislaus River.

I dialed the number and waited. After four rings, I left a message saying who I was and that I had something important to discuss with her. She called me back about a minute later.

"Hi, Mister Call. I'm returning your call."

"Please, call me Travis. How are you doing, Claudia?"

"Well, I was doing okay, but now I'm not so sure. What's Keith done now?"

I chuckled. "Well, I'm not sure, but you know I'm still doing some financial planning for him."

"No, but it doesn't surprise me. He always liked you."

"Thank you. So, he sent me a key in a letter, with your phone number, and he told me to ask you a strange question."

"What's that?"

"What's your maiden name—and where you were born?" I didn't feel I had the right to read the letter to her.

"He told you to do that?"

"Yes—I think it has something to do with the key."

"Well, does it look like it could go in a bank, you know, in one of those boxes?"

"Actually it does."

"Okay, I don't know why he's playing games with you, but my maiden name is Wells, and I'm from Fargo, North Dakota, so the key probably goes to a box at Wells Fargo."

"That would make sense."

"Do you know why's he doing this? I mean, why didn't he just tell you himself where the key went?"

"He says he didn't want the information to fall into the wrong hands—if the letter didn't reach me."

There was another pause. "This isn't something to get out of paying alimony, is it? I really need that money each month."

"To tell you the truth, I don't know what this is all about. But I'll make you a promise. If I see him again, I'll ask him what's going on—and I'll ask him to let you know why he wanted me to call you. Is that okay?"

"Of course. But if he's trying to get out of alimony—you know I didn't want to break things up. It wasn't my idea, until he started, you know—"

"Actually, Ms. Nelson, I *don't* know, and I really don't want to know, but I promise, I'll ask him to get back to you if I see him."

"You keep saying 'if.' Has something happened to him?"

"I don't know, but thank you so much for your time, Claudia, and for the information. I'll make sure and have him call you if I can. Good-bye now."

"Okay—good-bye."

I felt bad about the way I left her hanging, but I couldn't go into details without Keith's permission. I put the key back in the envelope and headed downtown. If I hurried, I should be able to get to the bank then make it to the office in time for my phone consultations.

Wells Fargo has several branches in Modesto, so I went to the one closest to his home. I presented the bank manager with the key and code, and presto, she led me into the vault where the safe deposit boxes were kept. The manager inserted her key and turned, and I inserted my key, turned, then I removed the box. She showed me a booth where I could study the contents in private.

What I found inside would change my life forever.

Chapter 3

Killer on the Road

Whislin Klah did not see himself as a bad man. He simply had gifts and skills that led him down a path that most would never understand. The logic was simple: He would do everything necessary to protect himself and his vital interests. He had learned this philosophy at the hands of a short-tempered father, and it had been reinforced in the military, where he served a country that was willing to bomb and destroy to protect its own interests. Pursuing this path had already earned him a degree of independence, and he would not abandon that path now that killing had become—how should he put it—more mercenary.

From the vantage of his black Jeep Wrangler, he waited for Travis Call to exit the bank. He thought he already knew everything Call was about to learn, and probably far more.

After the meeting with Nelson two nights ago at Dry Creek, he had gone to Nelson's home and searched for more artifacts. He found none, but he had found Nelson's laptop computer, still open and running. The man had actually left his computer on, expecting to be back that night. Klah looked at the last open document—a letter to his financial counselor, a man by the name of Travis Call. But the letter had little to do with finances and everything to do with the cave and its relics.

Klah used a set of thumb drives to download the contents of the computer's solid-state drive, including the encryption software Nelson had placed on it. Of course, the encryption software meant nothing, since the computer had been left on, with all its files fully exposed.

After assuring himself that no more artifacts were in the house, Klah took the computer to his room at a motel in Stockton, thirty miles to the north. No need to leave clues of his presence by staying in the same town where Nelson had died. He spent the rest of the night familiarizing himself with Nelson's computer activity, which included numerous visits to Kinkaid-related websites. In Nelson's second letter to Call, he also saw that Nelson referred to an old letter from Ephraim Wells. He searched the scanned downloads for a copy of it and found what he was looking for.

He searched the text of the scanned letter for clues as to how Nelson had found the cave. But no clues were there. Disappointing. Somehow Nelson had found a cave that had remained closed up for over a hundred years.

He called his contact at the Society and received instructions for the artifacts. He was to carefully package them and overnight them to his contact, then start monitoring Call. Klah said he would ship the parcel but that the surveillance wasn't part of the job. He had obtained the relics and, of course dispatched Nelson, which was already more than he had agreed to do. They negotiated until Klah finally agreed to monitor Call for up to two weeks, for an extra $25,000, unless Call went to the canyon, at which time the payment would increase to $50,000.

Though it was unsaid, both parties knew that much of the payment was for his continued silence, but even with that, Klah was getting an idea of just how desperate the Society was to close the matter.

Call came out of the bank, and Klah saw him blink against the sun, which had made a brief appearance. Call walked to his car, holding a sheaf of papers. The papers had not been in his hands when he went in, but Klah was almost sure that he knew what was in them. Of course, he would verify that later.

Chapter 4

A Cry From the Dead

Still going through the box in the bank's private room, I found a large envelope with my name on it, and under that I found a yellowed letter in cursive handwriting. Under that I found several printed pages from the internet. I opened the envelope and found a four-page typed letter meant for me.

Dear Travis,

This is going to sound strange, but if you are reading this, something bad has happened.

About five years ago my wife, I mean my ex-wife, inherited a bunch of stuff from her uncle. There wasn't anything valuable in it (you know me—always looking out for number 1). But there was a bunch of old books that we put on the shelf. Well when Claudia left me, she left those books too, and about six months ago I looked at them to see if I could get any money from them down at Yesterday's Bookstore—you know that bookstore? I figured ten or twenty bucks was better than nothing. I still don't know if they're worth anything, cause when I went through them an old letter fell out. It wasn't from Claudia's uncle, it was from <u>his</u> great uncle, a guy named Ephraim George Wells, and it was to his brother, Grant Wells. I had never heard of them before. I'm including it so you can read it for yourself.

It turns out that Claudia's great, great Uncle Ephraim was a miner from Idaho, and he took a trip down the Colorado River—he was like the second guy to do it and survive. Anyway, when he was going down the river in the Grand Canyon, he saw a cave up on one of the walls, and he climbed up there and went in.

Inside it he found a bunch of mummies and jewelry and other stuff. Pretty amazing.

Then he died.

No, wait, before that, he gave two interviews to a newspaper about the cave. The newspaper was in Phoenix.

(Sorry, this is getting kind of confusing—but hold on, it gets more interesting.)

So, anyway, great, great Uncle Ephraim found this amazing cave with all this stuff, and he told somebody back East about it and he even sent some of the stuff he found to the Smithsonian, and they came running out and made him show them where it was. So he took them up there, and the guy he showed the stuff to, (Something-something Jordan) started crying when he saw it, I guess, and they brought out a team of experts at digging those things up, only you don't need to dig them up cause they're only on the ground inside this cave, but the cave is kind of hidden and it's really hard to climb up to. But anyway, this team goes in there and starts hauling stuff out.

And that's when the problems started. Everybody today thinks this cave is a big hoax. They think a hundred years ago the newspaper just made up the story to gin up sales, but it's not a hoax. I followed the directions in the letter and found it myself.

Course, it about killed me, but I found the cave.

Only it's closed off. And just so you know, that whole part of the Grand Canyon is closed off. Nobody's supposed to go in there. Not even the rangers. But I snuck in cause I knew where to go, and believe me, it's really hard to get up to. And then when I got in the cave by the side way, just about everything was gone. BUT NOT EVERYTHING.

In the margin to the right of this, Keith had written in ink: "Closed off. Duct south of cave. Back of Well's Letter."

And here's the bad part. I took some of the stuff I found. I opened a mummy and found some beautiful jewelry, and got out, which was kind of hard cause that air duct is really narrow, and it loops up and down.

I don't have a wife anymore, and no pretty women want to date me, so what good is an old headband and necklace and bracelet gonna do me?

So I tried to sell it. They really are beautiful and have all kinds of gold and jewels in them, so I figured somebody somewhere would be willing to pay a lot of money. I know it's against the law—and I'm only telling you this because of two things: First, I know I can trust you, and 2, you said the Book of Mormon was written by Indians, so maybe that's who these mummies are? I don't know, but if they are, maybe they can prove that the Book of Mormon is true, ha-ha. What I do know is that old Ephraim thought these things were from Egypt, and I have to admit that some of the writing on the walls looks Egyptian, but the mummies and the jewelry look more Native American if you ask me.

Anyway, I know it's probably against the law to take stuff from the Grand Canyon, so I went on the dark web—you know what that is? And I found a possible buyer. It was really hard, because most of the people on the dark web don't want to be found by normal people like me, and it cost me a lot of money just to find the guy (I had to get a "consultant"), and then I lost $5,000 when the first guy I found blackmailed me and said he was going to turn me over to ICE, but he didn't know my name, so when I said I wasn't going to pay any more money, he sent a Trojan horse to my computer and fried it. Totally fried it. So I bought a new computer and got some encryption software and I went back on the dark web by myself and this time I found a legitimate buyer. At least I think he's legitimate. He says he's going to pay me 100 grand for the stuff—if I give him exact directions to the cave. But here's the deal, he's being very evasive and keeps changing what he wants me to do, and now he wants to meet me alone. He thinks I might be ICE or something, and he won't believe anything I say except that I have the jewelry and know where the cave is——cause I sent him pictures of everything.

I don't want to meet him alone. But I don't know what else to do, cause nobody else has offered to buy it, even on the dark web.

And that's why I'm telling you: Because if something happens to me, if, like, I'm suddenly GONE, I want you to do something for me.

I'm supposed to meet the guy tonight, so if you're reading this, that means I didn't get back to empty the box—or answer your phone call.

Oh wow, this is really getting weird!

But a hundred grand is a hundred grand.

Now you know that I committed a crime, but that probably doesn't matter so much. Besides, you don't really have any proof, except what I said here! And anyway, aren't you my counselor? Don't you have some kind of legal obligation to keep my information confidential?

When you read the other stuff inside the deposit box, you'll understand how big this is and maybe why someone would want to do something to me. So, if I'm gone, I'm asking you to figure out what happened. I don't know how you'll do it, cause I don't even know who the guy is, but I know you solved your wife's murder when the cops couldn't. And I know you really believe in the Book of Mormon, and maybe these mummies are from that time?

But listen, if you read this and it turns out that I'm okay, don't tell the cops and I'll give you a huge percent of the profits, maybe even 50%. But I'm going to try really hard to get back and answer your phone call and empty this box before you find out! Ha-ha!

Okay, I'm talking to myself now and this is really getting creepy, so—so long!

Good luck & Thanks,

Keith Nelson

I stared at the last few lines—it was definitely getting kind of creepy. I put the letter back in the envelope and lifted the other papers out of the box. As I did so, three 4x6 photographs fell out. The first was a picture of a side of a mountain, taken from a river—the Colorado I assumed. A long, winding ravine rose steeply from the river toward red vertical cliffs hundreds if not a thousand feet high. Above the immense red cliffs a pale blue sky hung above the canyon rim.

I picked up the next picture. It was of a vertical wall made up of hundreds of light-colored rocks and boulders. It appeared to be manmade and seemed to conform to the dimensions of a large cave's mouth. I turned it over. It said: "Kinkaid's (Ephraim's) cave. Sealed shut now." Whoever had sealed the cave had used boulders that must have weighed over a hundred pounds and cemented them with smaller rocks and mortar. I estimated the cave was maybe a dozen feet tall and about the same width.

I picked up the last picture. It was of a smaller hole in the cliff, maybe two feet in diameter. I turned the picture over. It said: "Air duct? South of cave. Tore some brush away."

I flipped the picture back over and noticed a thick, sturdy bush growing horizontally out of the pinkish rock, just left of the air duct. Part of it appeared to have been pulled away to allow access to the hole. So this is how he had entered the cave. I visualized Keith's short, slender frame and could see how he might slither into the narrow hole, but I doubted a larger man could do it. But more than that, I wondered how he had scaled the mountain to get up there.

I looked at the papers again. There appeared to be two sets, one was the old letter he had mentioned, definitely in cursive and probably from Ephraim Wells, and the rest was a small sheaf of papers printed from the internet. I looked at these first.

There were two articles. One was a single page about an article in the "Arizona Gazette" dated March 12, 1909. The other was a much longer article. I looked at my watch and saw that I had already been in the bank nearly half an hour. Perhaps it was the excitement from last night, but I found myself feeling a little weak. I closed the empty box and gathered up the papers and got the attention of the bank manager. She put the empty box back in its place, then I got my key and left the bank. Ten minutes later I was alone in my office, where I spread the letter and photos on a table. Then I lay down on the leather couch, with the two articles in my hand.

What had Keith gotten himself into? Who steals ancient relics from the Grand Canyon and tries to sell them on the internet? And who shares all this with his financial counselor, who does *not* have the legal privileges of an attorney? Yes, I had signed a nondisclosure agreement with him, as I did with every client, but that didn't shield him from legal consequences if he informed me of criminal actions. But then again, as he had said, I only had his letter as evidence. Maybe he had thought better of the whole thing. Maybe he was in the Grand Canyon right now replacing the booty. Maybe he was down at Captain Johnson's office, a certain officer of the law with whom I'd had some dealings, coming clean at this very moment. I wouldn't breach my contract with Keith until I knew more. A lot more.

The first article was a short piece from the *Arizona Gazette*.

ARIZONA GAZETTE - MARCH 12, 1909

G.E. KINCAID REACHES YUMA

G. E. Kincaid of Lewiston, Idaho, arrived in Yuma after a trip from Green River, Wyoming, down the entire course of the Colorado River. He is the second man to make this journey and came alone in a small skiff, stopping at his pleasure to investigate the surrounding country. He left Green River in October having a small covered boat with oars, and carrying a fine camera, with which he secured over 700 views of the river and canyons which were unsurpassed. Mr. Kincaid says one of the most interesting features of the trip was passing through the sluiceways at Laguna dam. He made this perilous passage with only the loss of an oar.

Some interesting archaeological discoveries were unearthed and altogether the trip was of such interest that he will repeat it next winter in the company of friends.

I wasn't sure what to make of this. The article mentioned "some interesting archaeological discoveries." It also mentioned that he planned to take another trip the following winter. I would have liked seeing some of the 700 "views" of the river, and especially of the artifacts he discovered, but none of them were published. I turned to the next article, which was much longer. The editors at the Gazette seemed more excited by the story now.

EXPLORATIONS IN GRAND CANYON

Mysteries of Immense Rich Cavern being brought to light

JORDAN IS ENTHUSED
Remarkable finds indicate ancient people migrated from Orient

The latest news of the progress of the explorations of what is now regarded by scientists as not only the oldest archaeological discovery in the United States, but one of the most valuable in the world, which was mentioned some time ago in the Gazette, was brought to the city yesterday by G.E. Kinkaid, the explorer who found the great underground citadel of the Grand Canyon during a trip from Green River, Wyoming, down the Colorado, in a wooden boat, to Yuma, several months ago.

According to the story related to the Gazette by Mr. Kinkaid, the archaeologists of the Smithsonian Institute, which is financing the expeditions, have made discoveries which almost conclusively prove that the race which inhabited this mysterious cavern, hewn in solid rock by human hands, was of oriental origin, possibly from Egypt, tracing back to Ramses. If their theories are borne out by the translation of the tablets engraved with hieroglyphics, the mystery of the prehistoric peoples of North America, their ancient arts, who they were and whence they came, will be solved. Egypt and the Nile, and Arizona and the Colorado will be linked by a historical chain running back to ages which staggers the wildest fancy of the fictionist.

A Thorough Examination
Under the direction of Prof. S. A.

Jordan, the Smithsonian Institute is now prosecuting the most thorough explorations, which will be continued until the last link in the chain is forged. Nearly a mile underground, about 1480 feet below the surface, the long main passage has been delved into, to find another mammoth chamber from which radiates scores of passageways, like the spokes of a wheel.

Several hundred rooms have been discovered, reached by passageways running from the main passage, one of them having been explored for 854 feet and another 634 feet. The recent finds include articles which have never been known as native to this country, and doubtless they had their origin in the orient. War weapons, copper instruments, sharp-edged and hard as steel, indicate the high state of civilization reached by these strange people. So interested have the scientists become that preparations are being made to equip the camp for extensive studies, and the force will be increased to thirty or forty persons.

Mr. Kinkaid's Report
Mr. Kinkaid was the first white child born in Idaho and has been an explorer and hunter all his life, thirty years having been in the service of the Smithsonian Institute. Even briefly recounted, his history sounds fabulous, almost grotesque.

"First, I would impress that the cavern is nearly inaccessible. The entrance is 1,486 feet down the sheer canyon wall. It is located on government land and no visitor will be allowed there under penalty of trespass. The scientists wish to work unmolested, without fear of archaeological discoveries being disturbed by curio or relic hunters. A trip there would be fruitless, and the visitor would be sent on his y. The story of how I found the cavern has been related, but in a paragraph: I was journeying down the Colorado river in a boat, alone, looking for mineral. Some forty-two miles up the river from the El Tovar Crystal canyon, I saw on the east wall, stains in the sedimentary formation about 2,000 feet above the river bed. There was no trail to this point, but I finally reached it with great difficulty.

Above a shelf which hid it from view from the river, was the mouth of the cave. There are steps leading from this entrance some thirty yards to what was, at the time the cavern was inhabited, the level of the river. When I saw the chisel marks on the wall inside the entrance, I became interested, securing my gun and went in. During that trip I went back several hundred feet along the main passage till I came to the crypt in which I discovered the mummies. One of these I stood up and photographed by flashlight. I gathered a number of relics, which I carried down the Colorado to Yuma, from whence I shipped them to Washington with details of the discovery. Following this, the explorations were undertaken.

The Passages

"The main passageway is about 12 feet wide, narrowing to nine feet toward the farther end. About 57 feet from the entrance, the first side-passages branch off to the right and left, along which, on both sides, are a number of rooms about the size of ordinary living rooms of today, though some are 30 by 40 feet square. These are entered by oval-shaped doors and are ventilated by round air spaces through the walls into the passages. The walls are about three feet six inches in thickness.

The passages are chiseled or hewn as straight as could be laid out by an engineer. The ceilings of many of the rooms converge to a center. The side-passages near the entrance run at a sharp angle from the main hall, but toward the rear they gradually reach a right angle in direction.

The Shrine

"Over a hundred feet from the entrance is the cross-hall, several hundred feet long, in which are found the idol, or image, of the people's god, sitting cross-legged, with a lotus flower or lily in each hand. The cast of the face is oriental, and the carving this cavern . . . [an apparent misprint]. The idol almost resembles Buddha, though the scientists are not certain as to what religious worship it represents. Taking into consideration everything found thus far, it is possible that this worship most resembles the ancient people of Tibet.

Surrounding this idol are smaller images, some very beautiful in form; others crooked-necked and distorted shapes, symbolical, probably, of good and evil. There are two large cactus with protruding arms, one on each side of the dais on which the god squats. All this is carved out of hard rock resembling marble. In the opposite corner of this cross-hall were found tools of all descriptions, made of copper. These people undoubtedly knew the lost art of hardening this metal, which has been sought by chemicals for centuries without result. On a bench running around the workroom was some charcoal and other material probably used in the process. There is also slag and stuff similar to matte, showing that these ancients smelted ores, but so far no trace of where or how this was done has been discovered, nor the origin of the ore.

"Among the other finds are vases or urns and cups of copper and gold, made very artistic in design. The pottery work includes enamelled ware and glazed vessels. Another passageway leads to granaries such as are found in the oriental temples. They contain seeds of various kinds. One very large storehouse has not yet been entered, as it is twelve feet high and can be reached only from above. Two copper hooks extend on the edge, which indicates that some sort of ladder was attached. These granaries are rounded, as the materials of which they are constructed, I think, is a very hard cement. A gray metal is also found in this cavern, which puzzles the scientists, for its identity has not been established. It resembles platinum. Strewn promiscuously over the floor everywhere are what people call "cats eyes", a yellow stone of no great value. Each one is engraved with the head of the Malay type.

The Hieroglyphics

"On all the urns, or walls over doorways, and tablets of stone which were found by the image are the mysterious hieroglyphics, the key to which the Smithsonian Institute hopes yet to discover. The engraving on the tables probably has something to do with the religion of the people. Similar hieroglyphics have been found in southern Arizona. Among the pictorial writings, only two animals are found. One is of prehistoric type.

The Crypt

"The tomb or crypt in which the mummies were found is one of the largest of the chambers, the walls slanting back at an angle of about 35 degrees. On these are tiers of mummies, each one occupying a separate hewn shelf. At the head of each is a small bench, on which is found copper cups and pieces of broken swords. Some of the mummies are covered with clay, and all are wrapped in a bark fabric.

The urns or cups on the lower tiers are crude, while as the higher shelves are reached, the urns are finer in design, showing a later stage of civilization. It is worthy of note that all the mummies examined so far have proved to be male, no children or females being buried here. This leads to the belief that this exterior section was the warriors' barracks.

"Among the discoveries no bones of animals have been found, no skins, no clothing, no bedding. Many of the rooms are bare but for water vessels. One room, about 40 by 700 feet, was probably the main dining hall, for cooking utensils are found here. What these people lived on is a problem, though it is presumed that they came south in the winter and farmed in the valleys, going back north in the summer.

Upwards of 50,000 people could have lived in the caverns comfortably. One theory is that the present Indian tribes found in Arizona are descendants of the serfs or slaves of the people which inhabited the cave. Undoubtedly a good many thousands of years before the Christian era, a people lived here which reached a high stage of civilization. The chronology of human history is full of gaps. Professor Jordan is much enthused over the discoveries and believes that the find will prove of incalculable value in archaeological work.

"One thing I have not spoken of, may be of interest. There is one chamber of the passageway to which is not ventilated, and when we approached it a deadly, snaky smell struck us. Our light would not penetrate the gloom, and until stronger ones are available we will not know what the chamber contains. Some say snakes, but others boo-hoo this idea and think it may contain a deadly gas or chemicals used by the ancients. No sounds are heard, but it smells snaky just the same. The whole underground installation gives one of shaky nerves the creeps. The gloom is like a weight on one's shoulders, and our flashlights and candles only make the darkness blacker. Imagination can revel in conjectures and ungodly daydreams back through the ages that have elapsed till the mind reels dizzily in space."

I lay the papers on the floor and closed my eyes. My mind was working in two ways at once: first, trying to dismiss these articles as a hoax, and second, not being able to do so because Keith said he'd actually been to this place.

Unless he was pulling some kind of hoax on me.

I wouldn't put it past him. He was a successful businessman, but his reputation left something to be desired. Some people I knew had made it a point *not* to purchase cars from him when he had his car lots, and now some called him a slumlord. He didn't have many friends that I knew of, and if I remembered right, his daughter had moved back east and rarely communicated with him. Yes, Keith had shown some interest in the Church the other night, but maybe he had ulterior motives, an angle that would enrich him while manipulating me.

I imagined a possible scheme: He goes missing after purporting to have found a lost treasure, a treasure that somebody wants to kill him for. Of course there is no evidence for this except the fact that he is gone and that his letters support this. But look at the origin of the main letter. I found it in his safe deposit box, making me, of course, his only "witness" of this fact. And then, consider the letter his ex-wife's great, great uncle wrote—a letter his ex-wife never saw. It appeared to be old, but old paper and ink can be purchased if you are willing to pay for it. And then, consider the pictures "he" took. Everything I have, all the possible evidence of an evil plot, came from his safe deposit box, to which I seemed to have the only key. This is very interesting, of course, but then nothing can be proved against me, because so far, no crime has been confirmed. Then, perhaps a year or so later, the IRS uncovers another scheme, a greater scheme, one of hidden assets and double books in Keith Nelson's portfolio, and the authorities rightly come back to me. What was my role in helping him disappear back then? Didn't I meet with him a week before his disappearance? What did I know and when did I know it? All the evidence would show that I was the last person to communicate with him, even to have opened his safe deposit box. And as far as that went, how did I get my name on the list of people approved to gain access to his box? When the investigation is over, maybe I look like the bad guy who was after him all along, since all roads seem to lead to Travis Call, erstwhile financial counselor, current murder suspect.

Redux.

I needed to be careful here.

I picked up the old, yellowed letter from great, great Uncle Ephraim, aka G.E. Kinkaid, or Kincaid (depending on which Gazette article you referenced). The handwriting coursed across the page in long, florid strokes in faded black ink that had feathered out, apparently with age. The paper was soft, crumbly, and had a musty smell. If it was a forgery, it was a good one.

April 16 1909
Phoenix, Arizona

To Grant Wells
Salt Lake City, Utah

My Dear Brother, Grant,

Please forgive me for not writing sooner. As you will see, I have been busy. Remember the expedition I launched myself upon last fall to discover new deposits of ore? I followed the Green River down to the Colorado and thence to the great canyon. While there, I spied the mouth of a cave far above the river just after a set of rapids. I beached my vessel to allow a time to rest. Thinking the cave might be the entrance to a Spanish mine, I climbed the slope, with much difficulty, until I came to a set of chiseled steps, which led me to the entrance of a cave.

And dear brother what I found there defies all description! Many ancient artifacts lay in the cavern, which was vast beyond all description. Whoever chiseled this cave must have used hardened tools of the finest steel. I found a cavern of mummies set upon three tiers of shelves, which lay back in a near reclining position. Inside one of the mummies I found a handful of ancient relics, which I removed to show the proper authorities. These included jewels of the greatest value. I also found a large statue of a strange deity carved out of stone. It seemed to be oriental in nature. But the hieroglyphics on the walls around it appeared to be of Egyptian origin.

As I said, I took some of the relics (unfortunately, as I could not take any images with my camera inside because of the awkwardness of carrying the camera up the slope, which by my calculations was some 2,000 feet above the river.) I took the relics down the slope and proceeded to navigate my vessel to Yuma. From thence, I mailed the relics in a parcel, with a letter of explanation, to the Smithsonian Institution in Washington, D.C. Then I went hunting ore in the district until receiving a response, which occurred in good time.

They said they were sending a Professor by the name of Sterling Jordan to the Grand Canyon railhead, and they asked if I could be there to join him to explore the cave. I replied that I would be honored and I traveled back to the plateau. He is (was?) a fine man, and I took an instant liking to him. We traveled by foot down into the great canyon and from thence up to the cavern. I had to help him by the hand up many parts of the very steep slope.

When he saw the artifacts inside and the mummies propped on their shelves, he wept copious tears and fell to his knees. (I thought we were praying to the Almighty and I dropped to the dirt as well, but, alas, he was only weeping in gratitude that such things existed.) He said that never had so great a find been discovered in all of North America. In his joy he suggested we call it the Wells Cave. I declined but very much appreciated his offer.

We took what artifacts we could safely carry and descended to the river and from thence to the Little Colorado and thence by trail up to the rim where a team was waiting for us. We then went back to the rail head where he shipped the artifacts to his superiors at the Institution.

I am sorry for the length of this letter, but I feel I must explain these things before you will take seriously the remainder of my report.

A month ago an exploration team arrived from Washington, and a person named Fletcher Winn swore us to secrecy. It was not a blood oath; however we were told to never reveal any parcel of the discovery to anyone, or our lives would be forfeit. We swore to "protect the knowledge of this site and its sacred treasures until such time as the President deems fit to promulgate its existence." The President, of course, is President Taft! Even my new friend, Jordan, had to take the oath, for which, I believe, he was very displeased.

Of course now I am telling you, but I believe I am justified in breaking my oath.

Fletcher Winn presided over the site and set about cleaning the cave out. He and his team of about 20 men constructed a narrow-gauge railway on the east plateau and began lifting artifacts out of the cave by rope to the rim, and from thence via the new railway to the main railroad at the Canyon village. They were destined, I believed, for the Smithsonian.

Several days after the shipments began, we were visited by a host of Indians—Hopis—who were bearing rifles and other arms. I counted over 100 of them on horses and burros. It was a frightful moment. I have always found the Hopi to be peaceful (it's the Navajo and Apache one must watch out for—along with the Utes), but this contingent was most exercised and demanded that we cease our activities. We had arms, but they were not available to us as we had been surprised by this "raid."

They claimed ownership of the cave and said it was where they first came from the Mother (Earth). Their great leaders and warriors from many generations are buried there (the mummies) and they called the place the Cave of the Dead.

Under the circumstances, Winn was obliged to agree to their terms, which obligated us to not touch the dead or anything in the room where they were found. But we had already confiscated most of the other artifacts, including the great statue, and were only waiting for the small train to come back before we brought the mummies to the surface. Their arrival (the Indians) probably saved their dead from being removed.

However, I had learned something beforehand that greatly disturbed me. On the previous shipment, I saw the trunks waiting for lading (which I was probably not authorized to see), and the address on them was not the Smithsonian Institution or anywhere else in Washington. They were being shipped to a place in New Haven, Connecticut. I memorized the address and soon after saw Sterling (my professor friend) and asked him about this. He said most soberly that he feared these precious relics were going to "feather someone's nest", and not to enrich the People. He was near tears when he spoke. He does not work for the Institution, but he does work for Secretary Walcott on special projects, and he was sick at heart for this loss—or probable loss. He said that our oaths were not to protect the "sacred treasures", but to protect "somebody's skin", maybe Winn's or somebody else's. I asked him if the President was involved in this theft, but he said it was his sense that Winn had been appointed by somebody under the President to see to this, probably a man named Grandin or Grander or some such. He believes the President to be a good honorable man.

Well, he may be a good honorable man, but he is blind, and the People are getting stolen blind. So I did something about it, and that is why I am writing this long tome to you. (My hand is sore, so I will take a rest but will come back forthwith.)

(I am back.) About two weeks ago I left the site and traveled to Phoenix on the train and spoke to a man at the newspaper that I had met previous, and he was only too happy to take my report again. (I had given him a report previous, after my first trip down the river.) Well, I spilled the beans, as they say—only I didn't mention any shenanigans. I only told about the cave and the artifacts and that men were excavating the cave with Professor Jordan. I didn't want to get anybody killed. But I hoped the newspaper people would get the word out and somebody would track down all the artifacts back East and get them into the museum in Washington. Since I made an oath, I didn't use my own name, but only my initials, E.G., which I transposed, and the name of my best friend in Lewiston—you remember him, Tommy Kinkaid. Only, when I saw the newspaper the next morning, I saw that I must have slipped and used the professor's name: "Jordan." I only meant to say "S.A.," but Jordan must have slipped from my tongue.

And now he is missing. The paper went all around the state, and I suppose Winn saw it and wanted to know who spilled the beans. Well, he must have seen the professor's name in the story, and maybe he figured the professor broke his oath. And now I heard from a man who just came down from the canyon that the professor is gone.

I am grieving for this, for I was a fool and broke my oath and perhaps caused a good man to die. But now I am feeling a concern for my own skin, and that is why I wrote this. If I suddenly turn up at your door, you will know why. And if I don't show up, ever, and if you never hear from me again, you will know that I am a lost soul— dead and lost for breaking my oath and getting a good man killed.

For now I think I will get myself down to Yuma, where my skiff is, and lay low. I have a little gold in the bank there, and will try to make do.

Many thanks for reading this. I didn't know I had a "book" in me. Maybe I missed my true office.

Your brother,
Ephraim Wells

On the front page in the right margin were two notes, written in a different hand:

> Inquired authorities
> at Phoenix
> "No work at canyon."
> 7/13/1909

Inquired at Smithsonian
No record of "Winn."
Sterling A. Jordan "left position."
8/2/1909

Eph. still "laying low"—or missing.
8/22/1909

I assumed these notes had been made by the brother, Grant. He had evidently made inquiries of the authorities and turned up nothing about Fletcher Winn or S.A. Jordan, or even about any "work" being done at the Grand Canyon. It appeared he had come up with dead ends.

I turned the last page over and saw more handwriting on the back: "Mouth sealed—South duct?"

I assumed "mouth" meant the mouth of the cave. From Grant's notes in the margin, however, it appeared that Grant had not gone to the canyon himself, but had simply relied on the "authorities" for the information he received.

Still reclining on the couch, I set everything on the floor and stared at the ceiling. After reading the letter, I couldn't see how this was a set-up. I supposed I could have the paper and ink tested for authenticity, but the fact that Ephraim, aka G.E. Kinkaid, had written it just days after the last Gazette article was published seemed to indicate that both articles, the one in March 1909 and the one a month later, were based on actual interviews. And therefore, unless Ephraim Wells had been lying about everything, there might be an actual cave in the Grand Canyon that, according to Keith Nelson, still harbored mummies and other artifacts. And if that were the case, then the three photos he included were probably authentic, as, probably, were his concerns for his safety.

My ears began buzzing, a common symptom when I became fatigued. I closed my eyes and tried to clear my mind.

For people with memory problems this is a surprisingly easy task.

My cell phone rang.

"Hey," Ross said, "just thought I'd check in. How's the buying going?"

"Well, to tell you the truth, I was just about to get on that."

Silence.

"Sorry, Ross, I've had a busy morning. But don't worry, the prices in these asset classes don't fluctuate much on a daily basis. You'll be fine. I'll let you know how it went when I get home."

"Okay. Sorry I bothered you."

"No bother. See you soon."

I had no sooner hung up when another client called on my office phone. I got up and answered it. Back to work. By the time I had finished that call and conducted a new-client phone interview, it was time for my lunch meeting. It ended up being more involved than expected, and I got back late. I managed to place five orders for Ross back East before markets closed at 2 p.m. Pacific Time. Hopefully, I could place the other five in the morning. When I finished, I saw the papers and three photos still lying on the table.

I called Keith again.

No answer.

I made copies of everything then spent the rest of the afternoon researching the Kinkaid story online. It had some believers, some disbelievers, but no finders, except, evidently, my friend Keith. Could he really have found it? If not, could he have fabricated all this?

When I left the building at five, I was surprised to see a mostly clear sky and a beautiful sunset over the Coast Range Mountains. I took my jacket off. Somehow spring had arrived between noon and five. I smiled, knowing how fast it could warm up in the valley. Summer might even appear next week.

I drove back to Keith's house. It was dark. Still no car in the driveway or garage. I knew I might have to call the police at some point. I wasn't anxious to visit with my old nemesis, Captain Johnson, again, but this was starting to seem serious.

Chapter 5

A Search for Truth and Wisdom

At home, a strange car was parked behind Ross's truck. I pulled into the garage and closed the door. Inside, I heard voices. After eight years of no contact with Captain Marcus Johnson, I was surprised at how quickly I identified his gruff voice. In our previous encounters he had been a lieutenant, but news reports indicated a promotion some years ago. Carrying a briefcase with the Keith Nelson documents and my unfinished homework inside, I entered the living room and found Anna on the love seat, phone in hand. Ross and Johnson sat on the chairs, forming a triangle with her.

"Hi, Honey," Anna said, standing up. She gave me a kiss. "I was just about to call you. An old friend just showed up."

Anna is about five-six, blond, blue-eyed, and exudes femininity. Somehow, though, she had acquired the ability to combine a Nordic chill with the warmest smile. When that chill comes my way, I want to head for the tropics.

"Good evening, Captain," I said. "It's good to see you again."

"Just when you think you'll never see somebody again," he said, "the opportunity just seems to come a'knockin'."

I set my briefcase and jacket down. "And what opportunity brings you here this time?"

I casually glanced around for my four children, but they were gone. Rosemary must have taken them upstairs. After the fiasco of eight years ago, when Johnson headed the investigation and at one point actually took Rosemary downtown for questioning, because of evidence I gave, I wouldn't have been surprised if she *had* absconded with the two kids we had at the time. I sat next to Anna.

"Actually," Johnson said, "I was hoping to speak with you in private." The captain was at least six-four, compactly built, and now, I discovered, was completely bald. The years had also contorted his face into a perpetual scowl. When he offered to take our conversation to a private setting, I was ready to jump up and run to the office. But Anna spoke first. "Oh, don't mind us. We're all family here. Right, Ross?"

"Well," Ross said, surprised, "I like to think so."

Yes, Ross was family, despite the fact that he hadn't lived with us in years.

"Besides," Anna added, "if Travis has a problem, then I have a problem, right? Since I've been his personal attorney for, how long is it now, Travis?"

"Seven years. No, eight."

"Well, seven years since we got married," she countered, "but, yes, I've been his attorney for eight years. So, maybe I should just stick around."

"So what can I do for you, Captain?" I asked.

He decided to go ahead. "After the fog lifted earlier today, we received a phone call, anonymous of course, reporting a body in the river under the Seventh Street Bridge. Our guys went down and fished it out. It had been snagged on a concrete piling, apparently for a couple of days. We're doing forensics to positively ID the body, but we already know who it is. I was just wondering if you, perhaps, might hazard a guess as well."

"Why do you ask me?" I said, having already done the math.

"He was a middle-aged man," Johnson continued, "and his wallet was still in his pocket, full of cash, so we know it wasn't a robbery. But of course he might not have been killed at all—he might have just fallen in—an accident. We only found two wounds, a bruise on his jaw and on his right shin. After we ID'ed him, we made a call to his closest kin—a daughter in Virginia. And shortly after our call, evidently, she called her mother, the victim's ex-wife, and gave her the bad news. And it turns out she, the ex-wife, lives in Fargo, North Dakota. Love the movie. Well, about two minutes later she called my office. And we had a very interesting conversation."

I was studying intricate designs cut into the rug at my feet, the complex patterns almost making my head spin. I looked up into Johnson's eyes. "Keith Nelson."

His great, bald head nodded. "You know what? I just *knew* you were going to say that. It's good to be on the same page with you again, Travis. Just like old times, isn't it?"

I felt Anna slide over to the other side of the world. When I glanced over, her eyes were conducting an inquisition of my soul.

"Travis?"

"Now, *see*?" Johnson interrupted. "That's what concerns me. If you were really his attorney, I don't think you would be asking him for an explanation right here in front of me. His real lawyer would be saying something like, 'That's all we have to say, Captain! Travis, not another word!' Or am I mistaken?"

Anna almost seemed to shrink—possibly for the first time in her life. "No, you're not mistaken. Thank you." She turned to me. "Travis, is there any reason we should let this continue?"

I thought about it. I knew exactly what information Johnson had, I thought, and though it might appear incriminating on the surface, it could actually be exonerating once somebody took time to understand it. I smiled. Not a care in the world. "There's no problem. Actually, it's all very simple."

They stared at me, waiting for my simple explanation, as I tried to organize it amid the swirling thoughts of the Grand Canyon, mummies, and a possible murder or two a hundred years ago.

"Well, I got a letter from him . . ."

"A letter?" Johnson asked. "And when was that?"

It seemed like a week ago. "Yesterday. But I only opened it this morning."

I paused, trying to verify this fact. It really did seem like last week.

"Okay, he sent you a letter. What was in it?"

I opened my briefcase and pulled out the single-page note. "This." I rummaged through the briefcase again and found the key to the safe deposit box. "And this."

Johnson came over, stepping around the coffee table. "May I?" He held out his hand.

I handed him the note and key. Standing before me, he read the note silently, then he looked more closely at the key.

"This looks like it goes to a safe deposit box."

"It does."

"And have you gone there and opened it?"

"Yes."

"All right, now I'm going to do what I should have done earlier. Is there a place where we can speak in private?" He turned to Anna. "Counselor, you're invited to join us if Mr. Call wishes. I seem to remember a nice office down the hall."

I closed my briefcase and stood up, and the three of us abandoned Ross, who remained motionless and silent.

In the office, the captain allowed Anna to read Keith's note.

"I read it this morning," I said. "I called Keith, but he didn't answer. So I went over to his house. He wasn't there, so I went back to my car and called Claudia, his ex-wife."

"Did you know her from before?" Johnson asked.

"Yes, I had met her once, in my office, when they had to sign for some joint holdings."

"All right, and then what?"

"I asked her about her maiden name and where she was from, like the letter said to, and it was obvious that the bank was Wells Fargo, so I went there and opened the box and found all this." I opened my brief case and produced the documents and pictures. I pushed them across the desk to him. He picked up the internet articles, and Anna, who sat beside him, began reading the withered letter from Ephraim Wells. A few minutes later they exchanged articles and read again.

Anna finished first, glanced at the photos, then smiled at me. At least that's the way I interpreted her rather cryptic look. When Johnson finished reading, he set the letter down.

"Now you know everything I do," I said. "Except, I went by his house on the way home, and he still wasn't there. I'm actually surprised I didn't see you guys there."

"They're there now," he said. "I spoke with his ex-wife," he looked at his watch, "less than an hour ago. They must have just missed you. I came directly here. When was the last time you saw Mr. Nelson?"

"Last week. He was at my office for a consultation about his portfolio."

"Was there a problem?"

"No."

"Did he say anything about any of this?"

"Not a word."

"Were there any concerns at all with his finances, anything that could have caused him to be a little more inclined, shall we say, to dabble in activities like removing artifacts from a national park?"

"No. His portfolio's doing fine. He seemed happy when he left."

"Was that meeting when you talked about the Book of Mormon?" This had been in Keith's letter.

"Yes, he asked some questions about my faith, and we talked about it, but he didn't say anything about any of *this*. I don't know what to think of it. In fact, when I left the office I had just decided to call you and turn all this over—even though I didn't know he was, you know—"

"Dead?"

"Yes."

Anna hadn't spoken since reading the letters, which surprised me because I recalled how quickly she had defended me at the slightest accusation eight years ago. Marsha, who had been a rising actress, had been dead for nine months by then, but her body had only just been found and I suddenly found myself at the center of a murder investigation. Anna had been recommended to me as a bright, hard-working lawyer who could ably see to my interests. Indeed, she had been very bright and very hard-working, and in the end she not only helped me find the true murderer but had saved my life. Over time she too had shown interest in my faith, investigated it, and eventually joined the Church. A year later we were married in the Oakland Temple. Now we had been married almost as long as Marsha and I had been, and with our four children and demanding occupations, we found spending time alone with each other getting more difficult.

"So, what do you think," Johnson said, "did he actually go to the canyon and find something?"

"I don't know, but it looks like it unless he fabricated everything. That old letter, the one from Ephraim Wells to his brother, it looks pretty convincing."

"We'll analyze the paper and ink—and any fingerprints. Might even find DNA."

"Well, you'll probably find mine."

"You say you got all this from the safe deposit box?"

"Everything except the note and the key."

"Were there any witnesses with you—at the bank?"

There it was, the first hint of an accusation. *Could I possibly have fabricated all this to mislead him?* I paused, waiting for Anna to protest, or at least interject, but she remained silent, probably as interested in the answer as he was.

"No, the bank manager left me alone when I opened it, but I suppose you could scan their surveillance footage and see me walking out this morning with a handful of documents—which I hadn't walked in with."

He nodded. "Do you have any idea who else Mr. Nelson might have been in contact with, who else he might have been worried about?"

"Not a clue."

"All right then." He rose from his chair, and Anna and I followed his lead. "If anything comes to mind, I'm sure you'll let me know. Here's my office number." He handed me a card. "What a coincidence that we're brought together again by unsavory circumstances. Who would have guessed? Have a nice day."

We led him to the front door and bid him farewell. The entire downstairs was empty.

Anna said, "You told him, didn't you?"

"Excuse me?"

"You told Keith what's-his-name, Nelson, that I didn't believe the Book of Mormon, didn't you?"

So that's what led to her cryptic smile.

"I'm sorry. Yes, I guess I did."

"Why would you do that?"

"Because when I shared my testimony with him, he said he didn't believe in angels and all that, and I just told him he was probably in good company, because you didn't really believe those things either. I was just trying to make him feel okay with things, you know, that I was still his friend."

"You shared my private feelings with him so you could be his friend? Travis, you told him things I haven't even told my best friends—that I haven't even told Rosemary."

"I'm sure she knows, after all the books I've brought home practically proving the Book of Mormon is true. She probably figured things out a long time ago."

We were still standing near the front door. I thought we were alone, but I caught a movement above us and saw Kevin and Kalley on the landing at the head of the stairs.

"Are you guys having a fight?" Kalley asked, truly curious.

"No, honey," I said. "We're just discussing something. Is Rosemary up there with the little kids?"

"Yeah, but they're in their room with Ross."

"Okay, you can tell them the coast is clear."

"Huh?"

Kevin laughed. "That was old man Johnson! I remember him. What happened, did somebody die?"

The boy had a preternatural gift. The last time he had seen Johnson, as I recollected, was at his mother's funeral, eight years before. He wasn't of my own progeny, as both Kevin and Kalley were adopted, but I had no doubt that one of his natural parents was extremely intelligent, and the other possibly criminally oriented. Of course, none of that explained Kalley, who was as sweet and guileless as a dove.

"Actually," Anna said, finally coming to my rescue, "somebody's gonna die if you don't stop eavesdropping. Now go tell Rosemary we're ready for dinner. And then come down and help set the table— after you've washed your hands."

"Who?" Kevin retorted with a malicious tone. "Me or both of us?"

"Well it was going to be both of you," Anna replied cooly, "but now it's just you—and it will be you for the rest of your life if you don't lose that attitude."

"Rest of my life! You won't even *live* for the rest of my life!" He turned and stomped off toward the little kids' room before I could deliver a final word. Anna snuck a hard look at me then went to the kitchen. I grabbed my briefcase and skedaddled down the hall to my office.

After dinner, Ross poked his head into the office as I scanned the Oriental markets. "Got a minute?" he asked.

"Sure. Come in. How's your leg?"

He sat across the desk from me, in the chair that Anna had been sitting in earlier. "Not bad—wanna see?" He rolled his pant leg up and showed me the lower bruise, which had grown beyond the bandage.

"You ought to go play basketball at the church and show it off."

"Yeah—the second one's just as good." He put his pant leg back down.

"So, what's on your mind?"

"I just thought I'd see how it went, you know, putting my portfolio together."

"Good. Great. I got five of the sectors purchased today, and I should get the others nailed down tomorrow."

"And so, you think it'll be good—I mean that it's going to be solid?"

"Of course. That's what I do, to the best of my ability. If you're having second thoughts, I can always sell and give you the funds back."

"No, it's not that. I know it'll be great. It's just that, well, to tell you the truth, I actually wanted to talk about something else."

"The thing with Johnson?"

"No, but, how often do you see him? I mean, I'm only back for a day, and here he is again."

"That's the first time I've seen him in eight years."

"Wow. I show up and he's back in our lives again."

"It has nothing to do with you. In fact, I doubt I'll see him again. It's just something with a client I have—*had*. But it's all in the cops' hands now."

"Did the guy try to steal something from you?"

"No, he died, under questionable circumstances. I don't know how much I can say, but he either drowned or was killed. They found him in the Tuolumne, and it turns out I was one of the last people to see him."

"Oh."

"Yeah. So, what's up?"

He brought a pamphlet from his back pocket. It was a three-fold tract about the Book of Mormon. "I found this downstairs." He handed it across the desk. "And when I went upstairs and asked Kevin and Kalley how things were going, they said their mom doesn't believe in the Church." He looked at me, waiting for a reply, but once again I wasn't sure how much to say, especially after my *faux pas* earlier. "Of course, it's none of my business," he added.

Maybe it wasn't, but as Anna had said, he was family. "Anna loves the Church, but she doesn't really have a testimony. She doesn't believe that God appeared to Joseph Smith or that an angel gave him the plates. The kids weren't supposed to know, but you can't really keep anything from Kevin. He probably knew before I did." I glanced at the pamphlet. "I got that for her, but I doubt she read it."

"Did she believe everything when she got baptized?"

"I thought so, but she said she'd had doubts all along, and they've just gotten stronger over the years. In fact, sometimes it seems like the more I try to convince her, the more she pulls away."

"What have you tried?"

"Everything. You know how logical she is, so for a long time I tried to prove the Book of Mormon was true. I showed her all the chiasms and Hebraisms that Joseph Smith couldn't have known about, but that just made her start reading anti-Mormon material to try to refute that. Then I tried historical stuff—how the ancient town of Nahom in the Arabian peninsula, where Ishmael was buried, is right where the Book of Mormon says it would be—but the town, with the same name, wasn't even discovered until recently. I just kept showing her all these impossible coincidences where Joseph Smith got things absolutely right, but she wouldn't accept it."

"Yeah, I've read about that stuff. It's amazing, but it seems that people who don't want to believe always find a reason not to."

"I should have just dropped it, but then something else happened, something kind of amazing."

"What?"

"I haven't told anybody but her, because it's so incredible, but I was down at the library doing some research on a county zoning law, and when I was done, I wandered around looking at books, and I came across this book about ancient Egyptian scripts and hieroglyphics. I had been interested in that stuff before, so I started looking through it."

"Okay—"

"I mean I was interested in the Anthon Transcript—you know, that piece of paper where Joseph Smith copied some characters from the Gold Plates?"

"Oh, yeah, right."

"For some reason, just a few weeks before, I had gotten curious about it and decided to study it—I guess because there's not much written about it. Well, there I was staring at that book, and I saw a character from the Anthon Transcript."

"What?"

"Well, not exactly. I mean, it was *close*. It's a character like a big letter Z, with some curlicues on top. The only reason I remembered it was because there were so many of them in the transcript—seven of them I think—and it's kind of big. But anyway, the one in the book was close enough that I started looking for other characters that could match those in the Anthon Transcript. I couldn't remember them all, so I got my phone and went online and found the transcript and started matching others I could find in the book."

"And? Did you find any others?"

"Three more. And right there in the book it had the English translations. And so guess what I did?"

"Called Salt Lake?"

I laughed. "I went home and found those same characters in the Anthon Transcript and counted exactly how many other characters were between them. So, remember that first character, like a big Z?"

"With a curlicue on top?"

"Yeah. Guess what the book says it means."

"I have no idea."

"It came and passed by."

"It came and . . .?" His eyes widened. "It came to pass?"

I smiled. "It was like finding the Rosetta Stone. So I got on my computer and created a couple of macros, you know, to search for patterns, and I started looking for any place in the Book of Mormon where that same sequence of 'and it came to pass' occurred. You know, because I knew exactly how many other characters occurred between them." I waited for him to grasp all of this, but he was already ahead of me.

"Don't tell me—you found it! You found where those same words happened in exactly the same sequence."

I smiled again.

"*Really?*"

"Yes. I couldn't have done it without a computer, but I found that sequence of "And it came to passes.""

"Where?"

"It's in the Book of Ether—the part where it says the stones shined when the Jaredites were going across the ocean, with the 'mountain waves' and all that. It's in chapter six. And it turns out that those characters, which only take up a small page in the transcript, take up almost a whole chapter in Ether."

He was staring at me with his mouth open. He said, "So, you know what those characters mean—not just 'and it came to pass,' but the others too?"

"Well, not exactly, because I doubt they're a perfect match, you know, one character for one word—but with some work I could probably get some ideas."

"Wow. Wait—and you haven't told anybody about this? Are you *crazy?*"

"How could I? I can't prove any of it—not really. And besides, I did tell Anna."

"What'd she say? How could she disprove *that?*"

"Well, first she asked me to show her the book where I found those characters." I paused.

"So? Did you?"

"No. I tried, but when I went back to the library to check it out, I couldn't find it."

"Somebody else checked it out?"

"I don't know, but it wasn't on the rack where I found it. I've gone back and checked like five times."

"Unbelievable."

"That's what she said."

"So, did you look for it in the catalog? Or on Amazon?"

Now came the truly embarrassing part.

"I tried, but—"

"But what?"

"I can't remember the title. It's like—it's just *gone.* I've looked up every title I can think of that had Egyptian characters or hieroglyphics in it, but I can't find it."

"You can't remember the title? Why? Because of the Lyme disease?"

"Who knows?"

"Weird."

"Yeah."

"Or maybe it was never there—when you went looking for it. Maybe the Three Nephites just put it there that day."

"Ross . . ."

"How do you know they didn't? They probably know where Modesto is. Maybe they put it in there, and took it out."

"Come on, it wasn't the Three Nephites. I probably just put it back on the wrong shelf, and then I forgot the title. Stuff like that happens to me all the time."

Disappointment crossed his face. "I don't know . . . But, hey, it doesn't matter, right? Because you can show how the exact sequence of those characters in the transcript matches those exact same words in the Book of Mormon!"

"Well, it's not a perfect match, because one character, like that big Z, can mean multiple words. But it's pretty close."

"And you haven't shown this to anybody else, except Anna?"

"Well, I just told *you* about it. It was only a couple of weeks ago."

"Unbelievable."

"Stop saying that."

"Whatever. So, what made you get into the Anthon stuff in the first place?"

"I don't know. It just kind of got in my head a few months ago."

"Maybe the Lord was preparing you—for when you saw the book that wasn't there."

"It was there, Ross." But I had to admit the thought had crossed my mind that the Lord somehow *had* had his hand in all of this, along with another thought. "So, Ross, you know how the Lord commands us to love him with all of our heart, might, mind, and strength?"

"Yeah."

"Sometimes I think studying things like this is part of loving him with our *minds*."

He thought about this. "I guess that makes sense. But too bad Anna won't use her mind the same way. She's like the smartest person I know."

"She didn't call me a liar; she just wanted to see the book with her own eyes. And besides, she's kind of hung up on the locations, like how the plates got up in New York, where Joseph Smith just happened to be living, if everything in the Book of Mormon happened in Central America."

"*If* it happened in Central America."

"Right. Nobody knows for sure where it happened, except . . ."

"*Except?*"

"Okay, this next thing's pretty cool even if it doesn't prove anything." I reached under the desk to a little shelf where I kept my non-work research and pulled out a folder with three pages I had printed from the internet, that repository of all things true, false and wacky.

"Two men who had known Joseph Smith in Nauvoo became local leaders in the Church in Utah; one of them was a stake patriarch. Both of them, independent of each other, told an amazing story, that Joseph Smith had told them that Moroni had come north from the land of Bountiful with a group of Nephites. Joseph told them that Bountiful was in Central America. And they said he even drew a map in the dirt—where Bountiful was and where Moroni and his men went. They said Joseph told them that after the wars at the end of the Book of Mormon, Moroni and a few men he found came north through Mexico and across the 'Sand Hills,' into Arizona, and from there they went north through Utah. And he said that while Moroni was in Utah, he stopped and dedicated future temple sites, like the one in St. George and one in Manti. And here's where it gets interesting; a few years after they told this story, Brigham Young confirmed that Moroni did in fact dedicate the temple site at Manti." I stopped to see if Ross was following this, but he just waited for me to go on.

"So, according to Joseph Smith, Moroni and his men were carrying some things with them; they had the gold plates, the Urim and Thummin, the breastplate, and the sword of Laban. And after they went up to the Salt Lake area, they turned east and traveled back to Missouri, where they dedicated more temple sites, including one at Adam-Ondi-Ahman. And they kept going east and dedicated another one at Nauvoo, then one at Kirtland. And finally, they went to New York, where Moroni buried the plates and Urim and Thummin at the Hill Cumorah."

"Moroni dedicated all those temple sites?" Ross asked.

"According to these men, he did. And they didn't stop there. In the Church archives, there are two maps that they drew of this account. It looks like both maps are basically the same, see?" I showed him copies of the maps that I had printed off.

As Ross studied them, I continued with the story. "These two maps are supposedly based on the map that Joseph Smith drew in the dirt. And it shows that after Moroni buried the plates at Cumorah, he came back and passed through Missouri again, and when he was there, it looks like he dedicated the temple site at Independence—the one that's supposed to be in the New Jerusalem."

Ross sat back in his chair. "So, what's all this mean? Do you believe it?"

"Yeah, I mean, how many Patriarchs do you know who lie? And remember, years later Brigham Young did say that Moroni actually dedicated that site at Manti."

"Did you show this to Anna?"

"I started to, but she wasn't interested. More revelation from Joseph Smith, you know." He nodded. "So, what are you going to do—about Anna?"

"Just what I've been doing—praying and hoping and having patience. I love her. She's a great wife, and a great mother, and sometimes I feel like the luckiest man in the world. And sometimes I wonder if we'll ever be together in eternity."

That put a chill in the room.

"Does she go to the temple?"

"Not very often, but sometimes."

"Well, I guess . . ."

"What?"

He was reluctant to go on, so I pressed him. "You guess what?"

"I was going to say, I guess you'll always have Marsha."

It jarred me, but he was right; I would always have Marsha, but the truth was I wanted both women, both wives, both mothers. I loved them both deeply, passionately, as fully as I could. I couldn't say it to Ross, or anybody else, but I felt that my life in eternity wouldn't be complete without both of them.

"You're a lot luckier than me," he said, "even if Anna doesn't believe everything."

"How's that?"

"At least you *have* a wife."

I put the papers back under the desk. "You'll have a wife someday, Ross—a very lucky one."

We left the office, my office work still undone, and joined the family in the family room, where they were all watching a movie.

"Aw, man!" Kevin said when we came in. "Does that mean we have to share the popcorn?"

I did some math. He wouldn't be eligible to go on a mission for another five years and three months.

Five years, three months, and thirteen days.

I took a large handful of popcorn and tried to enjoy the movie.

Chapter 6

A Denial of Truth

The next morning in the *Modesto Bee*, Keith Nelson's death was made public in an article saying that his body had been found in the river and that more details would be coming soon. The next day another article followed in which more details were released, but it suggested no cause of death. On the third morning a fuller article appeared with an old photo of Keith, probably provided by his daughter:

> As reported previously, the body of local businessman, Keith M. Nelson, was found Wednesday afternoon in the Tuolumne River.
>
> After receiving an anonymous tip, search and rescue personnel recovered the body from below the Seventh Street Bridge. According to a police department spokesperson, the body appeared to have been in the water for "up to 72 hours."
>
> Mr. Nelson was known for years as the owner of two local used car dealerships, both of which he sold in 2012. More recently he owned and managed a variety of real estate holdings, including nearly two dozen duplexes in southwest Modesto.
>
> Several complaints were filed in 2016 by tenants against Mr. Nelson. Those complaints, along with other grievances from tenants, were reported at the time. City officials claim that the complaints were "in the process of

being attended to." There is no word from the tenants on whether the complaints have been satisfactorily addressed.

According to a police department news release, an autopsy and initial investigation into the victim's death indicates "no sign of foul play." The release further states: "It appears that Mr. Nelson may have suffered an accidental drowning when he fell into the river and was swept off in the current, which was made more powerful than usual by heavy rains earlier this week."

Mr. Nelson's family has been notified. Funeral arrangements are pending.

It had been four days since Keith's body had been found, and during those four days the police, evidently, had come to the conclusion that there was "no sign of foul play."

I discussed this with Anna.

"Did they even look at the letters I gave them?" I asked.

"Of course they did—and they're probably still looking at them."

Maybe, but I didn't like where the investigation was going. I had the photocopies of the letters in front of me. "When you looked at these letters the other day, did you think they were fake? Did you think Keith was making it all up?"

She smiled patiently. "Since all of my dealings with Keith Nelson were in the courtroom, where I mostly knew him to lie or shade the truth, yes, I do think he could be making it all up—though this seems a little beyond his ability. But, Travis, the last thing we need is another murder investigation. Let the police handle it."

"But they're *wrong*!"

"Drop it, Travis."

"But he trusted *me*. Keith asked me to—let me see—" I searched the letter for his exact words, but Anna got there first.

"'Lead you on a quest to find justice.'"

I looked at her. "How did you know that? Did you have it memorized?"

"It kind of stuck out."

"Stuck out?"

"Yes, as in—Is my husband really crazy enough to seek justice for someone he barely knows, who may have been using him in some scheme, and who by his own account stole ancient artifacts and tried to sell them on the black market?"

"Well, that's one way to look at it. But personally . . ."

"What other way is there? Do you know more than Johnson? Did you keep anything from him?"

"No."

She visibly relaxed.

"*What?*" I asked. "Did you think I *had?*"

"Honey, I think sometimes you have an overdeveloped sense of right and wrong, and I was just praying, if I can use that word, that you hadn't done something really dumb like holding evidence back."

"You really don't trust me, do you?"

"Let me be honest," she said, still kind and patient. "I trust you ninety-nine percent of the time. But there's that one percent I wonder about sometimes."

The woman was ruthless. I tossed the letters on the table.

Anna came over to me. "You're an idealist, Travis. And frankly, that's part of what I love about you." She hugged me.

This would make arguing more difficult, but I was determined.

"All right, thanks, I think. But don't you think I should do something?"

"Like what?"

"Like, I don't know, call the captain?"

"And say what? Remind him about the letters? Do you think he forgot about them?"

"No, but . . ."

"Drop it, Travis."

"But it's not right. I know he was killed."

She took a step back and eyed me critically. "You *know?*"

"It's the only thing that makes sense."

"If it's the only thing that makes sense, don't you think it makes sense to the investigators too? Think about it. How many people have you talked to about this? And how many do you think Johnson's talked to? He actually knows more about this than you do because he knows everything you know *plus* what other people have told him. He has detectives investigating." She held up the paper again. "It says they're *investigating.* So, let them investigate. Meaning, stay out of it. *That's* what makes sense."

One of the drawbacks of marrying someone smarter than you is you spend a lot of time losing arguments.

We got ready for bed, and I asked if she would pray with me. She sighed, glanced at me forlornly, then came around to the bench at the foot of our bed and dropped to her knees. We held hands, and I prayed.

But that night I couldn't sleep, and in the morning, after taking care of business at the office, I went down to the station and asked for Captain Johnson. A phone call wouldn't do. I wanted to see his face when he explained the inexplicable to me.

Surprisingly, the busy man made time for me. After being scanned for weapons and then walking through a labyrinth of hallways, I sat in his office, which was a larger version of his old office we had met in eight years before.

His bald dome was motionless as he drilled me with steely blue eyes. "Are you here to confess, Call?"

I thought I detected a glint of humor in those icy eyes. "Not yet," I said, playing along, "but if it's a confession you're wanting, why did you tell the paper that Keith's death was an 'accidental drowning'?"

"Mmm," he said, his glare hardening. "I'm not sure which part of that sentence I should focus on first."

"The last part."

He opened the top drawer of his desk and produced a large, official-looking envelope. "This may surprise you, but I actually made inquiries of the National Park Service, the Smithsonian Institution, and ICE. You know what ICE is don't you?"

"Immigration and Customs Enforcement."

"*U.S.* Immigration and Customs Enforcement. And do you know why I bothered those good people?"

I sighed, once again recognizing the lofty signs of superior knowledge. Part of my mind was already ruing the fact that I had disregarded counsel from my chief council. "So you could tell them about the letters from Keith?"

"Not exactly, but that's close enough. I scanned and emailed the letters and documents that Keith gave you and asked them if there might, possibly, be anything to all of this." He pulled a letter from the envelope. "This is from the Smithsonian. Let me share part of it with you:

Not only do we receive numerous inquiries each year about this hoax, but we have begun sending form letters to those who make such inquiries. In your case, however, because you are a law enforcement officer, we are answering you personally. As we have said publicly on numerous occasions, there is not now nor ever has been an "Egyptian cave" in the Grand Canyon. We wish Mr. Kinkaid had never made such a claim. In fact, we are almost sure he never did, as no trace of a "Mr. Kinkaid" has ever been found. The purported letter (which we cannot examine because you sent us a scanned copy) indicates that he may have gone by a different name (Ephraim Wells), which is possible, but we still don't have any knowledge of a cave of the description he gave.

The letter to "Grant Wells" also mentions a Sterling A. Jordan. It will interest you to know that our personnel and financial records indicate that no man or contractor by that name ever worked for the Institution, not in the early 1900s, and not at any time since. Why this Ephraim Wells would state that such a man had "left position" from the Smithsonian Institution is a mystery to us—but perhaps not to those who deal in hoaxes.

Over the decades our archeologists, in conjunction with the National Parks Service, have sent several teams to that part of the Grand Canyon to investigate this rumor, along with any other archeological discoveries they may find, but nothing of the sort has been located. What those expeditions did discover, however, is that this rather remote area is very hazardous for exploration— which is why the officers at the park have made it off limits to rangers and patrons alike. Any qualified research team, however, is free to make expeditions there so long as they meet standard requirements, such as indemnifying the park for any accidents or casualties that may result from their explorations.

"The letter goes on," Johnson said, putting it away, "but I think you get the general tone. In my opinion, we won't be getting any help from them."

I sighed again. "Thanks, but, it's just that Keith asked me to do something if anything happened to him—and it did."

"And *you* did. You turned the evidence over to us, so we'll take care of it."

"Did you hear back from ICE or the national parks?"

"Sure. I got a call from ICE. They're very interested in things like this. In fact, I think they like these things more than drug busts. But, and I fully understand this, they said they can't dedicate assets to an investigation without some evidence of an actual crime. And, of course, the only evidence we have of a crime is a drowned body— and his letter that he stole some relics and tried to sell them. But we don't have the relics, or the person he contacted, or really much else. So, until we have something else, where's the crime?"

"You have his computer, don't you?"

"Glad you asked. It was fried. Cooked. Our forensics guys say nothing's coming off it."

"Wait—was that his first one? Keith said his first one got hacked, but he bought another one and loaded some heavy-duty encryption on it."

"There was only one computer in his house. And he doesn't have an outside office that we know of. If another computer existed, he took it somewhere, or another person has it."

"Did you find his phone?"

"No. It wasn't on his body, and we didn't find one at his home. It probably fell in the river, but even if we found it, it wouldn't be any good to us."

"So, did the National Park Service say the same thing?"

"Pretty much. It was another phone call, strictly a courtesy call because we're law enforcement. They said they'd be interested in the old letter if we can prove its authenticity. But, about the cave? They said it doesn't exist. Or if it does, they don't know where it is. Nobody has found it in over a hundred years."

"Nobody but Keith."

"Well, if he found it, he took his secret to a watery grave. So, you can see why the preliminary verdict is an accidental drowning. There were no marks on the body, except maybe bruises on the chin and his right shin, possibly from when he fell in. The autopsy shows that he had inhaled water, which again indicates drowning. Those riverbanks are like grease; our own guys were slipping and falling when they went after him."

I was disappointed. The letters left no doubt in my mind that the cave existed *somewhere*, because he said he had found it, but what could I say? Johnson had done everything I would have, except—

"Are you going to check the old letter for authenticity?"

He picked it up and looked at it again. "Frankly, I'm already satisfied that it's legitimate. I don't think Nelson would go to the trouble of forging something like this—unless he had a big payoff waiting on the back end. And if he had a big payoff waiting for him, we'll probably never know about it."

"So, if you think it's true, aren't you going to send somebody down there to check it out? You know what it said on the back, right? About the mouth of the cave being sealed."

"Are we going to send somebody down to the *Grand Canyon*?" he asked, surprised. "What are we going to find? A murderer? The person who may have killed Keith Nelson? I don't think so."

"But if you found the cave, it would prove that his fears that something bad might happen, that someone was after him, were right. And, you could tell Parks and ICE and the Smithsonian that it actually exists."

"Do you really expect us to spend thousands of dollars, which we don't have, on experts to go climbing around the Grand Canyon so they can find something the rangers say doesn't exist? I admire your dedication, Call. You're loyal to your friends, and that's in short supply today, but we've done about all we can, unless we get more information. We'll keep the investigation open, officially, but we can't dedicate many resources to it."

"But—the coincidences!"

"Tell me, if you were in my shoes, with my financial constraints, what would *you* do?"

He had me there. If he couldn't justify sending people to the canyon, he probably couldn't do much at all. I stood up and put my hand out. He took it.

"Thanks for explaining everything to me."

"Have you ever been there?"

"To the Grand Canyon?"

He nodded.

"Yeah, a couple of times."

"What was your first impression as you walked up to it?"

I thought back to when I first saw it as a teenager with my family. "At first, just how big it is, but when I think about it now, I think it was the silence, that all-consuming silence coming up from the maw of that thing."

He nodded. "'The maw of that thing.' I like that. For me, it was just the size. I go up to the high Sierras every summer and hike to secret fishing holes for golden trout, but I can't imagine trying to hike in the Grand Canyon. That would be impossible. If any clues to Keith Nelson's death are hiding down there somewhere, they'll probably stay hidden for a long time."

Chapter 7

Under Surveillance

Whislin Klah had already received his extra payment when the call came.

"The investigation's over," his contact said. "You can pack up and leave."

"How do you know?" Klah didn't really question the fact, but he wondered how his boss got his information.

"Our men in Washington have ways of knowing. The case is still open officially, but it isn't being pursued. The captain in charge, a Marcus Johnson, has hit too many dead-ends. Nice work, by the way, with the body. No marks. Accidental drowning is perfect."

"I'm worried about Call. He went to Johnson's office today."

There was a pause. "We didn't know that. What does he have?"

"You saw the letters."

"I saw the scanned copies. Does he have anything else?"

"I don't know."

There was a pause, and Whislin sensed again the importance of the case. "All right, continue the surveillance. We'll check our sources again to see if he brought anything else to the cops."

Klah didn't want to spend another day, let alone another two weeks, in Modesto surveilling a nobody businessman. But the pay had been good, and he prided himself on thoroughness.

"Somehow Nelson got in the cave," Klah said. "You've got to address that."

"Are you sure he actually got in?"

"How else did he get the artifacts? Do you have them yet?"

"Yes."

"So, what do you think? Are they real?"

"They're from the period, but Nelson could have gotten them from another source."

"But not likely," said Klah. "Not when you remember the pictures. He was there."

Silence.

"And if he was in the cave, other people can get in."

"All we can do now is continue the surveillance. We'll try to find out what he told the captain."

Klah hung up. It was the right decision, but he still didn't want to do it.

Chapter 8

Reeling in a Dangerous Direction

The morning of Keith's funeral dawned with a sky of pinks and baby blues. The weather had indeed gone from murkiest winter to spring in a single day. Keith's daughter, Saundra Flament, had flown out from Virginia to oversee the services and the disposition of Keith's estate.

Anna and I both attended, as she had been acquainted with Keith before our marriage. She had represented a complainant in a lawsuit over a car. Its transmission had ceased to work within two miles of leaving the lot. California's Lemon Law gave her an easy victory, but she fondly remembered Keith's fierce battle for his "rights," his position being that he had the constitutional right to sell whatever he wanted to whomever he wanted, as long as they were gullible enough to buy.

On the way to the funeral, Anna idly speculated on whether Keith was at this moment battling for another set of rights.

I was pleased that she still believed in eternity.

I thought we had arrived early, as there were only six people in the funeral home, but we were right on time. Saundra sat with her mother, Claudia, who had flown in from North Dakota. The service, which mercifully included a closed casket, was exceedingly brief, and in fifteen minutes Anna and I were offering our condolences to the bereaving family.

"Thank you for coming," Saundra said, letting me give her a half hug. Her eyes were rimmed with tears, indicating some genuine compassion for her father. Claudia's eyes, on the other hand, simply bore into mine, as if I harbored some surreptitious knowledge.

When the half hugs were done, she said, "Just so you know, I told the police about your call to me."

"Yes, I know. Captain Johnson came to our home and asked about it." I turned to Anna, who gave her silent affirmation.

"So, what was going on? Johnson wouldn't tell me since I'm not 'family' anymore."

"You were right," I said. "The key went to a safe deposit box, and inside were some documents about a 'business deal' he was working on."

"Did they have anything to do with his death? I mean, Keith never went down to the river in his life. He didn't even own a fishing pole. And the letter kept saying 'if' you saw me again, or something like that."

I chose my words judiciously. "It had to do with some Indian artifacts." I turned to Saundra. "Did your father ever say anything about having some Native American artifacts?"

Her eyes were dry now. "No. He never told me anything about *anything*."

"Why, are they valuable?" Claudia asked, her sense of fair play rising.

"I wouldn't know. I've never seen them, but that's what the documents in the box referred to. I suppose Johnson will turn everything over to you, Saundra, when the case is closed." I turned to Anna. "Johnson will probably give them to her, won't he?"

"Yes, if they're not pertinent to an investigation. He'll eventually turn everything over to the family."

"So Johnson has the artifacts?" Claudia asked. "What are they, like masks and tomahawks?"

"No, I think they're more like—" I felt Anna's eyes on me. "Maybe more like jewelry."

Both Mother and daughter seemed interested. "Ancient jewelry?" Claudia asked.

I wished I had heeded Anna's silent rebuke. "Like I said, I haven't seen it, and we're not even sure it exists."

"Well, *something* exists," Claudia said. "I mean, he told you about it, and he told you to talk to me about it. So, I think you better tell me *all* about it."

"How much is ancient Indian jewelry worth?" Saundra asked softly, as if vocalizing such things might scare off the whole shebang.

Anna took charge. "Like Travis said, nobody has seen them. Not even Captain Johnson, and, also like he said, they might not even exist, so we don't know any more than that. We really should be going now."

That sounded like an excellent idea.

"Wait!" Saundra said, suddenly asserting herself. "You were my father's financial counselor, right?"

"Yes."

"Then don't you have an obligation to tell me everything about his financial affairs, since his will left everything to me?"

I turned to Anna for help. Her face had a sudden reflective aspect, as of great contemplation. I had seen this look before. It seemed to mean I was on my own.

"Well, yes," I began, "but . . ."

"So, what did he leave me? What was in the box?"

Inspiration came to me, and I suggested we all go out to lunch. Claudia would have none of it. She wanted answers now. I explained that the box had contained several letters and documents and that laying everything out would take considerable time. Claudia suggested we go to my office for a "briefing," as if this were a legal matter. Which it very well might become if I didn't act wisely. So I told them we could meet at my office after I had gone home to retrieve the necessary documents.

"Wait a minute," Saundra said. "You have them at your house? I thought Johnson had them."

Ah, a sticky matter.

"Well, as I often do, I made copies of the documents before turning them over so I would have proof if anybody tried to alter anything."

"Anybody?" Claudia asked. "You mean the police? Do you think they're going to change the letters or something?"

"No, no. It was just a precaution."

"Is that legal?"

"Of course that's legal." I turned to Anna. "Right?"

Anna appeared to be pondering some grave matter.

"*Right?*" I repeated.

"Oh, yes," Anna finally said. "He'll go get the documents, and you and he can have your consultation. Is your schedule clear, dear?"

"Well, it's clear for lunch. I have until about one." It was almost eleven.

On the way home Anna said, "You had to open your mouth, didn't you?"

I had been expecting something like that and had prepared several answers—none of which, I now realized, would do.

"You're too open, too trusting. You've got to learn more reserve."

"I thought she had a right to know."

"The *daughter* had a right to know, and Johnson would have told her everything when he was ready. Those documents are his responsibility, not yours. After all, he has the originals."

"But don't I have a responsibility too?"

"It could be construed that way, in a court of law, if that's where you want her to take this. But, if you hadn't told her about the jewelry in the first place, she wouldn't have known, and you probably *wouldn't* have had a responsibility. It's her *knowing*, that gives her standing in this. The documents aren't currently part of her estate, since they're in the authorities' hands and may never be released. But once you told her about them, she had a right to ask about your knowledge of them, since they *might* have a financial bearing on her estate. You've got to know when to let sleeping dogs lie."

We got home without incident.

I collected the papers and was headed for the door when Anna met me. She was about to go to her office. "Just so you know," she said, "I still love you."

She kissed me.

I thought I had calmed down, but now my shoulders relaxed, and I realized how tense I had been. She took my arm and we went out into the sunshine together.

At the office I took mother and daughter into the conference room and tried to go over Keith's portfolio with them, but they would have none of it. They wanted facts about the jewelry. So, I put the folder down and retrieved the copies of the letters and photos from the canyon. They studied them for several minutes, then they began asking what I knew about this and that. Of course I had no answers for most of their questions. It was Mom—Claudia—who got to the heart of the matter.

"But wait, didn't Johnson say that Keith's death was an accident? How can it be an accident when he *knew* something might happen to him? Are they on drugs around here?"

I explained Johnson's point of view about there being no evidence of a crime except these letters, and that some supposedly smart people in Washington said that Keith's assertions were not true.

"But my own great, great uncle—what's his name . . ." Claudia searched the letters. "Ephraim said that the cave was there. He even wrote to my great grandfather, what's his name—Grant—about it."

"Yes."

"Can't they see that this *is* proof that he was there, especially when you combine it with the newspaper articles?"

"They're intrigued," I allowed, "but the problem is, according to the experts, there is no actual cave. And if there is no cave, there are no relics—at least not from the Grand Canyon. And if there are no relics from the Grand Canyon, then there was no crime. He died, yes, but there was no evidence of foul play. It was an accident—at least officially. Like I said, Johnson's intrigued by all this, but he can't justify the expense of an expedition to the canyon."

"Unless they get more evidence," said Saundra, who had been mostly quiet until now.

"Right—unless they get more evidence. So, if you've got any, let me know, or better yet, let Captain Johnson know."

Mom was getting upset, and she got up and began pacing the room. "So they think all this is just a coincidence? He said he was scared. He said his life was in danger—and then he accidentally died!"

I nodded, hoping silence would defuse the situation. I knew she wasn't concerned about his death—she hadn't shown much interest until she heard about the jewelry. The fact was, of course, that she was entitled to none of it. Because of the divorce, everything would go to her daughter, unless Mom sued the estate (meaning her daughter) to seek adjustments for her upkeep—and I didn't want to touch that subject.

"Mom, come sit down," Saundra said. "Let's think through this."

"Actually," I said, "I only have until one, so maybe we should discuss the rest of his holdings." I picked the other folder up. I liked that folder. I understood it. I could discuss it confidently.

"No," said Saundra, who continued to trip me up with her on-again, off-again interest. "That's just numbers. We can take care of that later. This is Dad's life. This is about who killed him."

Claudia sat down, and we both looked to the daughter. She thought for a moment, seemed to arrive at some conclusion, then turned to me. "Mr. Call, do you think he was murdered?"

"Well, I, uh, don't know, but, uh—it seems so."

Anna's words about sleeping dogs came hurtling back.

"He trusted you," Saundra added. "He asked you to do something for him, to fight for justice, for him."

"Yes."

"And he died."

I grew silent, dreading where this was going.

"You owe him."

I stared at her, Anna's words now mocking me.

"He trusted you more than he trusted me. He trusted you more than he trusted my mother, or even his lawyer. You're the only one he told about this. He knew he could trust you—*with his life*."

I tried another dose of silence.

"How much would an investigation cost?" she asked.

I mentally calculated what it might cost for a private investigator to go over all of this, try to reconfigure his computer, possibly even spend some time in the Grand Canyon. I came up with a number sure to scare her off: "At least fifty thousand. Maybe a hundred."

"Does he have that much?" She pointed at the other folder. "In his other investments?"

"Saundra!" Mother almost shouted. "What are you doing?"

"Does he?" she persisted.

"Yes, he does—or rather, you do. But I really should be discussing this with only you."

"It's okay. My mother knows this is my money now."

Her mother stared at a distant wall.

"But she also knows that I will take care of her if I can. So how much is in his, what do you call it, a portfolio?"

I nodded. "Over eight years he has invested about ten thousand dollars a year through my firm. We've been lucky. As the country came out of the recession, we acquired some excellent growth stocks, and the total of seventy-five thousand dollars that he invested has grown to about double that. Because the cost basis changed at your father's death, you should realize almost the full value of one hundred and fifty thousand dollars."

"One-fifty?" Mom exclaimed. "I know he's got more than *that!*"

"That's all he has with me." I let that sink in. "Of course he still has the twenty or so duplexes on top of that. I don't know how much they're worth after mortgages—maybe a couple of million."

Claudia blinked. "Oh, that's right. I forgot."

Saundra considered all this then said, "I'll cover your expenses."

"For an investigation?" I asked, clarifying. "You'll really need to talk to a private investigator. I was just estimating costs."

"No, for you. I want you to investigate. My father trusted you."

"I'm sorry. That's not what I do. There are some excellent investigators I can refer you to. Any of them would serve you well."

Her eyes drilled into mine with new intensity. "No. *You*. I know you can do it. I know what you did when your wife was murdered. The whole country knows. You know my father was murdered, and you're smart enough to find out who did it."

"Actually, Saundra, I'm not. That show they did about me? It didn't show that I almost died because my wife's killer found me before I found him." I hadn't actually seen the show, but my mother had seen it well over ten or twenty times.

"Yes, they did. They showed that—and it was the best part."

"It was?"

"Yeah, how you lured him into your home so you could kill him when he was threatening your family."

"But I didn't lure him in! He *snuck* in, and he didn't just threaten my family, he almost killed them—*all*. I can't do this."

"You owe him."

"I don't owe him *that*."

"He trusted you."

"He *should* have, I *earned* his trust. I earned him—*you*—eleven percent interest. Annually."

"He *asked* you."

"Yes, but I didn't answer. I don't know why he asked me. We never talked about it. Ever."

"He said he could trust you because of your faith, not because you made him a lot of money. I trust you for the same reason."

"Because of my faith?"

"Yes, because you *believe*. And because you have integrity. And because I know you can do it. Please, Mr. Call. Do this for us. Money is no object. Help us find his killer."

Her poor mother sighed loudly, but I tried to focus on the bigger problem—which was difficult because something strange was happening to me. Something surprising and terrifying.

Something way down inside me wanted to do this crazy, foolish, reckless, thing. I sat very still, hoping it didn't show.

"Please, Travis."

Somebody said, "Let me think about it."

Saundra smiled. "Of course you can think about it, but, when you come back and say you'll do it, I want your whole heart and soul. This is life or death to me, and I want it to be life or death for you."

I spent a long moment marveling at her. This woman who had seemed so timid just a few minutes ago had the strength of a lion. I couldn't have been more wrong about her. I would talk to Anna, but I already knew that unless she strongly disapproved, I would foolishly take the job. That's who I was. My unfortunate wife had married a naïve, reckless imbecile. It was my children who were innocent in the whole matter.

And then the thought hit me:

Anna will *strongly* disapprove. And she'll try to talk me out of it. Maybe she could save me.

But even then—

This thing surging to the surface, whatever it was, felt good. It felt almost *right*.

I began to despair—I would never be saved from myself.

Chapter 9

Embracing Danger

"Are you *insane*? Are you an imbecile? What's the matter with you?"

Anna was actually more subdued than I thought she'd be. We were behind closed doors, so only the closest neighbors could hear.

"It just means finding out if the cave is there," I explained, "because if the cave *is* there, then Keith was right, and it's not some elaborate hoax, and he probably took the relics and was probably murdered. So, if I can prove that the cave is there, the authorities, all of them, will have to pay more attention."

"Then use Saundra's money to hire an investigator. I know half a dozen who are desperate enough to take the job."

"She wants *me* to do it. She doesn't want an investigator."

"How will she know *who's* actually doing it if you don't tell her?—Oops there I go again, encouraging *discretion*."

"I'm going to be completely honest with her, like I am with everybody."

"Okay, let me ask you a question."

I thought she was about to say something logical, incisive, and possibly mind-changing, but a pleading look melted her face and she raised her voice again. "Did you learn *anything* from our nightmare eight years ago? We were right *there*." She pointed at a spot just inside the bedroom door. "You were on your knees, with a gun to your head. And I just happened to—" She stopped and choked up.

I went over and held her. She had saved my life that day, and probably the lives of my two oldest children. She had a right to care about the kind of business I got involved in. She had a right to protect our children. But, in my opinion, the odds of something like that happening again were remote. In the extreme.

"I won't ever put you in that situation again," I said, still holding her. "This is just a fact-finding trip. In fact, we can probably take the whole family and make a vacation of—"

She pulled away. "You *are* insane! Fact-finding? It's the *Grand Canyon*, Travis. It's a mile deep! It's bigger than entire states. And if there *is* a cave with mummies in it, you can be sure the government knows all about it and is keeping it a secret on purpose. And you want our kids to go with you? You need counseling."

"I don't need counseling."

"That's what they all say. Let's at least talk to the bishop. Will you talk to the bishop before you go?"

"Sure, and I'll even accept what he tells me."

Her eyes narrowed. She stepped forward. "And what is that supposed to mean?"

"What do you think it means?"

Playing coy with one's spouse is always a bad idea. But I wouldn't learn this lesson for several seconds.

"I think it means that you think I *won't* accept him, that I *don't* accept him, that I don't trust him because I don't have a testimony of the Church. I think you're mocking my honest beliefs."

"Or disbeliefs."

That was a mistake that I regret to this day. It was not only mean-spirited, it was dangerous. Her eyes widened and nostrils flared, and I thought I saw colors emanate from her flesh like an especially successful chameleon. I quickly raised my hands in a gentle pleading position. But the colors persisted, so I stepped forward to take her in my arms again—to hold her with love and affection and protection.

"Don't you touch me! How dare you! You want me to share your beliefs, but if your belief turns people into, into, THIS—" She flung her hands at me with impressive disdain. "Then I don't want any part of it!"

"I'm sorry."

"You're not sorry—you're pathetic!"

"Please forgive me."

"Forgive you? Why? You don't forgive me! You throw my doubts at me like a, like a grenade. My doubts are honest, Travis. They're even sacred—at least to me. And you use them to win an argument? Who does that?"

Evidently I did.

"So, if you really want to talk about beliefs, let's talk about yours."

"No, let's not. Please. I was out of line. I'll tell her I won't go. I'll call her tomorrow."

She paused. She was processing some vital information, probably something to shame me with.

"Why?"

I had no idea what she meant. "Why what?"

"Why aren't you going—because your wife won't let you? Is that what you're going to tell her?"

"I don't know—I . . ."

"Why not? You're blaming me for everything else, aren't you? Lack of faith, teaching the children false doctrine, not letting you be this woman's knight in shining armor."

"I didn't say that."

"You didn't have to. I just said, 'Let's go talk to the bishop,' and you threw my honest doubts in my face. They're obviously on your mind. *If my poor wife can't believe the Church, how can she believe the bishop?'* Right?"

"No, listen . . ."

"No, you listen. You go do what you want. I don't want to talk to the bishop or anybody else. Go knock yourself out. Get yourself killed. Just don't bring it home with you. I can't go through that again. And I won't let the children . . ."

"Anna, that's not going to happen. Nobody's coming after me. I just want to get some answers."

"Why? He wasn't even your friend."

"He trusted me."

"I don't know why."

I shrugged, then I sensed her energy change again. She knew she had gone too far, as I had. Wisely, perhaps for the first time in this conversation, I did the right thing and shut up.

"I'm sorry," she said. "I don't mean that."

Are there more healing words in the English language?

"I'm sorry too." I took a tentative step toward her again, but she put her hand up, stopping me. "You're going to do it, aren't you?"

"I haven't decided. I'm going to think about it." I held my arms out. "Can I hug you now?" I took a step forward, and when she didn't back off, I embraced her.

"I still love you," I said. "A lot."

Slowly, very slowly, her arms came up around me, and I put my face in her hair. I loved the smell of her, the feel of her.

I squeezed, and she squeezed me back, and at that moment I learned another lesson, that sometimes a good, long hug is better than any words.

After Anna went to sleep, I snuck out of bed and went into my closet and prayed. I needed answers—mostly about myself. Why did I want to move forward with this investigation? Keith had never really been my friend, and I hadn't met his daughter until today, so what was going on? I had expressed my feelings to her when I initially declined the offer, but then my feelings changed, suddenly, drastically. But though I prayed for nearly half an hour, no answer came. My knees and back ached, so I got up and paced the bedroom for a few minutes, still searching for answers, but again nothing came.

Anna was beautiful in her sleep, her blond hair laying helter-skelter over her face and neck. Her breathing was deep and regular, the hair near her mouth gently dancing up and down. I loved her and wanted to please her. She was right to want to avoid danger, but something was pushing me to move forward. Was it pride? Was it a delusion that I was someone's "knight in shining armor"? I hadn't seen the show about our family's tragedy, but as the horror of those days slowly wore off, the praise and esteem of others slowly bore in. Was I actually hungering for some kind of praise or, sadly, redemption? Did I need to make up for my earlier failures and try to be a hero?

I got hungry and went downstairs, where Ross was at the kitchen island with several courses of leftovers before him.

"Ross, do you ever get full?"

"Sure, when I eat enough."

I looked at the oozing mounds of mashed potatoes and gravy, the freshly microwaved fried chicken, the mixed vegetables, the beading glass of milk. I was in awe. "Do you ever get heartburn?"

"What's that?" He bit off a huge chunk of a drumstick and chewed with confidence.

I got a small glass of milk and a sliver of apple pie. I was twenty pounds overweight and feared every bite.

"Can't sleep?" he asked.

"Yeah."

He consumed a quarter pound of potatoes and gravy then spoke through the swarming mouthful. "What's the matter? Same thing Johnson was here about?"

Ross was always direct.

"Yes."

"Is that the same thing you and Anna were going on about upstairs?"

I was surprised then indignant. "Were you listening to us?"

"Not exactly," he said, lifting the large glass to his lips. He drank deeply, contentedly, then continued: "You remember that vent over there?" He pointed at an air vent above the counter. "Remember how we used to be able to hear you guys up in your bedroom through it?"

I was mortified. Eight years earlier that little vent had saved our lives, because people downstairs could hear the trouble upstairs. Afterwards I had planned to reroute the ducting so Anna and I could have more privacy, but procrastination had led to eventual forgetfulness.

"Weren't you going to fix that?" he asked.

"Yeah, I'm still going to."

He rolled his eyes. But I was still a little angry.

"What did you hear?"

"Not much. I went back upstairs when I heard Anna ask you if you were insane or an imbecile, or something like that. I figured it was a private thing. But actually, I probably could have heard it even without the vent."

How much had Rosemary heard over the years? Kevin? No wonder he knew everything about everybody.

"Ross, when you get married, you'll probably learn that private conversations can get kind of loud sometimes. Or maybe not. Maybe you'll have one of those perfect marriages we hear about in general conference."

"Not me. I always say what's on my mind—but I kind of don't like it when other people say what's on their minds, so, I figure I'm saving some woman a lot of misery by staying single." He plowed through another row of potatoes. I brought a pittance of pie to my watering lips.

"So, what do you want to talk about?"

"What makes you think I want to talk about something?"

"You couldn't sleep—and Anna's mad at you, right? And you're here. So, you better talk—or you might get heartburn!" He chuckled as he reloaded.

So again throwing discretion to the wind, I spilled the beans. I told him everything except Saundra's request. Soon the letters and internet articles were spread out on the table. He whipped out his phone and began checking websites about the Kinkaid cave. Lots of people had tried to find it, with no success. But then, when we really dug into their efforts, it appeared that none of them had actually climbed the steep talus slope to the infamous Redwall, and over it to the supposed site. The Redwall had a sheer drop of over a thousand feet, making any investigation problematic. One group said they had tried to rappel down from the rim but got hung up halfway down and almost got fried in the afternoon sun. The canyon runs north and south there, and the wall they hung from faced west, so they were receiving direct sunlight and its reflection off the rocks. Ants under a magnifying glass.

Ross's fingers were flying through the internet. "Huh, did you know that all the peaks around there have Egyptian names?"

"They do?"

He turned his phone toward me, but the picture was too small. He cleared his plate then ran upstairs and got his laptop. Soon we were gazing at pictures of Osiris Tower, a peak near the supposed cave that was named after the Egyptian God of the Dead. Then we checked out the Temple of Ra, a mesa named after the Egyptian Sun God. Other nearby peaks were called the Isis Temple, the Cheops Pyramid, and the Tower of Set—all Egyptian names.

"What does that mean?" Ross asked.

"I don't know. Why would they give them Egyptian names if they were trying to keep a cave full of Egyptian artifacts hidden?"

"Yeah. It doesn't make sense. But Kinkaid—wait, what's his real name?"

"Ephraim Wells."

"Right, Wells said that the Buddha thing looked Oriental."

"Yeah, but he thought most of the things were Egyptian."

Ross started to compare the two Arizona Gazette articles from 1909 then quickly changed subjects. "So, why does the first article spell Kinkaid with a K in the middle and the second one with a C?"

"I don't know, maybe Ephraim didn't know how to spell his friend's name, so he accidently changed the spelling in the second article."

"Yeah, or maybe the newspaper writer got it wrong." He put the articles down and changed the subject again. "But this is all a no-brainer. Someone killed Keith what's-his-name."

"Nelson."

"And you say Johnson's not going to do anything about it?"

Ross knew Johnson from the old days. I tried to explain the lack of a clear crime and the budgetary constraints.

"All right—but still, all of this can't be a coincidence."

I decided to share my dilemma. "So, Saundra, Keith's daughter, wants me to go find the cave."

He laughed. "Why? You're no expert." His lack of guile could almost be endearing.

"Well, actually she wants me to find his killer, but I figure that means finding the cave first, or not, to see if any of this makes sense. If there's no cave, there are no relics, right?"

"Unless he's trying to throw everybody off for some reason."

"By writing a fake letter from 1909—that probably isn't fake?"

He thought about this. "So, where's the actual letter? This is just a copy."

"Johnson kept it."

He nodded. "It would be nice to test the paper and everything."

"That's probably part of the expense they don't want to spend—unless someone can prove there's a cave out there."

He looked at the last page of Well's letter. "What's this? Why's it all by itself?"

"Oh, that's from the back of the last page." On a separate sheet I had photocopied the few words there: "Mouth sealed—South duct?"

"It sounds like somebody duct taped his mouth shut."

I smiled. "It probably has something to do with the mouth of the cave. It looks like he wrote it as an afterthought."

"Does Johnson have it?"

"Sure, he has the whole thing." Something occurred to me. "He has it, but I wonder if he scanned the back of that sheet when he emailed copies to the people in Washington. They may not have that information."

"So, how much would it cost," he asked, "to test everything?"

"I don't know, but she's willing to pay all the expenses."

"The daughter is?"

"Yeah, but only if I do it. She doesn't want an investigator."

Ross Keller can get fixated on things, and at this moment he was fixated on my eyes. Getting uncomfortable, I said, "I know—kind of dumb, huh?"

"No, it's great! No wonder I wanted to come out here so bad! She wants you to do this, and she's willing to pay the expenses?"

"What do you mean, that's why you wanted to come out here?"

"Maybe it's the reason I'm here."

"You didn't come because you wanted to place your investments?"

"*Right*." He couldn't have sounded more cynical. "Didn't you wonder why I keep hanging around? I mean, the money was invested last week, and even though my leg's mostly healed up, I keep sticking around."

"I thought you just liked us."

"Well, kinda. I mean, you guys are great. So, when do we go?"

"No, Ross. I haven't decided anything yet. I need to talk to Saundra again. And even if I do decide to go, I have other clients, and I'll need to wrap up some business before then."

"Like, when, in a day or two?"

"Maybe a week or two. Maybe longer. Besides, Anna doesn't want me to go."

"Ah, so that's why you're an imbecile. Totally makes sense. I mean if somebody killed Keith what's-his-name—"

"Nelson."

"They could kill you too."

"Or you, if you go with me." I tried to pin him down with a direct gaze, but it didn't work.

"Are you kidding? I wouldn't miss this for anything."

As the sky got lighter outside, we gathered our things, cleared the table, and did the dishes. I caught maybe two hours of sleep before getting up. When I came downstairs again, Ross was at the table, eating breakfast.

Chapter 10

Man Under Cover

Whislin Klah prided himself on his strength. He'd always been big, and now at nearly 6-5, 250, he admitted that he had packed on a few unnecessary pounds, but his strength was greater than ever.

In high school he had excelled in sports until his family's frequent moves precluded participation. His father worked on oil rigs, following the work to New Mexico, Texas, Oklahoma, and California. During his senior year in high school in Bakersfield, he dropped in at a mixed martial arts dojo and signed up for lessons. To pay for them, he worked at a car wash around the corner. His strength, endurance, and stealth led him to victories at several tournaments. The day after he graduated from high school, his father gave him a present: a thousand dollars and an order to leave the house. That afternoon, as he walked away from home for the last time, Whislin decided to turn professional. Over the next three months he won six consecutive fights, grossing a little over $11,000. After paying fees to his manager (20%), club (10%), trainer (10%), and expenses for medicals, taxes, and transportation, he netted less than $5,000. Bigger paydays were in the offing, but Whislin Klah, always one to calculate risk, didn't like the profit to pain ratio. His thick, black hair had been pulled out in bunches, his face was lacerated above and below both eyes, and his ears were turning knobby.

He banked his savings, and joined the Marines.

Still eighteen, he found himself in boot camp in San Diego where he once again excelled, both at the physical and emotional challenges. In his first day at boot camp, a short, feisty drill instructor in Echo Company laughed at him because of his name. Whislin responded that "Klah" was Navajo for left-handed, which coincidentally he was.

The drill instructor laughed again, formed his left hand into a grotesque claw, then said, "No, moron, I was laughing at your first name."

Whislin didn't respond, but one evening a week later he saw the D.I. walk into the restroom. As the man sat on the head reading a magazine, Klah silently stole into the adjoining stall, reached under the partition, and grabbed the D.I.'s left leg. The instructor suddenly found himself yanked off the head and onto his face by someone with enormous strength. Klah forced the man's leg into a reverse leg bar (over the shoulder) and squeezed until he felt the knee give way. When the screaming D.I. tried to reach under the partition for Klah's hands, Klah grabbed his left hand and broke some fingers. The vengeance was swift and satisfying. He exited the restroom before anyone could run in to see the cause of the hideous shrieks.

Each member of Klah's company was questioned, but there was no evidence to prove guilt. The drill instructor had not seen the attacker's face or heard his voice. The enormous strength required to commit such a feat, though, and the fact that only the left leg and left hand had been assaulted, left little doubt as to the perpetrator. Klah was singled out for punishing duties for the next twelve weeks, but he continued to excel and eventually graduated with his company.

Over his four years in the Marines several brave men asked about his first name, but he never confided that it came as a result of a condition at birth, that when he breathed through his nose as an infant, he whistled. His father, who was half Navajo and half white, only half-jokingly wanted to name him Whistling Pete. But his mother, who was half white and half Hopi, managed to forge a compromise.

At 22 the strapping man, now sporting a pair of shoulders that wouldn't fit most football shoulder pads, left the Marines and joined the Navy and quickly entered BUD/S—Basic Underwater Demolition/SEAL Training. Nothing about BUD/S is easy. More SEALs have died in training than in combat, but Klah managed the 15-mile runs, six-mile swims, and 20-mile "rucks" (carrying weighted packs) with less trouble than most, and he moved on to SQT—SEAL Qualification Training.

But he was Med-dropped halfway through, meaning he was dropped out of the program for health reasons.

A HALO is a high-altitude, low-opening parachute jump. He had done it before without injury, but on his final jump, from 15,000 feet, another free-falling parachuter had collided with him in mid-air, and Klah wasn't able to open his chute until too late. He hit an outcropping of granite at thirty to forty miles an hour, forcing his right knee to collapse the wrong way, producing the worst pain he had ever known (ironically the same kind of pain he'd given to the drill instructor). The damage included a severed anterior cruciate ligament, torn posterior cruciate ligament, and torn meniscus. After multiple surgeries and nearly a year of desk work, Klah knew his knee would never permit him to operate at the high levels demanded of a Navy SEAL again, so he submitted his request for permanent leave. It was granted, and Whislin Klah became a civilian again.

By then he had saved nearly $50,000. He used his Native heritage, SEAL experience, and natural smarts, to get himself admitted into a prestigious school in the eastern United States. It was there that he met Colin Richardson, a young bug-eyed professor of psychology. The man's eyes were the only thick things about him, unless you counted his glasses. He had a narrow face that led down to a narrow chin that sat atop a body so skinny that Klah looked twice to see if the man was standing sideways. Colin Richardson had a B.A. and M.A. from Yale and a Ph.D. from Harvard. He also had a father who had almost been a U.S. Senator. But more importantly, at least to Klah's future, he claimed to work for one of the most elite and secretive societies on earth.

After class one day, the professor, only six years older than Klah's 26, asked the young man if he had a minute. The professor had noticed the enormous man's quick eye and heavily muscled physique, along with his heavy, prematurely wizened Native features. He had also read three of the young man's papers, which were unusually clear in content and aggressive in tone. In one, Klah had shown an understanding of the oil business, especially in the Texas and California fields. Klah didn't really care for the professor and was about to reject his offer to meet, when the little man said something that made him reconsider.

"I'm intrigued that you're left-handed, as your name implies, but I'm more intrigued by your record in the SEAL qualifying program. Would you have a moment, perhaps this evening, to discuss your future?"

Klah didn't know how the young professor had learned of his service record, so he decided that he had a moment after all.

Over the next two months Klah met with Richardson several times, answering his surprising questions. They were surprising because they implied a knowledge that Whislin Klah had not given to him. The man was somehow gathering intelligence on him. Just after finals, the professor made an offer that seemed calculated to either end their relationship or propel it forward.

Whislin had come home that evening and found his door unlocked. He entered slowly, assuming the assault stance.

"Good evening, Whislin," Richardson said, sitting on a sofa with one of Klah's books in hand. "I hope you don't mind that I came in out of the cold."

Whislin eyed the professor. No apparent threat. He surveyed the room. Clear. He turned back to the professor, consciously slowing his breathing. "How'd you get in?"

"With these." The timid-looking professor, wearing dark slacks, button-up white shirt and blazer, produced a lock pick set. "They're much more convenient than trying to find master keys for all the doors in town." Sitting on the sofa, the man was almost humorously small, a stark contrast to Klah's massive presence, and although Richardson was barely in his thirties, his dark hair had already receded to a point just above his ears. A pair of gold, wire-rim spectacles sat on his nose.

"I could break your neck and tell the cops you tried to attack me when I came in."

The little professor set the book on an end table and stood up. "Which is precisely why I'm here." He held the lock pick set up again. "These are my tools. They are simple and elementary. Yours are of a more, shall we say, masculine nature. But they are also vital, and I have been authorized to seek their services—*your* services—in a vitally important matter."

"Why didn't you just meet me at a restaurant or something?"

"What I have to say is much too sensitive to discuss in public." He produced a fist-sized, yellow electronic device. "And just so you know, I have taken the liberty of sweeping your apartment for surveillance accouterments—for bugs."

"You've taken a lot of liberties."

"As will you, if you accept my proposition."

"Do you work for the government?"

"You might say that I work for the people who *oversee* the government. Please have a seat and I'll explain. And afterward, you can tell me to get lost, and I will—forever. Or you can ask me any question you want, and I may answer you."

Over the next hour Whislin learned of the existence of the Skull and Bones Society, a secret sect nearly 200 years old. Members of the sect, called Bonesmen, are either seniors or alumni of Yale University and have their headquarters in a building in downtown New Haven, Connecticut. Many of the activities, however, are conducted at private residences. Some prominent members have included President William Howard Taft, George H. W. Bush, George W. Bush, John Kerry, James Angleton (father of the CIA), Henry Stimson (Secretary of Defense during WWII), Henry Luce (founder of Time, Life, Fortune, and Sports Illustrated magazines). The Society's financial holdings have never been made public but are reportedly massive.

"So, you tell the government what to do?" Klah asked cynically.

Professor Richardson chuckled. "No, nothing so overt. You might say we nudge it from time to time, from within. We have our own agenda, and the government has theirs, and usually the two work together smoothly. But when the government takes an abrupt turn, as it has recently, we might suggest a correction or two."

"A correction or two?"

"Oh, nothing a reporter could point to, but a private, gentle, 'nudge' to the right person at the right time."

"For example."

"Well, perhaps one, just so you know we are able to conduct our business. You saw how a recent, rather liberal president came into office with both the House and a veto-proof senate behind him."

"Obama."

"Immensely talented, and with the congress he had the power to effect any legislation he desired. Given a strong enough inclination, he could have altered the language, and intent, of the constitution itself."

"You think so?"

"We'll never know, because at a key moment, in his first two years, he was given to know, or shall I use a stronger word, *persuaded* to know, that further radical shifts after the Affordable Care Act, were not desirable—or safe."

"You threatened the life of the president?"

"Oh, nothing so crass, but have you ever wondered why the most talented campaigner ever to occupy the White House, a president who owned both houses of congress, never really tried to accomplish anything beyond Obamacare?"

"Like I said, you threatened the life of the president."

Richardson sat still, his own steely glare driving an immutable fact home. He was serious. This mousy little man had a steel will. And the group he represented was powerful. Klah took a deep breath and got up from his seat, needing a moment to process this new orientation of the world. He walked into the kitchen. "Would you like a beverage? I'm afraid I only have . . ."

"No, thank you. I'll be leaving soon. Please come back here."

For the first time in Klah's memory, he obeyed a direct command without inner turmoil. He would consider this moment often in years ahead. He sat down. "So, what do you want me to do?"

"First, I want you to check out what I've told you, as much as you can. I want you to go on the internet and read about our little group. You won't learn much, but you'll find out that everything I've told you is true—except the part about affecting our recent president's administration. Sadly, for him, that never made it to the papers. Or maybe not so sadly. Can you imagine how history would have judged him if it were known that he had backed down from a small, obscure group of Yale philistines? No, that wouldn't do.

"Second if you're satisfied that we are who we purport to be, I want you to consider accepting a position as an independent contractor."

"Doing what?"

"Being a fixer of sorts."

"Would it include killing people?"

Richardson smiled. "I like the way you think. Always direct. Aggressive. Let me put it this way, if you ever find your life compromised, or if you find the Society itself compromised, then extreme measures may be justified. If that occurs, we will do all we can to protect you from the powers that be, both local and federal. We're actually very good at that. But more importantly, we will rely upon your powers of, shall we say, discretion, to keep your actions as veiled as possible. We will rely on your ability to operate in the dark, to veil your activities from exposure. Indeed, that is one of the reasons I have approached you. We believe in your ability to *resolve* issues with a minimum of fuss."

"We?"

"Naturally I am operating under the authority, and with the approval, of the highest sources."

"How high?"

"I can't reveal that, but they were high enough to get a president's personal attention—and acquiescence."

Whislin surprised himself by not doubting this. Though he was generally not a believer in conspiracies and global intrigues, he didn't kid himself about the existence of powerful men in secret places. The only thing that surprised him was that he himself was being considered for such a position.

"Why me?" he asked.

"Because you have the skills and, as I mentioned, the ability to keep quiet. We were especially impressed by your work with the drill instructor in San Diego."

Now Klah knew how deeply these men could dig into one's life.

"How much will it pay?" He knew this question essentially implied his acceptance of the position.

"It will be on a case-by-case basis, but you will find that you will be able to live rather comfortably. We want your availability at all times, on a moment's notice, so you will not need to worry about other employment. The first job we have for you will pay between fifty and one-hundred-fifty thousand dollars, depending on what is required."

For the next hour, Klah listened to the details of what might be required in a remote county in west Texas.

* * *

My office phone was ringing the next morning as I walked in. It was Saundra, and she was upset.

"Mr. Call, do you have a cell number? I've been trying to reach you all morning." I looked at my watch. It was 8:45. I considered giving her a homily on patience, but instead I gave her my cell number then told her that before I made any decision I wanted more information about Ephraim Wells. She said she didn't have any; she hadn't known he existed until she read the letter.

"Do you think your mom has some information, maybe some family records?"

"I don't know, but here, you can ask her." She gave the phone to her mother.

"Travis?"

"Yes, hi, Claudia. I was telling your daughter that before I make a decision, I want to learn all I can about Ephraim Wells. Do you have any family records or other letters I can look at?"

"No. I think my Uncle Jesse keeps all that."

"Can you ask him?"

"Yes, but why don't you ask him? I'll let him know you're going to call him, okay? Then you can ask him yourself."

I agreed, then I asked how much longer they planned to be in town. They didn't know. They were meeting with an estate attorney that afternoon, hoping to liquidate Keith's holdings soon.

After we hung up, I went through Keith's folder and made a quick list of all of his assets and the firms who handled them. I hoped to sell the securities as soon as I received permission from Saundra. Then I made a list of my other clients' most pressing needs and prioritized them. If I were leaving for a while, I would need to get ahead on my work. Business had been good, which meant the list was long.

At noon, as per my agreement with Claudia, I called her uncle, Jesse Wells. He lived in Salt Lake City, and I learned almost immediately that he was a fellow member of the Church. After introductions, I said: "Claudia may have told you that she wants me to check on some things about her second great uncle, Ephraim Wells. She thought you might have some information."

"Yes, she did, and I've gone online to remind myself of the facts. I've tried to put everything there, you know, in FamilySearch, all the records, letters, pictures—any memories we might have."

I winced. I hadn't done any of this with my own family records. But of course, I had an excuse; I had brain fog whenever I tried to do anything hard.

"That's great. Were you able to find anything?"

"Oh, yes. I have his birth and death dates and . . ."

"So, he actually lived?"

"Oh, yes. Did you doubt that?"

"Well, I wasn't sure. It seems he may have been part of something in Arizona that a lot of people think was a hoax."

"I don't know about that. A hoax about what?"

"A cave he found in the Grand Canyon."

"I didn't see anything about that. But it's interesting, he lived most of his life, from what I can tell, in Idaho, but he died in Yuma.

"When was that?"

"Just a minute." As he typed on a keyboard, he continued talking about his 2nd great grandfather. "I'm glad Claudia's asking about him. It turns out he was quite a character. He claims he was the first white person born in Idaho, but you know, some of the Mormons were up there in the 1840s, and since he wasn't born till 1852 or 3, it's hard to believe that he was the first white child." He typed some more. "Okay, here it is. We don't have an exact date of death. His body was found in the Colorado River on October 2nd, 1909, but his death was sometime before that. There was an investigation by the sheriff, and he deemed the death an accidental drowning. The estimated date of his death was, quote: 'Several days previous,' so he probably died sometime during the last week of September."

I did some quick math in my head. Grant's last note on his brother's letter had been dated August 22nd, about a month before the estimated date of Ephraim's death.

"Do you have a death certificate?"

"Yes, his brother Grant requested a copy from the county. They sent the certificate to him."

"Does it have any other information on it?"

"Well, let me scroll through it and see. It says his residence was a skiff."

"A what?"

"A skiff. I think that means a boat."

"He lived on a boat? Like a houseboat?"

"Well, when I think of a skiff, I think of a rowboat—probably not a houseboat. But I don't know what it meant then."

"Sounds uncomfortable."

"Yeah. It also says his body was discovered close to his skiff. That's what it says. Quote: 'Body discovered in water plants near skiff, south bank, Colorado River.'"

"And they think it was in the water for about a week?"

"That's what it says. 'Estimated.' And at the bottom it says he was buried in a pauper's grave—in Yuma."

"Do you know if he was disinterred and reburied somewhere else, in Idaho maybe?"

"I don't have any information about that. What I've told you is about all we know about Ephraim Wells, except that he was a miner of gold and silver and didn't marry or have children that we know of."

"So, there's nothing about him dealing in Indian artifacts or Egyptian jewelry?"

"No. One of the records we have is from a family Bible, and by Ephraim's name it says: 'Miner, gold and silver.' That's it." He paused for a moment. "But there is one other thing that I find interesting."

"What's that?"

"You're the second person to ask about him in the last few months."

"Really? Who else asked about him?" I was fairly sure I already knew the answer.

"My niece's ex-husband—the one I understand who just died. He called me out of the blue. I had only talked to him at family gatherings, so I was a little surprised. Kind of like today. Is there something going on I should know?"

I wasn't sure how I should answer that, so I tried to limit it to the facts I was aware of.

"I was Keith's financial counselor, and he left some papers about some Indian or Egyptian artifacts that he supposedly found and was trying to sell. I'm trying to determine if there was anything to this, but the fact is, we don't have any proof that he actually found them. He claims he found a letter in Claudia's things, from Ephraim to Grant Wells, the brother you mentioned, that led him to the artifacts."

"So that's why Claudia is interested—the value of the artifacts."

"I believe so."

"I see."

I didn't tell him that these artifacts may have led to Keith's death. Discretion, as Anna liked to say.

"Just one more thing," I said. "Do you happen to know if Ephraim was a member of the Church?"

"No, but I've wondered about that. His grandfather was a member. He came out with the Saints. And Ephraim's father was a member, but he had stopped participating in the Church when he moved to Idaho. There is no record of the children being baptized. My father joined the Church when he was a teenager, and that's how our line got back in. Claudia's line never rejoined as far as I know."

We chatted for another minute or so, then we said good-bye. I believed everything he said, but the only important thing I learned was that Ephraim Wells had been in Yuma, just like G.E. Kinkaid had been, and that he owned a boat on the Colorado, just like Kinkaid had. I didn't believe these were coincidences. I believed the two men were one in the same. And I now fully believed that Wells/Kinkaid had done everything he claimed he had done in the Arizona Gazette.

And as a result, I fully believed that his great, great grand nephew by marriage, Keith Nelson, had been killed for the relics he had found in the cave Ephraim had discovered—and which the government may have been hiding for over a hundred years.

Chapter 11

A Pronouncement

The next week, after spending a day in fasting and prayer, and after a frantic Monday trying to get ahead with my clients, I made an announcement. The children loved our family home evenings, which included a prayer, songs, a lesson, and fun. Anna seemed to like them too, as she tried to come home early on Mondays so she and Rosemary could help the kids make special treats. We were growing as a family, with eight people in the home. After our last game, right before a closing song and prayer, I asked for a moment.

Kevin, who had lost the last game, made his own comment first: "I hope it's about people *cheating* in our games."

"Actually, Kevin, it has nothing to do with cheating. And do you know why?"

"*Why?*" he said almost challengingly. He sat by himself in a corner chair with his arms folded.

"Because I don't think we have a problem with cheating in our family. I think people in our family are honest. Don't you, Kalley?"

Lawyers are taught to never ask a question in court that they don't know the answer to. I was about to learn why.

"Not too much," she said, "except for when Kevin cheats at school."

"*What?*" Kevin exploded. "I *never!*..." His arms flew open in a display of victimhood. He was standing, his eyes darting from his sister to his mother to Ross to Rosemary, and finally to me.

"Kevin, please sit down."

"But I don't cheat!"

"Yes, you do!" Kalley declared. "I saw you looking at Missy's paper in our test today!"

"Why would I do that? I don't even *have* to cheat. You're the one who gets F's!"

"That's enough," I said forcefully. "Kevin, sit down."

He did so, and I was about to move on, not because I wasn't interested in Kevin's cheating or Kalley's F's, neither of which I had known about, but because I hoped to avoid a further delay in my announcement, but then I heard muffled sniffling from Kalley. I looked to my left, where she was sitting on the sofa, crying into a pillow. I turned back to Kevin.

"Kevin, please apologize to your sister."

He glared across the room, unyielding. I looked to Anna for help, but she avoided my gaze with great success. I turned to Rosemary.

"Don't look at me," she said, pushing herself back into her plump, overstuffed chair and smoothing her short graying hair. "I don't cheat."

I took a deep breath and chanced a glance at Ross, who, sure enough, was smirking. I scooted over and put my arm around Kalley, and she cried harder.

"Honey, don't worry about what Kevin says. I believe you."

"*What?*" Kevin erupted, rising to his feet and throwing his arms open again. "You think I cheat?" The boy had a gift for drama.

"Sit down, Kevin."

"I don't *believe* this! Why would I cheat? I always get A's!"

Anna came to the rescue. "Kevin, did you look at Missy's paper today?"

He hesitated, and everyone in the room, possibly even Lucas and Mia, knew he was guilty.

"Probably."

"Why?" Anna asked.

"Because he *likes* her!" Kalley blurted, her face coming out from behind the pillow.

"I do not!"

"Do so!"

"Do not!"

"Do so!"

I had heard about family home evenings like this from several old and grizzled parents. I held Kalley a little tighter, still trying to calm her. Anna again spoke to the boy.

"Why did you look at her paper?"

"Because she always gets the wrong answers."

"And why do you care about that?"

"'Cause I always know what grade she's gonna get, and that makes her mad."

Who was this child? What kind of monster were we raising?

"Really?" I said. "You know what her grades will be before she gets her paper back?"

"Course. And I know what grades my grades will be too—A's!" He stared at Kalley, and she fell to sobbing again.

I couldn't remember the question that had started this fiasco. Oh, right, something about cheating.

"Kevin, do you ever cheat in class?"

"Oh, *riiiiight.*"

That seemed to settle it for him. And, frankly, for me too. The kid may be arrogant and mean, but he wasn't a cheater. I could only imagine what Lucas and Mia, both wide-eyed, were learning from this important lesson. I tried to take control again.

"Anyway, as I *mentioned*, I have an announcement to make— actually a question for you all." They looked at me. "I have been asked to investigate something for one of my clients, but it means that I might have to be gone for a while."

I waited for pleading entreaties. None came.

"So, I thought I would see how you feel about this. Are you okay if I have to leave for a few days, or maybe a week. Or two."

At these last words, Anna's eyes narrowed.

I expected a question from Rosemary, but she sat silently in her comfortable chair, unaffected by the prospect of my absence. It was then that I realized that she and Anna had been talking, that she probably knew I was going to leave before I did. I looked at Kevin, whose wheels were clearly spinning.

"Where are ya goin'?" he asked.

"To Arizona."

"How come?"

"Because I need to look for something."

The wheels still spun. "I looked at a map of Arizona last night on my phone. It's big. How do you know where to find it?"

"Arizona?"

"No, the thing you're lookin' for."

"Well, I know about where it's at. And why were you looking at a map of Arizona last night?"

He ignored the question. "Is it by the Grand Canyon?"

"Yes. And how did you know that?"

He glanced at his mother and said, "'Cause I heard Mom and Rosemary talkin' about it yesterday."

The two women were suddenly more interested in the discussion. "We'll talk about that later," I said. "So, how do you feel, are you kids okay with me leaving for a while?"

Kevin looked at Kalley, who looked at him, their dispute forgotten. "Yeah, sure," Kevin said, "but Mom will be mad."

"No, I think we've got that worked out, Kevin. Mom understands." I hadn't risked another look at her.

"I don't *think* so," Kevin said. "They were talkin' an' I heard her tell Rosemary that you're . . ."

"That's enough, Kevin!" Anna came to the rescue again. In this case, her own.

"But you said . . ."

"I know what I said," she uttered through clenched teeth.

"It's not nice to eavesdrop," Rosemary added. "You should never do that."

"Why not? You do it when Mom and Dad are talking. I seen you do it in the kitchen."

If I didn't stop this now, the lot of us would be filing for divorces. "Kevin, listen to me. Mom and I have got this worked out. She doesn't really want me to go, but she knows I might have to because of, well, I have obligations."

Calculations whirred in his head again. "Does 'obligations' mean ya can do anything ya want, and Mom can't stop you?"

Anna stepped in again. "We don't stop each other, Kevin. We give our opinions and let each other do what we think is right. Daddy thinks it's right for him to go to the Grand Canyon, so he's going to go."

His keen brain moved on, running circles around my own. "Are ya gonna take my wrist rocket?"

"I don't know. I haven't thought about it."

"It can kill things, ya know. I killed like nine . . ."

"Yes, we know what you did."

"But, if ya run into any Indians, and ya have to clear 'em out—"

"All, right, Kevin. Thank you for your advice." I turned to Anna. "Well, that seems settled. I guess I'm going."

She didn't respond, but Kevin, the wheels fairly steaming, said, "When I grow up and get married, I'm gonna get obligations too, so

I can do anything I want." He turned to Kalley with a sly grin. "And you better watch out, 'cause your husband's prob'ly gonna get obligations too."

That got her crying again, and I told her to ignore him again. Then we quickly had a closing song, "Count Your Blessings," and a prayer, a rather short one, and disbanded to the kitchen for treats and safety.

In retrospect, I was grateful that I had fasted and prayed that day.

Chapter 12

A Cover-Up of Truth & Light

Whislin Klah knew that the job in west Texas was his probation. If he succeeded, he would get paid. If he succeeded well, he would get future contracts. If he failed, he might get eliminated.

It was a messy situation. The Society, according to Richardson, owned majority shares in dozens of once-retired oil wells, but these wells were beginning to produce again because of a technology called hydraulic fracturing, or "fracking." By these methods the wells were about to start producing millions of dollars in profits. It was like discovering an old bank account you had forgotten about—and the interest had grown to seven, eight, or nine figures. But there was a problem: A local do-gooder on the county court of commissioners had been converted to the notion that fracking led to all sorts of maladies, including earthquakes and volcanoes. The last thing he wanted was his semi-desert prairie to be turned into an apocalyptic wasteland by the oil boys, so he got on his soap box and began converting the citizenry to the idea of strict regulations regarding hydraulic fracturing. His proposed regulations were so strict, in fact, that they made California's regulations look childlike.

Normally the big boys, like Exxon and Standard, took care of nuisances like this, but they didn't have many wells in the county, so it fell to the Society to protect their own interests. They had tried quiet, behind-the-scenes negotiations, Richardson said, then manipulation, but these attempts failed, mostly because the do-gooder didn't seem to have any vices they could leverage. So the Society decided to give Richardson's new boy a try.

Whislin moved to the county seat and quickly learned that the locals were not quite as anxious to straightjacket the oil industry as their sterling commissioner was. But unfortunately two of the other four members of the court had already been turned and would almost certainly vote with him. Whislin had less than thirty days to effect a change of heart in one of the three commissioners before a final vote was taken.

It took him less than ten—and the change of heart was final.

By careful surveillance he learned that one of the three commissioners had a drinking problem. Nothing severe, but three or four shots of whiskey each evening left the man slightly inebriated. Whislin slipped into the man's home when he and his wife were out and added a small dose of Tincture of Monkshood to the half empty bottle of whiskey. Monkshood, a beautiful ornamental flower found nearly everywhere, produces one of the more deadly toxins in the plant world. Whislin's father grew it and applied the tincture on his arrowheads when bow hunting each fall. In whiskey, three or four shots of the mixture should have been enough to make the man violently ill. As the man was recovering, Klah planned to leave a message in the house one night, something like: "Remember, fracking can be good for your health." But, according to the police report, the man and his wife got into an argument on the way home and he drank the half empty bottle. He was dead before midnight.

A day later Klah stole back into the house and removed the bottle. No reason to leave evidence behind—or allow collateral damage to the wife. He wasn't a merciless killer. A coroner's report declared the cause of death as a heart attack, which it had been, eventually.

Klah calculated the possible consequences of his action. He knew that if things went south and he were prosecuted, the charge would probably be reduced to manslaughter or criminally negligent homicide. But in the meantime, his bosses didn't know that the killing had been unintentional, and they would think he was willing to do anything for their fine organization. Plus, because he had just killed somebody while under contract to them, the Society was criminally liable as well, making them as beholden to him as he was to them. They were all in this together. Which meant, in the long run, his value to them had just increased.

Unless they chose to eliminate him as well.

Which he would be ever vigilant to prevent.

So, all in all, what did the killing mean? More than likely an increase of respect from his employers, possibly leading to an increase in pay. As long as he survived, there was no downside to it—unless one factored in the possibility of an afterlife. But though he respected his mother's belief that spirits rode on the wind, he didn't believe they were any stronger than he was. And the idea of a God greater than all the spirits? He had never seen any evidence of that, though there had been solemn moments at night when his conscience haunted him.

Back in Texas, the do-gooder couldn't convince any of the other county commissioners to vote for his regulations, so the cause died a quiet death. Within a fortnight Klah was paid in full, and three months later the Society was supposedly churning out money as fast as the crews could fracture the earth.

And it had all been done so quietly, so tidily, though somewhat accidentally, that, despite those solemn bouts of guilt, Klah wondered if he had a gift.

His future assignments didn't require such dire actions again until the foggy night when Keith Nelson went down. Whislin had actually been given the choice of eliminating the man or, if that was too dangerous, buy him off. But when Nelson had lied then mocked a medicine man, Klah had hit him, maybe a little too hard.

The accidental killer.

* * *

After graduation, Klah had moved to Flagstaff, which was close enough to his family that he could attend the occasional gathering but distant enough that he wouldn't have to answer too many questions about his career. He had kept Richardson informed of his movements, so he wasn't surprised when he came home one evening and found the door unlocked and Richardson inside.

Just like old times.

Richardson told him that something important had come up, more important than any job so far. They sat down in the living room and he got right to the point, mentioning the highlights of the cave, Ephraim Wells, and the artifacts.

Klah was skeptical. "A cave like that," he said, "people would know about it. You can't keep a mile-long cave a secret."

"Maybe the government can't, but we can. And we have. We shut it down completely, covered it up—with some help from key friends."

"Which friends?"

"First, let me explain something about Ephraim Wells. He had become a real problem, not just for the Smithsonian, but, in some ways, for science. And in some people's minds, he was even a far bigger threat than that."

"That's pretty big."

Richardson shook his head. "It sounds crazy now, but the people in the know were worried, very worried, about the future, not only of science, but of Christianity."

A laugh escaped Klah's lips. "Christianity?"

"You have to understand the times. Scientific skepticism wasn't as great back then. Religion still held sway in the halls of research. The President of the United States—Taft—like most presidents, was a devout Christian and tried to promote an environment for Christian values in the country. Others felt the same way, even scientists, like Charles Walcott, the secretary of the Smithsonian. He was a zealous believer, and unfortunately he wasn't above slighting a lesser truth to protect a greater truth."

Klah rolled his eyes.

"Try to suspend your disbelief, Whislin? This is important."

Klah willed himself to be patient. "So, what kind of truths are we talking about?"

"Let me give you an example. You've heard of the Wright Brothers? Built the first airplane?"

Whislin waved him onward.

"The truth was, they built the first heavier-than-air aircraft, but they didn't get the credit for decades. Their airplane, the one that made history, was rejected for display at the Smithsonian because the guy in charge, that same Charles Walcott, personally refused it. Why? Because he was trying to protect a friend's legacy."

"He kept the Wrights out of the Smithsonian?"

"Yep—he lied about man's greatest achievement to that date."

"But there are pictures of the first flight. I've seen them. Didn't What's-His-Name know that?"

"First, 'What's-His-Name' was an important man. Charles Walcott determined what science was and wasn't in his day. He was a close friend of the Wright brothers' main competitor, Samuel Langley. You've heard of Langley Field, right? CIA headquarters? It was named after him. Also, Walcott had the Smithsonian invest fifty-thousand dollars in Langley's venture. And Walcott felt that because the Smithsonian had helped finance the construction of Langley's plane, which had been catapulted off the earth for about three seconds before crashing into a river, that the institution could declare *that* plane the first to fly. So Langley's demolished plane was rebuilt and put in the Smithsonian as the first heavier-than-air flying machine. And there it sat, a bald-faced lie—for almost *fifty years*. The Wright Brothers' plane finally got displayed in some museum in London, but in the meantime, because of Walcott's lie, the Wright brothers almost lost all of their patents. It was literally a fifty-year legal struggle for their survival. In fact, one of the brothers, I don't remember which, died before the truth was finally recognized."

Klah hadn't heard this before, but he didn't doubt it. The professor, was, after all, a professor. "So, you're saying he was willing to lie to protect his friends."

"It was bigger than that—worse than that. He was willing to bury a truth if he thought it was necessary to protect a higher truth. And what was the highest truth in the world to Charles Walcott?

"Religion?"

Richardson nodded. "Christianity. And he was willing to protect that from anything, everything, even from the theory of evolution—which, by the way, he actually believed in."

Klah laughed. "He believed in evolution but was willing to protect Christianity from it? How'd that work?"

"Simple— he was one of the first scientists to blend the book of Genesis with Darwin's theory of natural selection. God still made the world in seven long days, but according to Walcott, he just used natural selection to create the animals and plant life. Evolution made perfect sense to him, once he could fit Christianity into it."

"So what's this got to do with the cave?"

Richardson raised a finger as if this were the most important thing to understand. "Ephraim Wells was either a Mormon, or he knew a lot about Mormonism, and he thought the hieroglyphics and the mummies in the cave were proof that the Book of Mormon was true, which meant, to him at least, that conventional Christianity was false."

Klah stared at him. "That's a big leap."

"Have you ever read the Book of Mormon?"

"No."

"According to the man who produced it, one Joseph Smith, it was originally written in Egyptian hieroglyphics on gold plates by Indians thousands of years ago. He said he got the plates from an 'angel' and translated them into English. But, of course, nobody has ever seen the plates or can even prove that any Indians ever knew Egyptian. But in 1909 all these Egyptian hieroglyphics show up in a cave in the

Grand Canyon. So, you can see Wells' reasoning: The cave was major ammunition for Mormonism, because if the Book of Mormon was true, then the Church was true, and all the other forms of Christianity were not, because there are some big differences between Mormon Christianity and other forms."

Klah thought about this. If any of it were true, if the cave actually held evidence that Native Americans wrote in ancient Egyptian, he could see why Christian believers might want to bury it.

"So Walcott ordered a cover-up?"

"Yes, and probably not just because of the Egyptian problem. When he was young, he had done a lot of field work in the canyon and was even considered one of the great experts on Marble Canyon, the part of the canyon where the cave supposedly was. But he never saw the cave. Not a trace. So, imagine his embarrassment a few years later when this itinerant miner comes along and spots it from two thousand feet below, and it's maybe the biggest archeological find in the Western Hemisphere."

"Yeah, that would rankle."

"I don't know how much he told the president, but at some point President Taft told him to talk to Gerald Grander, another Bonesman. Grander was a lawyer who had worked in Native American law, mostly with the provenance of graves and artifacts. Grander listened to Walcott and immediately saw the scope of the problem and recommended another Bonesman, Fletcher Winn, to take care of it. Winn was a real piece of work. He'd been involved in the latest Indian flare-up at Wounded Knee, about ten years before. Maybe you've heard of it. Major massacre. The way he put it: he helped 'clean the problem up.' The guy really knew how to protect important people and their interests, if they paid enough."

"Kind of like me, huh?"

Richardson saw his mistake but decided to double down on it. "That's right. Every important institution needs fixers. You've been a good one so far, and we've shown our appreciation. The Smithsonian needed a fixer then—a good one—but Winn made some mistakes. And frankly, that's why we need you now."

"What'd he do?"

"For starters, he put himself first. That's a big no-no. He saw a chance to make some money and pay off some debts. He went down there with a professor of archeology, Sterling Jordan, and a crew of about twenty men. They built a narrow-gauge railroad from the south rim above Marble Canyon to the Grand Canyon Railway. Then they lowered ropes and cables over the rim to the cave and began hauling stuff out."

"What kind of stuff?"

Richardson eyed him carefully. "Yeah, you'd be interested in this. Mostly it was stone statues and earthenware pottery, but they also pulled out swords and helmets and armor made of hardened copper. Some of the alloys, supposedly, were things we can't make today. They even pulled out a two-ton statue that looks like a Buddha—I've got pictures—but it's probably just a statue of one of their leaders. And pulling that out was no small feat. The rim is almost a third of a mile above the cave. Then they pulled out three of the mummies— before about two hundred of your people, the Hopis, showed up with loaded guns and basically threatened a battle if they didn't stop looting the cave. There was a big standoff, two dozen white men against two hundred Indians with guns. They told Winn how the cave had been hewed out of stone over centuries for protection from raiding parties from the south—and eventually as a holy sepulcher for their greatest leaders. I'm sure you've heard of the Emergence Hole—or Cave."

Klah paused before answering. He wasn't necessarily a believer in the old ways, but this was sacred ground to many of his people. He nodded.

"They told Winn the cave they were looting was their Emergence Hole, the origin of their entire people. They had come out of it when they were sure that the threats from the south were over. The other Emergence Cave, the one everyone knows about on the Little Colorado, is a ruse to mislead people. Winn wasn't a total fool, and he parleyed well. The Indians said he could keep what he had, but they had to stop. Right then. That moment. But, of course, by then almost everything was gone and sitting in a warehouse back east."

"The Smithsonian's warehouse?"

"Good question. Not a trinket. Most of it was sent to 64 High Street, New Haven, Connecticut."

"The Society's headquarters?"

"You've done your research. Yes. But his biggest mistake was that he also sent some of the more valuable pieces—of course they were *all* valuable—to his own rented warehouse in New Haven."

"And what happened to them?"

"Like I said, debts were paid by quietly selling the wares. The black market was just starting to heat up because of the Egyptian discoveries—the actual ones in Egypt. We don't know where the big statue went, but then Winn sold one of the mummies. We wish he hadn't done that."

"So, do you know where the stuff ended up?"

"We think the mummy Winn sold might be on display in southern Arizona. We did some checking, and it looks like it passed through several owners, but now it's under lock and key in a cheap, private museum."

"So, the Smithsonian never got the stuff?"

"Not that we know of. And if they did, it was only through the black market. So when they say they don't know anything about this—and, believe me, they get asked all the time because the story about Kinkaid's Cave is all over the internet—they're telling the truth. Their records were scrubbed by Walcott. In fact, you can't even find the name of Sterling Jordan anymore."

"And nobody talked? That's almost as hard to believe as anything."

"You're right about that, except—"

"Except somebody *did*?"

"Wells. He went to the press when he realized the artifacts were being sent to New Haven and not to Washington. You can read the whole interview online. Just look up Kinkaid's Cave."

"*Kinkaid*? I thought his name was Wells."

"He used a different name when he went to the paper. And he went to it twice, but the funny thing is, somebody spelled the name wrong the second time. Of course, he should have used a totally different name the second time because the story was a lot more detailed, and it ended up giving him away. The fool actually thought that by using the alias he could escape detection. You see, the whole crew had been put under oath not to talk about the cave, under threat of death. I don't know anything else about him, but he had to be something of a simpleton. He never would have made it as a crook."

"So, Kinkaid's Cave? I've never heard of it."

"When the second article came out, Walcott and Winn worked hard to make sure the whole thing looked like a hoax. They buried the story in the east, and it never appeared anywhere else. One of the first great examples of 'spin.'"

"And Kinkaid didn't talk again?"

"He couldn't."

"Why not?"

"He was dead. The same with Jordan, who's name showed up in the paper with Kinkaid's."

"Winn killed them?"

"More than likely he had them killed."

"And now the cave has been found again."

"Looks like it, and that's why I'm here. If it's the real deal, we need to know, and you'll need to shut it down, quickly, quietly, and completely. Remember, this isn't about profits, this is about survival. If it gets out that the Society had anything to do with the cover-up of maybe the greatest archeological discovery in the New World, we won't last."

"Neither will the Smithsonian."

Richardson considered this. "Like I said, they really don't know anything about it, so they have plausible deniability. But forget them. Take care of us. If you can meet this guy, find out if he's a genuine threat, and if he is, either buy his silence or create it. We need things to stay the way they are."

"Until somebody else finds the cave."

"Not likely. The fact is, we don't know how this guy could have found it. The cave was sealed shut by Winn's crew in 1909. Native stone and mortar. You can't even tell there's a cave there now. I'll show you pictures in a minute. The Hopis knew about it at one time, of course, but they weren't talking, and now, I don't know if any of them still know about it."

"They always pass their knowledge on. Someone knows."

"Maybe, but like I say, they're not talking. This other guy seems to be the only possible source of danger. Back in 1909, even the work crew didn't talk. They saw what happened to Wells and Jordan and understood the benefits of silence."

Klah understood the importance of the job, but he was wondering why it had come to this. "I still don't see why they didn't just let people know about the cave, take tours, show them the Egyptian stuff. I bet somebody would've come up with some way to save Christianity. I mean, really—the whole Church was going to fall?"

"Like I said, they made some mistakes—Walcott and Winn both. But here we are."

They discussed modes of procedure. Richardson opened a briefcase and gave Klah photos taken in 1909, both of the cave and the artifacts. One photo had been taken with a long lens from across the canyon, showing where the cave was on the east wall, but as

Richardson had said, the cave itself was indiscernible. No visible trace of it. They decided that Klah would go on the dark web as a potential buyer, meet with the seller, and determine if the artifacts were genuine. Then, if necessary, Klah would eliminate him, or less likely, buy him off. In exchange for these services, Whislin Klah would be paid $250,000.

When they finished, Klah understood the importance of his mission—and the consequences of failure.

* * *

But now, days after the killing, Whislin knew almost nothing more. Richardson had told him that the cops had basically dropped the investigation but that the guy's financial counselor, one Travis Call, might still be nosing around. Klah had seen Call and Nelson's ex-wife and daughter at the funeral, which was expected, but when they went to Call's office, that concerned him. Were they wrapping up Nelson's finances, or was it more ominous than that?

He had already placed a high-end GPS tracking device on Call's old Lexus so he could follow his movements in real time. But that had led nowhere, as Call basically went nowhere.

A year before, Klah had spent three weeks of intense training in high-tech surveillance. He had been given the best tools and had learned how to track everything from cars to computers to satellites, and he could break into anything from a glove box to a million-dollar safe.

Last Monday night he had used his skills to break into Call's office. Call's computer was password protected, of course, but Klah had just the answer for such obstructions, an 8-GPU Sagitta Brutalis. He connected the Brutalis to Call's computer, and Call's eight-character password was cracked in thirteen minutes. The Brutalis was pricy but worth the cost when time was short. But in this case the hacking didn't lead to much. A quick scan of the search history showed that Call had not used the computer for any searches relating to the Grand Canyon, Native artifacts, Egyptian relics, or even Kinkaid's Cave. If Call was still looking into Nelson's death, he hadn't done it on this machine.

Klah also installed tracing software on Call's computer and a bug on his office phone. The tracing software could even record verbal conversations in the office when the computer was on, and Klah could access all this information on his cell phone. Life in black-ops was getting easy.

But just because Call didn't use his office computer for searches on the cave didn't mean he had lost interest. If Klah could get access to Call's computers at home, especially his laptop, he might find out for sure whether Call was still nosing around.

For another week he surveilled the house but never found it unoccupied. If the nanny wasn't home with the two little kids, Ross Keller was there. But the truth was, even if Whislin had gotten in, it might not have led to anything, as Call had the annoying habit of taking his laptop wherever he went, even to church on Sundays. No, Klah would need to break in at night, which was risky with so many people inside—especially as one of those people was Ross Keller, who was almost as big as Klah and had, according to newspaper accounts, killed a previous intruder with his bare hands.

This would require some thought.

Klah had received half the money soon after dispensing with Nelson, but the rest had been held back until all parties were satisfied that no further investigations were being conducted. At this point it appeared that Travis Call was almost certainly the only possible threat—the last impediment to Klah receiving the final $125,000.

Chapter 13

Fearsome Breathings Out

Ross and I spent the next two weeks researching Marble Canyon, deep in the east end of the Grand Canyon where the cave supposedly lay. After studying 3-D images of online maps and watching several videos of cross country treks into the canyon, we began to realize the terrible vastness of the area and the complexity of the undertaking. The more I learned, the more my admiration for Keith Nelson grew. But it also suggested that if a slight, middle-aged man could reach the cave, so could we.

But the more I talked with Ross about this, the less Anna seemed to be talking to me. This would not do. I had an obligation to my wife and family before any other duty. On Friday night I took her out for a nice dinner and a live show at the Gallo Center that she wanted to see. When we came out, the night air was warm and clear. The fog was a distant memory. March in Modesto can be beautiful. While driving home, I thought I would say something provocative.

"I love you, Anna."

There was a long silence in which I realized my statement wasn't as provocative as I had hoped. "Did I say something wrong?"

"No, but I know you only said it because you're leaving on a fool's errand, and you want to get back in my good graces before you go."

That pretty much summed up the situation, but I thought I deserved some points for trying. "Isn't loving you enough?"

"Of course not." Her soft, beautiful lips could say just about anything and get away with it, while I, on the other hand, could say almost nothing without getting a silent rebuke. "I expect far more than that," she finally added. "Just like you do."

Well, at least we were past the silent treatment. "What do you mean?"

This opened the lid, so to speak, on a free-flow of information to which I was not previously privy—and frankly hope not to be again.

"Actually, I'm not sure anymore. I used to think marriage was about respect and honor, as well as love. I used to think it meant doing something for the other person just because the other person wanted it, or needed it—or not doing something because the other person didn't want you to do it. I didn't realize it meant giving the other person total freedom to do anything he wanted." She paused while obviously making a conscious decision to change the subject of her theme from "other person" to the third person singular. "I thought my feelings might be considered."

"Well, yes," I began, assuming that she wished me to speak. "I actually did . . ."

"I don't think you know what you did. I feel like a stranger in my own marriage. I feel like you and Ross are better partners than you and I are. I feel like if I said something like, 'The house is on fire,' you'd just look at me and say, 'Well, that's nice, Honey. Now can I get back to planning my big adventure with my best buddy?'"

"That's not fair."

"Oh, fair? You want fair? Think about how fair it is that Rosemary has to teach our children that, no, daddies aren't always the boss in every family, and, no, they can't always do whatever they want—that most daddies, most *good* daddies, try to work things out with their wife before going off to hunt for some killer in the Grand Canyon."

"Anna, we've been over this. We *have* worked it out. I'm just going there to find some evidence that what Keith said in his letter is true."

"No, we haven't worked it out. *You* worked it out."

"But I told you I wouldn't go, and you said I should."

"Of course I did. What did you expect me to say?"

This dumbfounded me, so I changed course. "But I told you I was going to fast and pray about it."

"That's right. You *told* me. Think about it. How would you like it if one of my clients asked me to personally investigate a possible murder, which by the way, isn't totally out of the question, because I actually represent murderers sometimes."

"I think I would under . . ."

"But that's not all. Then if they asked me to leave the state and go sneaking around somewhere that is *restricted by law*—not for long, just for a week or two or three."

Frankly I was glad she threw in the "week or two or three," because I had no answer for the "sneaking around" part.

"Just a week, or two—probably not even that long."

"All right—how would *you* feel?"

Ever the lawyer, she was asking a question that she already knew the answer to.

"Anna, a man is dead, and I seem to be his only chance at getting some justice. And his family . . ."

"You are not his only chance at justice, Counselor."

That was going too far. *She* was the real counselor; I was just a lowly financial advisor. I made a mistake and said as much.

"Oh, you're not a *high* counselor?" she retorted. "You don't represent the stake president? How do you think he would feel if he knew about this? Maybe we should give him a call."

Wisely, I fell silent—something I was learning to do with more frequency.

"But you didn't answer my question. How would you feel if the roles were reversed?"

I feigned seeing a near accident off to her side, said "Whoa!" and even jerked the wheel a little, but that didn't distract her. She had gone up against far better tacticians and knew what was important. And right now, her question was important. "Well, I said," glancing back, glad to see the imaginary accident fully avoided, "—Wait, what did you say?"

She exhaled loudly. "How would you feel? Can you see why I might feel the way I do?"

"Oh, well, yeah, sure."

We again fell into silence, and I waited for the expiration date on this conversation to pass—especially the part about sharing my plans with the stake president. Still driving down 9th Street, I idly watched several teenage waifs scurrying away from a store with mounds of unopened packages.

"*Yeah, sure?*" she repeated, recalling my line from what seemed like a previous conversation. "And that's supposed to—what? Make me feel better? Make this whole thing disappear?"

Her powers of discernment were unnerving.

"Of course not," I said. "It's just that, the man is *dead!* I feel like I have an obligation to him."

"Oh, and that was a wonderful word to teach our son. Now he has 'obligations' every time I ask him to do something."

I turned and looked at her in true, subject-changing disbelief. "He does? I'll speak to him as soon as we get home." Which, by my calculations, couldn't be soon enough. "I can't believe he's being defiant."

She stared at me like I was crazy. "You can't believe he's *defiant?* This is Kevin we're talking about, our twelve-year-old defiant genius."

"Has he been doing this for long?"

"What? No! Yes! Don't try to change the subject!" She continued staring at me, while my own eyes were focused, or rather unfocused, on the road.

"Travis, you're—you're, *unbelievable!*"

I detected a tremor in her voice, the beginnings of a new emotion. Anna was many things, most of them very good, but one of them was not a *crier*. I swallowed, humbled, and glanced at her again. She was staring out her window, perhaps also hoping that we could get home sooner.

What a disaster.

And all I had done was say, I love you.

"I'm sorry, Anna. I didn't know you felt so strongly about this. I won't go if you really don't want me to."

Silence. Dead silence. The kind that I had been praying for just a minute ago.

We pulled into the garage, and her door opened before we stopped. Then she stopped and turned and said, "You go. You both go. And if you get killed or get arrested or break your neck and get paralyzed, just remember—"

She didn't finish.

"Anna, I won't go."

"GO!" Her eyes were blazing. "You go, and every time I do something you don't like, just remember this. Just remember that I told you to go when you knew, absolutely knew, that I wanted you to stay home." She got out, slammed the door, and went inside.

For the next several minutes I mused over my ability to put myself in no-win situations. Then I transferred my guilt to Anna and mused over her ability to put me in those situations. Then, just to be fair, I recalled a time or two when Marsha had put me in some no-win situations. Then, purely by the grace of God, I realized that such thinking could only result in more no-win situations, and I bowed my head and said a brief prayer, one of contrition and penitence as well as supplication for wisdom.

Rosemary had already put the kids to bed and Ross was out with friends from church. It cheered me a little to know that he was making friends in the Young Adult ward he had begun attending. Rosemary went upstairs, and I went into the family room and watched the news for a while, but the stream of murder and mayhem depressed me so much that I turned it off. My options were to go upstairs and possibly dig myself into a worse no-win situation, or flee to my home office and do some work. By two that morning the work was done and the coast, I hoped, was clear. I snuck upstairs and got ready for bed in the dark, and I silently, oh so silently, slipped under the covers. Then I remembered my prayers, got out, went into the closet, and offered a desperate benediction on the day.

Chapter 14

Holding A Council

Over the next few weeks I got ahead on my work, while trying to find an honorable way to avoid the trip, but neither Anna nor Saundra Flament would have any of it. One Saturday on the way to the Bass Pro Shop in Manteca to get our supplies, Ross broached the subject.

"So, are you sure you should even be going?"

I spied him out of the corner of my eye. "How much have you heard?"

"First-hand, not very much, but from Kevin, a lot."

My head slumped ,and I had to will myself to look back at the road. "What does he know?"

"You probably don't want to know. I think the vent that goes to the kitchen must go to his bedroom too."

When our house was built, just before we moved to Modesto, about ten years ago, it was supposedly a contractor's house, with attention paid to every detail. Marsha and I could barely afford it, but we indulged, thinking the security of living in a well-built home was worth the sacrifice. Now if I could have found the supposed contractor, I would have given him the house back, along with a schematic of a professional ducting system.

I told Ross that Anna was insisting that I go kill myself.

He chuckled. "Yeah, we prob'ly will. The more I look at the 3-D maps, the more I think we're done for. There's a reason why they call it the *Grand* Canyon—because you can prob'ly fit all the other canyons in the world in it. Have you ever been to Yosemite?"

"Yeah, sure."

"Then you've seen El Capitan—three thousand feet of rock, straight up."

"Yeah."

"The north face of the Grand Canyon is *twice* that high. Think of El Capitan, on top of El Capitan."

I was about to turn around and go back, to go tell Anna that she was crazy—there was *no way* I was going to the canyon—but then a thought hit me. "Wait, we're not going up the north wall; we're going up the east wall, in Marble Canyon."

"Think of half of El Capitan on top of El Capitan."

I forged on to the store. Although I already owned a backpack and good boots, Ross had left his in Utah, so he produced the credit card that his former fiancé had been bragging about and ransacked the store. The old Lexus barely held everything on the way home. There was no way we could tote half of it on our backs.

Definitely, fools on an errand.

By mid-April I could find no more excuses to avoid the trip; my clients were as prepared for my absence as they could be, and we had all the supplies we could think of. We would be leaving on a Monday morning in Ross's truck. His lifted 4x4 should easily tackle whatever ruts we might find.

The Sunday before, our family gathered in the evening. I was moved by the sight—eight souls, all trying to live together in harmony. I told them that Ross and I would be going on our great adventure the next morning and that I wanted them to know how much I loved them. Kevin, of course, needed convincing.

"Then how come yer gonna go kill yourself in a sacred cave?"

I studied his blank face and marveled, briefly, at his skills. "We're not going down there to kill ourselves, Kevin. We're going down there to find evidence of a possible cover-up of a secret Egyptian cave."

"Then how come Mom says you're prob'ly gonna die?"

I turned to my wife to see if she wanted to address this, but her look was as defiant as Kevin's ever was. "Kevin," I said, "have you been listening to us through the vent in your room?"

His blue eyes shifted back and forth, then he said, "It's not my fault if you guys yell all the time."

"We don't yell all the time," I said in an even voice. "But sometimes we talk in our bedroom, and it's not polite to eavesdrop."

"Eavesdrop?" he said. "I gotta use ear plugs to get to *sleep*."

"Yeah," Kalley said. "I can hear you in my room too."

Demoralized, I turned to her. "Through the vent in your wall?"

She nodded. "It sounds like you're a long ways away, but I can still hear you."

There was a sudden motion to my right; Anna had bolted from the room and gone into the utility room, by the garage. We soon heard something ripping and drawers opening and closing. Then she reappeared and marched up the stairs with duck tape, a flat piece of cardboard, and scissors in her hands.

"Anna," I called out in what I thought was a kind voice, "I'll take care of it."

"You've had ten years to take care of it! *I'll* take care of it."

I was about to tell her that we needed that vent so we didn't suffocate, but then four-year-old Mia began crying. I scooted across the couch to comfort her. "It's all right. Mommy will be back soon." She jumped away from me and fled to Rosemary, who received her with open arms. I went back to my seat and glanced over at Lucas, who was the only child not to betray me in the last hour. He was a quiet, happy boy and was often protective of his younger sister. He returned my loving look of supplication with, perhaps, the first withering glare of his life.

Under the circumstances, I thought it best to suspend the meeting.

But then Anna came back and sat down. Emphatically. And, lo, the meeting was on again.

"So, anyway," I continued, "I just wanted to get together and go over a few things."

"Are ya gonna give us blessings?" Kevin asked.

"Um, well—would you like me to?"

"No, but you should prob'ly give Ross a blessing so he can help you get out of the canyon—ha-ha-ha."

I surveyed the room. If mutiny were truly in the air, I wanted to know it now. Rosemary tried to conceal a grin, and Anna turned her face away to do something with Mia's hair, who had chosen to sit on the *other* side of her mother. Kevin challenged me with his blank stare, and Kalley, with perhaps some envy, was watching her mother work on Mia's hair. Ross, my good *friend*, sat contentedly, a half smile on his face, daring me to continue.

And continue I did. "So, anyway, let's all kneel and have family prayer." I fell to my knees, and one by one they dropped to the floor. I called on Ross to pray.

Sure enough, he gave a splendid prayer, invoking the Lord's protection on us all, making me feel guilty for not doing it myself.

The next morning we were fifty miles down the road before the sun rose over the Sierras to our left. For entire minutes the whole sad affair of the night before was forgotten, partly because I was fretting over how my health would hold up over the days and possibly weeks to come as we scoured one of the mightiest holes in the world for something that might not exist.

Chapter 15

Casing the Joint

Klah was getting worried. When he arrived at 6:30 to watch Call's house, Keller's truck was already gone. Maybe he had left for home in Utah sometime after midnight, when Klah had gone back to Stockton, but more than likely, something else was up.

According to the GPS tracker, Call's car was still in the garage, but Call had only left for work after eight once, and usually he was gone by seven. Was Call sick? Had Klah missed him being picked up by someone else? Using his cell phone, he checked Call's computer at the office. No activity. He checked for phone conversations. Nope.

A knot formed in his stomach. Had he overlooked the obvious? If the two men were going to the canyon, they would probably take the four-wheel drive truck. And they would probably leave early. The knot twisted.

Should he leave now and try to get to the cave before they did, or should he stay and break into the house tonight? After all, they would probably never find the cave—but he wouldn't know for sure. Unless, of course, he bugged the house tonight and surveilled them when they came home.

He dreaded the next phone call with Richardson. He had lost them. But since he didn't know how long they had been gone, or if he could even find the cave himself, he decided to stay and bug the house tonight. What's more, he decided to go back to his room in Stockton and get some needed rest. He probably wouldn't get it tonight.

* * *

It was a little after two when he stalked up to the side of the house and used a pellet gun to break the lens of the camera above the gate. Then he disabled a window sensor connected to the house alarm by using a shaped neodymium magnet. After that it was easy to remove the screen and unclasp the window with a common burglary tool. Less than thirty seconds after walking through the gate Klah was in Call's home office.

As he had assumed, the truck had not returned, and Call had never shown up at work. They were almost certainly in Arizona, but the canyon was a big place, even the north end of it in Marble Canyon, and he knew the odds were still in his favor.

Earlier that day he had made the call to Richardson, reporting the two men's escape. Richardson was upset. "Bugging the place now won't accomplish anything if they get in the cave tomorrow. The damage will be done."

But Klah had thought through this. "They won't have time, especially if they get a call tomorrow telling them that their house got broken into. They'll race back here as fast as they can."

There was silence on the other end. Richardson had much to consider. Finally he said, "You better hope so. A *lot* is riding on this." *Including Whislin Klah's life.*

"This might be nothing," Klah said. "Maybe they're just out looking for a place for the family to camp on their vacation."

"Or there never was a vacation. It was always going to be a trip to the canyon."

In the end, they had decided that Klah should tap the phones and set up keyboard tracing software on the family's computers.

Now inside the home, he found a desktop computer in Travis's office, but no laptop. The man was *married* to that laptop. The computer was password protected, but rather than hook up the Brutalis and waiting fifteen minutes, he tried the password that had worked in the downtown office. Sure enough, it worked again. Before installing the tracing software, he checked the computer's recent online history.

And his heart sank.

There it was, pages and pages of searches for Kinkaid's Cave, hiking trails in Marble Canyon, camping supplies, rules and restrictions in the canyon, all within the past seventy-two hours. There was even a search for the best routes to Page, Arizona, along with gas stations to stop at along the way. Call and Keller were probably in

Arizona this very minute. He installed the software and bugged the phone.

He quietly went into the large living room. Call was doing well for himself, though he reminded himself that his wife might be making the real money. There were no sounds in the house, no indication of any alarms, though he wouldn't know if a silent alarm had been sent by Wifi to an outside agency.

He bugged the house phone in the kitchen then considered going upstairs to bug those phones, but that would be risky. He was mostly concerned about Anna and the oldest boy, about twelve or so. Klah had seen him earlier sneaking around the neighborhood with a slingshot, picking off birds. Klah would hate to hurt a kid with so much spirit.

He went back to the office, messed it up, gathered his tools, and exited, leaving the window open. Having worn gloves, he left no fingerprints, but he was sure that both Johnson and Travis Call would receive phone calls in the morning.

* * *

After six hours of sleep, Klah was back in position two blocks from Call's house. He had packed before leaving the motel room and had everything in the car, which made things cramped, as he generally conducted surveillance from the back seat. The rear and side windows were heavily tinted, which provided a degree of concealment. He had his cell phone in his hand and his computer in lap as he monitored the house phone and Travis's office computer. He had already made a decision about his next move—he would either move to a motel in Modesto, making his commute each morning and night shorter, or he would go to the canyon, but first he needed to see if Travis would come home.

A movement outside the Calls' house got his attention. The side gate swung open and the boy stepped out. Klah had learned from Travis's computer that the kid's name was Kevin. He had his slingshot again. He must have seen the open window and displaced screen and come out to find the culprit. His unruly blond hair stuck out in all directions. Klah grabbed his binoculars. The kid was barefoot and still in pajamas. The morning was clear but cool, and dew coated the lawn, but that didn't stop the kid from searching the bushes around the house, the slingshot loaded and pulled tight. Finding nothing, he scanned the street in both directions. He didn't seem to notice Klah's tan Wrangler 200 yards away. He lowered his weapon and trudged back to the gate, but just before going through, he stopped and looked up at the surveillance camera. He stepped back to view it from a different angle. Then he surveyed the length of the street again and went through the gate.

Two minutes later a ding from Klah's laptop told him that an outgoing call was being made from the house phone. He listened in.

"Nine-one-one, what is the nature of your problem?"

"I'm calling to report that someone broke into our house last night."

"What is your name?"

"I am Anna Call. That's C-A-L-L."

"Are you at the house at this moment?"

"Yes."

"Is there any threat to your safety?"

"I don't think so. We just looked around the house. The intruder seems to be gone."

"What is your address?"

Anna gave the address, and Klah listened to the rest of the call, which was brief and factual. It made sense that Anna had used the house phone to place the call, as a 911 call from her cell phone would go to the highway patrol and have to be redirected. She mentioned that not only was a side window left open, but it appeared that one of her home surveillance cameras was broken. The dispatcher took the details and said that an officer would be there soon.

Klah wondered how long it would take for her to make the next call. The thought had barely crossed his mind when his computer dinged. He checked the screen. Someone on the house phone was dialing Travis's number. The call went to message, and Anna's voice came on.

"Travis, someone broke into the house last night. They broke the camera by the gate—the same one that was broken last time. They came in through the window in your office. I called 911 and made a report, but I'm sure this has something to do with Nelson. The police should be here soon, but please call me when you get this."

She hung up, and his computer dinged again. The next call went to Ross's phone. She didn't leave a message. When no more calls were made, Whislin figured she started using her cell phone, which wasn't bugged.

He considered the reasons for Travis not answering—and kept coming back to an obvious one: there was no cell service in the canyon.

He reviewed his options. He could wait in town for the men to come back, then try to discover what they had learned, or he could go after them. The problem with going after them was that he had never been to the cave and didn't know exactly how to get there. He had the photos, and they would be helpful, but he knew that it would take at least a day of driving and two more days of hiking to reach the cave—and the men were well ahead of him. But there was a third option.

He opened a leather valise and took out the long-range photos of the cave that Richardson had given him. They had been taken from the west side of the canyon, which was usually called the North Rim. Maybe he could go there and use his telescope to watch the cave. He would need to go home and get his digital telescope, but that wouldn't be a problem. He called Richardson.

"They shouldn't be able to hike upriver till tomorrow," Klah said. "And they'll still have to climb up the Redwall, so they probably won't get to the area of the cave till Thursday."

"Where were they going in from?" Richardson asked.

"Lipan Point—that's where he was lookin online."

Klah heard computer keys clicking.

"Got it," Richardson said. "What is it, twenty miles to the site?"

"About that—but it looks like nobody really knows. I mean, nobody's actually made the hike."

"Except Nelson."

"Yeah—but he didn't put anything online about it."

"So how do you want to handle this?"

"I'll use glass to watch from the North Rim. If it looks like they find a way in, I'll get in my Jeep and go over Navajo Bridge and wait for them at Lipan Point. I figure they'll have to come out the same way they went in."

There was silence as Richardson considered the weaknesses of the plan. "They could go out to the north, up at Lee's Ferry."

"Why would they do that? They'll want to go back to the truck, at Lipan Point."

"You're sure they went in there?"

"It's the only entry point he was searching online."

"Who, Call? Maybe Keller was searching somewhere else."

"But this is the logical place to go in, unless they want to go down the Little Colorado, which is longer and probably harder, but I'll do something else first. Before I go around to the North Rim, I'll stop at Lipan Point and check for Keller's truck. If it's there, I'll bug it. Then I'll go around to the North Rim and watch through the glass. If they get to the cave, I'll see them, and if they find a way in, I'll know it, and I'll be waiting for them somewhere down on the trail—where there are no witnesses."

Richardson paused as he clicked through more sites on his computer. "There's another issue. The road getting to the North Rim from Utah is closed in the winter—snow. It won't open again until the middle of May."

"I already checked it out. They've had a heat wave, and the snow's gone. There's barricades at the closure site, but I can four-wheel around them—or I can go around the back way, behind all the buildings. It shouldn't be a problem—I'll do it at night."

"Just a minute; let me bring that up." A moment later they were looking at the same views of the closure site. "I see what you mean—yes, you can probably get around the barricades. Okay, listen, I don't know what kind of lens they used to take the pictures we gave you, but it's like eight miles across the canyon. Is your telescope strong enough?"

"Of course, I just need to go home and get it first."

"In Flagstaff?"

"Yep."

"That's out of the way."

"I'll drive through the night. I'll be on the North Rim tomorrow morning, before they can even get up the river that far."

"I hope you've had some sleep."

"Sleep's not an issue."

"Do you know where to look for the cave?"

"I've got your photos."

"You'll need to know where it is exactly. I'll email you the GPS coordinates."

"All right, thanks."

"Try to report in every day."

"I will if I can. It looks like there's no signal in the canyon—don't know about the north rim."

"Are you still monitoring calls from the house, in case he gets a signal and calls her?"

"Only from the house phone. I don't have a bug on the wife's cell."

Richardson paused again. As Klah continued watching the house, a patrol car rounded the far corner and parked in front of the house. An unmarked sedan followed and parked behind it.

"Johnson just showed up," Klah said, "and another cop."

"Can they see you?"

"Not unless they've got binoculars."

"All right—make this work. Everything is depending on it, Whislin. Everything."

Klah hung up. He had thought about asking for more money, but he had learned not to kill the golden goose. Future contracts could be worth millions. Rather than turn around, he broke one of his own rules and drove down the street in front of the house. As he passed it, he saw two cops walking up to the door, Johnson and a uniform, then he saw a movement above them and looked up. The kid was in a bedroom window watching. Klah saw black binoculars dangling around the kid's neck. Klah was wearing sunglasses, but they locked eyes as he passed. A cold chill ran down his back.

Chapter 16

The Canyon

Experts say there are three things you should avoid doing in the Grand Canyon:

1. Hiking in the heat.
2. Hiking off the main trails.
3. Hiking anywhere if you are over forty.

Ross was only breaking two of the rules. We had stopped at Grand Canyon Village to pick up our backcountry permit, which I had applied for online. The permit was good for seven nights, but they wouldn't know where to find us if we stayed longer.

We entered the canyon at Lipan Point, which people say has the most beautiful view from the South Rim. As Ross pulled into one of the many empty parking stalls, my gaze was locked on the mind-boggling, heart-stopping view before us. The chasm was much bigger, deeper, *vaster* than I remembered. *What were we doing?* We must have gotten out, because I was suddenly looking down over a precipice into the yawning cavity. In two miles the trail below us descended two thousand vertical feet. It would be like walking down a staircase for half a mile, with switchbacks, with harrowing ledges, with ball-bearings under us—with no guardrails.

A fool's errand.

I looked over at Ross, who already had his pack on and was adjusting his hip belt. A toothy smile lit his face. This did not give me courage. "Come on," he said, "time's a wastin'."

At this elevation, of over 7,400 feet, the air should have been cool, if not brisk, but the intense sunshine already radiating off the ground gave me pause. The forecast for Northern Arizona was record heat.

It was barely seven and I was already sweating. Of course, that may have been more from the ominous view.

With my first step off the concrete, my foot landed on a layer of loose dirt, causing jets of red dust to squirt out, form a cloud, and somehow land back on my boot. How long had that dust been sitting there? How dry was it down in the canyon? Everything below me looked hard and sharp and terrifyingly far down. A load landed on my shoulders, and I staggered forward. Ross was placing a pack on my back. I caught my breath—I wasn't that far from the edge.

"Thanks," I muttered.

Looking down into infinity, I realized again that if I fell there only two options: pain or death.

Or pain *and* death.

The world was about to swallow us whole.

We knew that I would be the slower one, so I set the pace, such as it was. Three steps down my foot slipped on some loose gravel on a sandstone block. I caught my balance, barely, and again peered over the edge. If I had gone forward just one more foot—

I couldn't even see the bottom where my body would be landing in a minute or so.

I took a deep breath and tried to take another step, but I couldn't. Ross was still holding my pack. He was the reason I had caught my balance.

Ross had come to our home two months before, not knowing exactly why, and a new, wholly unexpected reason had just been manifested.

"Ya okay?" he asked.

"Yeah, thanks. These rocks are slippery."

He may have just saved my life—something he had done before.

We continued our uncertain descent. A few minutes later the physics of the canyon seemed to be changing. The sun, which was still to our right, hit me from all sides at once as it glanced off protruding rock faces. I stopped again.

"Is there a problem?" Ross asked.

"No, I just thought I'd put some more sunscreen on." I took a long moment to lather more ointment on my face, neck, and arms, trying to conceal the fact that I was already breathing hard. I hoped it was just the elevation.

Down we went, toward some mysterious cave that may or may not exist somewhere in the crust of the earth.

The multi-colored cliffs were breathtaking, with green shrubs and occasional pinyon pines and junipers dotting the terraced cliffs. Several times we stopped to catch our breaths and found ourselves in a strangely beautiful world. The latticed sediments were mesmerizing, with their indefinable distances, wrinkled shapes, and enormous size.

Although the rocks in the canyon are ancient, the canyon itself is quite young, relatively speaking. Essentially the canyon was formed six or seven million years ago as the dusty plain through which the Colorado River flowed began rising. As it rose, pushed up by deep tectonic forces, the river, rather than sloughing to one side or the other, sliced down through the rock. Actually this was no great accomplishment, as the plain was only rising about a quarter of an inch a year. And since the upper layers of limestone and sandstone were soft enough to easily wear away, a river channel was formed, a channel that kept slicing into the rocks as the earth rose, and rose, and rose, over a mile. That's all it took—a combination of permeable, rising rock and incessant, rushing water.

I learned all this from my research before the trip, but frankly, it didn't mean as much to me now as my feet fought for purchase and I pled for strength to endure.

Finally, after what seemed hours, we got down to a place we recognized as Stegosaurus Rocks, a series of oddly shaped red pillars that reminded me of the monoliths on Easter Island. Most of the rocks were only ten or twenty feet high, but they did, in an odd way, resemble the serrated back of a stegosaurus. As per instructions, we cached two gallons of water for our return trip. Unfortunately that didn't lighten my pack, as Ross had been carrying the water. After another hour down the trail, we found a place to eat.

Even Ross was quiet. I had known it would be hard, but not this hard. After eating handfuls of trail mix and drinking until I wanted to throw up, I took my boots off and applied Moleskin to the soles of my flaming feet. Then I pulled my cell phone out to let Anna know I might expire any moment.

There was no reception. No wonder my phone had been silent this morning. No wonder Anna hadn't called me. I mentioned this to Ross.

"Oh, yeah," he said, finishing off half a gallon of water, "I read about that. No coverage down here."

"Thanks for telling me. I should've left this thing up in the truck. It feels like about five pounds now."

"Naw, don't worry about it. You're doin' great." He studied my face and frowned. "Did you put sunscreen on your face too?"

"Yeah, like half the tube."

"Okay. Good. Then you probably only have sunstroke. Ready to move on?"

I ignored him and tried to heave my pack onto my shoulders. It weighed less because I had emptied about four pounds of water down my throat, but the world of physics had again altered, making the pack impossible to hoist above my waist. Ross stepped over and raised it effortlessly. As he set it on my shoulders, my knees resumed their familiar quivering.

"How much farther?" I asked, though I already knew the answer.

"To the river? About five miles."

I eyed the sheer precipice to our left. "Do you think I could make it if I jumped?"

He took the question seriously. "Yeah. Sure. Eventually."

I willed one foot in front of the other and tried to take my mind off the pain in my feet, legs, and back by forcing myself to admire the layers of reddish brown limestone we were descending through. Knowing their history, I felt a sense of walking back in time. Although the canyon is relatively young, the rocks are extremely old. Geologists estimate that the rocks up at the rim are about 270 million years old. To put that in perspective, the Sierra Nevadas are relative newcomers, at about 40 million years. But the rocks at the rim are the *youngest* rocks in the Grand Canyon. As you descend, they get older, and at the bottom of the canyon at the far end they are nearly two billion years old—some of the oldest rocks on earth. Every foot of vertical drop, on average, takes you through a quarter million years of sediment. So, as you walk down the trail, you are essentially walking backward in history at the rate of a quarter million years a step.

Pretty fast walking if you think about it.

In that first step, when the dust squirted out from under my boot, I had already walked below dirt that had formed in Adam and Eve's time. In fact, I had done that in the first two millimeters of the first step.

Such facts are nearly incomprehensible. To put them in terms of a person's life, if a man were born at the same time the oldest rocks were formed at the bottom of the canyon, and he had a child thirty years later, and that child had a child thirty years later, and if a new generation came every thirty years, it would take 60 million generations to reach today.

I couldn't tell if I felt older or younger as I waddled into the past.

The slope eased as we dropped past the red and mauve limestone layers. By now even Ross was grunting. The shadows were growing longer and darker. I looked at my watch and saw that it was three in the afternoon. Then I noticed another phenomenon as we slipped over the edge into the inner gorge where the river itself lies; the sun had become invisible. I felt enveloped, even swallowed, by the earth. I stopped walking, not sure why, and saw blue sky directly overhead, but all around us dark walls loomed overhead. A sense of quiet oppression settled upon me. So far we had seen no other humans. In fact, now that I thought about it, we had seen no animals at all except a few jittery lizards on the scalding rocks.

When I was a teenager on a Boy Scout trip, I woke up one morning with my head at the wrong end of the sleeping bag. For a few panicky moments I didn't know where I was, and I thrust my arms and legs in all directions, trying to escape. I finally turned myself around and poked my head out and saw the welcome sight of our smoldering campfire. Now, slowly, I felt that panic making inroads again. But, with one disciplined thought at a time, I kept it at bay. I was in the belly of the beast and only a ten-mile hike, almost straight up, would free me from it.

At some point I lost track of time. Every step was an eternity. Every jolt on a stump or slip on a rock produced wincing pain.

We passed through a barren, nearly lifeless side canyon, and I briefly wondered if I had passed into the next life, then I thought I heard something, a hissing sound ahead of us. With the heat still growing, I wouldn't have been surprised to turn the corner and find the stunted trees on fire. As we rounded some mauve, domed rocks, I realized that I was hearing the muffled roar of the Colorado River— the Tanner Rapids. We had reached the bottom.

It's amazing how water can give a man hope. I trudged faster. The flood plain we approached was composed of sand and gravel, and, like the side canyon we had just exited, it was nearly lifeless. I dropped my pack to the ground, and although I was surprised by how light I suddenly was, *I* also dropped to the ground. Ross bounded by me with his pack still on, which was at least twenty pounds heavier than mine. The man was a two-legged Clydesdale. I found the strength to stand, and I somehow stumbled to the edge of the river. It ran clear and blue, which pleased and surprised me. I had always thought of the Colorado as muddy, which it probably had been until the Glen Canyon Dam, nearly a hundred miles upstream, impeded its flow and caused the silt to drop out in Lake Powell. Before I could tell Ross not to drink the unfiltered water, he had his filter out and was filling it. I hurried (perhaps too strong a word) back to my pack, got my own filter, and staggered back to the miraculous water. I filled the bottle, looked to see if any sediment was swirling in it, couldn't see any, and began sucking on the Life Straw. Let me say here and now that the water of the Grand Canyon is the sweetest, coolest, finest water on the planet, no question.

After satiating ourselves, we lay on our backs and stared at the darkening sky.

"We're alive," I said.

"Speak for yourself."

"When we're done, you know you'll have to climb out and send a team down to rescue me."

He turned his head and eyed me through narrow slits, and I realized that his own face was sunburned. "If I climb outta here, and you're not with me, I'm just gonna get in my truck and start drivin'."

"What a friend."

"The best you got, and don't forget it."

He rose to his feet and began surveying the wide beach around us. He found a place to camp—back under a rock ledge, in case it rained, I supposed. Fires were not legal in this part of the canyon, and we didn't want to raise untoward interest, so we made a cold dinner, rolled our sleeping bags out on ground cloths, and tucked our stuff away so snakes, scorpions, and other wildlife couldn't slip into our clothes during the night. We probably could have protected ourselves a little more by setting up the tent Ross had in his pack, but we were too tired to bother—and it was too hot anyway. We had another ten miles to go in the morning, and putting up a tent now just meant we would have to strike it and re-pack it tomorrow.

We positioned our sleeping bags so that our heads stuck out from under the overhang so we could watch the stars poke out one by one. That gave me hope, providing proof that we weren't in a mile-high tomb.

"So how are you and Anna doing?" Ross asked, his voice chipper. The man's recuperative powers were discouraging. "Do you think she's really going to be okay, you know, with you coming out here?"

"Yeah, as long as I don't die or anything."

"I was wondering about that today."

I turned and looked at him. He was watching the stars. "I wasn't kidding about how red you looked—like it was heat stroke or something. I'm kind of surprised you made it all the way down."

I didn't tell him how much I was praying those last couple of miles.

"So, how's she doing, anyway?"

"You see her about as much as I do."

"Yeah, but I don't talk to her about important stuff."

"Like what?"

He was quiet a minute, and I wondered if he had forgotten the question or was just ignoring it. He turned his head and said, "Spiritual stuff. Her testimony."

"Oh, actually I don't talk to her about that too much either. I mostly just pray that she can gain a testimony—especially of the Book of Mormon. I think that's the key. In the meantime, she's doing all the right things, just, maybe, not for all the right reasons."

"You love her a lot, don't you?"

I wanted to be as honest as possible. "I've never told anybody this, but I love her in a different way than I did Marsha. It's more physical, maybe more romantic, but just as strong. I don't like being away from her. With Marsha, we were apart for two or three months at a time when she was filming, and it didn't really bother me. Without Anna, this week will be hard."

"Wow. You've loved two women. I wish I could find *one* woman to love."

I would have laughed if I hadn't been so tired. "All I can say, Ross, is she's probably out there right now, looking at the same stars, thinking the same thing about you."

"Sure."

I was watching the Little Dipper crawl around Polaris. The stars were brilliant blue with a clear, almost blue light. "You're a good man, Ross. She'll be glad she waited for you."

I don't know if he said anything else, because moments later I was waking up and light was chasing shadows away. Eight hours of sleep felt like two seconds. I sat up and looked around, seeing my breath plume out in the chilled air. Ross and his sleeping bag were gone. Off to the side against a rock, his pack was standing upright, ready to go. I tried to get out of bed and discovered that my body had other ideas. If rising from the dead felt this bad, I may be the only man to go unresurrected at the last day. Sounds from behind me caused me to turn. Ross was adding filtered water to a baggy that contained granola, sugar, and powdered milk. Such would be our breakfasts for the duration.

"Check your bag before you get out," he said. "There was a scorpion on it when I got up."

My head snapped down to inspect my bag. "On my sleeping bag? Did you get it off?"

"Yeah, sure, but there's probably more—or maybe that one will come back. I don't know."

The sudden jolt of adrenalin helped me scramble out of bed, and after a cold breakfast, hiking didn't seem so impossible.

Chapter 17

The Serpentine Way

Ten hours after leaving Modesto, Klah pulled into his personal parking stall at his gated complex in Flagstaff. His body ached for rest, and he did a brief calculation to see if he could take a nap. It was six o'clock, Tuesday evening, still light, but the sun was dropping toward the horizon and the air was growing cold. He had grown soft in the California spring.

He climbed the stairs and went in. The condo was as he had left it. Paying a premium for gated security was worth the peace of mind. You never knew when an intruder might break in and steal your stuff. He smiled at the irony.

Whislin Klah prided himself on his substantial rise in society since his dad had kicked him out. An upper-middle-class condo, which would be paid off after this job, a new Jeep, already paid for, and all the other accouterments of life. He was living like a *bilagaana*—a white man—something his father had always sneered at (but secretly craved). He walked into the kitchen, which was clean but bare. He actually wouldn't mind having a woman around, though that could wait until after retirement, when she wouldn't complain about the source of his income. "I'm just a lucky investor, Honey. I'm half white and half Injun, and that makes me all smart."

He checked the canyon online again and satisfied himself that he would easily be in position on the North Rim before Call and Keller reached a position below the cave. After eating a microwaved chicken pot pie—he loved those things—he lay on his bed and closed his eyes. The alarm clock in his head woke him up four hours later.

Ten o'clock, time to get on the road again.

He went to his closet and pulled out his prized piece of surveillance gear—his digital telescope with motion detector. With its massive 70x magnification, it had won awards for best surveillance instrument. He loved taking it to the roof, setting it on his tripod, and zeroing in on life for miles around. He spotted deer out on the distant hills that hunters with scopes couldn't see. He loaded the telescope in his Jeep, along with his other gear and food, and departed.

An hour later he turned off Highway 89 onto Desert View Highway. A quick thirty minutes after that he pulled into the parking area at Lipan Point. Even in the dark, he spotted Ross Keller's truck, as it was the only vehicle in the lot. He parked behind it, keeping the truck in his headlights, and texted Richardson that the two subjects had indeed entered the canyon at Lipan. He waited to make sure the text went through, which it did, surprising him. Coverage had improved since the last time he'd been here. He crawled under the truck and planted a GPS bug glued to a neodymium magnet. It might be discovered by probing eyes, but it would never fall off, as the magnet grasped the pickup's steel frame with over twenty-five pounds of pull force. The hardest part of the operation had been separating it from another magnet he had accidentally put in the same bag.

Three hours later, after crossing the Colorado River east of the canyon at Navajo Bridge, then traveling west for another forty minutes, he approached the road closure at Jacob's Lake, which blocked traffic to the North Rim.

He had been here before, but not in the off-season or at night. It stood at nearly 8,000 feet, and the thermometer on his dash read 27 degrees. He hadn't seen another vehicle in over an hour, and the little community looked deserted. Towering Ponderosa Pines stood like sentinels in his peripheral light on both sides of the road. He pulled over, turned off his engine, and got out to listen. There was absolute silence except for the creaking noises coming from the cooling engine. The lack of sound was almost unnerving. In the faint light of the moon he could make out the dim line of barricades across the road a hundred yards ahead. He could probably just move one aside and go through, but he was still concerned about being heard by a ranger in a cabin and followed. An empty campground lay off to his left, and a darkened Chevron station sat on his right, but it also seemed deserted. He was more concerned about the Jacob Lake Inn, just ahead. It was dark, but he knew that forest rangers and state transportation workers sometimes stayed there. He pulled a U-turn in the deserted road and went back a mile then turned left onto a dirt trace that passed under some power lines. The dim path took him behind the inn and the other buildings then finally back to the main road, well beyond the barricades. He stopped again and got out to listen. He waited five minutes in a gentle breeze, until he was sure that no doors had opened or vehicles had started up.

Exhaustion hit him as he continued on down the dark, winding road toward the rim, but he fought it back. For the next fifty minutes he felt as if he were cocooned in a twisting tunnel of Ponderosa pines passing by on both sides.

When he finally reached the turn for Cape Royal Road, it felt as if he had been freed, mostly because he knew he was almost there, almost at the rim, almost at the end of the world. He gained elevation, going up over 8,500 feet, and his thermometer plunged to 17 degrees. Nearing the rim, he slowed down on the serpentine path, inching along as his headlights peered into the towering pines and scrubby junipers. Occasionally he glanced at the screen in his dash, which showed interminably slow progress on a GPS-tethered map.

Dawn was still just a hope when he finally pulled into the small, deserted parking area at Roosevelt Point, his headlights disappearing into a vast maw of blackness.

The canyon.

He set the parking brake, got out, and stood not three feet from the edge of death, gazing into the abyss. Even by the light of a partial moon, the sight was breathtaking. He wasn't a religious man, but standing before the massive, yawning fissure lurking in moonlit grays and browns, he nearly used the Lord's name in venerating prayer. Something inside him whispered that this was beyond erosion, beyond time, beyond geology. This was divinity at work.

He took a deep icy breath and forced himself to focus on the job at hand. He opened the back of his vehicle and unloaded his equipment. The last thing out was a black, carbon-fiber case containing his Glock 19 and threaded suppressor. He wrapped a tactical belt around his waist, removed the unsilenced gun from its case and holstered it. He was probably alone out here on the edge of nowhere, but it would pay to be prepared in case a shadow came bolting out from the trees. In a quiet but almost tangible way, he began to understand why the people on his grandmothers' sides sang songs to appease the spirits that restlessly wandered over this wonderful and mysterious land.

Chapter 18

Going Forth Along the River

Ross and I prayed each morning and night, and at meals, but this morning after learning about the scorpion I felt a greater yearning for protection. But more than that, something was nagging at me about the situation at home. Had I left something undone? Was somebody hurt? I hadn't felt this concern before leaving, so it gnawed at me. I couldn't call, but as Ross and I knelt in prayer that morning, I pled for the powers of heaven to descend upon my home and family.

Then I led us up the river.

Almost immediately I noticed something strange; the river seemed higher and more powerful. If we hadn't camped up by the rocks, we might have gotten flooded out or even swept away. I said as much to Ross.

"Oh, yeah," he said, coming up beside me, "didn't you hear it? The roar kept getting louder and louder, and I got up and watched the river tsunami go by us in the moonlight."

"Tsunami? Was there a flash flood or something?"

"Kind of. It happens all the time, especially when it gets hot. I read about it before we left. When they need to make more electricity, they let more water out of the Glen Canyon Dam, and it rushes down the river. With that record heat yesterday they probably opened the spigots to create more power. The surge didn't hit us till last night. I'd love to raft down it."

What was going on? Scorpions, tsunamis, sudden worries about my family.

Fortunately the water seemed to be dropping as we lumbered up the trail.

There is one constant in the Grand Canyon. It is not the heat, which probably goes away for a moment or two in the winter. It is not the suffocating dryness, which burns your eyes, chaps your lips, and makes your skin feel like leather, which may disappear in the rainy season.

It's the rocks.

They're everywhere. You cannot open your eyes without seeing a rock. You cannot walk without stepping around them, by them, or on them. Some limited stretches of beach do exist, but they too are composed of gravel and sand—decomposed rocks. There are some isolated places of mud by the water, but they're always right next to rocks.

There are millions of them. Billions. At first, I was fascinated by their age, but at this point, as we hiked north along the river from Tanner Canyon toward the Little Colorado, the rocks were so ubiquitous that I didn't care if they were older than the universe itself; I just wanted them out of the way. In the first ten minutes I had nearly turned my ankle five or six times. This would not have been good, as I had to use that ankle to get out of the canyon, eventually, so I might still enjoy a productive life. My boots helped, nay, saved me many times, but sometimes my ankles twisted and my knees gave and my body heaved as I tripped, slipped, hobbled, waddled, jumped, dodged, and finally fell down on the rocks. The Bible says that one of the Lord's greatest miracles was walking on water. A greater miracle might have been walking ten feet in this place without hitting a rock.

Off to my right, Ross said: "Why are you walking clear over there? Why don't you stay on the trail?"

I looked over at him and saw a smooth trail of dirt and sand. No rocks. I coughed up an explanation about studying the formations of sedimentary stones.

"Do you have to fall on them to study them?"

I didn't dignify this with a response, but I did sidle over his way. Without falling again, I managed to lead us up the Beamer Trail, a wonderful invention, past several dry creeks that must have flowed into the river during the rainy season. We also worked our way through voracious clumps of a green, scaly plant. I say voracious because this plant, which I later learned is the feared tamarisk, has limbs and leaves that reach out to molest you. They grope your face and armpits and legs, giving one flashbacks of apple trees in The Wizard of Oz. The tamarisk, by comparison, appears more innocent, with its narrow limbs and tiny cedar-like leaves that beguile you into a false sense of co-existence—and then they engulf you, and strangle you, and, of course, trip anything with only two legs.

Ross stopped and looked down at me with a quizzical expression. "Studying the rocks again?"

The tamarisk is dreaded, I later learned, because it's an invasive species, not native to the Promised Land at all. It sucks up valuable water and somehow leaves deposits of salt behind. It's a pariah, almost as pervasive in the river bottoms as rocks, making the Grand Canyon, I suppose, one of the most dangerous places on earth.

We resumed our journey up the trail until we came to the first large outcropping.

An outcropping is a portion of the canyon wall that extends all the way out to the river. Which means you can't get around it without swimming or climbing it. We chose to climb, of course, which in this case meant summiting a height of four hundred feet on a ledge no wider than—no, "wide" does not apply here. Wide connotes room, expanse, freedom to gaze upon the many possibilities of death around you. What we had here was the tiniest thread of a trail that even snakes caution their children about. As I looked down to make sure my left foot landed on the path and not on thin air, I became aware, of course, that the river and its associated *rocks* were the only things below the left side of my body. I was tempted to look up and try to focus on something ahead, until I noticed that someone had left rocks on the trail as big as my feet, with jagged edges and points sticking out that could catch a boot.

I was only moving about a yard per hour, but I managed to slow further to navigate these rocks, but as I did I failed to warn Ross, and he bumped into me, causing my foot to lodge against a rock, which made me stumble, which made me reach out with my right hand to grab the handrail that, of course, was not there. In slow but inevitable motion I began losing my balance over the edge of the cliff. In the next split second I prayed a lifetime of prayers. I prayed, for example, for Ross, who was right behind me, to grab me and pull me back. But he didn't. Then, just as I was gathering speed, just as I was tipping over the side and abandoning myself to a wholly new experience, a gust of wind, an updraft from the river, nudged me just enough to help me regain my balance.

My knees were quivering so hard I had to sit down. Ross took a seat too.

"Sorry," he whispered.

Speech, for me, was not possible. We sat like two riders on a children's train, in silence, and I was surprised by how cold it had become.

How had Keith Nelson done this?

A minute or so later Ross rose to his feet. "Well, I guess we should get going."

"Yeah," I croaked, still not quite ready. "Can you help me up?"

I felt my pack rise, and I carefully rose to a standing position. I didn't look down to my left at the river or at the sheer canyon wall across from us. I kept my gaze firmly on the trail, the trail I had once been grateful for, and I spotted every rock for the next two or three feet. Then, timidly, gingerly, prayerfully I put my right foot in front of my left. Then I put my left in front of my right. This continued for an unknown period of time, possibly some days, until we were off the outcropping and down by the river again.

I dropped my pack and sat down—permanently I hoped. Ross joined me.

"I didn't know you were going to slow down back there," he said.

"I know—I should have said something."

"No, it was my fault. I'm sorry." He paused and shook his head as if in remorse. "It's just that if I don't stay close, I can't catch you when you start to fall."

In that instant I realized how much of a burden I had become. He couldn't leave my side for fear of my falling off a cliff or getting stung by a scorpion or getting squished under my pack.

"Ross, I'm sorry. I had no idea it would be this hard."

"Yeah, me neither."

We were quiet a moment, and I was about to get my LifeStraw out to drink from the river, when he said, "How'd you—when you were starting to fall—how'd you stop? I mean, you were going over the cliff, and I couldn't grab you because I went backwards when I bumped you, and then you were just—coming back. How'd you do that?"

"The wind pushed me."

He gave me a quizzical look. "The wind?"

"You know, that gust that came up from the river."

"I didn't feel it."

"You didn't feel that wind that came up from the river and pushed me back?"

"Travis, there wasn't any wind. There still isn't."

I looked around. He was right. The world was still. A deep, trembling feeling seeped into me, and I looked at him again and thought I saw a tear welling in his eye. He turned away and got his own LifeStraw, then he closed his pack, wiped his face, and looked over at the river.

"I wasn't there for you," he said, "so God was."

"I think he's been with us both."

He nodded, and we made our way to the water and drank until our 23-ounce containers were empty.

After our break, I began to think more about Keith and how he had done this by himself. He hadn't looked like an athlete, and yet he had made it to the cave, so he said, without help. More and more, that was becoming something of a miracle.

Yelling and laughter came from the river to our left. I wheeled around and saw two large inflatable rafts passing by on a stretch of light rapids. The people in the rafts, all wearing life vests and helmets, waved and yelled at us, but I couldn't make out what they were saying. It might have been, "Why are you *walking*?" We watched until they disappeared around a bend.

"Mmm," Ross said, "maybe we should have floated down here."

"Yeah, it sure looked fun."

"And no cliffs to fall off of."

"Or scorpions."

"Or fifty-pound packs."

We continued on our trek toward the next outcropping.

Several hours later, after scaling many more outcroppings, we approached the confluence of the Little Colorado River, nine or ten miles above where we had started the day. My legs were rubber, and my heart was pounding like a hammer. As we neared the confluence, I seemed to have an epiphany—or was it a revelation? The smaller river looked impossibly blue, almost iridescent blue. I came down off the trail and walked down to the bank and put my hand in the brilliant water. I was surprised by how warm it was, especially compared to the Colorado which was decidedly chilly.

"Don't drink it," Ross warned.

"Don't worry, I'll use my filter," I said, shedding my pack.

"No, even with the filter. See how blue it is?"

"Yeah, which means it's clean."

"No, which means it's filled with calcium carbonate and copper sulfate. Filters won't get rid of it. You'll get sick."

I looked to see if he was joking. "How do you know?"

"I read about it."

"Where?"

"Online."

"When?"

"When you were at work."

Add this moment to all the other moments when he saved me from destruction. We still had water from an earlier stop, so we took off our packs and broke out some trail mix. As we ate, a party came floating down the Little Colorado in two more rafts, their feet dangling in the water. I looked accusingly at Ross.

"I didn't say you couldn't touch it," he said. "You just can't drink it."

The rafters waved as they went by, their rafts merging with the Colorado, where the brilliant blue water didn't fully assimilate with the darker water for hundreds of yards.

After eating, Ross stood up. "I'm going to go check out that old stone cabin."

I looked up the Little Colorado where he was headed. A broken-down relic stood by some rocks above the west bank. Finally he was talking about something I had read about. "What do they call it again—Beamer's Cabin?"

"Yeah, want to come?"

We stashed our packs in a copse of creosote and peaceful-looking tamarisk then hiked over to the cabin. A miner who lived there a hundred years before had built the ten-by-ten structure on the site of an ancient Pueblo shelter. It had a great view out the front window, which was framed with rough-hewn planks, but the all-stone walls, roof, and floor left something to be desired.

"Old Beamer sure knew how to rough it," I said, standing in the middle of the ruin.

"Yeah, but he was on his own. Free. Totally independent."

"And totally lonely."

"Maybe."

Ross almost seemed to identify with the hermit. He certainly admired his gumption in trying to make a go of it, which in this case meant surviving.

"I think I'll go back to the river and soak my feet," I said.

"Getting blisters?"

"No, I just want to feel something *good*."

He gazed out the door, up at the far canyon rim. "You know, there's parts of a plane wreck out there. People still find pieces of two planes that collided in the air back in the fifties. I read about a guy who found one of the wheels."

"Small planes?"

"Nope, airliners. A hundred and fifty people died." He surveyed the river bottoms. "I don't know if they ever found all of the bodies."

"Well, that's a pleasant thought," I said, heading out the door. "I'll just go up the river a bit and see if I can find a skeleton or two. Don't let the rattlesnakes bite."

Actually, I needed to use the john, which, of course, didn't exist.

After heeding nature's call, I went up the river a bit further, seeking a secluded place where I could remove more than my boots. I was hot, dirty, and exhausted, and I thought a bath in the warm, strangely iridescent water might refresh me. I figured if we couldn't drink it, but could touch it, maybe it had some powerful cleansing properties. A few hundred yards upstream, I found a sandy spot near a thicket of willows that looked tall and deep enough to conceal me up to my shoulders. Closer to the bank the foliage turned into greenish brown reeds. I pushed my way into the willows and removed my boots, socks, pants, and, yes, everything else. Then, remembering my own counsel, I did a careful survey for snakes. I didn't know if water snakes lived around here or if rattlesnakes lived along the river, but I was doubly vigilant now.

I came out of the willows and stepped into an open, sandy area close to the brilliant water.

The sand did something funny.

My first thought was *earthquake*, and I stopped. The sand was shaking, almost like jello, but then it seemed solid again. I took a few more steps with no issue; then it happened again. But this time water seeped up around my feet, and I started sinking. The river was still twenty yards away, but I was already in the water somehow.

Quicksand flashed through my mind, and I nervously fought to extricate my feet from the goo, but suction held them fast. In no time the quagmire was up to my shins, and I began panicking. I managed to pull one leg up, but as it almost came out, my other leg sank to my knee.

I screamed for Ross. My actions were instinctual now. Primal. I thrashed about, exhausting my strength and submerging both knees into the viscous sand. I yelled louder but heard only echoes off the canyon walls.

I forced myself to stop and think—and as I did so, I noticed that if I held perfectly still, I almost stopped sinking.

Almost.

Movement and agitation seemed to activate the quagmire. But remaining motionless was possibly the most counterintuitive thing I'd ever done, and deep down I knew that if I didn't exert some effort, I would never get out.

The empty river was in front of me, and I could only see behind me by twisting my body, which inevitably inched me farther down. The willows behind me had been about shoulder high when I was removing my clothes, but they were well over my head now. Ross would only find me if he heard my cries.

I looked down the river, trying to gauge my distance from the old cabin. I had come farther than I had thought, maybe a quarter of a mile. He would never hear me.

Turning back toward the cabin, I yelled as loud and long as I could—a long frantic "Ahhhhhh!!!!"

As my breath expended, I saw stars, and I had to put my hands on my thighs to clear my head. Then I noticed that the sand was touching my fingers, above my knees.

Then another, very real, epiphany came to me.

I had taken things for granted.

I knew I had a chronic illness, and yet I had supposed that I could make this trip simply because I felt an overriding obligation to do so, both to Keith and to the idea of justice. For some reason, it was up to me to solve a murder the police had already given up on.

I had a hero complex.

A wave of shame passed through me, but then another thought came, just as legitimate: I had prayed about the trip and had felt right in coming, even at the expense of crossing Anna.

Had I been mistaken?

As I sank another precious fraction of an inch, I contemplated my decisions and my pride, and my heart sank faster than my body. I had not prepared myself to come on this trip. I hadn't trained for it, and the hike yesterday had nearly killed me. What right did I have after being so cavalier to expect success, or even survival? And yet, what about the prayers before leaving? The apparent answer I had received? The peace?

Maybe I had done both right and wrong. The idea was good; the execution was flawed. I could have taken more time, been more prepared, built up my strength and somehow won Anna's approval.

But here I was, with my life in the balance—again. The living sand was crawling up my thighs, and I had no hope of escaping.

Had each saving moment earlier been a message that I should turn around? I hadn't felt that, exactly, but I could see the possibility, especially when the mysterious breath of wind had pushed me back onto the ledge.

I took a deep breath and yelled again, as long and loud as I could. I didn't try to face the cabin, as that only quickened my immersion. After yelling again, I was spent. And now I strangely lost the strength to stay upright. I needed to stay erect so Ross could see me, but my strength was gone. Too many hours hiking, too many hours in the burning sun.

I had a choice: I could bend forward at my waist and fall on my face, or I could try to bend at my knees and fall backwards. But my knees were already submerged, and I didn't know if the suction would allow my thighs to pull backwards through the sand.

Slowly I tried to force my knees to bend, so I could recline. It didn't happen at first, but over a long minute of slowly forcing my way back, oh so *gently*, the quicksand began to yield, and I began to fall back in slow motion. It probably would have looked comical to someone watching, but this was no laughing matter. As my back finally met the wet sand, my feet and lower legs rose the tiniest bit— just enough for my knees to rise to the surface. Then they fully bent— and I lay down in the quicksand.

Or, I should say *on* the quicksand, because at that moment I ceased sinking. I was floating. The sun was blinding, and I closed my eyes, and for a moment I actually worried about getting sunburned, but all my thrashing about had splashed liquefied sand over most of my body, even my face.

After resting a moment, I put my arms out to the sides and, like a swimmer doing a lazy backstroke, I tried to propel myself backward. No motion. I tried a few more times and found that if I pressed my hips down with the slightest force, my legs, with less weight on them, rose a little again, just enough that the suction began to give way. I tried the swimming motion again, pressing down with my hips, which arched my back up slightly, and caused my legs to rise a little higher. Then, as my legs rose that fraction of an inch, my body slid backward that same fraction of an inch.

I moved!

I tried harder, arching my back higher and my hips lower while pulling again with my arms—and I began to sink again. I fought back another wave of panic as the malleable sand began to ooze into my ears. This had to be done just right. It was an art, not an athletic event. A fraction of an inch was hope—maybe life itself. I calmed down and tried to achieve the proper balance of effort and stillness, pulling with my arms and hands while arching my back and lifting my legs ever so slightly.

And another millimeter was won.

I found that by forcing my legs outward a little, again very slowly, they became more buoyant, maybe because the outward motion allowed air to seep down along the inside of my thighs, releasing the tenacious grasp of the sand. But whatever motion I made, gentleness, easiness, kindness was the key. Quick motions provoked the monster, but soft, oh-so-minute movements allowed progress.

After what seemed an hour of worming backwards, I was almost where I had first noticed the jello-like movement in the sand, about six feet from where I had started. My body was floating a little higher now, and my ears were fully above the sand, so I tried pulling a little harder, and this time I didn't sink. I was gaining elevation, and the water was not seeping up as high. I pulled harder, very slowly, and gained a full inch. After making another foot of progress this way, I felt drier sand under my hands, and exerting all my strength, I pulled my body several inches. Then, slowly again, I turned and put my elbows in the firmer sand and pulled harder. My torso came out of the sand, and moments later my legs popped free with two sucking "pops."

I crawled into the willows, exhausted.

In the distance, I heard a muffled voice. Or was it the roar of the river?

But the river wasn't roaring. It was barely murmuring. I stuck a finger in one ear and found sand. I tilted my head and tried to clear it, then I heard Ross calling my name, so close that it startled me.

"Over here," I called, too tired to yell with much force.

He came through the willows. "I saw your clothes over there, and—"

He was staring down at me. "What are you doing?"

"Breathing."

He looked around and saw my sliding tracks in the wet sand. "Why were you crawling in the mud? Why'd you take your clothes off?"

Forfeiting all dignity, I rose to my full height, and said, "There's quicksand over there." I began to stumble back to my clothes.

"Quicksand? What were you doing—*swimming* in it?"

I rubbed some sand off my hands and face. "For a while."

The heat, which had now descended upon the canyon with oven-like ferocity, began drying me off, but I needed to get clean. I looked up and down the river for possible spectators, saw nary a soul, and began walking to where some boulders led me down to the water. As I reached the luminescent water, I was astonished at how soothing it felt, how warm and comforting. I submerged myself up to my neck, let the current flow around me, then went farther out and submerged myself fully. Down into the depths. I used my fingers to scrub my hair and scalp, to extract more sand from my ears, to cleanse my soul.

I came up several times during this process, and the last time I came up, I saw Ross on the rocks, removing his clothes, then he waded out to me. I sucked in a mouthful of the electric liquid and sprayed it on him. He looked at me astonished and said, "Did you forget what I said?"

I shot another jet at him and said, "Hey, ya gotta go sometime!"

He laughed and sunk his face in the sparkling water, came out, and shot a mouthful at me.

"Wow!" he shouted. "This feels great!"

For several minutes we bathed and lounged about, then he asked me about the quicksand again. I told him I had gotten stuck and had to work myself out by crawling backwards. He asked how long that had taken, and I told him I didn't know—I didn't have my watch on—but that I learned one thing.

"What's that?"

"Remember when we got our camping permit and they told us we weren't supposed to camp within a quarter mile of the Little Colorado?"

"Yeah."

"Now I know why. When you wake up, you're six feet under—and still going down."

He laughed and said I had probably found the only quicksand in
the whole park, which I doubted, then he said, "Hey, you know that
Hopi Sipapu we read about—the emergence cave?"

"Yeah."

"It's right up the river. Do you wanna go check it out? We can go
around the quicksand."

Hopis believe civilization began when their ancestors emerged
from the earth through a hole in the ground a few miles up the Little
Colorado from the mighty Colorado River. Supposedly the hole was
still visible in a vertical cave that went down into a forty-foot dome
of solid rock. I felt a little refreshed but didn't think I had the strength
to go sightseeing and still hike up the canyon. I looked up and saw
the sun beginning its descent toward the canyon wall.

"We should get going."

He checked the sun. "Yeah. How much farther do you think it is,
anyway?"

"Up where we want to go?"

"Yeah."

"I don't know—a few miles or so. We'll just have to go up to
where the area matches Nelson's pictures."

As we got dressed, I was surprised by how quickly we dried off,
and I wished I had brought a thermometer. It felt like it was over a
hundred degrees. "Ross, wasn't it cold this morning?"

"That's the way I remember it."

"Then why's it so hot now? These temperature swings must be
fifty or sixty degrees."

"At least. Probably because of how the canyon focuses the sun's
rays down to the bottom. It's like a magnifying glass."

"Lucky us."

"Yeah."

We ate more trail mix, filled our water bottles in the Colorado,
then saddled up. For the most part we were able to cross the
confluence by stepping on boulders. Our legs and feet got wet, but
the river bottom was solid, which, at the time, was all that mattered
to me.

Chapter 19

Watching From the Mountain

Klah woke with a start. He hadn't set up his tent, and now the sun bore down on him, and he knew he had slept longer than he should have. Thy icy chill had woken him twice during the night, interrupting the sleep his body craved. Through bleary eyes he looked at his watch. 9:03. He jumped from his sleeping bag and hurried over to the telescope he had set up the night before. He put his right eye to the frozen eyepiece and saw that the glass wasn't trained on the right spot---the moonlight had been insufficient to allow any focus on the rim eight or nine miles away. He quickly brought the far wall into focus and saw a cluster of rust-red broken rocks. He nudged the telescope downward, as the cave was supposedly below him, and saw only more rocks, then a copse of junipers.

With his heart racing, he ran back to the Jeep and got the photos Richardson had sent him. According to his boss, Roosevelt Point had been where the photos had been taken from two years earlier. Nothing should be different.

To his naked eye, the distant wall was just striations of rust-red, green, and tawny beige—layers of rock, interspersed with green foliage, but in the telescope's eyepiece, he could distinguish bunch grass from rabbitbrush. If the light were right, he'd be able to see a ringtail cat scamper to its haunt.

From the photos, he knew he needed to focus on a large cleft in the far wall, a V-shaped crevice that formed a deep indentation to the east. He found the cleft without trouble then started focusing on the area just above the Redwall. It was so high above the river, which was hidden below mesas in the canyon, that he couldn't imagine how anyone could climb to it without ropes. But then, he didn't have a three-dimensional view of the rock face, and it might have a gentler grade than it appeared.

He took a couple of minutes to scan the entire V-shaped cleft and saw no movement. Then he looked for the cave itself, which had been sealed shut over a hundred years ago. He couldn't find it. He studied the photographs again, one of which was a blown-up image of the artificial wall that had erased the cave from view. The manmade wall incorporated native stone from the site, causing it to blend in almost perfectly. It took him ten minutes, searching casually at first, then frantically, before he located it. The illusion was remarkable. Unless a person knew exactly where to look, they would never find it. His admiration for Keith Nelson increased.

But how did Nelson get in? Klah examined the stone wall again, looking for fissures in the manmade facade, but the telescope's magnification wasn't sufficient to distinguish little shadows from possible crevices. And, for all he knew, Nelson had repaired the hole after coming out of it.

He checked his watch again. 9:17. According to his calculations, Call and Keller should still be several miles away, maybe at the confluence of the Little Colorado. But his calculations could be wrong. They could have traveled farther than he figured on the first day. He had read of people hiking all the way to the Little Colorado in one day, which would mean they could be well upstream now, possibly even on the wall below the cave. He angled the telescope down further so he could see more of the vast Redwall, then he gradually scanned down, lower and lower, almost to the River, which was just out of sight.

Still no movement.

He went back to the Jeep and got his laptop, which was fully charged, and connected it to the digital telescope so he could see the magnified image on his 15-inch screen. He also set the motion detector to trigger his computer to begin recording at the slightest movement on the screen. He could leave it alone now.

He walked up a low rise and checked out the road as far back as he could see. Again, no movement. Because the North Rim was closed, he didn't expect any visitors, probably for days, maybe weeks. He went back to the Jeep, which was parked only ten feet from the rim, and he took a moment to take in the entire view of the canyon. With cloudless light seeping over the east rim, the shadows behind the pillars and spires protruding from the canyon graduated from light pinks to dark purples and husky blues. It was beautiful, breathtaking—but the sense of being watched, of someone lingering nearby that he had felt the night before, came back. This was part of a sixth sense that cropped up occasionally, an invisible voice that sometimes gave rise to more questions than answers. It usually told him when he was not alone, but over the years he had learned to pay less attention to it, choosing to follow his measurable senses instead.

This job, though, might require both kinds. It might be the most important job of his life. If he completed it well, who knew, he might be able to live a normal life, maybe even get to know his roots a little better.

He checked the computer screen again. No motion.

He reevaluated his current location. It was exposed to anyone who might come down the road, as unlikely as that was. He saw a trail leading out to an outcropping, farther below the rim, off to his left, and he followed it out onto a peninsula that projected a hundred yards or more out into the canyon. When he got as far as the trail would take him, he looked back and saw an overhang under the canyon's rim that would easily conceal his tent and equipment. He wouldn't be able to take the Jeep down there, but he knew he could hide that in some trees he had seen a quarter mile back.

He went up and checked the screen again, found no change, then began bringing his gear down to where he would be concealed from all but the occasionally annoying voice.

Chapter 20

Held Up by the Lord's Gentle Breath

Once past the Little Colorado, we were in a restricted part of the park. Neither of us knew why it was restricted but figured it probably had something to do with the Hopi Salt Mines a few miles up the Little Colorado. The trail, which had now become the Tonto Trail, continued on the other side of the Colorado, though there was no way to get to it from our side. So, technically, we were in a wilderness area, but as we looked across the Colorado it was plain to see that the "wilderness" extended in all directions. Virtually no hikers came this far up the canyon.

For the first mile or so the hike was on flat, relatively sandy ground near the river. Then we came to another outcropping. A thin beach of gravel ran along its base, but the water, which was moving swiftly here, was already rising again, thus making a trek around it unsafe. But the outcropping was several hundred feet high, which was also unsafe, as we had learned, so we decided to risk the water.

It wasn't as dangerous as we had thought, but by the time we got around it, our feet and legs were soaked; and, with two groans, we realized that there were more outcroppings ahead, and of course the gravel beaches below them were quickly disappearing. The ground from this point on was composed of loose shale, tilted at roughly a thirty-degree angle. But, once again, rather than hike over the next outcropping, we decided to stay close to the roaring, frothy river. The shale was surprisingly firm. We had only gone about a hundred yards when two large inflatable rafts came bouncing down the white water. The rafters waved at us, and we waved back, as if we were not trespassers in a restricted zone. Moments later they were gone, and we scampered to the next outcropping.

My ankles were getting fatigued from the constant leftward angle, and as we neared Sixty-mile Creek the gray-green slope got steeper, and soon I was wishing I could shorten my right leg. I even considered turning around and walking backwards to even out the fatigue, but we had to hurry on to escape the rising water.

After a few more minutes of the pegleg motion, I stopped for a breather, and I found Ross standing contentedly behind me.

"Doesn't it bother you," I said, "stepping up with your right leg and down with your left all the time?"

"Naw, I just follow the trail you're making. It's pretty flat."

I looked back and saw that I had indeed been forging a trail in the shale, so much so that he had almost been walking on a flat path the last half mile. I waved him by, and we continued our journey.

I now realized how much easier he'd had it. As long as I hadn't slipped or fallen, he had been able to take his mind off the trail and admire the rising heat, as I now did. It had been cold when we woke up, but the rays of both the direct and reflected light heated things up quickly.

We hiked into the afternoon, the afternoon light sparkling off the white water and the rapids rising and falling like a Wagnerian opera. The Redwall dominated the gorge on our right, soaring upwards half a mile to a ribbon of white cliffs, which finally, far above us, gave way to a brilliant blue sky. There was beauty in this oven—music, power— and Ross had been drinking it all in while I had plopped up and down, searching for my next lifesaving foothold. I was about to register an official complaint when I saw a reflection off a sheer rock ahead of us, a shimmering illusion of sun and rock that reminded me of a crimson and gold stained-glass window. The fiery incandescence literally took my breath away, made me marvel, and my complaint evaporated. This place, I was realizing, could be magical.

With Ross leading, we quickened our pace, skirting around more outcroppings and scaling a couple more, and gradually the sun began disappearing behind the wall to our left. I was about to suggest a break when Ross stopped. He was gazing up to his right.

"What?" I asked.

"I'm looking for the spot."

What?

I dropped my pack, not really caring if I'd ever be able to hoist it up again. We had studied Keith's photos in the morning, and the canyon wall here did look promising. Realizing that I might be more effective sitting down, I did so, using my pack as a backrest. Ross stayed upright, shouldering his pack the whole time, then said, "Nope," and began walking again.

I scrambled to my feet, turned and hefted my pack to my waist, where it stopped. I let it down, tried again, and failed again. I called out to my good friend.

He heard my cry and came back and dutifully lifted the pack over me, let me walk under it, then he let its full weight crash down on my weary shoulders. My knees buckled, and I almost tripped down the slope into the rapids, which would have meant sure death, after a refreshing dip. But did Ross care? Did my good friend apologize for nearly breaking my back, shoulders, and knees? No, he was twenty-five yards down the trail, which, of course, was no trail at all until he forged it, humming some Primary tune. It was possibly "Heads, Shoulders, Knees, and Toes," a fine song but inappropriate in the circumstances. After a dizzying, awkward, exhausting jog, I caught up to him and suggested we take another break. He pretended not hear me.

Much later, he stopped and set his pack down. Then he started helping me take mine off, or I thought he was, but it wouldn't seem to come off. Then I realized he had simply opened one of the flaps of my pack and was rummaging through it, all the while letting me bear the burden.

He came back around with the envelope of Nelson's pictures and took one out. We were in an area littered with brown and gray boulders at the mouth of a dry creek bed. He studied the picture again—while I prayed for power to remain upright.

"Oh," he said, feigning surprise that I still had my pack on, "you might as well take that off. I think we're here."

I grabbed the photo from his hand. Indeed, the picture of a riverbank and dry creek bed was a dead ringer for our surroundings.

"Wow," I said, "this place hasn't changed at all since he took these pictures."

"No, probably not for the last ten thousand years."

I gazed up at the white cliffs above the Redwall, astounded, no, terrified, at how high they were. "Wait, we don't have to go up there, above those red rocks, up to those white ones, next to the sky, do we?"

"Yep."

"That's impossible."

"That's what I was thinking."

We looked at each other. I dropped my pack, and without conviction, said, "Well, Keith Nelson did it."

This was insanity. I got my water bottle and poured a swig of molten liquid into my mouth then spat it out. "This is like two hundred degrees!"

Ross put his finger in his mouth then stuck it in the air. "Yeah, pretty close."

We walked around growths of prickly pear and short barrel cactus to the river. At the water's edge, a few stands of willows and the ever-present tamarisk offered some shade. We squatted at the edge of the water where a quick eddy swirled behind a boulder, and we let the cold water, which had recently been released from the chilled depths of Lake Powell, fill our bottles. We had to suck hard to pull the purified water up through our straws—which was a nuisance, but it was worth it if we wanted to filter out diarrhea-causing giardia.

There were some small rapids here, but we could hear the roar of larger ones a few hundred yards upstream.

We went back up the bank and found a nearly level area next to some boulders above where we thought the river might rise. After clearing stones and small sticks, we set up our tent, then, while Ross rolled out our pads and sleeping bags, I set up our lightweight butane stove and got some dinner going.

The light was fading, but we had already learned that dusk lingered for a couple of hours down here before full night came on. Ross was now looking up the dry creek bed angling up the little draw to our east. "I wonder if we can get up to that white strata by following this ravine."

I looked up from the pot of freeze-dried stew and saw that the ravine, which was nothing more than an eroded fissure in the rock, did indeed lead upward at a gentler grade than the outlying area. "It's probably the *only* way we'll get up there. What is the cave, two thousand feet higher than us?"

"That's what Kinkaid said—I mean Ephraim Wells."

"I wonder whatever made him want to climb up there in the first place."

"He wanted to get rich."

I followed Ross's gaze. "But how did he ever see a cave? I don't see anything but an unclimbable wall."

"Don't forget, he was out in the river and had a better angle, and, of course, the cave wasn't closed off then."

I studied the distant white cliffs two thousand feet above us. Wells must have had built-in binoculars.

Ross looked down at me. "You surprised me today."

"How?"

"Look at you. You were dead yesterday. Today you hiked even farther, and almost drowned in some quicksand, and you're still going strong."

"Don't let my good looks fool you. I died a couple of miles ago."

"No, you're different. You're stronger today."

I didn't say anything about how refreshed I had felt after bathing in the electric blue waters of the Little Colorado. I was still trying to determine if the water itself had re-energized me or just the hope that we were getting closer to the cave.

"You know," I said, stirring the stew. "Sometimes I think something's been trying to, I don't know, keep us away from here— or at least keep me away."

"Like what?"

"I don't know."

"The adversary?"

I shrugged. I didn't really want to talk about it, though I did want to understand it.

"All I know," he said, "is you're looking better today. Think you'll be ready to scale that monster in the morning?"

I looked up at the distant strata of white rock just below a floating veil of pink clouds. "Probably not. In fact, why don't you just go up there and check it out and come back and tell me about it?"

He didn't respond.

The stew was gooey and still boiling, almost as hot as the air, but it tasted great.

Chapter 21

Serpents in the Canyon

The way Klah figured it, this should be the day he saw two little figures scaling the far wall. He had risen from his cot beneath the overhang before dawn and made sure the motion detector on his digital telescope was operational. The battery on his laptop was low, but that was no problem, as he had two more. He replaced the battery and went about making breakfast. Later this evening, if he hadn't spotted Call and Keller, he would take the used batteries to his Jeep, hidden a quarter mile back, and charge them.

As he heated a pot of oatmeal over a camp stove, he glanced out from his perch at the far wall. At his level, a thousand feet higher than the east rim, the sun was actually below him as it crept over the horizon. A dazzling array of violets, blues, and pinks materialized over the Kaibito Plateau. Then he realized that these colors were matched and maybe even exceeded by the kaleidoscope in the canyon below. He had heard that the North Rim (actually the west rim at this location) had the better view. As the spires and mesas below caught the light, a kind of terrestrial rainbow billowed up from the gorge with layers of tints and hues defying description. The reds alone were staggering, the auburns and corals and russets at the top dancing over scarlets and crimsons and rubies in the depths. The bowels of the earth had caught fire. He longed for a vocabulary that would allow him to describe it, but words didn't come, partly because as the earth continued its eastward spin, the colors were already changing.

The oatmeal came to a boil, and he turned the stove off, eliminating the soft hiss from its jets, and the silence enveloped him—an absolute nullity of sound. The audio void exposed the emptiness, not of his soul, not of the canyon, but of the universe. There were no voices now, no murmuring whispers, only a spectacular vacuum of beautiful silence. He scraped his boot on a rock just to measure the rudeness of the report. He smiled. The canyon had carved out an existence of dumbfounding silence that had lasted longer than he could imagine, could ever imagine, but he still had the power to break it.

He was about to pick up a rock and throw it into the canyon just to follow its cascading echo, when he heard a "*ding*" behind him. He spun around, nearly slipping on the gritty sandstone.

His computer was alerting him to something on the far wall.

He hurried to the folding chair on which his computer sat and lifted the lid. An image from the telescope immediately filled the screen, a field of view of about a hundred yards all around the cave. At first he focused on the stone facade, but he saw nothing. Then he searched the glints and shadows nearby for motion, but again saw nothing. Then something down in the left corner shifted. He studied it, seeing something so perfectly blending with the terrain that it went invisible. Then it moved again. The concealment was nearly perfect, but as the tawny, sure-footed animal inched across a cliff below the cave, Klah relaxed. He went to the telescope which was positioned on the tripod at face level and carefully put his right eye to the eyepiece. There it was again, a bighorn sheep with its winter coat hanging in strips from its side. It was a smallish ewe foraging on a narrow ledge below and to the left of the sealed cave. Its movements were slow and deliberate, but the motion detector had caught it nonetheless.

This meant it should easily catch a man clambering over the rocks. Klah went back to his breakfast, satisfied that if Call and Keller found their way to the cave, he would see them.

* * *

I awoke to utter silence. Even the river was mute. Outside the tent a soft amber light illuminated the gorge. Because of the heat, we had left the tent flap open, and my sleeping bag was wide open. I checked my torso and arms for scorpions and insects, but saw none. Ross was still asleep, with his head near the open flap, on his bag rather than in it. A movement caught my attention just outside the tent, then I realized that it was both outside and inside the tent.

A pinkish stick was undulating out of the tent. As my vision cleared, or perhaps as my brained accepted reality, I saw that the stick was a snake nearly as thick as my arm, and about a foot from Ross's head.

My first instinct, fortunately, was to do nothing, and a moment later the snake's tail slipped out of the tent, two parallel rows of rattles silently trailing about two inches off the ground.

I breathed deeply, surprised that I had been holding my breath. I had seen videos of rattlesnakes before, but I had never seen a pink one. Ross must have heard my intake of air, and he rolled away from me, his right arm landing where the snake had just been.

I got on all fours and carefully peered around the corner of the tent, but the snake had vanished.

"Whatcha lookin' for?" Ross muttered, rolling onto his back.

I didn't answer. He sat up.

"Are you all right?"

"Yeah," I said, scooting back into the tent. "I think it's going to be an interesting day."

"Why?"

"Because I kind of believe in omens, and the snake that just crawled out of here could either be a good omen, like in Moses's day, or a bad omen, like in almost everyone else's day."

His head whipped to the front, and he looked out through the opening. "A snake was in here?" He got up on his hands and knees and poked his head outside. "Did you see it?"

I nodded. "It went right by your head." I looked out at a cluster of rocks where I thought the snake had gone. "I figured the best thing to do was to just let it go out, you know, since it wasn't rattling its tail or anything. I didn't want you to wake up and scare it."

He stared at me. "It had a rattle? How big was it?"

"About three feet long and almost as thick as my arm. It probably sensed our body heat and came in to look around."

He peered out of the tent again.

Instead of waiting until breakfast to have our morning prayers, we knelt right there and offered heartfelt oblations. I was voice, and I added numerous pleas for help, guidance, protection, safety, and wisdom for the rest of the day.

A few minutes later, the blessing on the granola was long and sincere as well.

When I told Ross that the snake was pink, his reaction surprised me.

"Aw, man! Ya shoulda woke me up! That was a Grand Canyon Rattlesnake! They're the only pink rattlesnakes in the world. I read about 'em."

"Don't tell me—on the internet—when I was working."

"Yeah, sure." He looked at the rock pile again, but the snake was gone. "Oh, *man!*"

"Believe me, Ross, when you die and see what actually happened, you'll be glad I didn't wake you up."

"Yeah, well, at least then maybe I'll actually *see* one!"

I dropped the subject.

It was already hot, but I was wearing long pants and a long-sleeved shirt. After breakfast I put on a pair of synthetic work gloves. Just looking up at the cleft in the wall told me we were going to be scrabbling hand over foot up rocks.

It looked like the climb up the dry ravine would be relatively easy for the first quarter-mile. Then the fun would begin when we faced a sheer wall. We had spotted it on Google Maps at home, and Ross had concluded that it would be impossible to scale, but I thought that if Keith had done it, so could we.

"But we don't know that he came this way," Ross said.

"Then how did he get these photos? He had to be right here, at the foot of that ravine."

Based on that flimsy logic, we were about to attempt the impossible. We took only one pack. Ross's pack would contain food and water, a first-aid kit, and a few tools, including a small LED flashlight, should we actually find the cave. Since we had seen no one else hiking in the canyon, we figured our tent and the rest of our gear would be safe where it stood.

The bottom of the ravine was composed of grayish-brown shale, dirt, and tamarisk. Ross led the way, going slower than he wished, but faster than I would have. In half an hour we had climbed about 400 feet and traveled the first quarter mile, which put us at the foot of the insurmountable wall, which was in fact steeper than the lying maps had indicated. There was no way Nelson had scaled this thing. It was like facing a cul-de-sac with sheer walls rising at right angles on three sides—and going up for another 700 feet. If someone had dropped a rope from the top and offered to pull me up, I would have turned it down.

"I don't think this is how he got up there," I said.

Ross, kind man that he usually is, didn't state the obvious—*I told you so*. We turned around and went back to the camp, which, because of the double-edge sword of gravity, took only ten minutes. We had just spent forty minutes and precious energy getting back to where we had started. We sucked some more water out of the mighty Colorado and discussed alternatives. Because we had no cell coverage, we had no online maps, but we *had* printed out three different angles of the area from Google Earth.

I pointed at another cleft in the wall, about half a mile away to our right. "It looks like there might, possibly, be a way up—*right there.*"

He looked at the place, scowled, then folded the map and put it back in his pack. "The problem is," he grumbled, "there isn't any other way that could possibly work." He shouldered his pack and led off to the south, not mentioning the fact that we were retracing steps we had taken yesterday to get here. Twenty minutes later we were at the mouth of the new ravine.

"I don't get it," I said. "If this is the place, why didn't he just take a picture here?"

"Probably because he did what we just did. He tried the obvious place, since it's right below the *supposed* cave, took pictures, then when it didn't work he came over here but didn't bother to get his camera out again. Hopefully, this ravine took him to the top."

I looked at my watch. It was eight. We had just wasted an hour.

We set off again. This ravine was narrower and steeper than the first one. After rising for several hundred feet, it snaked around to the left and led up at an even steeper angle. The draw was progressively narrowing. The same grayish-brown shale we had seen earlier littered the area, and footing was tricky. I asked Ross to slow down, which he did. It was probably getting steep even for him. But we hadn't run into an impassable wall yet, which kept our hopes alive for the moment.

We came around a series of boulders as big as houses then stopped. The draw bent farther around to our left and then led up a narrow chimney. The chimney, which was about twenty feet wide, was too steep to hike, but possibly passable on all fours. Distances were tricky here, but I estimated the chimney at about six hundred feet high.

We were about to climb, on all fours, the height of a sixty-story building.

Neither of us spoke.

Ross started climbing.

"Climbing" might be too positive a word. We were slowly, cautiously, placing one hand in front of the other, one foot in front of the other. Less than a minute into the climb, Ross found a small boulder to rest against and took his pack off. He dug down into a side pocket and found his gloves and put them on. The rocks in the direct sun were warming up, and most had sharp, jagged edges. They might be eons old, but time hadn't dulled them much. Falling—even sliding back down—would have been a very dangerous proposition.

I estimated the angle of the climb at about 40 degrees, with a couple of stretches approaching 60. On one of these stretches, I began to slide back then caught a football-sized rock and held on. If the rock had given way, I would have been gone. Several times Ross dislodged stones above me that tumbled into my hands and forearms. A smaller one, about the size of a baseball, glanced off another rock, bounced up, and hit my shoulder. He heard it but didn't see it, because turning to look might have caused even worse results.

The climb took an hour, but as we neared the top, our hopes of success increased. According to the map, this would be the steepest part of the ascent. We pulled ourselves over a set of smooth, rounded stones, which looked like the lip of a dried-out waterfall. It actually proved to be the most precarious moment so far, but once over it we saw that we were in a bowl. Still on hands and knees, we crawled into it, and Ross finally let his pack slide off. We lay on our backs, sprawled out on a small patch of gravel. The sun was fully overhead, baking our faces, but we didn't care, fatigue and gratitude overwhelming other thoughts.

But one idea kept nagging: we would have to go back down that chimney. Then, another thought, a familiar one, echoed through my brain: How had Keith Nelson ever done this?

The man had clearly been driven by manic greed, but even that seemed to be insufficient motivation.

I scooted over to the lip and looked back down the mountainside. I am tempted to say it was straight down, that it was as sheer and dangerous as the face of Half Dome, but it wasn't.

Not quite.

But it was close.

"Good climb, huh?" Ross said, sitting up now. "How are you feeling?"

I took stock of myself. "Surprisingly good."

He studied my face. In times past, simple stress could reduce me to vomiting and debilitating fatigue. Just two days ago, coming down the Tanner Trail, I had nearly collapsed.

So, where was this strength coming from? If I had known the journey would have been this hard, I wouldn't even have thought of coming. Was I cured or just temporarily strengthened?

To exit the bowl, we still had another steep scrabble up a pink limestone face, about thirty feet high, then, according to our map, we would be at the base of the Redwall. Fortunately it only seemed to rise at about a 30 to 40 degree angle. A piece of cake. I smiled at the thought. Every part of this climb was steeper than any trail or outcropping we had been on in the previous two days.

We drank some water and ate some trail mix, then we marched off toward the steep climb out of the bowl. It was slightly easier than the previous climb and took only a few minutes. Then, cresting a sharp bluff, we came out onto a broad slope of red talus.

The Redwall.

We turned to admire how high we had come and saw a world of stunning space and light. The river, now blue-green far below, snaked around mesas and outcroppings. Across the canyon a pinkish glow illuminated the void as if the canyon were lit from within. The sky was a sharp, azure blue, without clouds, without limit, and the distant peaks, most with Egyptian names, rose like ancient sentinels to guard the sacred ground we claimed—sacred not only because of the Natives who first claimed it, but because of the sacrifice required from *anybody* to conquer it. Standing on the shoulder of this immense red balustrade that ran the entire length of the canyon, we both felt some pride, but probably more humility. We were momentary giants lording over the earth, yet we were also tiny ants, swallowed up by the immensity of this fissure in the earth's crust.

We thought surmounting the Redwall would be a little easier, until I slipped on some loose rocks and barely arrested my slide before plunging a thousand feet. My respect and humility increased. We turned to our right and started up at an oblique angle across the massive Redwall.

First we turned westward to take us around another outcropping, a thousand-foot-long peninsula projecting out to a point almost directly above the river. With the shale so loose and the angle so steep, each step was a calculated risk between progress and death. We had been climbing in stagnant air, but now a warm wind rising from the canyon floor buffeted us. At one point as we traversed along the peak of a narrow ridge we held hands to stabilize each other in the wind. After twenty minutes of cautious travel, we came to the far end of the peninsula and lingered to take in the expanded view of the canyon. The pink and amber hues below and startling blues above left us breathless, but that may have been more because of the climb.

As we made our way back toward the cleft in the wall that we had started for in the morning, we continued angling upward, each step taking us both across and up the slope. As with the outcroppings earlier, our right legs were always lifting us, and our left legs were jamming down into the talus, trying to prevent slippage. But we were a little more used to it now.

We came to an area where a dozen or so boulders had wedged themselves into a gully and formed a level pad of gravel behind them. We climbed up it and took a break. The cloudless sky was both beautiful and brutal. The deep blue was stunning, but the solar oven of the gully was searing. After applying more sunscreen, we studied the map and Keith's photos again. It appeared that we were less than a quarter mile from the cave, but still three or four hundred feet below it.

We decided to go up the gully to claim the elevation we needed then skirt along the top of the Redwall to, hopefully, reach a point just below the cave.

Because of thousands of stones that had rolled into the gully through millions of years of erosion, we had a kind of staircase to walk on, and we surprised ourselves by reaching the top of the Redwall in less than fifteen minutes.

Now it was a straight shot across the face of the wall. We found a ledge about two feet wide and quickened our pace as our anticipation mounted. I stopped looking around. I stopped admiring the canyon. I became fixed on a spot ahead, just around Ross's left arm, where the cleft in the wall began to curl back into a cul-de-sac—the area where the cave was supposed to be.

The ledge suddenly steepened, and the terrain changed from solid rock to loose shale again. A final test. Every step became precarious. I glanced around Ross again to see if perchance a trail existed in the shale, thinking that if Keith had been here, his tracks might still be visible, but the talus gave way under my left foot, and I waved my arms out to catch my balance. Ross stopped and looked back. I didn't worry about finding a trail again. That was Ross's job.

He stopped. I tried to see what he was looking at but couldn't see anything. "What is it?"

"Look—just above that big rock." He pointed straight ahead. "On that little shelf up there, just above the boulder."

I followed his arm toward a dun-colored rock ledge, but I still couldn't see anything peculiar. A rock seemed to move. Then another. I had to bend my body to see around him. "What are they? Deer?"

"No, sheep—bighorns."

I stepped on the slope above him. The two animals were definitely shorter and stockier than deer—and the circular horns on the larger animal left no doubt.

"It looks like a male and a female," he said. "Pretty cool, huh?"

I glanced at him to see if he was serious. It was cool, but we were on a veritable slope of *death*, within yards, potentially, of one of the greatest archeological finds in *history*, and he wanted to watch the sheep? "Sure. Come on, let's go."

He watched a moment longer then said, "Wow, this would be a great place to work in. Maybe I'll be a ranger."

Frankly, at the moment, I didn't care. I was tired, getting hungry, and we were standing on a 30-degree slope of loose shale that could shift at any moment.

He started hiking again.

Chapter 22

Going to the Top

"Ding!"

Klah didn't run to his computer. He didn't stir from his cot. He didn't even bother to roll over. He had run to it the first few times, then, after seeing that it was the same ewe, he had begun checking only occasionally when the motion detector went off. Then about an hour ago, a ram had joined the ewe. The ram was larger, with impressive horns that curled symmetrically around its head, but the problem was the motion detector caught every movement. Lately Klah had stopped checking the screen at all. If Call and Keller had camped by the river the night before, there was no way they could reach the cave before noon, at the earliest. He checked his watch.

11:46.

No wonder he was getting hungry. He sat up and faced the canyon. The colors had shifted from blues and violets to pinks and ambers. By dusk he expected it to shift further toward the reds. Pinnacles and buttes he hadn't noticed just hours ago were prominent now, as if tectonic forces had created them in a single morning.

"Ding!"

He had grown so accustomed to the canyon's deafening silence that the persistent alerts began to annoy him. He decided to mute the sound while making some lunch.

"Ding!"

He flipped the screen open and saw the ram, still pursuing the reluctant ewe. The sheep were nearly in the center of the screen, well below the cave. Heat waves were beginning to obscure the resolution. He put his finger on the touchpad to click the sound off, when it dinged again. Only this time, because he was watching the sheep, he noticed that they hadn't moved.

"Ding!"

He looked around them, eventually lowering his eyes to the far right corner of the screen.

And he froze.

Two humans had just entered the screen, walking slowly, as if unsure of their footing. The cave was about two hundred feet above them to their left. They stopped moving, and the one in front, taller, it seemed, turned to face the other. Heat waves slued the image, but he knew the taller one had to be Ross Keller, and the shorter one was Travis Call. They hadn't found the cave yet, and being so far below it, there was still a chance they wouldn't. He looked up at the cave and was again impressed by the naturalness of the manmade facade. Though his view was almost constantly blurry from heat waves, it seemed that they might even stand right in front of it and not see it.

But something bothered him. How had they known where to go? He had read the same letters Call had received from Nelson. They hadn't been specific enough to lead anyone to within a mile of the place, let alone a hundred yards. Call must have found some other information.

He stepped around the telescope and looked into the eyepiece. The image was smaller—about four millimeters across where it reached his eye—but the resolution was clearer. Both men were wearing hats, which clouded their faces in shadow, but he was sure it was them. His pulse quickened. If they found the cave, he would have to pack up and drive back to the Lipan Point then go down into the canyon and wait for them on the trail.

Then kill them.

And this time it wouldn't be accidental.

* * *

The ledge led us up to a rust-stained limestone prominence, and our hearts sank. We could now see that we had been mistaken about being above the Redwall. We had reached a band of beige rock, which is what we were looking for, but this was just a temporary stratum, a kind of fool's gold. Now it was clear that we had at least another hundred vertical feet to climb, maybe two hundred, to get up to where the cave should be.

The heights were already ridiculous, so another couple hundred feet didn't bother us, but with fatigue making every step a life-and-death moment, the anticipation of more climbing was demoralizing.

Discouragement is an interesting phenomenon; it's emotional, but it affects the physical. I doubted we would turn around, not so close to the white rocks just a couple of hundred feet above us, but for the moment we were too tired and too disheartened to move forward. So we stood in our tracks and played mind games with fatigue, hoping our will and desire would eventually win out.

Off to our left and slightly above us rocks began tumbling down, and we turned to watch. They were mostly smallish stones, about the size of baseballs and softballs, but by the time they clattered by us, they had enough momentum to knock us over had we been in their way. I looked up to see what had caused the rock fall and saw the two sheep scamper across the ribbon-like cliff, as if a six-inch ledge were no more perilous than a broad pasture. The sheep rounded the base of an outcropping farther to our left and disappeared.

"Unbelievable," Ross whispered.

My own thoughts tended toward the worldly: *If you could make a climbing boot that replicated the soles of their cloven hooves, you could make a fortune.* Ross took a step upward. We were climbing again.

We angled leftward across the slope then rose onto a shelf, six to eight feet wide. The wind was stronger here, but a ledge with level ground was more than welcome. Ahead of us, a narrow gully rose upward, winding around, still to our left. Everything seemed to take us to the left, toward a huge cleft in the main wall that rose out of sight. The narrow gully attracted my attention, and even though my thighs were burning and I was blowing like a marathoner, I began to shuffle over to it across some loose shale. Ross had set his pack down and was getting food and water. I looked at my watch. It was 12:22.

Something seemed odd about the gully, mostly because it didn't continue down past us but stopped abruptly where the shale began. Also, it almost looked like it had a series of broken steps carved into the solid limestone, as if a staircase had been chiseled into the rock.

My pulse quickened as I thought back to the cryptic directions Kinkaid—Wells—had mentioned in the newspaper article.

"Ross! Come over here! Could this be the staircase Wells talked about?"

Ross left his pack and came over and looked up the ravine.

"The steps." He knelt and put his gloved hand on the ragged edge of the beige, almost pink stone protruding six or eight inches from the side of the gully. "It looks like someone hacked it out of the rock, then broke it off."

Both sides of the narrow ravine showed jagged, broken steps jutting out from the sides. They went up thirty or forty vertical feet to what might be another shelf. We turned and inspected the ledge we were on. It was wider than the other ledges we had followed and seemed to be almost perfectly level with the deep cul-de-sac the sheep had disappeared into. Above it, darker colorations marked the rock where water had deposited rust-colored minerals, like ancient watermarks. I could see how someone might call the discolorations stains, as Wells had.

"This ledge is what Wells thought was the water line a long time ago," Ross said.

"I know, but we're at least two thousand feet up from the river. If this was the water line, there must have been something blocking the river, damming it up. But that's crazy. A lake two-thousand feet deep? Filling two-thirds of the Grand Canyon? I don't think so."

Ross agreed. This was probably just a natural ledge made by different layers of rock stained by rust.

He looked back at his pack. "We should probably eat now. We may not get another chance for a long time."

We ate a fast lunch and probably drank too much water, leaving only about a gallon in a larger, collapsible container in Ross's pack. After he saddled up again, we went to the edge of the gully and looked up at the winding staircase. He motioned out to it with his hand. "After you."

* * *

Klah watched in disbelief as the two men began clambering hand-over-hand up the narrow draw. The big one, Keller, was powerful and confident, which was probably why he trailed the smaller one, Call; if the weaker man fell, Keller could catch him. But how had they known they were below the cave? There was no way they could see it below the upper shelf, which, now that he gauged its size against their bodies, almost looked wide enough for a vehicle. Dimensions were deceptive at this distance.

But that didn't matter. They were almost to the top, almost to the point of no return, and if they knew where the cave was, they would almost certainly see it when they got there. Thinking things through to their inevitable outcome, his eyes almost inadvertently fell to his folding chair, where his Glock 19 lay in its holster.

* * *

Our gloves had made the climb easier, protecting us from the unweathered edges protruding from the broken steps. It was clear that the fractures were relatively recent, at least in the geologic sense, within a hundred years or so. As I pulled myself over the last rise, I expected, or hoped, to see the cave, but what I found was a wide level area, much larger than the ledge we had rested on below. But even before I got up on the ledge, I spotted something I had been looking for earlier.

A footprint.

It was a boot-print in a layer of sand, right before my face. I got up on the ledge and saw more prints under a rock overhang where the weather couldn't reach them as easily. As Ross came up, I pointed to the first print.

He smiled. "I'd say about a size eight. Wasn't Nelson a small guy?"

Yes, these prints would have matched Keith Nelson just right.

We turned toward the cliff face, only a dozen feet in front of us. The cave had to be here, somewhere. The bench we were on was a couple of a hundred feet long, and the cave could have been anywhere along it. As I viewed the wall, it appeared to be a dividing zone between the Redwall, which we had just summited, and the light-colored Supai Formation, just above it. Quickly scanning it, I could see that the intersection of the two zones had several fissures in it, some up to a foot wide, any of which could have led into caves.

"Remember," I said, "it's supposed to be covered over, like in the picture."

Ross lowered his pack and pulled out the pictures. We compared the photo of the cave face to the wall in front of us.

Nothing.

I walked to our left, scanning the pink, red, and beige rocks that had been thrust up and twisted by gigantic forces. "I don't know. It should be right—"

I was staring at it.

Ten feet to my left the rock wall matched the picture exactly.

"Here it is!"

Ross came over and held the photo up. "That's amazing. You'd never think there was a cave here if you didn't know it."

Small boulders had been mortared together forming a remarkably natural-looking wall. Someone had taken a lot of time masking the cave. And bringing in the mortar couldn't have been easy.

Ross stepped back and looked at the whole facade. He sighed, and I thought he was going to laugh, but he seemed serious, almost angry. "All right, who's behind all this?" He took his hat off and put his hands on his hips. "I didn't ask before, because we didn't know if it was really here—but now I want to know! Who did this? The government? The Smithsonian? Goldman Sachs?"

I smiled at the name of the giant investment bank.

"I mean, it's *really here!*" he half yelled. "Kinkaid—Wells—whoever he was, he really found this place. And I believe everything he said, and I don't believe *anything* the government says. This wasn't done by one person. *Look* at it—the wall's twelve feet high! How many bags of mortar and how many barrels of water did that take? I'll tell you one thing, that stuff didn't come up from below. It did not come up the way we just came." He looked up to the top of the canyon wall. "It's over a thousand feet up there. How'd they get it down here?"

I just shook my head. "Wells said they used ropes, remember? He said some guy named Fletcher Winn had a group of men pull the artifacts out. Plus, he was supposedly feathering his own nest."

He looked at me, eyes blazing. "Yeah, I remember—but somebody's *still* doing it. Somebody killed Keith Nelson to keep this a secret. And they killed Wells—and whoever that professor was."

"S.A. Jordan."

"They killed him! It's a conspiracy! A hundred-year-old conspiracy."

He was right, but we weren't going to solve anything by getting mad. "Let's try to find a way in." I tugged on one of the stones. I might as well have been pulling on the great Redwall itself. Ross mule-kicked one about waist-high. His foot ricocheted off, causing him to stumble backwards. "Whoever built this knew what they were doing. There might even be rebar in there. It's pretty solid."

I pulled my phone out of my front pocket. "We should probably take more pictures of it."

"I guess," Ross said, "even though Johnson has Nelson's pictures—and he still didn't believe they showed the cave."

"Well, maybe he'll believe us if we show him different angles. Go stand in front of it, so we can get a perspective of the size."

He did, and I took some pictures, then he took his own phone out and took three pictures of me from different angles. We viewed them and had to admit they didn't prove much.

"We've got to find a way in," I said. "Let's look for the air duct."

Ross put the picture of the covered cave entrance back in the plastic bag and pulled out the one that showed a hole with the bush by it. After memorizing it, we each followed the bench in opposite directions. I went to the right, checking every possible crack and fissure, but I found nothing. I turned to see if Ross had found anything, but he was already staring at me, having completed his search. We started looking again. On my second pass, I decided to go out farther, along an even narrower ledge extending out past the bench. On my right, below this two-foot-wide ledge, was a thousand feet of empty air. I couldn't tell if the tiny ledge I was on was an animal trail, but it certainly wasn't made for humans. Loose rocks fell away as I shuffled along it, my stomach and hands pressed against the sheer cliff. I inched my way around a projection of stratified rock that bulged out over the canyon, a small outcropping. Without the experience of the last few days, I never would have tried it. After squeezing around the bulge, I was completely cut off from view of Ross, and I thought about stopping and waiting until he could join me, but off to my right I saw some bushes about twenty feet away, at head height. I shuffled over to inspect them.

A gnarly creosote bush was growing out of a crack between two shafts of rock that had been twisted apart by geologic pressures. The crack was about the width of my fist. I ducked under the bush and came up on the other side and saw a replica of the picture Keith had taken.

The air duct.

Along with the bush and rocks, everything appeared untouched since he had been here. Without his picture, I never would have found it. I certainly wouldn't have risked my life scooting around the little outcropping. And I doubt he would have done it without Well's handwritten notes on the back of his letter from a hundred years ago.

I still couldn't see or hear Ross, so I checked the opening further. As I faced the cliff, it was still a little off to my right. Some dead brush littered the ledge immediately below it. The hole started at about six feet above the ledge and was twenty-four to thirty inches in diameter. I was about to go back and get Ross, when I heard his voice.

"Did you find it?" He had squeezed around the outcropping and was shuffling sideways along the ledge toward me. We had both grown inured to the thousand-foot precipice we stood on.

"There's a hole over here, on the other side of the bush, and it looks just like the picture."

I tried to kick the brush on the ledge away so I could get under the hole itself, but my foot hit something, causing it to ricochet off and making me lose my balance. My left hand shot out and grabbed the creosote bush growing out of the wall, and I regained my balance. I didn't look down, because I knew there was nothing there.

"Are you okay?" Ross asked, wide-eyed.

"Yeah."

"What made you lose your balance?"

"I don't know." I bent down and checked the brush I had kicked and found a foot-high, boulder hidden under it. On the other side of that, there was another boulder, slightly larger. They were piled like a small pyramid directly under the hole. I wondered if Keith had stuck the brush there when he pulled it away from the hole.

"Hah, look! A step ladder!" Ross said. "Let me get up and take a look inside."

He obviously didn't trust me to take the first look. I carefully stepped to the far side to let Ross get under the hole. He pulled his flashlight from of his pocket.

It was on.

"Uh-oh," he said under his breath.

"What?"

"The flashlight was on. It might have been on the whole time."

The light seemed bright enough, but if it had been on since morning, the batteries could nearly be dead. "How many hours are the batteries supposed to last?" I asked.

"I don't know."

"Do you have the extras?"

He thought for a moment. "No. You do, remember? In your pack. We didn't think we'd need them right away, so we put them where they'd be out of the way."

We stared at each other. My pack, of course, was still down by the river. We had both forgotten them. I pulled my phone out of my pocket again and checked the battery. "Fifty-five percent." I hit the flashlight icon, and the light came on. "It should be good for an hour or so."

"Maybe," Ross said uncertainly.

He put his foot on the first stone, carefully shifted his weight onto it, put both feet on it, then stepped up on the second stone. His face was above the hole. He put the flashlight inside and dipped his head to look around.

He pulled his head out and stared back at me.

"What's the matter?"

"It'll be a tight fit, but you should be able to make it—at least part way."

"Part way?"

"The hole goes back about five feet, and then it angles up out of sight."

"Well, if it was big enough for Keith to get in, it should be big enough for me."

"Maybe, but it's not big enough for me. I won't even be able to squeeze in this first part." He lowered himself back down to the ledge and handed me the light. "It looks like you're going in by yourself, partner. Be careful."

Crawling into a cave that might be a mile long with dozens of passageways, was the last thing I wanted to do. Keeping one hand on the cliff-face, I stepped up on the rocks and peered inside. The round air duct was smooth on the bottom but rough on top where chiseled grooves ran its length. Indeed, Ross would have never fit in. Toward the back, the passageway did angle upward, like an elbow. "Why do you think they turned it up like that?" I asked, still probing it with the light.

"I don't know, but doesn't it look like the back of the hole is wider than it is here? And then, as it angles up, doesn't it look like the walls might angle in on themselves, like an inverted cone?"

I stuck my head in as far as I could without climbing in. The hole at the far back did indeed seem wider than the hole where I stood, and as it angled up, it did look like an inverted cone, getting narrower as it went up. "Yeah, it does," I said. "I wonder why they did that." As I studied it, a thought hit me. "I wonder if it's so animals couldn't crawl up in there. They wouldn't be able to hang onto the smooth walls upside down."

"Could be."

I got down off the rock. He looked at his watch. "It's almost one. What's the plan, boss?"

I tried to think of option B but couldn't come up with one. "I guess I'm going in. This is why we came here."

"All right, you've got the flashlight and your phone. Do you want my phone too? There's about forty percent power left." He held it out to me.

I wouldn't mind having another backup flashlight in the cave, but I didn't plan on being in that long. We needed to head back down to the river in a couple of hours, and since it might get dark before we got down, I figured we should keep his phone as fresh as possible. "No, you keep it. Who knows, you might even get a signal up here."

He looked as if he hadn't thought of that. Both our phones had zero bars at the moment. "Just a minute. Let me get something."

He shuffled back around the outcropping, far quicker than I would have, and came back with a bottle of water and two granola bars. "Take these, in case of an emergency."

I stared at him. An emergency. A broken ankle might doom me. Sliding down a chute that I couldn't climb out of would lead to a long, dark, agonizing death. "Whatever you do in there," he added, "just remember the way out. I've read about people who got lost in caves. Someone usually finds their bones about twenty years later—but not always."

I didn't thank him for the advice. I looked at the water bottle and two granola bars and wondered if I shouldn't take more—maybe twenty years' worth. But just trying to squeeze in would be tricky. The water probably wouldn't fit in my pocket, as it would make my hips too big, so I would have to hold it in my free hand. The granola bars and phone would have to get squished, and probably bent, in my pockets.

The magnitude of what I was doing hit me. "You know what?"

"What?"

"I think we should say a prayer."

His eyes narrowed. "Yeah—and you should say it, since you're the one who might die."

He had a wonderful childlike way about him.

We oh so carefully lowered ourselves to the 24-inch ledge above the breathtaking sky, then I offered a very heartfelt prayer.

* * *

Through distorting heat waves, Klah watched the two men look for something in the dirt, or were they praying? How odd. He couldn't remember the last time he had prayed. When the men rose to their feet, they seemed to pose for more pictures. He would definitely need to get their cameras and phones. Call stood up on something again, probably a platform of rocks, and started worming his way into the hole, with Keller helping him. A moment later Call had disappeared into the rock face. Klah expected Keller to follow, but he stayed outside, as if guarding the hole.

But how did they know that little hole was there? It hadn't been visible through the telescope until they had removed brush from it. This too merited investigation.

Keller seemed to yell something into the hole, then he turned and inched his way back to the wide bench where his pack was. He got some food and water from his pack then began walking back around to the cul-de-sac that angled deeper into the canyon. Where was he going? Looking for the sheep?

With the heat waves getting worse, Klah turned the telescope back to the hole and saw no movement. Call was alone inside.

He swung the instrument back to Keller and saw him walk into the cleft where the sheep had gone and was soon out of view. Klah had a choice: he could keep watching for Call to emerge from the hole, or he could adjust the telescope to try to follow Keller. The day was getting hotter, and the image was distorting further. Keller probably wasn't going far, as he wouldn't leave Call alone for long. Plus, he had left his backpack behind.

Klah already knew what he had to do. He checked the screen again but found it blurred beyond recognition, and he closed the laptop. It would take the men at least one long day to get back to Tanner Trail, if not two, and then another to get up to Lipan Point. All Klah had to do was drive around the canyon, park at the head of the trail, and wait for them somewhere down along the trail. All things considered, it would be one of his easier jobs.

It would mean killing in cold blood—committing premeditated murders, but the payoff would be huge—big enough to help him deal with his intermittent conscience later.

Chapter 23

Into the Cave

Years earlier, I had hurt my back playing church basketball and needed an MRI. It turned out nothing was seriously wrong, but as I lay motionless in the coffin-like scanner for an hour, I found myself praying away waves of panic. Since then, I had done all in my power to avoid claustrophobic situations—until now.

As Ross helped me get into the hole, which was almost certainly an air-duct (and *possibly* an escape hatch for the malnourished), I knew that I would be fighting feelings of panic until I found a larger chamber—and then only if I saw that that the roof was solid. The portal was just wide enough for my arms to reach forward and pull myself into the cave. My long-sleeved shirt prevented abrasions as my elbows and forearms dug into the gritty stone. When I reached the back of the narrow tube, where it angled up, I was relieved to find two things: first, that it was significantly cooler, and two, that the greater width in the inverted cone allowed more freedom of movement. I couldn't quite stand up, but I was able to maneuver with more ease, and I quickly got to the top, a few feet up, where it angled laterally again, deeper into the rock.

Almost standing up in the vertical section, I focused the light on the new passageway and saw that it emptied into a larger chamber about five feet away. I bent down as well as I could and yelled at Ross, to see if he could hear me.

He yelled back that he could, and I told him that I was now sure that I could make it into the main part of the cave. He said great and told me that he would be back as soon as he checked out the cul-de-sac where the sheep had gone.

I didn't argue, because we had already argued about it before I climbed into the tunnel. What was he going to find? We had seen no signs of water, so he couldn't refill our jugs, and even if he found a trail, our main purpose when I got out would be to go back down as quickly as possible, not deeper into the cleft of the canyon. I just hoped he didn't sprain an ankle or twist a knee on the way.

On my belly, I inched my way into the new passageway until I could poke my light into the larger chamber. Immediately I saw that it was a tall corridor, extending only ten or so feet to my left, but to my right it went for forty or fifty feet until it bent around to the left, again going deeper into the mountain. With my head still sticking out of the air duct, I looked down and saw another platform of stones below me. It was tricky, but I managed to wriggle my way out of the tube and onto the platform in the larger chamber. I looked up—and hit my head. The rock platform I was standing on put me about five feet above the chamber floor—too close to the ceiling to stand up.

A staircase of stones led down to the floor on my left. I tested each step as I made my way down it; they appeared to be locked together by shape and placement, rather than cement.

I took a moment to orient myself. I was in the cave that Ephraim Wells had told the world about, a cave that may have been hundreds or thousands of years old—a cave that may have been constructed, according to Wells, by Egyptian or Oriental laborers. And as I gazed around at the tunnel, I quickly saw that, indeed, it was not a natural cave. Chiseled markings appeared on the ceiling and walls. It may have begun as a natural orifice in the limestone, but it had clearly been enhanced into a semicircular arch, about ten feet across, by human hands.

As I began walking down the corridor to my right, I recalled Ross's counsel to remember my way out. I stopped and turned off the light. A few moments later as my eyes adjusted, I saw faint light filtering in through the portal. If I could find this corridor again, I should be able to find my way out—unless it was dark outside.

I turned my light back on and looked down. My eyes fell on footprints in the layer of dust on the rock floor, and I instantly recognized Keith's "size eight." His prints showed that he had walked in both directions. Then as I ranged over to the far side of the corridor I saw fainter footprints, or what might have been footprints. A thin layer of dust resting in these impressions told me they were old. A hundred years old? Older? They had the shape and texture of a flat sole without tread, but that probably meant little in terms of age, as I supposed that both ancient sandals and hundred-year-old boots were made with flat, leather soles. I saw only one set of these older prints leading away from the portal, going in the same direction I was now headed. Could they have been made by Ephraim Wells? Had he tested the portal as a possible entrance and exit before writing to his brother?

As my eyes adjusted, I saw that the walls were composed of the same pinkish-gray limestone that made up this entire canyon strata. I gently brushed the surface of one of the chisel marks and found that it was relatively smooth—finer than fine sandpaper. It was also hard. Whoever had hewed this impressive cavern had obviously used hardened tools. I began taking pictures.

My little LED flashlight produced more than enough light, but the question arose: why did the corridor lead away from the main entrance, which would have been to my left when I came in? I had no answer.

For the first fifty yards or so as it wound around to my left, I saw no rooms or corridors branching off. There were also no artifacts, no tools or pottery or scraps of wood. Then as it continued winding around to the left, it brought me to another passage, a little larger, about twelve by twelve. I probed it with my light and saw that it had several large indentations in the walls. Each of these turned out to be openings leading into rooms. Above each doorway were markings etched into the stone. Creeping inside one of these rooms, I took more pictures. It was perfectly empty. No furniture or hardware of any kind. It had smaller indentations in the walls, possibly for candles or small lanterns. The shape was square, perhaps 20-by-20 feet, with the same twelve-foot ceiling. This room led to other rooms on all three sides. Those rooms were smaller, about twelve-by-twelve. They had no outlets, but in each room, a round hole, about a foot across, was bored high into the walls lining the corridor for ventilation.

I went back out and followed the corridor to the next opening, one on the left, and found the same arrangement, a larger room leading to three smaller rooms. I checked the next six large rooms, alternating on each side down the corridor, and found them all identical. These seemed to be dwellings, or apartments for families. The fact that they were empty became startling, almost spooky, as it spoke to the efficiency of Fletcher Winn's team in looting the place. No doubt these dwellings had been furnished and possibly even comfortable at one time. Where had the furniture gone—the tables, benches, beds, water pots, chamber pots? I stood in the middle of this last room and felt a growing depression. My heart broke for the world's loss. I turned and left, determined to search every room.

But that soon proved impossible.

As the corridor bent around back toward the main entrance, I found dozens of rooms. Some were larger, and a few smaller. Most had smaller rooms branching off, some did not, and all were empty. After looking briefly in the first twenty or thirty rooms, I began passing them by. The cavern was proving to be enormous, almost beyond comprehension, and I only had a couple of hours left.

I came to what seemed like the main hallway, the one that must have come from the cave entrance. It was a little taller and wider than the previous corridor. I turned left, back to where I thought the walled-off entrance would be. It was farther away than I thought, but within a few minutes I found it. The men who had set the stones in mortar had not been as careful on this side, and gobs of hardened gray mortar lay like frozen lava behind the manmade wall. Many footprints etched their place in the dust, too many to count. I shined my light all around the facade, searching for weak spots, but found none. What I did find, though, stopped me.

Turning to my right from the mortared wall, my light fell on a picture etched into the rock at about head height. It was a diagram of a square maze about eighteen inches across, with an opening at the top and lines winding around to the center of the image. It was unlike anything I had ever seen. I touched it and found that it was etched into the stone about a quarter of an inch deep.

I turned and went back deeper into the cave, and now with my eye drawn to the walls, I found more etchings, though none like the maze. High on the left wall I found an image of what might be called a heart, though that seemed a stretch. It was turned slightly on its left side and looked more like two ears crudely joined together. Two others were of animals, a snake and a large, misshapen turtle. Most of the other images were of humans drawn as stick figures. Several of these had their arms upraised rather than down at their sides. A little farther in I found a mural that had several stick figures of a man playing a flute. And a little farther on, I found a series of designs, one of square coils, a single line coiling around itself, turning at right angles, moving from right to left. Then I saw a design that made me stop—a swastika with the arms bent to the right. I had read enough history to know that the swastika had not been created by the Nazis, but I was still surprised.

As I followed the main hallway deeper into the cave, back toward the corridor I had come in on, I found more petroglyphs. Whoever had made them had etched them deep enough that they would last for millennia.

When I arrived back at the corridor that I had come in through, I saw that almost straight across from it, to my left, another corridor angled off at about forty-five degrees. I quickly looked into it and saw that it was basically identical to the first corridor, with large rooms leading to smaller rooms, alternating on each side. I turned and continued walking down the main hallway.

Soon I found myself getting chilled. Whoever lived here must have worn long-sleeved shirts and pants, as I now did. I estimated the temperature at about sixty degrees, maybe a little cooler. I think the reason I became aware of the chill again was because of gentle, continuous air movement from one cross corridor to the other.

Twenty or thirty yards past these corridors, I came to what Wells had called the "Cross Hall." He said it was "several hundred feet long," which I took to mean longer than a football field. It was maybe twice that long. Although he said he had seen a statue here of a cross-legged god, I again found nothing. The floor was bare, with only a thin layer of dust and many footprints. I followed the Cross Hall to my left and found a large room that contained two tall structures that baffled me. They were perfectly circular and rose nearly to the ceiling. Near the bottom, about two feet from the floor, each structure had a metal door that slid open and shut. The doors were about eight inches high and a little over a foot wide, and they were all open. I put my light in, saw a scattering of dark kernels of corn, and instantly knew that these structures had been silos or granaries. I tried to find some steps leading to the top but saw none. Then I saw large indentations on the upper lip of each silo where a ladder could be hung. But there was no ladder. Then I realized that the granaries were not hewed out of stone but had been constructed out of a dark gray cement, which was of a different color (darker) than the mortar at the entrance. I ran my hand over one wall and found it perfectly smooth and expertly made. I marveled at the perfect plumb and integrity of the structures. I doubted they could be better made today.

Across the hall was a larger silo, maybe as big as the two smaller ones combined. This one was completely empty.

Continuing down the hall, I found more rooms, mostly dwellings, but some of these were larger, perhaps fifty to sixty feet square. All of them had air ducts high on the walls, about a foot across, connecting them to each other and to the corridor itself. I wondered how they found any privacy and wondered if they might have hung cloth or skins over the ducts to muffle sound.

More dwellings about the same size lay ahead. How many people had lived here? Hundreds, maybe thousands, and I had only just begun to investigate the place. I didn't follow this hall to its end, since it was so long that my light couldn't reach the end of it, but because of the press of time I went back to the main hallway and across it to follow the Cross Hall in that direction as well. It was identical to the other side except that it had no granaries, and after a few minutes I came back and continued deeper into the main hall.

I began jogging. After all the hiking and climbing and nearly dying that morning, the fact that I could still walk, let alone jog, was almost miraculous. Since getting up, I had climbed over 2,000 vertical feet from the river, had crossed two side canyons, and had done all this after hiking over twenty miles in two days. I slowed and gauged my energy level; I still felt remarkably good. Clearly I was being blessed.

Shortly after leaving the Cross Hall, I came to a larger than usual oval-shaped door on my right. Something was etched in the stone above it, something more elaborate than the etchings above the other doorways. I illuminated it and found writings over the entire length of the oval. I didn't recognize their origin and didn't know if they read from left to right or right to left.

And now I remembered something that made me want to kick myself. In my excitement, I had forgotten to take pictures. I pulled my phone out, set it for flash, and took pictures of the writings, then I backed up and took another picture of the large door itself. I considered going back to the granaries and other hieroglyphs on the walls but quickly decided to get those pictures on the way out.

Keeping my phone in my left hand as a reminder to take pictures, I stepped inside the room and froze. The room was the largest I had seen so far, perhaps a hundred feet square, with a ceiling that was at least thirty feet high. But the dimensions of the room had little to do with my amazement. I was staring at three tiers of what appeared to be mummies stacked around the room. I recalled Ephraim Wells' description of the "tomb or crypt," and I found the room to be exactly as he said it was. The walls slanted back at a fairly sharp angle, and each mummy stood on end, supported on its own shelf in a recess carved into the wall.

The mummies had no sarcophagi or coffins, but a heavy wrap of some kind covered them. Wells said it was bark, but I thought it was wool treated with a stiffening agent. The wrap had been covered in clay, giving each mummy a kind of protective shell. I didn't look closely at all the mummies, but it was obvious that the clay had fallen off some of them.

On my left were three empty recesses. Either these were spaces reserved for future mummies, or someone had removed mummies that had been there. In the fourth recess a mummy had been torn open. I went to it and found that the clay shell and cloth wrap around the head and torso had been pulled back to reveal the cadaver. I figured this was the work of Keith Nelson, as the tears in the cloth and deposits of broken clay on the floor appeared to be fairly new.

It appeared to be a male, perhaps a little over five feet tall. Its skin had desiccated to a hard, leathery state that was more gray than brown, possibly because the clay had permeated through the wrap and discolored it. There were no eyes. The facial skin had tightened and stretched back over the bones until it produced a tight grimace revealing two rows of crooked but mostly healthy-looking teeth. The hair was long and stringy and had probably been black before being matted with clay. The arms were thin and folded over the lower midsection. There was no jewelry or other adornments.

I wanted to repair the damage Keith had done. I wanted to put the wrap and clay back in place and make the mummy whole, but I hesitated, not because it was a dead body, but because it was sacred. Again, I was disappointed at the loss, at the callow desecration, all for the sake of greed. I knew Keith didn't need the money. He did it because he could, because he always wanted *more*. I supposed he would have looted the other mummies if he thought he could have packed more jewelry through the portal and lugged it down the canyon and up to the rim. I gently lay the wrap back around the body and face as well as I could. Then I took pictures.

There were 67 mummies, and when I was done, all of them were in one picture or another.

I found no other artifacts in the room, though I did find a bench hewn out of the wall on one side. All the urns, tools, and tablets that Wells had described a hundred years ago were gone.

I left the room and continued my march deeper into the cave, finding more doorways leading into rooms, and more hallways branching off the main corridor. Obviously it had taken decades, maybe centuries to hew all this out of rock, but why had they done it? I had read Wells' thoughts, that the complex was either the original Sipapu, the underground living quarters from which the Hopi had emerged, or a refuge from warring tribes. But now that I was in it, I couldn't see the motivation for this simply being a hideout from warring tribes. It was too elaborate, too big, too hard to make. A group of people who felt threatened would probably do what other threatened peoples have done—move to another place or fight to the death—or, if possible, assimilate into the stronger nation. But I knew of no other examples where a people had carved out an entire village, nay, city, in a mountain of solid rock. The only possible reason I could see for a people doing that was if they felt their god commanded it. I knew that people would go to remarkable extremes to please their gods, such as building a tower to heaven, or building pyramids for their deity-kings. If these people had developed steel or hardened copper tools that allowed them to penetrate the natural limestone, as they obviously had, then perhaps religious injunction pushed them to complete this mind-boggling task. I wondered how many lives, how many generations, had been sacrificed to the undertaking.

And how had they brought food and water in? We had only brought a gallon of water and a few handfuls of food, and it had been incredibly difficult. I thought of the children raised within the tomblike walls who rarely if ever saw the sun, or rain, or a tree. Surely they had heard about the sheep and deer and snakes outside, but did they see them?

I checked my watch and was startled. It was nearly 2:30. How many miles had I traveled? How deep had I come into the complex? I had retraced my steps many times exploring side passageways and corridors. I had always come back to the main corridor that led from the main entrance, but I didn't know how long it would take me to get back out. Fortunately my light was still strong.

Or was it?

I shined it on a nearby wall, and it looked as bright as ever. Then I realized that I couldn't quite make out the chiseled grooves in the wall that had been clear when I first came in. Over time my eyes had adjusted to the gradually failing light, deceiving me into thinking it was as bright as ever, that all was well.

But all was not well.

I had to put the light within three feet of the wall to make out the chiseled marks. It was producing almost no light at all. It was amazing how well my eyes had adjusted to the fading light.

I turned my phone back on and checked the battery level. 37%. All the pictures I had taken had required a flash. I should have accepted Ross's offer to take his phone. I turned on the flashlight app and turned off the LED flashlight. It was strong. Hopefully I had a few minutes of emergency light if I needed it. I still wanted to see the main hall, where, according to Wells, all the people had eaten as a group. It was supposedly longer than two football fields, and dozens of hallways spoked off it. In other words, I hadn't even reached the center of the complex yet.

I figured I had thirty minutes of light left on the phone and maybe half that on the flashlight. I hurried on.

Along the way I noticed that the hallway narrowed somewhat. Had the people grown weary of carving a hallway twelve feet wide and twelve feet high all the way? Had they discovered by this point that it didn't have to be so big? And now I found more narrow corridors branching off from time to time, but I didn't explore them. All of them had markings above their oval-shaped doorways. Then my light visibly dimmed. I shook my phone like I used to shake my old Boy Scout flashlight when it began failing. But the light wasn't the problem. The walls had suddenly gotten farther away, and there was less reflected light. A few steps later and I was in the main hall.

It was vast—yes, at least two football fields long, probably longer, and the extreme length made the width, which was only forty or fifty feet, seem narrow in comparison. The two dimensions seemed incongruous. There were no tables, chairs, benches, utensils, or anything else Wells had spoken of. It was wiped clean—a vast wasteland. If we ever discovered where the artifacts went, I would personally launch a crusade to bring them back.

I began jogging again. I wanted to see what lay beyond this ancient convention center.

My battery life was at 28%.

All the climbing and walking finally began to hit me, but a new surge of adrenalin pushed me onward. If I got stuck here with no light, I might die, but something drove me on to see what was next.

In five minutes, I had probably covered a quarter mile, finding more corridors and hallways branching off, then, almost abruptly, the walls began converging to where they were only eight feet across and maybe seven feet tall. I slowed down, waving the light along the walls, looking for more signs or markings, but found none.

Then I smelled it. The "snaky" odor that Wells had mentioned. I had always wondered what a snaky odor was. Now I knew—ammonia and rotten eggs, with maybe a little raw Sulphur tossed in. As I walked toward it, the floor began rising, like a ramp. The walls here looked rough and unfinished, and soon the appearance became that of an actual cave, with occasional limestone rocks jutting out. The floor was smooth but still gently rising. It had definitely been shaped by human hands and feet, but the walls and ceiling were totally natural-looking. The idea struck me again that most of the cave had once been a natural cavern that had been widened and improved to this point. The sulfurous stench of this back-end place became stronger as I approached a large boulder blocking my path. It seemed like it had been placed there as an intentional barrier to whatever lay beyond.

The rock was about six feet high, but I found that I could climb up its front, using little divots that had been carved into it, then I could squeeze around its right side. As I climbed up and around it, I noticed that the ceiling quickly rose beyond the boulder. On top of the boulder I was almost overwhelmed by the stench, which now combined the sulfur smell with a more rancid ammonia odor. Before I shined my light into the blackness beyond, I thought about ancient Native superstitions about lizard people, ant people, and skinwalkers. Maybe I didn't believe the myths, but the odor compelled reflection.

The ceiling rose enough that I could stand upright on the backside of the boulder. I turned my phone light into the void beyond—and saw nothing.

I checked my phone. The battery was down to 23%, but it still shone brightly. I turned it back into the pitch blackness and again saw nothing, no walls, no reflections, no floor. It was a maw of inestimable blackness. I thought back to Wells' account. If he had ventured past this place, he had not written about it.

I fished the LED flashlight out of my pocket, thought twice about what I was about to do, then turned it on. I pointed both lights into the black void.

Nothing.

The only reason I could think of for not seeing anything was that nothing was close enough for the light to reflect off.

How big was this place?

Earlier, when I had reached the main hall, which was at least two football fields long, my light was strong enough to faintly make out the back part of it. But not here. Was this a new complex? How distant did the walls need to be to not reflect my light?

Time was running out. I took another moment to check out the rocks around and above me, and, just as I was to turn away, I caught a flash of something on the ceiling, the last visible thing over the void. It was about ten feet in front of me and six feet above my head.

Someone had etched writings there, not on the ceiling proper, but on a ledge hanging below it. The ledge was only a couple of feet long, but the more I stared at it, the more the characters seemed familiar.

My light dimmed again. I had to hurry. I was over a mile into the cave, and both batteries were dying.

I pulled my LED light out again and shined it on the ledge, giving it all the light I could. Yes, the symbols were annoyingly familiar, but still I couldn't place them. An urgent thought came to me; I didn't have time to stay here and figure this out, but I could possibly take the writing with me—if I chanced another picture.

Every second was a step closer to doom, so I made a snap decision and kept the LED light on and hit the camera icon on my phone. Seconds later I used the flash to take a photograph, nearly blinding me. I moved two or three feet to my left, got as high on the boulder as I could, and took another picture.

I was momentarily blind, but I managed to turn both lights off. For a long minute, I sat down on the boulder, letting my eyes adjust, and when I turned the phone light back on and checked the battery level, a ring-tone issued from the phone.

15%.

I scrambled off the rock and began running down the ramp toward the main corridor, which would eventually lead me to the main room with the many passageways spoking off it, none of which I had scouted. Then, eventually, almost a mile later, I should find my way to the main entrance.

Which of course was sealed shut.

I didn't let myself to think about that now. If I had any light left by then, I should be able to find the hallway to the left leading to the air duct.

I stumbled as I ran, fatigue catching up with me. My legs were jello. I never should have ventured so far in.

I heard loud echoes bouncing off the walls and came to a stop, then I realized that they were echoes of my own ragged breathing. How fast could I run three-quarters of a mile? When I was eighteen, maybe in four minutes. Now, at forty, exhausted and of dubious health, I had no idea. My feet kept pounding the limestone floor, and I felt something bouncing in my right pocket. I slowed down to see what it was.

I had forgotten about the food and water. When I had taken the camera out of my pocket, I had placed the water bottle in it. The thought occurred to me that I should stop running and eat. But I knew I couldn't afford to waste the battery and kept running.

But the thought came again. *Stop and eat.*

This time I obeyed. I was breathing so hard that I literally couldn't drink any water or take a bite, so I turned the light off, sat down on the floor, and waited.

The absolute darkness created vertigo. Then a terrifying thought hit me. Maybe it wasn't vertigo, maybe it was the old sickness—which would debilitate me completely.

But I didn't feel the nausea now. Just hunger. I listened to other parts of my body, the glands in my throat that *always* became swollen and painful when the illness hit. But again, they were silent. When the headaches came, my head would feel like it might explode with internal pressure, even making my ears pop. A specialist in Lyme-induced Myalgic Encephalomyelitis (the official title of my disease), told me that the brain swelled during these episodes, forcing air out of the inner ear. This "popping" was similar to what happens when you rise or lower in elevation, except that with me it happened much more rapidly, like a staccato "pop-pop-pop-pop-pop-pop," rather than a hard single pop. This often hit me just before waking in the mornings, which my subconscious somehow often worked into a dream. The pre-awake poppings usually indicated I would have a hard day.

But my ears weren't popping now.

Maybe I *was* just tired.

I bowed my head in the zero light and offered a prayer of gratitude. It was incredible that I wasn't sick. I hadn't pushed myself physically so hard in years—literally, since getting sick.

My breathing finally slowed and my natural sense of balance returned. I opened the bottle of water and took a long drink. Then I opened a granola bar by feel and stuffed half of it into my mouth and washed it down with more water. I stood up and jammed the half-empty water bottle back into my pocket, along with the wrapper. I still had another granola bar in my pocket, but I would save that for later.

I turned on my camera light and began jogging again. As I took my first few steps, I checked the time. 3:16. It would still be light in the canyon, but the sun itself would have crossed the rim's horizon and begun its long descent in the west. By the time we got back to the gorge, the river would be in twilight, and finding safe footholds on the exposed ledges and half-trails would be almost impossible.

I picked up my pace, but only for a minute, as the pains in my legs and the burning in my lungs forced me to slow down again. I finally staggered into the main hall, but my light didn't illuminate the opposite wall. Where I had once been able to see hundreds of feet ahead, now I could now see less than fifty.

How much farther did I have to go? Was it four hundred yards? Eight hundred yards? Did I turn right or left at the main entrance? It seemed to take forever to cover the seven hundred feet of the main hall, then I floundered into the main hallway. I glanced up at the walls to see if I recognized the etchings, but everything was a blur. My phone beeped again. It was down to five percent. I staggered forward.

I came to an intersection branching off at right angles, and I nearly hit the wall on my right. Why had I veered so far toward the wall? Why wasn't I in the center of the hallway? The answer was terrifyingly clear: because I couldn't see the walls from the middle of the hallway.

They were only six feet away, and I couldn't see them.

I stopped and probed with the faint light in all directions and recognized that I had just entered the Cross Hall. I went down one branch of the hall and hurried to the closest oval doorway and saw hieroglyphics above it. I could barely make them out, but they were familiar. I had been here.

As I had no choice, I turned the phone off.

I began mumbling a prayer as I pulled the LED light out of my pocket. If it didn't work, I would be in real trouble. I flipped the switch and was answered with brighter light than I had been used to. I didn't wait for my eyes to adjust; I just started running.

If I recalled, the next big corridor would be the one that angled back into the cave sharply on both sides. Both sides would have many rooms, some large and some small. I couldn't remember how far this corridor had been from the Cross Hall, but it seemed like I should have reached it by now. The LED light was brighter, but now that I looked carefully, I realized that it too was failing. Had I passed the corridor?

I slowed down and started walking. Since the angled corridor would branch off on both sides of the hallway, I sidled closer to the left wall, so I would be sure to see it. The light faded to a dim glow, shocking me by how quickly it was dying. I put my left hand on the wall and began following it more by feel than sight.

A hollow opened up on my left. The wall was gone. I probed into it with the faint light while my left remained on the wall. It was indeed the angled corridor. Now I knew where I was.

But I still had a long way to go.

In near total darkness, I began walking across the intersection to the far side of the angled corridor. Halfway across, the light failed completely.

I had no wall to guide me, no light to orient me, but I knew that I only had another seven or eight feet before I got to the far side, where the corridor should continue—unless I began walking in a circle and missed the far side of the intersection completely.

I took a step forward, reached out with both hands, and felt nothing. I took another step.

Nothing.

I took another.

Nothing.

I had to consciously force myself to not start running. Where was the wall?

The sense of disorientation, even vertically, was becoming extreme—a floating nothingness. If I couldn't find the correct wall in this intersection, I was dead. I fought down panic, reasoning that the wall had to be somewhere close. I took another step, and another.

I stopped and remained absolutely still, and I verbally prayed. My words bounced off the walls, but I couldn't isolate them.

Then a strange thought occurred to me.

Check the time.

But what did the time matter at this point? I was desperate to escape the cave even if it was midnight.

But I decided to follow the idea, and I pushed the little button on my watch and was startled by a soft glow.

With my eyes attuned to absolute blackness, the smallest pinprick of light was welcome, and this was more than a pinprick. The time was 4:14, and I instantly knew what I had to do. I turned the face of my watch to the front and flashed it on again. The far wall of the angled hallway was not before me; it was off to my left. In the few moments of total darkness, I had somehow veered to my right and was walking in the circular fashion I had dreaded. It wasn't a total circle but was just enough that it had turned me nearly in the opposite direction, and I was halfway across the main hall. If I had continued walking as I had, I would have eventually hit the wall on the far side with my left hand, meaning I would have unknowingly done a one-eighty and would have begun retracing my steps, going deeper into the cave.

The little watch had saved me.

No—the prompting had saved me.

I let the light go off, and I shuffled mummy-like to the other side of the angled hallway. Then I moved past it, still following the wall on my left in the main corridor, knowing that at some point I would come to another passageway leading to my left—the one that led to the air duct.

While practically hugging the wall, I flashed my watch on every ten or fifteen seconds to make sure I was on course. It was amazing how insecure I had become without sight.

After several more minutes of cautious progress, I came to a passageway leading to my left. I was pretty sure it was the one leading to the air duct, but though I flashed my light several times on the walls, I saw no markings. I stopped and tried to remember if there had been a second passageway between the sealed off main entrance and the angled hallway leading to the air duct. I couldn't remember one, but my memory was often faulty, especially when I was fatigued. So, I could either follow this passage along its entire length to see if it were the right one, or I could pass it and continue on to the sealed-off main entrance. Then I could double back to this passageway. But that would take a lot of time.

I turned left and went down the passage, hoping to see some light leaking in from the air duct. If I remembered right, the passage would wind around to my right before reaching the air duct, which meant the light from the air duct probably would not reflect all the way back to here.

I checked the time again, and this time I focused on it. It was 4:42. Somehow I had spent half an hour getting lost and finding my way again.

An owl hooted faintly somewhere in front of me.

An owl?

I stopped and waited. I heard it again.

Not an owl. A voice, muffled by winding tunnels.

Ross was yelling my name.

How long had he been doing this? How desperate was he? Now knowing that this was the right passage to the air duct, I kept my watch light on and started running.

His voice was hoarse. As I rounded the long bend to the right, toward the exit, his calls became stronger. A muted glow reflected off the rock walls as I reached the chamber with the rock platform. I cupped my mouth and yelled up toward the portal I had come in on.

"I'm coming out!"

"Travis?"

"Yes! I'm coming out!"

I climbed up the stone stairs, got up on the platform and began inching my way into the hole. With each forward movement, the light intensified, and I had to squint. When I got to the cone that angled down, I was faced with a dilemma—either continue onward and land on my head, or scoot back, turn around, and go in feet-first. I wondered what Nelson had done. The man's bravery, or greed, was beyond astonishment now. I kept going forward, tried to slide gently down the chute, but the inverted cone-like structure gave me no purchase, and I fell headfirst. My hands were free, and since it was only about a three-foot fall, my hands and elbows broke my fall. Or so I thought.

"Travis!"

I turned toward the voice—and the blinding light—and saw Ross's face filling the exit at the end of the five-foot passage. My eyes stayed open only for a quick glimpse, but he didn't look happy. As I crawled toward the opening with my eyes still closed, I felt a pair of strong hands grab my shoulders and pull me into a baking oven.

"Hold on—hold on!" I gasped, still out of breath.

He pulled more gently and helped turn me right-side up, so I didn't land on my head again.

"What happened?" he asked, pushing my hair away from my forehead.

"Sorry," I said, still breathing hard. "It's a lot bigger in there... My batteries died... I was lost."

"No, what happened to your forehead—Wait, your batteries died?"

I cracked my eyes open, braving the daylight. He was staring at my forehead. I put my hand to it and came away with blood. "I must have cut myself when I fell down that last chute. I kind of landed on my head."

"Are you all right?"

"Yeah—just tired." I pulled a handkerchief out of my back pocket and pushed it against the cut. It wasn't bleeding much, but a trickle had run down my nose.

"Let me do that," Ross said, taking the handkerchief. "You're just smearing it." His voice was hoarse.

"I'm just so tired."

"You should be. You were in there over three hours. Here, hold it there."

I tried to keep the handkerchief pressed against the cut.

"So, your batteries died? Both lights?"

"Yeah. Thanks for calling to me. That told me I was in the right tunnel."

"You're shaking. Sit down." He took me by the shoulders and guided me back to the narrow ledge below the air duct.

"How long have you been out here, yelling?" I asked. "Your voice is hoarse."

"It's hoarse for two reasons. One, I ran all the way back here from the rim, and two, I've been calling for you for over an hour."

Had I heard him right? "You ran back from the rim?"

He smiled like he knew something I didn't.

"From the *rim*?" I asked again.

"You know how I said I was going to check out the end of the canyon—that cul-de-sac where the sheep went? When I got back in there, it wasn't so steep, and I just kept going, and, eventually, I found a way to the top, kind of like a chimney."

"*What?* That's impossible. We checked that out on Google Maps."

"Want to see my pictures?" He held out his phone, but I was too tired to focus on the photos. "But there's a problem," he added.

"What's that?"

"No, first you tell me what you found in there."

"No, how about first you get me some water."

"I don't have much left. I had to drink some of it when I got back. If you hadn't noticed, it's getting kind of hot out here." He took my water bottle and filled it up from the collapsible jug in his pack.

I *had* noticed. It was the hottest day so far. "Inside," I said, finally able to speak in a normal breath, "it was like sixty degrees, maybe colder."

He looked up at the air duct. "Really? Maybe next time we ought to open this thing up so I can squeeze in; then we can sleep inside."

I looked out into the canyon and saw deepening shadows. The sun was indeed behind the west rim. We needed to hurry.

"What's it like in there?" he asked. "What'd you find?"

"I'd show you some pictures, but my phone's dead. I found the room with the mummies. It looks like they're all there, except three. And one of them's been looted."

"Nelson?"

"Yeah—pretty sure." I took a drink, then I looked Ross in the eye. "Everything else is gone."

"What about the big statue—the Buddha thing?"

"It was supposed to be in the Cross Hall, but it was gone. Nothing's in there now. Oh, wait, in the silos where they kept grain, I saw some kernels of corn."

"That's it?"

"Yep, except the mummies."

"Wow."

"Winn's group must have worked fast. It's like somebody swept it with the besom of destruction."

He chuckled. "The old besom, huh? On my mission we used to say the besom was coming to sinners any day."

"Well, it came here first. But I did see some drawings, or some etchings, on the walls. I even found some writing, or it looked like writing. When we charge my phone, I'll show you." I finished the water and was already starting to feel a little better. My health was amazing.

"So," I said, "what's the problem?"

Ross hesitated then pulled his phone out of his pocket and looked at it. "Nope."

"Nope what?"

"No bars. When I got to the top, I got reception, like you said."

"Really?" I hadn't really been serious about getting reception.

"I didn't think about it at first, but after I'd been up there a few minutes, my phone buzzed, and I had a bunch of texts—and some voice messages. Most of them were from Anna."

I stared at him, waiting for the rest.

"Somebody broke into the house the night after we left. Kevin discovered it. The intruder came in through your office window. They called 911."

I got to my feet. "Are they all right?"

"They're fine. I actually talked to her up there."

"*To Anna?* What'd she say?"

"Well, they're scared, but they're all right. It hasn't happened again. And it doesn't look like anything was taken, but Kevin thinks he saw the guy who did it."

"Kevin saw the guy *break into the house?*" I was ready to grab Ross by the collar.

"Hey, sit down. We've got a long hike ahead of us."

"Just tell me what happened!"

"I will—just mellow out, okay?"

I realized that I had taken a step toward him. I stepped back and put a hand up as a peace offering. "Yeah—sorry."

Ross grinned, as if amused at my weak attempt to hurry him up. "Right after he saw that your office window was open that morning, Kevin went outside. Remember that video camera I was trying to fix when you shot me?"

"*Yeah.*"

"It was broken. Totally shot up. It's still broken."

"So we don't have the guy on video."

"Nope—they checked it. Anyway, Johnson came out, and he said they'd start patrolling the area and watching the house, and then Kevin went upstairs and looked out his window with your binoculars."

"My binoculars?"

"Yeah, and he says he saw some guy sitting in a car, maybe an SUV, about two blocks away, watching the house. And then the guy drove by. Kevin thinks he could identify the guy."

"What did Johnson think—what did Anna think? Did they believe him?"

"They don't know. Johnson had a couple of cops ask the neighbors, and they hadn't seen anybody. But, I don't think Kevin would lie about something like that."

I sat back down on the rocks. "At least they're okay."

"Yeah—but there's something else."

My heart dropped. "What?"

"Anna called a computer guy in and had all the computers in the house checked for bugs, you know, tracing software and stuff?"

I nodded, wondering why I hadn't thought of that before we left. "What'd they find?"

"Exactly what they were looking for, a bug on the downstairs family phone and keyboard tracing software on your desktop. We might as well face it, whoever is behind this knows everything you know about Keith and the cave."

"Were their cell phones bugged?"

"No."

"Well, we almost never use the house phone."

"Right, but they know everything you have on your computer. What did you have on it about coming out here?"

"Everything."

He sighed. "Well, anyway, there's something else—I told Anna about the cave. She was surprised, and she asked if we could be wrong. You know, mistaken identity. Wrong cave. She said she's been reading about this area and knows there are lots of caves around here."

"Yeah, but this is the right one."

"That's what I told her. And I told her that you were in there right then—and that I couldn't get in."

"I bet that went over well."

"She wasn't happy, but I won't tell her how long it took you to come out."

"Or about my lights going dead and then my getting turned around and almost going back in the wrong way."

"Naw, I won't tell her that either."

"Is she going to tell Johnson about this?"

"She said she'd wait till we got home, but I thought you should know that she knows we found the cave."

"Thanks." I thought about the situation. "The problem is, we've violated federal law just coming here."

"I know that—and so does she. But the family's more scared about the break-in. I think we ought to get back as soon as we can."

I thought about the snaky cavern. I still wanted to get all the way in there, and now that I had access to more batteries, I hoped to do it the next day.

"Like tomorrow," he said.

"Tomorrow? How can we get out of here tomorrow? It'll take two days at least just to get back to the truck."

"Maybe—maybe not."

"I'm really tired, Ross. I'm not going to hike through the night, especially not over those outcroppings. One of us would probably die, and it wouldn't be you."

"I don't plan to go back over the outcroppings."

"Then how would we—" I stared at him, letting the handkerchief drop from my head. "You're thinking about going out over the top? You want to go over the rim and hike a zillion miles back to the truck?"

He took my hand and guided the handkerchief back to my forehead. "Keep it still, you're making a mess. Now listen: I checked Google Maps on my phone up there. It's mostly flat up past the rim, or rolling ground, and there's lots of dirt roads. And, not too far away, there's a highway. I figure we can walk on the dirt roads and maybe catch a ride with somebody, or if we have to, we can walk to the highway and hitch a ride back to Lipan Point. It's not that far."

"How far is 'not that far'?"

"To the highway?"

"Yes."

"Nineteen or twenty miles."

"*WHAT?*"

"But it's all flat, and if we started now, we could be out of the canyon in an hour, and then, even if we didn't find a ride till we got to the highway, at three miles an hour we could be at the highway in like six or seven hours. That's like midnight."

"More like two or three, and only if we can go three miles an hour. I'm *exhausted.*"

"All right. Here's the alternative: we hike back down to the river tonight, and hopefully don't die, especially when we go back down that old waterfall thing, and then we leave camp in the morning. We spend two days getting back to Tanner Trail, and then another day going up Tanner Trail. Remember, that alone is over ten miles, almost straight up. And that's the third day. Then we get home on the fourth day. On the other hand, if we go straight up tonight, we'll be home tomorrow, probably in the afternoon."

"You want to leave our tent and stuff down by the river?"

"Not really, but I'm willing to if it means getting back to the family sooner. Anna's not too happy, and the kids are scared."

I could only imagine. She had been afraid of something happening. "Do they think the break-in had something to do with us coming here?"

Ross just stared at me.

"Yeah," I said. "I guess it only makes sense."

"She said that's why Johnson is putting so many resources on this—because it could be part of a murder case."

"He said that?"

"Well, I doubt he put it like that—but we all know it's a possibility."

As I thought about that, I reached into my front pocket and pulled out the other granola bar. It was squished beyond recognition but was still edible. I peeled back the wrapper and ate it, mostly licking the mushy contents off the wrapper.

"Here," Ross said, digging into his pack, "let me get you another one."

"Do we have enough food to get us through the night?"

"Well, it depends on how much we need. We've got four more granola bars and some trail mix. And a little over half a gallon of water."

"Not much to hike twenty miles on."

"Nope, but you can have it all. I just want to get back there. She really wasn't happy, Travis."

I was never going to win this argument. And come to think of it, I shouldn't win it. My wife and children were in danger. "All right, but can I just rest for a while? I'm *really* tired."

"Sure, take all the time you want. It just means we get back later."

"Just a few *minutes?*"

"Yeah, sure. I'll get everything ready. Whoops, I forgot. It's already ready." He held the strap to his pack, ready to fling the thing over his shoulder.

"Really, Ross, just a few minutes."

"All right. Take a nap. I'll just be back on the bench waiting for you." He picked up his pack and began shuffling along the narrow ledge around the big boulder. I lay down and tried to close my eyes.

But what seemed so easy, so *insistent*, when I came out of the cave just a few minutes ago wouldn't happen now. I couldn't rest. I would close my eyes for about two seconds, then I'd think of Kevin finding the window open, of Anna calling 911, of the guy, possibly the man who killed Keith Nelson, coming back tonight or tomorrow. I got up on weary, aching feet and began shuffling around the big boulder, not even noticing the narrow ledge and thousand foot drop.

I couldn't imagine walking a mile, let alone twenty, but death was death, no matter how it came.

And I didn't want it to come to my family because of me.

Chapter 24

On a Deadly Course

Whislin Klah didn't expect Call and Keller to come up the Tanner Trail until Saturday afternoon at the earliest. It was still Thursday afternoon, so he felt he had time to go home, catch some sleep, and prepare for the inevitable. Call and Keller must not reach the rim. They must not find a way to communicate what they had found, because if they did, he would lose all he had worked for, all he had dreamed of.

He continued to monitor Call's computer and home phone. As expected, nothing came from them. Nobody was using Call's computer, and, he figured, Anna was using her cell phone. He still considered bugging that line too, even if Travis and Ross were disposed of, just to make sure they hadn't somehow relayed vital information to her.

So tomorrow he would rest and prepare in Flagstaff, then early Saturday he would drive to Lipan Point, wait for them somewhere down on the trail, and kill them.

Business, after all, was business.

Chapter 25

A Long Journey Under the Moon

Ross had clearly said the words: "It wasn't so steep."

In my opinion, steep is anything over a ten or fifteen percent grade, something you might find on your steepest mountain roads. Very steep was what we had climbed earlier when we had scrambled hand over hand in death-defying summits of crags and mesas that made the world spin under us. This was ridiculous. This was beyond steep. We had navigated the narrow bench until it went around a long corner and led into the cul-de-sac, then we followed several other ledges up and down for the better part of half a mile until we came to the "not so steep" part. We would definitely have words when I found some oxygen.

The climb that actually took us up and out of the canyon was at least a thirty percent grade. Yes, it had solid rock for footing and good handholds, but that wasn't what I had been led to expect.

Altogether, the hike out of the canyon was less than a mile, and the total time spent was about two hours, but the total toll on my system was incalculable. What were we thinking? *We were climbing up the nearly sheer face of the South Rim of the Grand Canyon.* It was insane, but what else about this trip wasn't? I didn't see what geology existed in this part of the canyon, what types of flora or fauna, because in the first fifteen minutes everything was a blur. I was utterly spent, and the fact that I didn't fall to my death became, with each step, a growing inconvenience.

Somewhere along the way I must have lost touch with him, because when I finally approached the rim I found him sitting on the edge with his legs hanging over, gazing into one of the great wonders of the world. The sun was setting. It may have been a glorious sight.

Said he: "It really is beautiful."

Said I: "How long have you been here?"

"Oh, I don't know. Long enough to have dinner, I guess."

Granola bar wrappers were sticking out of his pants pocket. His water bottle lay by his side.

"You said I could have those."

"Well, you didn't say anything, so I thought we would split them."

I hoisted myself up and considered pushing him over the side. He probably would have survived and still beat me to the highway. I saw that we were on the rim of a large bowl, between the actual rim and the "chimney" we had just come up through. It seemed to be a kind of transition zone between the canyon and the rest of the world. Looking out over the canyon, I ate some trail mix and drank some water.

After a while, Ross stood up and stretched. "Well, we better get going."

"How much farther is it?"

"Nineteen or twenty miles, like I said."

"From here? I thought that was from where we were."

"No, from here. I said from the rim."

Injustice upon injustice. I made the mistake of standing up. Or tying to. My legs had gone to sleep while hanging over the rim. I collapsed back into a sitting position and looked up at him. "I'm afraid you're going to have to carry me."

He laughed. Give the man some food and water and he thinks everything is a big joke. He had his pack on, but that didn't stop him from stooping over and snagging me by an armpit and hauling me to my feet. The display of strength had a meliorating effect upon my indignation. He started walking east. Reluctantly, incredibly, I followed.

We walked what seemed several miles, and I asked, "Can we stop and have some more water?"

He looked at his watch. "It's been fifteen minutes. You've got to wait a little longer—like maybe five hours or so."

I couldn't tell if he was joking.

The land was indeed flat, like he had said. But what he hadn't said, or even alluded to, was that it was also a moonscape. It was as bleak and blighted as any land ever seen, on any number of planets, even in pictures. The fact that Indians lived here did not make it less so; it only made them more superhuman. I was convinced we were stepping on dust that had never known human contact. Nor should it have. It was bleak beyond description. It seemed purposeless, poisonous, malignant. I saw a weed growing in one spot and wondered what crime it had committed in the preexistence. We walked and walked and walked and walked.

Like the song.

Only farther.

Ross and I did not talk, which was good, because we were no longer on speaking terms. My legs went numb again, and I actually looked down to see if they were propelling me or if I had finally died and was floating along behind my former friend to torment him.

I've heard stories of soldiers falling asleep while they marched. Unfortunately, this didn't happen to me. Instead, it seemed that I fell into some sort of trance. It felt like I was traveling through space, then I realized that the stars had come out and surrounded us from horizon to horizon.

Ross stopped, looked over to his left, where a round knoll rose from the surface of the moon. He went that direction. I didn't follow. On he went, and on I stayed. Eventually I sat down. Sometime later, perhaps twenty minutes according to the rotation of the stars, he appeared again.

"Where'd you go?"

"Up that hill over there," he said.

"Why?"

"To see if I could see any headlights out here, you know, on the dirt roads."

"I haven't seen any roads."

"Oh, we've crossed a few. But they were empty."

"Too bad."

"Yeah."

"Did you see any lights?"

"No."

"Lucky thing the stars are out, so we can see in front of us." I hadn't seen the moon yet.

"Yeah."

"Do you know where we're going?"

"East, toward Highway 89."

I turned and looked up at the Big Dipper and found the North Star. Fortunately it was on our left, basically.

"How far do you think we've gone?" I reconsidered. "No, don't answer that." I stood up and started walking. Ross came with me.

Over the next hour I tried to recreate the zoned-out, coma-like state I had achieved earlier, but it eluded me, which meant I felt the bite of every step, the twinge of every muscle, the desperate cry of every thought.

Eventually I expressed one of these.

"Ross, how did you get rich?"

"Huh? You know, I just called all those colleges and made lists of what classes transferred to all the other colleges."

"No, I mean, did you become a liar?"

"A liar?"

"Yeah, like when you said that the path coming out of the canyon wasn't so steep. I wouldn't have come if I had known how steep it was."

"I know."

"So you lied."

"I massaged the facts. It really wasn't that steep to me. That's why I was waiting for you on the rim. I had been there a while. But I knew it would be steep to you."

"Do you feel good about paying tithing on the money you made?"

"Of course, because I didn't lie to get it."

"You just massaged the facts."

"Maybe. Sometimes. But not very often. I like to think of myself as basically an honest guy."

"Basically."

"Mostly."

"All right. I don't want to talk to you again. So be quiet. You might lie again. You might make me believe that there's a car coming down a road that doesn't exist, and I'll get my hopes up and then get them crushed, and then I'll cry until I die, just because you lied to me again, so just be quiet."

"Okay."

"All right."

We walked for another unknowable distance, perhaps two hundred miles, when another thought occurred to my incredibly shrinking brain. "Ross?"

"Are we talking now?"

"Just for a minute."

"Okay."

"You didn't break the camera by the gate before we left the house, did you?"

"No. I was trying to straighten it out, remember, when you tried to shoot my leg off?"

"I didn't try to shoot your leg off."

"You shot a ball bearing like three hundred miles an hour at my leg. That could have taken it off."

"Could not have."

"Could so have."

I forgot what question I had asked and had to recreate it in my mind. "Oh yeah. So, you promise that you didn't break it, and that's why Kevin found it broken, because somebody else broke it?"

"Yeah, I promise. Somebody else did it."

"Like who?"

"Like, I don't know. Like the killer probably."

"You think so?"

"Sure, who else would do it?"

"But why do they always break that camera?"

"You mean like what happened so many years ago?"

"Yeah—it was the same camera."

"Because that's the one that shows who's coming in through the gate."

"Oh, yeah."

"Do you trust me this time?"

"Yeah."

"Why?"

"I don't know."

We walked for a long time before I said, "Ross, I really need to stop. My legs are killing me."

"Yeah, mine too."

"Really?"

"Well, we've walked like fifteen miles today and climbed over five thousand feet—and remember, I went to the top twice."

"Yeah, but I walked like three miles in the cave."

"Maybe farther. You were in there for three hours—or four."

"I know."

"You can walk more than one mile per hour."

"Yeah, but I was just hugging the wall some of that time because I couldn't see, but you won't tell Anna, will you?"

"Prob'ly not."

"Thanks."

We were getting stupid.

"Was it scary?"

"When the light went out?"

"Yeah."

"Only when I got lost. I kind of got turned around and almost started walking back into the cave. So, that was scary."

"How'd you figure out the right way to go?"

"I checked the time."

He glanced over at me.

"I flicked my watch on to see what time it was, and the light came on. Then I knew I could flash my watch and see where I was going. That's how I got to the hallway where I heard you yelling."

"I thought you got stuck or were dead. My throat still hurts."

I put my hand on his shoulder. "You're a good friend, Ross. You're the best friend I got."

"Really?"

"Yep."

We must have forgotten about our legs being tired, because we walked for another hour before we stopped to eat. When we were done, so was the food and water.

"How many more miles do you think we have?" I asked.

"I don't know, maybe ten."

"Do you have any bars on your phone? Do you think you should call the cops to rescue us?"

"I thought about that when I was on the hill, but I didn't have any bars." He pulled his phone out and checked it. "Nope."

"It was strange that you had service on the rim."

"Yeah. Strange."

We started walking again.

A while later, I said, "Ross, when we get back, are you going to shave your beard off?" We hadn't shaved during the trip.

"I don't know. What about you?"

"I have to. I'm on the high council, and President Whiting doesn't like facial hair."

"Too bad."

"Yeah. But Anna doesn't like it either."

"Right. You need to keep her happy."

"Yeah."

"I wish I had a wife."

We trudged on in silence.

The moon came up on our left, a waning gibbous moon that brought a blue tint to the sky. We came to another hill, a little larger than the first. We stopped.

"Are you going to climb up there and look?" I asked.

"I don't know. It's a long way."

"Maybe you'll see lights from the highway."

"Yeah. Wanna come?"

"No."

He dropped the pack and started up the hill.

I don't know how long he was gone, because I was asleep when he got back. He was kind enough to wake me up with his boot. We started walking again.

"Did you see anything?"

"Maybe. I'm not sure. It seemed like there was a glow or something way off to our left."

"Do you think we should go that way?"

"Yeah, but it was really faint, so it's probably still a long ways away, and it isn't very big."

"But maybe there will be a phone there."

"And some water. I don't know about you, but I'm getting kinda thirsty."

"I passed thirsty a long time ago," I croaked. "My tongue is like one of those silica packages that dries things out. If my phone fell in the toilet right now, I could dry it out in my mouth."

That hit him as funny. Then, a while later he took me by the arm. I guess I had been weaving. Finally my legs gave out completely, and I fell to the sand and looked up, feeling remarkably peaceful. Blue stars were very close.

Ross came back and stood over me, blotting out the stars. "Are you going to be able to make it?" His voice was gritty and hoarse.

"Not now." It hurt to speak.

He dropped down beside me. My eyes were closed. When I opened them again, he was gone. I slowly turned my head and saw him lying on the sand. His eyes were closed and he was breathing heavily. Asleep. I didn't know what time it was, so I tried to raise my arms a little so I could push the button on my watch. I finally managed to do it, but nothing happened. I pushed again. No light. My watch was dead. I watched the stars for a while and was grateful it wasn't raining. It might have been cold, but I couldn't tell. A shooting star lit up the sky with a spectacular green and red trail. The sight was so beautiful I almost smiled.

A soft flutter of sand made me glance to my left. An old man was standing about five feet away. Even in the faint light, I could see that he was an Indian. His brown, deeply wrinkled face narrowed down to pointed chin with a cleft in it. He had long, grayish, braided hair and was wearing blue jeans and a red western shirt. His kind, taciturn look told me he wasn't a threat. He glanced at Ross then, using a tall walking stick, came over and knelt beside me.

A leather bag hung from his shoulder. He opened it and pulled out a leather water pouch, then he propped my head up with his left hand and put the pouch to my lips. The water was cool and sweet, and I wondered how he had kept it so cold. He pulled it away and let me breathe for a minute.

"Thank you," I said in my scratchy voice.

He put the pouch back to my lips and let me drink again. Then he dribbled some on his hand and cooled my face with it. When he was done, he looked over at Ross, who was still asleep.

Strength began to course into me, and I worked my way to a sitting position. He was still kneeling, so we were nearly eye to eye.

"Navajo?" I asked.

He shook his head. "This is Navajo land, but I am Hopi. I watch you come. Three nights."

"You watched us come for three nights?"

He looked up at the stars, as if that answered my question. Had he been following us through the canyon? Lowering his eyes to mine, he said, "You are welcome here, but you do not have the sacred corner."

I had no idea what he meant.

"I will find you when you come again." He smiled, and his teeth reminded me of the mummy's teeth I had seen in the cave. Then he looked up at the blazing sky again, and I did too and it made me feel good. The Milky Way hung just over his left shoulder. I turned to ask him what his name was.

But he was gone.

Then I was waking up.

Ross was sitting beside me.

"Ya know what?" he said, "I've been lugging this pack around for miles, and it doesn't have anything we need. I'm leaving it here." His voice was still hard and scratchy, but it sounded a little stronger. He looked down into my face. "Hey, you cleaned the blood off your face. How'd you do that?"

"Huh?"

"It was smeared on your forehead, but now it's gone."

I touched the cut with my finger. There was no blood.

"You must have wiped it off when you were asleep."

"I guess so."

"Ready to rumble?"

I had been awake, but now I was waking up again. What had happened? I looked all around but saw only shadows and wasteland. Ross got to his feet. "Here, let me help." He extended his hand and half lifted me to my feet. "I really needed that rest," he said, "but I'm good now. How about you?"

I tested my legs and took a couple of deep breaths. "Yeah, I'm good."

"Great." We took a few steps, then I stopped and turned back and looked. We were alone. I could see tracks in the sand, but it was impossible to know if any were from the old man.

"Don't worry about it. If we really want it, we can come back and get it later. But I bet that pack's going to become the property of some Indian someday."

I glanced at Ross to see if he meant anything by that, but he was already hiking.

After a mile or two, I saw a glow on the horizon to our left.

"Is that what you saw earlier?" I asked.

"I think so."

"What do you think it is?"

"Maybe a gas station or something."

"Way out here?"

He was silent, and we bent our direction toward the light.

"Ross?"

"Huh?"

"Did you hear anything back there?"

"Where?"

"Where we were resting."

"No. Did you?"

I thought about it. "Yeah, I think so."

He turned and looked at me while we walked. "What do you think it was?"

"I'm not sure. I may have been dreaming."

"Well—you sound a lot better."

I looked up and saw the fiery stars still enveloping us. Life was getting better.

We walked a long time, and my brain began working again, and I spent some time thinking. What had he meant that I was welcome? What was the sacred corner? Was he real?

We had almost finished hiking up a long mesa when a cool breeze made me shiver.

"Wow," Ross said, "it can get cold out here at night. I hope that place up there is open, whatever it is."

As we crested the mesa, and about a half mile away we saw a commercial establishment sitting like an island on the far side of a ribbon of highway. A pair of headlights appeared to our right, a semi-truck. We heard its engine power down as it came down a gentle grade. The truck slowed and turned right, into the parking lot. The place must be open. Our step quickened. Between us and the establishment, which we now saw was in fact a gas station, a set of low buildings sat in shadows. Ten minutes later we half-walked, half-stumbled around the buildings.

As we passed under an old sodium light illuminating the parking lot, the sudden entry into the bright lights of civilization was disorienting. Things looked fake. Ross looked taller. The pavement looked like dark light. Another truck rumbled by on the highway, behind us now, shattering the silence. Ross checked his phone. We thought we'd try to catch a ride over to Lipan Point before calling for a cab or Uber—not that one existed out here. It was almost four. We had covered twenty miles from the cave in eleven hours—almost two miles an hour—but some of that time had been spent sleeping. My hips and legs moaned but were still functioning.

We went into the store, and the garish lights hurt, but I manned up and squinted. For some reason, a corn dog rotisserie stood out to me. I slapped my back pocket and sighed with relief when I found my wallet still there. I had taken it out of my pack, along with my phone, when we left camp this morning—or yesterday morning.

"Ross, do you have your wallet?"

A panicked look crossed his face, and his hand shot back to his pocket. His face melted in relief as he pulled it out. We may not like everything about civilization, but it's nice to be prepared for it.

Integrated back into the ways of the world, we waddled to the fridge, where we each grabbed two large bottles of water. We hurried, no, shambled, over to the counter where the truck driver we had watched pull in was paying for his food. Ross didn't wait for him. He slapped a ten-dollar bill on the counter and opened his water and began guzzling. Nobody stopped him. I opened my water and did the same.

It was delicious, beyond description, but achingly cold. I had to stop before getting a brain freeze. Ross didn't stop. I noticed that the cashier, a Native in his twenties, probably a Navajo, and the truck driver, a grizzled middle-aged man with a big boiler hanging over his belt, were watching him as he finished the bottle. I looked down at mine, which was the same size, to see how many ounces he had just downed. Two liters. He put the empty bottle on the counter and began unscrewing the second one. The cap had just come off when he stopped and stared ahead, a concerned look on his face.

"Uh-oh. I think I drank that too fast."

"You boys seem a might thirsty," the truck driver said.

Ross put his hand on the counter to steady himself then put his other hand to his forehead and slowly slid to the floor.

"We just walked out of the canyon," I said. "We ran out of water a few miles back."

"The *canyon?*" the young cashier asked in disbelief. "The *Grand* Canyon?"

"Yeah, we climbed out of it this afternoon, well, yesterday. It was a long walk."

The two men shared a look, then the cashier uttered, "I never heard of that. You just climbed up the wall and came out?"

"Yeah. We're kind of in a hurry to get home. Are you okay, Ross?"

A low moan issued from the nether regions.

"You know what?" I said, "We're kind of hungry too. How much for ten corn dogs?"

The cashier looked over at the rotisserie. "We don't have corn dogs—those are just regular hot dogs."

I looked back at the rotisserie. He was right. The things rolling and rolling and rolling were desiccated hot dogs. The heat was awful around here.

"How much for ten hot dogs?"

"Two bucks each. Twenty bucks."

"Here." I handed him a credit card. "We might be here for a while."

The trucker laughed, then he looked out the window at the pumps. "Is your vehicle as thirsty as your friend?"

"We don't have a vehicle," I said. "We left it at Lipan Point. That's where we started hiking." I sidled over to the hot dogs. "Ross, do you want ketchup and mustard?"

He was swaying back and forth, his head cradled in his hands. "I got a headache. I got a *bad* headache."

"All right, you're getting both."

The cashier quickly ran my card as the trucker watched with evident pleasure.

"We're actually looking for a ride back to Lipan Point," I said, freely squirting condiments on the petrified hot dogs.

"I'm headed the other way," the trucker said, "but I'll tell you what, I'll put a call out and let the other boys know you're in need."

"Thanks."

I took a bite of the old dog and never tasted anything so pleasant. It was gone in ten seconds. Possibly less. Much less. I took one over to Ross. "Here, eat this. It'll fix your headache." He raised his head and eyed the hot dog and bun dripping with ketchup and mustard and a dollop of relish. He took it, smelled it, and ate it in two bites. Very impressive. "I'll get you another," I hurried back to the petrifying machine.

The trucker laughed and said good-bye, then said again he would get on the horn to the other ten-fifty-ones. I didn't know what he meant. The cashier said, "Other dudes comin' this way." I nodded and ate another tough, tasty dog.

Ten minutes later a dozen hot dogs were gone (only two eaten by myself), as were all four bottles of water, and several candy bars and two bags of chips. Five minutes after that a mammoth candy-red semi-truck pulled into the lot and a thick, squat figure with hair of a similar color stepped out. He came into the store, eyed us, and said, "You the dudes crawled out of the canyon?"

I corrected him. "We didn't actually crawl through most of it." He seemed suspicious and began asking for particulars, such as our home towns, destination, and places of worship.

"What?" Ross said, getting up off the floor. "You want to know where we go to church?"

"Sure do."

"Why?"

"Cuz ya out-number me. I gotta know if yer God-fearin' or if yer gonna attack me for my virtue."

I tried to laugh but was too tired. "We're both Mormons," I said. "Ross here served a mission in New York. I run a financial consulting firm in Modesto, California, where I'm on the stake high council. Do you want my bishop's phone number?"

The stubby man squinted, as if trying to read my words. "Bishop's number? Naw. I'd prob'ly start confessin'. So, I got two Mormons? Well, I'll take ya, but ya gotta promise not to preach at me. I just wanna hear your story."

Ross and I shared blank looks, then I said okay. The man was about five-five and weighed at least 250. He walked by us. "Gotta use the head. *Mormons*, comin' up outta the canyon! What'll they think of next?"

When we got out to the truck, Ross climbed up before me and scrambled into the bed in back and was asleep before I answered the man's first question. Ross saves my life one minute and leaves me alone with "Redbone" the next.

It took us an hour to get to Lipan Point, and by the time we arrived, my voice was talked out. The man asked questions I never would have thought of, but of course I never told him exactly *why* we were there, though he grilled me mercilessly. He never heard a word about the cave or Wells or a conspiracy, though he did hear a lot about the rich beauties of nature, the ways of bighorn sheep, and the mysteries of cell phone service. Finally, in a raspy, faltering voice I said, "Why do you want to know all this?"

"Gotta have facts or the crackerheads won't believe it."

"The crackerheads?"

"You know, all the sandbaggers out there."

I was lost.

He tapped the C.B. above his left ear. "You know, all the dumb truckers who laugh at ya behind your back cuz they don't believe nothin' ya say. I gotta have the facts or I'll get blown up. Ol' Redbone here's gonna be famous—at least for tonight."

We reached the turnoff to the point. He didn't think he could navigate the S-curves going up to the turnaround, so I woke Ross up, and Redbone dropped us off at the intersection of Desert View and Lipan Point. We shook his hand and thanked him and offered him money. He said he had payment enough. "Mormons, crawlin' up outta the canyon—wait till I tell 'em!"

His truck ratcheted through the gears as he drove away, and Ross and I began laboring up the hill. I was actually surprised that my legs responded to the synapses sent by my brain.

"Thanks for nothin'," I said.

"Hey, I needed some sleep. I'm driving, remember?"

It was after five-thirty when we crested the long hill and saw a glow in the eastern sky. We also saw Ross's truck. I stopped and turned to him. "Please tell me you remembered your keys too."

A panic-stricken look came to his eyes, and he patted his pockets furiously. After he got the desperate look he wanted from me, he pulled them out of his front pocket. "No way I'd leave them down by the river." He opened the truck, and we got in.

I plugged my phone into the charger before he did. As he backed and pulled away, I pushed Anna's speed dial number. The call went to message, not unusual at this hour, and I said something about being home in ten hours or so.

I fell asleep about five seconds later.

Chapter 26

On a Bad Course

Klah had almost forgotten how comfortable his $3,000 Sealy Posturepedic mattress was. A gift to himself after his second job, the sweet, king-sized mattress made the long hours of work, even camping, almost worth it when he got home. Knowing that this was his day off, he allowed himself the luxury of sleeping in until noon. When he finally hauled himself out of bed, he went to his laptop to check his email. Nothing showed up, so he checked the messages on his phone.

Just one.

The tracking software that followed Travis Call's car and Ross Keller's truck had sent him an email. He bolted upright. The subject line told him there had been a change in location. His heart stopped racing when he realized that someone at the house had probably driven Travis's car—but when he opened the email, he saw that it was Ross's truck.

Had it been towed away by the park service? Stolen?

He read the brief message, almost dismissed it, then forced himself to carefully reread it. The truck was currently moving north through central California—which, of course, was impossible. He clicked on the online map where he could follow it in real time and saw the green icon representing the truck crawling slowly up Highway 99, less than 200 miles south of Modesto.

Absolutely impossible—unless somebody had indeed stolen it. Or, maybe, it had been repossessed. Doubtful. Some of Travis's emails mentioned six-figure investments for Ross—no way he'd miss payments.

Had the two men reached the truck and driven it away?

His stomach turned. If Call and Keller had reached the rim early, they had undoubtedly found cell service, and if they had found cell service, they may have already called Johnson about the cave. And if that had happened, not only would Klah not get paid for the job, there might not be any more jobs. In fact, there might not be any more Klah. Richardson had made it clear how desperate the Society was to keep the cave a secret.

He had called Richardson on his way back from the canyon and told him that the men had found the cave and that Call had crawled in through what appeared to be an air hole. After a long pause, Richardson had asked Klah what his plan for containment was, though they had already discussed that earlier. Klah knew that his boss was simply emphasizing the point: Handle this, or else.

Now, as he watched the green icon pass the turnoff to Wasco, about 190 miles south of Modesto, he tried to think of other alternatives to the men having actually reached their truck. But there were no alternatives. Either the truck had been stolen or Call and Keller were in it—and the fact that it was making a straight line for Modesto tilted the odds in the wrong direction. As much as he dreaded the idea, he would have to call Richardson and deliver the bad news. He took a deep breath and punched speed dial.

Richardson answered immediately. "Is it good news or bad?"

"They're gone."

There was a long pause. Klah thought Richardson was thinking through the possible ramifications of this news, but he quickly learned otherwise.

"And you just now learned this?"

"Yes. From the tracking device. They're in California, on their way home."

"We had this information two hours ago. Don't worry about how—one of the benefits of having friends in high places. Now listen to me. From this moment on, you are off the case. Do not follow them. Do not go to California. Stay home and let us take it. A damage-control team is already on its way to manage the problem."

Whislin knew what a damage-control team was. "Colin," he said, "you can't take them out. Everyone will know there's a connection to the cave."

"Maybe—it depends on how it's done. We've got access to their communications now, so we'll know what they know and what they plan to do. But, I was wondering, how'd they get out of the canyon so fast?"

"I don't know. There are no other trails, except through the Little Colorado, and even that would take another day."

"Hmm."

"Maybe they just climbed out over the rim, but I didn't see any climbing gear on them, so I don't know how they could do that."

"All right. Don't worry about that now. Just sit tight."

"What's that mean?"

Richardson didn't answer.

"Are we done? For good?" Klah already knew the answer.

"Don't take things too far, Whislin. You just need some time off. You've been working too hard. You need some rest. We'll be in touch soon." Richardson clicked off, and Whislin was left staring through his living room window at the high desert landscape of southwest Flagstaff. A damage-control team. One would be going to Modesto soon—and another was probably on its way to Flagstaff. He was a loose end. He had seen the cave. He knew too much.

He made three trips to his car and was ready to roll. He looked up at his condo. He had almost done it, almost owned it outright, but chances were he would never see it again. He got in his Jeep. Richardson said they'd known about the pickup leaving the canyon two hours ago. But they hadn't called him; Richardson said they didn't want to spook him. He backed out of his parking space and pulled forward to the exit. He stopped and looked both ways, looking for a black SUV, which was what Richardson drove. He doubted Richardson would actually come here himself—but he might. And he might have actually been on the phone with Klah from the airport, or just down the road.

Klah turned toward a gas station down the street. From there, he didn't know where he would go, which gave him hope that a damage-control team, including Richardson, wouldn't know either.

But before getting gas, he drove around behind the gas station and parked, where he got out and got on the ground and carefully checked every square inch of the undercarriage. No devices. Breathing a little easier, he pulled the car around to the gas pumps and filled up while thinking things through.

Call and Keller were almost to Fresno by now, maybe an hour and a half from Modesto. Surely they had already told Anna about the cave, but she was supposedly a savvy lawyer, accustomed to keeping important knowledge confidential. All things considered, there was a chance the authorities still knew nothing, which meant there was still hope for him.

If he could convince the men not to go public about the cave, or even go privately to the authorities, maybe Richardson and his bosses would ultimately take no action. Maybe they would let the Calls and Keller live. Maybe they would even allow one Whislin Klah, former Navy SEAL, current transient, continue to breathe.

Chapter 27

The Eyes of the Lord See *Something*

As Ross and I pulled in front of the house a little after three on Friday afternoon, I saw a movement in a second-story window above the front door. Kevin stood with binoculars pressed against his eyes. A question occurred: was he scanning for threats—or opportunities?

I got out and nearly fell to the ground as my legs failed me. I pushed my way to a vertical position and saw Kalley come out through the front door.

"Daddy!" she squealed. "You're home!" She ran with open arms and threw herself against me. I absorbed the blow, and we embraced. I tried to lift her off the ground, but that didn't happen.

"Daddy! I missed you so much!"

It was just what the doctor ordered, my twelve-year-old girl, already over five feet tall and growing into a young woman, offering her all to me. I was her knight, her joy, her hope, and I would do all in my power to stay that way. She all but carried me into the house while Ross gathered up our few supplies, mostly fast food wrappers.

The whole family was home, including Anna, which surprised me. She gave me a hug and quick kiss then stood back to survey me. It was Rosemary who said the obvious:

"Looks like you've been eating your own cooking."

There was a large mirror just inside the front door, and I saw myself. I was startled by the beard, then the sunburned nose and hollow eyes. Then I noticed my wraithlike, nay, cadaverous body. I would find out later that I had dropped twenty pounds. And that was after consuming a pile of hotdogs, chips, and four liters of water. I looked at Rosemary in the mirror and said, "What's for dinner?"

After giving a brief summary of our trip ("It was really hot during the day and really cold at night, and Ross almost got bit by a pink rattlesnake, and I almost got stung by a scorpion.") I went up to the bedroom, followed by Anna. She hadn't said much, and I was too exhausted to ask about the intruder or police protection. I sat on the bed to take off my boots, then I slumped backward on the bed and closed my eyes. I could sleep forever.

Anna stood at the foot of the bed. "How are you feeling?"

"Kind of tired."

"And the illness?"

She meant the chronic Lyme, which, strangely, or blessedly, still hadn't recurred since the bath in the Little Colorado. "I'm fine," I said, "just tired. Ross and I walked about twenty miles last night. Then we drove straight home. Or, he did."

"You've lost some weight."

"One of the benefits of hiking the Grand Canyon. We went in the wrong way." She hadn't moved. "We probably should've just driven to the edge of the canyon above the cave and hiked down into it. That's how we came out. But we didn't know that then."

"Ross said you found it."

My eyes stayed closed. The fatigue made me feel like I was spinning on the bed. "The cave's there—just like Keith said."

"So, what's that mean?"

I opened my eyes and saw a beautiful woman before me. Knowing we were on our way home, she had gone to the office, worked hard, come home early, changed, and softened her appearance. She was wearing roomy, casual clothes in pastel colors that made her most inviting. Her makeup, always strong and exact, was muted now. But I thought I saw reservation, perhaps fear.

"For starters, it means Keith wasn't lying. I believe everything he said. For another, it means somebody, somewhere, *is* lying. They're covering up one of the biggest secrets in North America. Third, it means—" I let the sentence hang, not knowing how to finish it.

"What?" she asked.

"It means we have to talk." I gave her my phone. "Look in the gallery. You'll see."

She began thumbing through the pictures. When she got to the mummies, she paused. "How old are these? What are they wrapped in?"

"I don't know how old they are, but they're wrapped in some kind of cloth or bark, or both, and sealed in some kind of clay."

"Are they Native American?"

"I think so, but I didn't look at all of them. Some of them, up on the top tier, are too high to get to without a ladder, but you can see the one that Keith opened up. There's no jewelry left."

She studied it. "I wish he had never gone there." She continued scrolling through the pictures. "What's this?" she turned the phone to me and showed me one of the photos of the hieroglyphics above the dark portion of the cave where I had turned back.

"It's some kind of ancient writing. I want to see if it matches any other Native hieroglyphics."

She sat down next to me on the bed. I sat up, put my arm around her, and said, "Tell me about what happened after we left—about the break-in."

She told the same story that Ross had already shared.

"Has anything happened since then?"

"No. The police drive by every hour, but it's been quiet."

"I'll fix the camera again, the one that got broken."

"It's the same one that got broken before."

"Maybe I should put it in a different place."

"I don't think it matters. Anybody can knock it out if they want to. She turned and looked at me. "After the break-in, I let Kevin have the slingshot again. You should have seen him. He's like a little man, guarding the house all the time. I actually think we're safer with him here than with the cops."

I laughed then realized she wasn't joking.

"I saw him in the window when we drove up. He was checking out the neighborhood with binoculars."

"He does that for hours. And he may have seen somebody, but he says that guy hasn't come by again."

"I'll talk to him."

"So, Travis, what do *you* want to do?"

That was the big question, and the answer would determine our direction together from now on.

She stood up, and I stood up beside her. She looked at the bed, where a faint, tan outline of dust remained. My clothes were torn and soiled beyond repair. Just last night I had been lying on the desert, parched nearly beyond endurance, then, somehow, conversing with a pleasant Hopi gentleman who gave me cool water. The dirt from that experience had just ended up on our bed. I patted it off.

"Sorry. I guess I should shower and change."

"Don't worry about that. So, what are we going to do?"

We?

Dare I hope?

"I've been thinking about that all day. You'll probably think I'm a hypocrite, but I don't think I should tell Johnson—not yet anyway."

Her eyes turned up to me, big and blue and surprised. "Why?"

"A couple of reasons. First, I broke the law by going there, and even though that's a minor detail in the big picture, it might be a big detail for me. Second, somebody powerful is covering this up. I mean, maybe the National Parks Service honestly doesn't know about the cave, since it's probably been sealed shut for a hundred years and is really hard to find, but maybe they do know and just want it to stay hidden."

"Why would they do that?"

"I don't know. Maybe just to keep from being embarrassed after all these years. Maybe there's something about the mummies. Maybe there's something else."

"I don't know—something of this magnitude. It seems somebody would leak it. It actually makes more sense to me that they don't know about it."

"Yeah, I can see that, except—"

"What?"

"Then why did somebody kill Keith? Was it just for the jewels? And if it was, why did somebody break in here and bug our phone and put tracking software on my computer? They didn't steal anything, did they?"

Anna shook her head.

"Think about it; they could have taken my computer, or the big TV in the family room, or a lot of stuff. They wanted information, not stuff. They wanted to follow my movements. In fact—"

A thought occurred to me that, in retrospect, shamed me with its obviousness. I went to the bathroom and grabbed Anna's large handheld mirror.

"What are you doing?"

"They were tracking my computer and phone. It only makes sense they were tracking our cars too." She nodded, then she patted the rest of the dust off the bedspread and followed me downstairs. We found Ross in the kitchen, eating the last remnants of a rotisserie chicken.

"Hey, partner," he said, "you wouldn't believe how good this—"

I fixed him with a stare. "In the garage."

He exchanged a glance with Anna then followed us to the garage. I opened the big door, flooding the garage with light. I went to the rear of Anna's SUV, got on my hands and knees, and started examining the undercarriage with the mirror.

"What's going on?" Ross asked between mouthfuls of a drumstick.

"He's looking for a tracking device," Anna said. "I should have thought of that myself. No, the cops should have thought of that."

I circled the car but found nothing. I moved across the three-car garage to my old, trusty Lexus and found a tracking device about ten seconds later, behind the right rear wheel. I couldn't pry it off with my hands, so I got a large screwdriver vise grips and pried it off with some effort. I showed it to Ross and Anna.

"A neodymium magnet," Ross said. "It was never coming off without being forced." He grabbed the mirror and screwdriver from my hands and ran out to his truck. Behind the right rear wheel, he found a similar device.

"So, somebody knew we went to the canyon," he said, "and now they know we're home."

"And yet nobody stopped us," I added. "They waited till we were gone, then they broke into the house. What's going on? Who are they? What do they want?"

We stared at each other.

"Do you want to call Johnson now?" Anna asked.

I shook my head. "Not yet. We need to think about this, think through the ramifications."

"But we know Keith was murdered," Ross said. "We've got to do something about that."

"Yes, he was murdered," I said, "and we could be next. Anna was right all along; things have gotten very dangerous. Whatever we do, we've got to be smart. Maybe there's a way to use these tracking devices to flush these guys out—or at least to find out who they are."

"Can I help?"

We turned and saw Kevin standing in the doorway, binoculars hanging from his neck and slingshot in hand. I honestly didn't know how to respond. Rosemary came hurrying through the door. "Kevin! Be careful with that! You saw what your father did to—"

I raised a hand. "It's all right. Kevin, you'll only use that to defend the family, right?"

He smiled, changed the slingshot to his left hand and raised his right hand as if in a court of law. "I swear I will only defend the family, the house, and anything else those jerks come for."

Ross laughed. "Who needs Johnson now?

We all met in the living room, and I briefly explained what Ross and I had found, then I showed Rosemary and the twins the pictures. Kalley thought the mummies were gross. I assured her they were but that most of them probably had a fortune of jewelry on them. Kevin asked for the phone to examine the photos again.

"But the real reason they're priceless," I added, "is because of their historical value. According to the man who first found the cave, there used to be a lot of ancient Egyptian relics—or some other kind of relics—in the cave. Now it's empty except for the mummies. Somebody emptied it, and they've been hiding all this for over a hundred years. And worse than that, somebody may have killed one of my clients because he found the cave."

Kalley gasped. "They killed him?"

"It looks like it. And that's why Ross and I went to the canyon, to see if this cave actually exists. Well, it does."

"So, now what?" Kevin asked, handing the phone back to me.

Anna spoke. "That's what we're here to discuss, since whatever Daddy and Ross do now will affect all of us. We thought we should all make the decision."

Rosemary, sitting at the dining room table with Lucas and Mia, silently nodded agreement.

Once the facts were laid out, we discussed our options, which basically included just sitting on things, going to the authorities with the photos, or pursuing an investigation ourselves. I admitted that I was surprised by how much my attitude had changed. Defying the law to verify that the cave existed was one thing, but people breaking into my house and putting my family at risk was another. I wasn't willing to live with that and do nothing. Anna was still reluctant to share her feelings, which surprised me. The more I tried to draw her out, the less she seemed willing to speak. In the end, I said something that surprised everybody, even myself a little.

"Somebody killed Keith Nelson, either for the jewelry or because he knew about the cave, but right now there's no way to know which it was. They also know that Ross and I went to the canyon, and now they must know that we're home. If they want more jewelry, they may come here again, though we don't have any. The only thing we brought from the cave was photographs. And if government people are trying to keep the cave a secret, the fact that we have photos, even of the inside of the cave—may put us in danger. If they're trying to keep the cave a secret, the sooner they silence us, the better—for them."

Everyone seemed to be in agreement, except Lucas and Mia, who were happily making a mess of their snacks at the dining room table. Rosemary was between them, trying to corral the flying fruit and jello. But she had listened and now spoke up.

"I was here eight years ago. I don't ever want to go through that again. And I don't want to see the kids ever put in danger again."

"Of course," Anna now said, sitting on the couch, next to Kalley. "We've got to protect the family."

Even Ross was nodding.

"So I propose," I said, "that we not go to Captain Johnson or anyone else right now, because we don't know if somebody in authority is in on the conspiracy, or if the government has access to their information." Anna gave me a blank stare, and I couldn't tell if she agreed or not. "And I also propose that, Anna, you and Rosemary, take the kids to a hotel tonight, and maybe for a lot more nights, until we know that there's no threat."

Kevin spoke up. "What about you?"

"I think that Ross and I should stay here. It may be the only way to find out who's behind all this. But if they show up, we'll be ready."

"But I wanna stay here too!" Kevin wailed.

"Kevin, quiet," Anna ordered firmly. She turned to me. "That's a really bad idea, Travis."

"Look," I said, "Johnson doesn't know why we were gone, but I'll call him and make sure he knows we're home now and that we would like more surveillance the next couple of days. But whether he gives it to us or not, Ross and I will be prepared. I'll fix the camera by the gate, and one of us will be watching the surveillance monitor all night."

"But what if they have guns!" Kevin cried. "You don't have one."

"Not that you know of," I said.

He took a moment to consider this before looking at his mother for confirmation, who gave no indication one way or the other.

"And who says *I* don't have one, or two, or ten?" Ross said smiling. "They may come in and find an army waiting for them."

"I gotta stay!" Kevin yelled. "You said I could defend the house!"

"No, Kevin," I said, "I want you to defend the family. Remember, the bad guys could be watching the house right now, and they may follow you guys to the hotel. If that happens, I want you there to help the family."

Of course I didn't actually believe this, but as I said it, I realized that I didn't know if it was false either. The bad guys, whoever they were, might be about to break in on us at this very moment.

"Travis," Anna said, her tone still soft but firm, "I think the family should stay together."

Finally Ross spoke up. "I can handle it, Travis, if you need to go."

"No, if there's another break-in, or if they decide to make contact, I want to be here. Keith was my friend, and I made a commitment to his daughter to find who killed him. I can do that best here." I turned to Anna. "I'm sorry, Anna. I think you'll all be safer away from here. Ross and I are radioactive now. We've seen the cave. If they wanted to hurt you, they probably would have tried something by now. Please, I think you and Rosemary should go to a hotel—and only use cash because they might be able to track our credit cards."

She shook her head. "Even though they might be following us from here to the motel?" I didn't respond. "Travis, I think you should at least tell Captain Johnson about the cave and show him the pictures. He doesn't have jurisdiction there, so he can't go after you about that, but seeing proof of the cave will motivate him to push the investigation. He might even go to the FBI since this looks like an interstate crime. And, believe me, they can solve murder cases better than anyone, even you. And I really don't think they'll come after you, not after they realize that you've found one of the great archeological discoveries of the Western World."

I actually agreed with her, but something was bothering me. "I'm sure you're right, honey. I know I can't do what the FBI can do, but, for now, would it be all right if we tried it my way?"

"But why when the police and FBI can do it better—and safer?"

"I don't know, but—please? I just feel we should keep all this confidential."

She had a decision to make, to trust me, a chronically ill, wholly fallible man who had recently shot his best friend in the leg, or to trust her own almost perfect reasoning.

"How long do you want us to stay at the hotel?"

Her question implied that a decision had been made, and I was so surprised that I had to think twice before answering. "Well, until we know more—at least through the weekend." Today was Friday. I turned to Kalley. "Can you help your mother and Rosemary take care of Lucas and Mia while Ross and I are gone?"

"Yes, but, Daddy, are you sure you'll be safe?"

Sitting next to her, Kevin rolled his eyes. But my heart was melted. "Of course I'll be safe—Ross is the one who'd better watch out; criminals always go after the big guy first."

She laughed and got up and gave me a hug, and soon we were all standing. The decision had been made. Anna's decision had been swift and decisive, as usual, though in this case it was surprising as well. She quietly went up to help Kalley pack, and after a few minutes of pondering, I went up to Kevin's room and found his big duffel bag haphazardly stuffed with clothes and steel ball bearings. He was at the window again, surveying the neighborhood with the binoculars. "You'd better take those with you," I said. "Maybe you'll see something from the balcony."

"Balcony nothing—I'm going up to the roof!"

"Right."

"And if I see that guy with the binoculars again, I'm going to—"

"Wait, he had binoculars?"

"Yeah, I told Mom that."

"So, what did he look like?"

"I don't know—he had binoculars in his face most of the time. But when he drove by, I saw him better. I think he's big, even bigger than Ross. And he had really black hair, and he looked like a, like a Chinese man—or an Indian."

"An Indian? You mean like an American Indian?"

"Yeah, but he had short hair."

"Short black hair?"

"Yeah."

"Do you think he saw you?"

He thought about this. "Yeah, prob'ly, 'cause he looked up when he went by."

"And you're sure he had binoculars and was looking at the house."

"Yeah. That's why I started watching him."

"And what kind of car was he driving?"

"It was kind of like Mom's car, only not as nice."

"Like an SUV?"

"Yeah, but it had big tires, like a Jeep."

"What color was it?"

"Black, an' its tires made a lot of noise when it went by."

"Big, knobby tires, like for going off-road?"

"Yeah."

"Anything else?"

"No. I only saw him for a few seconds."

"Kevin, you did good. This is great. But do me a favor. If you see him again, just tell your mother. Don't try to do anything yourself, okay?"

"But I never miss. I can hit a cat from—"

"I know, but please, just go tell Mom or Rosemary."

He didn't answer. Which meant, of course, that he didn't agree to the terms.

"Kevin?"

"What?"

"Do you promise to do that?"

"Course not! What if he's running right at me? What if he has Kalley? What if . . ."

"Okay, but if he's not a clear threat, at that very moment, just go tell your mom. She's very smart, and she'll know how to *really* get him."

"You mean, she has a gun, like you?"

"I didn't say that, but trust me, she knows how to put men in jail."

"I thought she got men *out* of jail."

"She does that too, but she knows how to do both. Will you promise?"

"Maybe."

"What's that mean?"

The twelve-year-old prodigy was considering his words carefully. "If one thing happens, I'll do one thing. If something else happens, I'll do something else." He put the binoculars back to his eyes and peered out the window, looking as far up the street as he could. The conversation appeared to be over.

Many bags were packed in both Anna's SUV and Rosemary's minivan. They would take both vehicles, which would give both women independence.

At her door, I kissed Anna and gave her a quick hug, which was not returned with much enthusiasm.

"Don't you want to know where we're going?" she asked.

"Yes, but maybe I shouldn't know. What if they get us and try to squeeze the information out of us. It would be better if I didn't know."

She started to smile then grew concerned. "I thought you were joking, but who knows, maybe you're right. I'll call you."

"No, they may be able to triangulate on your phone. Or they may be authorized to just listen in. We don't know what they can do—except keep one of the greatest discoveries in North America secret for a hundred years."

"So, how will we be able to talk?"

"Maybe we won't."

"Are you sure that's wise?"

"Okay, let's agree to meet every day at a certain place, at a certain time."

"Really? How about if I just come home every day and see how you're doing?"

Her logic was always so true, so unassailable. "Oh, yeah, that might work. But be careful. Make sure you yell for us before you walk in the door—just in case we're being held hostage."

She smiled. "Just take care of yourselves, and I'll see you tomorrow."

"When?"

"Noon?"

"All right."

When both vehicles were gone, Ross came to me. "Hey, just so we're on the same page, do you really have any guns?"

"No. Do you?"

"No."

We went back in the house. A fine lot of detectives we were.

Ross went upstairs to shower and catch a few minutes of sleep while I went to Best Buy to get a new camera. I took my Lexus, which had no tracking sensor on it. I found the camera I needed outside and bought four of them, a replacement, a replacement for the replacement, and two replacements for any others. When I got home, I found Ross asleep on his bed. Our home did not appear to have been invaded yet, and since my rather astonishing run of good health and energy seemed to be continuing, I got up on the roof and replaced the broken camera, then I turned one of the cameras from the back left corner of the house toward the front, in a hope to catch somebody tampering with the camera by the gate. I went back in and watched the monitor for a few minutes and found that it worked.

I was getting sleepy, but I didn't think we should both be asleep at the same time, so I went to my office and turned on my laptop. The tracing software had been deleted from my office computer, but I still wondered how much privacy I had. I took out my phone and immediately loaded copies of my photos of the cave onto the laptop. Just to be safe, I planned to load them onto Ross's and Anna's computers as well.

Looking through them, I focused on the last two images of hieroglyphics, the cryptic lettering above the void leading into the darkest part of the cave. I enlarged the second photo, which was the clearest, and the feeling came again that I had seen the strange lettering before. I thought back to the other hieroglyphics above the doorways in the cave. Though I couldn't remember them all, they had seemed to be of a different type, more pictures than letters.

But these appeared to be all letters.

Reading from left to right, I saw two dots, side by side. Two dots. Then there was a space, and then there was another symbol, which was simply an upside down V. It actually looked like an A without the cross line. Then another space was followed by four flat horizontal lines stacked on each other. These symbols were followed by something resembling a capital H, but more ornate, with the left vertical line curling into an L at its base, and over that same vertical line there was a cap on it, making it look like a capital T. The second vertical line of the H, on the right side, was curved like a capital C. Maybe this was why the symbols seemed familiar—because one of them actually was—an ornate capital H. Those first four symbols were followed by three small boxes, almost as if they were bullet points at the end of a sentence.

Another wave of weariness swept over me, and I got up and went to the living room to lie down on the couch. I would check online for Native American hieroglyphics later. In the last twenty-four hours I had pushed myself almost beyond endurance, and now, although I had slept a few hours in the truck, I was again succumbing to fatigue.

Moments later I was asleep.

Chapter 28

Going Down an Evil Road

As Whislin raced west across the Mojave Desert at 80 miles an hour, he ran Richardson's words through his mind again. *We're sending a damage-control team to manage the problem.* He had never heard Richardson use the term before, but he imagined it was what it sounded like—a former military black-ops group with one objective, to remove a threat. He couldn't see how they could remove any threat, though, by removing an entire family. These were prominent people. A captain in the police force knew them well and also knew about Keith Nelson's mysterious death. Dots would be connected. More expeditions to the canyon would be made. The best the Society could hope for was a pledge of silence, enforced, perhaps by very real threats to the children.

But that was Klah's thinking, not the Society's. He had never met Richardson's handlers and had no idea how they thought, except that they were willing to pay large sums of American currency to hire people like *him.*

Another part of the conversation came to mind: *We've got access to their communications now.* Were they working with the phone companies? Access to private communications without a warrant violated federal laws. Did they have access to information gathered at the NSA Data Center in Utah, which supposedly stored every phone conversation in America? Did their access have no limits? And just who was opening these doors for them?

Of course, he had violated a few laws himself, but that was a different matter.

He had hoped to formulate a plan while driving, but the only plan he could come up with was to somehow convince Call and Keller not to go to the authorities with their information. If they would agree to this, and if he could somehow convince his bosses of their honorable intent, maybe they would all be allowed to live—especially since the hazards to the Society for committing more homicides might be even more costly.

But, what if Call and Keller went public immediately?

How could the Society eliminate all of them if they were internet celebrities with proof of "Kinkaid's Cave"? What would the Society do, knowing the ensuing investigation would likely include both ICE and the FBI?

Interesting. He had gone from would-be killer to supportive outsider in keeping them alive.

He would continue to ponder these complexities, and, if Call and Keller were still alive when he arrived at Modesto, he might even chance a meeting with them.

Of course, that assumed that he himself was still alive.

Klah didn't know that he was being followed until he pulled off 99 to get gas in Bakersfield.

Did the Society have access to satellite surveillance too?

He had exited to get gas, but the brand he preferred, Chevron, didn't exist where his phone told him it should be. As he searched for the station, he saw a maroon SUV exit the freeway about thirty seconds behind him. It slowed as it passed him then continued on. Klah had been trained to notice such things, but with his mind preoccupied he thought nothing of it. At the next exit, however, where he finally found his Chevron, the same maroon SUV got off again. Sure enough, it slowed as it passed him again then did a U-turn two blocks down and parked in front of a strip mall, positioned to follow him back onto the freeway. Interesting—the color was wrong for a surveillance vehicle. Red is easy to spot, and the high profile of an SUV would stand out on any street. But maybe that's what they wanted. Either they were hoping that he would dismiss the red SUV as a follow vehicle because it was all wrong, or they wanted him to spot it. Though, of course, it could just be that these guys were morons, the only contract guys Richardson could find on short notice.

He filled his tank, cleaned his windshield, paid with a fairly new credit card, then left the station. He drove by the maroon SUV without glancing at it. It was a 2017 GMC Yukon. Either these guys were highly paid pros, or they had run down to the nearest rent-a-car and got the last vehicle on the lot.

Instead of going back to the freeway, Klah continued on east, away from 99, then turned right at a major crossroad, going south, hoping to get back to the previous exit he had taken earlier. If the Yukon followed him, he would be waiting. He got back to the first road he had come in on, turned right toward the freeway, then pulled in at a restaurant and tucked in tight on the far side of the building. Sure enough, the deep red SUV came by fast, heading for the freeway. He pulled out behind it and followed it onto 99. It had been too easy. Now he knew—these guys were morons. Klah was half tempted to call Richardson and laugh out loud.

He followed them for a couple of minutes at over ninety as they raced to find him. When the lane on the right opened up, he pulled over and came up beside them and looked to his left. The front windows were less tinted, and he could see a passenger and driver in front, both men in their thirties. He couldn't see into the back.

A few moments later the passenger casually glanced over and saw Klah smiling at him. He feigned disregard, but his lips moved, then the driver looked over.

Klah increased his smile for the startled driver.

Then Klah touched his brake and pulled in behind them again. Both cars settled down to something near the speed limit, and Klah waited to see what they would do. A rabbit chasing the coyote.

He knew the status quo would be unacceptable to the contractors, so he expected them to make a move soon. But it came later than he expected, fifty miles away, at a rest stop just north of Pixley. The Yukon was still in the left lane when it suddenly swerved across the lanes and barely made the exit onto the off-ramp. They had cut off an 18-wheeler pulling bales of hay, which hit its brakes and sent up plumes of smoke. Klah didn't want these guys tailing him again, so he tried to make the off-ramp. He was too late to stay on the pavement, but he veered off the freeway just inside a chain-link fence dividing the freeway from the off-ramp. But his left side mirror swiped the exit sign as he lost purchase on the loose dirt. The right side of the sign bent backward and his mirror flung back against his door. As he slowed down, now fully on the off-ramp, he saw that his mirror was hanging by its electrical cords.

That angered him. It could cost north of five hundred bucks to get that mirror replaced, and that was only if his door didn't need to be repainted. He didn't know who these guys were or how they had found him, but he was determined to put an end to the pursuit.

He stayed behind the Yukon, which had slowed to thirty or so as it entered the rest area. He slowed further, allowing a gap to open between them, and he reached into the back and retrieved the black case holding his Glock. Slowing further and steering with his knees, he threaded the suppressor onto the gun's muzzle. The Yukon was crawling now, and the guys inside appeared to be arguing. Should they stop and deal with Klah or speed up and try to put distance between the two vehicles on the freeway? Eventually they would probably all meet up again, as both parties knew exactly where he was headed.

Near the end of the rest area, they pulled into a parking stall fifty yards or so from the nearest vehicle. Klah braked to a stop behind them, rolled down his passenger window, and methodically shot out both rear tires of the shiny red SUV. The report that escaped the suppressor was cancelled by freeway noise, and the back end of the Yukon sat down, first left then right, like it had been dropped from two jacks. Whislin hit the gas and was on the freeway before the men got out of the car. If they fired any shots, he didn't notice it.

He was still mad about his mirror, but he figured the money he would have to spend on it had bought him a few precious hours up in Modesto. He needed to reason with Call and Keller. The way he saw it, even now after several hours of contemplation, they had two options if they wanted to live: they could go public as quickly and loudly as possible, or, if they agreed to stay silent, they might be allowed to live with a threat over their heads.

Even with his mirror flapping against his door panel, Whislin pushed his speed up to 80. As young almond orchards became a blur on both sides, he checked the clock in the dash. Almost seven p.m. With any luck, he would be in front of Call's house in two hours.

Chapter 29

And it Came to Pass That
Truth and Light Emerged

It was getting dark outside—half past seven. As I came fully awake a growl of hunger stirred my belly. I had no idea what was in the fridge but I was anxious to find out. As I got up, several pieces of paper under the coffee table caught my eye, and I reached out and pulled them out. It was a printout of an article I had found weeks ago about the Anthon Transcript, detailing the characters that Joseph Smith had copied for Martin Harris to take to a professor in New York. I had printed the article out for Anna. I wondered how it had ended up here. Maybe Ross had found it and brought it into the living room. I doubted that Anna had done so.

I flipped through the pages and saw something that stopped me cold—a magnified copy of some of the characters, including a large, ornate H. It appeared to be written in an old, classic script. And now I realized that it looked exactly like the figure I had seen in the cave.

My breath came up short. Even in my fatigued state I realized the enormity of the coincidence.

I sat upright, my gaze remaining on the H, which was scripted in nearly the same style that I had seen in the cave—the same letter that I had been looking at on my computer. I scanned the rest of the page for more symbols, and almost immediately my eyes fell on a square box on the second line of symbols. In the cave I had definitely seen a box that looked something like this one. Like the ornate H, it had been part of the lettering above the "snaky" void of blackness. I pulled my phone out and brought up the photographs of the hieroglyphics. Thank goodness the light had been strong enough. Thank goodness I had chosen to risk the battery life and take the picture—because there it was, or rather, there they were, three identical boxes to those in the Anthon Transcript. And, as in the transcript, each box appeared to be filled in, or in this case, chiseled in. I couldn't imagine how long it had taken someone to chip out each flake of stone to hollow out the boxes. The similarity between the transcript and the carvings in the cave was uncanny.

Trying to remain calm, I compared other symbols from the cave with symbols in the Anthon Transcript, and within a minute I found three more, including the upside-down V. Then I found the symbol of just two dots. Remaining calm now was not a possibility. I hurried through the kitchen to my office and looked under my desk for my notes from Ether six. Fortunately, they were right where I had left them. Evidently whoever had broken in didn't want them. I pulled a Book of Mormon from the shelf to my left and opened to Ether six. I began comparing the symbols from the Anthon transcript with the words in chapter six, and within minutes had made several possible connections, allowing me to begin isolating the translation to possible individual words. I again compared my notes from the Anthon Transcript with the photos from the cave. They were almost certainly a match. Putting it all together, I began experimenting with matches, this symbol for that word, this one for that phrase. Within minutes I had a few possible translations for each character. Then, barely taking a moment to reflect on the enormity of what I was doing, I tried to put the English translations to the characters in the right order:

> With his two directing eyes, The Lord [the unknown symbol of the four horizontal lines] we had with us in the tight quarters of our vessel the light of day as we went forth. Holy Land. Holy Land. Holy Land.

It made almost no sense, but my excitement had to be shared. I went back out to the living room and shouted up the stairs.

"Ross! Ross! Come here!"

I scanned the paper again for more matches. There were only seven symbols on the ledge in the cave, and six of them were right there in Anthon Transcript. It was incredible.

I pulled out my phone and called Ross. He answered after the fifth ring.

"Ross, I need help."

He was instantly alert. "Are they here?"

"Who?"

"I don't know—the bad guys!"

"No. I need help with the pictures from the cave."

He groaned. "You couldn't let me sleep? Do you know how long I've been up? You woke me up so I could help you with pictures?"

"But it's amazing! You won't believe it!"

"I'm hanging up."

"No! Really. You know those symbols above the *snaky* part of the cave?"

"No."

"*Listen!* You know those two pictures I took of that ledge just above the really dark part of the cave?"

"Yeah."

"Those symbols, those *characters*, are in the Book of Mormon!"

He was quiet, and I waited a long moment for him to talk before realizing that he had hung up. I was dialing him again when he showed up on the stairs and bounded down. I met him with the evidence.

"Look!" I said, showing him my photograph of the seven symbols, "remember these?"

"Yeah, sure, but they're not in the Book of Mormon."

"No, but look—they are!" I showed him the Anthon Transcript so he could see all the characters. Then I pointed back to the photo. "See? These boxes on the ledge in the cave are also in the Anthon Transcript—and the Anthon Transcript is from the Book of Mormon."

"Yeah."

"I mean, how many languages use a box for one of their words?"

"I don't know—hundreds?"

"I doubt it—but look at this." I showed him the two dots, which almost certainly meant "eye" or "eyes," and the inverted V, which seemed to mean "God" or "The Lord."

"Look," I said, showing him the Anthon Transcript again. "These are identical matches. And look at this." I showed him the ornate H from the picture in the cave, then I showed him where it appeared several times in the transcript. "What are the odds that an H, with the same curlicues and everything, is going to show up in both places? They're perfect matches."

He took the paper and studied the characters, then he took my phone and looked at the pictures again. "Yeah, they kind of match. So, what does it mean?"

"It means that they're probably from the same language. And if they are, then Joseph Smith was copying actual characters from an actual ancient language when he made this transcript for Martin Harris."

He stared at the pictures again, letting this sink in. "Okay, they look like actual letters, or characters, or whatever, but what do they mean? Did you figure out the translation?"

"Well, kind of, but it doesn't make sense."

"So, that's not good."

"No, that's why I called you. I need you to help me figure it out."

He laughed. "You're the one who went to college. I'm just the dummy who made a few million bucks. Why do you think I can figure it out?"

"Come on, Ross. We both know you're smarter than me."

He scratched the back of his head. "I don't know—" I showed him my rough attempts at a translation, and he read it a few times.

"You're right; it doesn't make any sense."

He took the pencil and wrote variations of the translation, using the individual meanings from each character in the book. A minute or so later he put the pencil down. "Look, I'm tired. You figure it out." He went to the refrigerator. I had been tired and hungry myself just a few minutes ago, but now I was on fire. If these characters represented what I thought they did—proof that Joseph Smith had translated the Book of Mormon from an actual ancient language— the ramifications were incalculable. Anti-Mormons would never be able to explain away the book again. People who wanted to believe but couldn't would have more evidence to bolster their faith. It would be world-changing.

Except—

I slowed down to reconsider. I only had seven symbols here. Even though six of them were found in the Anthon Transcript, after a fashion, it wasn't exactly overwhelming proof that Joseph Smith had translated an early Native American language. I would need more evidence. And the only place I could think of to get more evidence was in the cave, *way back* in the cave, maybe in the dark void. Maybe these characters were some kind of blessing or invocation on whatever lay inside.

I sat down, ignoring the clanking of bowls from the kitchen. Of course, I knew firsthand that the only way to really know that the Book of Mormon is true is to receive a witness of it by the Holy

Ghost. That's when you receive not only knowledge of its truth but a desire to live its teachings. Was I trying to put the cart before the horse by trying to produce tangible proof of its truth? Was I putting the arm of flesh before the Spirit?

I looked at the transcript again, which was open to the page with each character listed in the order in which it appeared. I had numbered each character, from 1 to 213. Had Joseph Smith actually found these characters on ancient plates, as he claimed, or had he made them all up? And if he did, how much time and effort would that take? He had put them in a specific order, with some of the characters used multiple times, just as we might use the same words multiple times in a paragraph. I checked my attempt at a translation again. It simply made no sense.

I thought about Nephi and Mormon inscribing these characters in plates of gold or some other soft metal, and I tried to put myself in their place: How long would it take? How much pressure would be needed to make the indentations with a stylus? How much would it hurt one's finger after writing a line or two?

A humbling feeling came over me. There were over 500 pages in the Book of Mormon, and Joseph Smith said that this represented only a third of the pages in the plates. I sat on the couch and closed my eyes, realizing for the first time how much sacrifice this had taken. I had known most of my life that the book was true, but now I had evidence that hundreds of people, or thousands, maybe even millions, had wished they could have. It was right in my hands. And in my mind I saw Mormon engraving a character on a metal sheet with his right hand, painstakingly pressing into the metal, making sure the character was legible, then he moved on to make the next painful character. How long had it taken?

In my mind Mormon was writing from right to left, not from left to right. The Nephites spoke Hebrew, and Hebrew, which they could also write, was written from right to left. I looked down at the Anthon Transcript again and saw that it too could have been written from right to left. Then I looked at the photograph, read it from right to left, then looked at my poor attempt at a translation—and reversed it:

Holy land, Holy land, Holy land. In these tight quarters the light of day will shine on *[the four horizontal lines]*. The Lord's directing eyes—watching over us.

It made a little more sense. Maybe the cave was considered holy, and the Lord was watching over it. But what did the figure with the four horizontal lines mean? They looked like four pancakes stacked on top of each other. Did the figure represent a house? Layers of rock in the cave? Layers of knowledge? The more possibilities I considered, the more I realized that I couldn't solve the riddle without more knowledge.

And of course, I wasn't even sure that I had the grammar right. Hebrew used a different syntax than English. I didn't know much Hebrew, but I knew that sometimes the meanings of a word were altered by what preceded or followed it.

I looked up and saw Ross holding a plastic container over his mouth, letting the viscous contents slide down his throat. He swallowed as fast as he poured. I was in the presence of two miracles at once: modern proof of the Book of Mormon and a human black hole. He lowered the container, smacked his lips, and sighed loudly.

"Was it good?" I asked.

He put the container in the sink. "Are you kidding? Rosemary's peach cobbler? You're never getting rid of me now."

"You just *drank* her peach cobbler?"

"You get the goodness faster that way."

He wiped his mouth and came back to the counter.

"I think I've found something," I said. "We were reading the characters from left to right, like English, but the Nephites spoke Hebrew, remember, which is written from right to left. Maybe they wrote their reformed Egyptian characters the same way. So here's what I think it says now."

I showed him the new translation.

He took it and mumbled it aloud.

"Maybe, but what does that figure with the four lines mean?"

"I don't know. It's not in the transcript."

"It looks like a Menu sign for a website."

"I doubt that's it."

He handed the paper back to me. "So, if the symbols in the cave are the same ones Joseph Smith translated from, it means—" He paused.

"It means," I continued, "that he knew exactly which symbols ancient Americans used for their writing. Or, it means he had the plates."

He stared at me, the wheels turning. "Then it proves the Book of Mormon is true."

"Well, at a minimum it proves that the Book of Mormon is authentic—that it is what he said it is."

He stared at me again, his eyes almost fierce. "No—this is wrong! You can't know this. You're not a prophet. Why would *you* get this?"

"Ross, it doesn't take a prophet to match symbols in a cave to symbols on a piece of paper. It's not like I'm revealing anything new, except that now there's proof that he was translating from a real language."

"*Whatever.* So what are we going to do? Do you want to call the Prophet? With something like this I bet we could get his number."

I chuckled. "I think we need more information first."

"Like what?"

"Well, for one thing, we need to figure out the meaning of the four lines, and for another—" I didn't want to finish.

"What?"

"Think about it. These words were chiseled above the entrance to that part of the cave like a sign on a doorpost. You know, like the Jews use on their front doors."

"You mean a mezuzah?"

"Yeah—how'd you know that?"

He shrugged. "Like you said, I'm smarter than you. It's just something I learned on my mission."

"Anyway, if that's what this is, some kind of sign invoking the blessings of God, then I want to find out what's *inside that part of the cave.*"

He thought about this. "Wait, you want to go *back*?"

"Don't you?"

"Well—aren't we waiting for the bad guys to show up, so we can immobilize-slash-interrogate-slash-dispose of them?"

"How do we do that without a gun?"

He looked exasperated. "I don't know. It was *your* plan. I've been sleeping."

"Ok, but think about it. What would we do if they showed up?"

"You really don't have this figured out?"

I didn't answer.

He sighed then said, "Well, we can't offer them any food because I pretty much cleaned out the fridge." His eyes flashed back at me. "Wait—you're not thinking of going now, are you? Tonight?"

I didn't answer.

"We're exhausted!"

"No," I said, "*I'm* exhausted. You just took a nap."

"No, *you* slept all the way home."

"Not all the way."

He threw his hands in the air. "We just drove like ten hours—*after* walking twenty miles! We can't go back now."

"I'll drive."

"Forget it! You'd probably get more Lyme disease and drive us into the ocean."

"Then you drive. I just thought I'd offer."

"This is insane. Whatever's inside that cave will last for another day or century or two."

"Maybe, maybe not. Now that the adversary knows that we know about it, anything can happen. You know he'll be tempting people to go in there and steal everything."

"The adversary? And what *'everything'?* The mummies? He already knew they were there, and people left them alone all this time."

"Not Keith Nelson."

This stumped him for half a second. "So, are you saying that he was an emissary of the adversary?"

I found that not answering saved time, so I said nothing again. This was getting easier.

"And if he was an emissary of the adversary, what's that make us— I mean *you*? *I* didn't go in. You were the one breaking the law."

"We were both breaking it."

"But you broke it more. You're a bigger emissary."

"Am not."

"Are too."

I didn't see a future in this. "We were trying to right a wrong."

"And look how it's turned out. You're going to prove the Book of Mormon is true."

"And that's bad because? . . ."

"Because we're *not supposed to*. Because we're supposed to let the Spirit tell us it's true. Remember Moroni's Promise? Chapter ten, three through five?"

"So do you want to throw all this away and pretend we don't know it exists? Do you want to put your head in the sand?" He didn't answer. Hiding one's head in the sand was contrary to Ross Keller's core principles. "Or," I continued, "are we going to stand up like men and say we have new evidence that Joseph was right, that the Book is true and that the world needs to repent?"

Ross liked to see people repenting.

He paused to consider the options. "Well, before we tell the world to repent, maybe we should show this to the general authorities."

"Yeah—after we get more evidence. And remember, we could still get into a lot of trouble."

"For trespassing?"

"Yes, if the government finds out."

"They don't even think the cave is there."

"Or they do and don't want anyone else to know about it."

"We're going in circles here. Do you want to go back there or not?"

"Of course I do! We have to. We discovered maybe the greatest archeological find in the *world*, and also maybe the surest proof that Joseph Smith was a prophet. Who knows what else is in there!"

Ross's shoulders slumped, and I realized just how weary he was. The lines in his face were heavier than usual. "This has really got you, hasn't it?" he asked.

"Doesn't it have you?"

"Yeah, sure, but I want to sleep first."

But I was energized. Something was driving me forward. "Okay," I said, trying to sound logical, "We know the cave is being kept a secret, right?"

"Yeah."

"And we know that whoever is hiding it probably killed Keith Nelson, and that they're probably the same people who bugged our phone and started tracing my computer, right?"

"Right."

"And now we know that they know that we know that the cave is there, right?"

"Wait, I got lost."

"In other words, they're probably coming here to kill us, right?"

"I don't know. Maybe they're trying to sleep, like we should be." He shook his head. "Sorry, I can't even think."

"But you can sure eat."

"That doesn't take any energy. Why do you want to go now?"

"Because I think we should."

"You don't think we should rest first?"

"Actually, I think we should get out of this house first. And I think we should get a bunch of stuff we didn't have the first time, and we should take it inside the cave—both of us—and find out what's way back in there—see if there's any more proof of the Book of Mormon."

"Great idea, but I can't get in, remember?"

"Sure you can. We just need to make the hole bigger."

He smiled. Now I was speaking his language. "Do you mean—explosives?"

"I didn't say that."

"But how else are we going to widen it? It's not like we can take power tools up there."

"Why not? My cordless drill has a foot-long bit, and the batteries are both charged."

"A hand drill? Really? That would take hours."

"I doubt it. That stone is pretty soft."

A gleam came into his eyes. "Listen, we'll use the drill to make holes in the sides of the air duct, then we'll put explosives in the holes. And then we'll blow the whole thing wider!"

"Explosives?" I asked, growing more concerned. "What kind of explosives?"

"M-80s, what else? I bet I could go down to Ninth Street right now and buy ten packs of them."

"But we'll be destroying a cave in a national park. That's like twenty years."

"We won't be *destroying* it, we'll be *enhancing* it! They'll probably give us a medal. They'll probably give us a reward."

"Like I said, they'll probably give us twenty."

"It was *your* idea to widen the hole. What does it matter if we use drills or M-80s—or both?"

He had a point.

"Okay, look," I said, trying to make sense of things again, "I don't want to stay here tonight. I don't think it's safe. I just wanted to get the family out of here—and away from us because we're toxic. So let's go to a motel, get some sleep, then go back to the cave tomorrow. That'll give us some time to buy our supplies."

"Two problems."

"What?"

"One, what if we go to the same motel the family went to. You know Kevin will probably find us and rat us out."

I rolled my eyes.

"And two—" He paused.

"What?"

"I forgot. I'm so tired I can't even remember my own good ideas."

I waited for him to continue, but he finally shook his head. "It was a really good one too, but I can't remember it. Maybe I'm having a stupor of thought. All right, we'll go. I can't even believe I'm doing this. Most of our stuff is still in the canyon, so we'll have to buy a new tent and backpacks and . . ."

"No, let's just drive out to the rim, right above the cave, and hike down to it. We could be at the cave in an hour from when we get there—instead of three or four days. Then we'll widen the hole and go in. We can probably be back out and up in the truck before nightfall. Then we'll drive to a town and stay the night there."

His eyes drifted away as he thought about this. "You know, that might work. All right, where are we going tonight?"

"To a motel, on Ninth Street. We need M-80s, right?"

He just smiled.

Packing was easy, since we only needed clean clothes. We'd have to buy everything else. Before leaving I thought about the Anthon Transcript. We might need it. But instead of throwing this one in with my stuff, I went to my office and got a copy that had my English translations of each character on the back. Hopefully I'd be able to see the characters well enough to match them to any others we might find in the cave. I folded the paper and stuffed it in my shirt pocket.

As we were putting our bags and power tools in the truck's back seat, Ross said, "Oh, I remembered what my other objection was."

"What's that?"

"Aren't we supposed to meet Anna here tomorrow at noon?"

Now I was the one in a stupor. How had I forgotten? "Okay," I said, "change of plans. We'll spend the night in a motel, go buy everything we need in the morning, then come back here and meet her at noon. How's that sound?"

"It sounds like she'll talk us out of going."

"No. We're on a mission. We'll be firm."

"Ha! A mission probably to get arrested—or killed—or excommunicated."

I couldn't help but laugh again.

It was almost nine and fully dark outside when we drove off. As we made our way down the street, I wondered who would be the next person to enter our house.

* * *

Whislin saw Call and Keller carry their bags and laptops out the door to the pickup. From his vantage point two blocks away, with his vehicle hidden behind a panel van, he saw the men settle into the truck, but because of the darkness he could only make out the large items they carried. What were they up to?

There was no reason for him to go in the house once they were gone. He already knew where they had been and what they knew— that the cave existed and that it contained ancient mummies. Rather, he only needed to convince them to do something with their knowledge, to go public very quickly, that is, if he hoped to live another day.

And even then things would be dicey.

The Society might kill him just to make a point: *You fail us, and you pay a price.* Or they might simply want revenge for his negligence. So his first option was to get them to go public so that any more killings would be instantly treated as part of the conspiracy. His second option was to go dark immediately and stay dark for years. He had enough money for a few years, but he would eventually get desperate.

As the truck pulled away from the curb, he was tempted to stay put just to see who else visited the house. The thought had even occurred to him to dispatch his would-be dispatchers when they showed up. He doubted it would be the two goons from earlier in the day, who were quite possibly still in Pixley trying to talk the Society into paying for two new tires. No, it would probably be veterans, not necessarily of military service, though that was possible, but of the kind of service that is advertised only on the dark web, and even then, only in the most cryptic and deniable ways.

He was sure the Society was growing more desperate with each hour, paying entire teams of scanners to peruse the web, both light and dark, to see if any news of the cave or mummies was posted. Frankly, he didn't know if Call had posted anything, but he doubted so because there were no police or news hounds at the house.

Yes, he was tempted to stay and greet the new team coming to take his place, but with sudden alarm he realized that as the truck drove away down the street, the green icon on his laptop computer screen wasn't moving. It was staying put. At the house. Was the sensor not working, or had they removed it? He had two more sensors in his bag, but they did little good now.

As the lifted, silver F-150 turned right at the corner, Klah started the Jeep. He had to look back over his left shoulder to make sure no vehicles were coming behind him before he pulled into the road—something that drove him crazy—because his mirror was still hanging loose. He would have to get it fixed as soon as possible; the last thing he needed was a ticket, as he figured the Society would know about it somehow.

He raced down the residential street faster than he should have and barely caught a glimpse of the truck as it turned right onto Pelandale, a major crosstown artery. Keeping several cars between himself and the truck, he followed them onto the freeway heading south and was surprised six miles later when they exited at Crows Landing Road. He had spent an hour or so here a couple of weeks ago when surveilling Call. It was a Hispanic enclave, where business signs were in Spanish and most establishments looked like they were a used car lot or a decked-out food truck.

He followed Keller's truck to a low, sprawling motel, and pulled over to the right as the truck parked in front of the office. Did they know someone here? Surely they weren't booking themselves a room. He turned off the engine, got his binoculars, and awaited developments.

Call went into the office while Keller stayed in the truck, and he put two and two together. They had discovered the tracking sensors and knew someone was following them. They knew they had been tracked to the canyon, and thus to the cave, so now they were heading out of Dodge before the same fate that befell Nelson befell them. He smiled at the irony. He had killed Nelson, and now he was running for his life as surely as Call and Keller were.

The rabbit chasing the rabbit—with a big wolf somewhere behind them both.

Chapter 30

Stuck in a Cave

I still hadn't taken a shower since getting home, so I took the opportunity at the Sylvan Inn. The room had only cost thirty bucks, and I was beginning to learn why. The water ran hot and cold when any toilet in the complex flushed, the shower curtain was ripped and moldy, and the bar of soap in the shower was unwrapped and used. But compared to the canyon, this was indeed a sylvan paradise, even if I did have to open a window to let the steam out. A shower? Hot water? An actual bed that had no rocks or scorpions or rattlesnakes? Ah, civilization.

I had just gotten out of the hot/cold shower and was drying off with a towel the size of a washcloth when somebody knocked on the door. An alarm went off in the back of my mind, but I knew Ross could handle it. About ten seconds later he opened the bathroom door and said that we had a visitor who wanted to see us both. He opened the door a little wider to reveal a stranger behind him with a gun in his left hand. I stepped out and threw on some clothes.

The visitor was a large man, larger and stronger than Ross, though he appeared to be lithe and athletic. He had a military haircut and was almost certainly Native American. His face was lined with anger and experience. I knew this was the man Kevin had seen. Ross and I sat on the edge of a bed while the man pulled a wooden chair in front of the door and sat in it.

"First, you need to know that I will not use this gun unless you force me to. I am not here to harm you. I am here to ask you to do something."

"Ask or demand?" Ross said, unintimidated by the man or the weapon.

"When you hear what I have to say, I think you'll realize that it is in your best interests to do as I *suggest.*" He emphasized the last word, grimacing as he said it, implying that it was both a request and a demand. "I know you have been to the cave, so don't deny it. I watched you, Mr. Call, crawl in through a small passageway at the south side of the main entrance."

"Which is closed off," Ross declared.

"Which is closed off," the man repeated, "and has been for over a hundred years."

"But, how did you see us?" I asked. "We were alone on that cliff."

"I was watching you from the time you saw the bighorn sheep. Remember them?"

I nodded.

"I was across the canyon watching your movements through a digital telescope."

"That has to be six or seven miles away," Ross said.

"Eight or nine." He looked at Ross. "Why did you not go in?"

Ross glanced at me, silently inquiring if he should answer. I nodded.

"The hole was too small. I couldn't get in."

The man looked over and sized me up, then nodded, accepting this possibility. "I assume you found the mummies, Mr. Call?"

"Yes."

"Then you know how Keith Nelson got the artifacts."

"Yes. One of the mummies had been opened."

"You mean defiled."

"Yes—he should've left it alone."

"He shouldn't have gone in at all. But now we have a problem— bigger than you know."

"Who are you?" Ross demanded. "Who sent you?"

The man's mouth turned downward into something I would normally call a frown but soon learned was how he smiled. "You probably think it's the government. You probably think this is all a big conspiracy."

"Isn't it?" Ross replied.

The man shook his head and frowned/smiled again. "Not like you think—but because of you, I no longer have a job. Because of you, my life is in danger as much as yours is. The people who emptied the cave were from a private organization, but they had close ties with the government. One of their members was placed in charge of the cave by the secretary of the Smithsonian, who was acting under the authority of the president. This man saw an opportunity to satisfy some pressing personal needs, and he brought in a gang to empty the cave. Unfortunately, as far as I know, none of those artifacts ended up in the Smithsonian. That happened in 1909, and over the years most of the artifacts were sold on the black market. Maybe some remain with the group who did this, I don't know. What I do know is that this organization wants to keep the cave a secret, and they are willing to kill to do so."

"Are you the one," I asked, "who killed Keith Nelson?"

He didn't answer.

"And who bugged my phones and computer?"

He still didn't answer.

"And who put the tracking sensors on our vehicles?" Ross added.

"My bosses paid me to follow your movements. That's all I'll say."

"Did you bug my office downtown too?"

"Your life's an open book, Mr. Call. I was hired to prevent you from going to the authorities. So, did you go to the cops yet?"

Ross was going to let me answer this. I made a snap decision to be honest.

"No, we haven't told anybody."

"Except your family of course."

I didn't answer this, which was answer enough.

He stood up, went to the window, parted the curtain, and glanced through it. He walked to the door, made sure it was locked, then went back to the chair and stood behind it. The massive gun, which was all black, seemed to weigh heavily in his left hand. As I looked closer, I saw that it was elongated by a suppressor screwed onto the barrel.

"So, who's the organization that did all this?" Ross asked.

"I'm not going to tell you that. If all goes well, maybe they'll have use for me again. But I'll say this, as far as I know, the government, even the Smithsonian, knows nothing about this. The employees there today know nothing about the cave or the mummies or anything else, so if you asked them why they're keeping all this a secret, they'll say they don't know what you're talking about—which is the truth. People have been killed to keep this quiet. They were willing to pay me six figures to stop you from coming out of that canyon with the knowledge you have. If you had come out the way you went in, I would have been waiting for you on the trail below Lipan Point, and you wouldn't have known what hit you."

If Ross wasn't humbled before, that should have done it. It certainly did it for me.

"So, tell me, how'd you get out? Did you climb out over the rim above the cave?"

I nodded, and Ross said, "Yeah. There's, like, a hidden chimney in the back of the canyon. It's pretty steep, but you can do it."

"And then you walked—where? Not back to your truck. That's too far."

"No," Ross said, "to a gas station on the highway. Then we caught a ride back to the truck."

He almost produced a real smile, the creases around his mouth lifting slightly. "That's a long hike, but that maneuver saved your lives. But now we have a bigger problem."

"Bigger than saving our lives?" I asked.

"Now they want to kill me too—because I didn't kill you."

He let this hang in the air as he stepped around the chair and sat down again. He was a dozen feet away from us, with the other bed between us. Surprising him by leaping over it was not a possibility. I hoped Ross wouldn't try anything.

"They want to kill you," I said, "because you let us get out of the canyon with proof of the cave."

"Actually, they don't know what you have—just that you've been there. But they assume you have proof. Do you?"

Again, I decided to tell the truth, since he could easily check my phone and laptop. "Yes, I took pictures outside and inside the cave."

"Even of the mummies?"

"Yes."

"Let me see them."

As I went to the gallery in my phone, he said, "I've never seen inside it, and actually, I don't think the people I worked for have either. I don't think they even knew about the hole you guys found. So, how'd you find it?"

"Something on a letter that Ephraim Wells wrote to his brother," I said. "It gave us a clue."

He pointed to the bed between us. "Throw the phone there. You don't need to worry—I'm not going to hurt you, unless you try something stupid."

I tossed the phone on the bed, and he picked it up, and, using his thumb, scrolled through the pictures. "What are these symbols?" He showed me the screen with the hieroglyphics above the dark part of the cave.

"They were on a ledge way back inside the cave. They looked like they were Egyptian or something, so I took a couple of pictures of them."

"Egyptian—or Mormon?" he asked.

I was astonished. There was no way he could've known this. "Why do you ask?"

"I know you guys are Mormon. That nanny of yours runs down to the church with your kids about twice a day. And I'll tell you something else; one of the reasons, maybe the main reason, the Smithsonian guy wanted to shut the cave down and keep it secret was because the guy who found it, Kinkaid, thought some of the writings inside it proved that Mormonism was true. So, what do you think— are these some of those writings?"

Ross waited for me to answer. "I don't know. Somebody should go back and find out."

"Like you?"

I remained silent.

"Are these all the pictures you have?"

"Yes."

He underhanded the phone back to me, and I caught it with both hands.

"It's not much," he said, "but it might be enough."

"For what?" Ross asked.

"So, here's the deal." He looked at me, "I want you to go public as soon as possible. I want you to tell the cops, call the paper, go online. Give the world all the proof you have."

Ross and I exchanged a look. "Why?" I asked.

"Because," Ross now said, his mouth breaking into a grin, "he thinks if we go public, the dudes he works for won't be able to kill him."

"Or you. Or your family," the man said calmly. "The scrutiny would be too much. This will be a big story, and besides—" His mouth turned down into that strange half smile. "I don't even know why they care if people find out about it. As far as I know, nobody can link them to the cave—unless there are some documents hidden in a government vault somewhere. And things hidden in the government are usually lost forever. And if nobody can link my bosses to the cave, then people would just blame the government for keeping it secret, but that would die down after a while. And then they could set up a visitors' bureau and make billions. Of course, the Hopis wouldn't like that."

He stopped and stared into space, then a light seemed to come on. "No wonder they don't want it to get out—the Hopis know who did it. They have the knowledge."

"And so do you," Ross said.

"Yeah. Okay, so that's my plan, either you go public immediately or somebody, maybe even me, is going to eliminate your family. Will you do it, yes or no?"

I almost laughed. "Uh, *yes*, but I'd like to talk to my wife first and let her know. This will impact her and the whole family."

"Yes, it will—either way."

A sound in the parking lot caught his attention, and he turned toward the window. He was about to part the curtain again but stopped and went to the light switch and flicked the lights off. "Don't move."

He went to the far side of the window and peered through the curtain. A car door had closed, but it may have closed too softly for him.

"How'd they find me?" He was almost whispering to himself.

"Who? The government?" Ross asked.

"No—higher than the government."

He was still looking out the window, cracking the curtain open with one hand and holding the gun with the other. "What's in the bathroom?" he asked, still looking out the window.

"What do you mean?" Ross asked.

"Is there a window?"

"Yeah," I said, "I had to open it to let the steam out—but it's small."

He glanced back, and his eyes rested on Ross. "Hopefully not too small."

"Why?" Ross asked.

"Because a red Yukon just parked across the street, and it's the same Yukon that was following me today. And there's another vehicle that wasn't here when I drove up." Something outside the window caught his eye, and he turned that way. "Do you have any weapons?"

"No," I said.

He glanced back, either to see if I were lying or to shame me for my lack of preparedness. "Well, there are four men outside—that I know of. Two of them are the guys I ran into earlier. I don't know the other two, but they're probably smarter."

He turned and walked by us to the bathroom. He stopped in the doorway and stared at the window. "Yeah, it's small—but maybe big enough." He opened it all the way and looked out into the alley. A whiff of something foul came in through the window. He stepped on the toilet, which was about a foot from the wall, and bent over and stuck his head out the window. He looked both ways. "If you want to live, follow me. They're gonna come running around the corner in about thirty seconds."

Holding his gun in his left hand, he pushed himself out the window to his waist then stopped. There was nothing to break his fall. Ross went over and held his legs and eased him down until he was doing a handstand in some green foxtails under the window. Ross let go, and the man slowly, almost gracefully, settled to the ground. Moments later we heard a ZIP.

Ross looked down then jumped back. "He's shooting at something! They found him already!" Ross rushed by me and went back into the bedroom. I followed and saw him looking up at an access panel fitted into the ceiling. It was about three feet by eighteen inches and was positioned above and slightly to the left of a low dresser. Ross jumped up on the dresser, no small feat, and crouched under the ceiling, waiting to see if the old piece of furniture would crumble under his weight. Its four legs were thimble-sized, but somehow they held. He pushed up on the panel with his back and shoulder, grunted, and pushed harder. It had been painted shut, but it finally gave. Ross tossed it up into the attic then stood up and poked his head inside. Then he nodded at me, and, without saying a word, jumped up, grabbed an angled truss in the attic, and pulled himself through the hole.

Leaving me alone in the room.

Somebody knocked on the door.

Two more ZIPS ripped through the alley. I scrambled up on the dresser as fast as I could. My legs had been cramping from fatigue off and on, but they held up just fine now. I looked into the attic. Ross was standing on a cross beam on the far side of a truss, holding his hand out to me. I looked up to see what he had grabbed when he jumped, but it was too high for me to reach.

Another, more insistent, knock rattled the door.

I jumped and grabbed Ross's right hand, and he pulled me sideways, raking my side against the edge of the access panel. I quickly grabbed the truss with my other hand and pulled myself up.

The room shook. Somebody was trying to break the door down.

Ross pointed at the plywood panel he had tossed aside. It was by my feet. I grabbed it and fit it into the opening just as the door burst open.

It was dark, but I could make out old rafters and a thin layer of gray insulation at our feet. The place had been built in the fifties or sixties—old but solid. And probably laced with asbestos. It was also stiflingly hot.

A voice boomed out below. "Bathroom! Go!"

Another voice yelled from the bathroom, "He's gone!"

"Is he in the alley?"

"No. He's *gone!*"

So the big guy had escaped somehow, which didn't surprise me. Ross and I both knew what we had to do.

Stay absolutely still.

He was balancing on a 4-by-6 beam, which seemed sturdy enough, but he had to remain absolutely still to keep the old boards silent. I had one foot on the cross member of the truss, the lowest part of the triangle, and my other foot on the frame of the access panel. When I put all my weight on the access frame, it flexed, so I tried to keep most of my weight on the truss. Very awkward. I held onto the upper part of the truss with my right arm while balancing my weight, which, fortunately, was some twenty pounds lighter than it had been, between the truss and the access panel.

"How'd they get out?" the first voice cried.

"I don't know!"

"Look under the beds!"

A new voice came from the bathroom, probably shouting in through the window. "He was out here! He ran down the alley. Come on!"

"Did you shoot him?" the first voice called.

"No, he was shooting at *us!*"

"Hold on!" the first voice said. He seemed to be in charge. "What about the others?"

"There weren't any others."

"Were you *watching?*"

"Course! Till he started shooting! He had a silencer. We had to take cover. They prob'ly ran out with him."

I prayed that the men didn't see the access panel and get ideas. Moments later it sounded like they ran out of the room. The door shut, but we couldn't tell if it latched. We remained frozen in the nearly unbearable heat, both of us sweating and shifting our balance from foot to foot. When it had been quiet for a few minutes, Ross put his hand through the truss again and whispered, "Okay, come on over."

I took his hand and wormed my way through the truss, where my feet found relief on the flat, solid beam. Had I taken the opportunity to join Kalley in her gymnastics classes, I might have even lay on it. I rubbed my thighs with one hand while holding onto the truss with the other.

A minute later we heard muffled voices, too soft to make out. Then the door shut again. Our eyes were fully adjusted to the dark now, and we could make out tiny cracks under the eaves where light streamed in from streetlights. I checked the corners for rats and large spiders but saw only old boards and gray insulation.

"Ross," I whispered, "I gotta sit down. My legs are cramping."

"Yeah, I think we should get out of here anyway." He stepped through the truss and kneeled over the access panel. There was no handle or pull-rope on this side of it, so he had to work his fingers under it before lifting one corner and sneaking a peek. The room was empty, but we could still hear voices in the parking lot. He lay the panel back down and shook his head. *Not yet.*

I looked down at the beam I was on and the bottom of the truss, which was about two feet away, and wondered if I could lay myself across them, but I knew my weight would press on the insulation between them, which would put pressure on the sheet rock in the ceiling, which might cause the whole thing to fall into the room. Ross could see I was in pain, and he started marching through the trusses toward the far wall, where the attic joined another room. A moment later he waved me over, and I made my way through the trusses and saw what he had found—two beams joined together where the rooms met. It was almost a foot wide. I was about to sit down, but he held his hand up, then he grabbed some of the pieces of insulation and lay them across the two beams. He extended his hand toward the bed he had made. I gratefully sat down, felt relief spread through my legs and back. Then, slowly, I lay on my back.

It was heaven. For a while.

Maybe half an hour later we heard loud pounding on the door. They weren't knocking, they were nailing the broken door shut. More than likely the manager had called a maintenance guy to close it for the night.

It was after midnight before the room was silent again, and my back was aching from lying on the twelve-inch beam. Ross checked through the access panel again. The coast seemed to be clear. He waved me over, then he went down first. He checked the door, which was in fact nailed shut. He came back and helped me down to the dresser, then to the floor.

We hustled back to the bathroom and opened the window, which somebody had shut. The alley was empty. I helped him out first, then he helped me out. Whatever stunk up the alley was stronger than ever. I cast about, looking for a body. Nope. Hunching over, we made our way out of the alley, turned a corner, and, after watching the parking lot for a minute, walked over to the truck.

But would it work? Had the huge Indian disabled it? Ross turned the key and three hundred horses whinnied to life. He smiled. "Where to, boss?"

We drove a mile away and got another room in another cheap motel, where I once again used cash. The manager seemed suspicious.

"No credit card? So sorry, meester. That will be another feevteen bucks—cash."

I forked it over. My wallet was getting thinner.

Ross asked where we might find some M-80s.

The clerk pretended not to know, until Ross showed him his own wad of cash and promised that he was not a cop. But even then the man only suggested we go see his good friend next door. Ross took his cash next door, while I went to our room, wondering if we should go back home and get more clothes. We had left most of our possessions at the other place when we skedaddled. Half an hour later, Ross came back with both the ordnance and our stuff.

"Did you go back to the room?" I asked, surprised.

He gave me a Cheshire grin.

"How? Did you crawl back in through the window?"

"It was easier going back in. I didn't feel like donating my clothes to the motel."

The firecrackers consisted of twelve M-80s and six M-250s. "How much did it end up costing?" I asked.

"Too much. I had to get more cash from the ATM, but this should move some rocks." I was getting tired, but Ross seemed revived, almost hyper.

"I'm not sure we lost those guys."

"What—did you see them?"

"There's a couple of guys in a truck. But I don't know if it's the same guys."

"What do you want to do?"

"I don't know. We can't go home."

"Nope."

His eyes were clear, wide awake.

"Do you think we should just go," I offered.

"I don't know—what about Anna?"

"I'll text her."

"But that guy said they bugged everything."

"Even our cell phones?"

"Maybe."

"All right. I'll call Kevin—from the desk."

Ross nodded, and we walked down the sidewalk to the office, taking the opportunity to check the vehicles for occupants. Ross noted where the truck was. Two guys were in it, watching us, but they didn't get out. We got to the office, and I explained that I needed to use their phone, which, for twenty bucks, the guy allowed. Everything around here had a price. He brought the black rotary phone up from under the counter. Putting my finger in the holes and turning the dial was almost disorienting.

"Kevin," I said, after getting him on the fifth ring. He was probably playing a game. "Can I talk to Mom?"

"Did you find 'em yet?"

"No, well, yeah, but we didn't talk to them. Is your mom there?"

"Why didn't you call *her* phone?"

"Because I'm being sneaky. You know, so the bad guys can't listen in."

"Oh. Yeah. Here she is."

"Anna," I said when she answered, "Ross and I have already run into some guys who are after us. We can't go back home. And you shouldn't go there either."

"What? Where are you?"

"Don't worry. We're okay, but we had to evade some guys. Look, whatever you . . ."

261

"*What?* You had to *evade* some guys? Were they chasing you? Were guns involved?"

She always asked the tough questions.

"Don't worry about that. But we can't meet at the house tomorrow, okay? It's too dangerous. Just stay where you are. Ross and I have got to go back." *(I knew I had made a mistake.)*

"Go *back?* Where?" She paused, and I could tell that she was thinking up more hard questions. "To the *canyon?* Are you kidding? You just got back from there, and you lost, like, twenty pounds. Tell me what's going on."

"Actually, more like twenty-five now. I'm losing weight by the minute."

"Travis! Wake up!" The bad guys didn't need to tap our phones. Her voice probably carried to Turlock. "You two should not go to the canyon. I'm calling Johnson. This is *crazy!*"

"No! Do not call Johnson. That's the last thing you want to do."

"Why?"

"Because they may have a mole."

"Who?"

"The bad guys—who else?"

"Is Ross there? Let me talk to him."

I thought that was a valid idea, and I handed him the old Bakelite phone.

"Hello?" he said tentatively. A shrill voice came from the earpiece. I turned around, trying not to listen. Finally Ross said, "Yeah, you're right, we probably have all the proof we need, but he wants to get something else . . . I can't tell you what it is . . . No, it's not the jewelry. We don't need to get anything from the mummies . . . Anna, nobody's going to kill us." He listened to the tinny voice for another few moments, then said: "Hey, wait, I have a great idea—I'm going to let you talk to your husband again. Bye."

I was almost to the door when he caught me. I put the ancient earpiece to my ear but remained silent. It didn't fool her. "Why do you need to go to the canyon? Ross says you have all the proof you need."

"Yes, but . . ."

"No 'yes buts.' You two come to our motel."

"We don't know where you are."

"Guess what? We're on the phone—I can tell you." She had been reduced to sarcasm.

"No," I pleaded, "don't tell me where you are, just in case we get found again. But make sure Kevin and Kalley keep their phones charged. I doubt their phones are tapped."

"For that matter," she said, "Rosemary's phone is probably good too."

"Right. Probably. Well, I gotta go. I'm using somebody else's phone here, and it cost me, like, twenty bucks. We're going now. I'll call you when I can."

"Travis! Don't hang up." She paused. "Are you still there?"

"Yes."

"*Really?* You were just going to hang up and not let me know who these guys are or what happened?"

"I don't know who they are, except, they may not be from the government, and what they want is to keep everything quiet about the cave. Except one guy. He wants us to go public, because if we all go public, maybe they can't kill us all."

"*What!*"

"I mean, okay, we'll talk again later. But stay quiet for now. Don't go anywhere."

"Travis—"

"What?"

"Never mind. I was going to say, where would I be going, since there's probably a gang of cold-blooded murderers looking for us right now? But I won't say that. I'll just say, please be careful. And, Travis?"

"Yes?"

"I love you."

No finer words have ever been said.

"I love you, too, Anna. And thank you for understanding."

"I don't understand anything. Just, please, be careful."

We hung up.

The manager had a concerned look, and I gave him the phone. "Thanks." I began walking to the door.

"Wait!" he cried. "Will they come after me too? Do they have my number?"

"Who?"

"Whoever will kill you!"

"I hope not. They're bad news." I went out the door. Ross followed and shut the door firmly.

Things were getting out of control.

We checked for the truck with the two guys in it, but it was gone. Maybe it was just two random guys, but constantly checking our mirrors, we drove to a Walmart in Ceres and bought new supplies: Two new packs, flashlights, head lamps, batteries, water, food, sunscreen, and, on a notion, two digital cameras. Ross also bought a pair of heavy-duty cargo pants that had more pockets than a pool table. He put them on in the restroom, filled the pockets with half of our new stuff, and came out looking like an upside-down hot air balloon. He said he liked the versatile pants so much he might start wearing them all the time.

Things were definitely getting out of control.

Chapter 31

A Terrifying Light Within

It had been a close call. The two new guys after him were probably more competent than the goons on Highway 99, but still they should have covered the back window before approaching the room's front door. He got lucky; if the window hadn't been big enough to crawl through, there would have been a blood bath. Klah needed to figure out how they had tracked him.

He also needed to figure out where Call and Keller had gone. Initially he thought they had been captured by the four men, but later when he circled back he saw the four men out front —and no Call or Keller. Their truck was still in the lot, so they hadn't driven off, but somehow the two had disappeared. Fortunately before knocking on the door of their room, he had placed another tracking device on the steel frame of Ross Keller's F-150.

Whislin Klah always tried to think ahead.

And because he thought ahead, he doubled back to Call's house to see if they had gone there. The house was dark, and he thought it was empty, then he saw a dim light in one of the upstairs' windows. Then it traveled to another window. Somebody was searching the house.

He parked around the corner, figuring his pursuers would soon be following. He went in through the same gate and window he had snuck in through before. Once in Call's office, he stopped to listen but heard nothing. Gun in hand, he quietly stalked up the stairs.

A soft noise came from the room where the boy had been watching with binoculars. The door was open. He snuck a peek inside and saw a short, thin man wearing dark clothes and gloves, rummaging through a dresser drawer. When Whislin caught a glimpse of gold, wire-rim spectacles, he knew who it was.

"We meet again, professor."

Richardson wheeled around, surprised. But he recovered quickly. "Oh, it's just you. I was hoping you would show up."

Klah smiled with real amusement. "What a nice coincidence; I was hoping *you* would show up." He closed the door. "But tell me, professor, why did you want me to stay home in Flagstaff?"

Richardson closed the drawer and took a step back. If he had a weapon, Klah couldn't see it, but that meant nothing. He remembered that the man had picked the lock in his front door a couple of times. Richardson looked helpless, but Klah doubted the man would be here without some form of protection.

"Oh, that," Richardson said with a wry smile. "Like I said, we had another team coming in to mop up. We didn't want you to muddy the waters."

"So, you don't know who the two guys are who followed me up the freeway, or the two other guys who tried to shoot me a few minutes ago?"

Richardson took his glasses off and polished them on his sleeve. "Actually, I do. We've been following you from the beginning. We were following you even before you signed on. You don't think we would hire you without knowing where you went and what you did, do you? The second time you came to my office, I—we—because others were listening—I gave you a bottle of water to drink. Do you recall that?"

Klah thought back to his several visits to the professor's office. He had a little fridge in the corner where he kept snacks and drinks. He didn't recall the professor handing him a bottle of water, but he doubted the man was lying. "No."

"Well, you drank it all, finished it, for which we were grateful. Do you mind if I sit down?" Richardson pointed at a chair by a built-in desk in the corner. Klah motioned with the gun for him to sit down.

"So you gave me a bottle of water. What was in it?"

"Oh, nothing. But from the empty container we accessed your DNA. And with that, we developed a tracking device meant only for you."

A chill went up Klah's spine.

"It was our military's newest development at the time. I say military, but it actually originated with our intelligence services,

266

though the military had begun deploying it in sensitive areas. Have you heard of nanobots?"

"A micro-sized robot."

"Right. Our side has miniaturized them to the point that they can exist inside a person's blood stream—without the person knowing. They are less than one millionth of a meter in diameter. And this particular nanobot is designed to do something very unique—to draw electrical energy from your body and occasionally send pulses of high frequency light outward. One bot's pulse is very weak, but thousands create a pulse strong enough to be detected over a quarter mile away."

Klah dreaded where this was going. "Detected by what?"

"By any normal cell tower. Essentially, Whislin, every time you passed a cell tower, we knew where you were. And because the nanobots have been engineered to mesh with your DNA, your body will never expel them. Some will end up in your liver, some in your kidneys, some, who knows?"

Klah didn't doubt the professor. He had heard of such weapons while in the SEALS. "So, you're saying that your people know where I am right now."

"Yes, of course. They may be outside as we speak."

Klah kept the gun on him while he stepped to the window and peered out. Nothing. He went back to the door and cracked it open and listened for noises in the house. "All right," he said, motioning with the gun. "Let's go."

The professor stood up and went out the door ahead of Klah. They went down to Call's office, where the window was still open.

"Is this how you came in?" Richardson asked. "They have cameras, you know. They'll identify you."

"They already know me. Being identified is the least of my worries. Out. Now."

Richardson climbed out into the night, followed by Klah. They went to the gate, and Whislin scanned the front. Still no new cars. He pushed Richardson from behind then grabbed him by the sleeve of his dark coat and began running with him. They ran across the front yard and down around the corner. Still jogging, they reached the Jeep. Klah unlocked it and pushed him in, and moments later they were moving down the road. As Klah turned a corner, he saw headlights behind him, but they turned onto Call's street. A red SUV. The idiots still hadn't changed vehicles. He hoped they would search the house before checking their technology, if it was portable, to see where he was.

"Tell me," he said, "when you hired this second crew, where'd you find them?"

"I'm not at liberty to say."

"Well, just so you know, the first two are morons, and the other two are idiots."

"I don't doubt it—but they were the best we could find on short notice. You were one of our best, Whislin. If you just hadn't failed on such an important mission. And I mean that sincerely. To the extent that you failed, I failed. To the extent that you pay, I pay."

"So that's why you're out here—trying to patch things up."

"Trying to save my life."

"So, what's the deal, has Call gone to the cops?"

"Not that we know of. Nor have they gone public. Things are still quiet. And they need to stay that way. But we can't find the family, and we recently lost track of Call and Keller."

Klah got on his phone and pulled up the app that was tracking Ross Keller's truck. The green icon was motoring down 99 southbound. Fast.

"May I ask where we're going?" Richardson asked.

"Following Call and Keller."

"And where are they going?"

"Where do you think?"

Richardson studied Klah's inscrutable face. "Back to the canyon? Why?"

"Who knows? Maybe they forgot something. So, we've got some business to attend to, you and I. And we've got about ten hours to do it in."

"What's that?"

"First, when I was hunkered down on the North Rim, waiting for our two boys to find the cave, I had some time to do some thinking, and I could see the writing on the wall. I could see that something like this would eventually happen. Someday I'd screw up. So I made a decision and did some writing. And when the boys got away, I went home and put a small package together. You'll be interested to know that the package included photographs of the cave, complete with GPS coordinates, and a copy of Kinkaid's story, and, of course, my own account of what the Society—*your* Society—did to the cave in 1909, including the theft of thousands of artifacts. It also tells of a conspiracy to keep the cave secret. Your name is prominent, of course, since it's the only name I have. But to be fair, I tried to make it clear that most of the blame goes to the boys above you—the Bonesmen."

Richardson nodded his head. "And what did you do then?"

"What any good, self-interested criminal would do; I put it in an envelope and put that envelope in a bigger envelope, and then I stuck on a lot of stamps and addressed it to a lawyer—someone I knew in the service. Inside the big envelope is a cover letter. I bet you know what it says."

"Oh, let's see, something like 'In the event of my death, please open the enclosed envelope.'"

Klah raised his heavy, black eyebrows. "Very good, but it was more like, 'In the event you don't hear from me on any given Monday, please open the enclosed package and see that copies of it are sent to the FBI, the National Park Service, and ICE.'" Klah let that hang in the air as he checked his rearview mirror. He had ripped the side mirror off before going to Call's house.

"And what did you do with this time bomb?"

"I waited, mostly to see if my suspicions about you and the Society were correct. I mean, why solve a problem if it doesn't exist? Plus, the lawyer isn't doing this for free. Then when you told me to stay home, that another team was coming in to clean up the mess, I knew that *another* team was on its way to Flagstaff. You would have been proud of how fast I got out of that condo and down to the post office."

Richardson pursed his tiny lips and nodded again, as if pleased with the man's foresight. His thin, gold-rimmed glasses shined in the dashboard's amber light. "That was very resourceful of you."

"I thought so, and that's why it was so nice to find you in Call's house, so I could explain our new situation in person."

"I see. So, now what do you want to do?"

"That should be self-explanatory. I want you to make a call to your friends to explain the new situation."

"Yes, of course. When?"

"Now, if you don't mind. Why do you think I let you keep your phone?"

Richardson obediently pulled his phone from his pants' pocket, entered several numbers from memory then looked at Klah while it connected. "They'll want some proof, of course, that you actually mailed the package."

"I thought they might—which is why I sent it by registered mail. I have the receipt in my wallet. I'll be happy to text them a copy at the appropriate time."

"Of course even a receipt won't prove what was inside the envelope."

"They'll just have to trust me on that. Or not."

Someone answered the phone, and Richardson spoke into it.

"Yes, I know it's late . . . We have a problem . . . Yes, a bigger one. I'm with Klah right now, as his *guest*."

Klah listened carefully as Richardson explained the new situation. Whislin hadn't really mailed a "time bomb" to a lawyer, but it didn't really matter so long as they thought he had. As for the receipt, he would make sure no one ever looked in his wallet while he was alive. He looked at his speedometer; they were flying through the night at 84 miles an hour. Even if the hitmen didn't find him, the California Highway Patrol might. He backed off to 79. Richardson said good-bye and disconnected.

"They're getting the council together," he said. "But in the meantime, no promises."

Klah laughed. "Promises? I don't want promises. I want mutually assured destruction. I want them to know that they're dead if they kill me. I'll let you in on a little secret: A couple of hours ago I told Call and Keller to go public as soon as they can."

"You *what?*"

"I figured if the word is already out, why would the Society kill me?"

"Because you're an inside source—because you might be able to identify them. If Call and Keller go public, you just signed your own death warrant."

"Not necessarily. The public won't know who I am, and they won't know who you are, or who's behind the whole conspiracy to keep the cave secret. The only thing that would be public would be the cave, and the Society could stay in the dark forever. Think about it, what harm does it do? Haven't they already made their money from it?"

Richardson thought for a moment then said, "Maybe it would work, unless the Smithsonian has records of what happened."

"But that would implicate the Smithsonian as much as you guys. Even more so, since they were in charge of it. Besides, it's been over a hundred years. If they had any records, they probably would have produced them by now. I think you were right—Walcott, or whatever his name was, was so scared that his beloved religion might be compromised that he made sure there was no trail between the Institution and the Society. He protected himself on all fronts.

"Maybe. So, why haven't Call and Keller gone public?"

"Maybe they have. Maybe they're on the phone right now with the New York Times."

"We would know it if they were."

"Unless they went to Walmart and bought a burner phone."

Richardson said nothing.

"But," Klah continued, "I think they've been busy. So, maybe there's a better way to resolve our problem, our *mutual* problem."

Richardson glanced at him. "What are you thinking?"

"All in good time."

In Fresno they stopped to fill up. Klah figured he was still ahead of any men trailing him, since they would have to stop for gas too. But from his phone he could tell that he was at least an hour behind Call and Keller. He tried to anticipate their next moves. Had they left something behind in the canyon? Yes, their tent and gear, but that made no sense; they had money, and this was a hard, 24-hour round trip. They were going back for something important, something crucial. Did they want more evidence? He had seen their photos and knew they already had enough to get an investigation started. The pictures of the mummies alone would do that. Whatever the reason, he and Richardson would follow them as quickly as possible. The Society knew he had Richardson and could call in favors from law enforcement ahead. If vehicles came up behind him, he would have to act quickly—and wisely. He checked his gun, down in the door to his left—his good hand.

He had no illusions. If Call went public, or even if Klah eliminated both men and then intimidated the family into silence, his life would still be in jeopardy. The Society would always know his location, and, in spite of the supposed package, they would never trust him. They would monitor every phone call and text and communication he made, and when they discovered that he wasn't contacting a lawyer each week, he would be quietly eliminated. He had just obligated himself to call a lawyer every week. And he may have also just doomed that lawyer to an early death.

But in the meantime, maybe he could buy some time.

He noticed that Richardson was smiling, looking out the window. Klah checked to see if a vehicle had caught up with them. But they were alone on the road.

Then he saw a cell tower pass by on Richardson's side.

He pushed harder on the accelerator.

Chapter 32

Holy, Holy, Holy

We got gas and important fast foods in Bakersfield, then Ross handed me the keys. It was the first time I'd driven his truck. It handled just like a lifted 4x4 should—rough, loud, and loose. I drove into the dawn and got us to Flagstaff, where we turned left on Highway 89. About an hour later we turned into the parking lot at the gas station/store we had stumbled into half dead not forty-eight hours earlier. It was late morning, and the same clerk was there. I half expected him to run over to guard the hot dog rotisserie. But all we needed was some gas and a couple of cold Gatorades. When we paid, he asked, "Going back to the canyon?"

"Yeah," I said, "but we're driving this time."

His brow furrowed with concern. "Not over the rim?"

"No," I laughed. "That would be crazy."

His eyes narrowed as we exited. Crazy was a relative term.

We had already plotted a course westward over the dirt roads to the rim above Marble Canyon. There were dips and potholes and washouts aplenty, but since we had put everything in the back seat and had nothing bouncing around in the bed, we were able to make good time—especially since Ross was driving again. I never would have pounded the truck so hard.

The farther we drove into the dun-colored wasteland, the more I was impressed by two thoughts: first, that it was amazing that we had walked so far with almost no food or water in a single night, and, second, that if the truck broke down now, we'd have to do it all over again. The place was bleaker by the light of day.

Memories of my Hopi friend stole into my thoughts. Had he been real or a dream? And what did he mean by a sacred corner? Maybe I'd fall asleep again and he'd return and explain it all, but sleep was something I was getting precious little of lately.

The twenty miles that had taken all night to walk took less than an hour now.

We stopped on the last dirt road, about seventy yards from the rim. We couldn't see into the canyon, but we could see the red and green cliffs of the far wall almost ten miles away—red with ancient limestone and green with spring foliage. We got out, filled the packs with our supplies, locked the truck, said a prayer, and began walking back to the oven.

* * *

A few miles past Willow Springs, Klah had pulled to within a mile of the truck and forced himself to slow down. Soon he noticed that they had stopped again. He zoomed in on his GPS and saw that they had pulled in at a gas station. From a slight rise, he actually saw the tall roadside sign ahead. It made sense. They would get some last supplies and fill the tank before going cross-country. He pulled over to the shoulder and slowed to a stop. No sense in letting them see him.

Richardson had slept part of the way, which had left Klah free to do some thinking. He was in an unusual position. He was trailing two men—adversaries—who didn't know he was behind them. He had another adversary at his side, awake and alert now, and perhaps four more enemies behind him. He assumed they were close. Perhaps as close to him as he was to Call and Keller.

"What're we doing?" Richardson sat up straighter.

Klah didn't answer. The man had been docile so far, but Klah kept the Glock in the drink holder in his door, close by his left hand. He would not hesitate to shoot his old boss if he had to.

Richardson glanced out his window at the side mirror on the right, the one that worked, possibly looking for an SUV behind them.

"Don't worry," Klah said with a lilt in his voice, "they're not there." Without notice he pulled a U-turn across the road. "Change of plans," he said. "Now I know exactly where the boys are going and pretty much what they want to do, so I'll give them some time to get down to the cave, where you and I can have a little fun with them." He had rethought things again. With the four of them so close to the canyon, he saw a new solution to his problem—to a number of his problems.

He expanded the image on the GPS screen to see how long it would take to get to Tuba City. They had passed the turnoff several miles back. He had been there before and was pretty sure he knew where the hardware store was. He did some quick math and knew that the timing should be perfect.

* * *

As I had learned several times before, but had repeatedly forgotten, going down was often more dangerous than going up. The "chimney," as Ross had described it, was not a chimney at all, but a long, nearly vertical chute in the eastern wall that had random "steps" where erosion had gnawed away clumps of dirt. Some of these steps, of course, were only one or two years from eroding away themselves—and perhaps one or two seconds from collapsing when stepped on.

Ross descended into the time machine first, as I was lighter and could theoretically be stopped by his greater bulk if I fell. The truth was, of course, that we would both crash through any "step" he might be on at the moment and would scream in terror as we accelerated downward, and would continue screaming and writhing and seeing life reviews until we hit and discovered which reward we went to.

No wonder this place was off limits.

The trickiest part was figuring out whether to go down facing the wall or facing the great void. Ross went down facing the wall, but I attempted multiple positions, searching for the safest. In the end, I mostly slid down sideways.

When Ross got down to a small ledge, he reached up and helped me negotiate the steepest part of the drop. How had we come up this thing, in the dark?

"Thanks," I told him, "you probably saved some rocks down there from being crushed."

His lips almost parted into a smile.

The grade became gentler after that, and half an hour later we were at the cave. It was a little after one, and the sun had just discovered us and was focusing its attention on us. I began longing for the coolness of the cave.

But a thought had been bothering me all day.

The air portal had been hewed out of sheer stone by Native workers hundreds or thousands of years ago. Enlarging it so Ross could get through would not be an "enhancement," as Ross had suggested. It would, in fact, be a desecration. As we finally arrived at the sealed main entrance, I mentioned this moral crisis to Ross.

"I've been thinking the same thing."

We stood still, staring at the entrance that had been cemented shut with rocks and mortar. It was twelve feet tall, but we didn't know how thick it was. "Do you think it would be a desecration to take out part of *this* wall?" I asked. "I mean, it was made by murderers and thieves—not by Indians—and it's only a hundred years old."

"Yeah, I was wondering the same thing again."

"Good to know we're on the same page."

"Yeah—strange."

"Because I really want you in there with me. You won't believe how big it is."

"Then let's do this." He dug into his pack and found the cordless drill, along with the biggest masonry bit I owned. He inserted it and hit the trigger. A high-pitched whine, wholly foreign to these surroundings, except when somebody was falling through the atmosphere to his death, filled the upper reaches of Marble Canyon.

"Here goes—" He touched the spinning bit to the mortar and gave a gentle push. The bit sunk in like it was going through soft clay. The old mortar was more fragile than it looked. He inspected the hole then stepped back and unleashed a sudden mule kick to the stone next to the hole. The wall held. If he had kicked me like that, I might have gone *through* the wall.

"It has strong tensile strength," he said, "but it's easy to drill." He reached into one of his many pockets and pulled out an M-80. He measured it against the hole then put the spinning bit back in and worked it around to widen the hole. He was about to insert the firecracker, when I said, "Wait, drill more holes—try to weaken the mortar all the way around the stone first."

In less than a minute he had drilled a dozen more holes around a bowling ball-sized boulder. He put the firecracker in one of the holes and got the matches out.

"Wait," I said again. "Why don't you just drill around all the rocks you want to take out? Maybe more will get loose with just one explosion."

For the next ten minutes, he drilled holes twelve inches into the mortar around several small boulders. If they all fell out, we should have a hole big enough for us to crawl through.

Now he put the firecracker in a different hole, more central to the others, and lit the fuse. We stood back against the cliff, not knowing what to expect. The explosion was more muted than I expected, but we definitely saw movement in the rocks. After the dust and smoke cleared, Ross put his hands on one that was knee high and tried to shove it to one side. It budged, but not much. He shoved it the other way, and it moved again. He kicked it, and it moved a little more. After a few more kicks, it came out. He put his hands in the hole.

"Wow, feel that."

Cool air oozed out of the twelve-inch hole. "I know. We should've brought jackets."

It took three more firecrackers and another twenty minutes to create a hole large enough for Ross to crawl through.

We ate and drank some Gatorade, then we put our headlights on and made sure our packs were loaded properly. I turned my light on and was the first to crawl in, being careful not to cut myself on the jagged mortar. Ross pushed my pack in after me, then he pushed his in, which I pulled through. No need to leave our equipment out where an inquisitive sheep might try eating it. Ross stuck his head in and started squirming. It wasn't easy, but he got in.

He stood up and looked around. The illumination from our lights and daylight from the hole lit up the cave in a way I hadn't seen before. Ross's gaze immediately fell on the maze pictograph just inside the entrance.

"There's a lot of these," I said. Then I corrected myself. "Well, not a lot of pictures, but a lot of etchings and carvings. Most of them are letters or hieroglyphics above the doorways."

"That is," he said, searching for the right words, "absolutely beautiful." He stepped closer and felt the depth of the etching with his fingers. It was even more beautiful than I had recognized before, but we needed to hurry.

We started to saddle up, when Ross set his pack down and took out the drill and extra batteries. "No need to carry all this. We'll get it on the way back."

What a mistake.

We adjusted our headlamps and set off down the main hallway, walking briskly, ironically too briskly for Ross, who wanted to stop and take pictures of every image he found. We developed a routine where I slowed and he stopped and took a picture then hurried to catch up. I had one goal—to go to the deepest, darkest part of the cave, and we still had a mile or so to go.

One stop we had to make, however, was the room with the mummies. Once inside, I set my pack down and took out an electric lantern and set it in the middle of the large chamber. When Ross saw the tiers of mummies supported on individual ledges, he let out a low whistle.

"I saw the pictures, but I had no idea." He stood and stared, turning in a full circle. I went to the mummy Keith had opened. I had closed its dark wrapping before leaving, but I opened it again to show Ross what Keith had done.

"Do you know what's amazing?" he said. "That he didn't tear all of them apart to get as much loot as he could."

"I think he would have, but he had just climbed up from the river and knew what it would be like on the way down. If it was gold and silver, you know it weighed a ton."

I laid the flaps of the torn covering back across the mummy.

"Just a minute." Ross made an adjustment to his phone, then he began slowly turning in a circle again. I asked him if he was taking a video, but he said, "Yeah, that too, but it's also a 360-degree picture, you know, the kind you see online all the time."

I didn't know, but that was irrelevant. "If we want to get back to the truck before dark," I said, picking up the lantern, "we'd better hurry." I turned it off and put it back in my pack. Ross snapped his phone off and followed me out.

We went by the granaries, where he saw the kernels of corn, to the room over two football fields long that Ephraim Wells suggested was a dining room. We went deeper into the earth, and I showed him the many, many hallways branching off the main corridor, with hieroglyphics above most of the doorways. He stopped and took a few pictures, but we didn't explore them. Eventually the main passageway began to narrow, with the ceiling getting lower, and I experienced a palpable sense of claustrophobia that I hadn't noticed before, probably feeling it more this time because my light was stronger and I could sense the narrowing more clearly.

"What do you think happened?" Ross asked. "Do you think they just got tired of digging, or was there a purpose in making the tunnel smaller?"

"I think they found a natural cave back here when they were excavating, so they narrowed the corridor to match the width of the existing cave."

He sniffed the air. "What is that?"

"Wait till we get all the way back in there."

Our batteries were still strong, and we had new ones in the packs, so light would not be a problem unless we got stuck.

The walls began to converge more severely, and soon the floor began ramping up. Ross sniffed again and probed his light along the walls. "Ammonia and, what—sulfur?"

"Yep, but like I said, it gets stronger."

We were closer than I thought, and in another fifty yards we had to stop. The walls were completely unfinished, and in the brighter light I could see that it really was a natural cave, with the brownish walls laced with limestone and seams of beige-colored rock. The corridor was so narrow that Ross and I had to stand shoulder to shoulder. It had taken nearly an hour, but we finally faced the six-foot boulder blocking the path.

"The part that won't light up is just behind this rock." I found the little steps on the right side and went up first, still wearing my pack. Ross followed.

"Oh, wow!" he said when he reached the top. He was holding his hand over his mouth and nose. The ammonia-sulfur stench seemed stronger than when I had been here earlier, but it was probably just a factor of my being less exhausted.

"Don't worry," I said, "you don't get used to it."

Though I hoped we would.

"Now, watch this." I looked up, causing my headlamp to direct its light at the hieroglyphics chiseled into the stone ledge in front of us.

They stood out in bold relief, and again I realized how weak my light had been before. Then I realized that they weren't just chiseled into the stone, they were highlighted in faded gold, the color partially obscured by dust.

"Wow," he said softly, perhaps reverently. "They're beautiful—and they're bigger than I thought."

As our lights illuminated the characters above the chamber, they also threw light into the chamber beyond. It was still a well of blackness.

Granted, my headlamp only had three AA batteries and probably produced less than the 250 lumens the package warrantied, but the package also warrantied a beam that would reflect off a surface 110 meters away, or 360 feet, which is the distance of a football field including the end zones. How big was this place? I distinctly remembered my headlamp illuminating the far wall in the great hall, half a mile back, which was over two football fields in length.

Ross was still focusing on the characters. "You were right, some of those characters are almost *exactly* the same characters Joseph Smith wrote down."

I undid a Velcro flap over my shirt pocket and pulled out the paper I had grabbed in my office. A photocopy of the Anthon Transcript was on one side, and a copy of each character's translation was on the other.

I held it before us, and we compared it to the characters on the wall. "Yep, they're the same," Ross exclaimed, "except for—see the third one from the left, the four lines like pancakes on top of each other? Like you said, they're not in the transcript."

"So, are the others the same, are we just seeing what we want to see?"

Ross shook his head. "No, we're not making things up. Look at that H. Even its curlicues are the same in the transcript. And those two on the left, the two big dots that look like eyes, and the upside-down V—they're exactly the same. This would convince anybody that Joseph Smith was using the same language. I mean, how did he know which ancient Native American characters meant what he said they meant?" He turned and looked at me, his light pointing above my head so it didn't blind me. "You know what?"

"What?"

"I think the Church must be true."

We both laughed. Of course the Church was true—we both knew that by a process more convincing than mere historical proof—but these characters brought everything home in a way that was so simple and logical that it was almost *illogical*. A good member of the Church simply didn't expect to see actual proof of his faith chiseled in stone.

But we needed to find out what lay beyond. I put my pack down and pulled out the big lamp again. Ross pulled out two flashlights, and we turned them on and pointed them into the void.

And I almost stopped breathing.

And my knees began to buckle.

The cavern was indeed enormous, perhaps a quarter mile across, and perhaps half as deep, and half as high. Or, about a quarter mile wide and a quarter mile high. Icy blue stalagmites rose from the floor far below us and cream-colored stalactites hung from the ceiling in the far reaches above us. When my brain finally, almost unwillingly, accepted the distances involved, I realized that some of the formations had to be hundreds of feet tall—and perhaps a hundred feet across. I looked down, steeper, to an area just below us, and saw formations that looked like broad cups with fluted edges, some perhaps ten or even twenty feet across. I looked up to the ceiling above them and saw huge stalactites hanging down like inverted pyramids, streaked in creamy whites, pinks, and a few in icy blues, and I realized that large drops of mineral-rich water had dripped off and formed the massive splash "cups" below. Over eons the minerals had formed the rims of the cups. The fluted edges were the results of splashes going higher in some places and lower in others. In effect, the cups were the perfect results of billions of these heavy splashes. Even under our poor lights, over such distances, the sight was astonishing, beyond adequate description.

Was it possible that Ephraim Wells and those with him had never seen all this? I didn't know how strong their lamps had been, but I knew that no one had written about it.

At some point my knees did buckle, because I found myself kneeling, with tears wetting my face in the purest awe I have ever known. To see known physics rendered irrelevant by flowing giant curtains above you hundreds of yards long and hundreds of feet high, to see stalactites protruding from a roof like daggers the length of football fields, to see acres of calcium cups wide enough for trucks to park in, and to see all this and more as far as the light illuminated the cave, was both humbling and disorienting. I was pretty sure that when God pronounced his creations "good," this temple was at the top of his list.

The sight was so overwhelming that, for the moment, it muted the stench rising up from below. And, as I gazed into the miracle, the significance of the three boxes settled upon me. This place was indeed "Holy." Or, as it said on the ledge above us:

Holy, holy, holy.

Peaceable stirrings inside gave witness to silent truths. Everything before me was holy. It was a temple, the kind people might roll a huge stone in front of to protect. And I began to understand, in the slightest way, why I had felt not to make the cave public or even go to the authorities. This was sacred ground, not just to the Hopis, not just to Ephraim Wells, but to God.

Ross was stepping this way and that, looking over the sides. "How do we get down there?"

I wiped my face, composed myself, and joined him in the search for a way down. The cliff was nearly sheer, steeper than anything we had navigated so far. But again I looked into the cavern and was taken aback by it impossible size and beauty. "I never knew anything like this existed," I whispered, pointing to where the largest stalagmites stood like a forest. "Look at them—they're as tall as skyscrapers. And those stalactites hanging down are as long as redwoods. And did you see those cups down there? This place is a sacred, surreal, magical kingdom. It's what Yosemite and *Disneyland* could never be."

But he ignored me, and his eyes widened as he pointed down to our right. "Look!"

I followed his gaze down and saw a line of steps descending along the wall to our right, going down to the cavern floor. But the steps didn't come all the way up to us. They started about twenty-five feet below us and went down from there. And there didn't seem to be any way to them.

We put all the light we had on that area and saw that the steps were chiseled out of white limestone and appeared to be so pearly smooth that from this distance they resembled a marble staircase. And just a few feet above them, following them all the way down, we saw a handrail fixed in the wall. They went down until the steps eventually curled out of sight behind a giant stalagmite, the steps becoming miniaturized in the distance. Everything about this place defied logic.

But more important, how did we get down to the steps?

We had a hundred-foot coil of quarter-inch rope, which wasn't intended for climbing except in emergencies.

"I guess we could double up the rope and slide down it to the steps," I said, "but then we'd have to climb back up it to get out."

Ross said nothing for a moment, obviously considering the implications. *He* could climb up the rope—but what about his helpless friend? Whatever doubts he had, they were minor compared to my own.

"Okay," he said, "I'll lower you down so we can check it out. If you can't climb back up, I'll pull you up."

It sounded like a logical and foolish plan. If my hands slipped off the rope, or if his feet slipped off the rock, a quick trip to the Spirit World would surprise at least one of us.

I tried to formulate an alternate plan, but each idea required me to exercise faith to transport my middle-aged body hither and yon. I chose not to expose these ideas to Ross.

There was no place to tie the rope off, so we walked it back and wrapped it around the boulder, tying it off in a big loop. The boulder wouldn't move, but I kept staring at the knot. "Hold the rope," I said in a tight voice. "I don't want to rely on our lashing skills."

He looked at the knot, which was about six inches thick. "What? If you get down there and everything's cool, I'm coming down behind you."

"What? But what if I can't climb back up?"

"Then I'll climb back up then pull you up. I don't want to have to pull you up twice. And besides, you'll be more motivated then."

"And exhausted."

A foolhardy plan. The main reason I wanted him in the cave was to save my life if, no, when, necessary. How could he do that if the rope came untied and he was stuck down there with me?

Ross tied a series of knots in the doubled rope, each about a foot apart, as steps for our feet and hands. The he tied off a loop for me at the very end, where the rope doubled back on itself. The loop was so tight that I had to squeeze it around my chest, but I wouldn't fall out of it.

"Okay," he said, "Walk off the rock, and I'll lower you."

Walk off the rock?

I didn't know how Peter felt when he climbed overboard and took his first step on Galilee, but I doubted he had more butterflies than I now had. But then, his faith was founded on something more secure than a quarter-inch rope and a pair of strong hands. Facing the rock as I went lower, I tried to "walk" myself down, but the wall became concave just a few feet down, and I ended up hanging in open space, which caused me to begin spinning in mid-pungent air. I wasn't terrified. I was beyond terrified. I couldn't even scream. In the end, Ross lowered me down by sheer strength, and when I finally touched the wall again, about fifteen feet above a ledge where the steps began, I grabbed a protruding rock like it was salvation and turned myself around.

A greater surge of ammonia-sulfur assaulted me. Ross was still lowering me and the culmination of fear, stench, and fatigue caused a wave of vertigo.

No, not here.

Vertigo was one of the first indications of the Lyme returning. The ledge below me seemed to be moving and squirming. Then as I focused on the ledge below me, the vertigo was replaced by terror without measure. What I thought was the ground moving was actually a layer of squirming snakes.

"*Stop!*" I screamed.

The rope jerked to a stop.

"What's the matter?" he half yelled, half grunted in a strained voice. Yes, I had lost twenty pounds, but he was still holding a man in mid-air who weighed over a hundred and eighty pounds.

"There are snakes down here! Lots of them!"

"Snakes?"

"Yes! Snakes!"

Our voices sounded distant and muffled with virtually nothing to reflect them. Then several seconds later I heard the clear echo of the last several words, or screams. It was like hearing aliens.

"Are they rattlesnakes?" he called.

"I don't know! Take me back up!"

"You're getting heavy—try to climb up! Use the knots."

My heart tried to stop. "Can't you pull me up?"

"Hurry!"

This wasn't good.

I tried to climb up, but the problem was that I couldn't use my legs. I was hanging from the loop, which was digging into my armpits, and my legs were dangling free. I tried to do a pull-up to the knot above me, but I had been using my arms the whole time to take weight off my armpits, and they were exhausted.

I began descending again.

"What are you doing?!"

"I can't . . .hold . . .you!"

The snakes were getting closer.

And closer.

Panic began competing with hopeless resignation. I was wearing hiking boots, but my shins and calves were only protected by blue-jeans.

I tried again to pull myself up to the next knot, but I simply couldn't do it. Now I knew how a person felt who had just fallen off a cliff. Only I was doing it in slow motion.

I looked down, casting my headlight on the snakes to see if there was any possibility of surviving an encounter with them. And now, as the last echoes of "I can't . . .hold...you" faded away, I heard the increased stereophonic, nay, multi-phonic hissing of hundreds of snakes excited by the approach of a dangling dinner. Then I realized that the hissing wasn't hissing at all, but the furious rattling of hundreds of rattles.

The snakes were about three or four feet long and looked fat, healthy, strong, and pink. And now I saw a miracle. As I looked down at the snakes, I saw that they were crawling over themselves to *get away* from me. As I continued descending, they cleared a circle several feet across.

As Ross lost strength, I went down faster, and my feet hit the earth.

I stood very still.

The closest snakes were five or six feet from me and were still trying to get away. And now I realized that there may have been some logic to the miracle. These creatures were accustomed to total darkness, and my light was blinding them. I turned in a hundred-and-eighty-degree arc, from left to right, making sure the light fell on all of them. The sizzle of rattles was almost deafening.

"Are you all right?" Ross called.

"Yes! My light is scaring them away—and, yes, they are rattlesnakes!"

"Just stand still, and I'll let more rope down, and you can put your feet in the loop, and I'll try to pull you back up."

"No, I think it's okay. I'm going to check out the stairs."

"Really? Be careful!"

He let more rope out, and I stepped out of the loop. The snakes were all fleeing in the same general direction. I looked up and my light fell on a crevice leading back into the wall, about ten feet wide but narrowing as it went back farther. Some snakes were already slithering into it, and now I noticed that the crevice went deeper into the rock than my light could illuminate, which meant that it went way back, maybe over a hundred meters. This smaller cave seemed to travel basically in the same direction as the corridor we had come in on, but perhaps winding slightly to the right. I saw no ambient light, but I may have been seeing only a short portion of the crevice. The snakes, after all, had come from somewhere. And they had to eat something. And the fact that they could see the light told me that they had not been bred, generation after generation, in total darkness, because snakes living in caves almost always lost their eyesight.

I was a little more accustomed to the urine stench by now, and the rattling seemed to be decreasing. I turned back toward the cavern, then I stepped toward the stairway on my right, which, like so much of the previous cave, had been hewn out of the wall. I took hold of the brownish rail and found that it was metal, perhaps a brass or copper alloy, and I gave it a soft tug. It was fixed solidly in the wall.

I didn't intend to walk down into the vast reaches of the cavern, but I did take several steps down along its length to see if I could get a better angle to see Ross. After five or six steps, I spotted him and painted him with my light. He was standing in front of the boulder, still holding the rope.

"Hey, up there!"

As my words echoed back and forth, he looked down at me and let out a small laugh. "Did the snakes back off?"

"Yeah! The light scared them away."

He dropped the rope. "So, what do you want me to do?"

"I'm coming back up to the ledge. Let all the rope out, so I can test it while I'm down here. I want to see if the knot around the rock holds while I'm close to the ground."

By the time I got to the rope, several feet of rope lay limp on the ground. "Okay! I'm putting my weight on it!"

"Okay. I've still got my hands on it, so if it comes loose it won't go all the way down to you."

That was a good idea—since there was no other way back up.

I put half my weight on it. "How's that?"

"Looks good. The knot's holding."

I grabbed a knot above my head and put all my weight on it. "How's that?"

"Still good!"

I pulled my weight up a few inches so I could put my feet on a knot just above the ground, and I hopped on it. "How's that?"

"Still good! Really give it a good jerk!"

I did. "Any problems?" I called.

"No. It looks solid."

I got off the rope. This would be the moment of truth. Well, actually, the moment of truth would be when both of us tried to get back up, but at least I would be able to use my feet and legs then. And, hopefully, Ross could go up first and help me—if he had any strength left.

A long moment went by with nothing happening.

"What are you doing?" I called.

"Putting lights and batteries and food and stuff in my pockets. I don't want to bring a pack down."

Lucky thing one of us was thinking. And lucky thing he had those Cargo pants.

"And I'm going to leave the lantern on. Doesn't it have, like, entire hours of life on the batteries?"

"Yeah—I think so!"

He grabbed the rope and began lowering himself over the lip, descending faster than I had. He stopped about ten feet above me and let his headlamp shine on the swarm of snakes still retreating. He quickly swiveled his head in both directions.

"Unbelievable!" he shouted.

"What?"

"They really *are* pink!"

I marveled at his priorities.

He hit the ground and started digging into a pocket. "We've got to get pictures!" He got his phone out and started chasing them, snapping away. He wasn't scared. They were.

Ross lived in a world very different from my own.

* * *

On the way back to Tuba City, Klah watched for the crew coming in from California. The two lanes were divided by a turn lane, so the red SUV could easily pull a U-turn, as Klah had done, and follow him. But he never saw them.

Klah had been wondering how he would keep Richardson from escaping when he went in the store. He knew there was no way the man would stay peaceably kidnaped, so he pulled off the road and went four-wheeling into the desert. The mighty Jeep Wrangler barely noticed the sand and gravel. After pulling behind a low hill, he stopped, pulled out the keys, and went around to the back of the vehicle, while he told Richardson to stay put. What was the man going to do, run into the desert? A Glock 19 could put a bullet through his back from a hundred yards away. Klah got a length of heavy twine from a toolbox and brought it around to the passenger side. "Get out and put your hands behind you."

"You're tying me up?"

Klah stared at him as if he had just heard the dumbest question ever.

"Where are you going?"

"To Tuba to get some supplies—so, maybe you better eat and drink something. Looks like it'll be a scorcher."

According to the thermometer in the dash, it was already ninety, and the blazing sun was just reaching its apex. What a time for a record-setting heat wave. Klah let Richardson eat a bag of chips and drink all he could of a quart of cold Powerade, then he tied his hands behind his back and walked him over to the shade of a rock behind the hill. He made him lie down, then he tied his legs together at the knees and ankles.

"Why don't you just shoot me? You know you can't let me live.

"Relax. I'll be back in half an hour."

"But if the other crew finds you, you may not come back—and I'll die out here."

"I thought of that, but, we'll both just have to take our chances. But I think I'll be back. We haven't passed a cell tower in like ten miles."

Whislin got in the Jeep and motored through the sand and gravel to the main road, often checking his mirror. When he got to the highway, he hit the gas and was in Tuba City in ten minutes. A cell tower stood on a small bluff to his left as he came into town. They knew where he was now.

The hardware store was where he thought it was. He quickly walked through the store, and in ten minutes he had a bag of quick-dry cement, two backpacks, two flats of water, a three-gallon bucket, and some food. Ten minutes after that he turned off the road to the low hill in the distance. Only five vehicles had passed him going the other direction. None was a red SUV.

Where were those guys?

Richardson was where he had left him, still alive and more subdued than ever. It always impressed Klah how a little fear could motivate a person to toe the line.

Chapter 33

In This Sacred, Enclosed Space, The Lord's Light Will Always Shine On These Plates. May He Watch Over Them Forever.

We counted the stock of supplies in Ross's pockets: four small but powerful flashlights, forty-eight AA batteries, a multipurpose knife, a dozen energy bars, four bottles of water, a first-aid kit, and a small camera. We also wore headlamps, and I had more batteries, a camera, and extra energy bars in my pockets. If we got stuck, we would die very slowly.

The hissing and rattling had decreased, allowing us to talk in natural voices, but we always kept one light trained on the snakes. The closest ones were in the long crevice and were no threat.

"Where do you think that cave goes?" Ross asked, focusing a flashlight into the narrow cave above the snakes.

"I don't know, but see how it turns to the right?"

"Yeah."

"Think about it: the snakes have to get food from somewhere, so, I wonder if that narrow cave goes all the way out to the canyon."

"But that's like a mile away."

"Maybe not," I said. "If it keeps going to the right, maybe it ends up in the cul-de-sac, where the sheep went."

"You mean where we got out of the canyon."

"Yeah, if it goes there, it might be a lot shorter."

"Yeah, and it might mean they'll be waiting for us." He twisted the lens, narrowing the beam and making the light dig as far back as it could go. Then he put the light in his pocket and took out his camera. After snapping some pictures of the snakes, he took a deep breath.

"Smell that?" he said.

"Yeah, you can't help it."

"No, the fresh air, coming in from the cave."

Frankly, I didn't smell anything but snake poop, which was enough to keep me from trying to smell anything else. Ross turned his attention to the staircase. "It's obvious why they stopped the steps here, instead of carving them all the way up to the top."

"To use the snakes as a barrier."

"Yep, a deterrent to enemies—or looters."

We gazed into the enormous cavern again, perhaps a thousand feet of it above us, and hundreds more below. I was fairly sure that nothing like this existed anywhere else on, or in, the planet.

"After you, boss," Ross said, pointing toward the stairs. I grabbed the metal handrail with my right hand and began stepping down. Ross followed. "They're perfect," he said, "not too tall and not too short."

Whoever made them probably had the same length of stride as us, which meant they were close to our height. Which meant they probably weren't Hopis or Navajos, who averaged considerably less than six feet.

New features became visible as the wall curved around to our right, into an indentation in the cave that we hadn't seen before. As we entered it, we were amazed by a sight I still find difficult to accept. A tower of mineral deposits, a giant stalagmite, rose up from the floor, still far below us, and topped out slightly below our level, which made it hundreds of feet tall. And exactly above it another structure hung from the ceiling resembling a massive curtain seeming to ripple in a nonexistent breeze. This curtain hung down almost as far as the tower rose up. It seemed impossible that a structure so large could cleave to the ceiling with its enormous weight. But, there it was, after millions of years, still hanging above the tower. And it was no doubt still growing, fraction of a millimeter by fraction of a millimeter each year. The cavern had to be nearly as old as the rocks in the canyon, perhaps over a billion years.

Ross took more pictures. I thought we'd better have two witnesses, so I took out my camera and began taking pictures of everything I could see, including Ross with his camera held before his face, to give some perspective. I don't think we said a word for five minutes, probably with our mouths open, transfixed before the massive tower and gigantic flying curtain.

We put the cameras away and quickened our step, always holding the rail, and it only took another ten minutes or so to get down, which, upon reflection wasn't surprising. We had probably traveled half a mile between vertical and horizontal distance, and a person could easily cover that in fifteen minutes. Going up, though, would be a different story.

The stairs leveled out on a broad smooth flowstone gently rising from the floor to the base of the tower. The handrail ended at the first step, and, as if drawn by a magnet, we walked up the flowstone base toward the enormous tower.

It was called flowstone because it was formed when traces of water flowed over it for millions of years, depositing calcium and other minerals. It was light amber, and shiny, as if it were slippery, but it wasn't. Upon closer inspection, it seemed to be composed of millions of smooth bumps, like warts. When we neared the tower, the flowstone got steeper, and we realized that this natural ramp to the base of the giant stalagmite went higher than our heads, perhaps twenty feet above us—and that was just to the tower's base. We took more pictures then walked part way around it, using our slightly higher elevation as a vantage point to marvel at the rest of this part of the cavern. It was overwhelming. There was too much to see, too much to make sense of. The sizes and distances were ridiculous. It was like standing in Yosemite Valley—with a roof over it. The place would be a spelunker's delight, an archeologist's dream, a geologist's heaven. And it would be every normal person's indescribable wonderland.

It was already after three. There was plenty of daylight left above, but we had a long ways to go. And I still had some questions. I could understand why a people would spend years, maybe generations, carving a half-mile-long staircase to the bottom of this cave, but I wondered if there was something else down here besides the cavern floor. They had tried to hinder the entrance with the boulder and snakes. Was it just to protect the other-worldly beauty, or was there something "sacred" here, as the mezuzah at the entrance seemed to imply?

I turned and started walking down off the flowstone, but instead of turning back toward the stairs and the main part of the cave, I went the opposite way, toward a kind of box canyon that was hidden from the stairs and entrance above. After a few minutes, Ross said, "Are we going anywhere in particular?"

I gazed at the box canyon's sheer walls rising over a thousand feet. "I don't know—I just want to see everything."

"Well, just remember, the sun will set soon."

"Yeah—I'm just—I don't know, I'm looking for something else."

"You mean something else besides the most mind-blowing cave in the world?"

"Don't you feel it?"

"What?"

"I don't know. I just wonder if there's something else down here, since they wrote those words above the entrance—something holy."

"This whole place looks holy to me."

I pulled the paper out of my pocket again. "Those symbols mean something like, 'Holy land, holy land, holy land—or maybe, just 'Holy, holy, holy.'" I looked at him, and he nodded that it might be a possibility. "Okay," I continued, "then you add: 'In these tight quarters the light of day will shine on *something*. The Lord's directing eyes watching over us.' The *something* is the symbol with those four lines."

"Well, I bet the Lord's eyes are on this place all the time."

"Right. Maybe that's all it means."

"But you don't think so."

I didn't answer. Something was compelling me to explore this hidden part of the cave, and I started walking deeper into the box canyon, which, now that I thought about it, was like the cul-de-sac in the canyon, only much more spectacular. Its vertical cliffs were highlighted with drapery and flowstone everywhere. We hadn't spent much time studying the ceiling, mostly because it was so far above us, but the fact that this place was as big as the cul-de-sac in the canyon and *had* a ceiling was impressive enough. On this part of the floor there were fewer mineral formations, probably because there was less water here. As we got deeper into it, the box canyon appeared to be almost perfectly dry, like the bleak moonscape up on the plateau.

It was darker here because the light from our thousand-lumen lamp above the snakes didn't reach around the bend we had just come around. And so, as in the cave up above, our headlamps created a bubble of light that defined our world.

The silence in the canyon was nothing like the brooding, heavy silence here. Was this the silence of the grave? Of the void of space? Was this the haunt of the dead, or of the brilliantly alive? What was I feeling? What was I hearing?

I simply wanted to take more steps, to keep going.

We came to the dead end of the box canyon and stepped onto a short pile of talus at the base of the thousand-foot wall above us. Small rocks had broken off above and fallen down, but in contrast to the cliffs outside, there was remarkably little talus here. Without wind, rain, or ice, the rocks didn't weather nearly as quickly. I stepped up on the talus and put my hand against the wall. It was gray and smooth and cold. Behind me, Ross sat down on one of the larger rocks.

"You want some lunch?" He reached into a pocket on his thigh and produced a handful of power bars. Then he reached into a pocket on the other leg and found two bottles of water. Mary Poppins.

There were no other large rocks to sit on, so I sat cross-legged on the talus, and we ate the power bars and drank the water. After finishing, I lay on my back with my hands behind my head, and in moments I knew that if I didn't get up and move around, I would get chilled. Plus, exhaustion was beginning to seep into my bones. I had lost count of the miles we had hiked the past week, the hours of lost sleep, the cliffs climbed and descended. The effects of the Lyme seemed to have disappeared, but natural fatigue was still very real.

I stood up and backed off a little ways and let my eyes travel up the sheer, monolithic wall. It was like standing at the base of Half Dome, and I could feel myself getting dizzy, when I noticed something on the wall.

A protrusion of rock jutted out a hundred feet or so above us, and under the protrusion there was a dark hollow, almost like the shadow of a cave. If I hadn't been standing right there, with my headlamp pointing directly up, I never would have seen the strange protrusion, or, possibly, the shadow under it.

I pointed at it, and Ross looked up. He got up and focused his light on the same area. The protrusion and shadow were definitely anomalies. We backed off to get a better angle, and we saw that the shadow under the protruding rock was indeed some kind of cavity. No matter how far back we went, we couldn't see the back of the shadow.

I started walking to our left, where the back wall of the box canyon met the vast side wall of the cavern. I was attracted by another shadow there, a vertical discoloration in the corner. Ross followed me, and when we arrived at the vertical shadow, we found more loose rock, only these seemed less random, almost like they had been purposefully hewed out of the rock. I looked up into the shadow, bathing it in light. Ross pointed both his headlamp and flashlight into it, and we saw what appeared to be manmade marks, not hieroglyphics or drawings, but steps, maybe even handholds. They began about six feet above our heads.

"Those are steps, aren't they?" I said.

"If they're not, they're good imitations."

We got as close to the base as we could.

"Whoever made them," I said, "must have used a ladder to reach the first step."

"These people were interesting," Ross said. "They made a staircase that doesn't go all the way up, and they made these steps that don't go all the way down. It's like they were always making things hard to get to."

We piled some rocks to make a platform a couple of feet high, and Ross stood on them. "Okay, partner, time to get up." He crouched down, ready for me to get on his shoulders.

"But how will *you* get up there?"

"I guess I won't. I'll just be waiting down here for you. So make it quick or there won't be any dinner left." He patted his pockets.

I tried not to dig into his shoulders as I climbed aboard, and a few seconds later I was eye-level with the second step. I reached up to the third with both hands, said a little prayer, and pulled up as best I could. Immediately I saw why they had put the steps here; a natural fissure in the corner of the two walls angled back, allowing me to lean forward just enough to step into it. I climbed up the first six or seven steps.

"How's it going?" Ross called.

"It's easier than I thought!"

But a hundred feet, I learned, is a long way to climb up a steep wall. Out in the canyon Ross and I had scrambled over areas this steep, but only for ten or twenty feet, which was bad enough, but this was unrelenting. Most firetruck ladders were shorter than this, and I was climbing on rocks. My forearms began cramping, and I ended up taking several rests, letting my arms hang below me until the blood oozed back into them. A man could carry some food and water up here if he wanted, but he would need a rucksack, and of course, getting a rucksack down to this place would be a challenge in itself. It took a long ten minutes, but I finally reached a lateral shelf six or seven feet deep that wound around to the shadow on my right.

Again, my sense of scale had been off; the protrusion of rocks I had seen was twice as big as I had thought. So was the shadow. As I approached it, I saw that it was a cave, and I shined my light in.

There was a room before me.

It too was manmade, about ten by ten, and inside that, through a doorway cut into the back wall, there was another room, larger, maybe twenty by twenty. I went through the first room, into the second, larger room and was surprised to find furniture in it. There were two long benches constructed of hand-hewed planks locked together with hardened leather strips. That told me that someone very strong had been here, as they had hauled the heavy planks and supplies up here. I went to the nearest bench, along the wall on my right, and tested it. It did not wobble. I touched the leather lashings holding it together and found that they had almost metallic strength. The wood had a thick layer of dust on it. I rubbed it off and found that the wood was coated in some kind of durable resin. The layer of dust indicated that it had not been used in a long, long time.

The bench on the opposite wall was identical. The room appeared to be an antechamber, a waiting room that led into an even larger, third room. Above the opening leading into it, I saw more hieroglyphics, instantly recognizing two of them, the double dots, which meant the eyes of the Lord, and the four parallel lines stacked on each other. My heart, already pounding, sped up.

I went into this third room and initially thought it was a kitchen or pantry, because I saw three tiers of shelves lining the walls that were filled with various implements. *How wonderful,* I thought, *I got here before the looters!*

Then I saw what the "implements" were, and my mind staggered at the sight.

There was a table and bench in the middle of the room, but my headlamp was focused on a shelf on the far wall. I walked past the table and bench and reached out to something on the middle shelf.

It almost looked like a large, rectangular book.

I touched the surface, removing another thick layer of dust, and the color brightened into a shiny deep yellow. I touched it again.

It was metal.

My hand began to shake as I removed more dust and saw hieroglyphics.

It was a book of metal plates.

I took an audible breath, calming myself. The plates were very thin, and I used my forefinger and thumb to riffle their edges. They were like heavy tissue, solid but thin and pliable. I placed both hands on the plates' sides and tried to lift the book but found it almost impossible. Was it stuck to the shelf? I stepped as close as I could and tried again. They moved, but they must have weighed sixty pounds. I finally began to lift them, then I saw several engravings.

I put it back down, and, standing very still, scanned the engravings to see if I recognized any characters, but the first thing I noticed was that they were black. I looked closer. Each character had been stained black or very dark brown. Was it oxidation from years of exposure to the air? I lifted one corner and saw the same coloring on the second page—or rather, third page, because now I realized that the plates were engraved on both sides. The engravings on the back side were also stained a dark color—deliberately stained. And now that I looked at all the characters on both sheets I realized that they stood out, almost popped out, from the gold background. Some kind of dye had been rubbed into them to allow them to be seen more easily, even in a dim light.

Surprisingly, although the plates were almost paper thin, they appeared to be solid enough to prevent characters from showing through to the other side. These were made by an artist's hand, one that had pressed hard enough to make an indelible impression, but not hard enough to bleed through to the opposite side. They were consistent and uniform in size and shape, each line ruler-straight.

I worked the first sheet back over a set of three rings and laid it flat, and my eyes fell on an inverted V. It looked like an "A" without the cross line. According to my translation of the Anthon Transcript, this represented "The Creator" or "God."

I carried the heavy book to the table and set it down. When I heard the thud it made, I checked the table to see if it was sturdy enough. The table was solidly made and virtually immovable, and it too was coated in a thick, hard, yellow resin. And now, for the first time, I took a moment to look around the rest of the room.

It was about twenty-five feet square, and about ten feet tall. All four walls, except where the doorway was, held three tiers of shelves. And on each shelf sat many stacks of metal plates.

How could the shelves bear their weight? I looked under one and found six-inch-wide dowels protruding from the wall as horizontal supports. Each was fitted into holes in the stone and cemented in.

They could probably support a thousand pounds. Some of them may have been doing just that.

I went back to the plates on the table and inspected them more carefully. They were remarkably similar to images that artists had made of Joseph Smith's gold plates, except for the dark stain on every character. They had three rather tall, D-shaped rings holding the pages together on the right side.

On the right side.

Yes, they read from right to left, so the "binding" would be on the right side. I studied the rings to see if they had a latch of some kind to allow new pages to be inserted. I didn't see one. In fact, the rings seemed to be of solid construction, though I realized there might be a way of separating them on the inside, somewhere between the metal plates.

I looked more closely at the characters on the top page. There were only five, and I assumed it was a title. I recognized two of these characters. One, of course, was the symbol for *the Lord*, and the other was a character with nine short vertical lines over a long, single horizontal line. I had seen it before but couldn't recall its meaning. I took out my copy of the Anthon Transcript again and found the character quickly, as it was the largest character on the sheet. In comparing it to the words in Ether six, I thought it meant something like *Many days on this journey*. If these characters had the same meaning, this record probably had something to do with a long journey, probably a long journey for the Lord.

Obviously each character had been engraved with some sort of durable tool. I scanned the room but didn't see one.

I lifted the metal page and carefully brought it over to the right side. The leaf was flexible but moved easily. I almost laughed, and I lifted it again, enjoying the feel of the tissue-like metal. It was heavier than one would expect, but remarkably malleable.

I knew that the page was made of gold. Brass would be more rigid and not as heavy. And in that moment I knew what the mysterious character on the sign above the snakes meant, the character that looked like pancakes.

Plates.

I looked at the paper again where I had written my translation of the symbols. Now, inserting the new word, it read:

Holy, holy, holy.

> In these tight quarters the light of day will shine
> on these plates.
> The Lord's directing eyes watching over us.

This still seemed a little unwieldy, so I mentally modified the translation to:

> Holy, holy, holy!
> In this sacred, enclosed space
> The Lord's light will always shine on these plates.
> May He watch over them forever.

I didn't know if it was perfect, but it worked.

The second sheet was filled with characters, most of which I didn't recognize—but I did see one that I knew. It occurred several times: the large Z with the curlicue on top that meant "And it came to pass." This character appeared seven times in the Anthon Transcript, and, not coincidentally, the same phrase occurs seven times in the corresponding passage in Ether.

I ran my fingers over the characters as if they were brail. The engravings were smooth and uniform in size and depth. There were no rough edges, no slivers, just consistent, near perfect writing in a foreign language. I wished my penmanship were as beautiful.

I realized what I was doing, and I felt butterflies. Where had these plates come from? Who had created them and did anyone else know about them? If not, would they be decipherable? And finally, why did *I* find them? Had I become a tool in the Lord's hands? And if so, why didn't I know it? I hadn't received a calling, physically or spiritually, that I knew of—just a series of thoughts and notions and desires to do this or that. Shouldn't I have seen a light or heard a voice, or, at the very least, received a call from Salt Lake?

And now I did hear a voice, very distant and hollow. Ross was calling my name. I hurried out and, from the ledge, saw him far below. He had his hands cupped to his mouth.

"Are you okay?" he yelled.

"Yes! I found another cave! It has plates!"

"It has *what?*"

"Plates! Gold plates."

"*WHAT?*"

"It has gold plates!"

"Like the Book of Mormon?"
"Yes!"
He looked over at the steps.
"I'm coming up!"

Chapter 34

Covering the Cave

Checking his phone, Klah saw the route Call and Keller had taken to the rim. He could monitor the route on his phone, or he could just follow the fresh tracks in the rust-dun soil. He put the Jeep in four-wheel drive and set off after them.

At some point, Richardson figured out where they were going. "Is there access into the canyon out here?"

"There must be, since that's where our boys went about an hour ago."

"And you want to follow them all the way down to the cave?"

"No, I want *us* to follow them all the way down to the cave. You're going to help me solve our little problem."

Although Whislin had spent years in northern Arizona, he had never been four-wheeling on the Kaibito Plateau. If he survived the next few days, he would probably never do it again. The desert here was as bleak as any he had seen. And that was saying something. There was nothing here but scattered withered brush that may have been alive but looked dead. At one point he did see a dark lump off to the right that looked strangely like a backpack, but he ignored it.

He continued to follow the truck's tracks down a dirt road, which narrowed down to a series of trails, then to a trace of a trail, then to nothing but tire prints in the soft dirt. The ruts and washouts were impressive, and he knew he would never have been able to do this without four-wheel drive. He slowed down to keep the Jeep in working order—no telling when he'd be able to afford a new one.

Fifty minutes later he spotted Keller's silver F-150. He couldn't see the canyon, but he easily made out the higher north rim, several miles away. He'd been camped somewhere out there just a few days ago. He pulled alongside the pickup but kept the engine running. The outside thermometer registered 91. Of course, that wasn't in the shade, because there was no shade.

"Now, boss, it goes without saying that you'll do exactly as I say."

"Yes, of course," said Richardson, "but I'm no longer your boss."

"Well, maybe not now, since you probably don't plan to pay me even if I do keep my end of the bargain, but I'll always think of you as a good boss—until you decided to kill me. So, here's the deal." He looked at Richardson's clothing, which consisted of black pants, black shirt, black jacket, and black running shoes. "You might want to lose the jacket. No chance of getting a chill out here. We're going to take some backpacks and follow our friends' tracks down to the cave. And once we're there, you will continue to do exactly as I say." He lifted the gun out of the compartment in the door.

Whislin got out and filled the backpacks with things they would need. His would be the heaviest by far, as he couldn't expect the miniature Richardson to carry nearly eighty pounds. When he was done, he let Richardson out of the vehicle, set the little pack on him, and pointed him toward the shallow bowl below the rim. "After you."

As they trudged through reddish sand toward the canyon, a thought hit Klah, and he reached into his left pocket and pulled out his cell phone and checked it for cell service.

Two bars.

Two bars? He slowed and looked in all directions. Where was the cell tower? How could he possibly have two bars out here? He knew he had been painted with a signal back at Tuba City, but that was over thirty miles away. Could this signal be coming from Grand Canyon Village? Willow Springs? Cameron? Page? The fact was, it could have been coming from multiple sources. They could be triangulating on him right now. Clearly, in this thin air and without buildings, tall hills or mountains, the signal could travel farther than normal.

But the real question was, could the cell tower detect the weak radio signal constantly issuing from his body? Richardson said the tower had to be within a quarter mile before it could detect his signal, but maybe up here, with far, open horizons, the signal traveled farther.

Klah grabbed a corner of Richardson's pack and pulled him to a stop. "Tell me the truth; how far away can they detect my signal?"

Richardson was already breathing hard. His eyes flicked down and to the right, indicating, of course, that he was preparing a lie. Klah looked at the man's hands. They were both fidgeting, the fingers rubbing against each thumb—another tell.

Klah racked the slide of his gun, chambering a round.

Bullets don't lie.

Richardson's eyes went to the gun then came up to meet Klah's. His hands relaxed, and he spoke confidently, probably truthfully. "I really don't know. Sometimes in Flagstaff they followed you for a few miles when you went out of town on a road with no cell service."

Klah still didn't trust him. "A few miles?"

"Maybe several miles. It was hard to tell, especially if they couldn't triangulate with multiple towers."

Klah looked at his phone again. "I have two bars. Could they be tracking me now?"

Richardson thought about it, but his eyes were looking down and to his left, probably accessing his memory. "I doubt it, but I don't know where the nearest towers are." He looked around the horizon. "You're probably out of range, but there's no way to be sure, especially with the village being just down the canyon."

He figured they knew where he was, at least generally. He should develop a plan in case they came out here. But he couldn't hide the Jeep, again no big obstructions. He'd just have to play it by ear. While studying the path Call and Keller must have taken, he noticed that the eroded notch, or indentation, in the canyon wall led down into Marble Canyon, an extremely remote part of the bigger canyon. Some of it was off-limits except to rafters, and some of the side canyons were off-limits even to them.

They were only at the edge of the bowl, just above the chimney, and Richardson was already blowing like a horse—a broke-down, splayed, old nag. He'd seen a lot of them on reservations. "What's the matter?"

"What do you think?" Richardson said. "This thing weighs a ton."

"Forty pounds. Maybe fifty."

"Whatever. You can't expect me to carry it down *there*. That's the Grand Canyon. That's like a mile-high cliff!"

"A mile-high cliff? All I see is a little ravine that our forty-year-old friend, Travis Call, climbed *up* a few days ago, and if he could do that, you can do this. Time to get your hands dirty, Richardson. Get moving."

The little man stepped up to the edge apprehensively, looked down into the dizzying depths of the chimney, and carefully squatted down like he was going to sit on the edge of a building.

Klah snorted. "You're going to slide down?"

"Just—let me do it my way." Richardson nudged his weight over the edge and began scooting down into the chimney. When he had gone about ten feet, Klah, toting his eighty-pound pack, stepped into the same notch and forced the earth to compress beneath his boots. It was steep but navigable. Richardson stopped and rested several times, catching his breath and summoning more courage. Half an hour later they came to the steepest part, the part where Ross had helped Travis down earlier. In this case, though, Richardson was lower than Klah, and the chute was too steep to let Klah past him.

"Get moving," Klah demanded.

"It's too steep. I'll fall—and I don't even know when I'll stop."

"Look, boss, you got two choices, get down on your own or get pushed down."

Klah wasn't sure how far down the cave was from here, but it seemed like they had already come down several hundred feet in elevation. He could see that the angle of the chimney eased somewhat after this. All Richardson had to do was slide or fall ten or twelve feet, and they'd be home free, but Richardson wasn't budging.

And in the meantime, the eighty pounds was getting heavier.

"All right," Klah said, "take your pack off and hand it to me, then go on down."

Richardson tried to work his pack off, but the wall of the canyon was too close to his back, preventing him from getting his arms free. Klah tried to reach down to help, but the pack was below his feet, and the extra weight on his own back caused him to fall forward. He jabbed a foot out to arrest his fall, but that broke the earth loose, causing a rockfall to land on Richardson.

The little avalanche hit him just as he was leaning forward to get more room from the canyon wall, and he lost his balance and plunged forward, diving about eight feet down and landing face first with the backpack smashing into the back of his head. Richardson bounced, hit again several feet down, then tumbled to a stop against a rock about twenty-five feet below.

He didn't move.

Klah worked his way down with some effort until he reached the motionless form. He dropped his pack and knelt by Richardson's head, which was lower than the rest of his body. It was twisted to his left and looked like the neck might be broken. The face was severely scraped, but there didn't appear to be any teeth or eyes missing. The pack was still on his neck and shoulders, so Klah lifted it off and laid it on some rocks above them.

Klah had received extensive triage training and knew how to check the vital signs. He placed his first two fingers on the carotid artery to check for a pulse. He didn't feel one, but the angle was awkward. He gently probed around the neck but didn't feel any broken vertebrae, but again, he couldn't be sure. The man had taken a wicked fall, and the pack had come down on his neck and head with its full weight.

Carefully cradling Richardson's head, Klah turned him onto his back, letting the legs and body slide below his center of gravity. When the body was stabilized, he lifted the left eyelid. Sunlight was hitting Richardson full in the face, and the pupil should have contracted, but it didn't, or if it did, it was barely discernible. Klah checked the other eye. Same result.

Klah didn't know if the man was dead, but he couldn't wait for decomposition to remove all doubt. He pulled Richardson into the shade of a boulder then saddled up under his own eighty-pound nemesis, tested his footing, then lifted Richardson's pack and cradled it against his chest. It would be hard, but he had no choice. He needed everything in both packs—and time was getting short.

He figured the cave was somewhere to his left and probably still a few hundred feet below him. He tried to keep an eye out for it, but that proved unnecessary as he saw Call's and Keller's footprints branching off on a thin animal trail. After a hundred yards of doing more shuffling than hiking, he came to a long ledge that was five or six feet wide, which took him out of what now looked like a cul-de-sac in the canyon wall. His arms and back were exhausted, but he continued carrying both packs until he came to the wider platform that he recognized from earlier surveillance. The cave had to be just ahead, around an outcropping to his left.

When he came to the cave, he was both amazed and angered. Evidently the air portal had been too narrow for Keller to squeeze through, but rather than widen it, they had made a hole in the wall covering the cave's entrance. He studied the wound in the facade and found bore-holes in the mortar and blasting paper torn to shreds. He smiled in grudging admiration; the two city boys had toted power tools and blasting caps down here. He was impressed, but he was also perturbed because this created more work for him and might stretch his resources beyond what he had.

He set both packs down, saw a mess of footprints all around, then he opened a bottle of almost warm water and downed it. He crushed the empty bottle and set it back in the pack, then he checked out the new opening the men had made. It seemed large enough for him to squeeze through. He checked the sun overhead. He still had time. He got on his hands and knees and stuck his head into the cave and listened. Initially he was struck by its coolness, but he heard only silence, so he squeezed all the way in, trying not to rip his shirt or pants on the mortar's edges.

He saw the drill and batteries before he even flicked his small flashlight on. The boys had left their heavy tools here, but that was all. If they had packs, they had taken them with them.

He stood up and scouted a little more. He was again surprised by the coolness—then by the cave's size. From across the canyon he had seen that the facade was larger than the two men, but he didn't think it was this big—perhaps twice his height, and easily that wide. He looked closer at the inside walls. They weren't rough-hewn as he had expected but were finely worked and smoothed until the arcing sides and ceiling almost looked like they had been poured, not carved. He noticed something on the left wall and instantly recognized the square maze of the Mother Earth symbol. He had seen pictures of similar mazes, but something about this one was different. It was larger than usual, but what set it apart was the exactness of its angles, its perfect dimensions. It bore a beauty he had not seen in other mazes, most of which had seemed almost crude. He ran his fingers over the grooves, admiring the consistency of their depth and width. What kind of tools had they used? He tried to flake off some stone with his thumbnail but was unable to.

He trained the light deeper into the cave. Kinkaid had said that the cave went back over a mile. The thought chilled him with a vague uneasiness. A mile into solid rock. He had always been more comfortable in the certitude of open skies.

He crawled back out into the blinding light and searing heat, taking the drill and batteries with him. He didn't know how long it would be before Call and Keller returned to the entrance, but he didn't plan to leave them any supplies. He also emptied Richardson's pack, pulling out the two flats of water and some tools, then he removed a fifty-pound bag and a twenty-pound tub of fast-drying Quikrete from his own pack. He wouldn't miss those on the way back up. He pulled out the three-gallon plastic bucket that, fortunately, hadn't cracked under the weight of the Quikrete. This form of cement was formulated to dry in ten to fifteen minutes—probably less in such ultra-dry conditions.

Stones littered the area where the two men had blasted through the rocks. All he had to do was fit them back in place, like a puzzle, and fix them with new cement. As he got to work, he found that it was easy to figure out which stones went where, the big ones on the bottom and the smaller ones on top. When he was done, he would go over to the air portal and seal it shut too. He didn't have any illusions about the men inside suffocating; there was far too much air for that. But they would only last three or four days without water. As he fit another stone into place, he wondered which man would start eating the other first.

He had been an accidental killer before, but now he was doing it intentionally.

And he was surprised at how easy it was.

After all, it was either him or them.

Chapter 35

The Plates

Ross was coming up?

How?

"Ross, that's insane! You can't get up here!"

"Yes I can!"

"How?"

"I don't know. Come down and help me."

Well, this was a change—me helping Ross.

But I didn't like it because I had to go back down a hundred feet, then come back up to get back to the plates, then go back down again when we were done—when, of course, we would have to climb the eternal stairway *back* up to the snakes, then somehow climb the rope, then hike a mile (literally) through the first cave, then climb out of the canyon (the *Grand Canyon!*), shimmy up through the chimney which was not a chimney at all but a long, never-ending vertical chute, and finally hike back to the truck.

If I were still alive.

But, then, Ross had only saved my life half a dozen times—maybe I could do a little something for him.

I walked across the ledge to the top step and, turning to face the cliff, began going down backwards. When I reached the bottom step, my thighs were quivering, but I found that it was wide enough for me to turn around and face Ross, who was about five feet below. He put his arm up, but his hand was still three feet below my feet.

"Take your belt off," he said.

I always wore a belt, a residual habit from being pantsed in junior high. I undid it and wrapped the free end around my hand and dangled the buckle end down to him. It was still six inches or so above his hand.

"I'm going to jump and grab it and try to pull myself up."

"What if you pull me over?"

"No, don't let me do that! Squat down and lean back as far as you can. Then pull hard. If I get high enough, I'm going to try to grab that first step."

"Uh, okay."

I squatted per orders and leaned back.

"Okay," he said, "are you ready?"

"No, but whatever."

He grunted and I felt a massive tug on the belt before I was ready and found myself leaning forward, not backward.

"Pull!" he cried.

He was hanging onto the belt. I tried to pull backward, but his two-hundred pounds felt like two thousand, and I couldn't get my weight back again. But at least I wasn't falling forward any farther. He jerked hard on the belt, and I realized he was trying to climb up.

Moments later I saw his right hand slap against the first step next to my boot. I tried to slide my foot over to make room for his left hand, but his left hand landed there anyway. The belt suddenly went limp when he let go of it to grab my boot, and I fell back against the chiseled steps.

"Help!" he cried, dangling from the step with one hand and from my boot with the other.

I tried to grab his wrist, like they do in the movies when somebody is about to fall to his death, but that didn't do anything. He was too heavy. So I bent forward and looped the belt around his wrist below my boot then looped it through the buckle and cinched it tight.

Then I stood up and pulled as hard as I could.

"Ahhh!"

I could only imagine how his wrist felt.

His hand came off my boot, then he leaned outward, away from the rock, and his legs began scrambling up under him as he tried to run up the rock. Moments later he was indeed coming up, and he latched his left knee and foot over the ledge. I stopped pulling so he could use his hand to push himself up, which was a good thing because his hand was already turning purple.

He rolled up onto the ledge and immediately ripped off the belt and began rubbing his wrist. "You almost pulled my hand off!"

"Sorry, I didn't know what else to do."

He eyed me warily. "First you shoot me, then you try to rip my hand off—am I forgetting anything else? It's dangerous around you."

"Yeah, but you're up here—and you won't believe what's up in that cave."

He got to his feet, still rubbing his wrist, which, I noted, was already returning to its regular sunburned red. "There are really plates? Gold plates?"

"That's what it looks like."

"How many?"

"A lot. And, by the way, how are we getting back down?"

"*Not* the same way we came up! I'll jump first."

I started climbing up the steps. He waited until I was far enough away to not be a threat before following.

I had to rest a few times, but we eventually made it, and I took him through the first little empty room and into the second room, where we ignored the benches and went straight to the third room, with the plates. We both had our headlamps on, which brought the plates along the walls into sharp relief, and now I noticed more plates stacked on the ground under the shelves. He stared, taking in the whole room.

"Oh, wow! Oh, my goodness!"

After a long moment, he cautiously, almost reverently, walked to the table, where I had left the plates open to the second page.

"Can I touch them?"

"I did. That's how they got here."

He extended his hand tentatively, as if it might get singed, then he touched the second page. He lifted a corner, felt its weight and thinness, and said, "Wow" again. He looked at me with an incredulous smile, his eyes wide and disbelieving. He put the gold page back down then felt the engravings with his fingers. "They're so smooth. So perfect." He picked the thin, second sheet back up and looked on the back side. "Yep."

"Yep what?"

"I always wondered if Mormon wrote on both sides of the paper."

I laughed. The "paper" was literally worth its weight in gold. No, with these engravings, with this provenance, it was worth many times that.

Then I caught myself. I had fallen into the same trap Joseph had once succumbed to, seeing the plates as a source of income. I mentally upbraided myself. I would not do it again. Yes, I was a natural man given to bouts of greed, but I now determined that whether or not these plates contained sacred writings, I would never think of them as "gold" or wealth again. In my mind, I saw a flash of the sign above the snakes: *Holy, holy, holy.*

"Is this the back of the book?" Ross asked, seeing the three rings on the wrong side.

"No, they read from right to left, remember?"

"Oh, yeah." He turned to me. "Do you think this is the Nephite language?"

I looked down at the plates and pointed at the character that meant *And it came to pass,* or more accurately in their vernacular, *it came and passed by.* "See this? Do you remember it?"

"Yeah, I think so."

I took the paper with the Anthon Transcript on it and showed him the same character, a cross between a capital Z and the numeral 2 with an ornate curlicue across the top. The two forms of it, on the plate and on the sheet, were virtually identical. Then I showed him the upside down V on the first page.

"What are the odds," I said, "that the exact same characters show up in both places? And if you want more proof, I bet I can find more of Anthon's characters here in two minutes."

Before he could respond, I bent over and began searching. It didn't take two minutes, or even ten seconds. On that very page, right in the middle, I found four stacked horizontal lines. Plates. Then on the line below it I saw the filled-in box again, which meant holy. We now had three of the five characters from the Anthon Transcript *on the first page we looked at.*

Ross nodded in slow motion, then, still moving slowly, he reached into his pants pocket and pulled out his camera. "Don't move." He stepped back and took a flash picture of me and the open set of plates. The flash about blinded me. "Whoa!" I rubbed my eyes. "Why'd you do that?"

"Because you discovered all this. They're probably the same plates that Mormon and Moroni had, and you discovered them."

I could almost see again. "We don't know that Mormon or Moroni or anyone else from the Nephites put them here—and besides, *we* discovered them. Not me."

"No, we wouldn't be here if weren't for you. You're the one who found the sign above the snaky part of the canyon, and you're the one who just had to come back here into this box canyon, and you saw the opening up here, and then you came up and found the plates. And, don't forget, you're the first one to read any of these hieroglyphics." He took another picture, surprising me. "I am hereby naming this cave the Travis Call Cave."

"Stop it! And you're not naming this cave anything. I found it, and I forbid anyone from naming it after me. We'll call it—" I paused, searching for sight and the right words. "We'll call it the Plates Cave— no, the Plates Room. How's that? The Plates Room."

"Lame," Ross said, glancing around at the tons of plates. "We'll just call it the Call Cave."

"No, we will not call it the Call Cave. Anna wouldn't appreciate it. And neither would I."

But for a moment I considered the implications of all this for Anna—and for so many others who might need a little help with their faith. Good people who just need a little *evidence* to help them out. This could work miracles.

And it could work tragedies.

I stopped and reconsidered. Can a person be truly converted to the gospel if incontrovertible evidence proved it to them rather than a miracle? Doesn't true conversion imply a sort of miracle?

But if that were the case, why were we here?

"Okay, wait a minute," I said. "We don't know if these plates are from the Nephites. We don't even know they're scriptures. Just because they have some of the same characters doesn't mean anything."

"Well, don't forget the character that means *the Lord*," said Ross, stopping me, "and *holiness* and *It came to pass*. I mean, if these plates have *It came to pass*, then they've got to be scriptures."

"Actually, we don't know that yet, but do you know what?"

"What?"

"We need to find out. There's what, maybe a hundred sets of plates here?"

He looked around the room, glancing in the corners and under the shelves. "Yeah, maybe."

"We don't have time to look at them all, so let's take pictures of them, and try to figure it all out at home."

"'Figure it all out'?"

"I mean, try to find enough characters on them from the Anthon Transcript, maybe even in the same order, so that we can start to find out if, and I mean *if,* these plates might actually be scripture."

"You mean take pictures of every single *plate*? Every page?"

I nodded. "If our cameras have enough storage to hold it all."

We checked the storage devices in our cameras and found that they were both sixteen gigabytes. Ross, the digital expert, figured out the rest. "At six megapixels resolution, we should each be able to get about four or five thousand pictures. How many plates are there?" We looked around again and figured there were probably just less than a hundred sets, but each set was of a different size, with more or fewer pages. We estimated there were at least ten thousand plates to shoot, meaning we might not have enough capacity. But it would be close. "But don't forget," he added, "we have our phones too, but their resolution may not be as good."

"All right, let's just shoot with the cameras until we run out of storage, then we'll switch to the phones if we have to. And if we run out then—well, I guess we just stop."

It was now a little before four. There were only a few hours of daylight left outside. "Okay, let's set up a system and start shooting."

"So to speak."

"So to speak."

Using the table as our workstation, we set up four flashlights on shelves around the room to illuminate the books we put on the table. Along with our headlamps, it created good lighting. I started with the book of plates I had already opened, and Ross hefted another and brought it over and started taking pictures, no flashes required.

We went slowly at first, turning a page and taking a picture every ten seconds or so, then Ross said, "This isn't going to work. My book has at least a hundred pages, and if we take ten seconds a page, that will take a thousand seconds. How long is that?"

I did the math in my head. "Sixteen or seventeen minutes."

"Give us the benefit of the doubt—sixteen minutes. And if we each do fifty books—what's sixteen times fifty?"

That was a little harder, but I finally got it. "Eight hundred minutes. And if we divide that by sixty, we get, let me think, thirteen or fourteen hours."

"Right. It won't work, unless we want to be here till *tomorrow.* And I doubt our batteries will last that long."

But I had one big objection to taking shortcuts.

"We may never be able to come back here, Ross. Who knows what's going to happen when we get back on top, or get back home? I want to take everything with us, and the only way to do that is by taking pictures of *everything*. So, we can go faster, but we have to make every picture count. It may be the only record we'll ever get of it." I flipped a page, took a quick shot, flipped another, took a quick shot, then stopped and checked the two photos. I showed them to Ross. They were clear enough that we could both make out every character on the sheet.

"Okay," he said. "Afterburners!"

Eventually we got into a sustainable rhythm that produced a new picture every four or five seconds. Combined, we were taking a new picture every two seconds, which should take us five and a half hours. Still too long, but I was determined to preserve every character in this room, even if it meant sleeping here and hiking out the next morning.

Ross mentioned the cold, which was indeed becoming an issue.

"I know," I said, "We should have brought coats—but, oh well." I took another picture. It was probably between fifty-five or sixty degrees. We could tough it out.

After an hour, and a dozen or so books, my arms were getting fatigued. Just thirty or forty more to go—for me.

Some of the records were thicker than others, and some were slightly wider and taller, which meant we had to hold our cameras higher to fit the whole page in the frame, which meant two things: we had to check each photo to make sure it wasn't blurred or poorly framed, and, our arms were getting exhausted.

"So, why are we here?" Ross asked, still snapping pictures.

"What?"

"You know—why us? If these things are what we think they are, why didn't the Lord send an apostle, or at least some scholar from BYU?"

"I guess I have two answers. One, maybe the Lord has been trying for years, or generations, to get some leader here, but they were too level-headed to follow such bizarre promptings, or, two, how do we know we were even *chosen*?"

"Well, I *hope* we were, because if we're just two random people finding these things, it could have been *anybody*. I mean, it could have been Keith Nelson, and you know what he would've done with them."

I had no answers. But I had a strong belief: "All I know is, I'm going to treat all this like it's sacred, and I'm going to pray to know what to do, and I hope you do too."

"Of course I will. You know that." He seemed a little agitated.

"I know. I'm sorry, but I have the same questions, and no answers. But one thing I do know—I'm not going to be like Keith and try to make money from all this. And I'm *really* not going to try to become famous from it. So this is the Plates Room, right?"

"I still like the Call Cave."

"Forget it."

I was only a few pages into my current book, and my arms were already killing me. The plates were incredibly heavy when we moved them, and the constant raising and lowering the camera was getting old. "I've got to rest, Ross. My arms and shoulders are really burning."

Ross lowered his camera and rubbed both shoulders. "I was hoping you had to stop before I did."

We sat on the floor against a wall and ate a couple of power bars and drank some water. Thank goodness Ross had remembered to stuff his pants with food. Thank goodness he had remembered to wear those pants.

Five minutes later I got up and went back to the table, but before I could start photographing, Ross came behind me and started massaging my shoulders. I closed my eyes, lowered my head, and muttered, "You have exactly one hour to stop that."

"You know," he said, "I still can't believe we're actually doing this." He dug into my shoulders and the near-pain made me sigh in pleasure.

"You know," I managed to mutter, "even if these are just old Hopi records, or from the people before them, or even before *them*, it's still amazing. I just hope we know what to do with it all."

He stopped rubbing, and I cracked an eye open and saw the brilliant gold page before me. The metal looked absolutely pristine, and the characters were so clear, so fresh looking, that I marveled. "Look at this," I said, "It's like they were engraved yesterday. I know pure gold doesn't tarnish, but how hard was it to make it so pure?"

After having my eyes closed while Ross rubbed my shoulders, the light on the page was almost too bright, and I blinked, and as I did so, I noticed something unusual. The characters I was looking at were familiar. All of them. It was like I knew them.

Was I getting the gift of tongues?

Then, almost with relief, I realized that I recognized the characters because they actually were familiar.

They were the characters from the Anthon Transcript.

Then it hit me—if I was reading the same characters in the Anthon Transcript, then I was reading chapter six of the Book of Ether.

I stepped back and bumped into Ross, and he stepped away. I almost apologized, but then I looked at the hieroglyphics again. They were exactly the same characters, but more precise and easier to read. I pulled the paper from my pocket and compared the two. My vision blurred. My eyes began welling with tears.

Yes, they were identical.

I dropped the paper on the shimmering plate, just below the passage about the fearful voyage in the dome-shaped vessels, and I stepped to the side of the table.

Ross sensed something. "Are you okay?"

"Look at that."

He took my spot and looked at the paper. "Yeah, I've seen that before."

"So compare it to the characters right above it—on the plate."

He didn't move. He didn't speak. He simply stopped breathing.

Then he looked at the paper a little closer.

Then he checked the plate, a lot closer.

Then he stepped back and looked at me. In a hushed, quivering voice, he said, "Is this the Book of Mormon?"

"I don't know if it's the whole thing, but it's at least part of the Book of Ether."

He put his hand to his mouth, then to his eyes. "Oh, my goodness. *Oh, my goodness.*"

He ran his fingers delicately across the perfect, tiny characters. His hand was shaking.

"What do we do?" he whispered.

"I don't know."

I could not have been more alive if a hundred joules of electricity were coursing through me. I tried to think, to understand, to figure out what was happening. Finally I said, "I guess we just keep taking pictures—and don't stop until we're done."

I was about to start doing just that, when another thought hit me, almost as staggering as the other thoughts. I understood that by comparing the record on this plate with the actual Book of Ether I would be able to glean the meaning of every character on these plates, which might indeed include the entire book. And then, by following the line breaks and chapter breaks, I would be able to determine if this actually was the whole book or not. And then, of course, after that, I might be able to learn the translation of every character on every plate in every book in this room.

I might be able to teach myself reformed Egyptian.

My arms weren't as tired now. My legs felt almost young again. I raised the camera and photographed that page, that precious page, then I took a moment to bookmark it in my camera, then I continued photographing until the book was done. I was motivated now. I was "anxiously engaged."

I was on a mission.

I kept finding myself imagining new and vain things, like "If I'm here, working with sacred plates, then this must of course be a sacred work, which means, I guess, that I'm a chosen and sacred man."

Which, of course, was folly, but my inner "natural" man would not be silenced so easily. Grand assumptions were plausible. Even realistic. It was hard work to remind my inner demons that I was still Travis Call, the man who had shot my best friend, who threw up when he got tired, who routinely troubled one of the brightest women in the land.

This worked for a moment, but . . .

The coincidence of what had just happened was too much: my arms had grown too fatigued to keep photographing at exactly the right moment, when exactly the right text was in front of me. What were the odds? Wasn't *that* special?

Of course, maybe I would have found the same passage later when I was going through the plates, but maybe not. Probably not. Why would I examine every character when most of them looked Greek or Chinese or, possibly, Egyptian to me? Thus my fertile mind whispered while I was snapping away. The coincidence probably wasn't a coincidence at all, any more than my desire to walk to this part of the cave had been. Or my choice to lie down in the only spot where I could then stand up and see the shadow of the entrance to this room. The odds were fantastic, which meant that something was going on, something which, now that I thought about it, was becoming more uncomfortable by the second.

Maybe I *was* special.

Heaven forbid.

But what to do about it?

I should probably call the Brethren. I wasn't sure how to do that, but I figured it was possible. Or maybe I should call my bishop or stake president and let them do the heavy lifting. The last thing I wanted—and I could say this honestly—was to gain the attention of Church leaders. I had watched the Brethren operate from a distance and knew that I didn't have the spiritual powers they had—the goodness or knowledge or love or humility they all seemed to possess. Sometimes I couldn't even get my wife to like me. I stopped snapping pictures, now fully confused and depressed. Ross asked why I stopped.

"I'm thinking—about how all this can make our lives miserable."

"What?"

"Think about it, you have a good life now, right? Freedom, money, youth. The world lies before you."

"Yeah, all I need is a good wife and children and a home of my own."

"Yeah, but things could be worse, right?"

"Yeah, sure."

"And, maybe I'm not as young as you, but I have a pretty good life too, including a good wife and children and a nice home."

"Not to mention a nanny-slash-housekeeper who makes *great* dinners."

"Right, so, why would I want to change all that? Why would I want to get out in the public eye—again? Remember eight years ago when the media was camped on the street and we couldn't go to church without making headlines?"

He stopped flipping pages and stared at me.

"Do you want that again? Even from the Church? Even from the *prophet?* I mean, yeah, it'd be nice to hear the prophet say something like, 'Well done, thou good and faithful servant, but . . .'"

"Wait, I thought the Lord was supposed to say that."

"Whatever—but do you know what he, I mean the prophet, would probably say next?"

Ross waited to hear my next outlandish thought.

"Brother Keller, you seem to have a real facility with ancient records. How would you like to work in Church archives down in the basement? Let's make it a calling.'"

Ross's eyes grew wider.

"Or," I continued, "he might say, 'You have a lot of energy and seem to deal well with unusual situations; we have a mission in the

A GRAND CONSPIRACY

Amazon that's having some trouble—' Oh, wait, for that you'd have to be married first. Oh, and think about that! You've had women coming after you for your *money*? Wait till they find out you discovered the lost plates! The Church will have to bring polygamy back because a thousand returned sister missionaries will be blowing up your Facebook page. They'll mob your door. They'll be so thick you'll never be able to get married!"

"You make it sound like a bad thing."

"So, what do you think's going to happen?

"I don't know—maybe we can do everything anonymously—whatever it is we're going to do."

"Anonymously? You mean tell the Church that we found gold plates with the Book of Ether, maybe the whole Book of Mormon, maybe the *entire Large Plates* and the entire Nephite history, and they're not going to ask *who we are*? You see these cameras?" I held my camera up. "These will be holy relics. *We'll* be holy relics. We'll be bronzed and put in cold storage."

"So, what do you want to do?"

I thought for a moment, then I took another shot of another plate. "Keep taking pictures. Maybe we'll figure it out."

Ross took another picture and flipped another page. "Yeah, or maybe we won't even live long enough to tell anybody. Remember, there are some real bad guys out there."

"Right. With any luck maybe they'll solve all our problems."

Chapter 36

The Dead Entombed

He had come down with two flats of water, which was a little over eight gallons. It had taken five gallons to make enough mortar to seal the hole at the entrance. Now he was sizing up the air portal. It was so well concealed—around a bend, above a narrow ledge, behind a bush—that he never would have found it on his own. He yanked the bush out of the wall and looked around for stones large enough to fill the portal's two-foot diameter. Fortunately someone had built a rock platform below it, and the platform was composed of bowling-ball-sized boulders, which would be perfect.

He poured more ready mix into the bucket and was about to empty a bottle into it, when a thought came to him.

The body.

This was a perfect tomb. A perfect solution for many of his problems. He looked up to gauge the light. He didn't want to try to climb out through that interminable chimney in the dark. He still had a few hours. He put the cap back on the bottle and started walking along the ledge to the cul-de-sac.

Too bad the sheep were gone; he had actually enjoyed watching them through the glass; watching them up close would have been fun. But then, he may have had to deal with evil impulses to have some fun with his Glock too—evil because he hadn't brought the weighty suppressor with him.

He got back to Richardson's body and found that it hadn't moved. He checked for vital signs again, but he still wasn't sure. If the man were dead, maybe he was having a near death experience. Maybe he was comatose. Whatever he was, he was about to be cemented into a cave.

Then another thought hit him, and he almost laughed.

He was an accidental killer—again.

Well, almost accidental. If the man was alive now, plugging him in the cave with no way out was basically a long-term execution.

After taking Richardson's phone, he tossed the body over his shoulder. He was surprised by both its weight and flexibility. The little guy hardly weighed anything and you could bend him like a pretzel.

He made it back to the cave without mishap and laid the body down. He was glad he had thought of getting it before tearing the platform apart, because he would need to stand on the platform to hoist the body into the portal.

Using another quart of water, he carefully mixed the cement. His work at the entrance had taught him how much powder and water to use to create the right consistency. He learned to only make a small amount each time because it tended to harden after he had only laid a few stones. He picked Richardson up again and stuffed him head-first into the tomb. His head and torso fit easily, but his legs kept collapsing against his body when Klah tried to push them in. It took a little effort, but he finally got the whole thing inside. He lay the mortar along the bottom of the portal then pressed three large stones from the platform onto it. He mixed another batch and laid four more stones along the wider middle section, slapping the mortar in liberally and forcing it in crevices between the stones. The top section was the most difficult, both because it was higher and because he had used up some of the ladder. By the time he finished, the mortar at the bottom was already hard.

Klah sat in the dust and ate a granola bar and drank another bottle of water. He couldn't have planned it better. Yes, Richardson had freely admitted that he knew too much and that Klah would probably have to kill him, but Klah had hoped to find a way to allow them to still work together. He could never make the same money anywhere else. But Richardson was right; once he had put out a hit on Klah, Klah would never be able to trust him again.

All things considered, this was a natural solution to many of his problems, except for the guys behind him. But the stars had lined up for this issue; maybe they'd line up for that one.

He put the drill and batteries into Richardson's pack and flung it over the ledge. He never heard it hit. Then he flung his own pack over. The only remaining traces of his presence here were his boot prints. He filled his pockets with the few things he would need, then he took the bush he had pulled from the portal and swept the area clean. By the time he finished, he had erased all signs of human presence. Then he began the long climb up to the rim. It was already getting dark in the canyon.

He would need to remember to remove the tracking device from Keller's truck.

There must be no evidence left behind.

Chapter 37

Works of Gold

There were only eighty-three sets of plates, so we finished faster than expected, but it was still almost eight o'clock. The canyon had to be dark. Great, another night hike. Would there be a full moon? There had been a partial moon a few nights ago, but I couldn't remember if it was waxing or waning. I tried to remember which way the crescent was pointing, but, really, it didn't matter. We probably had all the flashlights and batteries we needed.

I was anxious to get cracking on the translation of the characters. Having bookmarked the photo of the Ether six plate, I planned to get on it right away. If sentence length, paragraph length, and chapter breaks corresponded to the same things in Ether six, I might be onto something. I was already kicking myself for not doing it for a few minutes here in the cave.

One thing I had noticed was how compressed the characters were compared to the English. Moroni said that his people used "reformed Egyptian" because their plates were not "sufficiently large" enough to allow the use of Hebrew. In other words, reformed Egyptian was a more compressed form of writing. He was also aware, however, that errors might be introduced in the translating process, probably for two reasons: one, because it was an unknown language outside their culture, and two, because of the concision itself, which seemed to require intuition to make sense of the syntax. For example, in the little I had gleaned from Ether six, I discovered no prepositions in the characters, which meant that one didn't know if someone was doing something *to* someone, or *for* them, or *with* them. Of course, I knew practically nothing about the language so far, so I may have been completely off-base, but it was becoming clear that a small section of reformed Egyptian, perhaps the size of a normal paragraph, could require a page or two of English.

We took one last look around the room to make sure everything was as we found it. We had been moving quickly and wanted to be sure we hadn't misplaced something. We had taken pains to move only one record at a time and then to replace it exactly where we had found it. Yes, we had dusted off the top plates and had undoubtedly left our fingerprints on the corner of each plate, but except for that and our footprints, the room looked untouched.

The important thing to me was, no matter what somebody else did with these plates, we would have a faithful copy of each page, each character. I would transfer all the photos from both cameras to my laptop later—after I had taken a good look at Ether six.

We were about to leave the room when Ross told me to go stand in the doorway. He pulled out his phone and began taking another 360 degree picture. As he was doing this I looked at the table in the center of the room. We had been standing beside it for hours but hadn't really checked it out.

"Ross, did you see if there's anything under the table?"

He put his phone away and glanced at the table. "Like what?"

"I don't know. A drawer or something."

"A drawer? No. Why?"

I didn't answer. I walked back and felt under the edges, looking for something, anything—but nothing was there. To be doubly sure, I knelt down and looked closer but again saw nothing. I got on my back and slid under it.

"Come on, Travis. It's getting dark out there."

"Just a minute. I just want to make sure."

"But there's nothing there."

I was about to crawl out when I spotted something in my peripheral vision. It looked like a triangular support joining a corner of the table to the leg under it. I checked the other corners and didn't see similar supports. I was instantly suspicious because it looked as if it had been finished to blend in with the grain of the table above it. I pulled on it to see if it would come out.

"What are you doing?" Ross was beside me now.

"I think I found something."

He bent down. "What is it?"

"I don't know. Maybe it's just a support."

"A support?"

"Yeah, it looks like the leg might have come loose, and they had to reinforce it at the joint, but—"

He sat down and tried to look up into the corner. "But what?"

"But it looks too big for that." The triangular support was about eight inches across at the front, which faced the center of the table. That was overkill if it was just a support for the leg, and the more I studied it, the more it looked like a triangular box. I knocked on it, and it sounded hollow. There wasn't a knob or handle to pull on, so I pushed in and pulled down, trying to slide it down, but nothing happened. I pushed and pulled harder.

"Be careful." He was on his back under the table now, watching.

"It's hollow. There's got to be something inside."

"Yeah, probably a baby snake."

That was a thought. Whoever had made this place was clearly willing to use snakes to protect things. I was only surprised they hadn't used them to protect the mummies. I pulled downward on the front panel again. It still didn't move. "What's with this thing?"

"Maybe it's been varnished shut."

"Maybe, but . . ."

Another idea hit me—to try to slide the bottom panel out toward the front. But if that worked, it meant that whatever was inside would fall out. I put one hand against the bottom panel and my other hand under it to catch whatever might fall, hoping it wasn't deadly, and I pulled outward. To my surprise, both the bottom and front panels slid forward. It was all joined together. A triangular top panel had stayed fixed against the table top. It had short grooves in it that allowed the lower box to slide out. I prepared to run if something alive jumped out.

The tray came out and rested in my hand. It weighed a few ounces. I looked inside and saw something flat and shiny in the glow of my headlamp.

"What is it?" Ross asked.

"I don't know. It looks like a little plate." I scooted out from under the table so Ross could see it.

A metal plate, about four inches square and probably made of gold, lay in the bottom of the tray. Several markings were on it. Touching only the edges, I lifted it out and held it up to the light. The plate was a little thicker than the other plates and thus was more rigid. I turned it over. The markings were only on one side. They appeared to be a picture of a tree with a little square near its base. But the tree had no top and no branches. But it did have markings of something flowing down its trunk, almost like cooled lava. In the upper righthand corner there was a curved line going from top to bottom, but the line was broken into many tiny sections, like steps—and a possibility occurred to me. The curved line might be the long stairway we had come down earlier, and the "tree" might be the massive stalagmite tower we had walked by. The hardened flowstone on the trunk of the tower did look like flowing lava. I focused on the little square at the tower's base. Along its perimeter it had two straight edges and two jagged edges.

"What is it?"

I gave it to Ross so he could look at it. "I think it's a map."

"No—it's a tree."

"Yeah, but I think the tree is really the big tower out in the cave, the one with the flowstone on its sides."

He looked at it more carefully. "Yeah, it could be. And so that's the staircase." He pointed at the winding line coming down from the upper right. "So, what's the little square?"

"I don't know. Let's go find out."

I was about to take the plate back, when Ross looked at it a little closer. "And look, what's this little line here?"

His eyes were better than mine. He had spotted a short vertical line just under the square. "I don't know. Hold it still, and I'll take a picture of it."

We took a couple of pictures, making sure the glare didn't blow out the image, then I put the plate back in the tray and slid the tray back into place. The tolerances of the tongue-in-groove construction were perfect.

We stood up and were about to leave again when Ross said, "What made you look under the table?"

"I don't know—I just wanted to make sure we weren't missing something. I got lucky, I guess."

"I guess."

We left the room, and Ross pulled out his last Power Bars and last two bottles of water. "There's more food in our packs, but maybe we should refuel here." We ate quickly.

The larger cave seemed a little dimmer now. Our headlamps were beginning to fade. We changed out the batteries from the stock in Ross's pockets then went over to the steps. Ross went down first, and I followed. At the bottom step, Ross hung from it then let go and landed on the talus, about five feet below. Then he turned around and helped me as I let go, landing half in his arms. Going down, it turned out, had been a lot easier than going up.

The main cave seemed dimmer too. "Ross, let's turn off our lights."

"Why?"

"Because I want to see how dim the lantern is up by the snakes."

We turned off our headlamps, and the cave shut down in almost total blackness, reminding me why no one had been able to see it before. Although the lantern above the snakes was not in a direct line of sight, we had seen its glow back in this box canyon, but now it was barely discernible. We turned our headlamps back on, illuminating the area around us. Thank goodness for the batteries in Ross's pocket.

We got two flashlights from our pockets and focused them as well as our headlamps on the spectacular tower, which soared upward about two hundred feet away. Above it, the amazing flying curtain hung hundreds of feet above us. Its size and frozen rippling beauty was almost scary, but we were on a mission now, and we kept our four lights trained on the tower. As we got closer, the brownish flowstone on its base began to sparkle like a city at night, as if diamonds were embedded in the stone.

We got to its base and found that the diamonds were thousands—millions—of glazed fractures along the bumpy, wart-like surface. The extra illumination from four lights lit them up in a way we hadn't seen before. We ascended the flowstone's gradual slope and made our way to the base of the tower, but we saw nothing that looked like a square. Ross turned and circumnavigated the "tree" one way, and I went the other. It was a couple of hundred feet around, so it took a while, but when we met again, neither of us had found anything. We got the camera out and looked at the map. I noticed that the little square was slightly higher than the base of the immense pillar.

"Doesn't it look like the little box is above the ground?"

"I don't know. If it is, it isn't much higher."

"I don't know—think about how tall this thing is. Even a little bit higher on the map could be twenty or thirty feet in real life."

We looked upward, trying to follow the smooth, fluted sides along the pillar for a sign, but we saw nothing. We went around it again, this time together. On the back side, the smooth, slightly fluted surface gave way to another fossilized structure, something that resembled Spanish moss frozen in place. It almost looked like tendrils, or hundreds of off-white tentacles, coming down the column. They stopped about five feet above us. We looked at the picture again, then Ross pointed up. "I wonder if that little line on the plate means one of these tentacle things coming down."

The problem was that the line seemed to come all the way down to the base—possibly to our level.

"Maybe it's a symbol for a ladder," I said. "Or a rope."

On the actual tower, some of the tentacles looked like they had pulled away from the base, possibly producing gaps of four or five inches between them and the pillar itself.

"I think we have to go up there," I said. "We need to check those gaps behind the tentacles."

"You mean, *you* need to check them out, because you also mean that *I* will have to lift you up."

"Well—I guess if you want to put it that way."

"What other way is there?"

"So, do you want me to take my boots off first?"

He shook his head in disgust. "What would you do without me?"

"Probably die."

"That's for sure. All right, take your boots off."

I took them off, and he crouched down, and I stepped onto his shoulders. Then, with my hands on the tower, he stood up and I was able to get up to a height of about ten or eleven feet, where I began searching in the gaps. The tendrils felt like calcified tree roots, though I knew they were mineral deposits. Again, I found nothing. Ross stepped to his left, and I searched more gaps and hidden openings.

"Hurry up," Ross said.

I weighed close to two-hundred pounds, but I knew he was as strong as a mule. "I need to be thorough. You don't want to do this again, do you?"

"Be thorough a little faster."

He stepped to the left again, before I had directed him to, and I was about to fall, when I grabbed one of the tendrils and stabilized myself. His little maneuver annoyed me, but I said nothing. Out of the corner of my eye I spotted something behind a root we had just passed, level with my waist. I had probably been looking above it. "Hey, go back to your right a little." He moved that way, and I was able to reach down and grasp a small but weighty object in the gap.

"Okay, let me down."

"How far?"

"All the way. I found something."

He lowered me to the ground, and both of our headlamps illuminated a square wooden box about three inches across. It was highly polished with the amber resin we had seen in the plates room. I tried to open it, but once again, it seemed stuck. I tried several different ways before it opened with an audible "crack."

"Did you break it?"

"I don't think so. I think it was just sealed shut." I slid the top off and saw a square rock inside. It was dark brown, about two-and-a-half inches across. It had jagged edges on two sides and smooth edges on the other two, like the picture on the plate. It was less than an inch thick, and it too had drawings on it. I carefully lifted it out and held it in our combined light.

"Is it a rock?" he asked.

"I think so, but it looks like it's been broken off of something."

"And it has pictures on it."

I flipped it over. There were pictures on both sides.

"Do you know what they . . . Whoa! Look!" Ross pointed at one of the symbols. It looked like a swastika, except the right angles were rounded instead of sharp. "Is that what I think it is?"

"Probably not," I said. "I doubt it has anything to do with World War Two. It probably has some spiritual meaning—probably all of these designs do."

I studied each one closely. Some of the drawings appeared to be broken off at the jagged edges, perhaps from a larger stone, a stone that apparently had a larger, fuller picture on it. On one side a line circled around the inside of the smooth outer edges, until it was broken off at the jagged edges where the stone had been broken off. It looked like it had been part of a border around the inside of a larger tablet. Inside that border were two other designs, one of which was the swastika with the rounded corners bent around to the right, and the other picture appeared to be a snake. It had two curves in it, like an S, but they were softer, straighter.

I turned it over again and saw four more pictures, which, again, appeared to have been broken off from a larger stone. One of the pictures, near where the stone had been broken off, was the head of a man, drawn in ink with three colors, white, gray, and black. If there was a body, it had been broken off. There was also another picture of a snake, or a curved path, and some kind of plant, possibly a corn stalk. The last picture was a simple right angle with a sun or moon inside it. I had no idea what they meant or what the larger picture might have looked like.

"What do you want to do with it?" Ross asked.

"I'm really tempted to take it with us."

"Do you think we should?"

I thought about it. "No, probably not. We didn't take any of the plates, or anything from the mummies. I guess we should just take some pictures and put it back."

Which is what we did, both of us taking several pictures of each side. In each picture I made sure that my hand holding the stone was in view for perspective. Then I put the stone back in its box and slid the top shut. Ross bent down, and I got back on his shoulders and put the box where it had come from.

I got down and put my boots back on.

"What do you think it is?" Ross asked.

"I have no idea, but it must have been important to whoever made that map in the plates room."

"Call Room—I mean Call Cave."

"Whatever."

As we walked away from the tower, I turned around occasionally to memorize where the box was on the pillar.

We arrived at the base of the staircase which wound a half a mile up and around to the snakes. I told Ross I was getting tired.

He turned my way, blinding me with his light. "Don't even *think* of asking me to carry you up those stairs."

So much for that.

We began trudging up, and I was struck once again by how perfect the steps were for men our size. Climbing them wasn't easy, but it could have been harder if they'd been smaller or shorter. It took twenty minutes, but we finally reached the snakes.

And they were waiting for us.

They were grouped between us and the rope. In fact, several of them were coiled up on part of the rope resting on the ground.

Well, I thought, this should be fun. But before I could say anything, Ross rushed them, waving his arms and screaming. Clearly he was tired of dealing with nuisances. He got closer than I thought he would, and the nearest snakes struck at him but missed. Then another snake sank its fangs into his pants. Ross jumped back, pulling the snake with him. I knew that rattlesnakes could strike at a hundred miles an hour, but now I wondered if that estimate was conservative.

It had been a blur. But Ross didn't hesitate; he reached down, grabbed the snake's body and yanked it outward, ripping its fangs out of his pants, then swirled it around his head and threw it back into the cave where they had gone to hide earlier. The buzz of hundreds of rattles filled the cave, but most were hurrying away again.

Ross checked his pants. "These were my favorites!" He showed me a tear in the fabric.

"Why'd you do that? You could have been bit!"

"It made me mad that they were trying to stop us!" He paused and looked at me. "When was the last time we slept?"

"I don't know. In the truck?"

"Maybe I'm not thinking straight." He looked back at the snakes, which were still putting space between us. "But why are they even here? I mean, what's down here except a bunch of cold air?"

"Maybe they evolved to like the cold. Or maybe they're hibernating and haven't decided to go outside for the spring yet."

"Why not? It's like a hundred degrees out there."

"Maybe that's why—too hot."

Putting his flashlight in his pocket, he walked to the rope, which was clear of snakes now, and grabbed it above a knot, then he jumped up and wrapped his legs around it and began climbing. It was at times like this when I admired his athleticism. He hadn't played sports in high school, but he clearly could have been a star. Six-three, two-hundred, with agility and quickness. High school had been a rough time for him, with both of his parents passing away.

Watching him manhandle the rope and fly to the top in less than ten seconds made me shake my head. There was no way I could do that.

After resting a few seconds, Ross asked what I was waiting for. I lied and said I was fighting off a pack of snakes.

"Then get on the rope. They can't get you there."

It was good advice, if I could take it.

I put my hands around a knot, a foot lower than the one he had taken, and grasped good and tight. Then I jumped up like he did and tried to get my knees around a lower knot, but the knots were small, and my legs kept slipping off. How had he done it? I let go and tried again, startling one or two of the snakes who had slowed down to watch me. I slipped off again.

"Hey, Ross! Can you just pull me up?"

He groaned. Loudly. "Really?"

I felt his disgust, and I determined to do better. I jumped again, this time grasping the same knot he had, because it obviously worked better, and pulled myself up a few inches. My legs wiggled free for a moment then found purchase on a knot. I pulled harder and defied gravity, by rising two inches.

This wasn't bad—only about three-hundred more inches to go.

I reached for another knot, caught it, and pulled up again. My legs wiggled free for a terrifying second before my knees found another knot and boosted me up. A minute later I had climbed five feet, maybe six, and had completely exhausted myself. But during quick glances below, I had noticed the snakes coming back, possibly for entertainment, possibly for something more.

"Hey, Ross! Are you sure you can't just pull me up?"

He didn't answer, but I soon felt myself rising, miraculously, wonderfully. We should have done this sooner. Sounds came from above, remarkably like a grizzly clearing its throat. Poor Ross, for all his strength, he was struggling. I decided to help again. I reached up, caught another knot, and succeeded in hoisting myself another foot or so.

"What are you doing?" he shrieked.

"Trying…to…climb!"

"Stop! It's making it harder!"

Well, if he was going to be like that.

I held my ground, or my rope, and mentally bade the levitation to continue.

When I reached the point where I could set my feet against the rock, I did so and tried to walk up its rounded face. It didn't work, so Ross yanked me over the edge. Then he collapsed.

"How much do you weigh?" he asked, not very nicely.

"Less than you! How much do you weigh?"

He just closed his eyes and continued grunting and groaning. I went to his pack and scavenged another Power Bar and bottle of cool water. They both tasted great. Ross eventually got to his feet and came over.

"You didn't eat them all, did you?"

I gave him some latitude because of his fatigue "No—and thank you." I spoke as sincerely as possible, but he still looked over to check for sarcasm.

"For what?"

"For saving my life. Again. I think I could've made it with a thicker rope, but, believe me, I know how much of a burden I've been."

He eyed me suspiciously then said, "Well, if we come down again, one of us needs to start working out first."

I just nodded, reached into the pack, and offered him a water and Power Bar. He finished both in about fifteen seconds.

I put the spent lantern in my pack, and after we had both mounted up, we set off. Because the packs were lighter, and because we were in a hurry, we increased our stride and made good time. It actually seemed that I *was* getting in shape, after a fashion. Which only made sense since I had walked fifty or sixty miles the past week, including a jaunt up and down the sides of the Grand Canyon.

Twenty minutes later we approached the entrance and saw that it was indeed dark outside. Very dark. Not even any moonlight.

"*It's gone*," Ross said, almost like a question.

We were ten feet from the wall, and now I realized what he meant. *The hole was gone.*

"Did some rocks fall into it?" I asked.

"I don't—" He walked to where the hole should have been and pushed on a rock. Nothing happened. He pushed harder, grunting. Still nothing happened. He took his pack off and knelt down.

"Look at this!"

I slipped my pack to the floor and knelt beside him. He was running his finger over a thin gray vein between rocks. Then I realized it wasn't a vein of rock, but a vein of mortar. I touched it and was surprised by its hard, sharp edges.

"Did somebody try to fix the hole?"

"No—somebody sealed it shut. And the drill and batteries are gone!"

He was right. A thrill of fear filled my chest.

Ross sat down facing the cemented wall and kicked at it as hard as he could. Nothing moved. He kicked again, and again, and again. Nothing budged.

"Let's go," I said and started jogging back into the cave through the corridor we had just come down. Ross knew exactly where I was going.

"Do you think it was the same guy?" Ross called as we ran. "I thought he wanted us to go public with everything."

"I don't know. Maybe he changed his mind—or maybe it was the other guys."

Speculation was futile.

We took the first right and followed it a long way, passing some doorways, and followed it around a bend to the right. It was farther than I remembered, but we eventually came to the tall platform below the hole, the one I had come in on a few days before. It was dark up there, but that was to be expected, as the passage beyond it wound up and down before leading to a narrow tube going out of the cave—too narrow for Ross.

I got up on the platform and stuck my head in the portal and was about to climb in, when I thought better of it. What if it was cemented shut too? Could I get stuck in the part where it bent down, where I had landed on my head the first time? I yelled into the hole and heard the echo instantly. Did that mean it was blocked? I wasn't sure.

"Do you need help?" Ross asked below the platform.

"I don't want to go inside it if it's sealed off too. I might not be able to get back out."

Ross joined me, but even with both lamps we couldn't see beyond the first hard turn.

"I'm afraid I won't be able to turn around," I said.

He went down off the platform and got the knotted, doubled rope out of his pack. "How about if we tie this to one of your feet? I should be able to pull you back out if I have to."

I looked in the hole again, trying to gauge the risk, but we had no other option. If only we had kept the drill. As it stood now, we were either getting out this way, or we were in serious trouble. We made the knot around my right ankle as secure as possible, as I would never be able to reach it if it came loose. Then I went in.

I had read stories about tunnel rats in Vietnam, men, not animals, who slid into enemy tunnels headfirst to root the enemy out. I never wanted to do that.

I navigated the turn without problem. Then I got to the inverted cone and immediately saw that if I went down it, I would never be able to get myself out.

"Ross!" I yelled. The sound must have somehow filtered back, because he answered. "If I keep going and can't get out, you'll have to pull me up through the upside down cone. And I won't be able to help!"

"What else is new?"

There are times to argue and times to turn the other cheek. I went forward, cheek first. Ross was keeping some tension on the rope, but not enough to hinder me. I started to slide over the edge into the cone and inched my way down a few inches until all my weight was on the rope. He couldn't see me, but he was almost perfectly lowering me into the hole. Moments later I was able to stick my hands out to the walls of the cone and turn myself around so I could see forward into the opening.

At first, I thought my vision had gone bad from being upside-down, because I saw a dark spot in front of me, as big as a bowling ball.

Then I realized that it was a head.

I tried to scramble back, but I was still mostly hanging in the air and ended up scrambling in place. Then I realized that I was still going down and the head wasn't moving. As my knees touched the bottom of the tunnel, I raised my head, with its lamp, and saw that the portal was walled off.

Whoever had buried us had buried this guy too.

But was he alive?

I felt the tension relax on my ankle as my foot hit the floor, and I yelled back over my shoulder: "Ross!"

"What?"

"There's somebody in here!"

"*What?*"

"There's somebody in here! He's unconscious. Or dead."

"Oh, wow." He was silent a moment then came the inevitable question. "Can you push him out? Is the portal open?"

"No! It's blocked off!"

Ross didn't respond, and I crawled over to the man. He was on his side, and I saw a nasty welt on his cheek. It looked more like a burn than a bruise. I put my left hand on his jaw to find his carotid artery, but I pulled my hand back. His face was warm. Either he had just been killed, or he was still alive. I put my hand back on him and felt for the artery. The positioning was awkward, but I thought I felt something. I tried to get my ear close to his face so I could hear his breathing, but my own pulse and breathing were so loud in the close confines that I couldn't hear anything else.

"Ross!"

"What?"

"I think he's still alive! Start pulling me back. I'm going to try to drag him back out!"

"Okay!"

I grabbed the guy's shoulders and tried to pull him toward me. It was hard, but I managed to straighten him out a little, then I used one hand to reach under his armpit and pull while I used the other to push myself backwards.

"Pull!" I yelled, and the rope tightened and I felt myself sliding backwards. Ross's strength was again being demonstrated—and was again being appreciated.

The hard part was keeping my hand over or under the man's armpit, and I kept pausing to reposition it. He was little, which helped, but it was still hard work, and my ankle was starting to burn.

We got to the cone, which I knew would be the moment of truth. Ross would have to literally pull me up by the ankle, and I would have to hoist all this dead weight. As my right leg came off the ground, I steadied myself for the increase in pain.

But I had no idea how great it would be.

Now I knew why Ross had screamed when I put the belt around his wrist and pulled.

As he lifted my leg and torso up, I gritted my teeth and tried to keep both legs together so my free one wouldn't hit the side of the cone. I got both hands under the guy's armpits and pulled him closer to me, putting my head next to his, allowing me to wrap my arms around him and clench my hands together at his chest.

Ross kept lifting, and soon I saw a serious flaw in our plan but had no idea how to fix it, or prevent what was about to happen.

When my foot got over the top of the cone, so that it was level with Ross and the rope, there was no way for my body to continue going up except for the front of my shin to slide over the edge of the stone.

I screamed from the pain and felt myself beginning to black out.

"Stop! Stop! Stop! Let me down!"

Ross quickly let some line out, and as my bone came off the rock I felt a measure of relief. I didn't want to see what it looked like. Using the man's body as leverage, I managed to turn myself around so the back of my calf would slide over the edge first.

"Okay! Try again!"

Ross pulled a little slower, and my foot, then my calf, began raking over the edge. The pain was sickening, but I didn't pass out. When the calf muscle finally slid over the top, so my knee could bend, some of the pressure was relieved, and I thought I might live.

Then I heard something below me, and I looked down past the man and saw a phone on the ground. My phone. It had fallen out of my pocket. I hadn't used it to take pictures of the plates, but it had other pictures from the days before, most importantly of the mummies. Of course, we now had other pictures of them, but I wanted these too.

"Let me back down! I dropped my phone!"

"Aw, *Travis!*"

He had a way of saying two things at once, because I knew what he really meant was *What kind of imbecile am I saddled with?*

Sometimes it's hard to be me.

He let me down, and the raking and excruciating pain repeated itself, and the man's body came to rest on the phone, and I wanted to cry, and maybe I did, because tears or blood or something was dripping from my face. I reached under him and forced him aside, all while being suspended by my ankle. Then I felt for the phone, found it, picked it up, stuck it deeply up into my shirt pocket, where I could Velcro the flap shut, then I took a deep breath and said, "Okay, pull us up!"

My pants legs had dropped down by my knees by this time, exposing the skin directly to the rock. And although the man's weight was still mostly on the ground, the pain on my calf was beyond belief. But Ross kept pulling, and I kept rising, then the man started rising, and I was dying a little more, until my right knee finally bent over the edge, which allowed my calf to lie flat on the shelf above me, which alleviated some of the pain, but not all of it, because the man was also rising, which put more weight on my leg, a lot more, and now the same raking thing happened to my hamstring. Each second became the worst moment of my life.

And all of this was compounded by thoughts that we might be stuck down here forever.

When my hips got to the edge, I called for a halt and managed to work myself around so that I bent naturally at the waist going over it. My hands began slipping from around the man's chest, but there was *no way* I was going down after him again, so I quickly let go of my lock around his chest and grabbed his armpits with both hands, digging my fingers into his muscles, tendons, or whatever else I might find.

And that's when he started screaming.

Which almost scared me to death.

"Shut up," I said, "and hold my hands!"

He was alert enough to follow directions, evidently, because I felt his hands grab mine. Of course, he may have just been trying to get my fingers out of his armpits. But I held on, and he held on, and we came out of the inverted cone more or less together.

When we were both on the level again, I told Ross to stop pulling, and I let go of the man and backed myself out. Ross held my legs and guided them to the floor. The man was no longer yelling, and I wondered if he had passed out again.

"Was it wet in there?" Ross asked, still holding my legs.

"It is now," I said. "With my blood."

He looked at his hands. They were red. "Oh, wow. Are you okay?"

I wasn't sure how to answer. I could have said, "Of course not, we're going to die in here." Or, "No, my legs just got ground up by that cheese grater somebody chiseled into the rock," or, "Please tell me you have another Power Bar in your pack, because I would like a last meal now." Instead, I just pulled my pant leg down over the raw meat and bone and looked back into the passageway at the man.

His face was pointed our way, and he quickly put a hand out to block the light.

"Come on!" Ross ordered. "We can't pull you anymore."

"Who are you?" he yelled. "Where am I?"

"We'll tell you when you get out! Come on."

He pulled himself forward until Ross could reach his shoulders.

"Don't grab my armpits!" he screamed. "I think they're ripped open."

"Ripped open?" Ross said. "Come here!" He was getting surly.

He helped the man down to the platform, then he put an arm around me and helped me down the steps to the ground. I collapsed when he let go of my arm. Ross looked up at the man to make sure he was staying put, then he got down next to me and checked my legs again. Both my right shin and calf were shredded and bleeding heavily. It looked like part of the bone may have been scraped off.

"We're out of water," he said, pulling a bandana out of one of his pockets. He dabbed my wounds to stanch the bleeding, then he wrapped the bandana around the leg and tied it off in a loose knot. When he was done, he pulled the pants leg down. "Are you going to be able to walk?"

I said I thought so, since some blood seemed to have stayed in my body.

The other guy was quiet but wide awake. Ross asked him if he could stand up, and the guy slowly got to his feet, and Ross helped him down off the platform. They both sat next to me.

The man saw the blood on my hands and boots, but remained silent.

"What happened to you?" I asked. "Who put you in the cave?"

He didn't speak.

"Are you okay?" Ross asked.

The man looked at him. "I fell and must have hit my head. I'm feeling sick to my stomach, and my face hurts," he touched the angry welt on his cheek, "but, I don't know—I think I'm okay."

He sounded intelligent, probably educated. His hands were soft, unaccustomed to hard work, but his eyes were quick, and I caught him stealing a glance at me before looking away.

"We're stuck in here," Ross said. "Somebody cemented the cave shut from the outside. Do you know anything about that?"

The man looked around. "There were some men out there. They may have been looking for you. When they came up to me, they accused me of helping two guys escape from them. We were up by the rim, and one of them pushed me down. That's all I remember. I guess they put me in here before they closed off the cave."

Ross and I shared a look. They were all up by the rim? We had been up there twice in three days and hadn't seen another human being within twenty miles, except, maybe, the old Indian.

"What were you doing up there?" I asked.

"I'm a geologist. I was gathering data for a survey on the age of Marble Canyon."

He was wearing all black, and none of his clothes seemed appropriate for work in the desert. No boots, no hat, no gloves. I could tell that Ross didn't believe him either.

"Well, we need to find a way out of here," Ross said, "or it won't matter who any of us are or what we're doing."

"But what *are* you guys doing here?" he asked unexpectedly, looking over at me.

"I'll make you a deal," I said. "When you tell us who you really are and why you're really here, I'll tell you why we're here."

He stared at me with dead eyes.

Ross stood up. "The way I see it, there's two options."

I didn't know there were any options, so this was good news.

"I remember feeling air moving in the main corridor, so I wonder if there's another air hole over on the other side of the entrance."

I thought back to the first day I came in; I had felt it then too, but I had figured it was simply air circulating from the air portal into deeper, colder regions of the cave.

"And in case there isn't, what's the other option?" I asked.

"The snaky cave. Those snakes have got to get out somehow. Maybe the opening's big enough for us."

"But how are we supposed to get past a hundred snakes?" I asked.

"What? A hundred snakes?" the man asked.

"Probably more than that," Ross said. "Rattlesnakes. And they're blocking the way out."

"But it's only the way out if it's big enough," I added. "Too bad we don't have more of those big firecrackers or maybe we could scare them off and try to widen it—if it's too narrow."

Ross stared at me, then his face seemed to sag in disappointment.

"What?" I said. "You don't have them?"

"No—I just got out-thought by somebody with a brain disease. Of course I have them. They're in my pocket." He shook his head. "And we don't have to try to scare the snakes; we just have to try to blow the wall open again. I'm really goin' downhill."

He stood up and peeled off a Velcro strap on his left pant leg and dug into a pocket and brought out a handful of M-250s. "I only used one of these, remember? 'Cause you made me drill all those holes. You're a genius. Maybe Kevin rubbed off on you. Come on, let's go back to the entrance."

"But we don't have the drill anymore. It probably won't work as good."

"All right, do you want to go back to the snakes?"

I stood up. He hadn't bothered to mention that going back to the snakes also meant going back to the rope.

"Where are we going?" the man said, rising to his feet. He swayed badly, and Ross and I grabbed him. "We're going to the main entrance," Ross said. "It's been cemented shut too, but we're going to try to blow some rocks loose."

The man nodded, and we began walking. He complained of nausea, which almost certainly indicated a concussion, but he kept walking.

"The guy who pushed you," I said, "was he a big guy, with short dark hair? Looked like a Native American?"

"I think so," he said. "He was strong, I remember that."

"It was probably him," Ross said. "He probably put another GPS tracker on my truck before he came to our room. I should have checked it before we left town."

We were in the main corridor now, and our lights illuminated the rock wall covering the entrance. As we approached it, the man saw the maze on the wall to our right. He wanted to look at it, so I took him over while Ross went to the cemented wall. Maybe he was a scientist after all.

He put his hand on it, just as Ross and I had done. "It's beautiful. Do you know who made it?"

I shook my head, causing the light to wiggle back and forth. He looked up at me. "Do you have more batteries?"

"Yes, but . . ."

"But hopefully we won't need them!" Ross interjected. "Fire in the hole!"

I covered my ears just before a brilliant light from the explosion filled the cave. Afterward, I could still hear, but I was almost blind.

"Did it work?" I asked.

Ross had turned away from it and could still see. He went back to check it out. "I stuffed it between two rocks as far in as it would go." My sight was coming back now, and I saw him blowing debris from the hole he had made.

"Yes!" He looked closer. "Kind of." He pushed the rock. It might have wiggled a fraction. "This new cement is strong." Still sitting down, he kicked it several times until I thought either his boot or the wall would fail. "The problem is," he said, catching his breath, "it feels like there's another rock behind this one, so I've got to loosen two or three of them at once."

"Can you get it loose enough so you can put two firecrackers in there?"

"Maybe."

He began kicking again, and I thought I could actually feel the shock waves in the floor of the cave. If this didn't work, nothing would. He stopped and examined the rock again.

"I knocked some of the new cement out. Maybe I can get two of them in there now."

He couldn't get two 250s into the hole, but he got a 250 and an M-80 in. He twisted the fuses so they would burn together and put a match to it. He jumped back and covered his ears. We did likewise and shut our eyes.

The explosion was formidable.

Ross jumped away as fragments of stone struck the back of his legs.

"Are you okay?" I asked.

"I don't know. Check."

He turned his back to me, and I saw several holes where rock chips had pierced his pants. He was bleeding in one hole, but it wasn't deep. "I think you'll live," I said, "but the pants are history."

"No! They're going piecemeal." He went back to the wall and tried to push the stone he had been kicking. It fell out of the wall.

He put the rock behind him and blew debris out of the hole that was left. "Okay, the other rocks are loose."

"I wonder if anybody outside could hear the explosion," I said.

"No way," Ross said. "It didn't blow all the way through."

As he positioned more firecrackers between two more rocks, I noticed that the little man's body was trembling. He almost looked like he wanted to turn and run, but he had no light so I didn't worry about that.

"What's the matter?" I asked. "Feeling sick again?"

"No. Just cold."

He didn't look 'just cold.' He looked terrified. "Really? So, you're not worried about what we might find out there?"

He was silent, then more firecrackers went off.

"Yes!" Ross exclaimed. "Progress!"

I turned back to the man. "When you want to tell me your name, go ahead, and I'll tell you mine—but I think you already know it."

His eyes flicked toward me, then away. "Why do you think that?"

"Because I can put two and two together. You're not dressed for work in hundred-degree heat. In fact, you look like a prowler, all dressed in black. There's only one reason I can think of for you to be out here—and that's to get us. You're with the Indian, aren't you?"

"You mean the big guy you were talking about?"

I rolled my eyes. "Just let me know when you're ready to talk. I've got a feeling we're going to run into him again."

Chapter 38

Betwixt and Between

Night had fully fallen by the time Klah approached the rim, which complicated matters because he didn't want to use his flashlight. Mostly, he didn't want to attract the attention of anyone waiting for him on the rim. He had finally reached the steep chimney-like ravine which led up to the bowl next to the rim. The starlight was fuller up here, he noticed, and he was startled by the bright gash of the Milky Way. At this elevation the stars' illumination almost doubled. Maybe he wouldn't need the flashlight.

He had Richardson's phone but didn't know which number would reach the Society. The man hadn't spoken of family or friends or colleagues at the university, though Klah figured he had some. He decided to redial the most recent numbers and see what happened. Hopefully he would eventually reach somebody in charge, then he would negotiate a deal. The deal would have to include full payment for the job, since, of course, he had actually completed it now; and it would also need to include a guarantee that they would never come after him again. If they did and he survived, he would make the cave public and reveal the Society's role in looting it and conspiring in the coverup.

He began the ascent up the steep ravine, trying to remain as quiet as possible. It was hard, tedious climbing, and chancy in the dark, but he couldn't risk being heard by others. He finally pulled himself over the last handhold that led into a semicircular bowl that in turn would lead up to the plateau where his Jeep should be. He climbed up into the bowl and made his way to the far edge, twenty or thirty yards away. His head cleared the horizon—and he ducked.

The red SUV was parked next to his Jeep. The nanobots' signal from his body *had* reached them. Keeping low, he worked his way to the right, around the nearly circular bowl, and raised his head again. All three vehicles were visible—his, the SUV, and Keller's truck—and he also saw outlines of at least two men in the front seat of the SUV.

He was almost certain there had been four at the motel, which meant there were probably two more in the back seat.

No doubt they were waiting for him or Call and Keller to emerge from the canyon, but they didn't know when that would be. They may have already been waiting for hours. Although he was outnumbered, Klah had the advantage. They had weapons and a vehicle, but he also had a weapon and the element of nighttime surprise.

The land above the bowl was level, but there was scrub brush and bunchgrass at roughly four-foot intervals. The brush was less than two feet high, but that was high enough for him to conceal himself as he crawled the seventy yards toward the SUV. He dropped the pack and took the gun out of his waistband, where it had been digging a divot in his lower back. He already knew it was fully loaded, but he checked nonetheless. 15 nine-millimeter cartridges were ready for duty.

He dropped to all fours and began crawling.

There was a voice, and he heard a door close.

In the desert, without obstructions, sound seemed to carry for miles, but he knew right where these sounds were coming from. Another door opened and closed, then two more. All four were here. He peeked around a bit of yellow rabbitbrush and saw them heading his way. Two had flashlights on.

He doubted they had seen him, but he hurried back into the bowl, and, taking no chances, slid back down into the chimney. Their voices came closer, calm, matter of fact. They hadn't seen him. Maybe they were coming over to the edge to see if a flashlight could be seen coming up the canyon. He was about to slide down farther into the chimney, to a large rock about fifteen feet below him, when he remembered the pack.

He froze. It was only about twenty yards away, but it was up by the horizon, where they would be at any moment. He turned away from it and let himself down to the large rock. His feet slipped and made a small rockslide, but it didn't seem too loud. He quickly reached the boulder and scrambled behind it. He was stuck now, the mile-deep canyon below him and the four men, probably with four guns, above him.

Their voices came closer. "Turn off your lights!" one of them commanded. "D'ya want him to see us before we see him?"

He looked up around the rock and saw a sharp glow of illumination go out. How far down would they come? How determined were they? How much money had they been offered to kill him? He heard nothing for a moment, then a littering of rocks cascaded into the chimney. They had come all the way across the bowl and were just above him. His gun was in his left hand, ready to fire. Outside of war he had never killed a man intentionally, but now he would do it with no regrets.

In fact, he would gladly do it four more times.

* * *

As Ross tore the wall apart, I did some thinking about our little friend. I was sure he had some connection to the others pursuing us, but I couldn't put the pieces together. It made no sense that they had entombed him in the portal and sealed it shut, unless they had had a falling out.

Ross was about to kick the last rock free of its mortar.

"Let me just tell you," I said to the man, "when we get out of here, you're free to do what you want. Even though I'm sure you're with the guys trying to kill us, we're not going to stop you. We don't even have a gun. But let me tell you something else. The big guy, the guy who held us at gunpoint in our motel room, he wants us to go public with everything we've found. He thinks it's the only way we can save ourselves."

I thought this might bring a response, but he remained silent.

"He thinks it might be the only way for him to survive too," I added, "because then the people behind all this would have no reason to silence him—the news would be out. But I've been thinking—maybe we won't do what he wants."

He looked up at me, and I noticed that Ross did the same thing from the wall.

"We have found things in here that I think are so sacred they shouldn't be disturbed. They're priceless, but if we went to the press or published it on the internet, every geologist, environmentalist, and politician in America would be here within a week—not to mention the crackpots and fortune-hunters who'd try to sneak in to make a quick buck. So, I'll tell you what we're going to do. Nothing. We're not going to say a word, and if you and the people I suspect you work for want to seal this place up again, be our guest. I'm sure it was done for the wrong reasons at first, but maybe it was the right move all along."

He watched my eyes carefully.

"We're outta here!" Ross had kicked out the last rock, and now he cautiously stuck his head and shoulders through it and looked around, then pulled himself back in. "Nobody's out there."

The man spoke. "What did you find?"

"Mister," I said, "this is probably the greatest cave in the world. There are formations in there that would humble anybody. Think of Yosemite, but with a roof over it. Think of the *Grand Canyon*, but with formations that nobody's ever seen and with a ceiling that's miles long and over a thousand feet high, and, it has hundreds of rooms and chambers, all perfectly engineered and carved by hand. Think of the mummies of Egypt, most of which got looted, but most of these, *most* of them, are untouched. There's ancient writings on the walls that would change the way historians see the world, not to mention religion."

An eyebrow went up. "Religion?"

"We've only seen a fraction of this place, but I'm sure it would change the way everybody sees the world. And maybe that's a good thing, but I don't want to be responsible for turning it into Disneyland." I looked at Ross, who had come back to us. "And I don't want to be responsible for changing the way people learn eternal truths."

Ross nodded in agreement. "Maybe the world's not ready for *everything* that's in here."

I turned back to the short, bald man. "So, we can get out of here now, and you can go where you want, do what you want, even try to kill us if you want. We don't have any weapons. But it seems to me that we'd all be better off if we teamed up. Who knows who's out there."

The man looked at the hole, seemed to consider something, then said: "I won't tell you who I am or who I represent, but, you're right, I'm with the men who have been sent to stop you from going public. And yes, you might say we had a falling out, but that's not how I got hurt. I had an accident on the way down, and it seems that the man who was with me—yes, the Indian—thought I was dead and tried to bury me."

"So, if he's out there," I said, "and we meet him again, is he going to welcome you or try to bury you again?"

"I don't know. But he does have a weapon—and if the others are out there, they'll have weapons too."

"Where do you think they are?" Ross asked.

"I don't know, but I'm sure they're following GPS trackers to your truck and the big guy."

Ross winced. "I knew I should've checked."

"So," the man continued, "they might be in the canyon, or maybe up by the rim. There's no way to tell."

"Do you want to stay here for the night," Ross asked. "or wait till we can see what's going on out there?"

It was a little after ten. The man still seemed to be cold, as were we.

"We've got plenty of lights," I said, "I vote for going outside and, if we don't see them, trying to get home."

"But maybe they'll see us before we see them," Ross said.

"So, no lights." I looked over at the man again. "What do you think?"

"I think I'm freezing. Can't we at least go out there and talk?"

Ross went out through the hole first, looked around again, then told us to come out. The man without a name went next, and I followed. The warmth felt wonderful. I heard stones knocking together and looked down and saw Ross putting the boulders back in place.

Anticipating our questions, he said, "If that big guy comes back, maybe he'll think we're still in there and won't come looking for us."

I scanned the area, but I couldn't see into the nooks and shadows. Four or five men could be hiding within fifty feet and we wouldn't have known it. But if they were, I doubt they would have let us come out of the cave so easily.

I was getting hungry. I asked the little guy if he had eaten anything recently.

"No, I'm starving."

"That's a good sign," Ross said. "Maybe you're getting better." He stood up. The hole in the wall appeared to be closed off again.

Ross and I threw on our packs, which were lighter now. "Why don't you stay between us?" I said to the man. He nodded, and Ross led us along the ledge toward the sheep trail, and minutes later we were rising rapidly into the cul-de-sac. This was my third trip here in three days, but it was no easier, especially as we only used one light. As we got higher, the walls closed in on us and the starlight became dimmer. We were aware that men above us might be waiting, but we needed to keep one light on, which Ross kept pooled around his feet. The little guy never complained, and fortunately he seemed to be doing a little better. We came to the bottom of the chimney, where we took a quiet break. We were getting closer to the rim and tried to be as quiet as possible.

* * *

Whislin Klah had a problem. The men had stopped no more than twenty feet above him, reluctant to come down farther without using their flashlights, but they also seemed content to stay where they were. He wished he had brought his suppressor. It would have been risky, but he could have tried to pick them off one at a time.

He turned his back to the boulder and faced the canyon. He had heard the men say something about "going down at dawn." So, should he sneak up there and try to get lucky, or wait for daylight and take them out as they came around the boulder?

He had decided to wait for daylight, when he saw a light below him.

It was just one light, so it was probably Richardson, but how had the man revived and escaped from the cave? But then another realization came; if Richardson could get out of the cave, so could Call and Keller. And then another realization hit him; Richardson did not have a flashlight or a phone with him.

Call and Keller had escaped from the cave, and for some reason they were only using one light. But more important, they were coming up the canyon toward him. In fact, they were just below the chimney.

There would be no avoiding them. There was no room to move left or right, and if he tried to slip around the boulder, the men above him would see him. Now he wondered if they had seen the light as well. As he studied the angles, he thought they might be blocked from it, barely, by the large rock shielding him from them. He thought about going back down before Call and Keller reached the chimney, but it was too late; he would practically land on them.

As the tiny light approached, he thought he saw the silhouettes of three men. They stepped into a small opening below him, and the light from the stars bathed them in a milky glow. Yes, three men.

Things were going from bad to worse. He had four enemies above him and three below him. In all his training he had never been prepared for a situation like this.

He heard soft voices below.

"Let's stop for a minute." It sounded like the big guy, Keller. Call answered: "All right. Do you think he left?"

No, Klah thought. He hadn't *left*. Nobody had.

And the night was still young.

Chapter 39

Stuck Below the Surface

As I sat down on a flat, square rock about a foot high, trying to catch my breath, I thought about the treasure we had with us. Explosive information was locked in our two cameras. Ancient people on this continent wrote on metal plates, just as Joseph Smith had said. And they didn't just write signs above entrances to rooms or a few do's and don'ts. They created a library of information, all in a wonderfully concise language. Maybe it held the secrets to their ability to hew an entire village out of stone. Maybe it told how to harden copper so it was stronger than steel. Maybe it held histories of their travels, where they had come from, where the land of the Book of Mormon was, and how they had come to this cave on an obscure cliff in the Grand Canyon. Maybe it foreshadowed where they went. And maybe, just maybe, it contained more scripture.

Maybe much more.

I stopped and again wrestled with the tormenting question: Who were we that such knowledge should be entrusted to us?

What was going on?

Whatever happened from this point on, I knew that I had to download the pictures onto multiple computers at the first opportunity. Then I needed to print it all out on premium photo paper, even if it cost me a fortune.

And then, at some point, when I actually knew what we had, I would need to make a final decision concerning the caves, the mummies, and the plates. Could I really hide all this away from the world and live with myself? Could I ask Ross to do so? Could I really trust everybody at the Church? Secretaries? Assistants? Wives or husbands?

I had spoken truth to Richardson and Ross: I couldn't abide the thought of the cave being trampled by others, even those with good intentions. And I especially couldn't abide the thought of ancient, sacred plates being confiscated by the government, maybe to never see the light of day again. We were only lucky, no, blessed, that Fletcher Winn and his crew hadn't discovered them.

"Okay," Ross said, "ready to climb this thing again?"

"Actually," the man said, "I've never climbed it before—and coming down here about killed me."

"Is this where you fell?" I asked.

"No, it was below here—but this looks just as steep."

"Steeper," said Ross, who stood up and threw his pack back on. "If you can climb this, you can climb anything."

"Let's just not get ourselves killed," I said as I saddled up again.

* * *

Klah listened to the entire conversation and was amazed that the men above him hadn't heard it, but they continued to drone on in their own quiet whispers, some of which he also picked up. They thought he was staying down by the cave until morning—and it was clear that they didn't know where the cave was.

The light appeared again, almost directly below him. The three men were coming up. They would be next to him soon. Klah stepped as far back as he could into the recess made by the large boulder, but he knew there would be no avoiding them. He had his gun ready.

A bluish-white light appeared at Klah's feet, then Ross Keller's head appeared. Klah had a choice; he could surprise Keller and push him back down the chimney then deal with the other two, which shouldn't be hard, or he could let them come on up. He knew, however, that if he pushed Keller, he would cry out, then Klah would be in a shooting match with the guys above him. So he let Ross Keller step up to the little ledge next to the boulder.

Ross didn't see him at first, but then he caught a glint of light on the barrel of Klah's Glock. He turned to his right and faced Klah, who was holding an index finger to his lips. Ross didn't speak. Richardson followed him up, and Ross pointed to Klah, who stood barely five feet away. Klah was still holding his finger to his lips. They crowded together and made room for Travis, who also saw Klah, the gun, and the universal sign for silence. The tiny area behind the boulder could have possibly held five men, but no more. As the four of them shuffled for space, it almost looked like they were close-dancing.

Klah removed his finger from his lips and pointed upward. In a tiny voice he had perfected in the SEALS, he said: "Four men up there, with guns."

He was quiet, then a voice above them said, "It's gettin' cold, man. Wasn't it like a hundred today?"

As the men above them talked, Klah put his hand out and whispered, "Give me your guns."

Ross said, "We don't have any. You can search us."

Klah knew that holding three men at gunpoint while patting them down would be tricky. "No," he said, "just keep your hands where I can see them—and turn the light off." Ross switched it off and put it in his pocket. Klah turned to Richardson. "I thought you were dead when you fell."

"Your triage skills must be great," Richardson said without humor. "I'm very much alive."

Klah smiled then pointed the gun at Travis. "How'd you get out?"

Travis shrugged. "We had some explosives."

"Explosives?"

Travis nodded toward Ross, who reached into his pocket.

"Careful," Klah ordered.

"I'm just going to show you these." Ross produced a handful of M-80s.

"Firecrackers?" Klah whispered. "I thought you guys had blasting caps, and I should have figured you still had something. What else do you have?"

"Huh?" Ross asked.

"In your pockets."

"Nothing, just our phones and stuff."

"Let me see."

Ross and Travis exchanged a long look.

Klah thrust the gun at Ross. "Right now. Both of you."

Ross and Travis produced what they had—wallets, keys, phones, cameras, and a couple of Power Bars. They held it all out to Klah.

"Give me your phones," he said, keeping the gun trained on the space between Ross and Travis, allowing him to shoot either one if necessary.

Both men handed him their phones.

"What're the cameras for?" Klah asked.

"We're in the Grand Canyon," Travis said. "We took some pictures."

"And you were in the cave," Klah thought about it then held out his empty hand. "Give 'em to me."

"*Come on*," Ross sighed. "They're just cameras."

"Keep your voice down. They're just cameras with *evidence*. You may not survive, but if images do, I'll still be a dead man. Give 'em to me."

Ross and Travis exchanged another despairing look.

"I have personal things on there," Travis said. "Please don't take them."

Klah smiled. "Personal things? What kind?" His look hardened, and he turned his gun to Travis. "Give it to me—*now.*"

Travis handed his camera over. Klah looked it over but didn't check the pictures, then he put it in his right pants' pocket. Ross gave his to Klah, which Klah quickly put in his other pocket. Between the phones and digital cameras, his pockets were full.

More chatter filtered down from above, and Klah said, "I could have shot you all ten minutes ago."

"Yeah, but if you did," Richardson said, "you would've been shot by those guys up there."

Klah turned the gun on Richardson. "That's *one* reason I didn't do it; the other is because there may be a way for us all to get out of this alive."

"What's that?" Richardson asked.

"You hired me, and you hired them. You fired me, and you can fire them. I want you to go up there and tell them they're off the job. Tell 'em they'll get paid, as long as they just go home."

"And after they're gone, what will you do to me?"

"Does it matter? You don't have a choice. If you don't do it, there's going to be a slaughter here. A prominent professor will be killed—and a couple of rich white boys. And maybe even a former Navy SEAL. And at least three of those guys up there too—I promise you that. State lines have been crossed so the FBI will get involved. The media will be all over this, going twenty-four hours a day until they figure out who your precious Society is. Is that what you want? Is that what your bosses want?"

Richardson remained silent.

Klah reiterated the obvious: "All you have to do is go up there and take them off the job."

Richardson chuckled softly. "Aren't you glad these guys saved me?"

Klah looked at Travis again. "I thought you guys were going public? What happened?"

"We decided to come back and check out the cave again," Travis said. "Ross hadn't seen it yet, and I only got to see part of it."

"All right, so, if I let you live, what are you going to do?"

Travis thought about this before answering. "I don't know. Maybe nothing. There are things in that cave that shouldn't be disturbed."

"The mummies?"

"Yes, and other things, maybe things we don't even know about yet."

Klah turned back to Richardson, who potentially held the solution for all of them.

"All right," Richardson said. "Help me get up there—and if we ever come down here again, let's take a *trail.*"

Klah waved the gun upward, indicating they were all to go ahead of him. Ross went out from behind the rock first, helping Richardson begin the arduous climb. Travis followed. Then Klah.

He yelled loudly: "Richardson is here, and he's coming up! We're all coming up!"

A scramble of feet above them started a small rockslide.

"Who's that!" came a voice from above.

"You know who I am!" Klah yelled back, "and you know who your boss is. Hold your fire. He has something to say!"

Four bright lights from above fell on the group clambering up the chimney. Richardson had a tough time of it, but with Ross's help from above and Travis's from below, he finally made it. Klah was the last one to emerge, and he stayed well behind the others, holding his gun on them.

They gathered in the bowl just below the level of the vehicles. The four men who had been waiting were about fifteen feet away and still slightly above those who had just come up.

"What's going on?" one of them demanded.

"Your boss wants to talk," Klah said.

Richardson took a step forward, showing his empty hands. "Gentlemen, there's been a change in plans. I know it looks like our friend behind me is holding me hostage, but the fact is, he's just making sure I do the right thing."

"And what's that?" the same guy, the apparent leader, demanded.

"You've never met me, but I'm the one who hired you. I gave you a verbal contract with a certain amount of money promised for completing your job, and I gave you certain names and instructions. As far as I'm concerned, you've fulfilled the contract, and I will pay you in full. So, I want you all to stand down."

One of the other men laughed. "He wants us to stand down. That's great. They're outgunned, so they dream up this little scam and expect us to let 'em go."

"Yeah," said the passenger Klah had seen in the red SUV, "It looks to me like three of our targets are right here. And they only have one gun. I say we shoot 'em and check out the 'boss' later. And if he can't pay, we shoot him too."

The man who had spoken first shined his light on Richardson. "If you're Richardson, I'm the guy you talked to. What were the terms?"

Richardson took a moment to look at all four men. "Are you sure you want everyone to know?"

"Yeah!" the man yelled who had suggested they shoot them. "We all want to know! Go ahead."

The leader seemed to grow uncertain, perhaps having second thoughts.

"All right," Richardson said to him. "You personally were going to receive twenty thousand dollars for taking out Whislin Klah, who has the gun pointed at my back, and your three friends were going to receive ten thousand each, for a total of fifty grand, but only if you took Klah out before he could do any harm to my superiors. And I believe that's the word I used—my 'superiors.'"

The man stood like a statue.

"*What?*" said the man from the SUV, who had wanted to kill all three. "You're getting twenty and we're only getting ten?"

"Yeah?" asked the man who had been silent until now. "You get ten grand more than us? This is Arizona—we all get the death penalty if we get caught."

The leader turned to face them. "The important thing right now is that we *all* get paid. We'll figure out the rest later."

"Yes, we will," said the third guy, "or maybe we'll take *you* out too. Let's see, twenty grand split three ways is . . ."

"Shut up!" said the leader. "I'll make it right!" He turned back to Richardson. "All right, you got the money?"

"I do—but not here. It's in a briefcase in my vehicle."

The leader looked back. From his vantage point he could probably see the tops of the vehicles. He said, "I see our car, and I see Klah's Jeep, and I see Keller's truck. But I don't see your car."

"It's where I left it—back at Call's house."

"In Modesto?" asked the leader in disbelief.

"I parked it around the corner from Call's house before I was escorted away by Mr. Klah."

Klah had been watching with interest, but now he said to Travis, loud enough that all could hear, "He was going through your son's things. I thought he should be stopped."

Travis said nothing. He already knew, of course, that Klah had broken into his home and office and sabotaged his phones and computers. And it didn't surprise him that the little man they had just called "Richardson," who was dressed in black, had also broken in.

But Klah wasn't finished. He came closer to the three, still using them as human shields. "Hey, boss," he said to Richardson, "I still need to get paid too. Maybe I didn't take out Call and Keller, like you wanted, but they're here now. And if you still want to keep the cave a secret, we could still throw them over the cliff, and then visit the beautiful Mrs. Call and her nanny to assure silence on their parts. That way, since these two gentlemen know our names now, they can never blackmail us." He turned his gun on Travis. "What do you say, boss? Do I get paid too?"

Richardson looked at Travis, then at Ross, then he squared off before Klah. "If these men disappear, when his wife, nanny, and children know he's here, somewhere, there will be an investigation. Then chances are we all lose, because chances are they'll figure out who *we* are." He glanced at Travis and Ross again, paused, then addressed Klah. "But that's not the only reason I don't want to kill them. They saved my life—after you tried to kill me. Believe it or not, that still means something to me. But," and now he held Travis's eyes, "I have an obligation to some very powerful people—people who won't hesitate to kill if they think it's in their best interest. So, I need to know what you plan to do, be silent or go public—and just remember, I may not come after you, but others will."

"Unbelievable!" Klah said. "You're going to trust them? Of course they'll say they'll be silent! All right, if that's your 'solution,' then I want to get paid whether they're silent or not. I've done my part. Here they are, right in front of you, and if you're going to pay those clowns over there, then you're going to pay me!"

"Who you callin' clowns?" the third guy yelled, taking a step toward Klah.

Travis saw Richardson roll his eyes, as if to say, *What was I thinking when I hired them?* He smiled at the irony, and he felt a gentle calm come over him. Then he spoke.

"You're right, Mr. Klah, we know your name now, and we know that 'Richardson' here is a 'professor,' and we know there's a 'Society' somewhere that has a long-term interest in the cave. And we know that you've all tried to kill us, but that doesn't change a thing. The fact is, we've crossed state lines, and if you kill us, there will be an FBI investigation. My wife knows exactly where we are. In fact, we're all getting cell service at this very moment, and the FBI will have no problem triangulating on the last known location of our phones. There are probably GPS tracking devices on at least two of the vehicles, and all that data has been collected by the tracking services. And don't forget the NSA. They collect all this "intelligence" and store it at the Data Center in Utah. If you kill us, each one of you will be easily located, incarcerated, and probably executed. My wife is an excellent lawyer and can be depended upon to seek justice, long-term justice. She and the family are already in hiding—*I* don't know where—so, after you pull the trigger, you better start running."

Klah and Richardson shared a long look. Klah knew that most of what Call said was true. The man was smart—and obviously brave enough to use those smarts.

"So," Call continued, "unless you intend to use those guns, Ross and I are going to leave. And I won't promise you anything, because even though I'm leaning toward *not* going public, I might change my mind. I can promise you that I won't do it for the money, but maybe somebody will talk me into making this place available to a world that has no idea it even exists. And believe me, it's something the world will *want* to know about. But we can talk about that later. You know where I live, and you have my number. You can call me any time you want." He turned to Richardson. "You know, somebody else is going to find this place eventually, so why not tear down that stupid false wall, open up the air portal, and let the inevitable happen? If it doesn't look like somebody tried to keep it a secret, there will only be rumors and suspicions about what happened a hundred years ago—but no proof that the Society was involved. I don't know where all the relics went, and it doesn't really matter now, because the men who stole them are long dead—even my friend, Keith Nelson. Maybe it's time to let the world know that thousands of years ago another great culture flourished here. Maybe it's time to let this whole grand conspiracy end. Maybe it's time to start trusting people again."

Travis turned to Ross. "Shall we?"

Call shouldered his pack and started walking toward the far end of the bowl. Ross did the same. They walked by the four men, all of whom held guns on them.

The two men didn't look back.

Whislin Klah actually smiled. He had just seen real bravery, and because of that, and perhaps because Call had made so much sense, he let his own gun drop a hair. After all, what was he going to do, kill them? Take them hostage? At this very moment his own body was betraying him to a cell tower somewhere in the distance.

Chapter 40

Death Under the Moon

I waited to hear the ratcheting of a gun's slide, but it didn't come. When we were out of the bowl, I whispered, "Please tell me you have the keys."

"I got 'em," he whispered back. "I kept 'em in my pocket when he took our stuff."

Not only did we not hear the cocking of a gun, we didn't hear any more talk. Either we had taken the words out of their mouths, or they didn't want us to hear what they were saying. And frankly, I didn't care. I was tired of living under a threat. I was ready to die right here, right now, to be free of all threats.

Ross unlocked the truck remotely and we climbed in. The truck was facing the men on the rim, and when the engine started, the headlights bathed the men's heads in light. The six of them hadn't moved. Maybe they were negotiating. Maybe they were in the middle of a Mexican standoff. I didn't know. I didn't care.

"That was amazing," Ross said. "You *stupefied* them."

"Give me a break."

"No, really! You put them in a stupor. Look—they still don't know what to do."

The men still faced each other. No one seemed to be talking.

"We lost everything," I said, beginning to feel sick to my stomach. "We lost the cameras. We lost the phones."

Ross let the truck idle. "Do you want to go out and wait somewhere? Let Klah go by and ambush him so we can get the cameras back?"

"Ross, he's the one with the gun, not us."

Ross put the truck in reverse, did a three-point turn, and headed back to the highway. I was feeling sicker by the minute.

The moon, a waning crescent, had just topped the horizon in front of us. The night was brilliant with stars. We bounced along the dirt trail, the truck's powerful high beams opening a tunnel before us, but I could think of nothing but the loss of the cameras and phones. Thousands of images, now in the wrong hands.

"We'll just come back," Ross said, almost defiantly. "We'll go buy new cameras and come back next week."

"Yeah, but Klah—what was his first name again? Whistling? Something like that? He'll still have the pictures of the plates. I can't stand that. Who knows what he'll do with them? Joseph Smith lost his 116 lost pages, but we lost a whole library!" I honestly thought I might throw up. I put the window down and saw an apparition to our right.

"What the heck . . .?" Ross said, slowing down.

"Don't worry. I know him." It was my friend, standing on the barren desert as if it were a downtown sidewalk. The walking stick in his right hand was at least four inches taller than he was. Ross brought the truck to a halt.

"You know him? *How?*"

"He came to us out here when we fell asleep, a few nights ago. He gave me water." I opened the door and got out.

"What?" Ross said, opening his door. "He gave you *water?*"

I had forgotten how thin the man was. His walking stick, etched with Native markings, almost looked thicker than he was. He wore the same clothes as before, a plaid, red western shirt and faded blue jeans. The same leather bag hung from his shoulder. In spite of our monumental loss, I smiled as I approached him.

"You want water," he said, anticipating me. He reached into his bag and brought out the pouch. "Sorry, not as much this time. I have been thirsty too." He opened it and handed it to me, and I brought it to my lips. The water was cold and sweet. I gave it to Ross. He hesitated then put it to his lips and took a long drink. He pulled it away from his mouth and looked at the nearly empty pouch.

"That's *great,*" he said. "Where'd it come from?"

"It is from my mesa. Good water."

"It sure is—like that stuff at the store." Ross took another long draught then handed it back to the mystified man.

"I don't know your name," I said. "But you seem to know me. Who are you?"

"I am your friend. I have watched you many nights. You struggle much, you and your friend." He turned to Ross and smiled, his perfect mummy teeth reflecting the ambient light. "You are a good friend to my friend. Maybe you will be my friend too."

A nervous look came to Ross's face. "Well, yeah, I mean if you're ever around . . ."

"No, I will stay here. But the spirits fight for you. Some help you. Some want to take your life. But still, here you are."

"Yes, we are here, but we lost what we came for," I said.

"You have lost the stone?"

"Stone?" Ross asked.

He looked back at me. "In my dreams I saw you in the Hidden World. You have the sacred corner of the Maasaw's stone—yes?"

"You mean the corner of the stone?" I held my thumb and forefinger about two inches apart. "The corner that looks like it was broken off from another stone?"

He showed his teeth in a broad smile. "It was prepared by Maasaw, the spirit who led us here. May I—" He seemed to grow nervous, touching his mouth then rubbing his nose. "May I see it?"

"I don't have it," I said.

His eyes widened. "But you had it. I saw this."

"Yes, but we left it behind. It wasn't our right to remove it."

He was silent.

"I'm sorry," I said, truly meaning it. "We felt it should stay there."

"And lucky thing we did, too," Ross added, "because everything we had got stolen."

He looked at Ross and studied his face. "But you have your truck."

"He didn't take our truck," Ross explained, "just the stuff we had in our pockets. He took our phones…"

"And our cameras," I whispered, my stomach rolling again. "Who did this?"

"A man back at the canyon," I said. "He's still there, with some other men. They all have guns."

"They let us go because Travis dared them to shoot us," Ross said, "and they figured they couldn't do it without getting in more trouble, so they let us go."

"On your phones and cameras," he said softly, "did you have pictures of the corner?"

"Yes," I said.

"And now it is in their hands?"

"Yes."

He looked at the truck, which was still idling. Then he looked up at the stars, the great Milky Way bathing us with its creamy glow. "My people have waited for the sacred corner for two thousand years. I knew it was in the Hidden World, but it was not for me to get." He took a deep breath, as if steadying himself. "And it is not for others— only those who are chosen. Maasaw told our people that two white brothers would bring it to us. One would be Pahana."

"Who is Pahana?" Ross asked.

"A man-angel. He will bring us a brotherhood of peace. He will bring us good laws to live by in the chaos to come. He will bring the stone parts together—and unite the Fire Clan tablet. He will repair the breach." His eyes bore into mine. "In my vision—" his voice trailed off, and he closed his eyes for a moment before continuing. "But my vision was wrong. You have no stone corner. And you put pictures of it in the hands of a man who would kill."

"I'm sorry," I said. "You are right, I put pictures of the corner in a very bad man's hands. I will try to get them back. I don't think he knows what they are. But, the corner itself is safe."

"Can any other man find it?"

I looked at Ross, seeking confirmation. He shook his head almost imperceptibly.

"No," I said. "It would be almost impossible to find."

"And it's protected by snakes," Ross said.

The old man nodded. "I know the snakes. They guard things well."

"And we found metal plates too," Ross said, "with writings on them. Do you know who put them there?"

"That language was lost to us many generations ago. It is for others to know." His eyes bore into mine again. "You must be very careful. You have beheld that which was created by the Maasaw. You are open to the spirits." He turned his attention to Ross. "You see but your eyes are closed. Your gift is also your weakness. Continue to grow in it, but be wise." He put the water bottle back in his bag and draped the bag over a shoulder. He looked at us again.

"I thought you had the sacred corner, but my vision was wrong."

He turned and walked behind a low rise, disappearing in its shadow so quickly that I wondered if he had fallen down.

"What'd he mean?" Ross asked, still trying to see the man who had disappeared.

"I think he meant what he said—that we need to be careful, and wise."

"Yeah, but I don't think I want to grow in a weakness."

I didn't respond, and Ross went to the back of his truck, turned on his flashlight and fell to his knees. I thought he was praying until he came up with a GPS tracking sensor. He set it on a rock and crushed it.

"I know it doesn't mean anything," he said, "since they already know where we live, but I don't like people tracking me."

I couldn't blame him. I was getting tired of it myself.

"In fact, I have a great idea," he said, coming back to the truck, "why don't we start tracking them? We need to get the cameras and phones back, and we can't get them back unless we know where they are."

We decided to go to the store to wait for whoever came out of the desert, and if it were Klah, we would tail him. But, then, as we bounced off toward the highway, fragmentary thoughts of the old Indian welled up, and a mournful weariness overcame me. Then, for some reason, perhaps because I was exhausted, perhaps because of our terrible loss, I began weeping.

* * *

Klah was in a tough spot. He had let Call and Keller go, but that was the least of his worries. All Richardson had to do was tell the men to shoot him, and they would.

Or, he could shoot Richardson first and take his chances with the others.

But those chances weren't very good.

He tried to intuit what the others were thinking, something he had always been good at, but there were too many lame minds to read—except for Richardson's.

But would Richardson do the smart thing?

Klah had lowered his gun, almost in disbelief, and partly in respect, when the two men had walked away, but now he raised it again, to Richardson's back. If Klah was going to shoot, this was the moment. But he let the moment pass.

The nanobots.

The four men still held their guns on Richardson and Klah, glancing at each other in tense anticipation.

Klah whispered to Richardson: "Don't forget the package I sent to the lawyer." He was sure Richardson recalled the little time bomb Klah had threatened the Society with earlier.

Richardson finally spoke. "So, boys, just remember, if you shoot us, you won't get paid. But if you do as I say, we will *all* walk away from this—and then I promise, you *will* get paid. The money is where I said it is." He turned back to Klah. "But I can't make that promise to you, because your payment has not been sent to me yet. However, I will do my best to see that you are paid in full."

The leader of the four men lowered his gun. "It seems like a no-brainer," he said. "I want to get paid."

The third man, the feisty one, did not lower his gun. "But I wanna get paid what *you* get paid. If you get twenty, I want twenty."

The second man to have spoken now turned to him, his gun also turning toward the feisty one. "But there's only fifty. If you guys get twenty, that only leaves ten for me and Jadon to split." Klah assumed the quiet one was Jadon.

All three men faced the feisty one, their guns also waving in his direction.

"Now, listen," said the leader, "I said we would work it…"

An explosion of gunfire made Klah jump—two quick shots, then a third. The leader fell, shot in the chest. Then the quiet man fell on his face, a blossom of blood protruding from his back. The feisty man had shot them both, but he had missed the last man, and that man now shot him. The feisty man rocked back on his heels then trained his gun on the other man again, and there were two new explosions. Both men dropped to the dirt.

Richardson had also dropped to the ground. Klah stood motionless, quickly assuring himself that the first four men weren't moving, then he looked down at Richardson, whose face was planted in the sandy soil. As the silence lingered, Richardson's head slowly came up and he stole a glance at the downed men. Klah realized that he had simply dropped for cover. Leaving him in the dirt, Klah walked over to the four men, all sprawled in various positions on the rust-red ground. He nudged each with his boot, turning the men over who were on their faces. Each was dead, all having been shot with 9mm rounds or larger. He looked down at his own clothing and checked for signs of gunfire, but he was intact. Klah went back to Richardson. On his way, he realized that he still had his pack on.

"Looks like you can pay me now—at least fifty grand."

Richardson raised his head a little higher. "Are they all dead?"

"They're eyes are open and they're not breathing. That means they're dead. Get up."

Richardson rose to his feet, still shaken. "Did you shoot any of them?"

"Nope. They took care of that themselves. Come on, we need to get back to Modesto before Call and Keller get to your car."

Richardson stared at the corpses with fascination. "What should we do with these—bodies?"

"Leave them where they are. Somebody will smell them and call it in, and when the cops come, I want it to look like exactly what it is—four guys who shot each other. We'll leave the SUV alone too. We don't want any of our fingerprints on it. Let's go."

He took Richardson by the arm, still holding his gun in his left hand. As they walked by the bodies, Richardson's legs nearly gave out on him.

"What's the matter?" Klah asked, "never seen a dead body before?"

They got by the bodies. "Not ones that had been murdered."

"Oh, that's right. You just pay for the murders—you don't dirty your hands with them."

Richardson was quiet as they got in the Jeep. Klah turned it on, illuminating the four bodies on the packed sand. He backed up, turned, and drove east toward the highway. "They'll see our tire prints," Richardson said.

"Yeah, and Keller's, but they'll have no idea who we are. And when they figure out that the four bullets—or five—in those four men all came from their own guns, they'll think it was a shootout, maybe a drug deal gone bad, and somebody else took off with the drugs."

"Maybe they'll go down in the canyon and see the cave."

"I couldn't find it if I didn't know where it was. How could they find it? We're in the clear."

As they got back on the dirt trace they had come in on, Klah almost smiled. Another accidental murder. Four of them. But this time he hadn't done a thing.

* * *

We silently sat in the truck on the side of the store, waiting for the other men's vehicles to come bounding out of the desert. We hadn't gone in the store, deciding that if Klah killed the other men, there would be an investigation and the clerk would almost certainly remember us. Fortunately we had filled the tank when we came through the day before.

Ross's stomach broke the silence.

"I'm starving," he said.

"Of course you are. You haven't eaten anything in four hours."

He glanced at me. "Maybe we could get a trucker to buy some hot dogs for us."

"You like those hot dogs, don't you?"

"Best things I ever tasted. Except for the water. But I drank that too fast."

We fell into silence again. The truck was running to heat the cab. I was still amazed at how cold the nights could get after a hot day. A land of extremes.

When Klah's Jeep appeared, it was alone—no red SUV.

"Uh-oh," Ross uttered.

"I only see two people in it," I said.

"So, do you want to wait around and see if the other guys come out?"

"No—we have to stay with Klah."

We expected the Jeep to pull into the gas station to fill up, but it got back on the highway and turned right, heading back toward California. Ross let half a mile get between us, then he pulled out.

"Memorize those taillights," Ross said, "because they're flying. I'm up to eighty, and they're still pulling away. Looks like they're fleeing a crime scene."

"What do you think happened?" I asked.

"No way to know. Maybe those guys are still coming. Maybe they're not coming at all."

I focused on the taillights. When they finally seemed to stop pulling away from us, we were going ninety-three.

"At least they'll get a ticket before we do," Ross muttered.

Twenty minutes later they pulled into Cameron to get gas. We cruised past them and waited behind a low hill.

"Glad we got gas on the way in," Ross said.

They screamed past us ten minutes later, and by the time we matched their speed, they were almost a mile ahead of us.

We almost ran out of gas before they pulled in again, at Barstow. They stopped at a Pilot to get gas, and we went across the street to a TA Mini/Mart. The sun was just peeking above the horizon. They showed no signs of having spotted us. I went inside to get supplies, and when I came out, Ross was just finishing up. "I think I know why they're going so fast." He was spying on them from behind his truck.

"Still trying to get away from a crime scene?"

"No, trying to get back to your house before we do, so they can get the money." He chuckled. "I bet they've been checking out every silver truck they passed—and they can't figure out why they haven't passed us yet. Hah! They're probably going to go a hundred from now on." But they stayed between eighty-five and ninety, which would still get them a ticket but not thrown in jail.

Ross let the Jeep pull away from us. Since we *probably* knew where they were headed, we decided to let them stay out of sight, and we would just creep up from time to time to make sure we hadn't passed them somewhere.

Somehow, blasting through the early morning, we both avoided getting pulled over.

Chapter 41

Following the Gold

As Klah drove down into the Central Valley just east of Bakersfield, he made a decision. He had been deliberating whether to take the fifty thousand and go into hiding or push for everything he was owed. He told Richardson to get on his phone and tell "the powers that be" that they needed to wire the rest of the money.

Richardson seemed to anticipate this. "I can't."

"Why not?"

"Because I don't have my phone. It must have fallen out when I fell."

Klah had forgotten that he had taken the phone before entombing the man. He tried to pull it out of his pocket but found it packed in with another phone and camera. He pulled everything out and set it on the console between them, then he leaned the other way and emptied the other pocket. Richardson saw his phone, gave Klah a glance, and picked it up.

"Nice of you to keep it safe for me."

"Least I could do."

Richardson turned the phone on, seemed surprised to get a signal, and punched in a number. He was soon in conversation. "Yeah, it's me. There's been some, uh, developments. The four we sent after Klah have been eliminated."

Whislin couldn't hear the other voice, but he assumed there was a moment of silence, because Richardson didn't speak again for a while.

"No, it wasn't Klah. And I didn't do it. It was up on the rim—they shot each other... Yes, one of them got greedy. No, it was fast—took about two seconds. And now, they're all out there... I don't know if anybody will ever find the bodies—it's very remote—but here's the deal, Call and Keller are still alive… I know. I'm sorry, but, well, we lost them. But we know that they have no evidence of the cave. Klah was able to get their phones and cameras, and they didn't have anything else. Besides, they're not going to the cops, or going public. They want to keep it all a secret… I don't really know why, just, they say there are things in there that shouldn't be disturbed." Richardson was quiet a moment while the other party spoke.

"Right, nothing is public yet, but there's another complication. Two of them actually: Klah is threatening to go public if he doesn't get the rest of his money—and he's holding a gun on me at this very moment. So, either you wire the money immediately, or I'm a dead man, and he goes public anyway."

Klah hadn't expected Richardson to share all that, but now that he had, it sounded good, certainly motivating. If this didn't get them to pay, he would have to find stronger measures. Richardson held the phone away from his ear as the other man raised his voice, allowing Whislin to make out the words: "What about the fifty thousand we already gave you?"

"Right, we're on our way to get that now. Klah is going to take it. So, technically, you'll only owe him one-twenty-five."

The other person raised his voice again. "We don't owe him anything! He's the one who got us into this mess! He should have taken care of everything at the beginning."

"Well, the fact is," said Richardson, who was trying to keep his voice level, "he did deliver Call and Keller, and they got away—from me." He glanced at Klah, who responded with a half-smile. "And nobody has gone public yet . . . Right, nobody that we know of. But, he says he's fulfilled his part of the contract, and technically, I guess he did." Klah heard laughing on the other end, then more words that he couldn't make out.

"I suppose that's true," Richardson said. "If you don't pay, you'll have one less problem, because I'll be gone. But you'll still have Klah—and he has all the evidence that Call and Keller found in the cave. Yes—two cameras and two phones."

Richardson listened for another minute then disconnected.

"He says you don't deserve it, but he's agreed to pay you another fifty, in a year, if nobody goes public."

Whislin didn't know who Richardson had just talked to, but he could get Richardson's phone back if he wanted it, and he should be able to get the man's address through a private investigator. He shook his head. He was getting tired, probably too tired to think clearly. He would need to come up with a better plan, but one thing was sure, he wasn't going to wait a year to get less than half the money, *if* everybody stayed silent, and *if* the man was true to his word. No, he would hurry things up. He told Richardson to try to get some sleep because they would have a big day when they got back to Modesto.

And he wanted Richardson asleep for another reason—so he didn't have to keep his hand so close to the gun in the door. The time to use it would come soon enough. Richardson appeared to be sleeping, and Klah's exhausted mind raced. Yes, he had probably botched things when he let Call and Keller go free, but he had felt something he couldn't really explain—a strange respect, even an admiration, for Travis Call.

If the money had been *right* there on the rim, and if Richardson had told him to shoot Call and Keller, would he have done it? He would have been tempted, but once Call pulled that stunt and walked away, all bets were off. It was one of the bravest, smartest, things he had ever seen.

* * *

As we pulled into town, not quite on fumes, we knew it would be harder to avoid detection, so we decided to go directly to the house. We took a shortcut and got there first. There were no unusual cars in front of the house, so we went around the block and, just before the last turn, saw a white mid-size car that had rental written all over it. We went back two blocks and waited.

* * *

The house looked empty when Klah drove up to it, which seemed right since he was almost sure that Anna and the rest of the family were holed up somewhere else. He reached over and nudged Richardson. "We're here. Where's your car?"

Richardson woke up and pointed down the street. "Go around the corner, to the left."

It was a white sedan of some amorphous type. Klah pulled a U-turn and parked behind it. No windows were broken. No tires slashed. People in this neighborhood must play by the rules. He told Richardson to get out as he stuffed the gun in his waistband and pulled his shirt over it. They walked to the car.

"If it's still here," Richardson said, pulling a set of keys out of his pocket, "it'll be in the trunk." He pressed the remote release, and the trunk popped open.

It was empty.

"Where is it?" Klah demanded, raising his voice.

Richardson lifted the cover off the wheel well, where the spare tire should have been, and from inside he lifted a brown briefcase. "The spare tire's in the back seat."

Klah stepped closer. "Open it."

Richardson turned the dials to the combination with his thumbs then unlatched it. The briefcase slowly opened.

Klah saw bundles of cash.

"At least we got here before they did," he sighed. The suppressor was still in the back of his Jeep. He should have screwed it onto the gun when they got gas. If Richardson were going to make a move, it would be now.

But Richardson simply closed the briefcase and the trunk, and they got back in the Jeep. It was all there, fifty thousand exactly. Richardson closed the briefcase and offered it to Klah. "I kept it on the combination, so you'll be able to open it." Klah took it in his right hand, still holding the gun in his left, and quickly memorized the combination. As he set the briefcase in the back seat, Richardson opened his door.

"Well, all good things must come to an end." Klah reached over and grabbed his arm.

"Not so fast."

The Jeep was still idling. A car passed them, the first they had seen since arriving. They were sitting a block away from Call's house, and around a corner, but it bothered him that he hadn't seen Keller's truck anywhere. He should have passed them in Arizona, but he hadn't, unless they had stopped somewhere. He had considered this for hours but had no answers. Almost certainly he had been driving fast enough that they couldn't have come up behind him.

"I know what you're thinking," Richardson said, closing his door again. "You don't want to wait a year to get less than half your money."

"You must have ESP."

"You're thinking you can get rid of me and get the man's address from my phone. But neither his name nor his address are there." He pulled it out. "You can check for yourself."

"There are reverse directories."

"Yes, but even if the phone isn't a burner, the number would only lead you to the address of a shell company, and that company, along with their other holding companies, are registered in Panama and the Caribbean. You'll never find the names of the principals. In fact, you'll never find the name of an actual human being on any of their records—even if you could access them. I've already tried. Sorry, but I'm the only access you'll ever have to them."

There was also no way of knowing if any of this were true. But it made sense.

"Let's say I don't kill you," Klah said, "what's your solution to my problem here?"

"I've been thinking about that."

"I bet you have."

"There are only two permanent solutions. One is that my bosses find you and eliminate you. The other is that you find them and convince them to pay you, and then you somehow convince them to leave you alone, because they will never hire you again. And by the way, how much do you think they owe you now?"

"Like you told them, one-hundred and twenty-five thousand."

Richardson nodded. "I wish I could cover that out of my own funds. That would make everything easier."

"Not to mention safer."

"Yes, remember my bosses don't exactly *need* me now. In their minds I've botched this up as much as you have."

Klah decided to press a point he had avoided earlier. "You say I can't find the men at the top, but I know exactly where they meet. I know the Society's address in New Haven. It might take some time, but I'll find the addresses of the men who go in and out."

Richardson thought for a considerable time, and Klah wondered what flaw there might be in his plan. The men at the top had to visit the office sometime. But even if he had to threaten underlings, he would get to the leadership.

Richardson looked him in the eye. "Whislin, you and I were friends once, before I introduced you to this whole mess, weren't we?"

"Maybe, but you were always above me, my teacher, then my boss."

"That's true, but believe me when I say that I've always admired something in you—and not just your ability to *fix* things. I admire your honesty. I know that's an incongruous thing to say at a time like this, but I mean it. I've never known you to lie to me. You have a worldview that allows you to protect your interests and those of your employer, but not dissimulate. However, I have not always been as truthful with you."

Whislin laughed. "You *think*? You hired those guys to kill me—and of course you forgot to tell me about it."

"My hands were tied. You had become a liability to my superiors. But, my superiors are not who you imagine them to be." Richardson let this sink in.

"What do you mean?"

"I told you about the Skull and Bones Society, and it's true that that's where the story began, with the cave and the Smithsonian, and even with the president. But that's also where it ended. I told you about Fletcher Winn, who was hired by the Smithsonian at the request of the president's advisor, Gerald Grander. At some point the Smithsonian gave Winn the authority to find out what was really going on in the canyon, especially to find out if Egyptian hieroglyphics were there, *anything* that might seem to *indicate* that the Book of Mormon was authentic. Wolcott was serious about that, and he gave Winn *carte blanche* to comb through the cave and remove everything. In his mind, he wasn't desecrating a national treasure, he was saving a religion."

"You told me all that—but what about your superiors?"

"So, Fletcher Winn cleaned out the cave, except for most of the mummies, because of the Hopis, but he didn't send all the artifacts to the Smithsonian. In fact, I doubt he sent anything to the Smithsonian."

"You said that before too."

"But he also didn't send most of them to the Skull and Bones Society."

"Right. He sent them to himself."

"He sent them to another group entirely. He could see that the treasures were vast, and some of them so *priceless*, that he created a new group, a new society, you might say, far more secret than Skull and Bones. The wealth they realized by occasionally selling the gold artifacts alone was staggering. And over the years, over the *generations*, they've quietly sold most of the antiquities to eager investors—and somehow Winn kept his alliances with the top people in Washington, probably made them partners, but Wolcott and the group at the Smithsonian were not among them. Skull and Bones may have suspected something, but over the hundred years since then it's all evaporated into history. If you go hunting for the leader of the Bonesmen, you'll find a man who knows nothing about any of this."

Another betrayal. He had been fed lies all along. Leaving the gun in his left hand, he reached across the middle console and grasped the man's throat. It was thin and feeble in his hand, and he knew he could snap it with a quick twist.

"You're going to tell me, right now, who your superiors are."

Richardson's eyelids fluttered, and his eyes began to roll up. Whislin relaxed his grip. Richardson tried to speak, and Klah relaxed his hand a little more. He leaned over and put his face in front of Richardson's. At this point he didn't care who might be driving by or stepping out of a door.

"Is there even a group, or is it all just you and the guy on the phone?"

Richardson coughed, spraying saliva on the dash. Klah let go of Richardson's throat and brought his gun to the man's side, letting it jab the little man's ribs.

"I'll tell you what I know," Richardson croaked.

Klah pulled the gun back an inch, letting Richardson breathe without pain. "You'll tell me everything."

"But I don't know everything. I'm just a middleman."

Klah was tempted to shoot the man in the leg. He might bleed to death, but he would probably divulge more information as more shots were administered. If the suppressor had been screwed on, he might have done it. But, even through the fog of anger and fatigue, he forced himself to calm down. He could wait until they got to a concealed area—out where Keith Nelson's life had ebbed away in the swirling waters of Dry Creek. "You're either going to talk—or die wishing you had."

He put the car in gear and pulled around the white rental. They drove by the Call's home again—still dark—then went out to the main road. Dry Creek was only minutes away.

* * *

From two blocks away, we couldn't tell what was happening in the Jeep. Richardson had brought a small bag or suitcase out of the trunk—probably the money—but after getting back in the Jeep they talked again, and when they finally left, they left together, leaving Richardson's car behind.

Strange doings.

"What do you think?" Ross asked.

"I think we need to follow them. Go!"

The Jeep had already disappeared around a corner. We took off and saw them turn another corner before they disappeared again.

"The other guys never showed up." Ross said. He glanced at me, but I didn't respond; we both knew that those four men would have never given up the money voluntarily.

We didn't dare let them get out of sight, figuring it would be better for Klah to confront us than to lose him. My stomach was twisted in a knot, knowing that nearly ten thousand images of ancient writings were in his Jeep. Of course, I didn't *know* that he still had them. He could have thrown the cameras into the canyon. He could have thrown them into the desert at ninety miles an hour. He could have dumped them in a garbage can at a gas station. But in that case, one of our big problems would be gone; Klah could never go public with them, and Ross and I could go back, even better prepared, and take pictures again. Anna may not be pleased, but surely she would see the value of getting those images and trying to decipher their meaning.

But how any of this would serve the interests of my client, one Saundra Flament, whom I had almost forgotten about and had completely neglected, quite escaped me. I certainly wasn't going to show her pictures of the plates in an attempt to prove that her father had been murdered. But first things first.

The Jeep turned right, toward the freeway, and I saw Ross glance at the gas gauge. "We've got like fifty miles left. I hope they're not going far."

"Well, they haven't filled up since we did."

He managed to navigate through two lights and two left turns while staying a few cars behind them. They led us onto a frontage road running parallel to the freeway, and in minutes we were entering the downtown area. I was amazed that we hadn't been discovered yet. Maybe they had other things on their minds.

* * *

Klah liked the symmetry. He had taken Richardson to the same bend in Dry Creek, even to the same tree, where he had killed Keith Nelson. He was almost surprised that he recognized the spot in the light of day. The fog had been so oppressive that night that he wasn't sure he'd be able to find it again. Surprisingly, there were no pedestrians about. Even the parking lot where he had left the Jeep was empty. He forced Richardson behind the three-foot trunk, just above the water. They were blocked on three sides by a jungle of foliage. He remembered how muddy the bank had been that night. But it hadn't rained since then, and the earth under the mat of dead leaves was dry and hard. He noticed greenery springing from its branches. New leaves. New life. Would Richardson actually have a chance today? That would depend on him.

"Give me your phone." Klah had connected the suppressor to his gun, and now its dull barrel prodded Richardson in the back. Richardson pulled his phone out and handed it over his shoulder to Klah. "Now," Klah continued, "look down at the water. This is where I killed Nelson. This is where I ended his lies. His body was found a day later, down past the confluence with the Tuolumne."

Richardson looked at the swirling eddies in the brownish water. The much larger river swept by on their right just yards away.

"You know what the book says," Klah continued, 'live by the sword, die by the sword.' You've made me your sword—but whether you die by me is up to you." He paused, letting this possibility sink in. "I'm prepared to let you live, just as I was prepared to let Nelson live, if you are completely honest with me. He wasn't—and paid the price."

Richardson turned toward Klah and stared him in the eye. He was scared—he clearly didn't want to die—but he was not the shaking, sniveling rodent Klah thought he might be. The man actually had some spine.

"I'll tell you what I can. I won't lie."

"All right, do you know who the man is that you work for?"

"I'm not certain—but I've made some deductions."

"Deductions?"

"The number I call him at changes. I'm almost sure he's using burners—at least most of the time. And the area code changes; sometimes it's in New Haven, sometimes in Hartford. But some things he's said lead me to believe he's in New Haven."

"Where in New Haven?"

Richardson paused for a long moment. "I've never met him, but I went there once, on a fact-finding mission."

"You went to New Haven? Doing what, searching for ammunition to blackmail him with?"

"Actually, yes. And I learned a few things. His predecessors, Winn and whoever came after him, stole the relics, like I said, but some of them are still in their possession. That's why they're so scared. They actually still have evidence on hand—and I'm almost sure they're still selling it. They avoid suspicion by liquidating them slowly, like every five years. And the prices keep rising. So, I figured the relics would need to be stored in a controlled climate. Temperature, humidity, ph, carbon dioxide."

"So you checked out the places that have those controls."

"Sure, but there are places like that everywhere. But I also deduced that they wouldn't store the relics in a public facility. They would keep them in private storage, maybe even somebody's home. So I checked the companies that specialized in building climate-controlled facilities for private use. It turns out there's only two within a fifty mile radius."

"So, you asked those companies where they'd built something like that?"

"Of course not, they'd never give me that information. I used other skills—skills that I was originally hired for. I hacked them."

Klah knew the professor was smart, but he didn't know the extent of his skill set. "So what did you learn?"

"Between those two companies, they'd built a lot of storage facilities in the area, but only thirteen in private homes. Of those thirteen, only five are in New Haven. Of those five, four were built in the last twenty years."

"Which means only one was built in a private home before that."

"Right, which would fit my boss's needs. He would have needed a controlled storage climate as soon as he could get it. So I figured I *might* have the address to my boss's home—or maybe his place of business."

"Which was it?"

"His home—I think."

"You think?"

"I know it was a home, but I'm still not sure it's him. I hacked into the owner's personal information, and it turned out he'd been on the dark web, but as far as I could tell, he never said a word about relics or mummies or secret societies. If it's him, he's very discreet."

"Discreet enough to hire someone like you to do his dirty work?"

"Probably. I waited outside his home, like you did with the Calls. I've seen him. I've got pictures and a name, but I'm still not sure it's him."

"Did you talk to him? Did his voice sound familiar?"

"No, I never talked to him."

Klah looked out over the creek, which was still full from spring runoff. There was no sound in the bushes, which surprised him. In the daytime it actually did look like a perfect hideout for the homeless. "I believe you. But you haven't given me the name or address."

"I'm not sure I should."

Klah's gaze jerked back to the small man.

"If I do," Richardson added, "what's to stop you from killing me? Keeping that information is the only insurance I have."

"Maybe. What if I hack the same places you did?"

"Good luck. They've all tightened up their online security since then."

"So you say."

"Be my guest—take a look. It's actually getting harder to hack now days. Lucky thing I've still got my teaching gig."

Klah chuckled. It was refreshing to see a sense of humor in a man who had a gun on him. "I didn't know you were still doing that."

"It's not the money. It's the perks. The insurances alone are worth teaching a class or two. Plus, do you know what it's like to be called 'professor' by a nineteen-year-old girl—and hold her fate in your hands?"

"All right, professor, when are we going out to New Haven?"

Richardson visibly relaxed. "If I were you, I wouldn't waste my money."

"Why?"

"Just something the man said the last time we talked."

"I was listening. I didn't hear anything."

"You only heard my side. I think he'll be out here soon. They're scared to death of what you and Call and Keller might do. They're scared of me too."

"So we just sit and wait?"

"It'd probably speed things up if we used a credit card that they could track."

Klah thought through this. "Why can't they just track the nanobots?"

"They can find your *general* location, but we want them to find the actual room." He turned around and faced Whislin. "Here's what I would do: we use a credit card for one room, and we use cash for an adjoining room. They break into the first room, and we ambush them from the other room."

This made sense. "I like the way you think."

"It's kept me alive so far."

Klah laughed and began unscrewing the suppressor from his gun. "All right, professor, let's go get a couple of rooms. We'll give it three days before we head out to Connecticut—and then, if you don't give me the name and address, maybe we'll have to see just how good your life insurance really is."

* * *

We lost them at a slowdown at 9th and I Streets, but I was almost sure I knew where they were going. "Go to Dry Creek," I said. "That's where Nelson's body got dumped."

"You think he drove him all the way here just to kill him?"

"I don't know, but if he did, it would be a good place to do it. No witnesses. No body to be found. No blood to clean up. The river takes care of everything."

Ross sped through a yellow light. A few minutes later we spotted the black Jeep in a parking lot above the creek. The vehicle was empty. We passed it and went down around a bend and turned around and parked a hundred yards or so from the Jeep.

"Think we should go help him?" Ross asked.

"How? We don't know where he is."

"Probably down by the river, like you said, with a big ol' Glock sticking in the professor's back."

I didn't move, and neither did he. We had walked away from that Glock once before and somehow survived. I didn't like our chances a second time.

When both men emerged from a stand of oaks a few minutes later, I let out a sigh of relief. The little man took quick, nimble steps in front of the large, powerful athlete. No gun was in sight, but no doubt it was close at hand. They got in the Jeep and drove off, going back the same way they had come. We followed them back through the downtown area then north to a motel near a Walmart. As they pulled into the parking lot, we slowed down and cruised by and saw them park near the office. We went down a block, did a U-turn and pulled up to the curb.

"Next time I'm getting a smaller truck," Ross said. "These U-turns are killing me."

When we got back, the truck was empty, meaning both men had probably gone inside. We drove to a corner by a back fence, concealing ourselves behind other vehicles. As we watched the door to the office, Ross became fidgety, finally opening his door.

"What are you doing?"

"No way he kept those cameras and our phones in his pockets. Maybe he left the truck unlocked."

He shut the door and sprinted across the parking lot.

I had been praying a lot lately, but I offered an especially fervent entreaty now. If he got caught, he would likely get shot by something worse than a slingshot. I thought back to the missing four men.

Ross reached the Jeep. The office door hadn't moved yet. He looked in the passenger-side window then got closer and cupped his hands around his face. He checked the office door again then tried to open the Jeep's door. It was locked. He tried the back door. Locked. He hustled around to the other side and tried both doors. Locked. He stepped back and looked like he might throw a haymaker at the driver's window with his fist, then he paused, checked the office door again, and turned and jogged back.

He got in and closed the door. "I saw the cameras and our phones on the console between the seats, but the doors are locked."

Five minutes later the two men came out, got in the Jeep, and drove to the far end of the complex and went into a room. Both men had stuff in their hands.

"What's going on?" Ross asked. "I mean, he's got $50,000, so why's he staying in Modesto? And why's Richardson still with him?"

"Right, and how are we going to get the cameras and phones back?"

We sat and watched.

And watched.

As the sun set over the Coast Range Mountains, I told Ross that I needed to find a way to contact Anna.

"Yeah," he said, "and I need to find a way to take care of business."

He got out and ran across the parking lot and turned down the frontage road. I waited, figuring he was finding a restroom at some business. When he came back, he had white bags with "In-N-Out Burger" printed on them. But most of them were empty. I sent him back on another mission to buy enough burgers and fries for both of us. The food was great. No wonder he had eaten so much on the first trip.

The door to their room hadn't moved, so I left on my own mission.

Walmart was only five minutes away in the other direction. As I walked north up the frontage road, almond nectar wafted in from nearby orchards. Thousands of trees were in full bloom, giving the northwest breeze a honey-jar aroma. My brief reverie was interrupted, however, upon entering Walmart's wilderness, where the sight of people clad in bizarre costumes sent me scurrying to a rack of prepaid phones. The sun had gone down and the local wildlife was beginning to make its nocturnal appearance. I selected two phones then went to the First-Aid rack and grabbed bandages and ointment for my leg, which was still oozing into my sock. Then I went to the food aisles, knowing Ross would need refueling soon. I tried to activate one of the phones on the way back to the truck, but I found that I needed two hands.

I got in the truck and asked if there had been any movement. "No," Ross said, "unless you count that bug crawling across the window. Whatcha got?"

While I watched a stinkbug zigzag its way across the windshield, stopping to probe occasional carcasses, Ross tore open a bag of Oreos and began eating. "Oh," he said, "I went over and looked in the Jeep again. The phones are gone. I guess they took them inside."

It took a few minutes, but I got the phone activated and called Anna. The call went to voicemail. Frustrated, I left a message. Then I fought to remember Rosemary's number, finally thought I had it, and called. It was Rosemary's number all right, but it too went to voicemail.

"Huh, nobody's answering," I said.

"Course not. It's a strange number. They probably think it's one of Klah's people trying to home in on them."

"Probably."

I called again.

Still no answer.

I called again and left a long message. We waited. Still no answer.

We watched until the bug was gone.

Stars came out. The moon rose in the east. The food was gone. Ross said, "Think we'll be here all night?"

"Could be."

He tried to stretch his legs by pushing himself back in the seat. "All right," he said. "I got an idea. How about we get a room and watch their door from a bed instead of from here? We could be here for days."

The complex was built in an L-shape, so theoretically we might be able to get a room that would allow us to watch their door. But we still didn't have a plan to get the cameras and phones. We temporarily tabled the idea.

I tried to stretch my own legs. I had bandaged my shin, but it was still on fire. "Isn't there some kind of sensor we could put on their Jeep that will alert us if it moves?"

Ross thought for a moment. "Yeah, but I got a better idea. Let's get a motion detector and put it on the overhang above their door. When it opens, it'll send us an alert, and we'll get a head start before they start the Jeep."

That sounded almost too easy. I tried to think through possible problems. Ross mistook my silence for assent and got out of the truck. "Be back soon!"

He hurried to the Jeep, looked in the windows again, lifted his arms in a helpless gesture, then began fast-walking out of the parking lot toward Walmart. I looked in the shopping bag for something to eat. But it was empty.

If we ever got home again, I'd have to start charging him for food. He could have the room for free, but the food bill was getting out of hand. Half an hour later he came back with a Stick Up surveillance camera, a GPS tracker, a laptop computer, batteries, and three kinds of super glue. Ross did nothing halfway. Half an hour later the laptop was online and the camera was functioning. We waited until no one was visible, then we went to Klah's room. Ross had the super glue ready to affix to the camera, but as we approached the door, we realized that the overhang was too high for Ross to reach. A car drove up and a man got out and walked toward the office, giving the two of us a look. We turned away from him, and I could only imagine what we looked like. If he was looking for drugs, he'd probably come around soon. He went into the office.

"All right," Ross whispered, looking around to make sure we were alone again. "Here." He handed the camera and glue to me. "I already turned it on. Just put some glue on it and get on my shoulders, and I'll hold you up until it sets." He knelt down on the concrete walkway.

Klah and the professor were separated from us by a flimsy door that could be opened at any time. There had to be a better way. But I couldn't think of one. We were close enough to the wall that, after squeezing glue onto the miniature camera, I could put a hand on the wall as he lifted me. I squirted the glue, capped it, and tried to climb on his shoulders.

Fortunately we'd had practice doing this in the cave. He slowly raised up, and I pressed the camera against the stucco ceiling in the place we determined would be most effective. I held it there for ten seconds or so, then the office door opened again and the same man came out. Ross and I, two stories tall, were facing him.

He saw us and paused, then he turned and sped forward again. Hear no evil, see no evil. I kept the camera clamped onto the ceiling.

"How long's it been?" Ross whispered.

"I don't know."

"Hurry up."

"What do you mean 'hurry up?' I'm waiting for it to dry."

We stood there, two stories tall, for several minutes.

The man in the car drove by, slowly. I didn't look at him, but I assumed he was gawking at us. He went around a corner. Ross began wobbling.

"Your boots are killing me."

I let go of the camera, and it miraculously stayed in place.

"Okay, let me down."

He knelt down, and I stepped off. The camera seemed to be angled in the right direction to catch the motion of the door. We were walking back to the truck when Ross veered off toward the Jeep.

"Where are you going?" I said under my breath.

"I might as well put this on now."

He pulled something out of his pocket and dove down behind the black Jeep. A moment later he came back up. "Ha! Now we're tracking *them*."

He had stuck the GPS tracker on the Jeep's frame. We got back in the truck.

"At least now I won't have to drive like a maniac to keep them in view."

"I didn't even know Walmart carried those things."

"Oh, yeah, lots of them. The battery lasts two weeks. That should be enough." He began rubbing his shoulder "Next time we go to the store, you're getting new shoes."

"Whatever. Let's check the camera. Can you see the door on the laptop?"

Ross checked it. "Yeah. It's great. You just better hope the glue holds, because next time I'm getting on *your* shoulders."

We also checked the tracker. It showed up bright and clear on the laptop. We put all the trash in an empty grocery bag and drove over to the office. We were almost out of cash now, but Ross had a credit card he'd only used a couple of times, so he went in to get the room while I alternated my gaze from the laptop to Klah's door.

Ross was back in less than a minute.

"Bad news."

"What?"

"They're out of rooms."

I turned and scanned the parking lot. It was almost full. "When did that happen?"

"Must have been when we were having all that fun watching the door. The guy said there's still one room available, but it's been reserved. He said we can have it if the people don't show up—at ten—because they didn't use a credit card to hold it. Mind if I go back to In-N-Out?"

"Ross, you've already eaten about five pounds of food."

"That's why I've got to go back."

He drove us back to our hiding spot in the back corner, then he left. The door hadn't moved. I looked down at the laptop. The glue still seemed to be holding; the image was firm. I tried to call Anna. No luck. I tried Rosemary's number. Nothing.

Ross came back with more hamburgers, shakes, and fries.

Just before ten a car drove up to the office, and a man and a woman got out. A few minutes later they got back in and drove over to a room at the end of the complex.

"Well, that's that," Ross said.

"That was the room that was available?"

"That was it. Looks like I just wasted a hundred bucks on a camera, since we can just watch them here all night."

We decided to take turns, but my leg was aching so much I couldn't sleep. Ross had no such problem.

Chapter 42

Hiding Beneath the Surface

Before preparing for a visitor, which he doubted would show up for hours, Klah had taken some time with the phones and cameras. On Call's phone he saw pictures of the canyon, then the entrance to the cave, which he was already familiar with, and then several things he hadn't seen before, including the maze on the wall, the swastika, and markings above empty doorways. He stopped when he came to the mummies. They were arranged in three tiers, and there were far more than he expected. He studied the one that Nelson had looted. The figure looked small and leathery but otherwise well preserved. He saw two pictures of the markings above the black void. They looked like hieroglyphics of some sort, but he had no idea what they represented. He handed the phone to Richardson, who rested against the headboard on the opposite bed. The man had shown no inclination to leave. Klah had not tied him up.

As Richardson thumbed through the photos, Klah turned on one of the cameras and began scrolling through the pictures. When he saw the images of the enormous cavern, he was in disbelief.

"Oh my—"

"Yeah," said Richardson, "these mummies are remarkable."

"No—look." He turned the camera's screen to Richardson.

"*What?* Is that the cave?"

Klah nodded.

Richardson grabbed the camera. "It's huge! It's massive. And look at those stalactites!" Richardson gave him the phone back and grabbed the other camera. Klah didn't stop him. For half an hour they showed each other photos of the impossibly vast and beautiful cave. Then they both came to the plate room. They saw the table and the open plates on the table. Then they began thumbing through frame after frame of pates.

"What are they?" Klah asked. "Brass books?"

"They're definitely metal, but I don't know about brass." Richardson responded.

"Gold?"

"I believe so. That's the only metal I know of that would allow such precise engravings to be made by hand. Though I suppose a brass alloy is possible."

"How many of these pictures are there?" Klah checked the metadata. There were well over four thousand, just on his camera.

Richardson found even more on his camera. If they were gold, and he was almost certain they were, they were worth a fortune. A hundred fortunes. "Winn must not have seen them," he said.

"No way he would have left them behind."

"So how did Call and Keller find them?"

Richardson and Klah looked at each other. There were no answers.

Klah went to the last image. It was not of plates, but of small piece of stone, apparently broken off from another larger piece of stone. He didn't recognize it. "What do you make of this?" he asked and showed Richardson the photo. Richardson studied it for a moment. "I don't know. It's just a piece of dark-colored stone with some drawings on it. It looks like it was broken off of a larger rock—or a tablet maybe."

That triggered a memory for Klah, something his mother had spoken of—a corner of a tablet that had been broken off by a guardian spirit, someone named Maasaw. The tablet had been given to the Fire Clan, supposedly, but the corner was broken off and lost. Someone was supposed to bring it back—someone special. As he lingered on the thought, a new idea came to him: Call and Keller knew where it was. They had seen it, taken pictures of it. Did they still have it?

After viewing the pictures, Klah put the phones and cameras in a cabinet under the TV. The men needed some rest.

After making sure the bathroom window was too small for Richardson to slither through, Klah put the man in there with blankets and a pillow, then he pulled a mattress off a bed and wedged it against the bathroom door so Richardson couldn't leave without waking him up. Klah slept deeply for five hours, calculating that it would be at least that long before anybody showed up.

He had timed it almost perfectly. Twenty minutes after his phone alarm woke him, he heard a noise. Someone was trying to work the lock in the next room.

As per the plan, Klah had taken adjoining rooms, paying with cash for their room and with a credit card for the other. He had mussed up the blankets in the empty room and threw some towels on the floor and turned on the bathroom light.

He grabbed his gun and went to the pass-through door, which was cracked open. In the silence, he heard the electronic door-lock beep and unlatch. Ever so slowly, the door opened. Klah almost wished he had pulled Richardson out of the bathroom at the first sound. Now he hoped the man didn't hear anything and make a noise trying to push his way out.

A large man poked a balloon of a head in. He was slipping a plastic key card into his shirt pocket. He had either stolen it or quickly had it counterfeited somewhere. The man stepped all the way in. A gun was in his hand.

The dark figure was obese. Who were they sending after him? The man waddled toward the first bed and looked at the strewn bedspread, blankets, and towels. Then he turned to the bathroom. Its light shone under the door.

The man's gun was elongated, obviously with a suppressor. He had a single purpose—and it wasn't to talk.

Klah had his own suppressor on his gun. He waited until the man inched closer to the bathroom, putting his back toward Klah.

Klah pushed the door open. "Don't turn around."

The man froze.

Klah stepped into the room and in three quick strides had the barrel of his silenced Glock in the folds of the man's back.

Klah whispered: "So nice of you to come calling. Now, very carefully, take your finger off the trigger and drop the weapon. And just so you know, the thing you feel in your back is a silenced Glock Nineteen."

The weapon hit the floor—a silver and black 32-caliber pocket pistol. Klah had seen them before, but never with a suppressor, which, now that he looked at it, was longer than the gun itself. He heard a noise behind him and saw Richardson in the doorway. Klah ducked down and picked the gun up. Keeping the Glock in the big man's back, he turned to Richardson. "Go back and sit on the bed."

Richardson did as ordered, and Klah inspected the little gun again. "A Colt thirty-two. Is the suppressor custom-made?"

The man started to turn, but Klah jabbed the gun in harder, arresting his movement. "Yes." the man said, squirming from the pain. "I just came to talk."

"Of course," said Klah. "You speak softly and carry a little stick with a big silencer. Now very slowly, turn around. I want my friend here to see you."

The man turned around. He was about five-ten and maybe three hundred. His dark hair was grooved into tight waves as if it had been permed. Strands of gray littered the temples and sides above the ears. He had the face of man in his mid-thirties but the body of an older man. As Klah looked him over, he saw strength in the chest and shoulders and realized the man was probably a former athlete gone to seed. His darting eyes seemed to miss nothing now, but he had missed Klah when it counted.

He looked up at Whislin, then down at Richardson. His eyes betrayed no recognition.

"Do you know him?" Klah asked Richardson.

Richardson turned on the light and came closer. "Never seen him before."

Klah told the man to get on the bed and lie down. The big man obeyed.

"Who sent you?"

The man was silent.

Klah chambered a round.

"If I tell you, you might as well shoot me—'cause I'll never be able to work again."

"I can accommodate that." He lowered the barrel toward the man's right thigh.

"No! Please!"

"Then talk. Tell me who you are."

"Jason."

"All right, Jason. Tell me who sent you."

"He wouldn't tell me who he was, but I like to know who I'm working for, so I had an associate do some digging. All I know is, he's local."

"Local? Where do you come from?"

"L.A, but the guy wasn't in L.A. He was local—from here."

"Modesto?"

"He called from a 209 area code, and it had a Modesto prefix. So, yeah."

Klah looked over at Richardson, who said, "Looks like our man's in town, and he got himself another burner."

Klah looked back down at the man. "So he's local. What'd your friend find out?"

The guy hitched himself up on the pillows so he could breathe a little easier. "So, my associate told me to ask my boss where he got the phone, 'cause it sounded so cheap."

"And did you?"

"Yeah, sure. When the guy called back, I gave him the line and asked where he got the phone, 'cause I never wanna get one there, and he said Best Buy. He even apologized for the bad sound. I told him I don't work for nothin'. I have a rep—ever since the Gulf War. He said I'd like the money."

"How much did he offer?" Richardson asked.

"Twenty grand."

"Come again?" Klah said. "I hear this guy pays twice that much—for professionals anyway."

"I'm top of the line—no body, no mess, no cops."

"All right, so the phone came from Best Buy. What's that mean?"

"It means my guy gets a look at the paperwork—'cause he can hack anything, for the right price. I figure it's worth three grand, so I offer it, but this kid—he's like eighteen or something—he says five. We settle on four, 'cause I wanna know who I'm dealin' with. So the kid gets in and searches for sales of burner phones at the Modesto Best Buy, and sure enough, he finds one that morning—yesterday. And then—you won't believe this—he hacks *their surveillance feed*. It's all on hard drive. No tape. And he searches for that exact time of day, and he literally *watches* the guy buy the phone. He downloaded it and said he'd send it to me for an extra grand. I said two-fifty. We settled on five, and the kid sends the video, and I see this old dude—looks like that actor, what's his name, played on Law and Order?"

"Jerry Orbach?" Richardson asked.

"No, the dude who was in politics. Ya see him in movies too."

"Fred Thompson?" Richardson asked.

"Yeah, that's it. But this guy's shorter. Anyway, he's right there buyin' the phone. We don't get his name or anything, but we got something better—his credit card number. The guy never thought he'd get hacked. The kid's amazing. I prob'ly shoulda paid him the whole five grand."

Richardson shook his head in disbelief. "Your guy cracked their credit card cryptology? That's hard to do. Even the Russians can't do that most of the time."

"That's what I thought. But this kid, he said he dropped out of UCLA 'cause it was boring—when he was sixteen! Anyway, I watched the video. The guy was there."

"But how do you know it's the right guy?" Richardson was interested now.

"'Cause it made sense."

"Hmm, so who is he?"

"We still don't know, 'cause the card's issued in the name of a company, and ya can't read the name he scrawled when he signed the paperwork. But we checked out the card, and it's always used for big amounts, and it always gets paid off each month. That's all I cared about, that he could pay."

"But you don't know who the guy is or where he comes from?"

"All we know is most of his activity is in Connecticut—some place called New Haven."

Richardson shared a look with Klah. This was their man.

"When are you supposed to talk to him again?" Klah asked.

"Right after I finish the job." He smiled ruefully. "But I guess I won't be calling him again."

"Wrong," said Klah. "That's exactly what you'll do, and you're going to tell him exactly what I tell you to tell him. Right?"

"Absolutely."

"All right, get comfortable, because you're going to be here for a while." Klah looked over at Richardson. "Let's go over what we want him to say. We've got to make this plan a little tighter."

Richardson nodded, with the hint of a little smile on his face.

* * *

Travis was just nodding off when he saw movement on the screen. He focused on the screen but saw nothing. No movement. So what had he seen? He looked up at the building and saw that Klah's door was still closed. He looked over at Klah's Jeep. It was still there. Nobody appeared to be in it.

He spotted a movement at the room next to Klah's. A heavyset man was trying to get his card into the slot to unlock the door. He seemed to be having trouble. At this hour, which was just after five, the man was probably drunk and had accidently waddled into the field of view of the Stick Up camera above the door. Travis looked over at Ross, who was sound asleep. The heavyset man finally got in, and Travis rubbed his legs then rearranged himself in the surprisingly uncomfortable seat.

* * *

A phone buzzed in Klah's pocket. It was Jason's phone. A local number appeared on the screen. Klah told Jason to put it on speaker and answer it.

"Yeah?" he said, letting everyone hear.

"Do you know who this is?"

"Of course."

"Are the subjects neutralized?"

"Not yet." Jason looked up at Klah, who shook his head in a silent warning.

"Have you located them?"

"Sure. I'm just waiting for the right moment. Too many witnesses right now."

There was a pause. "At five in the morning?"

"Busy town."

"I want it done this morning," the other man said. "I'll check back at noon." He clicked off.

* * *

We were eating take-out biscuits and gravy from the Black Bear Diner, just north of the hotel, watching maids go in and out of empty rooms. The food, once again, was great, but when Klah's door suddenly opened and three men came out, Ross almost dropped his breakfast.

"What? There's three of them?" He almost started the truck, then he decided to wait until the men had gotten into the Jeep.

"I think I saw that other guy," I said, "the heavy guy—he went into the room next door this morning, when it was still dark."

"Did you see him come back out and go into the other room?"

"No. There must be a door between the rooms. The guy looked like he was drunk."

The three men walked to the Jeep and got in. The little professor was driving, the heavyset guy was in the passenger seat, and Klah sat behind them. They left the parking lot, but rather than going after them, we followed their progress on the laptop. As long as the tracker was affixed to the Jeep, we would know where they were within ten feet.

"Okay, we should probably go now," I said, wondering how long he would wait.

Ross kept staring across the parking lot at Klah's room. The door was closed.

"I've got an idea," he said.

"Uh-oh. What's that?"

"I'm about Klah's height and size, right?"

"Yeah—but he has jet black hair, and yours is mostly blond."

"Yeah, but we both have short haircuts." He got out of the truck and went to the back seat and reached under it. "Where is it?" He fumbled under the seat until he found something. He pulled out a black baseball cap that had "Grime Wave" embroidered across the front. He patted off some dirt and lint and put it on.

"Grime Wave?" I asked.

"I was an extra in an independent film last summer. Don't bother to watch it." He pulled the cap lower over his face. "Do I look like Klah now?"

"No."

"Well, what do they know?" He looked over at the maids going from room to room. "I bet we all look alike to them."

"No, Klah looks like them, and you look like a big white guy with a hat on."

He laughed, as if I had just been funny, then he closed both doors and walked toward a room where a maid was working. I looked down at the laptop. The green icon representing the Jeep was making its way north up the frontage road, passing Walmart.

Ross stood in the doorway of the open room, talking to the maid. She shooed him out and came out to the sidewalk with him. He showed her his empty pockets and gestured toward Klah's room. She shook her head and pointed at the office, seeming to say that he would have to get a key at the office. Ross pulled his new phone out and looked at it, perhaps checking the time. A new shift had almost certainly come on since he had tried to check in last night. He strode boldly to the office. Ross never did anything halfway.

Five minutes later he emerged and walked directly to the room. Halfway there he pulled a plastic key card out of his pocket and waved it at me.

Unbelievable.

He put the card in the slot and went inside.

I glanced down at the laptop to see if our friends were truly gone. The green icon showed that they were on the freeway north of us, just south of the Stanislaus River. I hated that place. It was where my first wife had been buried after being murdered years ago. I looked back at the open doorway.

Ross came out with his hands full, then he set the items down on the sidewalk and suddenly jumped up and grabbed the camera. It came off with a shower of dust and debris. He dusted off his shoulders and stuffed the camera in his pocket, then he picked up the other items and came over to the truck. He opened the door and set our phones and cameras on the console. "So, where do you want to go?" he asked, getting in. "No need to follow those goons anymore."

Both phones and both cameras were on the console. Without the gospel, the man would have been a world-class thief.

"How'd you get the key?"

"I just asked for another key to Whistling Keller's room, because a third guy had the adjoining room and needed it."

"Whistling Keller?"

"I figured they'd believe his name was actually Keller, not Klah, or whatever his last name is, and the guy checked the computer and just looked at it for a long time. Then he said, 'It says Klah or Klay here.'"

"'Yeah, I get that a lot,' I said. 'But my name's Keller. See?' I showed him my license, but I may have had my finger over my first name. And he looked at it, and then he just went over and got a key for me. Here, I've still got it." He showed it to me. "I guess we can go back in whenever we want—but there's nothing there, just a messy room—now that I have these." He nodded at the phones and cameras.

I was too stunned to say anything else. I picked up my phone. I had missed two calls and two texts.

"You know what I'm most proud of?" he said.

"That you can break into motel rooms in broad daylight?"

"No, that I didn't lie. Everything I said was true, basically."

I took his word for that while I looked at the text messages. Both were from Anna. The first one said, "Call me." The second one was longer.

> The kids are bouncing off the walls. We're going somewhere where they can play. Remember where we vacationed last summer?

They were at Sunset State Park, at Monterey Bay. No wonder I hadn't been able to get her on the phone; there was no signal at the beach. I looked at the date and time. Two days ago.

"Let's go home," I said. "The family's at the beach."

"Yeah, I see that." He was looking at his own phone. "I got a text from Rosemary."

We listened to the voice messages, also from Anna and Rosemary.

Before leaving, we checked the laptop again. The green icon had stopped at the river. What was it about that place?

* * *

Whislin Klah stood waist-deep in the dark green water of the Stanislaus River, holding a gun in his left hand and a phone in his right. The phone was set to record. The gun was still silenced, though he doubted anyone could hear the report out here, as they were concealed by a thick canopy of trees and undergrowth miles from the nearest structure. Richardson and Jason stood near him, knee-deep in the water, a little closer to the bank. Klah had made them remove their shoes, socks, and pants, figuring that men with no shoes or pants would be less willing to make a break for the thickets of wild roses and blackberries fringing the bank. He was also reassured of their complacency by the remoteness of their location, east of Highway 99, surrounded by the tangles of vegetation and riparian forest.

They had decided that Jason would call his boss and tell him that Klah and Richardson were dead and to bring him the money. Richardson stood next to him, should Jason need prompting. Klah, now mostly submerged to prevent the microscopic nanobots from communicating with a cell tower, was behind them both with a phone in one hand and his gun in the other. Should the leader check the recent history of Klah's whereabouts, he would see that Klah had traveled from the motel, six miles away, to this remote spot, then disappeared. Hopefully that would signal that Klah's body had stopped producing the electric charge necessary to power the nanobots.

"Okay," Klah said, directing the men, "You know what you're going to say?"

Jason looked back at him. "Yeah, sure."

"Is it on speaker?" Klah asked.

"Yes."

"All right, go ahead, and remember, I'm recording the call." Klah lowered himself a few more inches in the cold but gentle water until only his head and hands were visible.

Jason hit the phone number, and all three men heard the phone ringing. A deep, male voice answered. "Talk to me."

Jason spoke loud enough for all to hear. "The targets are down."

There was a pause, then the voice said, "Where'd it happen?"

"Out by the river."

"Which river?"

"The Stanislaus."

"How do you know you weren't seen?"

"You're in town, right? Check the scanners. There are no one-eighty-sevens or ten fifty-fours."

A one-eighty-seven on the police scanner signified a murder. A ten fifty-four was a possible dead body. Klah knew that Jason was bluffing, that none of them had been listening to a scanner, but he also doubted that the other guy was listening either, or that he even knew what the codes meant.

"Sorry, I need visual confirmation."

"You want to see the bodies?"

Another pause. "Discretion please. Others could be listening."

Jason looked back at Richardson and Klah. Other people were indeed listening.

The deep voice was insistent. "I need *evidence*. Do you understand? *Proof.*"

"All right, I'll meet you out at the river. We can dig *things* up if you want. But bring the money. I need to see that first."

There was a long pause, perhaps ten seconds, and everyone grew anxious. Jason brought the phone closer to his mouth and said, "Are you still there?"

"Yes. Just checking on something."

Klah assumed the man was tracing the trail of nanobots. Hopefully he was pleased when he saw that the trail ended at the river.

"Okay," the man said. "What about the other men?"

"The other men?"

Jason was buying time. He had told Klah and Richardson that he had been hired to take them out first then find and eliminate Travis and Ross. The boss would take care of the women later—Anna and the babysitter. Klah and Richardson had been surprised by this, knowing that the authorities would realize that so many killings had to be coordinated and were almost certainly connected to Keith Nelson's death. The FBI would be brought in because the business in the canyon crossed state lines. The boss, or bosses, were truly desperate.

"Don't make me use names. You know who I mean."

"I couldn't find them," Jason said. "Do you show any activity on their cards?"

"No."

"All right, I want the first payment now, for these two. Then I'll go after them." There was a long pause, then Jason added. "Your choice—no money, no evidence."

"All right, where am I going?"

Klah smiled. The big guy knew perfectly well where to go. He could see on his computer screen where the nanobot's trail ended.

"You'll never find it," Jason said, managing to keep humor out of his tone. "I'll meet you at the corner of Pirrone Road and Hammett. East side of the freeway, just south of the Stanislaus River. There's a parking area there, but you need to go through the gate and follow the dirt road all the way to the river. I'll make sure the gate is open, then I'll take you to the, uh, evidence."

"Just a minute."

There was a pause. "All right, I see it. How will I be able to identify you?"

"I'll be waiting in a gray Crown Vic."

"A Crown Vic.?"

"A Crown Victoria. They have big trunks."

"Oh, right."

"Shall we say an hour from now?"

"Make it two," the man said.

"Why two? Need to pick up reinforcements?" Jason was ad-libbing now.

"Of course not. I assume we'll both be alone."

"Oh, sure, alone. But tell you what, let's make it half an hour. Then we both won't have time to bring in help."

The man considered this. "Very well. Pirrone and Hammett. Then down the dirt road. Thirty minutes." He clicked off.

Jason lowered the phone and looked at Klah.

Klah was about to speak when he winced from a sudden pain. He rose slightly and saw a six-inch black leech wriggling from his chest. He couldn't grab it because of the phone and gun in his hands, so he tossed the phone onto a tuft of long grass and grabbed the leech. It came off with a spattering of blood, and he flung it into a thicket of wild roses. He grabbed a handful of mud from the bank and patted it onto the wound. Then he looked at Richardson.

"Professor, are the bots supposed to stop working when I die?"

"Well, that would make sense, since they gather their power from the electric current produced by the body."

Klah grabbed more handfuls of mud and began patting his torso, legs, and arms. "All right," he finally said, "you guys get dressed and let's get over there before he does."

* * *

Upstairs I found the results of the professor's break-in. Drawers were open and items had been pulled from shelves. I cleaned it up and checked the rest of the rooms. Nothing seemed to be missing. Rosemary's room appeared to be untouched, as were the little kids' rooms. I let Ross take care of his room. It looked like Richardson had started in Kevin's room and quickly been stopped by the man named Klah. I took a shower then packed for a long stay at the beach. When I came downstairs, Ross was in the kitchen making sandwiches with flour tortillas, peanut butter and jelly.

"They took all the bread with them!" he exclaimed.

The sandwiches were massive circular things overflowing with peanut butter and jelly.

"Ross, how do you survive on fast Sundays?"

"Easy, I just load up the day before. Wait—what day is it?"

"Don't worry. Fast Sunday's not for another couple of weeks."

He relaxed and went back to work. I went to my office and found my desktop computer still there. But it had been left on. I opened the program that accessed the surveillance footage and went back to the night the two men had broken into the house. Sure enough, a little after midnight a small figure clad in black clothes stole in through the gate and forced open the window to my office. It was clearly Richardson. Less than fifteen minutes later Klah entered the screen, not bothering to hide his face. We might as well have left the doors open and put a welcome sign out.

A wave of weariness rocked me. I hadn't slept much, and it was catching up with me. I focused on my stomach, which often betrayed me when I became fatigued. It seemed to be holding up. How had I improved so much? Had the Little Colorado really cured me, or was this just a temporary lull? Although sitting down, I got dizzy and closed my eyes. Maybe I needed some rest after all.

Something was pushing my shoulder. I opened my eyes and saw Ross above me. "Sorry, man. I let you sleep for an hour, but I thought we should get out of here if we're still going to the beach."

I started to push up from the chair and felt a wave of vertigo take the floor out from under me. I sat back down and put my head in my hands.

"Hey, maybe we should just stick around for a few hours," Ross said. "You don't look so good."

I really wanted to get to Anna and the family, but Sunset State Park was over three hours away. I felt the first flip-flop of my stomach, though it may have just been all the rich food we had been eating.

"Really, man, you look like a ghost. Come on, I'll help you upstairs."

"But people may still be after us."

"Don't worry, I'll just wait here by your window and knock 'em all out when they come in." He was smiling. "I've been looking at the surveillance footage on your computer. I think we should put a door where your window is and make people sign in."

Ten minutes later I was sleeping like the dead in a wonderful, actual bed.

* * *

A vast, perfectly flat field was planted in young pumpkin vines. The California spring was pushing toward an early summer, and the meeting place was surrounded by river vegetation on one side and hundreds of acres of low vines on the other. Because of that, there was no cover for the two men. So while Jason stood in the open by his gray Crown Victoria on an empty corner of the dirt road, Klah and Richardson hid in the undergrowth not ten yards from the vehicle. Klah was still packed in clay, which was quickly drying out, making him look like one of the mummies in the cameras. The tangle of willows, wild roses, blackberries, and poison oak shielded them from view. Klah had carefully avoided the poison oak. And the blackberries. And the wild roses.

It looked beautiful, but it was a menacing place.

With the gun in one hand and his phone in the other, he monitored the situation, keeping an eye on both Richardson, next to him, and Jason, standing out in the open on the dirt road.

If things were going to go wrong, it would be very soon.

He looked at the phone then at the sun's position in the sky. It wasn't noon yet, but it was already heating up. The valley could hit a hundred in late April. It had been over half an hour since the phone call.

"He's late," Richardson said. "He should have been here ten minutes ago."

Klah no longer held the gun on him, though it was still in his hand. Not only had the gun grown heavy, but he sensed that Richardson had grown complicit in the arrangement. His former boss was on his side now—since *his* boss had clearly put a hit on him. Klah wasn't as sure of Jason, but so far the man had shown no sign of running. He seemed to only want to get out—and get paid if he could.

"Can you still hear me?" Klah said into the phone in his right hand.

"Loud and clear," said Jason, speaking loud enough for the phone in his shirt pocket to pick his voice up. "But you prob'ly don't wanna talk when he shows up. It's still on speaker, so he'll hear ya."

"Just stand close enough so I can hear *him*." Klah's own phone was also on speaker but was set low enough that it was barely a whisper.

The snap of a twig breaking behind them made both Klah and Richardson jump and turn around. They saw nothing.

"What was that?" Richardson said.

"I don't know, a deer maybe."

"Wouldn't we be able to see a deer?"

Klah didn't answer. He knew that a footbridge across the river was only fifty yards to their west. He couldn't see it through the heavy growth, but he knew that people occasionally crossed it. On the far side, where the bridge ended, a foot path led through the woods down to the opposite bank.

"Maybe it was just a branch falling," Richardson offered. "Or a small tree. Did you know that beavers live here?"

"Beavers?" Jason said over the phone. "Really?"

"Shut up," Klah ordered. He looked up. A distant sound, like the soft buzz of a bee, had become audible above them, but the canopy of oaks and cottonwoods blocked his view. Richardson noticed it and stepped into a slight clearing several feet away and gazed up. "Look at that. Someone's flying a drone—"

"Get back!" Klah ordered. Both of his hands were full, or he would have stepped over and grabbed the man. "Get out of sight!"

Richardson hurried back to the brush. "Do you think it's—"

"Of course it's him—checking the lay of the land. He's either on the other side of the river, or he's got someone over there controlling the drone. I should have thought of that! I should have *done* that." The drone had come across the river and passed overhead, flying from north to the south. Klah slowly snuck toward the clearing and looked up. The drone hoovered over the trees, perhaps a hundred and fifty feet high, rotating counterclockwise. A rectangular black box hung from its belly—the camera. Klah knew that if it had infrared capabilities, like his Flir-enhanced phone did, he had already been spotted.

"Jason, act like you don't see it. He's videoing the area."

Jason fortunately had not heard Richardson's words about the drone, and as he now began to turn toward them, he kept his gaze level rather than looking skyward. "What is it?"

"A drone. Your boss is scanning the area."

Jason's phone rang. It was a new number. He knew that if he answered it, it would disconnect the call he currently had with Klah. "What do you want me to do?" he called back.

"It might be him," said Klah. "Answer it—and move closer to us so I can hear."

Jason answered the call. The drone was now stationary above them.

"Hello?"

"I thought we were coming alone." It was the man who had hired him.

"I am." He sidled closer to the bushes and kept the phone on speaker so Klah could listen.

"Then who are those two men behind you?" the voice on the other end said.

"Where? There's nobody here."

"North of you, in the bushes."

"What? Wait—where are you? Can you see me?"

Klah rolled his eyes. Anybody within a hundred yards would be able to hear the drone.

"Look up," said the voice.

Jason looked up at the drone. "Oh, is that you? Where are you?"

"No, the question is, who are those two men in the bushes?"

Klah's heart sank. He and Richardson had been spotted.

"Just a minute—let me see." Jason maneuvered his heavy bulk into the bushes and looked at Klah and Richardson. Both men stayed mute. Jason covered the phone with his hand and whispered, "Run away."

Klah got the message and tugged on Richardson's arm, and they both scurried back toward the water.

"It's just some homeless guys," Jason said into the phone. "They just took off."

The drone changed position, following the two men.

Klah reached the river and waded back into it.

"Very interesting," the voice said over the phone. "I just watched Whislin Klah's signature disappear—at the same time one of the men ran into the water. Tell me, Jason, how does a dead man—a dead man who is buried—do that?"

"I don't know what you're talking about. Two homeless guys just ran away from me. What do you mean, his *signature*?"

The call ended.

Moments later the drone disappeared back over the river. In the new silence, Jason trudged through the undergrowth to the water, where he found Richardson standing on the muddy bank and Klah neck-deep in the brown current, holding both his gun and phone above the surface.

"Might as well come on out," Jason said. "He knows you're here."

Klah came out of the water, the liquified clay running off his body. He was about to speak when he threw his phone down and frantically reached under his left armpit and grabbed another leech. He threw it against a tree, where it burst in a spray of blood.

"Let's get outta here! These leeches can eat through anything. Let's go back to the motel let him come to us."

"I thought that's what we did last time," Richardson retorted.

"Do you have any better ideas?" Klah asked. "Do you want to just go home and take your chances?" He turned and looked at Jason, who was struggling as he waddled up the riverbank. "And how about you?

You just double-crossed him. He'll come after you too. Do you want to go home and just hope nothing happens?"

Neither man answered. Klah picked his phone up from the grass. The plan had been a total bust. In fact, the whole job had been one blunder after another. Maybe he should just get out now, kiss the money good-bye, and go hide out under an alias for as long as he could.

He washed the mud off at the riverside, keeping a keen eye out for the devious leeches. After getting dressed, he sat in the back on the way back to town and directed Jason to drive them to the In-N-Out by the motel. They hadn't eaten all morning and were starving. Klah used his card again, knowing it meant nothing. They could track him anywhere.

Chapter 43

Praying Unceasingly to God

A bighorn sheep was trying to push me off a vertical cliff into the Grand Canyon. I pushed against it and must have said something harsh, because a sad voice filtered into my brain: "Really, Travis? Do I deserve that?"

Ross was trying to wake me up again. Through the fog I remembered what I had said to the sheep. "Oh, sorry, Ross. I thought you were—never mind."

"Yeah, never mind. Here, Anna wants to talk to you. You didn't answer your phone, so she called me. And by the way, you've been asleep for almost twenty-four hours." He didn't look good, almost as if he hadn't slept in all that time. He left the phone on the nightstand and left the room.

"Hi, Anna."

"You didn't answer, and I thought something had happened. Thank goodness Ross is there."

"Yeah, thank goodness. Sorry, I must have crashed. Ross says I've been out for twenty-four hours."

"Are you sick again?"

"I don't think so. Actually, I'm feeling pretty good right now." I sat up higher in bed. "What's up? Where are you?"

"I'm at a Subway in Watsonville. Travis, something terrible has happened."

I was fully alert. "What? Are you all right?"

An involuntary sob issued from her throat. "Can we come home yet?"

"I don't know, but—" I considered everything about our situation and made a snap decision. "Yes, things are getting ridiculous. Please come home. We'll go to Johnson and get more protection. I'll hire personal security. I'll buy some guns. Tell me what happened."

"Are you sure we can come home?"

"Yes, come home, straight home. Or wait, should we come get you?"

"I—I don't know."

This didn't sound like Anna at all. "Anna, what happened?"

"There's not time—I've got to get back. But, we'll be out of cell service for a while. And, Travis?"

"*What?*"

"Pray for us. Pray for Kevin."

The phone clicked off.

Adrenalin coursed through me, and I shot out of bed.

"Ross!" There was no response. "Ross!" I ran down to his bedroom and found him sprawled on his bed sound asleep. Should I wake him up? He had probably been up all night watching the house. I thought about calling the Santa Cruz Sheriff's Department to have them check on the family, but it sounded like Anna and the family would probably be gone before anybody could get there. Ross and I could try to meet them halfway, but there was no guarantee we would find them until they left the mountains and got back into cell service.

I decided to let Ross sleep.

There was nothing I could do but wait. And pray.

I went down to my office and knelt and prayed with all my heart for Kevin and Anna and the family. I didn't know what exactly to pray for except safety and protection, so I prayed for that like I had never prayed before.

Afterwards, I got my camera and tried to look at the pictures of the plates again, but I couldn't focus, and in despair I kneeled and prayed again.

Chapter 44

Death by the Sea

Klah was getting sick of seeing the same two faces in front of him. They were still in the same two rooms, but none of them had a change of clothes, and, frankly, the room was getting rank. They could shower, and Klah had rinsed his muddy clothes in the bathtub again, but as their beards grew and their tempers soured, Klah was ready to send them both home. Let the new "society" take care of them. If it even existed.

Well, no, *somebody* existed, because somebody was still trying to kill them.

But no matter how often he used his card or exposed his body to cell towers, nobody showed up. He ordered out three times a day. Pizza. Chinese. Pizza. Chinese. Using the card each time. How often could he do that before the society finally sent someone to put them out of their misery?

On the evening of the second day he remembered the images on the cameras and decided to try to figure out where, exactly, the gold or brass books were in the cave. But when he looked in the cabinet under the television, they were gone.

His first thought was Richardson, and he confronted the little man, who even now appeared to be wasting away from malnutrition. The man had a strange constitution. He could eat meat like a cannibal and still lose weight. Richardson seemed genuinely surprised that the cameras and phones were gone. Together they looked everywhere for them. Even Jason helped, probably out of boredom, since he hadn't been told what secrets they contained.

Klah called the office and told them about the missing items, accusing the maid of stealing them to make a few hundred bucks. The

manager, a wispy man with long yellow hair, came in, took a look at
the room, and told them to open some windows. Then he listened to
Klah's report.

"I doubt she took them," he said, "because the maids know we
have video of them going in and out of the rooms."

"You have video?" Klah asked.

"Oh, yes, come look." Outside on the sidewalk he pointed out
four cameras, two in the parking lot, one near the office, and one at
the other end of the complex. "Every room is monitored. But, of
course, if the maid hid the items in her cart, we may not be able to see
them when they came out."

"How long will it take you to watch the footage?"

"You don't know if this happened yesterday or the day before, so
it could take hours."

"So what good are the cameras if you don't look at the footage?"

"Well, *you* could watch it if you want. But it's a very small room.
Only one of you could fit in there."

This sounded like some kind of violation of privacy, but if the man
was willing to let them—

"All right, I'll get back to you," Klah said.

The man left, and Klah tried to think of a way to make sure the
two men didn't escape while he spent hours reviewing surveillance
footage. But then, the two men didn't actually show much interest in
escaping; in fact, they seemed to want to stick together more and
more, no doubt so they could deal with an attack together when it
came. And surely it would come, wouldn't it? After all, they had
knowledge of the cave and could go public any time. Surely the
society, whoever it was, was still determined to keep their hundred-
year-old crime a secret.

But why hadn't any attacks come?

Was it possible that they would try to wait things out? In fact, was
it possible that the old arrangement could still be saved? Was it even
possible—*no way*—that he might still get paid?

But the rational voice in Whislin Klah told him that getting the
rest of his money was an impossibility. It had probably evaporated
when he let Call and Keller go, and for sure after the fiasco out by the
river. But maybe there was another way. The more he thought about
it, the more he realized that the gold books might bring even more
wealth, extreme wealth, if he could find them.

He tried to recall the sequence of photos in the phones and cameras. Had they revealed how to find the room with the books? But he couldn't recall. There had been too many pictures. He had to get those devices back. Especially the cameras.

Sitting here seemed to be getting him nowhere. For whatever reason, the men who wanted the three of them dead had not come back, and Whislin was tired of waiting. He made a decision and went to the front door and opened it.

"You're free to go," he said.

The two men looked at him in silence.

He waited, but they didn't move. Just as he had figured—they wanted to be with him when the hangman came.

He went to Jason and gave him his phone and keys. "Go on," he said. "You're on your own."

Jason seemed surprised, but he put his hand out and took his keys when Klah dropped them in his hand. "Ya know, I've been thinking," he said, "they've got my number, but they don't have my real name and address—maybe they can't find me."

"I'm sure they can find you if they want to," Klah said. "Wouldn't you agree, Professor?"

Richardson didn't hesitate. "Of course. But they may not care to. You don't know why we're wanted—the real reason they want us dead."

"And I don't want to know. Don't tell me a thing. Can I have my gun too?"

Klah took it out from behind his waist, removed the ammunition, and handed it to Jason. The man stuffed it in his own waist, suppressor and all, then took his phone and headed to the door. He stopped and looked back. "Good luck, boys. You'll probably need it." He exited and walked out to his gray Crown Vic. They watched him until he exited the parking lot and turned right, onto the frontage road, apparently heading to the freeway.

Richardson was still dressed in black. Klah laughed at him—the get-up had to be miserable. "I bet you can't wait to get out of those clothes."

"They were unwearable before, but after the river, it's been worse. But, Whislin, I'm not leaving."

Klah wasn't completely surprised. He had seen the wheels turning in Richardson's head. "You like your chances better with me?"

"Yes. Maybe they'll let Jason go, or whatever his name is, but they can't let us go. So, I figure we're stronger together than alone."

"So, why haven't they come back for us?"

"I don't know. It makes no sense."

"I agree. So what do you want to do?"

"Keep waiting. They know where we are. But if I can have my phone back, I'd like to do a search for any word on that shootout at the canyon. Maybe they're dealing with that."

With Richardson's fate inextricably linked to his, Klah didn't mind letting the man have his phone. "Let me know what you find. And one more thing—if we're going to stay here, let's do it in separate rooms. I'll take this one." Richardson went into the other, scratching both his leg and stomach.

Klah had mixed emotions about letting Richardson stay. He would like the extra hand if things got dicey, but pure greed dictated that Klah make his next move alone. Those gold books. Their weight in bullion alone would bring him a fortune, far more than he was owed. Maybe the writings were valuable too, but probably too traceable. He would just melt them down and liquidate the assets. The manager was right, the maid had probably concealed the cameras in a cart, but he had other means of extracting the truth. Maybe tomorrow morning he'd ask her some hard questions.

He cracked the door open and scanned the area. No one was lurking in a car or hiding behind a corner. He was alone, something he had missed the last few days. A pleasant, honey-like aroma captured his attention. He stepped out and looked across the freeway to the west and saw an almond orchard with thousands of loose petals fluttering to the ground. It was like snow. With the soft, orange sun setting over the orchard, and the honey-scent wafting across the land, the scene was beautiful—almost idyllic.

What was happening to him? *Idyllic? Letting enemies go free?*

Something caught his eye off to the right, and he looked over and saw a cell tower above the far corner of the orchard.

He went back into the dim, stinking room.

So much for idyllic.

* * *

Anna's van pulled into the driveway just as the sun set behind the mountains, and Ross and I hurried out to meet the family. The two little ones poured out first and ran over to give us hugs. Rosemary got out and looked over at me. I saw worry and sadness, but no harm, no injury. She went to the back of the van to get the luggage, and Ross went to help her. Anna shut her door and we locked eyes. Again, deep sadness, streaks of tears, but otherwise unharmed. I directed Mia and Lucas into the house and began walking toward Anna, still looking for Kevin.

Kalley got out and intercepted me with a mighty hug, squealing with delight. "Daddy! Daddy! It was so much fun!" The girl would never be allowed to leave me again. That was final. Anna told her to go back and get her bags, and Kalley pulled me down and kissed my cheek, then went to the back of the van. A gift from heaven. Before Anna could go back to her bags, I hurried over and embraced her. She was limp at first, then she clung tight, holding the back of my shirt. "Oh, Travis."

I looked through the windshield. "Where's Kevin?"

"He's still inside. He's—oh, Travis. He needs our love so much!"

I couldn't bear it; I broke free and went to the side door. He was in the corner, curled up on the back seat, staring at the seat in front of him. I helped him sit up. He looked much older than his twelve years.

"Kevin, are you all right?"

He didn't respond.

I was bent over in the van, so I gently pulled him to his feet and led him to the door. He didn't resist.

Anna was waiting for us. "Let's take him up to his room," she said. "He needs to rest."

I began walking him toward the house. He moved as if sleep walking. Ross was just coming out of the front door after taking in luggage. He stopped and looked at Kevin for a long moment, then he reached down and picked him up with an effortless grace. He put his face to Kevin's and whispered, "I love you." Kevin didn't resist. Ross set him down and went back to the van. Anna and I walked Kevin upstairs to his room.

As he sat on the edge of his bed, I asked him if he wanted anything, but he didn't answer. Anna went to him and lifted his legs onto the bed as if he were a paraplegic. As he lay there, staring at the ceiling, Anna invited me to go with her to our room. She sat on the edge of the bed and asked me to sit beside her.

They had been camping at the beach for a couple of days, having a good time, she said. But this morning there was a heavy marine layer, and the temperature was cool, but they went to the beach anyway. Their van was parked by some sand dunes, near a restroom. Kevin had his slingshot in a bag with his towel, along with a supply of steel balls. Within minutes of their laying out the towels on the beach and watching the surf through the thinning fog, Kevin said he had to go to the restroom. No other cars had been in the lot, so Anna didn't worry about him going back over the dunes to the restroom by himself.

But instead of going to the restroom, Kevin found a spot on a dune that was covered in waist-high grass. He made a little blind and got his weapon out. As seagulls strayed over him, he fired at them. He said he didn't hit any. But from his vantage point, he saw something on another dune about a hundred feet away. There had been a movement in the grass. He thought it was an animal and raised his slingshot, but then he saw that it was a man, crouching down, watching the family. Anna and Rosemary had their backs to him, watching the other three kids playing by the surf. The fog was continuing to lighten, and Kevin said he could make out everybody clearly, especially the man, whom he realized had made his way up from the parking lot and was using the dune and the grass to conceal himself.

With all that had gone on, Kevin was instantly alert. He saw the man take something out of his pocket and hold it in front of him and point it at his mother and Rosemary. It looked like a gun.

Without hesitation, Kevin raised his slingshot and shot at the man.

The shot missed, and Kevin quickly reloaded and fired another ball just as the man was turning to face him. The steel ball caught the man in the face, and he dropped instantly.

Kevin reloaded and waited for the man to get up, but he was still. Kevin cautiously made his way to the other dune and found the man on his back, with blood oozing from his eye socket. The eyeball was gone.

Kevin stood there for a while, not knowing what to do, then he walked down to his mother and stood by her with his back to the ocean, staring up at the sand dune. A minute or so later Anna asked him if everything was all right. He didn't answer.

He watched seagulls flying over the dune. Several landed.

"I think I killed somebody," he said.

Anna and Rosemary looked up at him, not sure they had heard him right.

"You what?" Anna asked.

"I think I killed a guy. He was lookin' at you guys, and he had this thing. I thought it was a gun."

Anna stood up. "What are you saying?"

Kevin pulled the slingshot out of his pocket. "I shot him with this. It went in his eye." He looked up at the sand dune again. More gulls landed.

"I think the seagulls are probably eating him."

"Ohhh!" Anna followed his gaze to the dune and saw dozens of seagulls jostling just above the dune to find a place to land. Rosemary began running up the hill. "Show us!"

Anna looked back at the other three children near the water and yelled at Kalley to watch the two younger ones. Kalley said she would.

As the three neared the top of the dune, the racket from the gulls sickened Anna, and she instinctively knew that this wasn't some dark creation from a boy just hitting puberty. This was the real thing. Kevin and Anna both stopped several feet from the body. Rosemary walked into the fray of the jostling birds.

"Get!" she yelled, waving her arms.

The birds gave way and the three of them saw what was left of a pulpy face. A minute more and the gulls would have been done with everything that wasn't covered.

"Where's the gun?" Rosemary asked.

Kevin stood mute, transfixed by the body.

Rosemary scouted around and found a spotting scope in the grass by the man's hand.

"Don't touch it," Anna said, stepping forward. She knelt by the man's mangled face and put her ear just above his mouth. Then, delicately, she took his wrist and checked for a pulse. There wasn't one. She went to the spotting scope and examined it more closely without touching it. Then she rose and put her arms around Kevin. "Have you seen him before?" she asked.

He shook his head, and she felt a wetness on her neck. He was crying. He was only five–three, but he was almost as tall as she was. She held him tighter.

The man was wearing a dark leather jacket, which had partially opened when he fell. Rosemary kneeled down and carefully lifted up a corner of the jacket.

"Be careful," Anna urged. "Leather holds fingerprints."

"I think he's got—" She looked at the outline of something in a pocket.

"What?" Anna asked.

"You can see it—a gun."

Anna pulled a piece of tissue from her pocket and knelt again and wiped the corner of the jacket that Rosemary had touched. Then she used it to lift the corner of the jacket a little higher. The handle of a handgun protruded from an interior pocket. She let the jacket down and stood up. Both women looked down at the beach. The kids were now frolicking in small waves streaming onto the sand, but more important, the family was alone. "I'm going to check out the parking lot," Rosemary said. "We were the only ones here when we drove up."

As Rosemary hurried down the backside of the dune, Anna held Kevin and wept with him. She didn't know what to do, though she was leaning toward not calling the police. Rosemary came back a minute later.

"There's a big van in the parking lot. And it looks like the fog's going to burn off soon. People might start coming."

Anna made her decision. "Rosemary, would you get Kalley and the little kids and take them to the van? I want to talk to Kevin."

Rosemary waved away several gulls fighting near the body then hurried down the dune toward the beach. Anna was surprised by the gulls' ravenous behavior. She stepped away from Kevin and kicked away as many of their footprints as she could, then she guided Kevin over to the dune and back to the parking lot. "Kevin, are you sure he was pointing that thing at us?"

"Yeah, I saw him."

"Why do you think he was doing it?"

"He was watching you guys. He was sneaking up in the grass."

"And you've never seen him before?"

"No. But I saw that other guy watching the house, remember?"

"Are you sure it's not the same man?"

"Yeah, that guy was an Indian or something, and he looked strong. But this guy, he's just white and old."

He wasn't that old, Anna thought. Maybe fifty. As they made their way down the trail toward the parking lot, she stopped and looked back up. Dozens of gulls were hovering over the dune, again fighting for a place to land. Any footprints the three of them had made would be scratched away soon. She had been tempted to search for a wallet in his pockets, but she knew better than to touch anything else.

As an officer of the court, not alerting the police would place her in legal jeopardy. If it was discovered that she had been here when the killing happened, she could be prosecuted for concealing information related to a homicide. No judge would look kindly on that, even if she had done it to protect her son.

Her son who had killed a man.

She checked her phone. No cell service.

"I think he was a bad man," Kevin said in a soft, halting voice. He wiped a tear away.

"Yes, he was. He wanted to hurt us. He had a gun in his pocket, and I'm sure he was with the people who were trying to hurt Daddy and Ross."

"But, I just wanted to scare him so he would stop sneaking up on you guys. I thought that thing was a gun."

They saw the large van that Rosemary had told them about. It was larger than a regular conversion van, and jet black. They went down to it and Anna looked through the heavily tinted windows. By shutting out the light with her hands she was able to see that it had twelve captain's chairs, each one with two armrests, and each armrest with a zip tie looped over it.

If she hadn't worked with clients who had their wrists cuffed to their seats while in transport, she might not have known what the zip ties were for. Each one was loose, ready for a hand to be pushed through the loop and tightened. A chill ran up her back. The man had planned to use his gun to herd them to the van then cuff them to their seats.

Bile rose in her throat, and she forced herself to calm down. The vehicle was a Mercedes Sprinter Passenger van. It looked like a rental. She looked toward the driver's seat and saw a canvas duffel bag on the floor. It was partially open, and she made out the collapsible stock of an assault rifle.

Kevin was behind her. "Is this his van?"

"Yes." Anna turned back to him. "Kevin, you never have to worry about what you did. He was a very bad man. Look inside at the seats."

Kevin cupped his hands and looked inside. "What?"

"Do you see those white plastic things on the armrests?"

"The zip ties?"

"Yes, do you know what they're for?"

Kevin stepped back from the window, wide-eyed. "He was gonna tie us to the seats."

"That's right, and up front, by his seat, there's a bag with guns in it."

Kevin looked through the window again. "He was gonna kill us."

"Probably, or he was going to use us to get Daddy and Ross to come to him. You did the right thing, Kevin. You saved us. Always remember that."

They walked around to their van, and Anna unlocked the door.

"Should we call the cops?" he asked.

"Not yet, but when we stop I'll call Daddy. I'm afraid—"

Kevin searched her face. "You're afraid of what?"

"I'm afraid that the police may not understand, or that news of this might leak out—and then more bad people might come after us." Anna heard voices and saw Rosemary and the three kids coming down the trail from the dunes. Lucas was crying, not wanting to leave the beach. Anna grasped Kevin by the shoulders and looked into his eyes. "You are not to tell Kalley or anybody else about this. Do you understand?"

"Why? Could they get in trouble too?"

"Yes, if you tell anyone, bad things could happen. Tell me you understand."

"I understand."

Kevin had stopped crying, but he was clearly shaken. As the others arrived, Kevin made his way to the back seat and sat in a corner. Anna went back to the big van and took pictures of everything, including the license plate.

Rosemary managed to get Lucas to stop crying and got everybody in seatbelts. Anna started the van and looked in the rearview mirror. Kalley was sitting next to Kevin, but he had turned away from her. Anna's heart was breaking.

They drove down to a Subway on Beach Road, and Rosemary took the kids in to eat lunch. Anna stayed in the van and called Travis. There was no answer. She called Ross and finally got to speak with me. And now, sitting on the bed, just hours after Kevin had killed a man, she asked me what we should do.

This was a moral decision, something that seemed higher than the law. I asked her to lie on the bed and rest, and I got my phone and Googled news reports from Monterey Bay. My quick search didn't reveal anything, but I knew it would only be a matter of hours before a story appeared. The body had probably already been found. I told Anna I was going downstairs to check in on the rest of the family. Her eyes were closed. She didn't speak.

Ross and Rosemary were in the kitchen making sandwiches for the other children.

"I know what happened," Ross said.

"What can we do?" Rosemary asked. Her eyes were red with tears.

"For now, just keep the kids happy. Kevin is resting, and Anna is lying down for a few minutes. I want to talk to him again before deciding what to do. Rosemary, do the other kids know anything about this?"

"No, nothing at all. It was amazing how she kept it so—contained. They think we came home because you and Ross were back."

"Good, let's keep it that way."

I wanted to let Anna and Kevin rest, but I needed help. I went to my office and locked the door and knelt down.

"Father, we need help—and we need it now. Please help me know what to do." A quiet peace came into me, but no answers. I prayed for a while longer but soon felt that I should be upstairs. I went out and told Rosemary and Ross that I would be with Kevin and Anna.

She was still lying down with her eyes closed, but she wasn't asleep. We spoke for a minute, then we went back to Kevin's room. He was still awake, with his arm over his eyes.

I asked him if he could sit up to talk to us. His arm came off his face, and he sat up against his pillow by the headboard. Anna sat on the edge of his bed and held his hand. I sat on a chair by a small desk that he used for homework.

"Kevin, I just wanted to say thank you."

He looked up at me. His eyes were swollen, but no tears were visible. "What for?"

"For saving the family. Mom told me what you did. It was a very brave thing you did, and if you hadn't done it, there's a good chance most of you, or all of you would be dead. Did you know that?"

His nod was almost imperceptible. "That's what Mom said."

"It's true."

"But I didn't know he was going to kill us. I just shot him 'cause I was scared—and kinda mad. He was sneaking up on 'em. But I thought I was just gonna scare him, or maybe hurt him a little, but I hit him in the eye. And then he died."

"I know it was an accident, Kevin, but sometimes accidents happen for a good reason. Let me ask you something. How far away was he from you?"

"I don't know."

"A hundred feet?"

"I guess."

"So, if you shot at a bull's-eye the size of that man's eye, from a hundred feet, could you hit it every time?"

"No."

"Half the time?"

He shook his head no.

"How about a tenth of the time?" I asked.

"Prob'ly not."

"It was kind of a miracle, wasn't it? And you hit him in the one place that would kill him, so he could never hurt us again." I wasn't sure if he was getting my point yet, which was that "accidents" can sometimes be divinely appointed. "Kevin, do you think it was just a coincidence that you hit that man in the one place that would kill him?"

"I don't know. Maybe."

"I don't think so. In fact, do you know who it reminds me of?"

He didn't answer.

"David—when he killed Goliath. Remember how David saved a whole nation? You saved our family, but I don't think you did it by yourself. I think you had help. Do you know what I mean?"

"You think God helped me?"

"I do. And because of that, I believe that you never have to worry if God will punish you for it."

He thought about this for a moment, then he said, "But I feel bad." His voice broke and a tear snuck out. His mother wiped it away and said, "Kevin, I've been doing a lot of thinking and praying about this. Do you know who this reminds *me* of?"

He shook his head no.

"This might surprise you, because you know how I feel about the Book of Mormon, but it reminds me of Nephi. Remember when he had to kill that rich man, Laban? Remember he was told that it was better that one man should die rather than a whole nation?"

He nodded.

"And do you remember how he felt about it?"

"He didn't want to do it."

415

"That's right, he didn't want to kill that man, but it was the right thing to do, and it let a whole nation have the word of God. You let our whole family live, because you were willing to fight for us, and I think God controlled your arm and made you hit that terrible man in the one place where it would kill him. And do you know why?"

"So you guys wouldn't die?"

"Yes, but more than that. Let's say you just wounded him, and we were able to call the police and they arrested him. Do you know what might have happened? He might have called other people, people he knows above the police, and they might have set him free, and then he might have hired somebody else to come after us all, and even more people might have been hurt. Do you know how we know that?"

"No."

"Because he was part of a group of very bad men who have been trying to kill Daddy and Ross."

"Like the guy I saw in front of the house?"

"Exactly like him," I said. "I met him later, and he told me that he had been hired to kill us because of something we found in the Grand Canyon. But for some reason he chose not to. I think that the man you killed was a very powerful man, maybe even powerful enough to make some of the police do things they wouldn't normally do. So if he got arrested, that wouldn't stop him from coming after us again. In a way, he had to die. So God let you do it because you were willing to protect the family."

"You mean, it's kinda like he used me?"

"Yes," said Anna, "just like he used Nephi and King David. You never, ever have to worry that you did a bad thing. It was time for that man to go home to God."

I wondered at Anna, who had just shown more faith in the Book of Mormon than she had ever expressed. The truth was we were all acting on faith. In our hearts we were all praying to a God we couldn't see and listening for answers that were only whispered.

I asked if they would join me, and I knelt to pray. We faced each other in a triangle, and I prayed for Kevin and the family with a force driven by desperation. I had experienced revelation in tender ways throughout my life, but now I needed it—*we* needed it—more than ever. Afterwards we stood and hugged, and I felt a sweet comfort that Kevin would be all right if we continued to follow the soft whispers.

Anna kissed him on the cheek, then she and I went to the bedroom to talk about what to do.

* * *

Richardson rushed into Klah's room without knocking. Klah was reaching for his gun, when he saw that the little scholar was holding his phone up, excited about something.

"Look at this," he said.

"Did they find the bodies?" he asked, sitting higher on his bed.

"No—they found *a* body."

Whislin took the phone and read an article from the Santa Cruz Sentinel.

Rodney Winn, Businessman, White House Insider, Murdered

The body of Rodney Winn, esq., a confidant of White House administrations and a successful businessman, was discovered Thursday morning at Sunset Beach, near Monterey Bay.

Mr. Winn spent his early career in the global antiquities and precious metals markets. Over the past two decades he gave time to advising both Republican and Democrat administrations on foreign and domestic affairs. Most recently he advised the Immigration and Customs Enforcement agency on establishing norms in trade and criteria by which stolen goods might be identified and recovered.

He was especially dedicated to helping ICE recover artifacts that had been illicitly removed from sacred Native American sites and other federal lands.

According to local authorities, he was shot once in the head by a "metal projectile."

"The projectile appears to be a steel ball bearing," the Santa Cruz County Sheriff Coroner's office stated in a release. "It entered the victim's right eye and did not exit the head. Death appears to have been instantaneous."

Inquiries for statements from the White House and ICE were not returned.

A spokesperson for the Santa Cruz Sheriff's Office added that it appears the projectile was shot by a "non-explosive device," perhaps a modified air gun or slingshot. Authorities are communicating with other agencies to determine if similar cases have occurred recently.

Mr. Winn once headed an extensive array of businesses centered on the importing and exporting of antiquities. He also traded successfully in gold, silver, and platinum markets. As his value grew as an inside adviser to administrations, however, he gradually transitioned out of most of his business activities.

He leaves behind one daughter, Fay Winn Cartwright, of Boston. Services in New Haven are pending.

"It's him," Whistlin said.

Richardson sighed in exasperation. "It never occurred to me to look for a 'Winn'—not after a hundred years. And his name never came up in my searches for private storage facilities."

"The only question is, was he alone?"

"And if he wasn't, how many are there behind him—or, like you said, was he the last of the line?"

"It says he has a daughter."

"Yeah, but a woman didn't call me," Richardson said. "A man did. I bet there's a good chance she doesn't know anything about the cave or the canyon."

Whislin looked at the article again, and a smile slowly came to his face. "I think I know who did it. I think I know who killed him."

"How? No—*who*?"

"The kid. Call's boy. What's his name—Kevin. He always carried a slingshot around. I saw him shoot a bird out of a tree. The kid was talented—and dangerous."

"Winn was killed over at Monterey Bay. What would the kid be doing there?"

"I don't know, but I can tell you why *Winn* was there. He was hunting Call's family. We know they've been gone for days. No wonder we couldn't find them. They've been laying low."

"Could be. And Winn, with all of his resources, found them. Maybe it was a credit card, or a facial recognition camera, or maybe their license plate got scanned in an HOV lane. He probably knew where they were going before they got there."

"Yeah, but the kid saw him before he could do anything about it." He laughed. "I want to go shake that kid's hand."

"So what do we do?" Richardson asked, getting his phone back.

"I was going to ask you the same question. You know those people, or that *person*, better than I do. Are we in the clear now?"

Richardson didn't answer for a long time. The man had always been a careful thinker.

"Here's what I think," he finally said. "Maybe we just go home. I doubt anything's going to happen right away, even if there are others. And, yes, I do think there are probably others. I doubt Winn dreamed up your nanobots by himself. At a minimum, he had connections in Intelligence. But right now there are too many bodies out there, too much risk. Plus, the Calls haven't gone public, and, neither have we— so, whoever's out there, maybe they'll just let the dust settle for a while." He stopped and considered things further. "Maybe they'll try to liquidate any other artifacts they have from the cave—or maybe just hold onto them for another five years or so and let the value go up. But, I do have to wonder, why did Winn come out here by himself? Why didn't he find another ex-SEAL, or just hire another

Jason? My guess, and it's only a guess, is that Rodney Winn's head was on the chopping block, just like mine and yours were—and he had to remove any threats to the group, or else. Yes, my guess is there's probably somebody else—very high up. But, really, who knows?"

Whislin didn't know if he could trust Richardson on this, but he could see the possibility that the threat had ceased for a short time.

"So, if that's the case, what do you want to do?" Klah asked. "Are you going to go home?"

Richardson grinned. "I made my mind up out at the river. There I was, half naked in leech-infested waters, with a gun on me. And that was after I had been cemented inside a cave. Right there I decided that if I survived, I'd go back and teach. I've done some terrible things in pursuit of money—and all for a man, or some group maybe, that I've come to despise."

"But what about the gold?"

"Too risky. I want something else now." His grin became a sheepish smile. "I'm kind of looking forward to getting in front of those nineteen-year-old girls again. Who knows, maybe one of them will think I'm worth spending some time with."

Klah wasn't sure about Richardson wooing somebody fifteen years younger than himself. But of course, they weren't *all* fifteen years younger, and a woman could do worse than marrying a professor. But, still, it didn't make sense.

"I don't know," Klah said, "getting a girl versus a ton of gold. I know which I'd take."

"All right, let's talk about the gold—if that's what it is. Remember, those metal books might be made of brass, and brass isn't worth the trouble of pulling it out of the canyon. But, really, the most valuable thing in the cave isn't the metal, or its amazing beauty, it's the hieroglyphics. No ancient writings of any length have ever been found in the Western Hemisphere. If the hieroglyphics on those pages are Native American, *and* pre-Columbian, the implications are staggering. Universities and museums would pay millions. But you have to be able to find them first, and then prove what they are, and then sell them. Good luck with that. And remember, Kinkaid never found them, and his professor friend, Jordan, didn't find them, and Winn didn't find them, and Nelson didn't find them. And all of them died because of their work in the cave. And, of course, don't forget the four guys who are probably still rotting out there. No, I think there's a reason why those plates are still safe in that cave."

Whislin was surprised. "Do you believe in omens and fate?"

"The jury's still out on that—but I don't disbelieve it."

Klah thought about this. Maybe they had more in common than he realized. "But don't forget, Call and Keller found them."

"They did, but they didn't take them, or even want to. If I really wanted to get those plates, I'd probably find Call and Keller and try to get them to help me—or at least give some directions. But I doubt they would. Like I said, they'd probably die first." He held his hand out to Klah, palm up. "So, if you don't mind, I'd like my keys. I want to go home."

The man's keys were still in Whislin's pocket. They were the last hold he had on the man. Richardson could still go to the cops about Nelson—and the guy in Texas. But then, Klah had something on him too, namely that Richardson had hired him to do those things. No, their common fear would keep them both quiet. He fished the keys out of his pocket and tossed them over. "Want a ride back to your car? It's probably a mile away."

"Yeah, sure—if it's still there."

Richardson had nothing else, no bags, not even extra clothes. Whislin locked the place up, and they went out to his Jeep. Once in the Jeep, Richardson had a question. "You seem more tempted by those metal plates than I am. Are you thinking about going back?"

Klah had his arm out the window, enjoying the fragrance flowing in from the orchards. It was a beautiful neighborhood. "Maybe. I'm not as opposed to getting rich as you are. But I've been thinking about things too. Like you said, a lot of guys have died poking around there. Maybe the spirits are against it."

"The *spirits*? You too?"

He nodded. "My mother taught me to respect coincidences—and maybe I'm starting to listen. But, still, if you ever hear of any new mummies or Southwestern gold showing up on the market, I trust you won't talk."

"Wouldn't think of it. I know how you get even with people who betray you."

"And I *will* get even."

Richardson's white rental was still there. This *was* a great neighborhood. "If I get rich," Klah said, "maybe I'll come back here and buddy up with Call. Seems like a nice place to live."

Richardson stepped out and took a long look around the block. "No bad guys."

"It's about time."

Richardson turned back to Klah. "Thanks for the ride—but mostly for not killing me."

Klah chuckled. "It could still happen, ya know. See ya later."

"Frankly," Richardson said, "I hope not."

Klah was still surprised when the little rental started right up. Great neighborhood.

He drove back to the motel. He knew what his next job was.

* * *

The man's name was Rodney Winn—an advisor to multiple government administrations. According to the article that Anna found online, the dead man had been "especially dedicated to helping ICE recover artifacts that had been illicitly removed from sacred Native American sites and other federal lands."

I bet he was. And no doubt he specialized in keeping ICE away from his own clandestine dealings.

So now we had an identity—and a big decision to make. If Anna went to the authorities, Kevin could face criminal charges and greater trauma from dealing with the court system. If she didn't disclose the family's involvement in the killing, she could face criminal charges of her own. After we prayed together, she went to bed, and I went to deal with the cameras and phones. I wanted Ross's help, but at his door I heard him snoring contentedly. I went down to my office to start protecting the thousands of photos.

* * *

Klah had gotten something to eat, as he knew he might be up all night, then he went to the manager's office and asked to see the surveillance videos. The closet-size room would give most people claustrophobia, but Klah had won that battle years ago during his SEAL training. Now he just had to find the right camera angle to watch—and win the battle to keep his eyes open.

Even though the footage was accelerated ten times, virtually nothing happened, and he dozed off while watching the first camera angle, but he opened his eyes in time to see the maid entering and exiting the two rooms that first morning. He zoomed in on her but saw nothing in her hands—because she clearly had nothing in them.

She had left the cart out on the sidewalk, and the two times she came back out to get supplies, her hands were empty. He watched the rest of that angle's footage, which covered the next fifty hours, which took five hours, and still he saw nothing. He was about to give up—obviously the maid hadn't taken anything—but with no other hope of finding the cameras, he loaded footage from another angle and forced his eyes to stay open.

The revelation came in the first hour. Incredulously, he watched Travis Call and Ross Keller enter the frame. Then Travis stood on Keller's shoulders and *glued a camera* to the ceiling above the sidewalk. They left as suddenly as they came. The next morning before the maid showed up, he saw Jason, Richardson, and himself exit the room to get a real breakfast. He watched closely. They had walked under the camera and never seen it. His skills were definitely slipping. Moments later Keller entered the frame again, tried the door, and left. Then he come back *with a card key* and let himself in. How'd he get that?

Keller came out of the room moments later with two cameras and two phones. Klah had put them right where anybody would look for them, in a cabinet under the TV. Definitely slipping. Then he watched Keller put the cameras and phones down and jump up and grab the camera on the ceiling outside. A shower of white stucco fell all around him. Keller picked up the other items and made his way across the parking lot then out of view.

And they had done all this while Klah and his band of professionals were mere feet away. Slipping! Slipping!

And, of course, Klah had missed all of this while viewing the first camera's footage because he had *fallen asleep.*

He should retire.

He should get a job as a janitor.

Angry, he called the manager in and showed him the footage.

The manager, the same pasty fellow with the long yellow hair, somehow went paler. He played it again, perhaps to be sure he had seen it correctly, and stopped the footage as Keller walked out of sight with his booty.

Klah said his lawyer would be in touch with the motel's lawyer, and the manager's personal lawyer, very soon. He demanded the manager's name, address, and cell number and wrote the information down very carefully. He then forced himself to smile and said, "I always wanted to get rich. Thank you."

The trembling man still at the playback console could not stand as Klah walked out the door.

* * *

I had been up late and now was dragging. After talking with Anna about Kevin, I had spent hours with the cameras and phones, downloading the images onto my laptop and also onto a separate solid-state hard drive. Then, after sleeping for a couple of hours, I got up for scriptures and prayer with the family and spent some more time alone with Kevin. Anna let the school know that he would probably be staying home for a few more days. At nine, when the bank opened, I took the hard drive to a bank and secured it in a newly rented safe deposit box. On the way to work, I almost relaxed: the photos were in a safe place, and the man behind the threats appeared to be dead.

But a jolt of adrenalin shot through me when I turned the doorknob to my office and found it unlocked. I stepped inside and saw the big guy at my desk.

Whistling Klah. Or something like that.

His jet black, close-cut hair seemed a little longer and unrulier. His dark eyes were sullen and bloodshot. But still, the bulges under his tight shirt represented potential harm. Potential great harm. He invited me to take a seat, which I did.

He swung his long, thick legs toward me. "We meet again."

"You should expect that when you break into my office."

"I could have broken into your home."

I let it go.

"He did it, didn't he?" Klah said. "He killed the guy." There was the faint accent again. If he hadn't been sitting before me, I would have guessed Middle Eastern, but now I recognized it as a Native American thickness, heavy on the consonants. I was pretty sure that I knew what he meant. "If you're talking about the man at the beach, that was an accident."

"Sure—I saw him kill a bird once from fifty feet. The kid's got a gift."

Hearing that your son has a gift is normally a compliment.

"Been to the cops yet?"

"No."

"Of course not. So, we have something on each other. Actually a lot of things. I know that your son killed Rodney Winn—of course I knew that already—and I know you've been to a part of the canyon you shouldn't have been at and found some "items" you should have told the authorities about."

"If you mean the mummies, I—"

"I mean the gold books."

My heart sank. He had seen it all.

"And of course," he continued, "you know far too much about my activities to leave me with any degree of comfort."

"So, what do you want?" I asked.

"What do you think I want?"

"Are you here to kill me?"

"Maybe. It depends."

"On what?"

"On if you'll give me the cameras back—or agree to take me to that room in the cave."

I knew that my children needed a father, and my wife wanted a living husband, but in an instant I knew how to react.

"I can't do that."

His tired face darkened. "Why?"

"Because I don't want you to have the plates. I don't want anyone to have them. I don't even want me to have them, or Ross. They belong where they are."

"Are you willing to die for that belief?"

"Absolutely."

He stared at me for what seemed a long time. There was a bag at his feet. He reached down and pulled out the Glock I had seen in the canyon. The massive suppressor was affixed to the barrel, making the unit look like either a long handgun or a sawed-off rifle. "That's what the professor said you'd say." He stood up. Ross is big, but this man would make Ross look normal—and make me look as small as I felt.

"I'm not sure I'd trust him," I said. "There was something about that guy I didn't like."

"I get that. But he was right this time. So, I have a question for you."

"I'll answer it if you'll answer one of mine."

He chuckled. "Go ahead."

"What happened back on the rim, after we left? We didn't see those four guys come out with you and the professor."

"You saw us come out?"

"Of course. We followed you all the way back here. We saw you get the bag from the professor—what's his name again?"

"Richardson."

"Yeah, we saw you get the bag with the money from the car by my house."

Klah chuckled and kicked the bag with his foot. "Still got it."

"You should put it in the bank. People might get ideas."

"I can see that."

"Anyway, what happened to those guys?"

"They got killed." He let that hang in the air.

"But I didn't do it," he continued. "Didn't have to. They got greedy and ended up shooting each other. Took about three seconds."

"Are they still there?"

"Far as I know. Now I've got a question for you. Who are you? What service were you in? I've never seen anybody so—and I'm going to use a big word here—cavalier about facing death."

"I'm not cavalier. I have a lot of respect for that gun. And I respect you, mostly because you have it, but also because you didn't shoot me in the canyon. That showed something—I don't know, a conscience maybe, a goodness hiding inside you. And I respect that. But, no, I wasn't in the service, except as a missionary—I was in the service of God. And the reason I don't want you or anyone else to get those plates is because I believe they're God's property. I think the men who put them there were prophets, and the information they contain may become a great blessing to humanity."

"How do you know? Can you read them?"

"I recognized some of the characters—from a book I read once. I'm guessing about the rest."

Klah was quiet for a while. He looked at the floor, then he seemed to notice the gun in his hand and slowly put it back in the bag.

"I never killed anyone intentionally," he said. "Except in the war. But I mean here—I never..." His voice trailed off.

This was becoming a most interesting conversation.

"Not even Nelson?"

He shook his head. "That was an accident—like with your son. I hit him because he lied to me, and he fell in the water and drowned."

I thought back to my dealings with Nelson, to the trust he had placed in me. I still owed him. "Where's your friend?" I asked. "The professor?"

"He wasn't my friend, he was my boss. He went home, back to his old job. Your son probably saved his life."

"And yours?"

"Maybe. They came after us, after we got back here. That's why we were at the motel—waiting for them."

"But, do you think Winn was the only one?"

"Don't know. We'll see. So, do you know why I came here?"

"Sure, to find out how to get to the plates."

"Not really. I didn't think you'd tell me, not after your stunt on the rim. I came here to get to Keller. I know how rich he is—or I know how much money you invested for him. I had access to your computer, remember?"

"Don't worry. I'll change the password."

"Don't worry. I'll crack it again."

A standoff. With him in charge. "So what were you going to do, take me hostage?"

"If necessary."

"Is it necessary?"

He didn't answer.

"Anyway," I continued, "he's more stubborn than I am. He'd probably let me die before you got any money."

"A couple of guys with principles."

"Sometimes. Maybe that's why we get along."

Something else seemed to be on his mind. I took a moment to search his features, the heavy lines in his face, the thick brow and slightly hooked nose. He wasn't exactly a handsome man, but his face commanded attention. "You're Native, aren't you?"

"Half," he said.

"What tribe?"

"My father was half Navajo. My mother was half Hopi. The rest is mongrel white."

"You look Native, but your words are—where'd you go to school?"

"Nowhere special. I just learned that if you want to survive in a white world, you gotta learn the white talk."

"Nowhere special? Somewhere back East maybe?"

He shrugged. "Maybe."

"Ivy League?"

"Maybe."

"That's what I thought. How did you ever get mixed up in all this?"

Again he went quiet, his eyes darting around, stopping on photos and meaningless plaques. Then he surprised me by bringing up something totally unexpected, though in retrospect it shouldn't have been.

"You have the corner, don't you?" His eyes were fixed on mine with a new intensity. Not anger. Not a threat.

"What do you mean?"

"The Maasaw's corner. The one Pahana is supposed to bring back. There was a picture on your camera."

I gave him the truth. "No, I don't have it. But I think I saw it. At least, that's what an old Hopi elder told me."

"An old Hopi elder?"

"I met him outside the canyon, after you let us go. But I had seen him before, out by the rim. He asked me if I had the corner."

"But you didn't?"

"No, we left it in the cave—like the plates."

"Did he tell you that a white man is supposed to bring it back to us?"

"Yes, he even expected me to have it, and when I didn't, he was upset. He said his vision was wrong."

"Do you still know where it is?"

"Sure, but I don't ever expect to go back and get it. The Hopi elder said the same man who brings it back will be 'the repairer of the breach.' That's not me. I don't know anything about your people."

"Does Keller know where it is?"

"Yes, but he hasn't talked about it since we got back. I doubt he's interested in it either. But who knows?"

He stared at a wall, thinking. I suspected I knew what was racing through his mind.

"I can tell you this," I added. "It's protected. The wrong person will never be allowed to take it."

"What—is it like Indiana Jones? I'll die if I look at it?"

"I'm not kidding. They're always watching it."

Of course I didn't actually know this was true, but it seemed plausible. After all, the old man had been watching me for days, he said, so why wouldn't he be watching the corner, or even me, right now? "I think the power protecting that stone is greater than anything most people have ever dreamed of. If you trespass against it, it will destroy you. Listen, Klah—wait, what is your name? Is it really Klah?"

He nodded. "Whistlin Klah. Without the 'g.' When I was a baby, I whistled through my nose." He looked at his left hand. "And I happen to be left handed, like my dad, which is what Klah means."

"The left hand of God."

"Huh?"

"The ancient Jews thought the left hand of God represented his destroying power."

"Huh." He paused again, the gears still turning, his elbows on his knees, his head hanging. "But maybe—maybe I don't want to be a left hand anymore. Maybe I want to get on the right side."

His head came up, and his eyes were softer. He seemed to be entreating me, hoping I'd understand.

"Then maybe it's time you changed professions."

He nodded almost imperceptibly. "Maybe it is." His voice was softer than before. A moment later he whispered, "The tablet. That's big medicine."

He grabbed his bag and stood up. Native Americans, Hopis especially, are generally angular and slightly built, but this man was larger than some NFL football players. It was a shame he hadn't played somewhere—it might have kept him out of trouble and made him the fortune he wanted.

"I never could kill you."

"It seemed like you never wanted to, except when you cemented us in the cave."

"Even then, if I'd really wanted to, I would have gone inside and found you." He walked to the door. "Maybe I'll check in again," he said. "I like your neighborhood."

He opened the door. It was a clear day with a breeze riffling the leaves of young Chinese Pistache trees out front. "Or maybe I'll sell my place and go back to my people. Problem is, they're not really my people." He faced me with an ironic smile. "You're as much my people as they are." He walked out to a silver Jeep at the curb and got in and drove away.

I got up and locked the door and called Anna and told her of my strange interview. Then I tried to get some work done.

Chapter 45

A Terrifying Fall

Within a few days I contacted all of my clients and, after a few buys and sells, had them in good shape again. Some had forgotten that I had even been gone, but most were grateful to hear from me. Rising tides, like rising markets, lift all boats.

We began seeing new behaviors in Kevin. For other boys his age, retreating into silence for hours or even days might be normal, but not for Kevin. The next evening after dinner I broached the subject with Anna. As before, she was concerned with the collateral damage inherent in going to the authorities.

"Well, maybe we don't start with them," I said.

"What do you have in mind?"

"Maybe we start with the bishop—and then, maybe, go to Johnson."

"Johnson?" she said in disbelief. "He's probably the last person we want to talk to."

"I think, if he's given the right understanding of the situation, he'll do the right thing."

"The right thing? Travis, let me tell you about the right thing. The right thing was for me to stay with the body while Rosemary got cell service and called the Santa Cruz Sheriff's Department. But I chose to protect our son instead. For three days I've been withholding evidence of a homicide—obstructing justice. For that I can get, let me remember now, oh yeah, five years. And I'm an officer of the court, so they'll be sure to push for every minute of it. And if Johnson doesn't turn Kevin over to the sheriff, he'll be complicit, and that'll be five years for him. So I doubt he'll want to do 'the right thing.'"

"Well, I guess it could go to court, but I doubt that, as long as the judge has any common sense."

"Don't count on that."

"But I do think it's important that we do the right thing here."

"The right thing again. Let me ask you, Travis, did Nephi do the right thing?"

I didn't answer. Anna's reputation as a clever lawyer was growing in town because she was exactly that.

"When he lopped off the head of Laban, one of the most powerful men in Jerusalem, did Nephi throw himself on the mercy of the court?"

"No—he followed the Spirit."

"Of course, and who's going to decide what that is?"

This was getting tricky. I was concerned about Kevin carrying a debilitating secret for the rest of his life—and I suspected that homicides were the worst kind of secrets to carry. He couldn't tell his sister. He couldn't tell his friends. He wouldn't even be able to tell his wife. Common sense indicated that we get this out in the open.

"Look," I said, "Johnson and everyone else will want to do the right thing for Kevin. He's only twelve. And they'll know he was protecting his family. I'm sure the sheriff saw the zip ties in the van."

"All right, let's say they decline to prosecute. But what about Winn's family? If they don't get justice in criminal court, they could sue in civil court. Are you willing to lose everything we have for peace of mind?"

"For Kevin's peace of mind? Yes."

She started to say something then stopped, then she bowed her head. A moment later I heard a sniffle. Being a mother was harder than being a lawyer.

I put my hand on hers. "Are you all right?"

Almost in a whisper, she said, "I found his slingshot in the garbage barrel yesterday. And I heard him crying in his room last night. It broke my heart. Maybe you're right. He should definitely talk to someone. But Johnson? I don't know—the risks are so great."

I held her hands. "Let's talk to Kevin about it—about going to the bishop at least."

We found him alone in his room with his earbuds in, listening to music that definitely was not conducive to the Spirit. We told him the name of the man he had killed, then we reemphasized that we were sure this man was responsible for all the threats that had been made on our family. After making sure that Kevin understood that he had saved our lives, I asked how he felt.

He didn't respond.

Anna sat down next to him, putting an arm around him, "Kevin, we love you so much. We won't make you talk to anybody, but if this is really bothering you, what would you think about going in to see the bishop, and then if he thinks so, maybe we could go talk to Captain Johnson. Your father is sure that he'll understand that everything you did was in self-defense."

Kevin glanced up at her. "What do you think?"

"I think the bishop will understand. He's a good man."

Kevin stared back at the floor.

"How about we go in and see the bishop first," I suggested. "We'll see what he says, then we can decide what to do."

"Will he kick me out of the Church?"

Anna held him closer. "Oh, no, Kevin. He'll just help us make the right decision. And he won't tell the police if we don't want him to."

Kevin decided that might be okay, and I immediately called the bishop on his cell phone. When I mentioned that it was serious, he said he would meet us at his office in thirty minutes.

How does one tell his bishop that his son has killed another human being and that you and his mother have been keeping it a secret? I may have been more scared than Kevin. There was actually a chance I could lose both of them. The bishop was waiting for us, and after handshakes I basically blurted out the facts:

"A man has been after us, Bishop, because of my work, and he's been sending people out to try to kill us, and while Ross and I were gone, my wife took the kids to the beach, and when they were there, one of the men showed up with a gun, and my son, Kevin, saw him and shot him in the eye with his slingshot, which killed him, and now the authorities are looking for the killer, but we haven't wanted Kevin to confess because he was basically just protecting the family and we're not sure the sheriff and prosecutor over there will understand. They may want to prosecute, so we've kept this to ourselves until now."

He looked from me to the others. "Say that again?"

Anna took a turn, explaining things with improved clarity.

"I see," Bishop Quinn said. He was in his sixties, at least twenty years older than us. His large bald head sat on an even larger round body. He was quite intelligent and had a sweet, friendly disposition.

The story was that his father had been a mission president, and one day, a visiting apostle saw the teenager and asked him how old he was. "Seventeen," he replied. "Young man," the apostle said, "You are to serve a mission immediately. Let's find your parents, and I will ordain you an elder and see that you receive your call soon." Within a month, Elder Stephen Quinn, still seventeen, left for a two-year mission to Tahiti. Despite this extraordinary background, or perhaps because of it, he was generally quiet, very compassionate, but could be surprisingly decisive.

"I see," he said. "I think."

"Basically, we're here," I said, "to seek your counsel, so we can do the right thing and hopefully get Kevin any help he needs."

He turned his attention to Kevin. "So, Kevin, would you like to tell me what happened?"

"No." Kevin was silent, perhaps reconsidering his answer. "But, in a way, I guess so."

The bishop smiled. "I think I understand. I actually get that a lot. So, could you tell me, in your own words, what happened?" He was sitting behind his desk, his benevolent expression unmoved by the bizarre facts before him. Kevin didn't speak, so the bishop said, "Kevin, here's what I think we should do. First, I think we should kneel and have a prayer, and then, if you can, I'd like you to try to tell me what happened. Is that all right?"

Kevin agreed, and the bishop came around and we knelt in prayer, with the bishop as voice. When we stood up he put his arm around Kevin. "I really think the Lord would like you to share what happened over at the beach. Do you think you can do that now?" Kevin nodded. "Good." The bishop went around and sat in his chair. "All right, Kevin, what were you doing when you saw the man?"

"I was just—well." He stopped and looked down.

"Go ahead and tell him, Kevin," I said.

"Well, I was trying to shoot some seagulls with my slingshot—but I didn't hit any."

"I see. Then what happened?"

"Well, I was on a sand dune, and I looked over and saw a man on another sand dune, but he was on his stomach and was hiding in some grass, and he was watching my Mom and Rosemary."

"Was he behind them?"

"Yeah."

"How far?"

433

"I don't know, maybe about a hundred feet." He looked at Anna, who nodded. "Kalley and Lucas and Mia were over by the water, but he could see them too."

"So, when you saw him spying on your family, what did you do?"

"I don't know, nothing at first—I just watched him. But then he picked something up and put it in front of him. It was black, and I thought it was a gun."

"Was it a gun?"

Kevin shook his head slowly. "No, it was just a telescope thing, like a hunting scope, but I thought it was a gun."

"Did he hold it like a gun, or did he put it to his face?"

"I couldn't tell for sure, because he was just looking at it, like he was doing something to it with his hands."

"Adjusting it," Anna said, helping him.

He nodded. "I guess so. But—it wasn't a gun." He looked down at his hands, which were quiet in his lap. I put my hand on them, and he looked up at me. I smiled and nodded at him, trying to let him know that I was pleased with him.

"So, what happened then?" the bishop asked.

"I already had a steel shot in my slingshot, so when I thought he had a gun, I just lifted it up and shot at him."

"Did you hit him?"

"No. I missed him. But then he started turning toward me."

"Were you scared?"

"Yeah, but—"

"But what?"

"Mostly I was mad. I thought he wanted to hurt my mom." He burst into tears, and Anna and I quickly put our arms around him. He had been calm to this point, so the sudden emotion surprised me.

The bishop pushed a box of tissues toward him and let him cry.

Nobody said a word for a long moment.

When Kevin had stopped crying, the bishop said, "You love your mother, don't you?"

Kevin nodded.

"You wanted to protect her, didn't you?"

Kevin was still staring at his hands. "I had to protect her. Because somebody else killed my other mom. And my first mom didn't want me."

I threw my arm around him and pressed my face against his. "Oh, Kevin, no!" I couldn't do or say anything more, except hold him and cry. Anna was clinging to him on the other side, saying, "Oh, Kevin, we love you so much. We'll never go away. We'll never go away!"

How could he have been so broken and I not know it? How could his trauma have been so deep and seethed for so long that he was willing to kill birds, cats, possibly even human beings—and I not know a thing? How cold and distant was I?

But I could say nothing. My own wound had suddenly grown as wide as the canyon I had spent so much time in. We both needed help.

The bishop stood up and came around to us. He knew that Kevin and Kalley had been adopted shortly after birth, when their mother gave them up through LDS Social Services. He also knew that Marsha, my first wife, had been killed when they were four. He gave a handful of tissues to Anna, who was closest to him, then to Kevin. I looked up at him and saw that he had a tissue to his own eye.

We were sitting too close to his desk for him to come in front of us, but he went around behind Kevin and put his face close to his, and Anna and I gave him some room.

"Kevin, your parents love you very much. We all love you. And I feel strongly that God loves you. You don't ever have to worry about that."

Kevin didn't respond.

"We will try to always be here. Do you believe that God loves you?"

Kevin looked down, took a quivering breath and said, "I guess so, but he didn't let me stay with my real mom, and he didn't let my other mom live. And sometimes—"

"Sometimes what?"

"Sometimes I get mad at him."

The bishop took a knee behind him but put his hands on Kevin's shoulders. "Sometimes I get mad at him too, Kevin. Sometimes we all do, because we don't understand him."

"But I was mad at him when I shot that guy, and I wanted to hurt him, just like Dad hurt Ross, only worse. So I aimed for his head."

Anna looked at me over Kevin's bowed head, her eyes wide, stricken with surprise. My own heart was breaking. So many wounds, so many revelations.

The bishop stood up and went back to his chair and sat down. Anna and I put our arms around Kevin again.

"Kevin," the bishop said, "can you look at me?"

His blond head came up.

"I can understand how you were mad at God. I think a lot of people would be. But I have to ask you, did you mean to kill that man?"

Kevin spoke in a flat, slow tone. "I don't know. I was just mad at him for sneaking up on us with that thing in his hand—and I think I was scared too, because I thought it was a gun."

"I see. I think a lot of people would have been scared—and mad. But, Kevin, you didn't want to hurt God, too, did you?"

Kevin thought about this, then said, "No, I just don't want him to hurt me anymore."

Deep, terrible wounds.

By the time he was four he had been abandoned by his birth mother and then lost the only mother he had ever known. I had suspected that these events had led to his aggression, and possibly to Kalley's strong opposite reactions of cleaving to her parents—especially to me—but I had never realized how deep these feelings were, that Kevin thought that his Eternal Father didn't like him, didn't want him to be happy, or even safe. Kevin had grown up thinking the universe was against him and that he could only find happiness by hurting those who hurt him. His aggression had been on display when he killed the cats, but I had only been confused and embarrassed by that, when I should have been alarmed. I should have talked to him then the way the bishop was talking to him now. Kevin was a gift to me, an eternal gift, and I had let him down.

Kevin spoke again. "I just don't want my mom to leave."

"I'll never leave you, Kevin," she said again, softly, keeping her arm around him. "I love you with all my heart." This was a commitment I knew she would sacrifice all to keep. Another revelation. I knew she loved all four children as if they had always been hers, but now I saw the depth of that love, the fierce tenacity of it, and I was humbled by it.

"Kevin," Bishop Quinn said, "can you tell me what happened after you shot that man?"

"He just stayed there, on the ground."

"He didn't move?"

"No. So I went over, and his eye was gone. And I could tell he was probably dead. And I could tell that the thing in his hand wasn't a gun, and I got scared."

"Did you look around to see if anybody else was there?"

"You mean to hurt us?"

"Yes."

"No. I couldn't really think about anything else. And the next thing I knew, I was standing by Mom, and I told her that, you know, that maybe I killed somebody."

The bishop looked at Anna. "Sister Call, when did you let Travis know?"

"As soon as we got into cell range, in Watsonville. But first, I saw the zip ties in the man's van. And the guns. He had an assault rifle in his van, and Rosemary and I saw a gun in his coat, when we went up to see what Kevin was talking about. He had a hunting scope and a handgun. And he probably had more weapons than just the rifle in his van. We didn't look inside the bag that was by the driver's seat."

"Thank you. And have the authorities found the body? Have they identified it?"

"Yes," I said. "And we're sure that it was the man who had been trying to kill me and Ross." I hadn't told him about the canyon or the cave or the plates. I hadn't told him about Klah or Richardson or the four guys who came after us. It all seemed too surreal. And somehow earlier today I had been as cool as could be when confronted by Klah and his massive Glock.

The bishop asked for more information about the people trying to kill me and Ross, and I gave him an abbreviated version of the facts—all true—but with no names and certainly no mention of the cave or the plates. I wasn't ready to dive into all that now. He asked if I had gone to the police about any of it, and I said that I had talked to Captain Johnson, downtown, twice, and that I would probably talk to him again, even though the threat seemed to be over.

"I would highly recommend that," he said. He looked over at Anna. "Sister Call, what do you think should happen now?"

"I agree with Travis. I think we should talk to the authorities, but I want Kevin to know what that means before we do it."

"I think that's a good idea. Kevin, do you know what will happen if your parents call the police and tell them you did this?"

"I guess—I could go to jail."

"Well," the bishop said, "I don't think they put twelve-year-old boys in jail. But they could remand you—that means put you in a home for boys who have done bad things. Sister Call, you know that world better than any of us. What do you think will happen?"

"I honestly don't know. It's an unusual case. So much will depend on the prosecutor and the judge they assign to it. I can't imagine they'll try him as an adult, so it will probably go to Juvenile Court, but I'm not even sure about that. They may not even bring charges. If it were me, I wouldn't."

The bishop looked at Kevin again. "I wouldn't either. Kevin, I want you to know that our Heavenly Father is very pleased with your decision to talk to me. He loves you. He loves you very much, and he doesn't want you to be sad or angry. He tells us that he created us that we 'might have joy.' But he also wants us to grow, and sometimes growth requires us to go through hard things. And when we do, he wants us to be honest with ourselves and others. I think you should let your mother and father call the authorities and explain what happened, and I think you should tell those authorities what you've told me today, and answer any of their questions. Can you do that?"

"I think so."

"Good."

I was grateful that we had come to the bishop before going to the authorities. How wisely he had handled it—especially for Kevin.

"Now, Sister Call, just so I have this right, you and Rosemary brought the kids home, where you told Travis, but you haven't told anyone else, right?"

"Just Ross—and now you."

"I see."

"Like I said, I'm concerned about what the law can do to somebody if things aren't presented just right. I know how little discretion judges have with mandatory sentencing laws today. If a person is found guilty, the law doesn't always make allowances for extenuating circumstances."

"Yes, but you deal with this all the time, don't you?"

"Yes."

"And aren't you under some obligation to tell law enforcement what you know?"

"Yes—technically."

He studied her face again, perhaps searching for the right words. "The handbook, and the Spirit, I might add, are clear on this. If a potential felony has been committed, then a confession, or at least an admission of the facts to the pertinent authorities is in order. You've done the right thing by coming to see me, Sister Call, but I'm concerned that if you don't share what you know very soon, you may be guilty of a crime yourself. Now, I'm not saying that a crime has been committed, but I'm giving you the same counsel I gave Kevin: Go to the appropriate authorities—you know who they are—and give a full report of all that happened. I believe if you do, you will be blessed with greater peace—and protection."

Anna sat stoically, returning the bishop's gaze. Personally, I agreed with him, but this would have to come from her. After the moment of silence and hard deliberation, I thought I detected some resignation on her face. "Yes, Bishop, I know you're right, but now I understand like I've never understood before why some of my clients refuse to trust the process. From this side of the ledger, it's terrifying. I really hope that the peace and protection you mentioned will come."

"Would you like a blessing?"

She nodded, but said, "I think Kevin might like one first."

The bishop invited me to assist him in giving the blessings. Although I was the patriarch of the family, he was the father of the ward, and I willingly acquiesced to his authority. The blessings were very tender and, I am convinced, inspired. When he finished, we embraced with tearful thanks and went our way.

Kevin went to bed and surprisingly fell asleep within minutes. The blessing had its intended effect. Anna made plans to call the sheriff in Santa Cruz County the next morning.

I slept well, between two long prayers. I don't know how well Anna slept.

She called her office the next morning to let her staff know that she wouldn't be in again. Somehow she had continued to serve her clients during these grave gyrations, mostly by checking in with her staff and giving them daily directions. After talking to them, she called the Santa Cruz County Sheriff's Office and briefly explained the situation. They quickly altered their schedules to accommodate an appointment later that day for both her and Kevin.

The ride over was quiet. If Kevin was concerned, and I was sure he was, he didn't show it. The boy wasn't just smart; he could be as tough as nails when he wanted to be. By leaving a little later in the morning, we avoided the heaviest traffic through Livermore and San Jose and got there in just over two hours.

At the sheriff's office we were led by a deputy to a conference room, where we were joined by Sheriff John Rowley, the district attorney, and a couple of assistants. Anna's call that morning had changed many schedules. As we sat around a large rectangular conference table, the district attorney stated that this would be an informal interview, but that a legal deposition could follow. Anna produced the slingshot she had recovered from the garbage and presented it to the sheriff, along with a small bag of steel balls. Sheriff Rowley was about fifty, with keen blue eyes and short dark hair. He was all business. After examining the weapons, he glared at Kevin. "Did you know that slingshots are illegal in state parks in California?"

"No," Kevin said.

From there the interview seemed to go downhill. We had chosen not to hire a lawyer, hoping our transparency would lend to our appearance of innocence. If we felt later that we needed a lawyer, we could call competent counsel from Anna's contacts in San Francisco.

Yes, Kevin had broken a law by using the slingshot in a state park, but that was quickly dispensed with as the conversation turned to more serious issues: Why did Kevin think the man was a threat to the family? Did the man show his gun? Did either Anna or I have any previous contact with the man? Was there a history between us, and if not, why was he stalking the family? Why did we think he was carrying the gun? We answered honestly that we had never seen or spoken to the man before. Like Kevin, both Anna and I kept our answers brief and straightforward. When asked if the man had shown his gun, Kevin told them about the "black thing" he held in front of him when sneaking up on the family. Kevin said he thought it was a gun at first, but that he didn't mean to kill the man—"I just wanted to stop him from shooting my mother." This last statement brought silence to the room, and soon they circled back to other matters.

Such as why Anna didn't report the incident immediately.

It was pure fear for her family, Anna said. Once she saw that the man had a gun in his pocket and zip ties over the armrests in his vehicle, she piled her children into their vehicle and got away, as she didn't know if there were any accomplices nearby. And once she was on the road, all she could think about was that somebody was hunting them and that she should call her husband right away, which she did as soon as she got in cell range. She said she now knew what her clients meant when they said they were paralyzed by fear. But, she was here now, she said, hoping this terrible incident could be cleared up. She also explained that part of our reason for coming forward was that we wanted complete closure for Kevin, who had been through emotional trauma since that day.

I felt as helpless and insignificant as the chair I was sitting on. The only questions asked of me were to confirm Anna's statements.

Both the sheriff and D.A. admitted that they were at a loss about Winn's motivations. There was little possibility, they had already concluded, that it was simply a case of a man surreptitiously watching a family on the beach, given the guns and zip ties, all of which bore his fingerprints.

After three hours of questioning, the authorities left the room to conference, and an assistant asked us if we would like anything to eat or drink. We asked for soft drinks and water but no food. After Sheriff Rowley's initial hard questions, Anna and I had almost despaired of getting any consideration or leniency, and our stomachs were still tied in knots. Only Kevin seemed at ease, remaining mostly quiet. I had expected them to interview each of us separately, but that, gratefully, hadn't happened.

After another hour, the team came back in and took their places around the table.

The sheriff remained silent, but the D.A. informed us that they would not be pressing charges against any of us. They considered the killing a justifiable homicide committed by a minor, and the only potential case they saw against Kevin was the weapons charge, but he personally felt that the twelve-year-old was sufficiently remorseful and had suffered enough for that. This was the kind of consideration and leniency we had been praying for. Although they had a case against Anna for not immediately reporting the killing, they understood why she had delayed, though they wished she hadn't taken so long. Also, the D.A. admitted, no jury in California would find her guilty of anything but protecting her family and, possibly, taking too long to come to her senses. He added that because of Kevin's age they would do all in their power to maintain his anonymity in the media. With that, the meeting was over. The sheriff picked up the slingshot, glared again at Kevin, then at me, then left the room. Evidently the decision not to bring charges had not been unanimous.

As we left Santa Cruz, going by an alternate route through the mountains, a sweet spirit of peace confirmed Bishop Quinn's blessings upon us. Before losing cell coverage in the mountains, we called the good bishop and shared our experience. He was grateful. "As the saying goes," he admitted, "you hope for the best but prepare for the worst. I must admit to having just the tiniest bit of doubt this morning—you know, after I went to work and the Spirit left me." We laughed, and were grateful that we could. He asked Kevin how he was doing, and Kevin said he was hungry. We took that as a positive sign. We stopped at Casa De Fruta, in the hills east of Hollister, where we gratefully indulged in too many of the finest local delicacies.

* * *

With morning sunlight warming his back, Colin Richardson, Ph.D., stood a foot back from the rim at the cleft above the south wall, gazing into the nine-mile-wide fissure in the earth's crust. When his mind actually accepted what it was seeing, which was not easy, the sight was mind-boggling. It was awesome, as his students would have said. But he didn't trust it. The brooding silence shrouded the colossal danger. The fact that one misstep could lead to instant death, or a lingering, parched death at the bottom of a thousand-foot ravine, aroused real respect—and fear. If he fell now, no one would know, and if he survived and lay paralyzed somewhere below, well, he didn't want to think about that.

His little rental car stood a couple hundred yards back, just above the little bowl. Frankly, he was surprised it had made it across the twenty miles of dirt roads and washed-out traces. It had bottomed out more than once, but it was still running when he parked it. *They don't make them like they used to.*

But where were the bodies? Where was the red SUV?

The four dead men had either not been dead, or they had been moved, because there was no trace of them now, not even bloodstains in the rusty earth. Before leaving Tuba City a couple of hours ago, after picking up a backpack and supplies, he had checked the internet for news of the men. There was nothing. Not a word. Not a hint of a word.

Something strange was afoot.

Still staring into the abyss, he smiled with a new thought. Whislin Klah had actually believed his tale about going home to teach again. The credulous fool. Did he not wonder why the professor had become a trouble-shooter for the society in the first place? He taught psychology, not archeology. He didn't care about the details of fracking or Texas politics or the historical niceties of American mummies. He cared about the money, which promised to relieve him forever from reading inane student papers and worrying about his inability to publish. Once he had tested the deep male voice on the other end of the line by performing a minor favor and receiving his first check for fifty thousand dollars, he was sold. Though the man claimed to be working for the Bonesmen, Richardson had always been doubtful. And sure enough, upon scrutiny he discovered that the man was either working for himself or for another even more furtive group. But he didn't care. Again, it was the money that drew him forward as if by a magnet to greater and greater paydays, until, at last, he got the mysterious voice to agree to pay someone else to do the dirty work while he, Colin Richardson, PhD., served as middle man, which conveniently buffered the money man with another level of plausible deniability. So he hired Klah and took a sabbatical from school. It wasn't exactly that he hated teaching, but he was getting tired of the game—bored students bargaining for better grades, department chairmen throwing their weight around, brain-dead editors telling him why his papers weren't good enough to publish. Soon the game would be over for good. *Nineteen-year-old girls! Hah!* The fact was, he knew the secret society, whoever they were, could not allow him to continue to live. He knew too much. They couldn't let a smart boy like him run free—he might discover who they were and begin blackmailing them.

He had no choice, he had to go underground, and that meant finding a way to support himself independently, but he was also ready to indulge in the riches he had fantasized about for years. His father, almost a senator once, had found a degree of wealth through underhanded, back-channel means. Most of the money was now parked offshore awaiting his retirement—his father's, not his. Dad had been annoyingly narrow-minded when it came to sharing his wealth with his offspring, and according to the old man's recent physicals, and as evidenced by the many octogenarians in his family, the old scoundrel may live for decades to come.

Which was too long for a bright young man like himself.

Wealth, true wealth, *extreme* wealth, was just half a mile away. Yes, it was down a precarious trail—well, almost a trail—but if he could negotiate it while carrying his pack of small tools, lights, batteries, food, water, and sleeping bag, and then come back up with verifiably ancient jewelry, he could go on the dark web and become wealthy beyond the imaginings of even his corrupt father's corrupt friends, most of whom thought twenty or thirty million was sufficient. With dozens of mummies to loot over time, and thousands of ancient writings to quietly sell to foreign buyers, there would be no end to the riches.

He took a step, and a tuft of powdery red dirt puffed out from under his boot. This place was old. More ancient, probably, than the cave itself. He descended into the furnace, one well-considered step at a time. He didn't have a deadline. He could sleep in the cave if necessary and come back up tomorrow or the next day. He was dressed for the heat of the canyon and had a jacket and gloves for the cave. No black garb this time.

He arrived at the steep chute where he had fallen before, but his pack was lighter now and his legs fresher. He scooted to the bottom with only a slight tear in his pants and a small cut on his hand, where a razor-like rock had sliced through his glove. The hike was almost easy after that.

Loose boulders filled the hole that Keller had made in the cave's entrance. Richardson had almost been entombed here. If he hadn't been found by Call and Keller, he might still be wandering around in absolute blackness, dying of thirst.

He put his hand on one of the loose stones to remove it, but he stopped when he heard a noise behind him. The pack made turning awkward, but he knew bighorn sheep were down here, and the last thing he wanted was to be butted by a territorial ram. But instead of a ram, he saw an old Indian several feet away. The man was smaller and somehow thinner than himself, and he was grasping a chiseled walking stick that was taller than himself. How had he gotten there? Coming up the sheer cliff seemed unlikely, though he knew that Call and Keller had done it. The old man, wearing a red cowboy shirt and blue jeans, must have been hiding somewhere along the ledge. White braids looped behind his large and gnarly ears. His dark eyes were like two little caves.

"You should have listened." The old man's tinny voice crackled with a Native accent.

"Listened to what?" Richardson asked, casting a quick glance to either side.

"To your conscience." The old man looked out over the edge. "But there's plenty of room down there. Your friends won't mind."

Richardson quickly put two and two together. "You moved the bodies! That's why the police don't know about them." Now Richardson followed the old man's gaze over the edge. "You threw them into the canyon?"

"The coyotes are just as hungry down there."

Something about the old man generated new fear and respect. They were about the same height, but that was the end of their similarities. The Indian did not wear spectacles, and he had a full head of peppery gray hair. His brown, wrinkled face sloped down to a pointed jaw sporting a deep cleft. Something about the easy way the man handled the walking stick gave Richardson pause. Leaping at him could prove grievous. No, wisdom dictated that he keep the man talking until he knew how to resolve the bizarre situation.

"What about their car?"

"It was left out by the highway. I think it is gone now."

"But then, how'd you get back here?"

The man was silent.

"How'd you get behind me?"

The old man's lips pursed into a scowl. "You do not listen. And it is too late to learn how. Your pack will protect your back—but not for long."

"Protect my back? From what?"

"My own friends."

Richardson had his back to the cave. He turned, looking both ways again. Nobody there. "Your friends must be invisible."

The old man seemed to consider this. "Yes, some of them are. But not these."

Richardson heard a rustling sound and spun back toward the cave. Again he saw nothing.

"There's nobody . . ."

He heard the sound again, like pebbles in a shaker below him, and he saw a mass of pink slithering snakes racing toward his feet. Some were already coiling themselves to strike. Many more were slithering his way from around a bend in the ledge.

He jumped back, the pack on his back making his movements unwieldy and absurd. He smashed two of the snakes under his boots, but many more began striking at him with unbelievable quickness. Two latched onto his calves, just above his boots. The searing heat from their venom was already working into his legs. He grabbed them both and yanked, ripping out flesh where the fangs had embedded themselves. But more were springing at him, piercing his hands, his arms, his face, engulfing him in writhing, searing pain. He ripped a snake from his cheek and threw it over the ledge, not sensing the pain of the torn flesh because of the overwhelming white-hot explosions of other double injections. He fell to his knees, which allowed more snakes to find targets. He swung at them wildly, clawing, pulling, throwing, but they found his neck, shoulders, armpits, the inside of his thighs. He fell backwards, landing on his pack, which had indeed protected his back, but now they were slithering under it too. He rolled forward and backward, trying to smash them, but too many were engulfing him, the angry serpents charging him, the searing pain driving him mad. The melee of man and snakes rolled closer to the edge, and the old Indian casually stepped back to let them by.

As Richardson's face disappeared under the furious snakes, his body became still, already freezing in paralysis. Through one eye he saw the wide maw of the canyon inches away, and slowly, painfully, he nudged toward it. At the edge, the writhing mound of man and serpents seemed to pause, as if he were reconsidering, but he found new strength, and, with a roar of effort and resignation, he slipped over the edge.

The Hopi elder listened to the primal scream fade as it descended into the void. He waited but heard no thud, no crashing over ridges and pinnacles, just a whisper of breeze oozing up with warm thermals. He took a step closer to the precipice, and his keen eyes caught the pinpoint of the still-writhing, pinkish mound disappearing as it fell backward in time.

The snakes on the ledge grew still and stopped rattling. Some looked up at the old man. He thumped his walking stick on the ground twice and uttered a guttural command, two syllables, and the snakes retreated back along the ledge and disappeared around the bend to their narrow crevice in the cave.

The man went back to the cave and examined the wall of stones at its entrance. Some were loose, but the realism was convincing. He looked down at the river, nearly a mile away, and could see it clearly, which meant that anybody down there could see the cave. But even damaged, its realism would keep the cave concealed—which was very good because he couldn't see himself packing fifty pounds of mortar and water down here to repair it. With the spirits' help, maybe no one would spot it for another hundred years. Which would mean, hopefully, that the precious corner would remain safe within the bowels of the vast cavern.

He hiked back toward the cleft in the canyon wall, following the nearly invisible trace that sheep used, that the Ancient Ones had called the Old Trail, a trail that, hopefully, few would walk again.

As he shuffled along, his legs tiring, he thought again about his vision of the white man and his friend. He had seen them bringing the corner of the tablet to him before they took it to its rightful owners. But the spirits had deceived him.

Or had they?

Maybe only the timing was off. Time in this place slipped forward and backward with the wind. He began the difficult ascent to the rim, wondering if he would ever see the white man with dark hair and his tall friend with the yellow hair again.

If he did, he hoped it would be soon.

He wasn't getting any younger.

Chapter 46

Truth Emerges

I called Saundra Flaument and told her that I had news about her father. She was back in Virginia, and her mother, Claudia, was home in Fargo. I gave her an abbreviated report over the phone.

"First, just so you know, I'm not going to charge you for anything. Everything I've done is on my own bill. I wanted to find out how your father died, and now I have an idea of what happened."

She caught her breath then said, "Go on."

"Saundra, your father's death was probably an accident, but not the way the police think. I'm fairly sure he was accidently killed by a man who had been hired by a collector of ancient American artifacts."

"Wait—he was killed?"

"Yes, but I can't prove it. I spoke to the man who did it, and he said it was an accident. He tried to buy the jewelry that your father took from the Grand Canyon, but your father lied to him, and the man hit him, and your father fell into the river and drowned. But again, I can't prove any of this. There were no witnesses, and the man who told me this won't confess to the police. Plus, I have no idea where he is or where his family is. The only reason I talked to him was because he came hunting me when I started snooping around."

She was quiet a moment, then she came back to the one thing I didn't want to talk about. "You say my dad took the jewelry, like he said he did, so does the cave really exist?"

Ironically, I was now the one hoping to keep the cave a secret. "It exists, but I'm convinced the park service doesn't know anything about it. Your father was able to find it from information he got from the letters that your mother's great, great uncle wrote, but the cave is extremely hard to get to—and very dangerous. Also, it's in a restricted area, a place that's off limits even to park rangers, so I don't think there's any way you would be able to find it."

"But *you* found it, didn't you?"

"Saundra, it's illegal to go there, so I don't want to admit to possibly snooping around a bit. But I'm satisfied that the cave exists and that your father was killed, accidently, by someone trying to keep it a secret. And just as important, I believe that the man behind it all, the man who was going to pay the man who did it, is now dead."

"The man behind everything is dead? Who is he? What's his name?"

"His name is Rodney Winn. He was killed near Monterey Bay a few days ago. He was shot in the head. But again, I can't prove that he was the man behind your father's killing. I can't even prove that he did anything wrong."

"Why not?"

"Because he used surrogates, and I only have hearsay evidence— one man said this, another said that. But I believe Winn did it, because I'm pretty sure he also tried to kill me and my family."

Again she went quiet, probably putting two and two together. She said, "Are you the one who killed him?"

"No."

"Do you know who did?"

"I'm afraid I can't answer that. In my opinion, Rodney Winn was a threat to a lot of people, and I'm not about to ruin somebody else's life who may have saved my own."

"Oh. I see."

I had laid a lot on her, more than I wanted to. Hedging on the truth is not my specialty. Fortunately, though, like Ross when he hedged on the truth with the motel manager, I was pretty sure that what I had said was true.

"Okay," she said, "what about the man who killed my father? Do you know who he is?"

"Saundra, I have no proof that anybody killed your father. But the man who I believe did it, who I'm almost sure did it, is a professional trouble-shooter. If you or anyone else were to go after him, we wouldn't be able to prove anything, and worse, it would put your own lives in danger."

"So you're not going to tell me who he is?"

I didn't answer.

"But I *hired* you!"

"But I'm not going to take your money. I'm sorry, Saundra, but I think you should let it go. Your father stole some valuable things from the Hopis. Have you heard of them?"

"The Hopi Indians? Of course."

"The jewelry he got was theirs, from an ancient tomb. He desecrated a mummy and tried to sell its jewelry on the black market. I've never seen it, and I doubt it can ever be retrieved. So we don't even have any evidence of an actual crime—his crime or your father's killer's. I believe all this, but, again, I can't prove it, so please, let it go. If I ever have a chance to talk to the killer again, I'll try to get him to confess to the authorities, but I'm afraid that's the only way any of this can be proven."

"Did the man who killed my father take the jewelry?"

"I believe so."

"Do you know where it went?"

"I have some thoughts, but I'll probably never know for sure. And I'm not going to pursue it. I believe there is a knowledge and power greater than all of this, greater than all of us. This may not mean anything to you, but I believe there's a grand design, a *divine* design, that will sort everything out and set it straight at the right time. And because I believe this, I'm going to stop searching for someone's ultimate guilt. This is my report to you, Saundra. Your father did something he shouldn't have, and he was killed while trying to profit from it. The man who accidentally killed him is gone, and the man who hired that man is dead. The cave is sacred to the Hopis, and I think we should keep it that way, sacred and undefiled, so I don't intend to go public with any of this. You can if you want, but you'll never find any proof unless somebody confesses. You'll never find the cave. It's just too hard to get to, and the Hopis are always watching it. So, please, let it go. Let it all go."

I hadn't planned to give a speech.

"So, what? I should just trust in this divine *design*?"

"That's what I'm doing."

"Listen, I don't even know if there *is* a God, but I know I had a father, and now I know that someone killed him, and I want justice."

"Saundra, sometimes justice isn't available when we want it. Sometimes we have to wait for it."

"Forever?"

I didn't reply.

"Mr. Call, my father trusted you—but now you say you don't know anything."

"I know some things, but not enough to prove anything. I'm saying that you will have to wait for justice, just like I will have to wait for justice for someone who tried to kill me, and who tried to kill my family. Saundra, I already lost one wife, and I had to wait almost a year to find justice, and that justice almost cost me the rest of my family. The other day I almost lost my current wife and family because of this work. I want justice too. I don't know if it will ever come in this life, but I have faith that it *will* come."

"I'm sorry. I didn't mean that you don't understand. I just—I guess I just wish that I had your kind of faith."

"So lean on mine for a while. Lean on me. I *know* God is there, watching over all of us, even your father, even the men who conspired against him. Seek *Him*. I promise you'll find greater peace that way, because you're part of that divine design too."

"You ought to be a missionary."

I laughed. "Well, maybe I'll repent and try to be one someday."

"All right, Mister Call, I'll try to let it go, because I don't know what else to do, but I can't promise that it'll last—and I really can't promise what my mother will do."

I almost laughed again. "I'm sure about that. Maybe we should pray for her."

"You know, when I do pray, and that's not very often, I usually *do* pray for her." Her voice was softer, kinder now.

"Saundra, I have a question for you, but you don't have to answer it."

"What's that?"

"Your father's estate. Did you get it all figured out?"

"I think so. It was kind of complex."

"So, then it was larger than the portfolio he had with me?"

"Oh, yes. Maybe I shouldn't say this, but I think he may have stolen other things too. So, some of the money is going to charity, though I know I'll hear about that from my mother too."

"You know, I think of charity as another word for love—and love never fails. Charity never fails to be the answer. Be generous."

"Be generous, even after losing my father. You really ought to think about being a missionary or a preacher or something."

We said good-bye, and as we hung up, I thought that she was exactly the kind of investor I would like to work for.

* * *

Before you can receive a new gift, you must empty your hands of old encumbrances. That's what had happened. When the threats of Winn, Klah and Richardson evaporated, I became available to new possibilities. When my wife and son became free from possible incarceration, I became open to new ideas. Old ways of thinking gave way to new truths.

I hadn't told Anna anything about the cave or the plates or the sacred corner, or even about the old Hopi elder wandering about the Kaibito Plateau on beautiful, clear nights. I hadn't shared any of this for two reasons: one, because we both had other matters on our minds when she came back from the beach, and two, because I didn't know how she would react to it. She had been opposed to exposing ourselves to danger, and that's exactly what I had brought upon the family. Ross and I had been cemented in the cave and left for dead. Four men who had been paid to kill us had evidently used their guns on each other, fortunately, but those bullets had been intended for us.

Mostly, though, it was her lack of faith that kept me quiet. I could show her, right now, that a section in Ether, the section Joseph Smith had transcribed for Martin Harris, also existed in a hidden cave in the Grand Canyon. And I could show her that thousands of other plates containing the same characters existed there as well. But I knew what this would do to her. It would not make her believe the Book of Mormon was true; it would make her *know* it was true. And that would be a problem when other issues of faith arose. How would that knowledge serve her when the words of the living prophet defied everything she thought was fair and equitable concerning people with same-sex attraction? How would knowing Joseph had actually translated the Book of Mormon from ancient plates serve her when she found out that he had later instituted polygamy and had been sealed to several young women against Emma's wishes? And on and on.

She didn't just need to know that the Book of Mormon was true; she needed to know for herself, by personal witness, that God lived, that the prophet of the Church was his mouthpiece on earth, that despite all the chaos surrounding history, policy, and doctrine, the Church was still the only true and living church upon the face of the whole earth. She needed to learn how to speak with God and receive his answers.

Her words about Nephi killing Laban, however, had given me hope. Maybe something was changing.

That evening after Klah left, I had some time to myself, as Anna and the twins were at Young Mens and Young Womens, where she served as an advisor. I got the cameras and downloaded the images to my laptop so I could study them on a larger screen wherever I wanted to. After they were downloaded, I found the bookmarked page in Ether.

Alone in my office, I opened my own Book of Mormon to Ether and set it next to the monitor to look for matches. I figured that if sentence and paragraph length and chapter breaks corresponded to those in Ether six, I might be onto something.

I lined up the picture of the plate on my computer with the photocopied Anthon Transcript, and with the words in Ether. They were perfect matches. The transcript began with verse three, which made sense, as Joseph Smith had probably chosen the text at random to copy for Martin Harris. As I already knew, the characters did not line up exactly with their English counterparts; they were in a different order, which also made sense as their grammar was based on Hebrew, not English.

I had intended to look for consistent sentence lengths, but as I studied the characters, I saw no sentences. The text appeared as a run-on sentence, like a stream of thought, without periods or natural breaks. I was confused. How could I know if the text that followed matched the text that followed in Ether? I saw a character I knew well—the large Z with the squiggly line at the top. This had become my favorite character, as it both looked funny and meant something all readers of the Book of Mormon know: "And it came to pass." It was evidently a symbol the Book of Mormon writers used to indicate that a new thought was coming. There were seven of these characters in the Anthon Transcript, and, of course, there were seven in the corresponding passage in Ether six. I decided to look for more on the plate and see if they more or less lined up with the corresponding text in Ether.

The characters in the Anthon Transcript take up seven lines, or about a paragraph's worth of space. The corresponding text in the Book of Ether fills almost a full page. Therefore, the length of a sentence in the Book of Mormon would be three or four times longer than the text on the plates. I scanned the verses following verse 13 and found another "And it came to pass" at the beginning of verse

18. I went to the plate and searched for the big Z. I found it two lines down. My pulse quickened.

I scanned the rest of the chapter in the Book of Mormon and found six more "And it came to passes," in verses 21, 22, 25, 26, 27, and 30. Meaning, there were seven more "And it came to passes" after the section found in the Anthon Transcript. Almost holding my breath, I went back to the image of the plate and began counting the number of times the big Z occurred after the transcript text. When I got to five, I knew the two would match. When I got to seven, I exhaled. Again, they matched perfectly. And the last one came just before a vertical break in the text, indicating the end of the chapter, exactly as it appeared in Ether six.

Each symbol was where it belonged.

I went back to the beginning of the chapter and saw one more occurrence of the phrase, in verse 2, and moments later I found it on the plate, in exactly the right spot.

Tears were forming in my eyes. An original copy of the Book of Ether was before me, in the original Nephite language—the reformed Egyptian.

Who had left these plates in the canyon?

And who was I that I should find them—and now read them?

I wanted to tell Ross, but he was out with the Young Single Adults. I wanted to tell Anna, but that would have to wait.

I wiped my eyes and went back three pages in the plates and found the beginning of the book. There appeared to be a brief paragraph at its beginning. I went to my Book of Mormon and found a two-line preface at the beginning of chapter one that said:

> The record of the Jaredites, taken from the twenty-four
> plates found by the people of Limhi in the days of King
> Mosiah.

I knew that this chapter heading had been written by Moroni, and here it was before me, perhaps in his own hand. Adrenalin coursed through me. My fingers began trembling. This wasn't just an obscure copy of a copy of Ether's words. This was a copy of Moroni's writings. And just as this thought began to make me weak, a second thought hit me, that I should compare the symbols in the preface of the English translation to learn what they meant. Then, if I could do the same for verse one, two, three, and so on, maybe I could begin teaching myself the ancient language of reformed Egyptian.

If I could do this, then, maybe, I would be able to read every single character on every single plate.

This thought was crushing. The plates and this new knowledge had come into my possession for a reason. The responsibility was awesome.

I needed to think.

No, I needed to pray.

I bowed my head and began a prayer, half expecting a revelation of some kind, but nothing came; however, as I continued to pray, a new peace eased into me, slowing my pulse and relaxing my nerves. I then asked for understanding as to why I had been allowed to find the plates, but again nothing came except a continuation of the peace. I ended my prayer and looked back at the Book of Mormon.

The first words were "And now I, Moroni…" I looked at the picture of the plate and saw a small character followed by a larger character. I wondered if the small character represented "And now I." I looked down at the second verse in the Book of Mormon and saw the words "And I." Going back to the plates, I found what appeared to be the second sentence of the chapter and saw that it began with the same two characters, but without one of its lines along the base of the character. Perhaps this modified character meant "And I," instead of "And now I." And if it did, then it made sense that the next character, the large one, meant "Moroni." I stared at his name, or what I thought was his name, and realized that he may have written it with his own hand. The feeling of peace intensified, accompanied by a sense of joy, and I quietly realized that I had just translated the two new characters correctly, including the character for "Moroni."

I moved on, going from right to left on the plate, matching characters to words, though struggling because the order was rarely the same. A great help came in the second verse when I saw three characters I already knew. First, I saw the four lines stacked upon each other, which I knew represented "plates," and toward the end of the verse I saw the characters for "Book of Ether." Those same characters stood boldly at the top of the plate, where the title was, and now I knew that this was indeed "The Book of Ether."

A sense of awe overcame me. This was Moroni's translation of Ether's 24 gold plates, which Ether had originally written in the pure

Adamic language. This was the handiwork of Ether, Moroni, and of God.

And I had held it in the cave.

And now I was translating it.

The next four verses were more difficult, as there were fewer characters I already knew. But by seeing their English translations in the Book of Mormon, I was able to make assumptions, some of which were confirmed by seeing the same characters in subsequent verses, and some of which I had to alter. This took time, but verses 7 through 32 were almost easy, as the same characters appeared repeatedly in a list of fathers and sons. Each name appeared at least twice, which allowed me to confirm their translations. As I came to verse 33, which read, "Which Jared came forth with his brother..." the door to my office opened and Ross came in. With my head still in another world, I almost said, "And Ross came forth with his brother."

"Oh, sorry," he said, stepping back out. He began to close the door.

"Wait, why are you sorry?"

He poked his head back in. "Because it looks like you've been crying."

I asked him to sit down. "I have been. Ross, do you know what we have here?"

He saw the open book on my desk. "The Book of Mormon?"

I turned my screen toward him. "Maybe. But I know for sure that we have the Book of Ether, chapters one and six, and probably all the chapters in between."

He looked at the characters on the screen then back at me. "Right, we know that because we saw the characters from the Anthon Transcript on the plates in the cave."

"No, we know that because I can translate it."

That brought him up short, and he got up and came around to see the screen better. "You mean you know how to read the characters?"

"I don't know how to pronounce them, but I'm learning what they mean. The Anthon Transcript was the primer." I was about to invite him to pull up a chair so I could show him how it was done, when I heard the twins come in the house. The lesson would have to wait.

I closed the computer, and we went out to be with the family.

The question now was, when would I tell Anna?

* * *

Whislin Klah stood on the edge of to be or not to be in more ways than one. He didn't know it yet, but the winds of change were blowing.

He had locked up his condo before sunrise and driven to the rim above the ravine that led down to the cave. Initially he had hesitated because of Call's warning, but he had finally made his decision: he would secure his financial future. Then, if necessary, he would deal with the consequences.

But now, standing on the brink of riches, he paused again. The sun had just crested the low, tawny horizon behind him, and the heat was already building. If he was going to do this, he had better get on with it before the furnace really fired up. He gazed at the ancient, striated rocks layered in pinks, lavenders, and gold. The shadows were working their wandering magic so quickly that he could actually trace their movement across the towers and mesas.

Then something whispered: "Turn around."

A spirit? Maybe it was from one of the mummies he was about to loot. Or, as Call had suggested, one of the ancient elders reaching out to him.

What else did Call know? The man was a puzzle—foolish but successful. And so was Keller. Worth millions but like a child. When Call had warned Klah to stay away from the cave, he had spoken with conviction, with authority, as if he too possessed an ancient wisdom.

As if he knew something that only the ancients knew.

But, all that gold was just below him, waiting for him.

Of course, it didn't matter what Richardson planned to do. If he wanted to go home and teach, that was fine. But Klah needed money, enough to pay off his condo and set him up for life. And he needed it now. But while standing on the rim with a full pack digging into his shoulders, something had struck him, something quiet but loud, something soft but startling.

Turn around.

A movement caught his eye. A man stood off to his right, also near the edge of the bowl leading down into the canyon. He was an old man, tiny, with pepper-gray braids dangling behind his shoulders. He wore a red shirt and faded jeans and had a hearty walking stick in his right hand. This area was as remote as any place in North America, so where had he come from? But there he stood on spindly legs, watching Whislin, about fifty yards away. Klah could see that the old man was a Hopi; he knew the subtle differences between the more

Oriental features of the Navajos and the more Aztecan faces of the Hopi.

Klah's unease increased. If he walked down into the ravine, the old man would know that he was going there for some *reason*. Nobody hiked into the cave from here; there were no trails, no water until you hit the river miles away, no famous features that he knew of. Klah was pretty sure that he was on Navajo land, but that mattered little. The Hopis thought of this land as theirs by ancient right. What would the old man do? The two stared at each other in silence. The man might have a gun in his waistband, though Klah doubted it. His own gun was in his pack, but he could quickly set the pack down and pull it out, but, again, that might lead to unintended consequences.

One more accidental murder.

Which he didn't want. He'd been thinking about the deaths. Though none were intentional, each could have been prevented with quick action. Especially in Keith Nelson's case; Klah hadn't needed to let the unconscious man drown.

A breeze, soft and cool, brushed by, evaporating the heat waves, and Klah recalled Call's statement that the Hopis were always watching. Maybe he should go back home. Maybe he should forget all of this. The breeze freshened, kicked up some dust and sent a little whirlwind spinning across the poor soil—and with a sigh of resignation, Whislin knew what he should do.

He nodded to the old man, a polite tip of his head, then he began the hundred-yard walk back to his truck. When he got there, he turned around, and the old man was gone.

Klah decided to take the long way back to Flagstaff, through the Painted Desert. Turning left at Tuba City, he took Highway 264 southeast by the Three Mesas, the ancient homes of his mother's people. His heart ached as he saw their poverty, the erosion of both land and spirit. He would never understand the pride which led some of his people to bask in silent superiority while wallowing in hopeless desolation. How could a people feel that they would rise again when they crawled in the dust, living on government handouts? The ragged mobile homes, broken shacks, and rutted dirt roads depressed him, and he depressed the accelerator. His mother had come from this place, had escaped it, though she always spoke of it with reverence.

He turned right at 77 and crossed back into Navajo land—the land not much better here, though the little community of White Cone hinted at the possibility of a future for the kids, with a modern gymnasium and skateboard park. He continued south on 77, renamed Navajo Service Road 6, and found himself diving into the heart of the Painted Desert. The sun was full high by now, and the undulating land glowed in a luminescence of purples, reds, and blues, with splashes of greens and yellows dappled in. He had once known what caused this wonderful, almost living, borealis in the earth—something to do with the way an ancient seabed was laid down—but what he knew now was that it soothed his spirit as he drove through the ocean of pastels, marine greens, and vivid purples flowing by in three-dimensional peace. Ahead, he saw a gray lump of something waddling along the shoulder. At the last second he saw that it was a porcupine.

Fortunately, it stayed in its own lane.

As Whislin should have done. As he should have done years ago.

But what *was* his lane? He had no family to speak of, no friends. Wealth had been his goal and violence his companion for years, but where had they gotten him? He was running from everyone, going nowhere. He had some money but not enough to secure his future. It was clear that he had to change careers. He was in the middle of nowhere, going nowhere—but the scenery, at least, soothed something inside.

His mother called it a spirit. She said there were more spirits than people. His father hadn't believed in anything except the power of his hands, or fists, to produce cold hard cash. Whislin winced as he realized that he had followed in his father's path in more ways than one. The violence. The false pride. The hunger for money. In his own way, he had become his father. He thought about the differences between his father and mother and saw at once that most of them stemmed from his father's lack of belief in something greater—a higher goal, and accountability. Without a belief in the next world, without that *faith*, he had succumbed to the brute level of physical wants and needs. He had lived like an animal from day to day, like a badger snarling at invisible threats, like a squirrel hording too many nuts for the winter, like a coyote wandering from kill to kill, from sunset to sunset. Whislin's father had been a terror because he lived in fear of things he couldn't control. His mother had been a woman of life, of *qatsi*. She had lived in her heart, believing the truth of the good things she could not see. And because of that, she had been the only compass of peace he had ever known.

And, then, of course, he had turned his back on her to follow his father's path.

Just as Travis Call had turned his back on him and followed his own path of truth.

Real strength, he now realized, lay in peace, not violence. Real purpose came in believing things you could not see but knew were true. Real life happened in the invisible, as well as the visible. Happiness was found in the balance of both worlds.

But Whislin had become *Koyaanisqatsi*, a life out of balance. Whislin had become the father he feared.

Only his father had never killed anybody—as far as he knew.

He passed a sign for the Petrified Forest and thought of the old ways. These reddened stone logs were solid, unchanging from year to year, from millennium to millennium. But still, at only two hundred million years old, they were relative newcomers out here. They had been given a birth and a life and would eventually know a death. The unseen world was greater than the known world because it lasted longer.

It lasted forever.

Was he petrified, or could he change? Could he get a new birth? Could he get a new life, a new forever?

His compass was gone, and he only see by the light of his eyes, but maybe his heart could whisper a new way.

In the hazy blue distance he made out the snow-capped San Francisco Peaks, the two-mile high pinnacles presiding over Flagstaff. Still nearly a hundred miles away, the peaks meant home—such as it was, empty, gated, lonely. He came to Interstate 40 and turned right at the Hopi Travel Plaza. Except for the far-off peaks and a low, distant mesa to the north, the land around him had become as flat and bleak as any he had known. Even the occasional tuft of yellow bunch grass bending in the arid breeze was forlorn and wistful.

Over the next hour and a half, as the distant peaks gradually filled his windshield, his mind drifted back to the puzzling figure of Travis Call. What did the man know? Was the Pahana's tablet really in the cave? Was Travis Call, possibly, the Pahana himself?

No way.

And what, exactly, *was* the Pahana? He vaguely recalled legends about this mythical person, saying he was supposed to be the Hopis' long lost white brother who would deliver them from a merciless enemy and lead them to a permanent brotherhood of peace.

There was that word again.

Klah had been raised in a White man's world of oil fields, steel, and street brawls, in a world where he fought for everything he got—even deliverance from his father's temper. But today he seemed to live in a no-man's land, a world of gray light. He had learned the white man's ways, even excelled at them, but they weren't *his* ways.

His mother's words from long ago walked into his head:

> *Listen to the spirits floating by, like a hummingbird.*
> *The ancient land holds the mystery of the future.*
> *In death you are born.*

He drove to his condominium complex, remotely opened the gate, and pulled into his parking spot below his condo. He turned the engine off. *In death you are born.* He wanted to find that birth. Something inside was letting go. Something in his heart was searching for the mystery of a new future.

He unlatched his seatbelt and got out. He had no boss, no income, no hope. He would have to find a new way of living.

As he went around to the tailgate to get his pack, he saw two men in suits coming down the stairs from where his condo was. His initial reaction was to run. Strangers rarely showed up here. Were they FBI? Then, he saw the face of the first one, young, innocent, tired. Then he saw the flash of a black and white nameplate on his lapel.

Missionaries.

No threat.

He was about to pull out his pack when a thought hit him: *Travis Call went to that church.* He and his family went there *a lot.* Klah had known other members of that church too, even in the SEALS, and it seemed that they went to church every chance they got. But it was Travis who lingered in his mind, the man who had found the corner of the sacred tablet, the man who had walked away from the mummies and jewelry, who had walked away from five guns, the man who had talked his way out of near-death situations more than once—the man who had told Klah that the Hopis were always watching.

Which, evidently, was true.

The two young men unlocked their bikes at the foot of the stairs and were about to ride off, when a new thought came to him—a thought he drove away. He would not talk to them. He didn't care who Travis Call was or wasn't, he would not consider opening the door to religion. If there was one thing he knew, it was that no organized religion spoke for the Creator. He had read too much history and seen too much pain to even consider the possibility.

His mother believed *something*, but her faith was not so much in religion as it was in a people, on both sides, bonded by belief.

He heard footsteps behind him and turned. The boy looked like he was about seventeen, the shine on his white face making him look like he had just been scrubbed by an SOS pad. These people could zero in on you like a TALON rocket, even the ones who weren't missionaries. The second one seemed a bit more timid.

"Hello!" the first said, too cheerfully. He thrust out his hand. "How're ya doin'?"

The kid sounded like he came from the South. Klah didn't take his hand; instead, he drilled the kid with dead eyes and waited for the kid's companion to reach them, then he drilled him. But the first kid's smile only got bigger.

They were too full of blind enthusiasm to notice that they were approaching a hardened killer—or so Whislin told himself.

The first one spoke again as if Klah were an old friend. "We were just in the area, and we were wonderin' if you'd like to know more about what happens after this life."

Letting the muscles in his face go completely limp, Klah said, "No."

But the kid didn't flinch, didn't get the unspoken warning. "We have a wonderful message of God's plan of happiness that we'd like to share with you."

Now Klah got serious. "I have just one question."

"Yes?"

"Can a murderer go to heaven?"

The second kid took a step back and glanced at Klah's hands, probably looking for weapons. Smart boy. But the first one, with "Timmons" on the name badge, rushed in where angels and companions feared to tread.

"Of course! You need to read the Book of Mormon. It has entire groups of cold-blooded murderers becoming God's people. Why? Ya got a friend?"

Klah smiled, which made him mad, but he couldn't help it. The kid's gumption was likeable. "Entire groups, huh?"

"Oh, yeah! One of 'em's about the Ammonites, who murdered like a thousand of God's people, but then they felt bad about what they'd done, and they changed and repented, and before you know it, they're God's people too!"

"Yeah," the second one ventured, having seen no guns or knives, "and then other people were tryin' to kill *them!* It's great!"

"God loves you," added Timmons. "But ya gotta repent. I mean, ya really gotta change. Ya gotta *return* to God. And ya know why? 'Cause he doesn't let any unclean thing get into heaven. But he still wants you there, right there with him—so ya just gotta repent, that's all. And then all of your sins, I mean *all* of 'em, will be washed away. We could tell ya all about that. In fact, that's why we're here!"

It was a waterfall of good news, and Klah felt drenched. Which made him even less happy.

"So, let's say a guy kills two, three, four people—like you said, cold-blooded murders—you're sayin' he can still get to heaven?"

"Not as a murderer, he can't, of course," replied Timmons with a half smile. "But as a *repentant* murderer he can!"

"A born-again murderer, huh?"

"Exactly!" said the second, whose name was Sawyer. These people teamed up on you, got you looking one way then hit you from the blindside. Good tactics. "Ya really gotta repent, totally change and be baptized by one having authority, and then it's just like the Lord says, you're born again of the water and the Spirit."

"But, mister," said Timmons, completing the whiplash, "ya really gotta change. It's gotta be deep down and all the way to your toes. And ya can never go back. It's all or nothin' with God."

They stared at him, and he tried to stare back, but his toughness was failing, his defenses withering, his heart softening and wandering into dangerous, mysterious moors. Who *were* these people? Evidently their confidence wasn't peculiar to Call; it was peculiar to all of them. "Okay, look," he said, fighting for some control, "I'm really not interested. I don't believe in organized religion. I just . . . *don't believe.*"

"Yeah," said Timmons, as if he had just apprehended a key fact, "but you don't *disbelieve* either. You think there *might* be somethin', or ya wouldn't be here talkin' to us. D'ya know what I think? I think you really do wanna change, you just don't know it yet."

These people didn't give up.

"Okay, we'll make ya a deal," Timmons continued. "Ya give us thirty minutes—" He looked around the complex. "Do you live here?"

Klah pointed helplessly up the stairs they had just come down.

"Great. You give us thirty minutes, and we'll either convince you that there's something here," he patted his chest, "something *real*, or you can tell us to leave and we'll never come back. How's that?"

Klah almost laughed. "You guys *always* come back."

The two kids looked at each other then broke into sheepish grins. "Yeah, well, *somebody* probably will, but it won't be us. Promise."

Klah tried to change the subject. "How'd you get in here? It's a gated community."

"Oh," said Timmons, "we got the code from a friend. He lives up there by you. We were supposed to meet him, but he's not home."

"Imagine that. I bet if *I* knocked he'd come out."

"Naw, we pounded on it for like five minutes," said Sawyer, showing some nerve now. "So, whadaya think? Ya got thirty minutes to see if you can really get into heaven?"

If Klah hadn't been impressed with Call, and if he hadn't just seen the old Hopi elder, *after* Call had told him the Hopis were always watching, he never would have entertained *these* elders, never would have given them two seconds, but he *had* felt something when he talked to Call, and he had seen the wraithlike man floating in the undulating waves of heat, and then, of course, he had felt the solemn emptiness of his life, the utter aloneness of a porcupine waddling along on an empty highway.

And now, here he was, thinking about actually letting these two *kids* in.

Unbelievable.

Unless, of course, it wasn't.

"All right. Thirty minutes. Starting now." He turned to get his pack out of the car, but two other hands grabbed it first.

"Here, let us help!" said Sawyer, now convinced that no harm was coming and unaware that the pack held a loaded Glock with a threaded suppressor. Klah let him take the pack to hump it upstairs. Maybe the gun would go off and solve a problem or two.

The Accidental Killer strikes again.

But it didn't go off. And they did go inside. And they did sit down and talk.

And thirty minutes later his head was spinning—that Ammonite story really *was* great, and what's more, according to Sawyer, they might be his ancestors.

Could it have been them, the spirits of his ancestors, dancing in the breeze that first night on the far canyon wall? Had they warned him away from the cave just this morning? Were they with him now?

All he knew was, he was feeling something exciting—and very, very dangerous.

Chapter 47

Their Brightness Preserved

Over the next few weeks I went through Ether verse by verse, memorizing each new character. By the time I reached Ether six, where the Anthon Transcript came from, I had learned 243 characters by rote, meaning I could read them without referring to my notes. I figured I was almost as smart as a Nephite first-grader.

I still hadn't told Anna about the plates. Not only was I uncertain about her testimony, but we were still dealing with Kevin's issues. One day he'd be crying over what he had done, and the next he would want to tell his friends about it. He said living with a secret was like living with a lie. When we suggested counseling, he became defiant. "I don't need anybody getting into my head. The guy deserved to die!" It would take time, maybe years, before he found lasting peace.

By the time I finished the Book of Ether, I felt a change come over me, a quiet confidence with the language—and with the Spirit. I had found a schedule that worked. I went to the office an hour early, immediately after scriptures and prayer with the family, and dove into the markets back East. When the largest markets closed in the afternoon, I would kneel and offer another prayer then open up the plates. Amazingly, I found that I could juggle incoming phone calls from clients with my translation of the plates almost seamlessly. When a phone call ended, I could go right back to the verse I had been working on as if I had never left it.

After finishing Ether, I decided to go back through the images of the plates to see if I could find First Nephi—the beginning of the Book of Mormon. I began my search the next afternoon, and almost immediately something extraordinary happened.

I found a new language.

It was not reformed Egyptian, but something altogether different, on larger plates.

Looking at it, I recalled Ross telling me in the cave that two sets of plates he photographed were larger than the others, and one of those two books was larger than the other one. I recalled looking over and seeing him raise his camera a little higher to get the pages in view. Studying the larger one now, I noticed that not only were the characters wholly different from the reformed Egyptian, but the plates themselves were a different color. They were still bright, but they shone with a darker hue, a light brown instead of gold.

Although I didn't recognize the characters, it was obvious that the writing went from right to left, like the reformed Egyptian. Since I couldn't read it, I was about to scroll through more photos to hopefully find some plates with the word Nephi in them, when a thought occurred to me. Although I'm sure many languages are written from right to left, I was only aware of one other one.

Hebrew.

Something clicked in my mind, and a connection was made. My pulse quickened. I only knew of one other set of plates that were written in Hebrew. I got on my work computer to find a Hebrew version of the Old Testament. When I found it, I turned to the first page of Genesis. It looked familiar. I went back to the first page of these larger plates and compared the two.

Verse one was a perfect match.

Verse two, likewise. I raced ahead to chapter two. Again, perfect matches in verse after verse. I didn't know exactly what they said, because they were in Hebrew and I hadn't memorized Genesis, but I was becoming certain that this was a copy of the Hebrew Old Testament. I went ahead to Exodus and found more exact matches. I decided to make the ultimate test. I found Isaiah in both versions— and came to a halt.

They didn't match.

There had been no problem in chapter one, but in chapter two, verse five, the corresponding verse on the plates was almost twice as long. I went to the next verse. Again the verse on the plates was longer than the one in the online Hebrew Old Testament. But the next verse matched again, as did several others, until I got to verse ten.

I grabbed a Bible from my shelf and opened it to Isaiah, chapter two. Then I opened my Book of Mormon to Second Nephi, chapter twelve, where the Brass Plates version of Isaiah Two was. Then, for the first time in my life, I compared the two. Sure enough, verses five, six, and eleven in the Book of Mormon were longer than the corresponding verses in the Old Testament. They were more complete, no doubt more true and faithful to the original.

I sat back in astonishment. Had I found the Brass Plates?

And, if so, were these copies or the original Plates of Brass? Brass tarnishes, but these appeared to be bright and clear. I opened my Book of Mormon to 1 Nephi 5:19, and read: "Wherefore, he [Lehi] said that these plates of brass should never perish; neither should they be dimmed any more by time…" Then I followed the footnote to Alma 37:3-5:

> And these plates of brass, which contain these engravings, which have the records of the holy scriptures upon them, which have the genealogy of our forefathers, even from the beginning—Behold, it has been prophesied by our fathers, that they should be kept and handed down from one generation to another, and be kept and preserved by the hand of the Lord until they should go forth unto every nation, kindred, tongue, and people, that they shall know of the mysteries contained thereon. And now behold, if they are kept they must retain their brightness; yea, and they will retain their brightness; yea, and also shall all the plates which do contain that which is holy writ.

I scrolled through page after page of these larger plates, searching for signs of oxidation or any other kind of corruption, but saw nothing. I went online and found pictures of newly smelted brass and compared it to the photos of the plates. The color and luminosity matched. These plates appeared to be brass, not gold. And they looked new. And the markings were written in Hebrew, not reformed Egyptian. Could these be the plates that Nephi had spilled blood over to save a nation from unbelief? I tried to recall if I had actually touched them when Ross brought them to the table, but I couldn't recall doing so. Mine eyes had seen, but I had not hefted. Or touched. Or even looked closely at. I had been remiss and would now always regret it—unless I went back to the cave someday.

In comparison to gold, brass is harder and more brittle, and I wondered what kind of strength it had taken to emboss thousands of

Hebrew letters on hundreds of these plates. Also, the plates appeared to be thicker than the others. I didn't recall Ross saying anything about their thickness or hardness at the time, but we were moving so quickly that we probably missed many details that would have intrigued us.

As I pondered all this, questioning if these could be the actual plates that Nephi had brought back to Lehi, another thought came to me again. From the moment I had seen the plates in the cave I had wondered if I should tell the authorities in Salt Lake about them. When I saw the plate that matched the Anthon Transcript, I figured it would just be a matter of time. But there were two issues: one, I wasn't sure what we had until recently, when I discovered that we had the entire Book of Ether, and two, Anna still didn't know about them. If I called Salt Lake, surely they would want to meet with me and see my proof. How would I explain that to Anna?

But perhaps the time was coming to make a phone call.

The plates may have once been the rightful property of the Hopis, but they seemed to take no ownership of them now except to protect them. Legally, I figured, the plates actually belonged to the federal government, since it owned the land they had been found on. But perhaps the Church had a finer, higher claim. The plates seemed to prove the spiritual provenance of the Book of Mormon—unless some clever man had engraved the characters on the plates after the Book of Mormon had been published, making sure to use the Anthon Transcript as a template, and then hauled 83 sets of them to the cave and left them there for some unsuspecting rube like myself to find them. No, that didn't happen. These plates stood as literal proof that Joseph Smith had translated the Book of Mormon from an ancient record, and had done so *without a primer*. In his day there were no books listing the Egyptian hieroglyphics along with possible English translations. Most of these characters had been unknown then, and many probably still were. So the Church certainly had a right to know about them. Plus, they had linguists who would soon be able to translate the plates faster and with greater accuracy than I ever could.

And, of course, they had Seers.

I considered the power and value of this discovery. The books of Zenos and Zenock could be read in full. I even wondered if I could find them, but since I couldn't read Hebrew, translating them would take months.

But the question was, did I know for a certainty that I had the actual Brass Plates, and if I did, when should I let the brethren know?

Then a strange thing happened.

Over the years I had wondered why Laman and Lemuel had stayed with Lehi's family in the wilderness rather than abandoning the group and going back home. They clearly hated the idea of wandering around with their "visionary" father while their home, and perhaps some remaining treasure, awaited them in Jerusalem. They were certainly old enough to live on their own, as they were old enough to marry Ishmael's daughters, yet they had stuck with the family, wandering around the Arabian Peninsula for eight years. Now, as I sat pondering, the reason came clear: They had stayed in the wilderness because they had no choice. When Nephi had killed Laban, he wasn't the only one who became a wanted man. People in Jerusalem had certainly known that the four brothers had come to Laban to get the plates, but he had first refused Laman, then the rest of them, then had taken their gold and silver. Many of Laban's people, at a minimum, knew about the brothers and their quest for the plates. And now Laban was dead and the plates were missing. When Nephi had killed Laban, he had made them all wanted men. And of course this became another reason for the older brothers to hate Nephi. And with this understanding, I began to understand another reason for the Lord setting up the slaying of Laban; he needed Laman and Lemuel, who "knew not the dealings" of God, to go with the family to the promised land so that their seed would become a "scourge" to the seed of Nephi, to stir them up unto the remembrance of God. Laman and Lemuel hadn't gone back to Jerusalem because they couldn't. Nephi had locked them in to God's work.

As I realized this, inwardly smiling at the power of God to accomplish his designs by using both our strengths and weaknesses, a new thought came: the Lord had given me this understanding as a sign that I might know that the plates open before me were indeed the Brass Plates. This was *his* work and I could share it with his anointed servants.

I texted Ross and asked if he could come to my office. I thought he was home, since he was now an unemployed bum, but no, he was out with some of the YSA crowd again. I was annoyed. It was the middle of the afternoon—didn't those people work? And now that I thought about it, how old did they let people get in that organization? Thirty? He was on the fringe. An old man. Ancient. I told him to get over here so we could discuss more important matters than his current frivolities. He said he was on his way.

I might have been annoyed, but I empathized with him. How would it be to hang out with fellow Saints but not be able to share anything about these amazing discoveries? He had held gold plates covered in reformed Egyptian, but he couldn't share that with anybody. They certainly weren't the same plates that Joseph Smith had held, but they were ancient plates with Book of Mormon writings on them, and some even appeared to be from the hand of Moroni. How could a single man trying to impress young women, and maybe a few guy friends, bite his tongue and say *nothing*?

But of course, I was doing basically the same thing with Anna. We did it because we had to, because we felt that it was the right thing to do.

Ross came into the office about fifteen minutes later and plopped down in a chair and ran his hands through his short blond hair. He had been sweating. "Thanks for rescuing me!"

"I rescued you?"

"Have you ever been the dead carcass at a feeding frenzy?"

The image precluded a response.

"We were supposed to be playing softball today, right? You know—"

"Wait—why are you guys playing softball in the middle of the afternoon? Doesn't anybody work?"

"It's a holiday, Call. Most people take Memorial Day off."

"Oh, yeah, right." I hadn't exactly forgotten that Memorial Day was coming, I just forgot that it came today.

"Anyway, every girl wants to be on my side. Well, not every girl, but a lot of them, most of them. So, it was like me and eight girls."

"You mean women. They're adults now."

"Whatever. It was scary. First of all, we got killed, because all the guys were on the other team. But every time I said something, eight girls laughed. And you know me; I'm not funny. I felt terrible for the other guys. They're probably more glad for your call than I was."

"Well, it's your own fault."

"Huh?"

"You're the one who got tall, blond, and rich."

"Well, I may be tall and blond, but I'm ready to give the money to the poor and hunker down in some monastery. Wait. Why don't we have monasteries? I could use one right now."

"Don't missions kind of serve that purpose?"

"Yeah, but only for a couple of years. They probably wouldn't take me again."

I changed the subject. "I found something."

"What's that?"

"Actually, you found it, but you didn't know it. Remember that set of big, heavy plates you found in the cave?"

He paused then nodded. "Yeah, they were wider and heavier, and they had a lot more plates. What were they, more scripture?"

"Yes, but, think about their color."

He thought for a moment. "They were darker, weren't they?"

"Yes, because they weren't gold."

"Then, what were they?" His eyes widened, and he got still. "Brass?"

I turned my screen toward him. "This is the first plate. See how it's in a different language—not in reformed Egyptian? See those characters?"

He nodded in silence.

I changed tabs and brought up the Hebrew Old Testament. "And see how these characters match those other ones perfectly?" I hit a couple of keys and put the two images side by side.

His eyes went from right to left. "They're the same. *Exactly* the same."

"Right. They're both from Genesis, chapter one. But look at this." I changed both windows to the images of Isaiah, chapter two. "Look at verses five, six, and eleven."

He got closer. "They're different."

"Now look at this." I slid hard copies of the Bible and Book of Mormon across to him, opened to the same pages. "Look at verses five, six, and eleven again."

He took a moment to compare them, then he sat back in his chair. "They're the same. I know, the Book of Mormon Isaiah has some changes."

"Right—the exact same changes that the plates in the cave have. These aren't just plates of brass—they're *Brass Plates*."

"*The* Brass Plates?"

"I think so."

He sat back, eyes wide in astonishment. "First we find Ether—and we weren't struck down by lightning—and now we find the Brass Plates?" A smile spread slowly across his face. "It's time, isn't it?"

"For what?"

"To make the call."

"That's why I wanted you here."

"So, who's going to make it? No, wait, *you* have to, because you can actually read the plates. What if they ask me questions about their grammar or something?"

"Actually, I think the first question is, *who* do we call?"

"The Brethren."

"There's like a hundred of them. Which one?"

He started to speak then paused, probably running into the same roadblock I had. We couldn't just pick up the phone and call a member of the First Presidency, or one of the Quorum of the Twelve, or even one of the Seventy. We had to call somebody who would take our call.

"I think we need to call President Whiting," I said. I knew our stake president fairly well, having met with him every other week for the past three years. "Better yet, we should probably show him the pictures of the plates, then tell him the whole story. Then he can call the Area Authorities if he wants to, and *they* can call Salt Lake."

"Right. Which will give us enough time to clear out of Dodge."

"Huh?"

"If we tell them the whole story, everyone will know where these plates are, and what we did—*illegally*—to find them."

"Not everyone. Not if they keep the knowledge to themselves."

"And not tell their wives? Or fellow general authorities? Come on, Travis, it's been killing me to keep this whole thing a secret. It's on my mind *all the time*. I don't know how you keep it from Anna. Don't you think one of them will tell his wife? I mean, this is bigger than a Three Nephites story."

The Brethren were supposed to be above reproach. They were men who knew how to keep confidences, but if one, *just one*, told a wife or friend or colleague, and that person told a wife or friend or colleague . . .

"So, what do you suggest?"

"Okay," he said, beginning to pace the twelve feet between walls, "Maybe we go to President Whiting and tell him that we found some plates that *might* have some ancient American writings, maybe even some of the characters from the Anthon Transcript, and that we think he should call Salt Lake. That should be enough, don't you think?"

"Ross, we have plates that have *all* of the characters from the Anthon Transcript, and we *know* we have 'ancient American writings' on these plates. I don't want to equivocate."

"No, don't equivocate—just be concise. Church leaders love brevity. Tell him what he needs to know so he makes the call."

I sat back. Maybe he was right. I knew we had to protect the plates, but we also had to tell him enough to get him to make a call he'd rather not make. "First," I said, "what do you say we pray about it?" I started sliding off my chair to my knees.

"Now?" He looked around, as if searching for clients.

"Ross, I know this is work, but I pray a lot here too."

He dropped to his knees.

I prayed. It wasn't long, but it was heartfelt. We still needed protection for ourselves and family. We needed to know how to protect the plates from bureaucrats, lawmakers, and well-meaning curiosity-seekers. We needed guidance, and we probably needed it soon. We finished and sat down again. Ross said, "I think you should just call President Whiting and ask for an interview and then follow the Spirit. You'll know what to say."

He was right. I pulled out my phone. I had his cell number because he had called me from it to inquire about the slaughter of the cats. He'd probably see my name come up and wonder if they were back—or if Kevin had killed something else.

Please, not that.

The phone clicked in my ear. "Brother Call?"

"Yes, uh, hi, President. I have a question that probably can't wait. And, actually, I didn't think I should go through Brother Donaldson either." Donaldson was the executive secretary.

"Travis? Hello? Are you okay?"

"Oh, yes. Of course. Do you have a minute?"

"A minute or two."

"Okay. Well, Ross—you remember Ross Keller, right?"

"Oh, sure, all the girls are talking about him—at least all the girls in our family."

He had three daughters, a recently returned missionary, a freshman at BYU who had just come back for the summer, and a high school senior.

"Well, Ross and I had some work that took us out to a—I mean, to a cave."

"What was that? Sorry, it sounded like you said 'a cave.' It's kind of loud here. I'm at Walmart with my wife. How about that? I finally get a day off, and we spend it at Walmart."

I offered a chuckle, a polite ha-ha, but the fact was, I was so nervous that I struggled to put two words together.

"So, anyway, we went to a cave, and, well, I don't know how to say this, but we found some plates, really *old* plates, and it looks like they have some of the characters from the Anthon Transcript on them." *(Guile! Shading the truth! Equivocating!)* Guilt welled up so fast inside me that I suddenly had to go to the bathroom.

But first things first. He was quiet, perhaps out of kindness, perhaps out of confusion. Then a woman's voice called out the price of green onions. It may have been Sister Whiting. I could only imagine the poor man's dilemma. "From the *what?*" he asked.

"From the Anthon Transcript—the paper that Joseph Smith wrote the reformed Egyptian characters on."

After a beat, he said, "You found *that?*"

"No, we found the plates—I mean, plates that look like gold, and brass, and they have engravings on them that look like the same ones from the Anthon Transcript."

A drop of sweat seeped out from under my right arm and trickled down my side. For some reason I had turned my back to Ross, but I was pretty sure he hadn't left the room. I didn't want him to see my guilty face.

"Where was this cave?"

Fortunately I didn't have to answer, as he spoke to his wife: "No, Honey, it's Travis Call . . . No, I don't know what cave. Travis, did you say *cave?*"

Great. His wife was listening in. "Uh, yes, President, maybe it would be better if we got together. Could we meet somewhere? Soon?"

"You mean you want to take me away from Walmart?"

"No, we could wait till you . . ."

"I'll be there in twenty minutes. Where are you?"

"At my office, but I just remembered, I need to get home."

Not only had I remembered that it was Memorial Day, but now I recalled that we had a barbecue planned. Thank goodness Ross had come over.

"Honey, we gotta go. I gotta see the Calls . . . No, they're not in a cave . . . Travis, are you still there?"

"Yes."

"At home you say?"

"No, but I will be. But maybe we should . . ."

"Okay, great. See you soon. No, honey, they *went* to a cave . . ."

I clicked off. I didn't want him to go to the house because it would be hard to explain to Anna, who was off work today, or to Rosemary, who was probably already kneading onion soup mix into the hamburger, or, for that matter, to Kevin, who could see through prevarications like they were so much hot air. I stood up to go to the bathroom, then realized I didn't have to anymore, so I sat back down and pushed speed dial for Anna. She answered.

"I'll be home soon, Honey. Just finishing up a few things here. Oh, and by the way, President Whiting is coming over."

"Oh, that's wonderful. Rosemary, President Whiting is coming over! Better make a few more hamburgers!"

"No, he's not coming over to eat. He just wants to—"

My brain froze. *He just wants to what?*

But Anna spared me further equivocation, which was good because she was a living, walking lie-detector. Kevin had nothing on her. "Of course he's going to eat," she said. "Just hurry up and come home. We're almost ready."

I hung up.

"That was short," Ross said.

"This is not going to be good."

"Why not?"

"Have you ever wondered why Abinadi wore a disguise the second time he went to King Noah, just to take it off and inform the King that he was, in fact, Abinadi?"

"No."

"Well, maybe you should start thinking about it, because I think we're both about to take our disguises off." I stood up. "Come on, let's get going. If I'm going to have an Abinadi moment, I'd rather get it over with fast."

* * *

Anna and I had an unspoken agreement: She wouldn't ask me about my work for Saundra Nelson, which she thought was clearly finished, and I wouldn't bring it up. Or, that's what I thought our agreement was until she instituted a new agreement; to wit, that she would ask all manner of questions and I would answer them under penalty of perjury.

Ross and I walked in, and Anna stepped out of the kitchen and asked if I could visit with her in my office. Ross walked past her then looked back at me and winked.

A match was being struck.

She closed the door behind us. "What's going on, Travis?"

"Huh?" *My disguise was slipping away.*

"President Whiting has never been here before. Why's he coming over now?"

"Oh, well, I guess we'll see."

"You don't know?"

Getting warmer. "Well, if you have to know, I think he wants to talk to me about my work."

"Your work? Are you investing for him?"

"Not yet." (And probably not ever.)

"So, what work? Is it about Kevin?"

"No, of course not. You know that I'd let you know if it was about any of the children. Anna, please. I don't ask you for space very often, but I'm asking for it now."

She eyed me narrowly. "You don't ask for space because you just take it when I say no. You almost got us all killed a month ago when I said no, and just so I'm on the record, I don't plan to go through that again."

I said nothing, and she turned and walked out. As the door closed behind her, the image of Abinadi fled, and an image of Lehi stole into my mind, the careworn man subjected to endless doubts and cross examinations. No doubt he loved his wife, as I loved Anna, but there were times when a higher responsibility prevailed.

Through the door I heard her voice again: "Oh, hi, President. We're so glad you could come by. You're just in time for some barbecue."

I didn't hear President Whiting's reply as I stepped out and went into the kitchen. Ross was waiting for me. "Do you still want me to join you? It might look suspicious to Anna."

"Yes, of course."

By the application of common sense, I made myself calm down. The common sense went something like this: I have done nothing to be ashamed of (except making my family hide out for days), nothing illegal (except long-term trespassing and blowing up parts of a cave in a National Park), nothing foolish (except trying to walk on quicksand, or hunting down a murderer, or turning my back on five men with loaded guns). Thus composed, I walked into the living room to greet the stake president.

He was just explaining how he couldn't stay for dinner. "I promised Martha that I would make it to our kids' barbecue, across town." He turned to me. "So I guess we should get this interview going."

As Ross and I led him to my office, I could have hugged him for using the word "interview," which carried the weight of officialdom and confidentiality. Perhaps the fire at my feet would flicker out.

We stepped into the room. They sat in the two chairs before my desk, while I went around it to my own seat.

"President, thank you for coming over so fast. I didn't really expect—"

He raised a hand. "No, I'm glad to be out of there. Walmart at rush hour—whew! So, what's up? You boys were in a cave or something?"

President Gerald Whiting was a tall, middle aged man with no hair on his head whatsoever. For years I thought he shaved it, then one day I overheard him joking that he had thrown his razors out years ago, which made no sense because his face was as shiny as his head. Maybe he used an electric razor. He had recently retired after a long and profitable career as an oral surgeon.

Facing them from across the desk, I explained the facts about Kinkaid's Cave, Keith Nelson, his ex-wife and daughter, and our trip to the canyon. I omitted the parts about Klah, Richardson, and Winn. When I told him about the enormous cavern where we found the plates, Ross raised his eyebrows in surprise. I raised mine back at him. It was his idea to talk to the president and he could live with the consequences. President Whiting asked if I had any pictures. As I moved the scriptures out of the way to turn my screen toward him, Ross showed him his phone, where he had already brought up the plates. The president looked at them while I enlarged some of the characters on my screen.

"You found these in the Grand Canyon?"

"Yes," said Ross.

"But you don't have any of the actual, um, plates, with you, do you? You didn't bring any home?"

"No," I said, "we felt we shouldn't take any."

"Good, because you probably would have broken several laws. Do you have any pictures of the room where you found the plates?"

Ross brought up a picture. While the President looked at it, I got to the heart of the matter.

"We think—no, we *know*—that we found some plates that have at least parts of the Book of Mormon on them."

His kind face became deadly serious, almost angry. "How do you know that?"

I handed him the old dog-eared Anthon article and had him open it to the page where the characters were line up.

"Oh, is this what you were talking about on the phone? I've seen this before. 'I cannot read a sealed book,' right?"

"Right—but I can."

His glare intensified. A terrible swift sword. "Please explain that."

"President, I've studied the characters on those plates and learned the language. I can read them—almost all of them."

"Almost?"

"Well, there are two sets of plates, the biggest ones, that are written in Hebrew. I can't read those."

Ross thumbed through the images on his phone. "See? These are the Brass Plates." He gave the phone back to President Whiting. "See how the writing's in a different language? That's Hebrew. Travis can't read Hebrew. Not yet."

"*What?* You're telling me that you found the *Brass Plates*? The plates that Nephi had?"

"Yeah," Ross answered before I could soften the blow, "and we found like eighty other sets of plates—and who knows what's on them!"

Maybe I should've had Ross wait outside. Nuclear blasts should always be delivered with delicacy, one impossible fact at a time. The president turned his gaze back to me, his once trusted high councilman.

"Is that right?"

"President, that's why we called you. Somebody else is going to go in that cave and find these plates, and we thought it should be someone from the Church."

He glanced at the images on Ross's phone again, sniffed like he had a cold, then said, "But, just to be clear, you don't actually have them."

"No, we left them there." I hadn't told him about the mummies yet, but, knowing they might come up sooner or later, I did now. Ross helped him find the pictures of the mummies on his phone. The good man looked at them for a long time, saying nothing.

He handed the phone back to Ross and sat motionless, staring at the floor. Then he buried his face in his hands. I didn't know if he was crying or pondering my imminent retirement from Church service—or both.

"There's lots of pictures, if you don't believe us," Ross said, scrolling through more images. "We've got the mummies, and we've got the plates with the Anthon stuff on them—and, oh, by the way, that's from Ether. And we've got stuff from—"

"Ross, I don't think he needs more proof."

The president's head slowly came up, and he looked at me with the eyes of a weary traveler. "No, I believe you." I thought he might cry, but he proved stronger than that. "This is unbelievable, absolutely unbelievable. This is *crazy*. No offense, Travis, but why, *why*, would the Lord let *you* see those plates?"

"Offense taken," Ross muttered under his breath.

The two were sitting side by side, with Ross half turned in his chair toward the president. If President Whiting didn't know before, he knew now that Ross feared nobody. I should have interjected, but I was so surprised by Ross that I was speechless. Then Ross made matters worse.

"Travis is, like, a genius. He figured out the language all by himself. You ought to hear him read it. It's like he's reading a children's book. He can—"

The president raised a hand. "Ross, I'm sorry. I believe you, really. I just don't know *why* any of this is happening. It doesn't make sense."

"It does if you know that other men, bad men, are after the plates too," Ross said. "They might even be there right now. And the Lord wants the Church to have them."

I could almost hear the man's thoughts: *I must get the high council together, and maybe a general authority, and hold a council . . .*

But he didn't say this, so I pressed forward. "I have the same question, President? Why me? And the truth is, I have no idea. But there is no question that we have all of these things: the Book of Mormon, the Brass Plates, and a lot more. It's all in that cave."

The president shook his head as if still not able to accept this. "Is there anything else? Did you find the Sword of Laban too? The Urim and Thummin?"

"Naw," Ross said. "Just the plates."

I saw no need to mention the Hopi tablet.

But I did mention the story of Moroni and a small band of Nephites taking the sacred records to New York. "According to this stake patriarch and one other brother who knew Joseph Smith in Nauvoo, Joseph told them that Moroni went up from Central America and through Arizona to what is now Utah, and he dedicated temple sites at St. George and Manti. And then he traveled east to the Hill Cumorah in New York, where he deposited the Gold Plates. But, when he went through Arizona, he probably saw the Grand Canyon, and maybe the Indians showed him the cave. Legend has it that those Indians were descendants of the Ammonites who had moved north to get away from persecution. Maybe Moroni saw a perfect place to deposit all the other records, and when he got back from the Hill Cumorah, he got the rest of the plates and moved them there."

"I have never heard that story before," he said.

"The maps that the stake patriarch and other brother drew are in the Church archives," I said. "They're not a secret. You can even pull them up on the internet."

The president took a deep breath and exhaled slowly. Then in a soft voice, perhaps trembling a bit, he said, "Who among us needs faith anymore?"

"Well, here's how I figure it," Ross declared. "The Lord knew all this stuff would get out soon, so he's just giving the Church a heads-up. We had a chance to learn by faith, but those days are over, well, almost over, and now we have to deal with sure knowledge. Know what I mean?"

I was quite sure that *I* didn't know what he meant.

"But," the President looked at me again, "you're not even a—"

"A prophet?" I finished for him.

"No, an apostle. A stake president. A *bishop*."

"I know. That's why we called you. We think we should tell the Brethren, but we're trying to follow proper priesthood channels."

"Well, that's a relief, since this doesn't seem to follow any other priesthood channels that I know of."

He was right. This defied precedent, reason, and, as I had earlier discovered, common sense.

"May I see those plates that have the characters from the Anthon Transcript again? And would you please translate them for me, in your own words?"

I brought up the characters on my computer and invited him to come around to follow along. "We took this picture in the cave. This one is of the plate where we found the characters from the Anthon Transcript. See? They're exactly the same, as in the transcript." I showed him the photocopy of the transcript again. Then, back on the screen, I moved my finger to the left across it as I began translating the characters in my own words.

> We were on a fearful voyage, and the Lord took control of our course. We were in dome-shaped vessels and were encompassed about by many waters. The sea swallowed us, and we did submerge beneath billows of waves as big as mountains. We cried with anguish of soul, and the Lord did hear our cries and bear us up. And he did deliver us out of the sea, and we did thank and praise him . . .

I felt a hand on my shoulder, and I turned and looked up. He was weeping.

"Thank you."

He went back to his seat, wiping his eyes, then he looked at me as if he had never known me, but he said nothing more. I handed him some tissues. Then, with a softer look, he said: "Travis, I know these characters are from the Book of Mormon—and I can see that you can read them. And I can even say that I feel the truth of—"

He was almost afraid to go on. "But, why, Travis? Why you? What's going on? I mean it. *Why you?*"

"I honestly don't know, President."

He nodded, seemingly resigned to this strange new reality. He turned to Ross. "I'm sorry, Brother Keller. I didn't mean to insult you or Travis. I just don't understand. This changes everything. Nobody has to have faith anymore. Anybody can see the truth for themselves. It'll be obvious that Joseph Smith translated the Book of Mormon from an ancient record, like he said. And if people can't accept that, they can't accept the very truth before their eyes." He turned back to me. "How can this be right?"

"That's why we have to let the Brethren know before other people find the plates."

He nodded. "Yes, they need to know—immediately. How many other people know about them?"

"We don't know for sure," I said. "There were two men who were hired to protect the cave the plates are in, and they've seen these pictures, but they don't know exactly where the plates are in the cave—it's really big. And there's this old Hopi elder. He knows about them, but he doesn't seem to know what's on them. And he says that his people are protecting the cave too."

"You talked to this Hopi elder in the cave?"

"No, outside it, above the rim. He says his people are the caretakers of the cave. Those mummies I told you about are their dead ancestors—their former leaders."

He exhaled loudly again, shaking his head. "This is amazing. Absolutely amazing."

"Yeah," Ross said. "So are you going to call the prophet?"

Between Ross, Anna, and Kevin, I knew little subtlety in my life.

"Yes, well, I can't call the *prophet*, but I can call someone who *can*." He looked at his watch. "It's too late now, but first thing in the morning. In fact, I'd like to do it from here, so you can answer any questions they might have. Is that all right?"

I wondered how I would explain *that* to Anna. "Actually, it might be better if we did it from your office. Anna doesn't know about any of this, and with your being here right now, she's already suspicious that something strange is going on."

"Very perceptive of her. Why haven't you told her?"

"Because, to be honest, she doesn't even know the Book of Mormon is true. Not really. And like you said, I didn't think it would be fair to prove it to her."

He started to speak then just nodded his head.

"All right, then shall we say eight o'clock at the stake center tomorrow morning?"

Ross and I looked at each other, then Ross said, "I'll get him there. He likes to sleep in, you know. He'll probably miss the Second Coming if I'm not around to wake him up."

The president smiled, but it seemed to hurt. He stood up. "I doubt I'll be able to sleep tonight." He looked at me again. "How have *you* been able to sleep? How have you been able to keep all this to yourself? Have you told anyone, besides Ross?"

"No. Just you and Ross."

"But he didn't have to tell me," Ross said, "because I was there. And if I hadn't been there, he wouldn't be *here*."

"What?"

"He would've been killed by snakes, but only if he hadn't already fallen off a cliff, or got stung by a scorpion, or maybe drowned in quicksand—and that was *before* we found the plates—when the *real* fun started."

President Whiting slowly shook his head again, in despair or disbelief, then opened the door and went into the hallway leading to the kitchen. Ross and I followed him to the living room, where Anna and Rosemary had strategically positioned themselves. The hamburgers were getting cold somewhere. The president, wise man that he was, went to Anna and shook her hand.

"Sister Call, I hate to say this, but I'm almost grateful that your son took matters into his own hands."

Anna almost pulled back, stricken, but the president didn't notice because he was turning to Rosemary. "My entire high council couldn't find a solution to that cat problem, including your husband, but that boy did. Now I'm not saying we want him to solve *any more* problems, but everybody knows that the cultural hall smells a lot better now. Well, I'd best be on my way. I made Martha leave Walmart early, and I have penance to offer." He shook Rosemary's hand. "I wish I could stay; I hear you're the best chef in the stake."

Anna had recovered, but I suspected that I would have to pay penance as well.

As soon as the door shut behind President Whiting, Anna turned to me. "Was he crying? His eyes were red."

I shrugged. "I think he felt the Spirit witnessing something to him—but he probably didn't want to talk about it."

"Was it about Kevin?"

"No, probably something sacred—just for him."

"Hmm." She walked to the family room, where the children were waiting. The Lord must have blessed her. And me. And everyone else.

Rosemary's hamburgers were indeed championship material, and we had a great time as a family, all eight of us, together, just having a good time.

And I am pleased to say that I actually did sleep well that night.

Chapter 48

And the Truth Shall Set You Free

Ross and I drove to the stake center separately, which allowed me to not have to tell Anna where we were going—after breakfast I simply left for the office. She just didn't know which office.

President Whiting was waiting for us. His bloodshot eyes evidenced a long night. But he had shaved, because his glistening face matched his glistening head. He shook our hands and sat down.

"All right, brethren, I've already taken the opportunity to make some calls so I could find out who we really need to talk to, and I've got a number here." He abruptly stopped. "Maybe we should have a prayer. I think we should." He came around the desk and knelt by us, and Ross and I followed suit. In the prayer, President Whiting pled for guidance and the Spirit. Then he made a special, fervent plea for the brethren to know how to respond, that the Lord would be with them "at this special time." When he finished, he went back to his chair.

"Thank you. I had a long night of prayer. It's not every day somebody comes to me with Ether in the reformed Egyptian and the Brass Plates, and whatever else you have. Martha asked me if I was sick, but I told her that it was just—*just*—a Church matter. Anyway, I made some calls this morning—they open pretty early back there—and I've got a number." He motioned to a pad of paper. "This is the number for one of the secretaries to the First Presidency. His name is Ted Whitford. My contact back there, Elder Simpson, said this man will be able to relay our message to a member of the First Presidency if he feels it's appropriate."

"How much does Elder Simpson know?" I asked.

"Well, not as much as I *wanted* to tell him, but more than you'd probably be comfortable with. I had to tell him why I wanted the number of a member of the Council of Twelve or First Presidency. When I told him that two men in my stake had found ancient records that might have reformed Egyptian writing on them, he asked me most of the same questions I asked you yesterday, then he gave me this number. Brother Whitford is expecting our call. Is there anything else you want to tell me, or shall we just go ahead and change our lives forever?"

"They're already changed," Ross said.

President Whiting made the call on his desk phone, but not on speaker.

"Hello?" he said. "Brother Whitford? . . . Yes, this is Gerald Whiting . . . Right—stake president . . . Thank you so much for taking my call . . . Oh, yes, we're doing fine out here, not quite Zion but, you know, we're trying. Anyway, I've got two brothers here, and they'd like to share something with you, something that I think is quite extraordinary. Would you mind if I put them on speaker-phone? . . ." He pushed a button and put the phone back in its cradle. "Hello? Can you hear us?" he said.

"Yes."

"All right. First, let me introduce Travis Call. He's a high councilman in our stake, very faithful. You might remember him from several years back with that terrible tragedy out here, when his former wife, Marsha Call, the actress—you may remember that she was killed by . . ."

"Oh, yes, we all followed that on the news. I'm sorry for your loss, Brother Call."

"Thank you," I said. "I'm very happily remarried and we have four children now. Life is good."

"Wonderful."

"And," the president added, "his good friend, Ross Keller, is here with us too. You may remember that he was part of that affair back then."

"Oh, Brother Keller! How are you? If I remember right, you served a mission after that."

"I did."

"And, if I remember right," Brother Whitford continued, "you were the one who put an end to that whole 'affair.'"

"Well, not really. We both—and Anna . . ."

"Oh, that's right. It's good to hear you're all doing well. So, how can I help you?"

He sounded like a good man, a brother I could trust.

"I'm going to let Brother Call tell his story," said President Whiting. He looked at me and sat back in his chair, no doubt relieved that this part of his job was done.

"Brother Whitford," I began, "I'm a financial counselor out here in Modesto, and a client of mine sent me some materials about a discovery he made in the Grand Canyon. Then he was killed. His family came to me and asked if I would investigate his death, because the police kind of ran into a brick wall, and the family knew that I had helped solve my first wife's murder. So, anyway, I went to investigate, which means that Ross and I went to the Grand Canyon and found the thing that my client said was hidden there—a large cave over a thousand feet above the Colorado River."

"A cave? A thousand feet above the river?"

"Yes."

"How'd you get to it?"

"It wasn't easy, believe me, and without Ross's help, I wouldn't have made it—he's a little younger than I am."

"A *lot* younger!" Ross added.

"But we found a path on a ledge, probably just an old sheep trail, and when we got there we found that somebody had sealed the cave shut with rocks and cement, but my client had said there was another way in, and we found it."

"And may I ask what he was doing up there in the first place?"

"Well, basically he learned about the cave from an old letter that a relative of his wife's had written about a hundred years ago. So, anyway, he found another way into the cave, and then he found some old Indian mummies in there, and he looted the jewelry from one of them. And then he was killed for the jewelry by someone who wanted to keep the cave a secret for his own purposes."

"This is getting complicated. So somebody else knew about the cave?"

"Yes, but—you're right, it is complicated—so, several people eventually found out about it, and they pursued us as well. But none of them, as far as we know, knows where the plates are."

"Plates?"

"Yes, that's what we're here for."

"Don't forget the old Hopi guy," Ross added.

"Old *Hopi* guy?" Whitford asked, with an air of exasperation.

"Like I said," I continued, "it's complicated, but there's an old Hopi elder who knows about the cave and the plates, but he says the plates weren't for his people, so they leave them alone. But they also guard the cave, because of the mummies—at least sometimes."

"And, just so I understand, what do the park personnel say about all of this?"

"Nothing."

"Yeah," added Ross, "they don't even think the cave exists, because it's written up in an old newspaper story you can find online, so they think it's just a hoax."

There was silence for a moment. "But you're saying it isn't a hoax."

"No," said Ross. "Like Travis said, we've been there. We've seen the whole thing, and it's *amazing.*"

More silence.

The stake president nodded at me to continue.

"So, anyway, we found a room with metal plates in it, just like Joseph Smith described. Dozens of sets of plates, and most of them have a strange form of writing on them. And, using the old Anthon Transcript, you know, that piece of paper with the characters that Joseph . . ."

"I know what the Anthon Transcript is."

"Okay, well, this is kind of hard to believe, but using that, and another book that had translations of some of the characters, I was able to . . ."

"Wait, you said you had translations of some of the characters *in the Anthon Transcript?* You said they were translated?"

"Just a few of the characters, in a book about ancient Egyptian hieroglyphics, that, unfortunately, I can't find anymore. But, it's okay, because I used some algorithms in my computer to match character patterns in the Anthon Transcript with word patterns in the Book of Mormon, and, when I found where the transcript came from, which is in the Book of Ether, I was able to start matching characters to words and phrases, and after a while I could just start reading the plates. And guess what? They made sense. In fact, they sounded just like the Book of Mormon."

There was a long pause in which I knew that I had said too much too fast.

"Okay," he finally said. "Let's back up. You used algorithms to match patterns in the Anthon Transcript with patterns in the Book of Mormon?"

"Yes."

"And you found out where those characters were taken from?"

"Yes, in Ether six."

"And you can prove this?"

"Yes, now I can, because we found the plate that it was taken from, and I can read it."

"You found the plate? And you can read it? Out loud? You know the language?"

I gave a nervous little laugh. "No, no—I just know what they mean, not the actual sounds of the words."

"Okay, but it sounds like there's lots of these plates."

"Yes, lots of *sets* of plates."

"Sets of plates?"

"You know, books of plates."

"*Eighty-three* of them," Ross said.

President Whiting's bald head was perspiring.

"Eighty-three of them? And you got them all? How much do they weigh?"

"No, we didn't take them. We left them there, but we took pictures of them, of each plate, each page. We had cameras with us."

"And then, you learned how to read them."

"Yes, at home."

"And they have the Book of Mormon on them."

"Yes."

I could have said that I hadn't found the entire Book of Mormon yet, but I was becoming sure that that was only because I hadn't read all the plates yet. President Whiting was silently urging me to move on.

But Ross beat me to it. "So we're afraid that other people who know about the cave are going to spill the beans, and then the rangers will probably find the plates, and then who knows what will happen? So we thought we should tell the general authorities first, you know, before all of that happens."

There was another long pause, then Brother Whitford went back to the first major hurdle, and we were back to square one. "Wait, you found the Book of Mormon? How? I thought Moroni took the plates from Joseph Smith."

"No, we didn't find the *Gold Plates*, not the ones that Joseph Smith had. Not that I know of, anyway. We found other plates that are copies—you know, that have same words. But we did find something else that Joseph *didn't* have."

"What's that?"

"The Brass Plates."

Silence.

"Brother Whitford," the stake president said, interjecting, "I know all of this is hard to accept, but . . ."

"Try impossible! Because God doesn't leave his scriptures lying around in caves for just anybody to find. There is no way you boys found the Brass Plates."

"That just shows what *you* know," Ross blurted. "Didn't Joseph Smith find the Gold Plates *under a rock*? And didn't the Dead Sea Scrolls—you know what they are?—weren't they literally hidden in a cave? We may not be geniuses, but we're not liars, and we did find the real Brass Plates, and we can prove it!"

The room became very still, as President Whiting and I stared at the mad man next to me. I could only imagine what Whitford was thinking. I doubt he'd been chastised like that since grade school.

"Look," Ross said in a softer more humane tone, "if you don't believe us, let us show you. Just give Travis a chance to show you what he found—and how he can translate the plates."

"Oh my . . ." Whitford sighed again.

"Brother Whitford?" President Whiting said.

There was no response.

"I know this all sounds too fantastic to be true," the president persisted, "but I've seen the pictures of the plates, some of them anyway, and Travis can indeed read them. Unless . . ." He stared hard at me. "Unless he's amazingly good at faking reformed Egyptian. But I've seen the plate that corresponds to the Anthon Transcript, and it's all there, only it looks a little different, a little more *ancient*, I suppose."

"No offense, President, but what if Brother Call and Brother Keller made their own metal plate and embossed it with the characters they showed you?"

"That's a possibility, but I saw lots of pictures of lots of plates, and they look legitimate to me. Thousands of them, more than anyone would make for some hoax." He glanced at me again. "And, they're not asking for money. They're offering all of this to the Church for nothing, just so we can protect them. And there's one more thing. I know Brother Call, and I trust him. And there's something else—" The president's voice trailed off.

"Yes?"

"When he was translating the plates to me, actually reading them, I felt the Spirit. I received a witness that these records are true. Brother Whitford, these things are exactly what these men say they are—and I know that Travis can in fact read them."

"Oh my . . ."

"That's really why I called you," the president said. "I believe him. He found ancient plates that contain the Book of Mormon, or at least parts of it, so I thought it would be wise to share this with the Brethren. What do you think?"

"I think all this is the most incredible thing I've ever heard. Why would the Lord do this? Why would he allow these two men to—"

"We've already asked that," Ross said, interrupting him again, "and nobody knows. Even Travis doesn't know."

I reached over and touched his arm. We had said enough. There was a long moment of silence when everything hung in the balance.

"President Whiting?"

"Yes."

"I'm not comfortable with this, not at *all*, but I feel I have no choice but to refer you to someone higher up. Maybe a member of the First Presidency, if I can arrange it."

"Thank you."

"I don't know which one, or if any of them will speak with these brethren; they're very busy, but I'll pass this on." He took a deep breath. "Incredible. Just *incredible*."

"Thank you, Brother Whitford. Should I expect a call from you first, or from . . ."

"If one of them contacts you, you probably won't hear from me first. But if they don't, I may call you again."

"Very good. Thank you again for taking our call."

"Yes, well, good-bye, brethren. I almost can't tell you what I hope for the most—that you're wrong, or that you're right."

We said good-bye and the president hung up. The president's head was fully beaded with sweat, which he patted away with a white handkerchief. I looked at Ross and saw a smile on his face. No sweat at all.

"This is *amazing*," he said. "Even a guy who's inspired in the First Presidency's office doesn't know what to make of this."

"Don't look at me," I said, putting up my hands in defense. "I didn't ask for any of this to happen."

"Maybe," the president offered, "but you'd better ask for the right things to happen now. Shall we pray again? And Brother Call, would you offer the prayer?"

We knelt and I prayed and they said, "Amen," then Ross and I took our leave. Frankly, nobody knew what to expect.

* * *

Anna wasn't surprised to find Kevin reading the Book of Mormon in his room a few nights later—he was a curious boy—but she certainly hadn't expected it. She told me that she had gone to check on him because she hadn't heard from him in a few hours, and when she knocked and entered his room she found him sitting on his bed with his back against the wall, reading the Book of Mormon. She asked if everything was okay.

He lifted the book and said, "You don't believe this, do you?"

Anna is always honest. "I don't know, Kevin. I want it to be true. Do you think that's enough?"

He slowly shook his head. "No, 'cause if it's true, then it means the Church is true. And if it's fake, then the Church is fake. So you have to know—for sure."

She sat on the edge of the bed. "That makes sense. So, what part are you reading?"

Kevin turned the book toward her, and she saw that it was 1 Nephi 4—the story about Nephi killing Laban. Later that evening as she shared this with me, she teared up.

"I asked him why he was reading about Nephi and Laban, and he said he wanted to know if he was going to hell. I told him that the bishop had already promised him that God loved him and wouldn't hold him guilty for protecting the family—but he said, 'Yeah, that's what you all say, but I want to know for myself.'"

Anna and I were alone in our bedroom, sitting on the bed against the headboard. "He's braver than I am," she said. "He's willing to confront it. I just want it to go away."

"So," I asked, "what'd you do?"

"We read it together, the whole chapter." There was a break in her voice. Something important was happening. I looked over. A tear was in her eye.

"That young man did it," she said. "He killed a man."

492

I thought she meant Kevin.

She continued: "I don't know how old he was, but he was probably still a teenager. And he killed that man."

I dared not speak. She was speaking as if the event had actually happened, as if there had really been a Nephi and a Laban.

"We sat there and read that whole story together—and it made no sense at all. Think about it, why would Joseph Smith write that particular story if he was trying to win converts? You have a young man, Nephi, and you set him up to murder a man for a book? I don't know who Joseph Smith was, but even a country rube knows better than to have his main character start off by killing innocent people for their property."

"Well," I finally ventured, "the Bible has David killing Goliath."

"Yeah, but that was *Goliath*, who was going to lead an army to destroy their nation. Of course David killed him. But this was a helpless man lying in the street. And Nephi just *killed* him. Cut off his head. I mean, what was Joseph Smith thinking? And then it hit me— Joseph Smith didn't write it. I've read the Doctrine and Covenants and other things he wrote, and he's either very intelligent or he received it all by revelation. And if he was very intelligent, he wouldn't have started his book by having his main character kill an innocent man so he could rob him of his property. It makes no sense. And so—" Her voice trailed off.

"And so?" I asked.

"And so it hit me—Joseph Smith didn't actually write it. It happened the way he said it did—an angel gave the plates to him, and he translated them by the power of God. That's the best possible explanation. And then other proofs came to me. The whole notion of Christ appearing in America after his death, and then Joseph Smith quoting long passages in Christ's voice. I mean, who does that? Long *original* passages in the voice of Jesus Christ? And they hold up! They sound plausible. More than that—they sound right. And then it hit me again—really hit me—*this is true. This is all true.*"

Her hand was on the bed between us. I covered it with mine.

She was staring into space. "I was just sitting there, and this power came over me and filled me with warmth and happiness, and I knew. I mean, I absolutely *knew* it was true. And I just started crying. I couldn't help it, because . . . Travis, it's *all* true. Everything. It's just like Kevin said—if the Book of Mormon is true, then everything's true. And I knew it was true. Travis, I know that it *is* true."

She looked at me and took her hand from beneath mine and tenderly wiped away a tear that had run down my own cheek. "How does this happen?" she asked. "It's a miracle. That's all there is to it. And you know what? It's the only way you *can* know. It's the only way to really *know*. I've never felt anything like this in my life."

I didn't dare speak.

"The Holy Ghost is real," she continued. "Everything is real—all of it. Who would have guessed?" She smiled and shook her head. "I've never felt so much love and happiness wrapped up in one thing in my life. It's a whole new language."

When Anna got something, she really got it.

"So, what did Kevin think?"

"Oh, he believes it. When he saw me crying, he said he had been crying too, before I came in. And then before I left he said, 'You know now, don't you, Mom? You know it's true.' And I just said, 'Yes.' And then do you know what he did?"

"What?"

She took a moment to regain her composure. "He said, 'You're a good mom.'"

Anna and I both cried a little. For any mother to hear this was a treasure, but for a step mother it was almost beyond hope. I didn't say another word. I was full of love—full of gratitude for the Lord's grace, for Anna's conversion, for Kevin's perfect help.

For everything.

Chapter 49

Confession

Whislin Klah was lost. His world was turning upside down. One moment he felt sheer joy, but five minutes later he felt terror and panic. This book was killing him, but he couldn't put it down.

A memory kept stealing into his thoughts. In high school one day, he had been walking home when another kid walking with him had said something that made him angry. He didn't remember what the kid had said, only that it made his blood boil. He had turned to the kid with his left fist cocked—the Whistlin' Claw—but the kid had quickly thrown his hand up like a traffic cop and said, "Stop."

And Klah had stopped.

The kid said, "C'mon, I don't wanna fight. Let's just be friends."

Whislin never hit the kid, and had never been mad at him again, though they hadn't exactly been friends either. And now that had happened with Call; the man had put his hand out and said "Stop." And once again, he had stopped. He wondered if there was a way to find out if that other kid was a part of the same church. But more important than that was the *thing* that had made Klah stop and listen. What *was* that thing? Whatever it was, he was sure that it had also stopped him from going down into the canyon when he saw the old man.

And he felt that same power now, as he read the Book of Mormon. It was hard to understand in places (the Isaiah chapters made no sense *at all*), the language was archaic, and some of the stories were bizarre (people falling unconscious because they heard good things), but he couldn't deny the power that possessed him each time he opened it. More than once he had been brought to tears. What was going on?

By the time he finished the Book of Mosiah, he knew the book was true. The panic attacks had subsided, and he was acquiescing to this feeling of peace and truth, fearing it less and being willing to go where it took him. He wondered if this feeling, this power, was where Call had gotten his confidence to walk away from the five guns.

Now Klah wanted that peace forever, but there was a condition.

He had to share—"confess" was their word—his serious sins to someone with more authority than the "elders" had. Of course, he had been wondering since the day they met how the Church would react when they knew he had killed people. He had implied as much on that first day, but had never actually said it, so he had accepted a meeting with the mission president, who would come up from Phoenix to see him.

They sat in a small classroom on beige plastic chairs with shiny metal legs. President Cloward was a middle-aged man in a middle-sized body, partially bald, with wire-rimmed glasses perched on a thin nose. In his white shirt, blue tie, and gray suit, he looked like an accountant, which didn't bother Klah; he had known officers in the service who looked like accountants but could take your head off if you crossed them. What counted was on the inside.

President Cloward offered a prayer to open the interview, then he said, "So, you want to be baptized. That's a wonderful thing. Even Jesus was baptized. But you need to be prepared. You need to be willing to repent of all your sins, because when you go down into the water and come forth, you will be clean, as if you had never sinned before—so long as you are prepared. And that preparation involves confessing your serious sins to someone in authority."

Things were happening fast, but Klah didn't want to slow them down. Every time he opened that book he felt alive. And the one time he had been to church, just last week, another kind of revelatory experience came. People were friendly, but that didn't matter; closed-minded people could appear friendly at first, and kind people could come across as shy or reserved. Plus, he wasn't so kind himself. No, he just liked what he heard. A "Relief Society"? Yep, that sounded like something "Saints" might have. A day for fasting? No problem; he had gone three days without food twice in the SEALS. Serving your fellow man was only serving your God? Well, that made sense, if you believed in a loving God, which the writers of the Book of Mormon did. But more than that he had felt a quiet sincerity and power in the members' words, like when Call talked. A quiet but immovable confidence. Sincere truth.

So he was about to confess, and he wasn't going to cut corners. If this Church were true, if it were organized and led by God, if Jesus Christ really presided over it as the missionaries said, then he would do all in his power to become a member.

"Well," Klah said, "I suppose I do have a few serious sins to my credit. Maybe more than serious. I've killed people."

The president didn't flinch. Maybe he'd heard that before.

"All right, please tell me about it," he said, more kindly than Klah expected.

So, Klah told him about the killings in Iraq, which, after a few careful questions, the president cleared up as "part of the burden of war." Then he told President Cloward about the county official in Texas who had held up fracking operations.

The president sat back, appearing to reevaluate things. "Did you intend to kill him?" he asked, although Klah had already stated that he only meant to make the man sick, to scare him.

"No."

"Were you ever held accountable for this in any way?"

"No. Nobody knew what happened, except maybe my boss. But I didn't tell him either. But he's a smart guy, so he probably figured it out."

"And where is he now?"

"Well, I thought he was back East, teaching school, but when I did a search on him last week, just to make sure, it turned out he never showed up at school. They're still looking for him; so I don't know where he is."

"And, did he have a boss? Someone who paid him to pay you to do this thing?"

"Yes. But that guy's dead now. Someone else killed him. Of course, there could be others, but I don't know."

"And you had no involvement in that killing?"

"No."

"All right. Is there anything else?"

Klah told him about Keith Nelson, and how he had let Keith stay in the water longer than he should have.

The president sat back again and took a deep breath. "This is a serious problem, Whislin. "Did you intend to kill him?"

497

"No, but I meant to hurt him. I was mad. He was lying to me. Plus, he was making fun of my people."

"And did you ever confess this to the authorities? Do they know you did it?"

"No."

"So, basically, you just got away with it."

"Yes."

They were both quiet for a long moment, Klah wondering if this would be when he found out, once again, that organized religion was not for him, no matter how right it seemed.

"Mr. Klah," the president began, "You did the right thing in sharing this with me. It couldn't have been easy, and I'm sure you were tempted to keep this to yourself. Now, I can't go to the police and tell them what you've done. I have an obligation of confidentiality, but I think I know what the First Presidency of the Church will say when I ask them for permission to baptize you. They'll almost certainly tell me to tell you to make a full confession to the authorities, and when you have paid your debt to society, you will be able to apply for baptism again."

Klah didn't move. This was it. How well did he know that book was true? Was it all just good feelings, or were those feelings, as the missionaries had said, the Holy Ghost speaking to him? He consulted his heart and felt nothing but fear as he pondered the possibility of serving thirty years in prison.

"So, in order to get baptized, I have to go to the cops and tell them what I did."

"Yes, I'm certain that's what will be required."

"And if I do that, and they put me in prison, will I be able to get baptized then?"

The president shook his head, and for the first time a sadness fell across his face. "No, probably not until you've finished serving your sentence."

"But that might never happen. They might send me up for life."

"Yes—though I doubt it; not if you confess voluntarily."

Klah took a deep breath.

"I'm sorry," the president said. "I know this will be a difficult decision, and I'm willing to go to the First Presidency and ask for permission anyway, but I think I know what their decision will be."

Klah nodded, letting the impact of this sink in.

"But I want to stay in touch with you. You seem like a man of extraordinary honesty and courage—"

"Except when it comes to going to the cops about my murders."

"No, Brother Klah—may I call you 'brother'?"

Klah nodded.

"Maybe you didn't do the right thing then. I think we can safely say you didn't. But you are showing courage and honesty by sharing this now." His face softened, and a new light seemed to come into his eyes. "I'm going to encourage you to fast and pray about this. The scriptures are clear; we cannot gain entrance into the Kingdom of Heaven without baptism, so if you choose not to confess to the authorities, you cannot gain the salvation you now know is available through Christ. The way is strait and narrow, but it *is* the way—the only way. So think carefully about this. Now that you know that your Savior lives and loves you, you have to decide how much you love him and want to be with him." The president stopped speaking, and Klah saw tears in the man's eyes. "Brother Klah, I will be praying for you to make the right decision."

A new idea struck Klah, but he didn't feel he could share it with this good man now. He stood up and was embarrassed by how much taller he was than the little man with the big love. He put his hand out, and the president stood up to shake it.

"I thought we might have a closing prayer," the president said.

"Right. I'll do it. The missionaries showed me how." Klah folded his arms and closed his eyes. "Heavenly Father, President Cloward just said that I need to confess my crimes to the police, even if I have to go to jail. Please tell me what to do and please give me the courage to do the right thing. I want to go to heaven, but I don't want to go to prison. I just want to feel the same feelings I get when I read the Book of Mormon. In the name of Jesus, amen."

President Cloward put out his hand, and they shook again. "So, would you like me to appeal to the First Presidency, or do you want to go to the police, or do you just want to wait for a while?"

Klah had already made up his mind. "Let's wait. I think I have something else to do first."

He didn't say what it was, and the president didn't ask, but he added, "And I will fast and pray, like you said. Thanks for your help."

As they parted, Klah almost felt like he had made a new friend. A tough one, but a good one.

* * *

The night after Anna told me about her experience with the Book of Mormon, I found her upstairs reading it. We had put the kids to bed an hour earlier.

We both had to work the next day, so I would have to keep things short. She set the Book of Mormon on her lap and said, "It's like a new book—like I've never read it before. I just didn't get it."

I knew what she was talking about. The first time I had read the Book of Mormon, before my mission, I already believed it was the word of God, but it still had a sweet power that changed the way I looked at things. It put a new perspective on almost everything in my life.

There was a stuffed chair beside me, but I remained standing.

"It's a miracle, isn't it?" I said. "When the Spirit opens your eyes, you see everything differently."

"And more clearly." She looked at me almost wistfully. "And you knew this all along."

"Yes, I did."

"But you didn't, I mean you couldn't—" She didn't finish the sentence.

"No, I couldn't give that knowledge to you. Nobody could. Only God."

"Everybody should know this."

"Well," I said, "that's why I went on a mission." I let her think about that for a moment, about our obligations as bearers of a testimony, then I said, "There have been other miracles too."

"I know, Kevin—"

"Yes—but there are other things too. More than you know."

She cocked her head. "Oh?"

"I haven't told you everything about our trips to the Grand Canyon. I'm sorry, but I really haven't even scratched the surface. A lot happened there, and things are still happening, amazing things."

She set the book on the bed. "Oh?"

"I'm sorry. I just didn't feel it was the right time."

"But you think it is now?"

"I know it is. But it might take a while."

"Well, then, you better get started."

I hemmed and hawed for a moment then just launched into it. "When we were in the cave, we found some metal plates, a whole room of them, and they, well, they had writing on them that I recognized from the Anthon Transcript."

She thought about it, "You mean that paper with those symbols that you showed me?"

"Yes."

"Wait—you went to the canyon and found metal plates with writing on them?"

"Yes."

"Like the Gold Plates?"

"Sort of—pretty much. And then I started reading them, and I found . . ."

"Hold on." She sat up a little straighter. "You started *reading* them?"

I had to back up. Slowing down, I told her how Ross and I had taken thousands of pictures of the plates, and that in doing so we had found the page in the Book of Mormon that the Anthon Transcript had come from, and that by studying that page and following along in the Book of Mormon, I had been able to learn which characters stood for which word, more or less, and that eventually I was able to grasp the grammar and see how the language worked. "I seem to have a kind of gift for it," I said.

"You have a gift for something else. Understatement. Where are these pictures now?"

"Different places. On my laptop, and on hard drives in the bank."

She was quiet, and I had no idea what she was thinking—probably how crazy I must be, how crazy all of this was, but I wasn't about to stop.

"And so I called the stake president. Remember when President Whiting came over?"

She nodded.

"I told him about the plates, and I showed him the pictures, and the next day he called Salt Lake, and, well, anyway, we spoke to a secretary for the First Presidency."

"A secretary for the prophet?"

"Yes."

"And when were you going to tell me about all of this?"

"I know. I'm sorry. But I felt it wouldn't be right to tell you about this until, well, you know—"

"No, what?"

"Anna, I felt it wouldn't be right to show you proof of the Book of Mormon before you knew it was true for yourself. I think we all need to learn spiritual things by the Spirit, or we can always second guess ourselves—even question what we thought to be true. And so I've been praying for you to receive a witness—for a lot of reasons."

She quietly looked down at her hands, and I continued.

"When I think of the early Church leaders who fell away, like Oliver Cowdery, who actually saw the plates, and Sidney Rigdon, who had wonderful revelations, I realize just how fragile our knowledge can be. We can always doubt. We can always lose our faith. But the best way to maintain our faith is to place it upon the surest foundation, which is always the Spirit. I wanted you to have that foundation before you received a knowledge."

I half expected her to become upset, but she just raised a hand and motioned for me to come over, which I did. "I think you were right. It's better this way. It's stronger. But, what about everyone else? What about the people who see the proof you have?"

"We haven't shown the plates to anyone but President Whiting, though there are a couple of other people who know about them— but they don't know what's on them. But, you're right, I don't know what will happen to other people who see these things. Maybe no one else *will* see them. The secretary for the First Presidency didn't even believe us at first. Probably still doesn't. But he said he'd get back to us. So, we'll just have to see what happens."

"Where are the plates now? Where did you put them?"

"We didn't take them. They're still in the cave. We just took pictures of them."

"You left them in the cave? So, what, somebody else can take them?"

"Anna, they're really hard to find. And besides, that's why we called the Church, so the Brethren can decide what to do with them. But I don't think anybody else will be able to find them, even if we give them directions. Like I said, they're really hard to find."

"All right. When can I see them? The pictures, I mean."

"Right now if you want. They're on my computer downstairs, but I have some pictures on my phone too." I took it out of my pocket and began opening the gallery.

"Wait, you're walking around with pictures of the Golden Plates on your phone? What if you lost it?"

"They're not the Golden Plates, not the ones Joseph Smith had, but, I know. I've been careful."

I gave the phone to her, with a picture of the entrance to the cave. I had also loaded some pictures of the larger cave itself, as well as the plates. She began thumbing through them, and when she got to the first image of the massive cavern, she gasped.

"I know," I said. "It's incredible. It goes on forever. And look at those pictures of the roof. See that hanging curtain? You can't tell how big it is—it's bigger than, I don't know, a church. A big church."

"A temple."

"Yeah, it's that big—and it's *hanging from the ceiling*."

There were only a few pictures of the cave, and she soon got to the plates. She zoomed in on one of the pages.

"Wow. They do look like that transcript. Travis, this is amazing. This is incredible!" She got to the last picture. "How many are there?"

"Almost ten thousand."

She stared at me. Sometimes I think I can see the wheels turning in her head, her brilliant mind working through things, but this time I think I saw her brain stop, her computer-like mind overloaded.

"And you can read these things?"

"Yes, a lot of them. But there are eighty-three sets of plates, and I've only looked through two of them—oh, and some of them are in Hebrew. That's when we decided to call President Whiting. We think we found the Brass Plates, and they're in Hebrew, and—"

"Stop." She got up and stared at me. I had been standing next to her, but now she walked past me and started pacing toward the closet. She stopped, turned around, and looked at me again, then came back. She was walking in circles. I guided her to the edge of the bed, and we sat down. I put my arm around her. I remembered her doing the same for Kevin a few nights ago.

"I know, Honey. It's too much. And I have no idea why I found it. All I know is, we've been protected from people who want to harm us, even to kill us, and now I can read the plates. I can read reformed Egyptian. And they're just what Joseph Smith said they were—all these plates seem to be ancient records from the inhabitants of this continent. But Anna . . . I haven't told you everything yet."

She looked at me again, perhaps with some fear. "What—are you seeing angels too?"

"No, but I found a piece of an ancient stone that had been broken off, supposedly by an angel or a messenger, maybe even by Jesus himself when he was on the continent after his resurrection."

A low moan came from deep in her throat.

"Anyway, an old Hopi elder found me out there, and he said he'd been watching us, in his dreams I guess, and he said that it was from the Maasaw, who is this messenger, maybe Christ, and that there was a prophecy that someone would find it and bring it back to his people."

"And you're him?"

"No, no. I left it in the cave. He said his vision was wrong. So, I'm probably not the one they're waiting for. And besides, I don't know anything about them, and I really don't want anything to do with all that. But I thought you should know."

She stood up again, as if she needed space from me. She turned and looked down at me. "Travis, *what's going on?*"

"I wish I knew." I stood up and embraced her and was pleased that she didn't try to pull away. "I just hope somebody from the Church calls back soon. I can't wait to get this off my shoulders."

She leaned back and stared in my face. "You found these plates. You can read them—translate them. You know where this corner thing is. You're not getting out of this. You're right in the middle of it, and we both know that you're there for a reason."

My heart sank and my spirits lifted. Although I enjoyed translating the plates, I truly did want to put the burden on someone else, preferably the anointed servants of God who are actually called to be seers and revelators. But at the same time, I inwardly rejoiced that Anna understood and *believed*. She was with me. I could trust her. She *knew*.

I tried to hug her again, but she stepped back again. "So, what does Ross think about all this?"

"Ross? He's okay with it, but he says it's been hard not to talk about it, you know, not to show off a little to his friends."

"Show off? He might as well say he's the new prophet. Nobody's going to believe him anyway—unless . . ."

"Right, unless he shows them the pictures. Like we did with President Whiting. And *he* didn't sleep that night. And now we're trying to show them to the general authorities, maybe even the First Presidency. But then what? They *have* to believe us. We have *proof*. What's going to happen then?"

She stepped back into my arms.

"I'm scared, Travis."

"You think *you're* scared?"

We held each other, then, after a minute, we knelt and prayed. Then we tried to get to sleep, because, after all, we had work the next day. But we ended up talking long into the night, and I told her more about our trip through the canyon, and how my Lyme disease had diminished since my dip in the Little Colorado, or in the quicksand, or *somewhere along the way*, and how a gust of wind had saved me when I almost fell off a 400-foot outcropping above the Colorado River, and how I had once dangled over a seething pile of pink rattlesnakes, and how Ross had saved me more than once, and that he was clearly part of this whole thing too—thank goodness.

During this long monologue Anna occasionally broke in to ask things like "Travis, what now?" "Travis, do you think the Church will actually call you—and why haven't they already?" "Travis, what am *I* supposed to do?" And, finally, "Travis, what about the kids? Are they safe?"

All to which I answered, "I don't know."

Chapter 50

The Prophet of the Lord

The next day I was at work, half asleep, trying to bring my clients up to date on their portfolios, when the door opened.

Whislin Klah.

His dark hair was recently trimmed, and he had shaved. I looked at his hands but saw no gun. Of course, with those enormous hands he could just wring my little neck.

I didn't stand. "Good morning, Mr. Klah. It is *Klah*, isn't it?"

"You have a good memory."

"Not really, but I'll never forget *you*."

He came in and closed the door. "May I sit down?"

I had just gotten off the phone with a client and was about to compose an email to him explaining the finer points of a wonderful new portfolio some bright people in Nevada had just invented, but that could wait. "Absolutely, you can do anything you want."

He sat heavily, and I glanced at his hands again as they came together in his lap. His fingers were like thick ropes; his wrists were bigger than two-by-fours. A random thought popped into my mind about phone books.

"Three things," he said, reminding me that he always got to the point. "First, you can let me remove the software I put on your computer. I don't need it anymore."

I almost laughed. "By all means. I wouldn't want to keep something that's not mine."

He didn't smile.

"And something else. I want you to forgive me."

This caused a bit of alarm.

"I did wrong by you," he said. "I surveilled your house, and got inside and put bugs in there too, and then I tried to cement you inside the cave."

"Yes, you did," I said, wondering what new offense he was about to launch.

"And I did it for money, which is the worst thing. I didn't even hate you. In fact, if you want to know the truth, I kind of like you—even respect you."

I tried to appear as if I were pondering this somberly, when in fact I was wildly scanning the possibilities of new attacks. "Thank you. Does that mean those sorts of things have been, shall we say, terminated?"

He smiled. "Yeah, of course. At least one of the guys who hired my boss is dead, and my boss is missing. But besides, I decided to change course—I mean I decided to change."

My radar was still up. "Mr. Klah, if we hadn't found your friend, Richardson, he would have died in the cave. Then you'd be guilty of murder."

He nodded. "Right, so, that brings me to the other reason I'm here."

"What's that? But wait, first, how'd you get software on my computer? It's password protected."

"I used an eight-core Brutalis to crack it. No problem. It's kind of pricey, but it's worth it when time's of the essence."

"An eight-core Brutalis—whatever that is."

"You know, now that I think about it, I probably ought to get rid of that thing too."

"Good idea. So, what was the other reason you're here?"

He paused for a moment as if searching for the right way to say it. "You're a Mormon, right?"

That took me aback, but it was an easy question. "Yes, though we prefer to say member of the Church of Jesus Christ of Latter-day Saints."

"Right—I've been reading your book—the Book of Mormon. And I have some questions."

There are moments when you hope, nay, *expect*, the Spirit to come to your aid and whisper sweet answers to your mind. But that hadn't happened yet. I had absolutely no idea what was going on.

"Okay . . ."

"So, if somebody wants to get baptized, because they know the Book of Mormon is from God, but they've done some bad things, like killing people, but they want to repent, why can't they join the Church?"

"What?"

"I'm talking about me."

The man was almost as guileless as Ross, which was scary in itself. A murderer who was completely open about his work.

"Forgive me," I said. "I don't have the foggiest notion of what you're talking about."

"Okay, let me start over." He crossed one huge boot over the other. "When I was surveilling your family, I saw how often they went to church, and, well, that didn't mean too much, but then I saw how you guys lived, and then I met you—you know, out at the canyon."

"Yeah, believe me, I remember that."

"And your kid. What's his name—Kevin? He's great, but he killed that guy. What happened, did the old guy try something?"

I was now getting annoyed. "What can I do for you again?"

"Anyway, I saw how you—you know, you had a confidence about you, like some of the guys in the SEALS, and I couldn't intimidate you. You weren't scared. You know what I mean?"

"You mean I didn't *look* scared. I was terrified. You had that gun, remember? I didn't know what was going to happen."

"Yeah, but you didn't show fear, and neither did Keller. And I've thought about that. And remember, I was reading your emails, and you were always honest and straight with people. I liked that. That's what I try to do—even if I'm doing something they don't like. And then what you said, last time we met, about the Hopis watching. And you know what?"

"No. I know almost nothing."

"You were right. I went back there, and I was going to go down to the cave, but this old Hopi guy was watching me, probably an elder, like you said. He just showed up out of nowhere. And I knew I shouldn't go down there. I felt it in my bones, so I went back home, and guess who I ran into?"

I didn't attempt to answer. Just listening to the man was work enough.

"Your missionaries. And I started putting two and two together, you know, like this was a sign, 'cause the old man was there, like you said, and so I talked to them. And they had that same confidence you had. And then I, uh . . ."

He paused, but I didn't try to hurry him along. It was an opportunity for me to take stock and maybe catch up a little. He didn't appear to be a threat, but he also didn't seem wholly possessed of his faculties. We sat in silence, I trying to read his mind, and he likely doing the same with me, then he said, "I took their book and started reading about the Ammonites. You know who they are?"

"In the Book of Mormon?"

"Right."

"Okay—yes."

"So, anyway, I read the whole book, and something told me it was real, you know, that it was true, 'cause every time I opened it and started reading I felt that same good feeling, like it's from God, and so I took the lessons they said I had to take, and I told them I wanted to get baptized, but they said I had to confess my sins, so I did, to their mission president, and he said I couldn't get baptized until I confessed to the cops and paid my debt to society. But, I just don't get it."

If he had walked in and told me that he was an alien from Kolob, I couldn't have been more astonished. "What don't you get?"

"I read that part again, about the Ammonites, and how a bunch of the Lamanites came over and started killing them, just slaughtering them, and then some of the Lamanites felt bad about it, and they stopped killing people, and they were allowed to join the Church. Here, I marked it." He pulled his phone out and opened up to a screen with the scriptures on it. "Listen:

> "Now when the people saw that they were coming against them they went out to meet them, and prostrated themselves before them to the earth, and began to call on the name of the Lord; and thus they were in this attitude when the Lamanites began to fall upon them, and began to slay them with the sword. And thus without meeting any resistance, they did slay a thousand and five of them; and we know that they are blessed, for they have gone to dwell with their God. Now when the Lamanites saw that their brethren would not flee from the sword, neither would they turn aside to the right hand or to the left, but that they would lie down and perish, and praised God even in the very act of perishing under the sword— Now

when the Lamanites saw this they did forbear from slaying them; and there were many whose hearts had swollen in them for those of their brethren who had fallen under the sword, for they repented of the things which they had done. And it came to pass that they threw down their weapons of war, and they would not take them again, for they were stung for the murders which they had committed; and they came down even as their brethren, relying upon the mercies of those whose arms were lifted to slay them. And it came to pass that the people of God were joined that day by more than the number who had been slain; and those who had been slain were righteous people, therefore we have no reason to doubt but what they were saved. And there was not a wicked man slain among them; but there were more than a thousand brought to the knowledge of the truth; thus we see that the Lord worketh in many ways to the salvation of his people."

He looked up at me—as if I should say something.

"So?" I asked, and I meant it.

"So these murderers, the Lamanites, killed a thousand and five innocent people, but then a lot of them repented, and they joined the Ammonites—even more of them than the thousand and five they killed. So, I'm just wondering, why did they get to join the Church—but now that I want to, I have to go to the cops and maybe go to prison for the rest of my life?"

I grasped his dilemma, which was one I had never considered. "You're serious about this, aren't you? You know that God lives and that this is his Church."

He nodded. "Yes, I do. I've been fasting for, let me think—for just two days I guess, and I've been praying for help to know what to do. And I keep thinking I should come here and ask you. That's what came to me when I was talking to the mission president. So here I am."

This self-avowed murderer was now as childlike as any adult I knew, and he wanted answers with eternal truth, the kind any member of the Church should be able to offer. But the fact was, I didn't have the answers. "So, the mission president told you that you had to confess your crimes to the police?"

510

"Yeah, but he said he could ask the people in the First Presidency, and they would know for sure. But I told him not to do that, until I talked to you."

Not in a million years could I have anticipated this situation. But that was no surprise; my whole life had become one big unanticipated situation.

"Well," I said, hoping to tread water until an inspired thought showed up, "just so you know, my wife is an excellent defense attorney, so if you're going to go to the police about the incident with Keith Nelson, maybe you should talk to her first. But, first, what do you say we say a prayer?"

"Right now?"

"Yes." I came around my desk, and dropped to my knees.

He slipped out of his chair. Even kneeling he made me feel small. "You say it," he suggested.

It was as heartfelt as any prayer I had offered recently, which meant *very*. Toward the end Anna's face came to mind—and I ended the prayer. We both stood up, and I said, "I think the mission president is right. If you really want to join the Church, you'll have to confess first."

We sat down in front of my desk, in chairs half turned to face each other.

"Why?"

"Because the Lord expects it now. Society is different, and the Church needs to be able to work within the society. But the Lord will bless you. 'Blessed are the peacemakers, for they shall be called the children of God.' If you want to become one of the covenant children of God, you'll need to prove that you are a peacemaker by making peace with the families you hurt, and that will mean going to the authorities and accepting their judgment."

"That's going to be hard."

"Yes, but remember, also 'Blessed are the meek.' We all have to bend the knee in humility before we can learn to live in righteousness. Now, I have a suggestion for you, actually a couple of them."

"Besides giving myself up?"

"Yes. First, I think you should prepare yourself to pay restitution. You've taken the lives of people who had loved ones and were participating in society. You've taken them away from us, and I think you should be prepared to pay restitution. I don't know how much money you have, but you should be prepared to offer it as a poor recompense to society."

"But I'll be broke."

I almost smiled. "Don't worry, I think the state will be taking care of your needs for a while." I was surprised by how well he took this. "And second, I think you should talk to my wife. She's a great defense lawyer, and she'll be able to get you the best possible deal."

"How much does she cost?"

"Don't worry about that."

He hung his head over his clasped hands. He had come for two reasons; one, because he felt impressed to, and two, because he was hoping I would give him easier counsel than the mission president had. But the counsel of truth is always consistent. What I didn't know was how Anna would react to my offer to him.

So I took a moment and texted Anna at work and asked her to give me a call when she could. The call came almost right away. I stepped into my conference room and closed the door and told her what was happening. She was amazed, but not totally surprised. Very little surprised us now days.

"I told him to be prepared to give everything he has in restitution," I said.

"How much does he have?"

"I don't know, but I saw him get fifty-thousand dollars from Richardson's car."

"Are you convinced he's sincere?"

"Yes, but I guess we'll know for sure if he's willing to give everything up, even his freedom, to do the right thing."

"All right, tell him I'll talk to him. But, Travis, be careful. People in his situation can have wild mood swings."

"All right, but I think his mood will improve when he eats something. He's been fasting for two days."

"Amazing."

We hung up, and I went back to Whislin. "Where are you staying?" I asked.

"I don't know. I came right here. I drove all night."

I pondered the nuances of the situation. Did I dare offer him a place to stay? Could I possibly justify that to Anna or the rest of my family?

Of course not.

"What do you think about paying restitution?" I asked.

"Mr. Call. I just want to do the right thing. I've always fought for myself—for everything I got. But everything that's happened—and that book—it's changed me. I've never felt anything like this. So, if they want all my money, they can have it. If they want my condo and my Jeep, they can have it all. I just want to get things right in my life."

We had a large house, six bedrooms. But they were all full. Ross had been staying in the guest room for over a month, and he was welcome to it as long as he wanted.

"You're welcome to stay with us," I said, "but you'd have to share a room with Ross."

"Keller?"

"Yes."

Before I knew it, he was standing up and grabbing me, either in a death embrace, or a love embrace, but either way it was painful.

"Thank you," he said, fairly lifting me off the floor. He relaxed his grip, and I inhaled a lungful of air. "I just felt like I should come here, because I wanted to get to know you better. You're a good man, Mr. Call."

I straightened my shirt. "And when did you start calling me Mr. Call? I'm Travis to you, and next time warn me before you try to give me an adjustment."

"Oh, sorry." He backed up a step. "It's just that, there's something special about your family, even Keller, I mean Ross. You guys live by different rules—and it *works*."

I asked for another minute alone, and I went back into the conference room and called Anna. Belatedly now, I asked her if Whislin Klah could stay with us. After a long silence, she said no. Now I had a dilemma. But I said nothing. This was her call.

After another long silence, she said, "Travis, are you sure?"

I told her I was sure that he was sincere and that he would need a place to stay while she worked out some kind of deal with district attorneys in two different states.

"Travis, this is hard. Our children—"

"Yes, and Rosemary. And Ross will have to share a room with him. But you know what keeps coming to mind, besides that you should represent him?"

"What?"

"The parable of the Good Samaritan. In a way, we're kind of picking him up off the road."

"The road to sin and death," she said.

"Yes, that too."

"Do you know what this reminds me of?"

"No."

"Eight years ago. Remember?"

I would never forget. Ross had been accused of murdering my wife—and to the astonishment of all concerned, including my new lawyer, Anna Kohlberg, and the media, and the world watching, I had let him stay with us.

"They're even about the same size," she said.

"Right, they've both got the hearts of giants."

She agreed that we could give him shelter and food and whatever hospitality we could muster, as long as he didn't try to kill us again. I thanked her and went back in to see Klah.

"Well," I said, "I haven't spoken to Ross yet, but I think he'll be okay—you're welcome to stay with us."

He hung his head again, still sitting, and I saw a tear fall from his face. The man had become a child, and I knew I would never underestimate the power of God, or the Book of Mormon, again.

As Whislin sat and waited, I wrote the email to my client, and then, as I was about to shut down the computer, Whislin said, "No, I gotta take that software off before you close out."

So, I got up and let him take over my computer. As he sat down and started digging into the software, he said, "So, I guess this means you forgive me?"

I laughed and said yes.

"Thank you. That means a lot."

He typed and clicked the mouse for a while, and I texted Ross with the news.

He texted back: "I always wanted a roommate, but I hoped it would be a woman. LOL."

He was onboard.

"Okay, it's off," Whislin said, pushing back from the desk. "I don't ever plan to use that software again."

"Good."

"Yeah, and it's a good thing we're going over to your house, 'cause I'm *really* starving. Fasting is hard work."

This was going to be very interesting.

* * *

Kevin recognized him immediately.

"You're the dude who watched our house!"

"Yeah," said Klah. "That was me. And you're the kid that shot that bird out front. You're a good shot." We had just come in and were standing in the living room. Anna wasn't home yet, and Mia and Lucas were in the family room watching a show.

Kevin got quiet. Being a good shot entailed things he'd rather forget. But Kalley looked at him with a resolve I hadn't seen in her eyes before. "Are you the man who tried to hurt my Daddy?"

He nodded silently.

"But why? He's my Daddy."

Klah stole a glance at me, but I figured the kids deserved an answer.

"Because somebody paid me to watch your dad and make sure he didn't go to the Grand Canyon."

"Yeah, but he did it anyway. You couldn't stop him."

"I know. He was too smart. He kept getting away when I wasn't looking."

"And sometimes when you were looking," Ross added.

Whislin smiled. "Yeah."

"So, how come ya didn't want him to go to the Grand Canyon?" Kalley persisted.

"Because the guy I was working for wanted to protect some things that your dad knew about, but that's all over now. Nobody's trying to hurt your dad now—or anyone else. And if they do, I'll stop them. I just want to be friends now." He put his enormous hand out to her. "Can we be friends?"

She looked over at me. I nodded.

She took his hand and let him shake it.

"Whislin is going to stay with us for a while," I said. "if that's all right with everybody." Kevin kept his eyes on Whislin but didn't answer.

"How do you feel about that, Kevin?" I had no idea what he was thinking until he said, "I threw the slingshot out. I don't shoot things anymore."

Whislin sat on the edge of the couch and looked Kevin in the eye. "Neither do I, because I threw my gun out. Here—" He offered his huge hand to Kevin, who paused before taking it. "Can we be friends too?"

"Yeah, I guess so."

515

"Good." They shook.

Then Whislin stood up and turned to Ross. "Thank you for understanding—and for forgiving me. I have a long road ahead of me." He held his hand out. Ross stepped over to him and engulfed him in an awkward embrace that looked like two grizzly bears trying to dance.

"Hey," I said, "Whislin is hungry. Do you think we can find something for him to eat before dinner?"

Rosemary had been watching the scene with a critical eye. Anna had told me that she would explain everything to her, but I still didn't know what her reaction would be.

As Ross led the others into the kitchen, I stayed behind with Rosemary. "He's taken the missionary lessons," I said, "and he wants to be baptized. He's about to lose all of his money, and he needed a place to stay."

"That's what Anna said, but can he be trusted? He's going to prison, isn't he?"

"Yes, almost for sure. But he's been fasting for two days, and I thought we could help him out. But if you're not comfortable, I'm sure we can make arrangements—"

"What? Kick me out of my own house? No, if anybody's leaving, it's you, because you keep picking up strangers." She turned and went into the kitchen to supervise the mayhem Whislin and Ross were about to perpetrate.

Anna came home at her regular time, met Whislin for the first time, and remained gracious and soft-spoken as the family sat down for Whislin's second dinner. After the kids went to bed, Ross and I sat with Whislin and answered questions about the Book of Mormon, the Church, and the hereafter. He knew about the plates but didn't understand their significance to the Book of Mormon or the Church—and we left it at that.

All in good time—maybe.

Upstairs, Ross had already inflated an air mattress, and he insisted on Whislin taking the queen bed. Whislin argued, saying that he was used to sleeping on the ground, but Ross would have none of it. "I don't care if you *are* an Indian, it's my room, and I get the floor!"

As a chagrined Whislin Klah got ready for bed, Ross came out into the hallway with me.

"He's changed. He really means it," Ross said under his breath.

"I know. It's wonderful. And the thing is, I think the miracles are just beginning."

* * *

Neither Salt Lake nor President Whiting had called back, so I had no idea where things stood, or if they stood anywhere at all. For all I knew, I had been dismissed as a fringe element, which I probably was. That night, after Anna was asleep, I pulled my laptop over and began scrolling through the pictures again. I went past the Brass Plates and began opening new sets. I loved this ability to read so many of the characters, and occasionally I would stop to try to tease out the meaning of an unfamiliar character, but unless I could see a translation in the Book of Mormon, it was usually impossible.

It was almost midnight when I opened yet another set of plates. The first character stopped me. It looked familiar, but I couldn't recall its meaning. I went on to the second character and saw another familiar character, one I knew: "First." Over the course of translating I had begun drawing each new character as I came to it. After drawing it two or three times, each character stuck in my mind. I went on to the third character and thought I recognized it as "Book," but I wasn't sure. I got out of bed, put on my robe, and went down to my office, where my notebook of characters was.

There it was, on the first page—"Book." It was the second character in the first line on the plate: "The Book of Ether," or, as the characters were arranged on the plate, "Ether Book," or "Ether's Book." I went back to the computer and saw three characters on the first line, not two: "[Something] First Book." I turned back to my notebook. I knew I had seen that first character before, but where? I began flipping through the pages, scanning the characters and their translations. After going through a dozen pages, I began growing tired. It was getting late, but I persisted. I was almost sure I had seen it before, which meant I had written its translation somewhere in the notebook. I kept scanning the pages, using my forefinger to make sure I focused on every character. My eyes were getting heavy when I saw the familiar markings at the bottom of page 19—the very last character of Ether 8:21:

> And they have caused the destruction of this people
> of whom I am now speaking, and also the destruction
> of the people of Nephi.

The character was "Nephi," a word I had seen twice in the Book of Ether.

A rush of adrenalin brought me fully awake. The first character at the top of the plate was "Nephi." The second was "First." And the third and last character was "Book."

Nephi First Book.

Or:

"The First Book of Nephi."

I stared at it, the characters on my screen almost blurring in my emotions. The second line was just as short: "His Reign and—" I didn't recognize the third character, but I didn't need to. I opened my Book of Mormon to the first page of First Nephi, and read the second line: "HIS REIGN AND MINISTRY."

I had found the first book of the Book of Mormon.

My eyes raced down the plate, looking for assurance of this. Familiar characters stood out: "Nephi...good parents... taught... father...having seen many [unknown]...I make a record of my [unknown] in my days." It was clearly the first verse of First Nephi, chapter one. But when I looked back at my Book of Mormon, I stopped. Something was wrong. The introduction was missing. The entire paragraph that either Nephi or Mormon, or, possibly, Moroni had written, was missing. The text on the plate, reading from right to left, went: "THE FIRST BOOK OF NEPHI / HIS REIGN AND MINSTRY / I, Nephi, having been born of goodly parents..."

So this was an *altered* copy of the book, not the same version given to Joseph Smith by the Angel Moroni. Clearly, then (and almost gratefully), these were not the actual plates that Joseph had translated from.

But it was still the First Book of Nephi, which meant the Second Book of Nephi would probably follow, and the Book of Jacob, and so on. I bookmarked the page and scrolled forward, plate after plate, until I came to the words: "Nephi Second Book." There it was, "The Second Book of Nephi." I continued scrolling until I came to another chapter heading. It said: "[Unknown] Book," or "The Book of [Unknown]." I quickly raced through my notes and discovered that I had never come across the character for "Jacob." I read the next sentence on the plate: "For behold, it came to pass that fifty and [unknown] years…" I checked it against the Book of Mormon, which said, "For behold, it came to pass that fifty and five years had passed away from the time that Lehi left Jerusalem…" I had now clearly found the Book of Jacob, which followed the Second Book of Nephi, which followed the First Book of Nephi. I went ahead and found the Book of Enos, and all the other books, until coming to the Words of Mormon. For some reason, the Book of Ether was on another set of plates I had already been through. Also, the Book of Moroni was missing.

Perhaps this was a copy of the records made by Mormon, before his son Moroni began adding to them. I would have to go through in greater detail, which meant I had many more characters to learn, which meant I would have to spend many, many more hours of diligent searching.

I pushed back from the computer and thought about this. Joseph Smith had translated all this, and more, in two months. It was beyond comprehension.

But not belief.

I looked at the clock.

3:15.

I had to get to bed. I shut everything down and turned off the light. As I was going upstairs, I thought about opening the door to Ross's room and seeing how the two men were doing. But I chose to leave them alone. Everything had been quiet, and Whislin had endured a very long day. He needed his sleep.

* * *

Whislin hadn't asked about the plates, what they meant and why I felt so strongly about them. That changed the next morning after we read from the Book of Mormon as a family. I had hoped to get to the office early again, to continue serving my clients again, yes, but mostly to begin digging into First Nephi, but, being fatigued, I had been slow, and Whislin grabbed me before I could get out the door.

"Hey, I was just wondering—those plates you guys took pictures of, are they like the plates that Joseph Smith had?"

There it was. With a prayer in my heart, I said. "We think they are. We think they might be from your people, from a couple of thousand years ago. We're still learning about them."

"No wonder you don't want anybody messing with them."

"That's right. If they're what we think they are, they're incredibly important—far more valuable than their weight in gold."

"So, what are you going to do with the pictures?"

"For now, I'm just studying them, trying to learn what they are for sure." I was afraid he was going to ask me if I had learned how to read them, which would require a very delicate answer, as I didn't want to shade his own testimony of the Book of Mormon. I spoke again before he could ask anything.

"Whislin, how do you feel about the Book of Mormon now, I mean after you've had a chance to think about it—and after you've had a chance to think about what the mission president told you? Do you still think it's true?"

Anna had just joined us, with briefcase in hand. He looked at Anna then back at me. "It has to be, right? It changed me. I mean, look where I'm at. I locked you in a cave. I killed people—accidentally—but still, they're dead because of me, and look where I am now. I'm in your home, trying to learn more, trying to get stronger. I know that book is true."

Anna set her briefcase down. "So, how do you feel about following the mission president's counsel to go to the police?"

"You mean going to prison for the rest of my life?" He still had his Book of Mormon in his hand. "Sometimes I still think about the Ammonites. They didn't have to go to prison. Of course, I get it that it was during a war, and killing in war is different, but still—" We were in the living room, which was near the front door. He lowered himself to a chair, as if weak from the prospect before him.

Anna sat on a couch across from him, and I joined her. Work, and translation, could wait.

"Listen to me, Whislin," Anna said. "You don't know how long your sentence will be. You don't know if it will be for the rest of your life. The police don't have any evidence that you killed Keith Nelson. We could ask for a deal in exchange for a confession. If you want me to represent you, I'll keep your name confidential as long as I can."

His great head remained motionless, the lines heavy in his face, his short black hair as thick as wires. "Eternity is a long time," he said. Then, after a pause he added, "Too long to spend in hell. Alma the Younger spent three days there and wanted to be extinguished, both body and soul. I guess I'd rather spend a long time here in prison rather than even three days in hell."

This was Anna's invitation to make her offer. "So, Whislin, I'd like to represent you—*pro bono*, of course. I do think there's a good chance we can get a deal."

He didn't move, his face inscrutable, his massive body a block of stone. I couldn't imagine what was going through his mind—indeed, what had been going through it for days.

Anna continued: "I know the prosecutors here, and I know what they want. The D.A. is running for office in Sacramento this fall, so he'll want to show some muscle, but then what else is new? We'll just tell him he can have something, or he can have nothing. It's his choice. He can have a conviction to wave before the public, or he can continue to have an unsolved murder case. When I present the deal to him, I won't tell him anything about you, except that you are willing to confess for reasons of conscience. If you want, I can also tell him that you committed another unintentional homicide in Texas, but I won't tell him where or when. I'll let him stew on that. He can break two cases, or none. But if he wants the conviction, he'll have to agree to our terms."

"Which are?" Whislin's voice, usually full and direct, had nearly cracked.

"Which are: First, you will stipulate to the homicide, or homicides, and offer any evidence you may have, which will probably be nothing more than a knowledge of the killings, including details nobody else has. Then they'll know you're not a kook out for some twisted publicity. Second, you'll turn over the names of those who employed you, and why. Basically, you'll give these people up so their offices can go after bigger fish."

"If I do that, they'll know about the cave—and the plates."

Anna looked back at me.

"He's seen the pictures of the plates and knows how valuable they are." I turned to Whislin. "We're concerned about that, but we want what's best for you. Maybe there will be a way to do this without revealing too much about the cave. I think—I hope—the Lord will open a way for us to do both, to help you and protect the plates."

"Maybe He'll put his blessing on it," he said. "Like when nobody could find the Gold Plates except Joseph Smith—for over a thousand years."

He had definitely done his homework.

"Yes, I hope so. After all, the plates in the cave have been protected this long so far."

Anna said, "Whislin, is there anything else you can offer to them?"

"Well, tell them I'll empty my bank accounts and sell my condominium and Jeep and everything else and give the money to the families."

"Just so we know," she asked, "how much might that amount to?"

"I'm not sure, but it's over a quarter million. It would have been a hundred thousand more if I'd been paid for my last job."

I stared at him. "You were going to get a hundred thousand for killing me?"

"And Keller. Actually more." He smiled, and his big rack of healthy white incisors set me back. "But let them know that I'll tell them where the accounts are, and they can have it all."

The financial counselor in me suddenly reared its ugly head. "Now, Whislin, you know that if you give them everything you have, you'll have nothing left when you get out."

"That's not true," he said, growing pensive. "I'll have my life back. I'll have eternity back. I'll have everything."

Maybe the man was more converted than I was. At a minimum, he had a perspective I would do well to achieve.

Anna touched his arm and gave him a smile of her own. "We can do that, Klah. If you'll authorize me to represent you, we can make a solid case for accidental manslaughter—man one."

He considered this. "How much time?"

"We'll ask for five years on each," Anna said, "to be served concurrently. The two prosecutors, here and in Texas, will have to agree, or no deal."

"Five years?" he said. "Is that all? Is that enough?"

That surprised me. "Enough for what?"

"For me to be forgiven?"

Again I was guilty of thinking temporally when Klah was thinking eternally. "All the Church demands," I replied, "is that you pay your debt to society, whatever that is. If you're sentenced to five years, or something less than that for good behavior, that's what you will be expected to serve. Of course, on top of that, you'll have to show continuing contrition and penitence for what you've done, then a bishop will review your case and it will be sent to the First Presidency's Office."

"No, I mean is it enough for God? Is it enough for the men, and their families, to forgive me?"

Anna spoke. "Don't worry about that. God will forgive you. Maybe the families won't, not in this life, but once they get to the other side and realize that forgiveness is the key to lasting peace, I'm sure they will."

He almost seemed surprised by this. "Do you know that?"

"It only makes sense," she said, "because if they don't, they will be guilty of the greater sin. The scriptures are clear—forgive people their trespasses, all of them, or you'll be guilty of the greater offense." Anna had been doing her homework too.

"Five years?" he said, almost under his breath. "Do you think they'll go for it?"

"Not at first. But they might come around."

"Why?"

"Because they have no choice. They have absolutely nothing right now. Your confession would be a gift. Plus, according to your own admission, both crimes were in fact *accidental.* You didn't intend to kill either man."

"No, but what I did wasn't an accident—just the results were."

"A point they will be sure to make, but again, they can take the offer or leave it."

"In which case I do what?"

"If they don't go for it?"

"Yes."

"Let's cross that bridge when we come to it."

He looked at her, perhaps thinking through the ramifications of confessing and spending years in prison, or of a life outside God's covenant if he didn't. Then he turned to me. "What would you do, Travis?" The softness in his voice touched me, sounding more like friendship than desperation.

"I would do it, because I think it's the right thing to do."

He rose to his feet. "All right, then, let's go."

The man didn't let grass grow under his feet.

Anna laughed. "No, Whislin. It doesn't work like that. First, I'll prepare our agreement, allowing me to represent you, then I'll write up the offer for the D.A. Give me a few hours, okay?"

"Oh, sorry."

"First, I'll call Johnson and make sure he's in. He'll want to be a part of this, and he might even provide the muscle we need to get the D.A.'s office to bite." Whislin didn't respond, silently urging her on.

She hurried out of the room. "I'll call the office and tell them I have an emergency."

Maybe this had been an emergency, but it almost felt as if the fire had already been put out.

Whislin looked around the room. "You know, the night I let myself in here, it seemed a lot bigger."

"I find that if I keep my wants and desires small, people don't try to take them from me."

The large toothy grin flashed again. "I'm going to tell you something: You're a good guy, but you have an even better wife. How'd you get her?"

"We killed someone together."

He laughed out loud, a huge bellowing laugh, louder, perhaps, than anyone had ever laughed in my home, and I marveled that it came from a condemned man. Maybe he had read old media reports of what Anna and Ross and I had done, but he didn't ask about it. Instead, he put his hand out, and I gave him my hand, hoping he wouldn't crush it. "Yep, you're a good man, Brother Call! And you just wait. In five years, I'll be asking you to baptize me!"

Rosemary stuck her head in the room, a scowl on her face. I still wasn't sure how keen she was on Whislin staying with us. "Is everything okay in here? It sounds like a couple of children carrying on."

Whislin laughed. "Everything's fine."

* * *

Anna went down to the District Attorney's office that afternoon and met with Price Moffat, the man with political ambitions. Anna adroitly introduced the offer, which Moffat quickly declined. If she had the murderer, he said, she was duty-bound as an officer of the court to produce him. She agreed, adding that since she represented him she also was duty-bound to get him the best deal she could, and if the geniuses in Modesto were too proud to play ball, she would take her offer to a court in Texas, where she was sure a D.A. would be happy to close a case that no one even knew existed, thereby making *that* D.A. a hero whom the locals could vote for again. Moffat said he would get back to her when he had more information, meaning that he would frantically search for the killer's identification so he would have more leverage.

He called back two days later. I wasn't there, but she told me the story.

Certain pressures, he said, demanded that he consider the deal—if she would agree to seven years. She informed him that she would have to hang up because she was about to buy two tickets for Midland, Texas. (This location was all she would give him about the Texas crime.) Moffat asked her to hold on. She gave him fifteen seconds. He came back in thirty saying he didn't know how she could live with herself, what with four young children and a nice home to think about—how could she justify putting a murderer back on the street in just five years. She said she actually expected him to spend only three to four years after good behavior. He moaned. He whimpered. He made the deal.

Of course, part of it was that the D.A. in Texas agreed to the same arrangement, but Anna had already spoken with him and knew that Klah's confession would be welcome there since the Midland D.A.'s office didn't even know what mysterious crime she was referring to. The death of the county commissioner had been declared a natural death by heart attack, which meant she and Klah were about to rewrite local history. She spent fifteen minutes on the phone with the Midland D.A., received a fax from him to the effect that he agreed to her terms, she told him the details. He didn't moan or whimper; he just whistled a long, shrill Texas whistle, then said, "You know, I always thought there was something fishy about that one, but the coroner gave it a clean bill of health—so to speak."

She told me to come home early, and I did, which was becoming all too common, and she and I went up to Ross's bedroom to inform Klah of the deal. I was enjoying watching her work. She was a bulldog—polite, kind, tactful—but always unrelenting. It was heartening to see her exercising her formidable gifts on someone else.

I knocked on Ross's door and entered at Klah's husky bidding. Ross was out. Klah was sitting on the bed reading *The Miracle of Forgiveness.* I raised an eyebrow. "Be careful, Klah. You might find that you've committed more crimes than you thought."

He thumbed back a few pages. "Yeah, there's a list here of all the sins you can commit. I'm pretty sure I'm guilty of all of them."

"Thank goodness for baptism," Anna said, stepping in behind me. "Believe me, I know."

I raised my eyebrows. She just smiled.

Klah already had his bags packed—to be put in storage. His Jeep was at a local consignment lot that would take 10% of the sales price. Just that morning he had DocuSigned papers giving a realtor in Flagstaff authority to sell his condo. He had previously signed over a power of attorney to Anna to handle the income from all the sales. She would place it in an escrow account and distribute it as the judge dictated.

Anna gave him the news.

He started to stand up, then he sat back down. He put his head in his hands. "So, it's really happening."

I couldn't tell if he was happy or sad.

"I'm really going to jail today."

He wasn't happy.

"Jail today," Anna said, "but prison soon. But like I told Moffat, I expect you to get out early."

"Early to you is still three or four years to me."

It was a humbling thought.

"When do we go?"

"Now. As soon as you're ready. Moffat's waiting."

He sighed and raised his head. There were tears in his eyes. "Okay, let's do it. The sooner I get in, the sooner I get out. And the Book of Mormon is still true." He stood up. "They'll let me have a copy, won't they?"

"I'll make sure you get one," Anna said.

The man was a giant in more ways than one. He took nothing but the clothes he was wearing. On the way downtown, Anna rehearsed what was going to happen—but it basically came down to confess and go to jail.

When we got to the District Attorney's office, Captain Johnson was a no-show.

"We caught a break," Anna whispered. "Johnson left yesterday for a two-week vacation to Hawaii—with his new wife."

I hadn't kept up. Evidently the man had his own life to attend to. "Why's that a break?"

A court stenographer was setting up for the hastily called interview. I wouldn't be allowed in, but I intended to wait as long as possible in a nearby waiting area. "Because," Anna whispered, "I don't know if Moffat knows about the cave. Johnson may have kept all that to himself, because he couldn't find any evidence that it existed. I've told Whislin to let me help him if Moffat brings it up."

She and Klah were ushered into the room, which had also been hooked up for a Skype connection with Midland, Texas. I was ushered into the waiting area. I had my phone and tablet to keep me busy. It was a little after two.

Over the next three hours I called clients, trying to reassure them that I was still monitoring their portfolios. Most of the calls were pleasant and positive, no doubt helped by the continuing bull market.

When Anna came out, she was alone. I looked for Whislin through the door but didn't see him.

"Come in," she said.

He was standing at the back of the room, with two deputies flanking him. His hands were cuffed behind him, which surprised me.

"Why's he cuffed? He came in voluntarily." I myopically walked past Anna and went to Whislin. He spoke before she did.

"It's all right—it's a compliment. They think I'm stronger than them. And they're right."

"Yes," I said, "but you're not a flight risk."

"Not now, but who knows when I get out in the hallway." He looked at Moffat, a few feet away, and wiggled his eyebrows. I would have laughed if things weren't so serious."

"This is interesting," Moffat said. "I thought Klah was your wife's client. What brings you here?"

This told me all I needed to know. Klah hadn't said anything about my involvement, which meant he might not have said anything about the cave. My mind raced for an answer. "Come on, counselor, not all of my wife's clients are bad men."

"That's true. Some of them are bad women—and I think she's even had a few bad juveniles. How do you feel about murderers going free after a few years?"

I sensed a movement from Whislin, but he managed to restrain himself from talking.

"I think some people change, especially if they have a conscience. Tell me, how many murderers do you know who offer to give all they have in restitution?"

He glanced at Klah, perhaps making sure he had remained constrained. "It looks good now, but we'll see if he still has a conscience when he's out on the streets again."

I turned away from the man who made his living by condemning others—most, of course, who deserved it, but some, no doubt, who didn't. I couldn't shake Whislin's hand, and embracing him would have been awkward, so I just stood in front of him. "You're a better man than I am, Whislin. I'm not sure I could do this."

When he spoke, his voice cracked. Either it was emotions, or his voice was giving out after hours of interrogations. "I'm not as good as you think. Like I said, it's probably a good thing these cuffs are on me."

"I'll visit you often."

"No, you take care of business. But when I'm out, you and I have an appointment, right?"

"Right, just as soon as we get approval from above." I didn't care if Moffat possibly thought some mischief was going on. I stepped over to Whislin and decided to finally squeeze his enormous torso, which actually didn't work, because his torso, when combined with his two arms, was far too much for me to reach around.

A tear landed on my face. It wasn't mine.

"I'm glad—" he said.

I let go and looked into his red eyes. "You're glad?"

"I'm glad you're still alive." He glanced at Anna then back at me. "You're the best people I've ever known."

Anna came over and tried to help me hug him again.

The two guards stepped in and each took an arm, separating him from us.

"I'll be by tomorrow," Anna said, with a stronger voice. "And I'll make sure you're being treated right."

"Don't worry," said Moffat, closing his briefcase. "We'll be on our best behavior too. Don't want to mistreat our local murderers." I wondered if the man had an ounce of empathy.

Klah was taken out of the room.

On the way home, the car felt empty.

"It's hard to believe he's gone for years," I said. "He won't be coming home until the twins are in high school."

Anna glanced over at me, a question in her eyes. "Home?"

I was beginning to see Whislin Klah, former murderer, as part of the clan now. He was ours, or we were his. He had been quiet at times, but he hadn't been moody. He hadn't laughed much, but he hadn't been melancholy either. And when he discovered that the gospel was true, he had been as straight and true as any man I knew in striving for its blessings, no matter the cost. The Ammonites had once laid their lives down rather than risk their eternal lives by hurting others. Whislin Klah, possibly a distant son, was willing to do likewise, to lay his own body down for the demands of justice, and when that law was fulfilled, the waters of baptism would be waiting for him.

"In the confession," I asked, "did he say anything about the cave?"

"It never came up," Anna said. "Like I thought, Moffat didn't know anything about it. He asked why Rodney Winn had paid Richardson to pay Klah to kill Nelson, and Klah said they weren't paid to kill Nelson; they were paid to get the jewelry that Nelson was selling online. He said he killed Nelson by accident when Nelson made some crack about a medicine man. And he said that he didn't realize that Nelson was unconscious when he rolled into the water."

"So the police—Johnson—didn't tell Moffat about the jewelry coming from the canyon?"

"If they did, he didn't bring it up. I think Johnson just kept it to himself because he just didn't believe it."

"Maybe he'll bring it up to Moffat when he gets back."

"Maybe. But remember, Nelson's death was officially ruled an accident. Why would Johnson be thinking about it two months later? In two weeks even the D.A.'s office won't be thinking about it."

I was driving. The sun had just set and soft pastels were painting the sky.

"Do you know what I think?" she said.

"What?"

"I think the Lord is still protecting the cave. I think Moffat's mind was clouded about the whole thing—the jewelry, where Nelson got it, and why he was selling it on the dark web."

That made sense. In the Lord's perfect timing, where there is only now, his protection always existed.

"Travis?"

"Yes."

"Do you think there's anyone else?"

"Besides Whislin? Besides Winn?"

"Yes."

"I don't know, but if there is, he's taking a long time showing up."

"Maybe he's just waiting to see if we talk about the cave."

"Maybe. And maybe it's not a 'he.' Maybe it's a they."

This brought a sobering chill to the conversation. We truly had no idea what the future would bring. But we all saw the need for discretion in speaking of the cave.

"When do you think the Church will get back to you?" she asked.

"Actually, I've been surprised that they haven't gotten back already—that is, until I saw a story from the Church this morning."

"What did it say?"

"That the prophet and other leaders just got back from a tour of the Far East. Maybe they needed to wait until the prophet got back. Maybe the matter has gone that high."

There was a sense of finality when she spoke: "Well, it should. This is big medicine." A sigh escaped her lips. "I'm starting to think like Whislin now."

We drove past the stake center. The parking lot was empty. No cats.

"You know," she said, "I think I'm really going to miss that guy."

* * *

I studied the plates for too long that night. Many of the characters in Nephi's book were new to me, which was proof that the man who had written them was not the same man who had written the Book of Ether. There were different phrases, different patterns of speech, even, at times, different nuances of grammar. As I came to recognize the differences, I felt the ancientness of Ether's text, which was a little strange considering that Nephi's writings were themselves 2,700 years old. The Book of Mormon was a marvelous work—indeed a marvelous work and a wonder—and the more I dug into this great, first book, the more marvelous it became.

* * *

The phone call came the next morning, just after we had finished scriptures and said family prayer. It didn't come from President Whiting, or Brother Whitford, but from another secretary, who simply said, "Brother Call?"

"Yes."

"This is Brother Sanders in the Office of the First Presidency. Could you please hold for the president?"

My mind was trying to grasp the meaning of the request, so it took me a moment to say, "Yes."

I had wondered how I would react if the call ever came—but I had been completely wrong. Instead of shaking in fear, I felt a wave of soothing peace wash over me.

"Brother Call?" an older but energetic voice came into my ear. I recognized it immediately as that of our beloved prophet.

"Yes?"

"Good morning!"

"Good morning, President. It's good to hear from you."

"And it's good to hear from *you*. It looks like the Lord has given us both another day."

"Yes," I said. "Lucky us." I was immediately mortified by my light-minded reply. *This was the prophet.*

"Hah! Yes, lucky us! Now, I hear that you have some interesting news. Do you have a minute, or should I call back later?"

I almost laughed. I would have put the president of the United States on hold for this. And Congress. And the Joint Chiefs of Staff.

"President, I have all the time you need."

And with this phone call a door opened that has affected every moment of my life since. If I thought the process of getting the plates was dangerous and unique and thrilling, it didn't begin to compare to the work that followed. As Oliver Cowdery once wrote: "These were days never to be forgotten . . ."

But that's another story.

About the Author

Curtis Taylor was raised in Modesto, California, where much of his fiction is based. After serving a mission for the Church of Jesus Christ of Latter-day Saints in Tokyo, he married Janet E. Scott, whom he met on the BYU track team. They are the parents of seven children. Curtis has served as managing editor of three publishing companies, Randall Book Company, Aspen Books, and Gold Leaf Press. After taking a break to overcome a chronic case of Lyme disease, he is writing and publishing again. He currently lives in Utah County, where his family runs an organic farm. Besides farming, writing, and publishing, he also makes the occasional film and video.